MASTERS OF MYSTERY

Ellery Queen

MASTERS
OF MYSTERY

Galahad Books   New York

Published in 1987 by
Galahad Books
166 Fifth Avenue
New York, New York 10010

By arrangement with Davis Publications, Inc.

Library of Congress Catalog Card Number: 87-80894

ISBN: 0-88365-719-8

Printed in the United States of America

ACKNOWLEDGMENTS

"The Bizarre Case Expert" by William Arden, Copyright © 1970 by Davis Publications, Inc. Reprinted by permission of the author.

"The Long Glass Man" by Rosalind Ashe, Copyright © 1976 by Rosalind Ashe. Reprinted by permission of Curtis Brown, Ltd.

"The Final Twist" by William Bankier, Copyright © 1976 by William Bankier. Reprinted by permission of Curtis Brown, Ltd.

"Miss Phipps Discovers America" by Phyllis Bentley, Copyright © 1963 by Davis Publications, Inc. Reprinted by permission of Harold Matson Company, Inc.

"Miss Phipps Exercises Her Metier" by Phyllis Bentley, Copyright © 1970 by Phyllis Bentley. Reprinted by permission of Harold Matson Company, Inc.

"Dr. Coffee and the Whiz Kid" by Lawrence G. Blochman, Copyright © 1972 by Lawrence G. Blochman. Reprinted by permission of Curtis Brown Associates.

"Missing: One Stage-Struck Hippie" by Lawrence G. Blochman, Copyright © 1970 by Lawrence G. Blochman. Reprinted by permission of Curtis Brown Associates.

"Gentlemen's Agreement" by Lawrence Block, Copyright © 1977 by Lawrence Block. Reprinted by permission of the author.

"A Kind of Madness" by David Bradt, Copyright © 1976 by David Bradt. Reprinted by permission of the author.

"Clever and Quick" by Christianna Brand, Copyright © 1974 by Christianna Brand. Reprinted by permission of Brandt & Brandt Literary Agents, Inc.

"The Second Reason" by William Brittain, Copyright © 1976 by William Brittain. Reprinted by permission of the author.

"Don't Cry, Sally Shy" by Barbara Callahan, Copyright © 1977 by Barbara Callahan. Reprinted by permission of the author.

"Baskets of Apples and Roses" by Victor Canning, Copyright © 1965 by Davis Publications, Inc. Reprinted by permission of Curtis Brown, Ltd.

"Never to be Lost Again" by Jean Darling, Copyright © 1975 by Jean Darling. Reprinted by permission of the author.

"Bread Upon the Waters" by Robert Edward Eckels, Copyright © 1973 by Robert Edward Eckels. Reprinted by permission of the author.

"The Great Bread Swindle" by Robert Edward Eckels, Copyright © 1975 by Robert Edward Eckels. Reprinted by permission of the author.

"My Brother's Keeper" by Charles Einstein, Copyright © 1970 by Charles Einstein. Reprinted by permission of Blassingame, McCauley & Wood.

"The Rose Murders" by E. X. Ferrars, Copyright © 1977 by E. X. Ferrars. Reprinted by permission of Harold Ober Associates, Inc.

"Double Entry" by Robert L. Fish, Copyright © 1968 by Robert L. Fish. Reprinted by permission of the Estate for Robert L. Fish.

CONTENTS

MASTERS OF MYSTERY

NEDRA TYRE

The Murder Game

It was time for the murder game.

To play it, my brothers and sisters and I, all six of us, were gathered as usual on the first Tuesday night of the month in our Aunt Felicity's huge and impressive bedroom which was big enough for a royal levee. From its high stuccoed ceiling hung two Venetian chandeliers. A vast canopied bed dominated one end of the room. We were sitting in the other end at small candlelit tables set in the bay window that overlooked the rolling expanse of lawn that swept down to the river.

We had finished eating a simple but superbly cooked dinner. Our three tables were grouped in a semicircle around the Recamier sofa on which Aunt Felicity, beautiful and elegant but badly crippled from arthritis, had half reclined as she ate from a tray.

I didn't like the foolish game, nor as far as I could see did my brothers and sisters; but five months previously Aunt Felicity had proposed it out of the blue, and she had been so kind to us, so loving and generous, that none of us dared protest at first, and by now it had become a monthly ritual.

Five of us were not the least bit good at parlor games. As children we hadn't played them. My three brothers were competitive and excellent sportsmen, and competitive in business and spectacular successes for such young men—Carl and Matthew were lawyers, but not partners, and Andrew was an investment banker. Alicia, our oldest sister, was competitive socially and the most prominent young hostess in the city; her parties were famous—people literally clawed each other for invitations to her balls.

However competitive my brothers and Alicia were in the professional and social worlds they were inept at Aunt Felicity's murder game.

Jeanine—next to me the youngest girl—always won the game. Always.

She was the scholar among us, the bright one. I don't think she had a competitive bone in her body, and she discounted the prodigious store of knowledge that she possessed. She was genuinely modest about it. Her attitude seemed to be that she could not take pride in having mastered some information when there was so much more to be acquired. All the same, I think it irked my brothers that the murder game was so easy for her.

I will describe the game as we played it. Perhaps it's a variation of a well-

1

known game. As I say, we hadn't played parlor games either as children or adults. Previously we had only talked when we had dinner together on the first Tuesday of each month. We never ran out of things to say to each other. It was our one night together when there were no outsiders; not even our brothers' wives or Alicia's husband joined us.

When we had finished eating, Jeanine and I would clear away the dishes and pile them in the dumbwaiter and send them down to the kitchen where Mr. and Mrs. Finch were waiting for them. Our brothers would draw up chairs around Aunt Felicity. Alicia and I sat together on a loveseat, and Jeanine, as if to hide herself and her brightness and her inevitable triumph, sat in a small Louis XV chair behind our brothers.

The game began when Aunt Felicity reached into the drawer of a table near her and took out six sheets of rather ratty-looking scratch paper on which she had inscribed with a red nylon-tipped pen the first names of the persons suspected of murder; then she would tell us that the murdered person, before expiring, had been able to write something which indicated the name of the murderer, but that the murderer himself, or herself, intent on getting away from the scene of the crime, was not aware of having been incriminated, since the clever victim had been able to point to the murderer in an oblique way.

Aunt Felicity handed the sheets to Carl and he distributed them.

We read the names of the suspects: Horace, Llewellyn, Mary Ann, Joan, Louise, Margaret, Lawrence.

Before the victim died he had been able to scrawl one word: George.

Again Carl rose. Again he took six sheets from Aunt Felicity and handed them around to us. We now held a sheet with the names of the suspects in red and a sheet with the one word George in black.

We all—except for Jeanine, of course—began to frown in disgruntled perplexity.

Aunt Felicity asked if anyone had the solution. No one answered. She quizzed us in turn beginning with Carl who was nearest to her. When my time came I said I had no idea who was guilty. Occasionally Alicia would make a stab, but it was always a futile, incorrect one. And our brothers invariably became jocular, charming, bluffing, willing to take a chance, and on rare occasions one of them made a lucky guess, but he could never prove it by evidence or any sort of clue.

Aunt Felicity didn't let the game drag on or permit our brothers to become too rollicking with their random guesses. She would suddenly say, "Jeanine, who is the murderer?"

Tonight, as usual, Jeanine was neither coy nor hesitant in answering. Her voice was clear but modest. "The murderer is Mary Ann."

"That's right," Aunt Felicity said. "Now tell us why Mary Ann is the guilty one."

"Well, the victim wrote down George. George Eliot is the name under which Mary Ann Evans published her novels. Therefore George equals Mary Ann."

"Good lord," Matthew said. "I haven't thought about George Eliot since I was a freshman in high school and had to read *Silas Marner* and *The Mill on the Floss.*"

With Jeanine's naming the murderer our evening together was over. I gathered up the twelve pieces of paper we had used in the game and threw them into the wastebasket. My brothers and sisters lined up around the sofa and kissed Aunt Felicity good night and then they left me alone with her. We were an affectionate family, in touch with each other two or three times a day by telephone, and my brothers and their wives and Alicia and her husband and Jeanine, who wasn't married but lived on campus at a nearby university where she was an assistant curator in the Museum of Fine Arts, made numerous brief visits nearly every week.

My brothers relied on Aunt Felicity's advice and counsel and she relied on theirs. She had been our guardian ever since our parents had been killed in a plane crash, the same crash that had killed Aunt Felicity's husband. At the time of that tragedy Carl, the oldest child, had been twelve and I, Sue, the youngest, five. Aunt Felicity had taken us into her large house copied from an English manor and had given us a wonderful life, and by shrewd investments had made a substantial fortune for us out of our parents' estate, so that we were all well off financially when we came of age.

I had neither my brothers' drive for professional success nor Jeanine's brains nor Alicia's flair for society, and so I stayed with Aunt Felicity. She needed me, especially after she was stricken with arthritis. I found it satisfying to give back a little of the care and devotion she had given us. I did her errands and her telephoning. She found it difficult to dial or to hold the telephone, but liked to be in immediate and constant touch with people. I made dozens, sometimes scores, of calls for her every day. I invited her continuous flow of guests. She was a witty and informed conversationalist who liked to have witty people around her. I bought books for her to read, sent presents and flowers for her, got up at dawn to go to the farmers' market when Aunt Felicity wanted special food to prepare for a gourmet friend. I searched the shops for kaftans and long elegant dressing gowns that would hide Aunt Felicity's crippled body.

That night when my brothers and sisters had left after Jeanine had said that Mary Ann was the name of the murderer, I wanted to say as I helped Aunt Felicity make the painful, labored journey from the sofa to her bed, "Why do you have us play that silly game? Don't you see that none of us really likes it? And it embarrasses Jeanine to win all the time. I've never known you to make other guests ill at ease. Why don't you stop insisting that we play it?"

But I didn't complain.

And the game did end soon.

Or at least we were to be given a respite when Jeanine left town at the end of the semester. She took a brief leave from the university to spend the spring in Italy studying art in churches and museums.

I had thought that perhaps at our last gathering before Jeanine left, Aunt Felicity wouldn't make us play the game, but I was wrong.

As always, when our meal was finished and the dishes were cleared away, Aunt Felicity told us to take our places for the game, and once we were settled she reached into the drawer and handed Carl the slips with the names of the suspects. Carl handed a slip to each of us and we read the names: Cleo, Annette, Josephine, Melissa, Maude, Frank, James, Warren.

Then came the sheet with the clue: a serpentine line, an irregular, lopsided S.

Andrew was brash and even before Aunt Felicity asked for volunteer answers he said, "The guilty person is Cleo. The clue that looks like an S is a serpent, the asp that caused Cleopatra's death. Cleopatra equals Cleo. Sorry, Jeanine, to end your unbroken streak of victories, especially on your last night."

"A very good guess," Aunt Felicity said. "But the name on the list of suspects is Cleo, not Cleopatra. Your answer is wrong."

After Andrew's gaffe no one else guessed or offered any kind of comment. It was, I think, the shortest game on record.

As always, Aunt Felicity turned to Jeanine and asked for the answer.

"The murderer is Josephine," Jeanine said. "The clue—the S—is the outline of a swan. The swan was Empress Josephine's motif or emblem or whatever you want to call it. She had swans embossed everywhere. So the swan equals Josephine and Josephine is the guilty one."

Aunt Felicity gave Jeanine a congratulatory smile.

Then we all kissed one another good night and wished Jeanine a wonderful trip.

And that, as it happened, was the last time that we ever played the game of murder.

The next week was frantic for me. Even more than usual the telephone was like an appendage, an extra limb I'd grown in order to function. Aunt Felicity gave a large reception for the curator taking Jeanine's place and introduced him to the young painters and writers in town. Then a famous conductor, an old friend of Aunt Felicity, arrived for a concert and Aunt Felicity invited him and his entire orchestra to a late supper party.

I had never made so many telephone calls or done so many errands, and the night after the supper party when I handed Aunt Felicity her dinner on a tray she insisted that I go to bed immediately.

"You look dead-tired," Aunt Felicity said, "I've imposed on you too much. I don't need you tonight. I'll have Finch come up for the tray and he can send any callers upstairs. If any of the children"—she still referred to my brothers and sisters and me as children—"come they have their own keys."

I glanced at the bedside table to be sure everything she needed was at hand. Two books of her two favorite poets—Keats and Gerard Manley Hopkins— were there; the sherry decanter beside them was full—Aunt Felicity liked to sip sherry as she read, the last thing she did before going to sleep.

"Sue, darling, everything I can possibly want is within reach," she said. "Now go and get some rest." She lifted her forehead toward me and I kissed it and we said good night.

Twelve hours of sleep was all I needed to give me back my energy.

I woke up the next morning feeling equal to a hundred telephone calls and errands. I bathed and dressed quickly, then went as usual into Aunt Felicity's room. I tidied up a bit and picked up the Hopkins book that had fallen to the floor and set it in its accustomed place beside the volume of Keats. I often found a book on the floor where it had fallen out of Aunt Felicity's hand when she had dozed off to sleep. I adjusted the shutters so that the sunlight streamed in.

Then I went to the bathroom and moistened a washcloth so that Aunt Felicity could sponge her face and hands. I leaned under the canopy and pushed back the heavy curtains of the bed and called to Aunt Felicity.

Her alert eyes did not look up at me.

She did not give me her usual radiant smile.

She was turned so that she seemed to be submerged, drowned in the deep mound of pillows.

I realized then that she was dead, but that did not keep me from repeating her name again and again, as if I might somehow arouse her; and then I compelled myself to do what must be done.

I made one telephone call after another that morning. The first one was to Dr. Cowan who came to the house immediately.

"Don't grieve for Felicity," he said as we stood beside her dead body, and even as he ordered me not to grieve I saw that he was weeping for his dear friend. "Every moment of her life was pain." He wiped his eyes and recovered his professionalism. "Her death seems a perfectly natural one. I'll examine her, of course. When you call your family and friends, just say that Felicity died in her sleep."

As I left the room to make the sad announcement, I saw Dr. Cowan stoop over her body.

Whatever he had said to me about not grieving for Aunt Felicity, I mourned for her. I knew that life was precious to her and that however acute her pain and the inconvenience of being an invalid, she considered them a small price to pay for the pleasure and exhilaration of living.

Carl and Andrew and Matthew and their wives and Alicia and her husband arrived within minutes after I telephoned them, a prelude to an invasion of friends and acquaintances. Soon the house was crowded with people. After some delay I had reached Jeanine in Florence and managed to convince her that there was no reason for her to come home for the funeral—Aunt Felicity wouldn't have wanted her to interrupt her studies.

Late that morning I went to the kitchen to brew more tea for the guests and Matthew was coming up from the cellar with four bottles of sherry to replenish the supply. He motioned me into the pantry out of hearing of Mrs. Finch and the maids preparing refreshments.

"Sue," he whispered, "she didn't leave one of those pieces of paper with a clue on it, did she?"

"What do you mean?"

"That game of murder meant so much to Aunt Felicity. Maybe she had a premonition that she was going to be killed. Maybe that's why she made us play it so that we could discover her murderer."

I couldn't answer Matthew. I stared at him. He might have said an obscenity over Aunt Felicity's body.

My lack of answer was evidently answer enough for Matthew. "I know it's far-fetched," he said. "I—well, my God, I suppose I'm crazy but I thought maybe she had been murdered. Whatever you do, don't mention my suspicions to the others."

And then Carl and Andrew in turn stalked me, each cornering me privately in that house teeming with callers and prodding me to learn whether Aunt Felicity had left a clue that might point to her murderer. My shock and disbelief made them back away with apologies. The suspicions appalled me; and each swore me to secrecy, none of them wanting his dark mistrust to be told to the others.

But when Alicia grabbed my arm and pulled me into the downstairs powder room and locked the door behind us and asked if Aunt Felicity had left a clue I was less shocked. I now had questions of my own.

"Who would be the suspects, Alicia?"

"Any of us. All of us."

"But why? Why on earth would any of us want to murder Aunt Felicity?"

"Money," Alicia said. "Aunt Felicity was very, very rich and she left her fortune to us."

"Money? We all have money of our own. We don't need Aunt Felicity's money."

"Don't be naive, Sue. No one ever has enough money. I happen to know that Andrew is desperate for ready cash, and Carl has a new love affair but his wife won't give him a divorce without stripping him of everything he owns. And Matthew—"

I held up my hand for her to stop talking.

"Little baby sister," she said, "you're much too unworldly. You've spent your adult life being an errand girl and making telephone calls. I didn't mean to upset you or to make monsters out of our brothers. Someone could have murdered Aunt Felicity out of pity. It was unbearable sometimes to watch her hopeless fight against pain. I've longed for her to die so that her suffering would be over."

"But, Alicia, how could she have been murdered?"

"I don't know. Maybe an overdose of sleeping pills or something else put into her sherry. We all knew she drank it before going to sleep."

I slumped into the chair at the dressing table.

"Stop looking so horror-struck," Alicia ordered. "And get up out of that chair. We've guests to attend to. Come on."

At last Aunt Felicity's house was empty of all the callers; my brothers and sister, about to leave, insisted I not spend the night alone; each invited me to be an overnight guest.

"Alone?" I said. "I'm not alone. Mr. and Mrs. Finch are here. I want to stay where I belong—in Aunt Felicity's house."

I had no intention of leaving, and I was relieved finally to close the front door on my brothers and Alicia and go to my room.

It had been a long difficult day and the night was almost over. I needed rest for the approaching funeral and all the details that would precede and follow it.

But I could not sleep.

Seemingly the only thing alive in that dark and silent house was my small bedside clock and its regular tick and its illuminated hands that kept circling around and around as the slow and sleepless hours marched past.

Then a breeze swirled up from the front door and ascended the stairway and turned the corridor and swept into my room, and the most cautious footsteps I ever heard mounted the stairs and eased into Aunt Felicity's room.

And I knew that Carl or Matthew or Andrew or Alicia was searching there for a sheet of paper bearing a clue that would point to Aunt Felicity's murderer. They had been right to be suspicious. I was, as Alicia had said, the naive one.

Aunt Felicity's game of murder had been played all along for a real purpose.

But I tried to persuade myself that the darkness and my tiredness had exaggerated everything, that I had only imagined the breeze that had entered with the opening of the front door. I could not have heard any footsteps—the chatter of the clock would have muffled them.

But perhaps I ought to make sure.

Perhaps I ought to get up and look into Aunt Felicity's room.

Then above the ticking of the clock I heard descending footsteps and then the front door opened and closed.

There was still time for me to find out who had come in. I could rush to the entrance and see whose car was driving away.

Then I told myself that surely our loving family had not bred a murderer. Whoever had entered had only wanted to check to be sure that Aunt Felicity had not left a clue; it was not a murderer intent on destroying a clue. Aunt Felicity's game of murder had only been an innocent pastime with the slight moral purpose of proving Jeanine's superiority over Matthew's and Carl's and Andrew's and Alicia's worldliness and my aimlessness.

That idea reassured me and I managed to fall asleep.

But I was not reassured when I awoke. My one resolution was to play out the murder game.

I had never liked the game, but that didn't matter now. For once I must be adept at it. Jeanine, the only one good at the game, was thousands of miles away, and if Aunt Felicity had left a clue she would have meant it for me. She knew I wasn't subtle like Jeanine, so she would have left a clue easy for me to decipher.

I went resolutely into Aunt Felicity's room.

The last time I had been in there, I had discovered her dead body.

But before I had discovered she was dead I had gone about the ordinary morning routine. I had picked up a book of poetry from the floor and had set it on the bedside table where it was now. I had opened the shutters and had gone to the bathroom to dampen a washcloth.

I looked around me.

Nothing about the room resembled itself. The bed with its hangings seemed almost pretentious, the tambour organdy curtains looked too stiff, the French sofas and armchairs belonged to a stage set, the chandeliers should light a palace ballroom, the paintings ought to hang in a museum.

Without Aunt Felicity's presence the room had lost its elegance, all its personality.

I walked over to the small table near the Recamier sofa from which Aunt Felicity had taken, as she began the murder game, the sheets listing the names of the suspects. The drawer contained pads of scratch paper. I fluttered through them, but I could find nothing written on any sheet.

Then I realized that if Aunt Felicity were in the last moments of her life and aware of her predicament she must certainly have been in bed, and would have had no way to make the arduous journey from her bed to the table and back again without help, which she could surely not have requested of her murderer.

So she would have left the clue near or in the bed.

But the bedside table had nothing to offer. The books of poetry and the sherry decanter and wine glasses were on it. Inside the top drawer were my aunt's cosmetics and medicines. The bottom drawer held stationery and various pens and pencils, but everything was innocent of the clue in Aunt Felicity's handwriting for which I was searching.

I pulled back the bedcovers. No doubt Mrs. Finch had changed the sheets after Aunt Felicity's death and had dislodged the clue if Aunt Felicity had left it in the bed. Mrs. Finch would have thrown it in the trash if it had fluttered out at her. I found nothing in the bedsheets or stuffed under the mattress or in any of the pillowcases.

There was no clue.

Or if there had been one the early morning visitor had found it and removed it.

But I would not give up.

I looked again at the collections of poetry. I picked up the Keats book and riffled its pages. There was nothing in it. I put it back and took up the Hopkins book; the only extraneous thing in it was a small piece of paper that marked Aunt Felicity's reading place.

I snatched the paper. It was not identical in size to the pads of scratch paper which Aunt Felicity used for the murder game, but it did not need to be. A single word was written on it with the black nylon-tipped pen that Aunt Felicity always used when she wrote down the clues.

The word was TERENCE.

I said the name aloud. It was vaguely familiar. Terence was a writer of antiquity, wasn't he? I didn't know. I didn't have Jeanine's fund of information. Holding the sheet of paper, I ran downstairs to the library and pulled a biographical dictionary from a shelf. "'Terence,' I read. 'Publius Terentius Afer. 190-159 B.C.'" My eyes raced down the rest of the entry but I paid no attention to what I was reading. It was of no use to me. Aunt Felicity would have known I couldn't make deductions from a literary reference. She would have made it easier for me.

But however simple or easy she might have thought she was making it she had not made it simple enough or clear enough for me.

Terence.

Terence.

Terence.

It meant absolutely nothing.

The telephone rang, summoning me to all the duties and details attendant on Aunt Felicity's funeral.

It was Mr. Frame, Aunt Felicity's attorney, telling me that the undertaker had tentatively arranged for the service to be held at two the next afternoon if it would be satisfactory with us. He asked me to telephone Alicia and my brothers and then to let the undertaker know.

I would telephone them and then I would call Dr. Cowan and ask if Aunt Felicity could possibly have been murdered. I would tell him I thought that as Aunt Felicity had grown drowsier and drowsier after her last caller had left she realized that the caller had put something lethal in her sherry when it was poured out for her, and that just before she died she had managed to write something that incriminated the caller and had put the slip of paper in a book just before it fell out of her hand.

First, though, I must telephone about the time of the funeral.

As always I began with Carl, since he was the oldest.

His telephone was busy, so I called Matthew. Two o'clock was satisfactory with him. I called Carl again, but his line was still busy. So I dialed Alicia and then Andrew; each said the hour was agreeable.

Carl was the only one left to question and his line was still busy; I kept dialing.

And then I realized that Aunt Felicity *had* made it simple for me.

Terence.

My finger, plucking at numbers, had also been dialing letters of the alphabet, and Carl's number was 837-3623.

I wanted the line to stay busy forever, but on my next try Carl answered. I told him the proposed hour of Aunt Felicity's funeral and, as with the others, it was all right with him.

Then I said, "Carl, Aunt Felicity did leave a clue. I found it a little while ago. The clue she wrote was Terence. It was directed at me because I use the telephone so much. When I dialed your number—837-3623—I also dialed T-E-R-E-N-C-E. As Jeanine would say, Terence equals Carl. You killed Aunt Felicity."

There was a long pause and then a sound I had never heard on a telephone. I thought at first that a door might have slammed, but then I heard my sister-in-law scream and I knew that Carl had shot himself.

JACOB HAY

The K. Mission

Chicago, Dec. 1, Inter-Press—Dagbur Agradamian, the fabulously wealthy British oil magnate, stunned financial circles here and in New York by a near-miraculous surprise appearance at the annual meeting of Eurasian Petroleum where he successfully prevented a take-over by Imperial Holdings, Inc., and safely preserved his own close control of Eurasian Petroleum.

How the hugely bearded, always impeccably attired—a gardenia in his lapel is his trademark—multimillionaire managed to escape the attentions of reporters remains a mystery. Financial observers here declared that if word of his coming had gotten out, Imperial Holdings might have obtained the necessary bank assurances to insure his defeat. As it was, Imperial was caught with its guard down, and Agradamian added another victory to his long list of business triumphs.

Long a flamboyantly elegant figure in British business and society, Agradamian is known, however, to have a passion for personal privacy, and in this respect has been compared with American multimillionaire Howard Hughes. He declined to discuss any details of his astonishing appearance here, and has again vanished to one or another of the several homes he maintains in Britain and on the Continent.

Reading the dispatch in his copy of *The Telegraph,* Vice-Admiral Sir Richard Appleyard, R.N. (Ret.), known to his friends as "Boy," grinned cheerfully and took another eminently satisfactory swallow of his pint of John Courage in the saloon bar of The Gallant Sailorman, just off the High Street in Budleigh Salterton.

Omega had done it again. "Omega" was the name that the press had bestowed on Mr. Agradamian when it was considered amusing to describe one of his vast talents as "the living end, my dear," and the name had clung so tenaciously that, on one of the rare occasions in his career, Agradamian had bowed to popular fancy and caused to be painted on the gleaming white funnel of his gleaming white yacht a golden Greek omega. The same design was shortly applied to the far-flung fleet of Agradamian tankers.

Once, in the not too distant past, Mr. Omega had done a very personal favor for Boy Appleyard, before the latter's retirement from what is euphemistically called "a very sensitive post," and the two were old friends, dating their friendship from Dagbur Agradamian's wildly reckless and vastly effective days as a Royal Naval Volunteer Reserve corvette commander.

Actually, it is not entirely accurate to describe Sir Richard Appleyard as "retired"—not in the strict sense of the word. Men who have held jobs like his never really retire. They may give the appearance of lounging around lovely old country houses in shabby tweeds and doing a bit of pottering with the roses and having the odd pint at the local, but they remain in touch. Very much in touch, you may be sure.

This business of Agradamian in Chicago, now. How had one of the best-known figures in the world of international oil operations succeeded in penetrating to the American heartland without anyone being the wiser? Appleyard dismissed the idea of a chartered private plane. Nor would Agradamian have descended to disguise—assuming it were possible to do anything whatsoever with that great iron-gray spade beard and the ferocious mustaches that he wore in grave tribute to his Armenian ancestors. He would have died before shaving them off.

Yet only a few days before, the society pages of the London, Paris, and New York papers had Mr. Agradamian entertaining the cast of an American film company at his villa on Corfu.

Thoughtfully, Sir Richard tamped a battered black briar full of Rattray's. Clearly, his old friend must have traveled by air—but how? Almost certainly some greedy soul working in a plane-chartering service would have tipped off the newspapers, as would some crew member on a commercial flight. Of course, Agradamian might have his own plane, although this hardly seemed likely, since he hated to fly and had frequently declared so in public. Although, Appleyard mused, if it meant protecting his own vast empire, Dagbur Agradamian would venture into the jaws of hell without a second's hesitation. Dilettante and international playboy he might choose to appear—but a fool he most certainly wasn't.

Yet there was something here worth pondering, and Appleyard had been doing a lot of pondering since his last visit to London. Not only on the fact that somebody had at last managed to get a measure of decent heating into his old office, and that Miss Shaw-Jones had finally taken the giant step and got herself married. She'd been a damned fine secretary and would make some lucky chap a damned fine wife.

It was Hawker who had handed him the headache. Hawker was still vaguely embarrassed whenever he called his former superior Boy.

"This is a tricky one," Hawker said unhappily, "and we're stuck with it. What it amounts to is simple. On this coming January fifteenth, General Evgeny Kornetsov will be in West Berlin for some kind of memorial service for Russian troops killed in the battle there. He will, of course, be staying in East Berlin at the Russian headquarters—"

"Kornetsov?" Appleyard had interrupted. "The logistics genius, isn't he?"

Hawker nodded. "Precisely. No reason why, as one of the Russian army's senior top brass, he shouldn't attend a memorial service in West Berlin, of course, but that's not his real reason for being there. Instead, he's coming here to visit us."

"Here!" Appleyard was genuinely startled.

"You'll understand why when I explain the purpose of his visit. What he's coming to discuss are the procedures for supplies from the West in the event of a war with China—how many transport aircraft might be available, what quantities of munitions, et cetera. The whole business has to be kept absolutely secret; if it leaked it might even precipitate the Chinese into a preventive war, which is the last thing any of us wants." Hawker smiled wanly. "Kornetsov won't hear of the meeting being held anywhere on the Continent. He seems to have formed a somewhat exaggerated admiration for our security measures. So now all we have to do is get him from West Berlin to England and back again, with no one the wiser."

"Why not a Russian plane, landing at one of our Air Force bases?" Appleyard countered. "Passenger in civvies descends, is bustled into the customary sinister black limousine, and is whisked off into the night."

"Bound to attract attention. Other ranks see; they go to pubs; they get to nattering. No, we've got to come up with some means of getting the package here and back, and so far nobody's come up with a solution. And time is running out."

A damned sticky situation, Appleyard thought as he drove his elderly Rover sedately away from The Gallant Sailorman toward the mellowed stone home a few miles inland, where his wife, Joan, would probably be readying tea. Turning into his lane he was dumfounded to see one of the more astonishing automobiles in the United Kingdom parked in his drive—Dagbur Agradamian's precisely authentic reproduction of a 1929 Duesenberg phaeton in British racing-green.

"Well, I'm damned," Appleyard muttered as he parked and walked swiftly into the house. There was no mistaking the great rumbling laugh coming from the library. This was positively eerie.

There was a bit more gray in the beard these days, but the big man was as imposing as ever, despite his country tweeds and boots. You would never mistake Mr. Omega for a gamekeeper.

"I've had a tiring few days in the States," Agradamian said as they shook hands, "so I thought I'd run down and impose on you and Joan for a bit of relaxation. This place always does wonders for my morale."

"By all means, Dag. But I confess that I'm astounded. You should be somewhere in the middle of the Atlantic by my reckoning. Apparently you've finally acquired a magic carpet."

Mr. Omega chuckled, pleased. "No magic, my dear Boy. Simple logistics."

At which point Joan Appleyard entered, followed by old Mrs. Wheelwright, bearing tea and her customary expression of solicitude for her mistress.

"Devonshire cream," cried Mr. Omega joyously. "The true food of the gods, I swear."

Thus it was not until after dinner, when Joan had gone upstairs to finish

reading the latest in the series of detective novels of which she never seemed to
tire, that Appleyard had the opportunity to discuss, in the most general of terms,
his problem. Typically, Agradamian made no effort to probe deeper.

"So there it is, Dag. We've a very important Very Important Person to get
from West Berlin to Ealingham Hall, which, as you probably don't know, is by
way of being what's called a 'safe house,' staffed entirely by our own people, all
of whom can be trusted absolutely."

"This Ealingham Hall—has it a courtyard?"

"As a matter of fact, yes. Quite a large one, too."

Mr. Agradamian nodded, his expression thoughtful. "That will be a help."

"Then you think it's possible?"

"Of course it's possible, Boy. Quite simple, really."

"But how?" There was a hint of exasperation in Appleyard's question, and
Agradamian grinned.

"Why not let me take care of it?"

"You know quite well I can't ask you to undertake this sort of operation."

"You haven't asked. I've just volunteered. After all the dull financial types and
their proxies I've been dealing with lately, a bit of sport would be just the thing."

"Dammit, Dag, this is not sport! It's a deadly serious affair—just how serious
I can't begin to tell you."

"The more reason to succeed, then. My dear chap, I don't know who your
VIP is, and I don't want to know. You say this meeting is scheduled for January
sixteenth, one day after your person arrives in Berlin. That should present no
problem—if he will be good enough to cooperate fully. You say there is to be a
reception at the Grand Europe Hotel following this memorial ceremony. That
would be at about four, shall we say? If your 'package,' as you keep calling him,
can be at the tradesmen's delivery entrance of the hotel at four thirty, we'll
accommodate him."

This was terribly irregular, Appleyard thought, but Dagbur Agradamian had
a genius for the irregular. Hawker would be desperately unhappy with the arrangement, and there was no point whatsoever in telling the Americans about
the affair. The Americans operated by the book, and Mr. Omega wasn't in any
book yet published, publicly or privately. But if Dagbur Agradamian could
make himself vanish from view completely, perhaps he could do as much for
somebody else.

"At precisely four thirty-five a large van will back up to the delivery entrance
of the Berlin hotel. It will bear the legend *Nettleton's Glasswares* on its sides.
The driver will come around to the back and open the rear doors. Meanwhile,
his mate will enter the delivery way itself and set off a smoke bomb. In the
ensuing seconds your package will enter the van which, naturally, will drive
rapidly away to avoid catching fire. He will reappear in the courtyard of your
Ealingham Hall," Mr. Omega concluded triumphantly.

Well, no one else had come up with an idea, Appleyard thought unhappily.

And what, he wondered, would the world think of one of its wealthiest
capitalists going to the rescue of a Russian general? Not that the world would

ever know, he hoped fervently, and if it ever did learn, it might not be around long enough to relish the irony.

As Appleyard had anticipated, Hawker was, to say the least, distressed when the bare bones of the scheme were presented to him.

"Confound it, man, do you suppose I would have come all the way from Devon to London if I didn't think there was a hope?" Appleyard finally exploded. "I grant you, Kornetsov has handed us a set of damn near impossible conditions, but think of the alternative—the possibility of a Red Chinese army looking across the Channel towards Dover."

"We're taking the very devil of a chance, you know."

"Do we have a choice?"

Hawker shrugged his concession.

"The finest Christmas present of my life," Mr. Agradamian boomed when Appleyard dropped by the sumptuous flat in Belgravia that the bearded giant called home when he was in London. Spence, his manservant, was pouring a bottle of a sweet Armenian wine which Appleyard secretly disliked. "Have a glass of my sugar-water, Boy, and when this is all over I'll tell you how it all works."

"*If* it works," Appleyard replied soberly.

"It will," came the confident answer.

Appleyard spent a particularly wretched Christmas, made the more so by Joan's absence. They had planned to spend the holiday with their only daughter in Copenhagen, where she was married to a promising youngster with the British Embassy there. Appleyard insisted that Joan keep the date, and pleaded urgent business in Britain. With 25 years of marriage behind her, Joan had recognized the tone of his voice and hadn't argued.

Meantime, there was not a blessed word from Dagbur Agradamian during the difficult period of working out the details of General Kornetsov's visit with the Russians in Berlin; and the Russians, as usual, were difficult—even more so, in fact, since only one of them, the KGB station chief, knew the real nature of the situation. It is not every day that the Russian staff in Berlin is ordered to turn one of its army's top generals over to British Intelligence for a couple of days. To add to the difficulties, the Americans were getting restive. If the Kornetsov mission became known, it could mean even worse problems in Korea and Vietnam. Was this meeting really necessary?

Now the security precautions at Ealingham Hall, which stands in its own vast park in a part of the United Kingdom which need not concern us here, are such that only a microbe can penetrate freely; but these security precautions are largely invisible, since one does not wish to arouse the curiosity of one's neighbors. Much better that one's neighbors be under the impression that Ealingham Hall housed nothing more exciting than a Ministry of Agriculture Experimental Station. Under the circumstances, then, Appleyard had taken all the necessary steps to insure that should Mr. Agradamian's Duesenberg show itself at the gatekeeper's lodge it should be admitted immediately.

But at 11:00 P.M. on January 16th there was still no sign of Mr. Agradamian or his Duesenberg at Ealingham Hall. What there was a sign of was panic, subdued but very real. The handful of NATO officers who would brief General Kornetsov had arrived and were comfortably established in the library where a well-supplied bar was in operation, but of the Russian they had come to brief not a word.

Outside in the cobbled courtyard Hawker paced feverishly while Appleyard smoked his pipe in grim silence. Hawker was not the man to lower himself to an "I told you so," and Appleyard was not yet ready to concede that Mr. Omega had failed. The telegram had been unmistakable in its meaning when it had arrived at Appleyard's home that morning: EXPECT DELIVERY SHIPMENT NETTLE-TON'S GLASSWARES TODAY. Minutes later, Appleyard was pushing the elderly Rover hard across the British countryside in the direction of Ealingham Hall.

It was 11:45 P.M. when the gatekeeper at the Hall, whose worn corduroys belied his status as a sergeant of the Welsh Regiment, phoned that Nettleton's van had arrived. It was 11:48 P.M. when the big trailer rig rumbled into the courtyard and ground to a halt. Its engine fell silent and the driver climbed down and approached Hawker and Appleyard.

"Admiral Appleyard, sir?" Appleyard nodded. "Receipt, sir. If you'll just sign here." The driver held a flashlight over the flimsy form.

"Received from Nettleton's Glasswares one important package," Appleyard read, and for the first time in many days he grinned as he signed. Then, to his astonishment, the driver and his mate silently proceeded to unhitch the boxlike trailer and then drive off down the lane into the night. Now what the bloody hell?

At which juncture the rear double doors of the trailer swung silently open and Appleyard stared up from the dimly lighted courtyard to perceive that the trailer was full of plywood cartons. Even as he stared, the center tier of cartons swung smoothly outward and to one side. In the glowing rectangle of light that now appeared loomed the large figure of Dagbur Agradamian.

"Your package, gentlemen," he announced amiably, "and one of the finest gin-rummy players it's been my pleasure to meet." He jumped down from the trailer nimbly, as befitted a squash player in excellent condition, to make way for General Evgeny Kornetsov, who was wearing the sort of civilian suit that only Russian tailors seem able to produce.

While Hawker led the General into the vast entry hall of the manor house of Ealingham, Dagbur Agradamian hauled himself back aboard the trailer and led the fascinated Appleyard into its interior, which might have been mistaken for the mahogany-paneled owner's cabin of a luxurious motor cruiser, complete with an enclosed john and a minuscule electric galley. Along one side was a comfortable-looking berth; ranged against the other were an armchair and a table. Several etchings adorned the windowless walls. As Appleyard gaped in amazement, Agradamian opened a cupboard and removed from their specially padded racks a bottle, with which he proceeded to do the proper things.

"Highly efficient, my dear Boy, wouldn't you say?" he asked genially, lifting his own glass.

"But you couldn't have driven—I mean, the time element—" Appleyard broke off.

"Of course I didn't drive, old son. I flew. Or, rather, I should say that we—your guest and I—were flown."

"Impossible! Not a trailer this size!"

"Not quite, actually, But this, Boy, is not really a trailer. It's what is called a 'container.' You should spend more time at Tilbury Docks, old son. Containers are all the rage these days." Mr. Omega took a satisfied sip of his brandy.

"What you do, in essence, is take a simple steel or aluminum box, twenty feet long, roughly eight feet wide and eight feet high, and load it up with whatever you choose at your factory. Then you put it aboard a flatcar, you see, ship it to the nearest docks or airport, send it wherever you choose by ship or plane, have it unloaded onto a freight car, and have it arrive intact wherever you want it to arrive.

"As you well know, I despise flying. Simply looking out of a plane's window, even when it's on the ground, gives me vertigo. But all passenger planes have windows. So when these containers began appearing on the scene a few years back, I sensed that here might be the solution to my problem, because it has become increasingly necessary for me to fly, yet at the same time avoiding the publicity involved, alas, with a commercial flight. What could be more comfortable, then, than a *personal* container?"

"What, indeed?" Appleyard murmured.

"But it is forbidden to commercial freight airlines to carry people, right? So the answer was to charter my own cargo plane. What could be more anonymous than the arrival of a cargo plane and its anonymous container? You understand, naturally, that this is no ordinary container: certain modifications were necessary, such as soundproofing—I cannot abide the noise of jet engines—emergency oxygen, provision for internal pressurization."

"But the expense must have been fantastic," Appleyard protested weakly.

"A trifle when you consider the results."

"So that was how you managed the Chicago business?"

Agradamian nodded happily. "I simply had myself shipped to Chicago. There's no messing about in air terminals when you fly air freight. All the comforts of home, and, apart from a few uncomfortable seconds during take-off, no vertigo, because there are no windows. I mix myself a drink, read an improving paperback detective novel, and hey, presto!—I arrive safe and sound. After which a bloody great forklift or something deposits my giant shoebox aboard a trailer and off we go."

"But emigration and customs—" Appleyard argued. "All the formalities, the regulations?"

"When it is convenient, these matters can be tactfully arranged, and quite legally. When it is not convenient—as, shall we say, this evening—well, again, these things can be arranged." Mr. Agradamian's smile would have made his Armenian ancestors proud.

"And when this conference is over—?" But Appleyard already knew the answer.

"Simple. *Nettleton's Glasswares* will make another delivery to the tradesmen's entrance of the Grand Europe Hotel in Berlin." Dagbur Agradamian's smile was beatific. "After which it might be best if *Nettleton's Glasswares* ceased to send its containerized cargoes to the Continent for a time. I think I could travel quite as comfortably as *Spooner's Marmalade.*"

"D'you know, Dag," Appleyard said slowly as he finished the last sip of his brandy, "I'm damned glad you're on our side."

He would, Appleyard thought to himself as the brandy warmed his innards, have to get cracking with a memo to the right people: *Containers: Possibilities for Illegal Shipments and Suggestions for Prevention Thereof.*

No. On second thought, let the Customs people figure it out for themselves. They were, after all, expected to be abreast of all new developments in transportation. Meanwhile, Mr. Agradamian's container might prove quite useful. One had heard reports that the Rumanian deputy chief of counterespionage desired to defect to more tolerant climes. But did the Rumanians eat *that* much marmalade?

Appleyard was still chuckling when Hawker rejoined him in the courtyard. Above them loomed the dark, silent bulk of the container on its trailer. Mr. Agradamian had retired for the night.

HUGH PENTECOST

Blood-Red in the Morning

She wasn't where I hoped she would be, the place we had met for so many dawns so long ago. I stood by the swiftly moving stream and looked down at the literally hundreds of trout, anchored behind the rocks, some of them trying to fight their way upstream. Laura and I used to try to fish some of them out by hand, and more than once we succeeded.

When I was 16 and Laura was 15 we met here almost every fair summer morning. We had fishing rods, but mostly we didn't fish. I would bring sandwiches and she would bring a thermos of coffee or milk, depending on the weather, from the big stone house that frowned down on us from the hilltop.

We would sit together on the bank of the stream, without embarrassment, holding hands. The future was quite clear to both of us. I had a year of high school to finish, and then college. After that we would be married, in spite of the stone house and all it stood for. We were irrevocably, totally, peacefully in love.

One morning when I met her in the gray dawn light she showed me a splinter she'd got in the palm of her hand. I tried to pry it loose with the small blade in what had been my Boy Scout knife. Our heads were close together. Suddenly we were looking at each other intently, her blue eyes very bright. I found it hard to breathe. She smelled like clover, like flowers, warm and sweet. And then she was in my arms for the first time, and then, without words or preamble, we were making love on the bank of the stream. It was the most natural thing in the world, because she and I were forever.

Later a shadow fell across us and I turned my head to see what it was. The Old Man was standing over us, like a colossus. He was about six feet five inches tall and 240 pounds of solid bone and muscle. He had a grizzled beard and mustache. In town we called him Big Daddy, after Tennessee Williams' character. He was what the big stone house stood for. He was Laura's father.

He picked me up by the back of the neck as though I were a bag of scrap. Holding me with one hand, he beat me with the other fist, back and forth, until the earth turned into a dark fog. Then he threw me on the ground. He was breathing hard—not from effort, but from pure rage.

"If I ever see you on this property again, John, I'll shoot you down in cold blood for trespassing," he roared at me.

I looked at Laura. She lay with her face buried in the dew-wet grass. What had been perfect had been turned into something shameful. I crawled away, over what seemed like miles of fields, and then under the white wooden fence that surrounded the property.

That was seven years ago.

Until three days ago I had not seen Laura again, except once or twice when she had been driven through town in the family Cadillac. I had written to her, but my letters had been returned, unopened, probably by the Old Man or some other member of the family. I had tried to phone her, but she was never at home. I had been too frightened to walk up to the front door of the stone house and demand to see her. I was just a kid.

I didn't blame the Old Man any more. Any father who found his fifteen-year-old daughter lying with a no-good neighborhood kid might have reacted as he had. He could have brought a legal action against me, but he didn't because, I suppose, he didn't want any public scandal to touch Laura.

So I went on, through high school and college, and then into the Army and the jungles of Vietnam. There was never another girl who remotely interested me. Any kind of permanent relationship seemed impossible. I got a letter from my brother when I was only a few months away from my discharge. Secretly I didn't think I would live that long, but I did.

"You remember Laura Gibney?" my brother Eddie wrote. Did I remember her! "She flew the coop about two months ago—took off for Hippieville, I guess. The Old Man had the cops and private detectives and God-knows-who-else looking for her in New York. They finally found her in the East Village living in a pad with half a dozen long-haired goons. She refused to come home and they couldn't make her—she's over twenty-one. She's singing in some kind of night spot in the Village."

I couldn't believe it: Laura living in some dive with half a dozen men, divorced from the luxury and care she'd always had.

I did live out those months in Vietnam, I did get discharged from the Marine Corps, and I did wind up in New York, even before I went home to my family in Connecticut. I wanted to find Laura. She had been on my mind ever since the letter. I fancied myself some kind of hero who would save her from "a fate worse than death."

I had no great trouble finding her. She was singing in a supper club called The Night People's Thing. Her picture was in a glass frame outside the front door. She was singing when I first saw her, accompanying herself on a guitar. Her voice was sweet and clear, and somehow it got you by the throat. She was good.

Her long golden hair hung down her back, beautiful—older but beautiful. The place was crowded with kids, most of the boys long-haired and bearded, most of the girls miniskirted and barelegged. All were intent on Laura and when she finished on a high plaintive note they stamped and applauded and demanded more. I didn't think she'd seen me, but she put down her guitar and came straight toward me where I was standing at the bar.

"Hello, Johnny," she said.

"Hi." It was a croaking sound.

"Strange accident, your coming in here," she said.

"It wasn't an accident."

"You were looking for me?" Her blue eyes had changed. They were more sophisticated, wiser, hiding some kind of pain, I thought.

"Yes."

"I would think that was a mistake," she said.

"Can we go some place to talk?" I asked.

"I'm afraid not. I have two more shows to do. And I'm here with friends."

I saw a dark-bearded young man giving me the evil eye from a few yards away. My uniform marked me as part of the unthinkable Establishment.

"When, then?" I asked.

"Oh, I don't know, Johnny." She sounded tired. "Shouldn't we skip it?"

"No."

"Do you expect to go up to your family's place in Lakeview?"

"After I've had a chance to talk to you," I said.

"Did you know I'd run away from home?"

"Eddie wrote me."

"Saturday is my father's seventieth birthday. My mother has persuaded me to come home for the celebration. It's a mistake but—well, it means a great deal to her. I'm going to give it a try, but I may turn around and come straight back to town. But if I stay, and if you're in Lakeview, perhaps we could get together."

"Where? When?"

"I'll have to see," she said.

Then she was surrounded by admirers and they quickly crowded me out.

"See you around, Johnny," she called to me.

So that was that.

And now it was just a little after five on Sunday morning. I hadn't heard from her. I thought maybe she'd remember the old days and come to the old place; but she hadn't.

The August dawn was blood-red, reminding me of the old doggerel about "Sailor take warning." I looked up at the stone house, four stories high, with its ironwork doorways, its terraces and verandas, its hugh cupola in which a great brass bell reflected the first rays of the sun. She was there, or maybe she wasn't. It seemed impossible she wouldn't have sensed that this was the moment and the place for us to meet.

I walked up to the house, to the terrace that overlooked the sloping gardens. There were two especially grotesque gargoyles at the ends of a stone wall, spewing water into a marble chute that emptied into a pool below. I stood on the wall to get a better view of the gardens which I hadn't seen for so long.—And I froze.

The water that ran down the chute was pure and clear, but the water in the pond at the bottom was clouded with the dark red of blood. Floating face down was the body of a man, naked except for a pair of swimming trunks. His hair waved away from his head like some sort of sea grass. There was a gaping red hole just below his left shoulder blade.

On the bank of the pond sat a girl. It was Laura, her blonde Alice-in-

Wonderland hair hanging down her back and gleaming in the sunlight. She had on a flimsy thing in dark-blue polkadots that left her back bare and reached only halfway down her thighs. Her legs and feet were bare, and her knees were drawn up under her chin, her arms wrapped around them. She stared at the dead man without moving.

A yard or two away on the damp grass there was a large pair of pruning shears, the long-bladed kind used for cutting the boxwood hedges that surrounded the garden. The blades were stained. They had almost certainly been used to make that hole in the man's back.

"God Almighty!" I said, and jumped down off the wall.

I half ran, half slid down the grass bank to where Laura sat, her concentration on the dead man so intense that she didn't seem to hear my breathless arrival.

I squatted beside her, unable to speak, not daring to touch her. The dead man was a stranger to me. Blood still oozed slowly out of the hole in his back.

Then Laura turned her head to me. She looked totally blank for a moment, as if she'd never seen me before in her life. Then her blue eyes widened and she recognized me. Two large tears ran down her cheeks. Her arms were suddenly around my neck, her wet cheek pressed hard against my cheek.

"Oh, Johnny, Johnny, Johnny!" she whispered.

A voice like thunder seemed to shake the ground under us.

"Palmer! Johnny Palmer!"

I turned my head, still holding Laura close. She was crying softly. Up above us, standing on the wall between the two spitting gargoyles, was T. J. Gibney, the Old Man himself. He looked like some giant Gothic warrior. At that distance you would never have guessed his seventy years.

Let the old tyrant just try to manhandle me this time. I could break him into a dozen small pieces without half trying. I had learned how to fight to kill in the Marine Corps. . .

The Gibney mansion in Lakeview was built more than 130 years ago by T. J. Gibney's grandfather. It had been owned by only three men in that time: Horace Gibney who built it; Nathan Hale Gibney, Horace's oldest son; and Thomas Jefferson Gibney, Nathan's heir, who had, the night before that red August dawn, celebrated his 70th birthday.

The fabulous old house was a museum containing priceless paintings and sculptures, rugs and tapestries, along with carved paneling and huge marble-manteled fireplaces. The entrance hall alone was big enough for an inaugural ball. In an age of self-help, a small army of servants, indoor and outdoor servants, kept the house, the gardens, the outlying grounds in perfect condition. It was the last of something that belonged in another era.

When you think of vast fortunes in American history you conjure up such names as Carnegie, Mellon, Astor, Morgan, Rockefeller, Ford. And Gibney. The Gibneys had gone West in covered wagons, had become cattle barons, had found oil under their grazing lands, had bought more and more land—and then industries and portions of great cities and patents and processes. And now there was The Gibney Foundation, which supported research in science and medicine, which underwrote the creative arts in a hundred cities, and which was devoted to urban redevelopment—paying for the cost of obliterating city slums and replacing them with decent modern housing.

And that was far from all. There were hospitals that bore the Gibney name, and clinics and laboratories. To God they had contributed everything from stained-glass windows to whole cathedrals. Publicly the name T. J. Gibney was associated with goodness, charity, and compassion. And T.J. had a public-relations man whose only job was to keep that image intact.

Privately, and particularly in our small town, we knew T.J. to be a shrewd, cruel, hard-drinking, lusty old buzzard. There were a lot of people who admired just those qualities in him. Huge fortunes are not amassed and increased without violence, ruthlessness, and even treachery. The Gibneys had apologized to the people they'd crushed along the way by building hospitals to take care of their families.

I think what I had come to hate most about T. J. Gibney was not so much the way his family had amassed its fortune. That kind of thing was part of our pioneer history. It was how he used the power that went with great wealth. Maybe I should have thought he had treated me with some leniency seven years ago. From his point of view a beating was a small price for me to have paid. From my point of view—well, there had been no hearing, no chance to explain that Laura and I had not been involved in some cheap affair, no chance to explain that we were truly in love.

It had been simple for him to make any further contact between Laura and me impossible. He had servants who were paid well to make sure he had his way. He could pay a man in six figures to make his public image warm and lovable. And he could buy his way out of any jam he might ever get into . . .

As he started down the path toward where I sat on the edge of the pool with Laura in my arms I felt like shouting at him, "How are you going to buy your way out of this one, Old Man?"

Do you know that it never occurred to me that Laura could be involved? No, not Laura.

"What happened?" I asked her.

She shook her head from side to side, unable to speak because of what was now convulsive sobbing.

As the clean water came into the pond from the marble chute, the bloody film seemed to drift away from the dead man toward the outlet at the far end.

The Old Man came across the lawn toward us. He towered over me and for a moment all my adolescent fears of him rose up in me. He was Power. He was Authority.

"The last time you were on my land, John," he said in a shaking voice, "I told you what I would do if you ever came back. Just one thing. Did Laura invite you here?"

"No, sir," I said. I had learned to say "sir" automatically since our last meeting.

"You came here uninvited?"

"Have you looked in the pond, sir?"

"What about the pond?" He turned, and suddenly he turned to stone. After a long moment he looked back at me and his mouth had gone slack. "What happened?"

"I don't know, sir," I said, still holding the sobbing girl in my arms. "I only got here seconds before you called out to me. If you let Laura get hold of herself she should be able to tell us."

"Laura!" he shouted.

"Don't yell at her," I said.

He gave me an odd look as though he couldn't believe I had the nerve to give him orders. I put my head down and whispered to Laura, "We have to know, baby. We have to know what happened."

I could feel her whole body go tense as she struggled for control. Finally she lifted her tear-stained face, making no effort to get out of my embrace.

"I don't know, Johnny," she said. She didn't look at the Old Man.

"You found him this way? You know who he is?"

"Of course she knows who he is," T.J. said. "He's Julian Traynor, a writer who's been living here for months and working on a history of the Gibney family. He's part of our household."

"I was coming to meet you, Johnny. I was going to the old place," Laura said, as if she hadn't heard T.J. "What time is it, Johnny?"

I could look at my wrist watch without taking my arm away from her. "A quarter to six," I said.

"Oh, my God!" she said, and began to shake again from head to foot.

"Easy," I said, "You can't start that all over again."

"I've lost an hour," she said.

T.J. and I looked at each other. We were suddenly allied in confusion.

"What do you mean?" I said.

"I came out of the house about an hour ago," she said. "I planned to be at our meeting place a little before five—the way we always used to, Johnny. I came out onto the terrace and then—and then I was sitting on the edge of the pond here, looking at Julian."

"What did you see when you first came out on the terrace?"

She turned in my arms and her hands gripped the lapels of my blue linen jacket. "I don't know, Johnny. That's what I'm trying to tell you. I've lost an hour somewhere, I've drawn some kind of blank. I was on the terrace—and then I was sitting here."

"You expect me to believe that?" T.J. demanded.

"I don't expect anything from you, Father," Laura said. She put her face on my shoulder and the quiet weeping started again.

The Old Man straightened his massive shoulders. "Will you be good enough to help me get Julian out of the water, John?"

"You shouldn't touch him, sir—or those garden shears. It's a matter for the police."

"Oh, God," he said. He turned to look at the body in the water again. "You're sure he's dead?"

"I've seen a lot of dead men in the last two years, sir."

He looked at me as though he were really seeing me for the first time in his life. "So you have," he said. He watched me stroking Laura's golden hair. I thought he had shrunk just a little. "You believe she's drawn some kind of a blank? Amnesia?"

"If she says so," I said. "Something else I've seen in the last two years—a lot of memory blocks like this. When a man has seen something too horrible to bear, the mind simply shuts off all the memory processes relating to it. It's not at all uncommon when people are being blown to pieces all around you. If Laura saw someone ram those shears through Traynor's body—"

He nodded slowly. "Will you try to get her up to the house?" he asked.

Believe it or not, I had been asked to help T. J. Gibney! I watched him walk up the path, his broad shoulders drooping. The big stone house seemed to have taken on a reddish tinge from the sunrise. And as I watched I saw a curl of black smoke rising from one of the half dozen chimneys. It must have been in the high seventies at six o'clock that morning. It was going to be a scorcher of a day. I thought: no matter what happened the orderly efficiency of the household would go on. Someone must be burning refuse from last night's party in the incinerator.

Laura seemed to have regained control. She slipped out of my arms and sat there, looking first at the body in the pool, then at me.

"Johnny, get out of here," she said suddenly. "Go as far away as you can. I should never have said I might see you. It's gone, it's dead, it's our lost childhood. It's Dreamsville."

"An every-day all-day dream," I said.

"Oh, Johnny!"

"I want to tell you something," I said. "I was involved with Intelligence in the Marine Corps in Vietnam. Part of my job was to debrief our commandos when they came back from a raid, and prisoners who had been rescued from the Vietcong forces. Every day I talked to men who'd been through some kind of unbelievable hell. What's happened to you—a lost hour, even lost days—was a common thing. The mind provides a kind of anesthetic for the unbearable. You may not remember for a long time what you saw this morning."

"Oh, God." She covered her face with her hands.

"The harder you try, the more impenetrable the block is likely to be. So just take it easy. Sooner or later, unpleasant as it may prove to be, it will all come back to you. The police are apt to pressure you to remember. I'll try to get them to understand."

"The world isn't the way we thought it was, Johnny," she said. "It's nothing like what we thought. Go away, Johnny. Try to develop a block of your own. Forget you ever knew the Gibneys."

"I love you," I said, trying not to sound romantic. "I hope you're going to marry me."

Her body seemed to writhe inside that polkadot nothing she was wearing. She cried out, "No, Johnny! Oh, no, no, no!"

She sprang up, and before I could stop her she began to run barefoot up the path to the house. Above her the black curl of smoke from the chimney was subsiding. The sun was well up above the hills behind the house now, hot and oppressive. I could feel little trickles of sweat running down my back.

I looked down into the pool. A faint red froth seemed to float on the surface above the dead man.

Growing up is a strange business. Was it Mark Twain who said that as a boy he thought his father was a complete idiot, but by the time he was thirty he was surprised to realize how much his father had learned with the passing of the years?

The first time I thought I was grownup was that dawn by the trout stream when Laura and I discovered that we were in love. Right after that, when I'd crawled away whimpering, after the Old Man had beaten me, I knew I was still an inadequate kid. When I was 20 they put a rifle in my hands and sent me off to basic training and I thought: Now I am a man. But I learned I couldn't even vote and there were a lot of places where I couldn't even buy a drink. Some grownup!

And then I saw death and destruction—little children blown to pieces, old men and women burned to death; and I thought: you have to be grownup to see this and still retain your sanity. And then I thought: I couldn't be very grownup because I couldn't get it through my head exactly what we were fighting for. I couldn't think of any noble reasons for being in Asia where some sniper whom I didn't know and who didn't know me, someone I had nothing against, was trying to blow my brains out from behind a rock. I knew what *I* was fighting for. I was fighting to survive—so I could come home and find Laura.

So I had come home, having started as a private and ended up as a Lieutenant with decorations and medals, and people on the streets of my town, seeing me in civilian clothes, said, "You're little Johnny Palmer, aren't you?" Grownup? I was still the same kid who lived with his mother and brother at the north end of Maple Road in Lakeview, Connecticut, U.S.A.

And Laura had run away from the simple mention of anything so grownup and adult as marriage.

In the pond a man lay face down, his dead mouth open in the bloodstained water. He had been born, lived, grown up, and died. Or had he grown up? The thousands of dead people I'd seen in the last two years had all seemed so helpless, so childlike in death . . .

Someone was coming down the path now, a blond man wearing a yellow sports shirt, yellow slacks, and yellow sandals on bare feet. He had a magnificent tan. He moved with the lithe grace of a conditioned athlete.

I knew he was Bob Gibney, Laura's brother—the younger of T.J.'s two sons, but ten years older than Laura. Bob was what the townspeople called "a wild one," as opposed to his brother Emerson who was a church deacon and whose owlish spectacles made him look like a third-rate bookkeeper. Bob Gibney drove foreign sports cars, climbed mountains, and had been saved from a dozen scandals with women by T.J.'s pocketbook. He had finally married a girl he found dancing naked in a cage in a Hollywood discotheque. Sheila Connors had obviously played for higher stakes, people said at first. She wanted the works, not a payoff. But later people changed their minds. Bob and Sheila were apparently devoted to each other. They were never separated. They dressed alike, strictly on the "mod" side. Someone had dubbed them "The Bobbsey Twins." But Bob Gibney hadn't settled down. He simply had a perpetual companion in his comet course across the sky.

He stopped at the edge of the pond, not looking at me for a few moments, and concentrated on the dead man.

"It took some strength to run those shears clean through him," he said.

"Frail people can generate a lot of strength if they're angry enough," I said.

Then he looked at me. He had the brightest blue eyes I can ever remember seeing—blue, laughing, heartless, I thought. "You said it, not me, brother," he said. "You're Johnny Palmer, aren't you?"

"Yes."

"You seem to have chosen an unlucky moment to renew your love life," he said. "You see it happen?"

"No," I said.

"That's right, man," he said. "Keep saying no. Because anything you say can be used against you."

"Now look here, Mr. Gibney—" I began.

"Call me Bob," he said, grinning at me. "There's only one *Mister* Gibney around here—the Old Man." He looked back at the body and his eyes seemed to grow even brighter, as though they were being provided with a special excitement. He glanced at an expensive gold wrist watch. "The last time I saw him was less than three hours ago," he said. "He was laying siege to one of the better-looking broads of the evening. Oh, yes, Johnny, I was watching. There's a bit of the Peeping Tom in all males, wouldn't you say? That's why the new naked movies please us so much and outrage the lady critics. Oh, well, as the fellow said, 'What a way to go'—flushed with success, your manhood verified."

He fished a cigarette out of a shirt pocket and produced a gold lighter from his trousers pocket. He stared directly at me through the flame. "You should of stood in bed, kid," he said. "I think we should get up to the house. The fuzz will be along any minute."

"You're trying to tell me something," I said.

"A fact of life," he said. His smile was mockery. "You grew up in this town, didn't you, man? Then you know the Gibneys never take the rap for anything."

Someone hailed us from the top of the bank. It was startling, because it was Bob Gibney's double—or almost. Same yellow shirt and slacks and sandals, same lithe body; only the hair was different. It was cut almost the same. Bob wore his longish, with sideburns brushed back over his ears and a thick mane down his neck—but expertly cut and styled. I understand that kind of haircut costs about twenty-five bucks on Madison Avenue. Sheila Gibney's hair was styled the same way, but it was henna-red.

"I don't think I'll come down," she called out to us.

"Good idea," Bob said. "We're coming up, anyhow."

As we came close to her I saw that her eyes were bright, like her husband's, but cat-green. She looked at me quizzically. I've been sized up by women before, and I knew I wasn't displeasing to her; but I also knew Bob would notice it, and I felt uncomfortable.

"You're Johnny Palmer, aren't you?" she said. "I'm Sheila."

"Hi," I said.

"Poor Julian," she sighed. "He was riding so high last night. What's this about Laura's sudden amnesia?"

"Shock," I said.

She gave a little shudder. "I think I'd like to head out of town, Bob. After all, they don't need us. We were together, so we alibi each other."

"That's why I married you," Bob said. "To have a perpetual alibi. No, we'll stick around and tell the cops what we were doing."

The green eyes widened. "You mean, blow by blow?"

Bob laughed. "That might constitute a delaying action," he said. "Seriously, we have to stay, Duck—for Lydia's sake. She'll need support while T.J. tells the cops how to do their job."

Lydia was Laura's mother. People had remarked in town how odd it was the two boys had always called her by her first name. But if you saw her riding one of her hunters over a stone wall, or driving her Ferrari around town, her blonde hair streaming out behind her, you'd take her to be of their generation and not of her own.

As we walked toward the house I saw that a white-coated servant was laying out a sort of buffet breakfast on the screened terrace that faced the spitting gargoyles. The whole family must be up by now, even though it was still only a quarter past six. Sheila was between Bob Gibney and me, and she ran her scarlet-tipped fingers along the sleeve of my jacket.

"A rough reunion for you, Johnny," she said.

"Not exactly what I'd hoped."

"Laura was expecting you?"

"Yes, she was expecting me."

"Too bad you waited so long, Johnny. Our Laura isn't exactly the girl you once made love to on a morning like this—what was it, six years ago?"

"Seven years ago, and what are you talking about?" I said.

"Oh, come on, Johnny, don't play stupid," she said.

"Johnny's been in Vietnam for the last two years saving the world for Democracy—or whatever we're saving it for," Bob said.

"Don't tell me the local bigmouths haven't kept you filled in on our Laura," Sheila said.

"Oh, shut up, Duck," Bob said. He looked at me and grinned. "As a small girl Sheila used to stick pins in insects just to watch them wriggle."

"That's not fair," Sheila said. "I just thought Johnny ought to be prepared for what's bound to come out in the open. We don't want two cases of amnesia, do we?"

They both thought that was a hell of a joke. I was developing a slow burn but there was no chance for it to intensify, because we'd arrived at the terrace and Bob opened the screen door. Inside, the servant was in conference with Lydia Gibney. She was something. She had to be in her middle fifties because Bob was in his early thirties and Emerson a couple of years older. But you wouldn't have believed it if you didn't know the facts.

Her hair was a golden blonde, like Laura's and Bob's. Her shoulders were broad, her hips narrow. Her eyes were large, a darker blue than the children's, and she had a wide generous mouth. I suppose the hair was carefully tinted; I know the mouth was expertly painted. But the figure was a young woman's, and her skin was tanned but not leathery. I thought of a blonde version of the present-day Joan Crawford. Vitality and excitement radiated from her. She had been married to T.J. for at least 35 years and there was no sign that he'd been able to crush her. It was an experience just to look at her.

She turned to face us. A little nerve twitched under a high cheekbone. "You've seen—it?" she asked.

"It's not very pleasant, darling," Bob said. "By the way, you remember Johnny Palmer?"

The dark blue eyes had an almost hypnotic effect on me. A kind of hardness faded from them and they became warm pools. She took a step toward me and held out her hand. Her grip was firm as a man's.

"I've owed you an apology for a long time, Johnny," she said. Her voice was low and husky.

"I can't think what for, Mrs. Gibney," I said.

"There was a time when I should have stood up for you," she said, "but I was too much of a coward. I hope this isn't the day I have to pay for that cowardice."

Cowardice was the last thing in the world you would connect with her. I supposed she meant she should have fought the Old Man over me. I could understand her holding back from that. He could crush you with sheer sound and fury.

There wasn't an opportunity for me to say anything because the Old Man and Emerson came out of the house to join us. T.J. had changed into a tent-sized seersucker suit, with a red ascot tied under his grizzled beard.

Emerson Gibney was as dark as his brother and sister were fair. His sports jacket looked as though it had been made for someone else. His dark eyes peered at me through horn-rimmed glasses, and they were openly hostile.

"Hello, Palmer," he said.

I said hello. I was still standing next to Lydia Gibney. "Is Laura all right?" I asked her.

"She's up in her room," Lydia said. "Marcia—Emerson's wife—is looking after her. Have you met Marcia?"

"No, I don't think so."

I heard Sheila laugh. "There's always something unexpected around the corner, Johnny."

"I think you should all have some coffee and something to eat," Lydia said. "The police will be here presently and heaven knows when we'll have another chance. Won't you help yourself, Johnny?"

The Old Man had crossed to the door and was looking out at the spitting gargoyles. "They're sending Zack along from the County Attorney's office," he said casually.

Bob echoed Sheila's laughter. "Didn't I tell you, Johnny? The Gibneys never take the rap for anything."

Manuel Zack.

Item: He was a former F.B.I. man.

Item: He had been involved in an antitrust case brought by the Government against the Gibneys. At the trial he had failed to give the expected testimony. The Gibneys were acquitted.

Item: The F.B.I. dropped him immediately after the trial. He promptly got a job as special investigator for the Prosecutor's Office in our county. Everybody knew T.J. had used his influence. Manuel Zack was T.J.'s boy.

Item: Everybody said he was as mean as they come.

I had just got down a cup of coffee and half an English muffin with some grape jelly on it when the two green-and-white State Police cars wheeled up the driveway spraying bluestone onto the grass borders. Manuel Zack and a trooper wearing green-tinted glasses got out of the first car. Two more troopers with cameras and other equipment got out of the second car.

Zack, wearing a tropical worsted in charcoal-gray, came up the path to the terrace. His white shirt was unbuttoned at the neck and a red-and-blue-striped tie was pulled loose and a little to one side. His egg-bald head was sunburned and peeling a little. He had a wide thin mouth like the edge of a carving knife. When his black eyes looked at you, you felt he could read the label on the inside of your shirt collar.

"Come in, Zack," T.J. said, opening the screen door. "Glad you could make yourself available."

"My pleasure," Zack said, looking quickly from face to face. He wound up glaring at me. "House guest?" he asked.

"John Palmer is a neighbor in the village, Mr. Zack," Lydia said.

Zack's eyes narrowed. "Oh, yes," he said. "Local war hero. You spend the night here, Palmer?"

"No."

"Then how do you happen to be here at this time of day?"

"I came to call on Miss Laura Gibney," I said.

"At six o'clock in the morning?"

It was Lydia who stepped into the breach for me. "Johnny and Laura were childhood sweethearts," she said. "They used to go on early-morning fishing trips in the old days. This was the first chance they'd had to meet since Johnny got back from the war. For sentimental reasons, I suppose, they chose to meet as they'd been accustomed to do when they were children."

Zack glanced at T.J. "He's the one you told me about?"

The Old Man nodded.

"So tell me what time you got here and how you came," Zack said to me.

"I walked," I said. "My family lives on Maple Road, which is less than a mile from the borders of Mr. Gibney's property. I came over the fence at the north end and walked through the woods and across the fields to the place where Laura and I used to meet. She wasn't there."

"So?"

"So I came up here to look for her, just outside there between the fountains. I saw Laura sitting on the bank of the pond. And I saw a body floating in the water."

"You didn't see anything happen? You didn't see this Julian Traynor before he was a dead body?"

"No. So far as I know I've never seen Traynor before that."

Zack dropped me for a moment. "You told me on the phone, T.J., that your daughter has some kind of memory block about what happened—what she may have seen."

"That's what she says," T.J. said.

"You have any reason to doubt it?"

T.J. drew a deep breath. "You know Laura's history, Zack. You helped look for her when she ran away from home. I don't know her any more."

I heard a sharp little intake of breath from Lydia. She was standing by the buffet table, a cup of coffee in her hand. The cup rattled slightly in the saucer. Emerson had wandered to the far end of the terrace as though he didn't want to be a part of this. "The Bobbsey Twins" were sitting on a wicker sofa, watching with a kind of bright excitement. I found myself thinking they looked like a couple of bloodthirsty spectators at a bullfight.

"Let's get this Traynor character straight," Zack said. "He's been living here for how long?"

"Nearly six months," T.J. said. He took a long thin cigar out of the breast pocket of his seersucker jacket and lit it. "He's doing—was doing—a history of the Gibney family. I spent several hours a day with him making tapes—talking into a tape recorder. He was just about ready to begin the actual writing."

"Get along well with everyone?"

T.J. looked around at his family. "Just fine," he said. "Nice fellow, pleasant sense of humor." He smiled a wry smile. "He stood up under my bullying very well. He'd come to seem like one of the family."

"I know he helped with your daughter when she was finally located in New York," Zack said. "Acted as a sort of go-between, didn't he?"

"She refused to see any of the family," T.J. said, his voice harsh. "There was nothing we could do about it—legally, that is. She's over twenty-one. Julian volunteered to talk to her—on Mrs. Gibney's behalf."

Lydia put down her unsteady coffee cup. "We had all made mistakes with Laura, knowingly and unknowingly," she said. Her wide eyes shifted to T.J. and quickly away again. "I wanted her to know that we still loved her, that nothing else mattered, that there'd be no recriminations, no demands. Julian went to New York to see her—four or five times before she agreed to let me talk with her. Julian had done a wonderful job, because when Laura and I met there were no barriers, no angers."

"But she wouldn't see T.J.?"

"No. But I kept at her, hoping somehow that the wounds could be healed. I finally persuaded her to come here yesterday for my husband's birthday party. Julian drove in to New York and brought her out here."

"You think Traynor had romanced your daughter?" Zack asked.

"I don't know what you mean," Lydia said.

"We can't play this with gloves on, Mrs. Gibney," Zack said. "Your daughter has been carrying on with everybody in New York. We know that. Do you think Traynor's scalp was added to her list of trophies?"

There was a kind of giggling laugh from Sheila.

"I think I very much resent your way of putting things, Mr. Zack," Lydia said.

"Lydia, we've got to face the facts," T.J. said.

"Yes, facts, Mrs. Gibney," Zack said. "We have to believe that someone murdered Traynor in a rage, running him through with those shears. Of course we may get lucky. There may be some good clear prints on the handles of the shears, and that will be that. But I seldom get that lucky. So we have to consider who could have developed a murderous hatred for this nice young man who had come to seem 'like one of the family.' We don't know, at the moment, what your daughter's relationship with him was. And we don't know about Palmer here."

"I told you I'd never laid eyes on him," I said.

"Until this morning," Zack said.

"Until this morning when I saw him dead in the pond."

"So you say." Zack took a handkerchief out of his pocket and blotted his bald head. It was oppressively hot. "Just what was your current relationship with Laura Gibney? I know what happened seven years ago. You were lucky that T.J. didn't have your hide then. What about now?"

I could feel an angry pulse beating in my temples. "Since that time you're talking about I had never seen or had any contact with Laura until three days ago. I went to see her at the place in New York where she sings. She told me she was coming here yesterday for her father's birthday party. It was left that we'd try to meet sometime today."

"Did you live with her three days ago in New York?"

"No, you cheap jerk, I didn't," I said.

The knife-edge mouth widened in a satisfied little smile. I realized he wanted me to blow my top.

"But you planned to resume the old relationship when you met at the old place this morning?"

"I planned to ask her to marry me," I said, fighting for control.

"Oh, Johnny!" Lydia whispered.

"You and Laura Gibney had agreed to meet at the place where it all started?" Zack asked.

"No. We hadn't agreed to any time or place. I just thought she might—might come there."

"At dawn? After an all-night party?"

"Yes."

"But she hadn't actually promised?"

"No."

"Evidently she planned to meet *someone* at dawn," Zack said. "Suppose it could have been Traynor and not you?"

I was still fighting to keep my voice steady. "She told me that she'd started out to meet me—at the old place—where I'd expected her. And then she found herself sitting on the edge of the pond staring at Traynor's dead body."

"And you bought that?" He looked around at the others. "You all bought it?" No one spoke. Zack came back to me.

"This girl you say you want to marry," he said. "If you saw her run a man through with a pair of garden shears, would you admit you saw it?"

I just stared at him.

"And if you caught her with Traynor and you killed him—you've been trained to kill on the spot, haven't you—would your girl friend tell on you, do you think?"

When I didn't answer he turned away from me with a little gesture of disgust and addressed himself to T.J. "In my experience," he said, "ninety-nine percent of all these sudden amnesia cases are fakes. I think I'd better talk to your daughter, T.J."

"Will you get Laura down here?" T.J. said to his wife.

I was wet all over with sweat. It was hot, but anger was mainly responsible for it. I saw what was happening, what Zack's and T.J.'s plan was. Laura, the black sheep of the family, and I were to be thrown to the wolves, one way or another.

I looked at the Old Man and I don't think I ever hated anyone so much in my life, not even that sniper behind a rock in a swamp in Vietnam. This was a man who never forgave. Laura had shamed him by her escape into Hippieland. She had further shamed him by her refusal to come meekly home and submit once more to his authority after she'd been found. She had shamed him long ago with me. Now she was to be thrown to the wolves—to Zack specifically. I was to be used any way that was convenient to implement that punishment. If I was destroyed in the Gibney stonecrusher, that would be only proper punishment for my adolescent crime.

Lydia had gone to find Laura. Zack had helped himself to a cup of coffee and a slice of cold ham made into a sandwich on homemade bread. He was a noisy chewer.

I went over to T.J. who had finished some kind of whispered consultation with the owlish Emerson and was now staring out across the lawn at the gargoyles.

"You're not going to let Zack put Laura through that kind of dirty-minded grilling in front of everyone, are you?" I asked him.

His strong white teeth showed in a bearded smile. "I'm going to let Zack handle this case in his own way," he said. "He's a top-flight investigator."

"I've had some experience with the kind of mental block that Laura has suffered," I said. "I've watched psychiatrists in the service handle dozens of cases. Zack's kind of pressure could prolong the block indefinitely. It might even do Laura permanent damage."

"When Zack needs your psychiatric skill I'll tell him to talk to you," T.J. said.

"I won't stand for it," I said.

His shaggy eyebrows rose. "*You* won't stand for it? You really are a presumptuous young twerp, Palmer."

Whatever I might have said—and I have to admit I was groping for words— was stalled by the arrival on the terrace of Laura, followed by Lydia and a woman I supposed to be Emerson's wife, Marcia. She was a tall bony young woman, with her hair drawn back in a severe knot at the nape of her neck, and she wore no makeup. She was like a Sunday School teacher I'd once had whom I remembered without pleasure.

Zack put down the remnant of his ham sandwich and wiped his mouth with the back of his hand. I saw Sheila huddle closer to Bob on the wicker couch, her green eyes glittering. This was to be the main event for the *voyeurs*, I thought.

Laura had changed out of the polkadot shift. She was wearing a black cotton turtlenecked sweater, the sleeves rolled up above her elbows. There was a red miniskirt and matching red sandals. She looked at me as if I was the only person present she'd ever seen before. I felt my heart thump against my ribs.

"This is Mr. Zack," Lydia said to Laura. "He's in charge and he has to ask you some questions, darling."

"Sit down, Miss Gibney," Zack said, in a surprisingly gentle voice. "Have some coffee?"

"No, thank you," Laura said.

She sat down in one of the porch chairs facing Zack, her arms wrapped around her as though she were suffering some sort of internal pain.

"Your family tells me that you've drawn some sort of memory blank," Zack said.

"Yes." It was scarcely audible.

"Suppose you tell me what you do remember," Zack said. He watched her as he lit a cigarette.

"I got up shortly before five o'clock," Laura said slowly. "I was going to meet Johnny Palmer at the trout stream." She glanced at me.

"But Palmer says you had no specific date, no agreed-upon time or place to meet."

"That's true. But I was sure Johnny would be there."

"And he says he was sure you would be there," Zack said. "You two have some sort of special ESP with each other?"

"Perhaps."

"So you planned to go the trout stream?"

"Yes."

"What changed your mind?"

She looked straight at him. "I don't know."

"Oh, come now, Miss Gibney, shouldn't we stop playing games?" Zack said.

"I came onto the lawn out there near the fountains," Laura said. "The next thing I remember is sitting on the edge of the pool, and Julian was—was dead in the water."

"My, my," Zack said, "how convenient not to remember what happened in between."

"It's torture not to remember," Laura said sharply.

"Maybe I can help you relieve that torture," Zack said. "Palmer had asked you to marry him, right? And you had things to straighten out before you could say yes, right?"

"I hadn't asked her to marry me," I said. "I told you I planned to ask her. I never got the chance—not till afterwards. I said then I hoped she was going to marry me. She couldn't have known about it beforehand."

"With all that ESP going for both of you?" Zack's laugh was short. "Did you know Palmer was going to ask you to marry him, Miss Gibney?"

Laura's china-blue eyes rested on me for a moment. "Yes, I knew he was going to ask me."

"And you had to straighten things out with Traynor before you could say yes?"

"I didn't have to straighten anything out with anyone," Laura said. "I was going to say no."

"You had to say no because you were already committed to Julian Traynor?"

"I was committed to no one," Laura said. She didn't look at me again.

"But you had an affair going with Traynor, didn't you, while he was being the diplomatic representative of your family?"

She took a frighteningly long time to answer, I thought. "I didn't have an affair with him," she said. Somehow it sounded evasive.

"I suggest you did," Zack said. "I think I could prove it if I have to. I suggest you planned to meet Traynor before you joined your friend Johnny at the trout stream. I suggest you and Traynor had an argument. I suggest you agreed to let Traynor have one more fling, or he tried to force himself on you. I suggest that Palmer, who'd gotten impatient, came up to the house to look for you and found you and Traynor together. I suggest he blew his stack, picked up the garden shears, and rammed them through Traynor. I suggest all that is what you so conveniently can't remember, Miss Gibney. I suggest it's best for you not to remember because there aren't many men who would want to marry you after Hippieville and Traynor and God-knows-who-else."

I was standing close enough to him to grab him by the shoulder and spin him around. I wasn't thinking about killing him. I just wanted to punish him. I hit him on the jaw with everything I had in my left and was ready to bring over the crusher with my right when I was swarmed on from behind by T.J. and Bob and Emerson.

Zack's face was a blur as he came toward me, smiling. While the others held me armlocked, Zack slapped me dizzy, back and forth with his open hand. Then he stepped back.

"Let him go," he said. His eyes were angry black gimlets. "They trained us in the F.B.I. how to hand-to-hand fight a killer. I think I know tricks they never taught you in the service, Palmer."

If T.J. and Bob, who were still holding my arms, had let go I'd have leaped at him. I wanted to wipe that smile off his mean face. It was Laura who changed things. She had come quickly to me, her cool fingers touching my cheek, which must have been red from the slapping.

"Please, Johnny, please!" she said. "I can stand it if you can. What he says doesn't really matter."

The screen door slammed behind us. The trooper with the green-tinted glasses had come up from the pool. He took in the scene and his right hand rested lightly on his holstered revolver.

"You okay, Mr. Zack?" he asked.

"I'm just fine," Zack said.

"I think you better have a look at things down there before we move him," the trooper said.

It turned out that I knew this fellow with the sergeant's stripes on his shirt sleeve and the green glasses. He was a local. His name was Mike Sayers. He'd been two years ahead of me in school, college, and Vietnam. We'd never been chums, but we always said hello and exchanged small talk. He looked at me as though he'd never seen me before, with that deadpan expression the state troopers develop when they say, "Can I see your driver's license?"

Zack gave me a crooked smile. "So it's recess time, Palmer. But school's not out. Nobody's to leave the premises, and that goes double for you, war hero."

Zack and Sayers went out through the screen door and disappeared down the grass bank toward the pool. The atmosphere on the terrace was highly charged, and yet no one said anything for a moment. Emerson had joined his Marcia and they were whispering together in a far corner. Laura had turned away from me and was watching the disappearing law. "The Bobbsey Twins" still sat together on the couch, bright-eyed, watching eagerly. Lydia made a quick exit into the house, almost running.

The Old Man came over to the buffet table, cut himself a thick slice of ham, and popped an English muffin into the hotel-sized toaster. While he waited he turned toward Laura.

"Would you like to tell us what happened, Laura?" he asked in a flat voice. She didn't speak or move.

"I've been in touch with my lawyer," T.J. said. "Maxwell's already on his way up from New York. I'll see to it you have the very best advice and help."

Laura whirled around. "So that the Gibney name won't be damaged, Father?"

"There isn't much more you can do to damage it," he said. "But we all have to stand together at a time like this."

"And the best way to stand together is to pin it on me or on Johnny or on both of us?"

"It would simplify matters if you'd stop pretending you don't know what happened," T.J. said.

"Has anybody ever had the courage to tell you, Father, that you're a miserable excuse for a man?" Laura said, her voice shaking.

The toaster made a popping noise. From the wicker couch came the sound of mocking applause, provided by Bob and Sheila.

"I think I'd like a little fresh air," Laura said. "Will you come with me, Johnny?"

She went out the screen door without waiting for me to answer. I followed her. She walked around the corner of the house in the opposite direction from the pool, past the sloping cellar doors.

There was a small flower garden surrounded by a two-foot stone wall that I remembered was Lydia's particular pleasure. I'd seen her in the early mornings when I was a kid. She'd be wearing a bright-colored smock, weeding and cutting. There were columbines with hummingbirds, tame as pets, already fluttering around the blossoms.

Laura sat down on the wall and behind her was a blaze of oriental poppies. She looked up at me, and her face was pale and her blue eyes were dark with pain.

"You're entitled to some sort of explanation," she said.

"There's nothing to explain," I said, "unless you want to." I sat down on the wall, facing her, and lit a cigarette. "I was an idiot to suppose you would even think of marrying me after all these years. It just happens that nothing has changed for me, but my life has been different from yours—fenced in by the disciplines of schools and war. There's been nothing new to change the way I've always felt about you."

"Dear Johnny, that was a very nice speech," she said. She reached out and touched my hand, then looked away across the scarlet bed of poppies. "I didn't change for a long time, Johnny. I loved you as totally as any young girl ever loves. I kept waiting for you to come back and— and carry me away. But you never did."

"I was a stupid kid. I was afraid."

"And rightly," she said. "You've had a taste of how they operate this morning. I was a coward, too, Johnny. I knew they were intercepting letters and phone calls from you. I never had the courage to try to get in touch with you myself. I was literally a prisoner for so very long, Johnny. I knew what really mattered to T.J. All he cared about was the family reputation. Not even that, really—he cared only about his own reputation. He kept insisting that the only reason he wasn't prosecuting you was to save *my* reputation, *my* future. . .

"I expected all the things I'd been brought up to expect—that you would be my husband, the father of my children, my whole life. This was every woman's dream, I'd been told, and I dreamed it. But month after month, year after year passed, and nothing happened. So I began to think it was all a phony."

She hesitated, then went on, "I watched my mother. Her dream had come true, I thought. She had her man—a big powerful man. She had her children, her home, her luxurious life. I watched her and I saw that it was all a phony. She was driven by anxieties and tensions I didn't understand, but I knew they were there. Everyone always said what a wonderful horsewoman she was, how daring, how expert. I began to realize that she was taking chances in the hope that some day she'd break her neck! The way she drove a sports car—and then the way she'd shut herself up for days on end and try to drink herself to death."

"Your mother?" I could hardly believe it.

"My mother," Laura said. "I began to realize that the greatest villain in the world was T.J. He had destroyed all of Lydia's romantic notions about living, he'd smothered Emerson and Bob, paying them off with gobs of money. We were all his puppets and we would do what he said whenever he chose to pull the strings."

"My God," I said.

"But even my father couldn't shut me away from the world like some Bronte heroine," Laura said. "There were newspapers and magazines and television and books. I was locked away from you and from life as I thought it was going to be, but I began to understand that out there a revolution was going on, Johnny— the revolution of the young people of my generation against the Establishment. It sounded like just words at first—fancy talk to justify throwing off discipline, to excuse self-indulgence in unheard-of freedoms. Then I began to believe in it. You were lost, Johnny—you and all the young men like you who were fighting a war that didn't mean anything—to me, an immoral war. You'd been sold a bill of goods, and there was a good chance you wouldn't live to find it out.

"I listened to T.J. raging about these perverted young people with their long hair and their beads and their crazy talk about Love and Peace—and then I heard a famous woman quoted as saying that all the crazy clothes and the long hair and the beards were simply a way of crying out, 'Look at us, listen to us— before it's too late!'"

She glanced at me. "You don't believe a word of that, do you, Johnny? You fought your war for T.J.'s kind of world and you were lucky enough to come out of it whole; and now you're one of T.J.'s boys."

"I don't know," I said. "I would hate to think I am."

She drew a deep breath. "Well, Johnny, I joined the revolution. You know something? I was already old. I was past twenty-one." She laughed. "The kids I joined thought I was pretty long in the tooth, but I believed in them with all my heart. Not the rabble rousers and the building burners, but the kids who believed in Love and in Peace."

I saw that her hands were locked together in front of her, so tightly that her knuckles were bone-white.

"You don't have to tell me about it," I said. The truth was I didn't want to hear it.

"One of the things they believed was that living together was as natural a part of life as breathing or eating. It didn't have to be wrapped around with T.J.'s concepts of honor and decency and propriety. It was just a thing that people did and felt better for having done—without promises or pledges or long-range selectivity."

"So you lived that way," I said in a tight voice.

"Freely," she said, but without looking at me. "With almost anyone." She looked at me with a kind of pity in her eyes. "So you see, Johnny, why I had to say no if you asked me to marry you. You could never understand. You would try, but you would think of me just as T.J. thinks of me."

"No!"

"Poor Johnny. You know what's so terrible about it? When I saw you the other night in New York I had the crazy notion that I could wipe the slate clean and we could take up where we'd left off. I wanted to, Johnny. And then I realized I'd be walking right back into T.J.'s world. Worse than that, I'd already been tempted. I'd agreed to come back here for T.J.'s seventieth birthday before I knew you were back in the land of the living. I told myself that I'd come because Lydia wanted it so much. She hadn't been able to break away and I think I mean a great deal to her. I told myself I was being noble, but the truth is, Johnny, I was tempted."

"By Julian Traynor?"

She looked at me with that same pity in her eyes. "Poor Johnny, you see how it would always be? Every man who ever looked at me would be a suspect."

"Was Traynor one of them?" I asked. "Can Zack prove it?"

"Do you know something, Johnny? Zack, with T.J. behind him, can prove anything. T.J., with an army of Zacks working for him, is our world today. They run our economics, our politics, our wars, our ghettos, our starvation areas. You cry out about injustice and the Zacks of the world, supported by the T.J.'s of the world, will prove beyond a doubt that you're actually protesting against Justice."

"What about Traynor?" I asked, with a dogged stupidity.

"The T.J.'s of the world, with their Zacks, write our history. Their counterparts write all the other histories. They obliterate truth whenever it serves their interests." She gave a small mirthless laugh. "So much for my stump speech. No, Johnny, not Traynor, although he very much wanted it. You see, from where he sat I was a round heels, and therefore available. T.J. sits in that same seat, and God help me so do you, Johnny. I'm sorry if I've hurt you, but you had to know why there's no future for us. I've lived in another world with another set of values, and there's no way to make it match yours."

There was no time to protest, even if I'd known how to protest or been sure that I wanted to protest. Mike Sayers came around the corner of the house, his green-tinted glasses glittering in the sunlight.

"Back inside, please," he said.

I stood up, and every bone in my body seemed to ache. Laura stood very close to me. "Don't try to fight for me, Johnny," she said softly. "It's a battle you can't win—not against the likes of Zack and T.J." She kissed me on the check and I felt as if I'd been burned.

"You truly don't remember what happened this morning?" I asked.

"Before God, I don't," she whispered.

"Then I'll fight," I said.

I took her cool hand in mine and led her toward the terrace. We hadn't quite reached the corner of the house when I heard the sound of a heavy vehicle coming up the driveway. I turned and saw the red truck that belonged to the local sanitation department. They'd come to collect the trash and garbage. Then I remembered the dark smoke I'd seen coming from one' of the chimneys.

What had someone been burning on such a hot day?

I don't know that I can describe exactly how I felt. There was a pain in my gut like a hot ball. I hadn't gone ten yards toward the terrace before I was blaming myself for everything that had happened to Laura. At the age of 16 I should have come charging back on a white horse and carried her away. I knew I couldn't have done it, but I should have tried.

She had painted a vivid picture for me. I'd have been faced by T.J. and an army of servants and gardeners and chauffeurs, all looking like Manuel Zack, and they'd have beaten my brains out. But at least I'd have tried, and then maybe she wouldn't have run away and—and done everything she had done.

Laura was right. I was one of T.J.'s boys and I played by his rules. I had surrendered Laura to the Vandals. I could forgive her anything because, damn it, I still loved her.

And just as I was feeling very noble about that decision I remembered my brother Eddie's letter: "They finally found her in the East Village living in a pad with half a dozen long-haired goons." I began to have visions of what that had been like, and I felt sick and ice-cold in spite of the August heat.

You could recall things about yourself and write them off without any feeling of loathing or horror. There had been a gaudy place in Saigon where I'd spent the better part of two leaves. That was an exigency of war, I told myself, to be forgiven and forgotten. But Laura? A small voice told me that was an exigency of war, too—a war against the T.J.'s and the Zacks, a war against what she thought of as the Establishment, a war against indecent use of power. . .

Someone had produced an ice cooler while we were gone, and Zack was making himself an iced coffee, laced with thick fresh cream. He gave us a knowing little smile as we rejoined the family, positioned almost as they had been when we left.

"Got your story all nicely arranged between you?" Zack asked.

Sergeant Sayers was a spectator at the far end of the terrace.

I felt myself figuratively tightening my belt. I was going to fight this battle right down to the last man, even if that last man was me. I looked around at the rest of T.J.'s army. One son and his wife stood in the corner, dark and gloomy; the other son and his wife sat on the wicker couch, waiting avidly for Round Two. Lydia had come back from inside the house and was sitting in an armchair at the head of the buffet table, still the perfect hostess. There was one change. She had put on a pair of black-lensed glasses that completely hid anything she might be thinking. She was now a kind of glamorous sphinx. T.J. stood across from her, watching her as though he expected she might go to pieces.

"Some facts for all of you," Zack said, "just so you'll know where we stand. There are no fingerprints on the murder weapon. Sayers found a pair of cotton gardening gloves thrown away in the lilac bush just beyond the pond. We assume the murderer wore them." He sipped his creamy drink, the ice tinkling against the side of the glass. "The garden tools are kept in a shed about fifty yards from the pond. Swenson, the head gardener, runs a neat ship. Tools are not left lying around. There is an exact place on the wall of the shed where those garden shears usually hang. On a table a few feet away there is a workbasket full of gardening gloves—like the pair we found in the lilacs. It paints a kind of different picture from the one I first had." He put his glass down and lit a cigarette.

"I thought of a quarrel, an explosion, and someone grabbing up the shears which just happened to be there and striking with them. There might be an excuse for that—intolerable provocation, self-defense. Even"—and he looked at Laura—"temporary insanity. Now we have to picture it another way. Traynor goes down to the pool sometime before five in the morning, perhaps to swim, probably to meet someone. You, Miss Gibney?"

Laura shook her head.

"Then someone else," Zack said. His dark eyes moved almost hungrily to Sheila, then to Lydia, then to the stone-faced Marcia. "Traynor meets this someone at the pool and they engage in some sort of dalliance. Miss Gibney comes out and sees it. She's infuriated because Traynor is her property."

"That's pure fiction," I said.

"I know," Zack said, grinning at me. "We're inventing a story. So—Miss Gibney sees this thing taking place and she blows her stack. She conveniently doesn't remember it now, but she moves swiftly down the top side of the garden to the tool shed, puts on a pair of gloves, and takes the shears from its place on the wall. Then she comes stealthily back along the low side of the garden to the pool. Traynor's companion has by now retired to the house, and Miss Gibney— temporarily insane, we may say out of kindness—runs the shears through her false lover. She tosses away the gloves, but she has no time to escape because Palmer has appeared on the wall between the gargoyle fountains and is looking down at her. She can't invent a story to satisfy him on the spur of the moment, so she invents amnesia."

"I'm not sure you have the legal right to indulge in this kind of fantasying," I said.

"I sure do, boy," Zack said. "Under the law it's called inference from the facts. I have the right to infer anything I please from the facts. The weak spot in my inference is the sudden disappearance of the third party. It would be more watertight if we assume that the dalliance at the pool was between Traynor and Miss Gibney, and that you, Palmer, were the enraged witness. You knew very well where the tool shed was from your boyhood days around here. You armed yourself with the shears and you killed Traynor. Miss Gibney could have been shocked out of remembering by the violence of it, and because it was you, Palmer. Or because it was you she's decided to protect you at any cost."

"You keep going round and round in the same circle," I said. "Do I get a turn at inventing a story?"

"You must have sweated out a dozen of 'em in the last few hours," Zack said. "If you've got a good one, why not try it on us?"

I reached out and touched Laura's hand—for luck. And then I turned toward Mike Sayers who was studying me with a blank expression through his green glasses.

"I want to be sure Sergeant Sayers is listening," I said. "I've known him since we were kids. We've been through just about the same mill. I only hope he hasn't sold out."

"Meaning?" Zack asked, his eyebrows contracting.

"Meaning that everybody knows you sold out long ago, Zack. T.J. took you to the mountaintop and showed you the world, and you lied for him and he paid you off with a job—and probably with a substantial bank account."

"Do we have to listen to a rehash of this dreary small-town gossip?" T.J. asked in a tired but dangerous voice.

"Let him go on," Zack said. The glitter in his black eyes told me that if we ever met alone it was going to be him or me.

"I just want to be sure that someone listens who hasn't been brainwashed by T. J. Gibney's world," I said. "Are you listening, Mike?"

A little nerve twitched high up on Sayers' bronzed cheek, but he didn't speak or make any sign. There was no way to tell about him.

"There are a number of reasons for killing a man," I said. "You kill because somebody orders you to; I've done that too many times. You kill out of jealousy; that's the one Zack's bugged with. You kill for greed; no one here needs anything that a dead Julian Traynor could give. Finally, you kill because the person threatens you, places you in danger, might even destroy you. So I draw *my* inference, Zack. I infer that there was no reason for anyone to kill Julian Traynor except that he was a threat. So—who could he threaten and how?"

I turned to look straight at T.J. "For months Traynor has been digging into the history of the Gibney family and particularly into the personal life of T. J. Gibney. I infer that somehow, somewhere—under some stone or from behind the woodwork—Traynor came up with something that T. J. Gibney and the Gibney family couldn't afford to have made public. After months of discovering how the world is really run, I infer that Julian Traynor put the heat on T. J. Gibney or on some other member of the family. Pay up or face the music. I infer that Traynor had a strong hand and that the Gibneys knew they were hooked for life. The one flaw in Traynor's scheme was that he underestimated just how far the Gibney family would go to prevent being hooked. They would go the limit, the whole way."

"Now ain't that something," Zack said sarcastically.

"I infer further that Traynor had evidence, that the evidence is somewhere in his notes, in the tapes he made, or even locked away in a safety-deposit box somewhere. I infer that if you go through Traynor's possessions you will find what you need to wrap up this case, Zack. Unless—"

"Unless what, buster?" Zack said, and his tone was menacing.

"Unless it's too late," I said.

"It's just a matter of routine to go through Traynor's belongings," Mike Sayers said. Everybody turned to look at him. I think they'd all forgotten he was there. "To back up *your* theory, Mr. Zack, there could be letters from Miss Gibney to Traynor."

"There's just one more thing I'd like to make clear," I said. "You've chosen Laura and me as your pigeons. Neither one of us is going to answer any more questions without the advice of a lawyer."

"Well, I don't know about you, Palmer," T.J. said, "but Guy Maxwell should be here soon. He will, of course, represent Laura."

"You have to be kidding," I said. "You don't think I'd let Laura be represented by your lawyer, do you?"

T.J. seemed to swell up and I thought he was going to burst. "*You* won't let!"

"Laura isn't a Gibney any more," I said. "She's joined the opposition."

"Oh, my God," Lydia said softly. "Oh, my God."

For better or for worse I'd accomplished one thing. Zack and Sayers went upstairs to go through Traynor's bedroom and study. I'd been guessing, but if I'd guessed right I might have blown the ball game then and there. If there was anything damaging to T. J. Gibney upstairs it was a sure thing Zack would try to cover for him. If Mike Sayers had sold out too, then Traynor's secret—if he'd uncovered one—would stay a secret.

The moment the law headed upstairs, T.J. gave a little signal to his sons and the three of them disappeared into the house, leaving me on the terrace with the four women.

It was Marcia Gibney who broke the strained silence. "Coffee, Mr. Palmer?" she asked. She'd crossed to the buffet to pour herself a cup.

I didn't want coffee or anything else. I wanted out. I wanted a chance to think. I kept looking at Laura and that brought on visions I wanted to destroy.

"I don't suppose you and Laura can ever forgive T.J. for what happened long ago," Marcia said. She produced a bottle of saccharine from the pocket of her dress to sweeten her coffee. "But he is a fine man, a fair man, a decent man. His only problem is his temper. Don't try him beyond his capacity to control it, Mr. Palmer. Do you really think we won't do everything we can to protect Laura?"

"Protect her from what?" I asked.

"Why—why, the consequences of what she's done!" Marcia said. "Surely no one can believe that she was in possession of her faculties when she—when she did what she did."

"Please, Johnny, there's no point," Laura said before I could answer. "Don't you see, I'm being offered a Gibney kindness. I'm to be shipped to a mental institution instead of the deathhouse."

"Laura!" Lydia protested. She leaned her head back against her chair. I suspected the blue eyes were closed behind the black lenses. "For the love of God, tell me the truth, Laura."

"The truth about what, Mother?"

Lydia suddenly leaned forward, gripping the arms of her chair. "*What did you see this morning?*"

Laura shook her head from side to side. "I've told the truth, Mother. I don't know. I keep struggling to remember—but I don't know! It won't come back."

Sheila got into the act then with her high harsh voice. "Is there any way you can take her away from here, Johnny, so she can think without being badgered?"

"How?"

"My car's by the front door—the red Mercedes." She held out a set of keys to me. "Take it and get the hell out of here as fast as you can. You see what's going to happen, don't you? Zack will build up a case against one or both of you and then when Laura *does* remember it will be too late. They'll simply say she's inventing something to clear herself—or you, Johnny."

"I doubt we'd get fifty yards away from the house," I said. "There are other troopers. And running would make things look worse for us."

"Then don't let Laura out of your sight," Sheila said. Her usually laughing face was now a hard mask. "Somebody knows what Laura will remember, when and if she does."

Marcia stared at her sister-in-law. "Sheila! Are you trying to say that someone in the family might harm Laura to—to *keep* her from remembering?"

"That's exactly what I'm saying, my dear innocent dope! And God forbid it should be my man. Get away from here, Laura. Take the temptation away from them."

There was an anguished cry from Lydia as she covered her face with her hands.

"Tell her not to talk that way, Mother Gibney," Marcia said.

"Lydia knows how they are," Sheila said.

"Not murder," Lydia whispered. "Oh, please, not *murder*!"

"You think it was a passing tramp who killed Julian?" Sheila said. "Do you really believe it was Laura or Johnny?" She turned to us and the green cat's-eyes were brilliant. "If it was Bob, I warn you I'll lie you both into the electric chair if I have to." She tossed the car keys on the buffet and headed for the house. "I need a large slug of bourbon."

The trickle of sweat that ran down my back was cold. Someone must be choked with fear that Laura would remember the truth. Traynor's death had been planned, but one thing had gone wrong. Laura, who should have been asleep, had been an eyewitness to the murder.

"It's not as monstrous as Sheila paints it, or as you think it is, Laura," Lydia said. She sounded exhausted.

"You've defended Father all the years of your marriage," Laura said. "Don't try to whitewash him to me, Mother, I know him."

"I don't think you do. I don't think you could," Lydia said. "You haven't ever loved him."

Laura's wide blue eyes contracted. "Have you forgotten, Mother? Have you forgotten what every little girl feels about her father? Oh, I loved him—until he stamped it out, like someone putting out a fire."

"Was there ever anything you wanted that he didn't give you?" Lydia asked, a note of pleading in her throaty voice.

"Yes." The blue eyes flicked my way. "Understanding about Johnny Palmer."

"Truly, Laura, can you imagine any father who wouldn't have been outraged?"

"There's no use discussing it, Mother. You've been here this morning. You've watched the way he and Zack work together. It's clear, isn't it, that he's chosen me, or my friend Johnny, to pay for whatever's happened here. For God's sake, Mother, don't you understand what's going on? A man has been murdered, brutally, coldbloodedly. What does Father do? Does he ask who is guilty? No, he just wonders how it will come out best for him. Ideally it should be Johnny, an outsider, who did it. But if that won't stick, then it will be me, the daughter who has already publicly shamed him, who is clearly some kind of a rotten nut."

"You say you can't remember what happened!" Lydia's voice rose. "Perhaps Johnny—perhaps you—"

"Listen, Mother, I'll say it once for you, and also in a way for Johnny," Laura said. "I had no reason in the world to want Julian Traynor dead. There is nothing he could have done to me that would have made me want him dead. He came to see me in New York after Father's detectives found me. He was kind and sympathetic and he had the saving grace of being able to find some humor in the situation. A twenty-two-year-old girl fighting the Gibney powerhouse, not without success, amused him.

"But he pleaded your case well, Mother. He made me see that you weren't responsible for the things against which I'd rebelled. He convinced me that it would be a loving gesture to you if I came back here for Father's seventieth birthday. Would I want Julian dead for that? I love you, Mother. I was glad to come to the birthday party if it would make you happy."

"Laura!"

"Julian's attitude was modern—not like yours or Father's or even Johnny's. When he came to see me—three times I think it was—he realized I was living in a different world with different values. He took me somewhere and bought me a drink, then suggested, quite casually, that it would be fun if we went somewhere and made love. I said no, not because he was unattractive, but because of his close association with Father. I would be secretly doing it to hurt Father, and that would have been for the wrong reason. He understood. He said, 'Thanks anyway,' and 'See you around'—and that was that. I liked him for understanding. I had no reason on earth for wanting him hurt, let alone brutally murdered."

"If what you've forgotten is that he tried to force himself on you—?"

"Mother, I'm a big girl! Just maybe you can begin to understand that. Father doesn't want to. He decided long ago that I was a—I guess his words would be 'wanton' and 'jezebel.' It suits his dilemma this morning."

Marcia broke in, her gaunt face set in lines of tension. "Do you believe there's anything to Mr. Palmer's theory that Julian was trying to blackmail T.J.?"

"Or Emerson or Bob or the family image in general. What other reason on earth can there be? My God, Marcia, haven't we lived with that all our lives? Isn't there an entire office in New York staffed with people who do nothing but see to it that the Gibney name has a perpetually glowing halo over it? If Julian found out something that would ruin that image overnight and decided to use it to benefit himself, can you imagine the Gibneys hesitating one minute to stop him?"

"Emerson would never be involved in such a thing," Marcia said.

"My dear sister-in-law," Laura said bitterly, "Emerson is the most cold-blooded of the lot, because he's the weakest. Some day he will be king of the Gibney empire, and he can't risk having anything spoil that dream. He's put up with too much, been a glorified errand boy for too long."

I found myself looking at the keys that Sheila had left on the buffet. I moved casually toward the far end of the terrace to where I could see a part of the circular driveway in front of the house. I could see the red Mercedes and I knew it offered no escape for us. A trooper was leaning against it, talking to a second trooper and to Dr. Fred Marshall, the town health officer. It would have been necessary for him to view the body before it was removed. The doctor was a pleasant youngish man whom I'd known ever since I could remember. Somehow it was a relief to see him there. He was his own man and I knew nobody could buy him. I stepped outside the screen door where he could see me and signaled to him.

He came up the path, his black bag tucked under one arm, wiping the sweat band of his Panama hat with a handkerchief.

"Pretty rugged situation, Johnny," he said. "I'm not the Gibney family doctor, but I was going to offer my services. I understand that Laura is in some kind of shock." As he spoke he could see her with Lydia and Marcia, through the screen.

I guess he'd already been brought up to date but I told him how things were with Laura and about my own experiences with that kind of shock case.

"If Zack keeps hammering at her," I said, "it may close the door tight. Meanwhile—"

"She may be in real danger," Marshall said. He looked at the women. "Logically she should go to the hospital, be carefully sedated, and given a chance to come out of it with her nerve ends less raw."

"So take her to the hospital. She could be protected there." Even as I said it I thought, bitterly, the name of the hospital was The Horace Gibney Memorial Hospital.

"I can't take her out of here against her will, and I can't take her out of here without Zack's approval," Marshall said.

"Not if staying here endangers her health and sanity?"

"We can give it a try," Marshall said.

He led the way back into the screened area. He put his hat and medical bag on a table by the door. He wore his grayish hair crewcut. He reminded me of a colonel I'd had in Vietnam, a tough but compassionate man.

"I'm so sorry for your trouble, Mrs. Gibney," he said to Lydia. He nodded to the others. "Marcia—Laura."

"Hello, Dr. Fred," Laura said.

"I had to come here in my official capacity as the town health officer," Marshall said. "I wondered, Mrs. Gibney, if there is any way I could be helpful to you. Unofficially, I mean."

"It's very nice of you, Doctor," Lydia said.

He smiled at Laura. "I understand you have some problems, young lady."
I saw that her lips were trembling.

"It's a pretty terrifying experience, Dr. Fred," she said, "not remembering something that happened just a little while ago and—*and not really wanting to remember*!"

"That's why you're not remembering—because you don't want to," he said, as casually as though he were discussing the weather. "You got up, you walked out into the garden, and you saw something so shocking that your mind had to blot it out. Since then you haven't relaxed for an instant. Your nerves must be tight as piano wires. There may be the simplest kind of way out of it. Let me take you to the hospital, place you under sedation that'll let you sleep around the clock and relax all your tensions. When you wake up it's two-to-one you'll remember everything just as clearly as though you'd never forgotten it."

Her eyelids fluttered. "I'm not sure—"

"You'll have to face it sooner or later," he said. His smile was gentle. "It would put an end to all the uncertainty here."

Laura looked at me and her eyes were brimming with tears. I could guess what she was thinking. For all her bitterness, for all her rebellion and anger, she didn't want to be the one to point a finger at anyone, friend or enemy.

"There are no uncertainties here, Doctor, that we aren't quite competent to handle," T.J.'s harsh voice said from the doorway. Emerson and Bob were just behind him. The council of war was over. "Dr. Von Glahn is on his way here. He'll look after Laura."

Von Glahn, I knew, was the Gibneys' doctor. He had recently retired as chief surgeon of The Horace Gibney Memorial Hospital.

"I prefer to have Dr. Fred take care of me," Laura said.

"Whoever takes care of you, Miss Gibney, is going to have to do it here," Zack said. He had come up behind Bob and Emerson. "Unless Dr. Marshall is prepared to state that it's actually dangerous for you to be treated here. And wherever you go, Miss Gibney, one of my men is going to be with you, in the room where you are. That memory of yours could pop back just as quickly as it popped away. I want someone on hand when that happens."

T.J. turned to Zack. "You find anything of interest among Traynor's effects?"

Zack shrugged. "Take days to go through all his notes and tapes." He looked back at Laura. "Just tell me where you'd like to settle in, Miss Gibney, so I can station a man there with you."

"You ought to go to bed," Marshall said. "You ought to take something that will relax you and let you sleep."

"Von Glahn will take care of that, thank you, Doctor," T.J. said.

"I don't want Dr. Von Glahn!" Laura said. "Have you got any legal right to keep me here, Mr. Zack?"

"Yes, ma'am," Zack said. "Material witness to a homicide. Here, in the hospital, or in the county jail." He grinned at me. "Same goes for you, Palmer. It would be better here, I should think—more chance that Miss Gibney's memory may stop troubling her—here, where it happened."

My mouth began to feel dry and cottony. They'd worked it out, I thought. Laura would be taken somewhere into the upper regions of the house, put to sleep, guarded by Zack, attended by Von Glahn. How simple for them! "Poor girl, she just never woke up!"

"Well, since I can't be of any help—" Dr. Marshall said. He turned toward his hat and medical bag.

"Wait!" My voice sounded so loud it startled me. "Wait, Dr. Fred!"

He looked back at me. I thought he was a little irritated at the way T.J. had brushed off his offer.

"Dr. Fred, listen to me," I said. I was aware that the entire household was staring at me. I imagined there was something diabolical about the group in the doorway—T.J., Emerson, Bob and Zack. "There is someone here, perhaps the whole family, who can't afford to have Laura remember what she saw this morning. Do you understand that?"

"Yes, Johnny," he said quietly. "But if you're concerned for her safety, Mr. Zack has indicated she'll be under guard at all times. There'll be a trooper with her."

"Can a trooper prevent a medical murder, Dr. Fred?" I shouted at him. "Can a trooper prevent them from fixing it so that she'll never wake up? Dr. Von Glahn is T.J.'s man. Mr. Zack is T.J.'s man. These are all T.J.'s people, and they can't afford to have Laura remember. Don't you understand that?"

"Why, you crazy—" I heard Zack say softly.

For just a moment I thought there was a cloud of doubt in Dr. Marshall's eyes. Then it cleared away. He came over and put a steadying hand on my arm.

"You've got yourself worked up into hysteria, Johnny," he said. "Dr. Von Glahn is a highly reputable man. If you think he'd be a party to—oh, no, Johnny. Better take it easy."

He picked up his hat and bag and walked out into the hot sunshine. And Laura and I were now alone with the enemy.

They worked it like a well-tuned motor.

Dr. Von Glahn must have passed Dr. Fred on the driveway as he came in. He was a handsome old gent with silver-white hair and white mustache and goatee. He'd evidently been well briefed on the phone before he'd started out. His attitude toward Laura was deferential and kindly. His suggestion for treatment was perfectly sound: rest under sedation with the hope that, properly relaxed after a period of sleep, the memory block would vanish.

"If you will get this young lady ready for bed, Lydia—" He was an old friend, I imagined, a frequent social guest. His bedside manner was calculated to make you feel complete trust in him. I almost convinced myself that Dr. Fred had been right. Von Glahn was a man of integrity; he couldn't be bought. Laura would be safe in his care and with a trooper on guard—

Almost.

I looked around at the stonefaced T.J., at Bob who had lost all vestiges of his normal, macabre good humor, at Emerson, pale as ashes. This was not a concerned family—not concerned for Laura's safety. They were only concerned—nearly panicked—by what it was she could remember.

Lydia, moving like an automaton, put her arm around Laura and led her into the house. Laura offered no resistance. She had thrown in the towel, I thought.

Zack gave orders to Sayers in my presence. One of the troopers in the yard, a man named Getliffe, was to be placed on guard, either in or just outside Laura's room.

Marcia tagged along to help with Laura, and T.J. and his two sons and Zack retired once more to the Old Man's study. I was left alone with Mike Sayers.

"You think I'm off my rocker, don't you, Mike?"

The green tinted glasses swiveled past me toward the study door at the far end of the great entrance hall.

"I agree with you that the Old Man is just what you think he is," he said, "but I think you're way off your rocker when you suggest that he—and the rest of the family—would harm a daughter just to keep her from remembering. And I know you're way off your rocker when you suggest that Von Glahn might be a party to it. As for Zack, he's mean, tough, sadistic—but he's a first-class investigator. Maybe he's accepted a favor here and there, but I don't think he can be bought."

"You trust this trooper Getliffe?"

"All the way," Sayers said. He took off his green glasses, blew on them, and began to wipe them with a clean handkerchief. For the first time I got a look at his level gray eyes. "You and I have seen what the top brass is like in the Service," he said. "Singletrack minds. That's how they get to be generals. And that's how you get to be rich, I guess. Ruthless and headed only in one direction. But murder your own flesh and blood?" He put his glasses back on. "I've got to get a report written up."

"No one ever understands how far they'll go," I said. He wasn't listening. "One thing. When you first got here this morning did you notice smoke coming out of one of the chimneys?"

"No, I didn't notice. Probably burning trash."

"At five in the morning?"

"Big birthday party last night. The cleanup lasted till after daylight, according to the help."

I didn't mention the sanitation truck to him. You may ask why not. I didn't go to Simmons, who had been the Gibney's butler for years and who was in charge of the domestic corps, and ask him what they had been burning in the cellar incinerator at dawn. You may ask why not. So maybe I was off my rocker, but I had a feeling that there would be carefully prepared answers to everything.

I was convinced that Julian Traynor had died because he had something on somebody in this big stone fortress. If there had been notes or tapes covering that "something," there was a good chance that's what had been hurriedly burned at dawn. There was a good chance too that there might be remnants of whatever it had been still in the incinerator. If I suggested that to anyone I would be guaranteeing that someone would make certain those remnants would never be found.

When we were kids we used to call the cellar under the big stone house The Catacombs. There were endless corridors and rooms, old coal bins transformed into storage areas, a carpenter shop which was a hobby of Emerson's, enormous brass boilers, furnaces, a garden room where Lydia grew seedlings under fluorescent lights, a paneled game room where there was still, I imagined, a ping-pong table and a billiard table, laundry rooms, the machinery for an elevator that had been built in when some Gibney developed a heart condition, and two hand-operated dumb-waiters that came down from the kitchen area. You could actually get lost in The Catacombs if you didn't know your way around.

One of the old coal furnaces, installed before modern conversion to oil heat, had been left for use as an incinerator. I wanted to have a look at it—just in case. I wanted to find out if someone in a hurry had neglected to make certain that everything burned in that incinerator this morning had not been reduced to ashes.

I remembered that on the north side of the house there was an outside entrance to The Catacombs. To try to go down from inside the house was to risk a head-on encounter with a member of the family, or with one of the horde of servants milling around in the kitchen area where the inside stairway went down into the cellar.

I opened the screen door and walked off the terrace into the now blazing sunlight. There was the faint sound of a radio going somewhere, and I saw that it came from a trooper car now parked just behind Sheila's Mercedes. A trooper, his wide-brimmed hat pulled down to shield his eyes from the sun, was slumped down behind the wheel listening to the short-wave calls, presumably from his barracks. It was obviously his job to see that none of the family cars left the grounds. There was a shiny black Cadillac parked just beyond the trooper, its license plate indicating that it was Dr. Von Glahn's.

I turned right, walking as casually and aimlessly as I could in case the trooper was watching me. A glittering reflection on the flagstone path in front of me made me look up. The sun was striking full on the big brass bell in the cupola. Horace Gibney had installed that bell almost a century ago, I remembered being told, before there were telephones in the big house, as an alarm system in case help was needed from the village.

I rounded the corner of the house. There didn't seem to be anyone in sight. From some distance away I heard the whir of a power lawn mower but no one was visible on this side of the house. A few yards away I saw the pair of heavy cellar doors, painted green. I'd have to lift them and go down a flight of stone steps to the main cellar door. If that was locked it would take a medieval battering ram to force it open.

I got to the surface doors and lifted one of them. It appeared nobody had opened them for a long time. The crevices were caked with leaves and dirt. It took all the strength I had to loosen the door and then lift it. A blast of damp cool air came up out of the stairwell.

I looked around. Still no one in sight. I went down the steps to the heavy iron-bound main door. It was almost wide enough to drive a truck through. There was an antique wrought-iron latch which stubbornly resisted being moved, but finally I worked it free, put my shoulder against the door, and pushed. After a few moments of strong pressure it gave reluctantly.

I went back up the steps and pulled the open outer door down over my head so that no one from the outside could notice that The Catacombs had been entered. As the door thudded down above me I was suddenly in pitch-darkness.

I made my way down again, my hands feeling along the damp stone wall. I had to push open the big inner door a little wider to make enough room for me to squeeze through into the cellar. It was still totally dark, but I could hear the hum of some sort of machinery and the faint sound of water in the pipes overhead.

There was a certain logic to the idea that there would be a light switch somewhere just inside the door, and presently I found it. One low-watt electric bulb went on in the ceiling a few yards away from me. Stacked around the walls were snow shovels, garden tools, an old toboggan and sleds which probably hadn't been used since the children had grown up. It looked like a neat attic stored with things that would never be used again in a lifetime.

But I got my bearings. A sort of wide corridor would lead the underground length of the house, with rooms opening off both sides. On the left would be Emerson's workshop, the tools, the special stacks of plywood and lumber, all kept in precise order. On the right would be the game room, with the billiard table and the ping-pong gear. On the left again would be Lydia's indoor greenhouse with its fluorescent lights beaming down on the red-clay flowerpots with their eager seedlings.

As I moved along the corridor I saw the glow of that artificial sunlight throwing a cone of light across my path. Just beyond that I knew the corridor opened into a huge room which contained the converted oil burners, the hot-water tanks—and the incinerator-furnace.

I moved quickly, not bothering with lights until I passed the greenhouse and realized I was in the big utility room. I found the light switch, flipped it on, and stood facing my objective. Somehow, in the cold glare of the naked light bulbs, the pipes and furnace looked like a monstrous Rube Goldberg invention.

I touched the outer surface of the old incinerator-furnace. The surface was warm, not hot. The fire that had burned something not long ago was dead. I opened the firebox door but I couldn't see anything inside. I put my face close to the opening and clicked on my cigarette lighter, and suddenly was aware of the odor of burned cloth.

I was looking for scraps of paper—notes—or bits of tape that Traynor had used in his recording machine. I couldn't see any such remains, but in one corner of the firebox my lighter disclosed a small piece of something white. I reached in and retrieved it. It was a piece of cloth, about the size of an old-fashioned pocket watch, charred around the edges.

When I looked at it closely it appeared to be a piece of toweling, or perhaps terrycloth from a robe. I stood scowling at it as my light slowly faded and went out. I turned to move closer to the electric-light bulb which would give me a better light, and the bulb went out leaving me in darkness. I spun the flint wheel on my lighter and got only sputtering sparks.

And then, instinctively, I did a rolling dive to my right across the floor.

I wasn't alone. Someone, breathing hard, had charged straight at my sparking lighter.

"Lights!" a voice said sharply.

The naked bulb came on again. On his hands and knees, at about the spot where I'd been before I rolled away, was Bob Gibney, a smear of dirt on his yellow shirtfront and on the knees of his yellow slacks.

At the door to this area, his hand on the light switch, was Emerson, squinting at me through his owlish glasses. And blocking the exit behind me, looking like a prehistoric giant, was T. J. Gibney.

"What did he find?" T.J. asked.

"Must have been a piece of cloth left," Bob said, rising and brushing the knees of his slacks. He was smiling at me but it was a smile totally lacking in humor. "You stupid cluck!" he said. "Why couldn't you mind your own business?"

I still had the little piece of white cloth clutched in my right hand. My lighter had skidded away across the floor. I got to my feet, stuffing the piece of cloth into my jacket pocket. My right shoulder hurt where I'd banged it against the concrete floor.

Not so many months ago I'd walked into a clearing in a South Vietnam swampland and suddenly found myself surrounded by a squad of Vietcong. I knew then that I was dead. I had the same heart-clutching certainty now. In Vietnam a miracle had happened. A 'copter had swept in out of nowhere, spraying the enemy with machine-gun fire. I'd made a headlong dive into a gully, and then the chopper landed and picked me up.

There was going to be no chopper to save me here.

"Is there any point in trying to reason with him?" Emerson asked.

"Never reason with an honest man," Bob said bitterly.

"If you hadn't been an idiot and burned the damn thing, Emerson," T.J. said. He was clenching his huge fists. The cellar was cool but I could see the beads of sweat on his forehead.

"Whatever you have in mind," I heard myself say, "you know you can't get away with it. How would you explain my disappearance, if that's what it's to be?"

"Suppose we ask you, Johnny," Bob said. He took a couple of tentative steps toward me. "We want that piece of cloth you found. We want your silence. We want Laura's silence. How do we get those things?"

"There's a price," Emerson said. "There has to be a price."

"So name it, Johnny," Bob said.

"Economic security," Emerson said. "Freedom to make a life with Laura—if she'll promise to keep on forgetting."

"All he wants," T.J. said in a bitter voice, "is to get out of this cellar in one piece and start blabbing. You can't buy anything from his kind. I tell you, he'll promise anything and talk his head off the minute he's safe."

"I'm sorry, Johnny," Bob said. "I have to agree with T.J. You're a hopeless case."

It came to me like a sudden tornado. Bob launched himself at me, a yellow streak in the semidarkness. I should have guessed how rough he could be. He'd spent his whole life staying in shape, learning the arts of violence just for the fun of it. I should have guessed he would know the techniques of karate—and of killing.

True, I had learned the countermoves by heart in special guerilla warfare training, but you have to be a special kind of person to use them without any hesitation. You temporize for just a split second, thinking that what's happening can't be true—and then it's too late.

I went hurtling over Bob Gibney's shoulder to smash into the concrete wall. He was on me almost before I could struggle to my knees. And now he wasn't alone.

T.J. had my right arm, twisting it into an agonizing lock behind my back, and I saw Emerson coming at me with some sort of iron bar or poker in his hands. Bob, directly in front of me, smashed at my face with bone-crushing fists. The pain was unbelievable. I tasted blood and my vision was a red fog.

I managed somehow to twist to one side and launch a kick at the Old Man's groin with everything I had left. I heard him scream out in agony and the paralyzing armlock was released. I saw him reel away, double over, grab at himself.

My head nearly came off my neck as Bob Gibney caught me with a haymaker right to the jaw and then I was caught in another karate chop and thrown violently against the wall again. I slid down to a sitting position, making some kind of animal sounds in an almost paralyzed throat. I saw Emerson standing over me, the iron bar raised to smash my skull. I remember covering my head with my arms in a futile gesture of defense.

And then I heard it. The bell! The great brass bell in the cupola was ringing wildly. I saw Emerson freeze, his face turned away and up. Bob, whose hand was drawn back ready for a lethal throat chop at my Adam's apple, was a yellow statue. A few yards away T.J. was down on his knees moaning, "Oh, my God! Oh, my God!"

Then there were women's voices, loud and hysterical, and the clatter of feet on the wooden stairway leading down from the kitchen, and then, of all things, the glistening bald head of Manuel Zack as he leaned over me.

"What the holy hell is going on here?" I heard him ask, before I slipped away into blackness and void. . .

I opened my eyes to look up into the pale face of Dr. Von Glahn. I could feel him gently touching the bruises on my face and head, and his hands weren't steady. Sunlight was pouring through an open window, and the sun felt warm and reassuring. I tried moving and let out a yelp. There wasn't an inch of my body that wasn't in agony, but my legs and arms moved. I saw the red tip of Von Glahn's tongue moisten his lips.

"He's coming around," he said.

"Thank God," I heard a voice say; I recognized it as Sheila Gibney's.

"Don't try to sit up," Von Glahn said, as I made the effort.

But I made it. They'd stretched me out on a couch in the high-ceilinged living room, just inside from the terrace. I reached in my pocket and felt for the little piece of cloth I'd found in the incinerator. Whatever it meant, the Gibney men had been prepared to murder me in cold blood to get it.

Sheila Gibney was standing just behind the doctor. Her cat's-eyes had lost their brilliance, but, like her husband just before he'd tried to kill me, she was forcing a smile.

"I told you I'd lie you into the electric chair, Johnny, if Bob was involved," she said. "You know what happened? I turned into a Swiss bellringer."

"*You* rang the bell?" I sounded as though I had a bad laryngitis. One of Bob Gibney's chopping blows had caught me in the neck.

"I had to get you help somehow," she said.

"Why?"

"Before Bob was in this mess beyond recall," she said.

My own smile was internal. I couldn't move my swollen lips enough to show it. "How much deeper do you want him to get than attempted homicide?" I asked. "Those three meant to kill me. I'm not likely to let them off that hook. I was within one bell-ring of having my skull smashed in like an eggshell." I looked at Von Glahn. "Laura?"

"Asleep. Safe," Von Glahn said.

"Can I talk to her?"

"In six or eight hours. She won't come around before that."

I looked back at Sheila. "I'd like it if someone would tell me what this is all about," I said.

"Zack's got everyone in T.J.'s study," she said. "I was to let them know if you were able to join them."

"I can make it." I wished I hadn't tried when I stood up.

I walked across what seemed like miles of entrance hall to the door of the study. Sheila knocked and Mike Sayers promptly opened it from the inside.

It was a beautiful book-lined room, furnished with heavy green-leather furniture—couches and armchairs—and a huge flat-topped desk carved by some Florentine artist.

Bob and Emerson were sitting side by side on one of the couches, like two schoolboys called into the principal's office. I noticed, with some satisfaction, that Bob's handsome face was a little chewed up.

T.J., looking a little green, was sitting in the tremendous armchair behind his desk, his heavy eyelids almost closed. I knew he was aware of my entrance but he made no sign, spoke no words. Lydia, her eyes shielded by the black glasses against the sunlight that streamed through the east windows, sat like a motionless statue in a straight-backed chair across the room from her husband. A little nerve kept jerking under one cheekbone.

Manuel Zack stood just behind T.J.'s chair, his face deadpan. Off to the right of the desk a trooper sat in front of a stenotype machine. Mike Sayers guarded the door.

Zack looked at me. "You okay?"

"Guess again," I said.

"Find yourself a place to sit," he said.

Sheila, who had come in with me, touched my arm and we sat down together on the empty couch which faced her husband and Emerson.

"We're just getting started here," Zack said. "Read back from the beginning."

The stenotype operator fingered the paper tape. "Question: You care to make a statement, Mr. Gibney? T. J. Gibney: I'm ready. Mr. Zack: Go ahead then. T. J. Gibney: I killed Julian Traynor. I arranged to meet him at the pool during the party. When everybody was in bed he went down for a swim and I followed him a few minutes later. Mr. Zack: Was it daylight? T. J. Gibney: It was just getting light."

There was something eerie about listening to the words read in the trooper's monotone voice.

"Mr. Zack: You went down to the pool prepared to kill him? T. J. Gibney: I was prepared to kill him. I went to the tool shed first and got those garden shears. Unless I could make Traynor listen to reason I meant to kill him. Mr. Zack: Reason with him about what?" The trooper looked up. "That's as far as we'd gotten, Mr. Zack."

"All right, I repeat the question, T.J.," Zack said. "Reason with him about what?"

The heavy eyelids lifted. "He was blackmailing me," T.J. said. "I had to arrange for a payoff that I knew he would honor, or get rid of him, permanently."

"What did he have on you?"

"Don't be a fool, Zack. If I would risk killing him to keep it a secret, am I likely to tell you what it was now? We talked about a money payoff and he just laughed at me. He wanted more than money. He wanted power and position. I saw that I was saddled with him for the rest of my life, so—so I ran him through with the shears."

"And then?"

"I threw away the gloves I was wearing, left the shears there on the grass, and came back to the house."

"Were you aware that Miss Laura Gibney had seen you?"

T.J.'s mouth twitched. "No, I wasn't."

"What happened then?"

"I woke my two sons and told them what I'd done. I needed their help."

"Help to do what?"

"To get rid of Traynor's body, for one thing. He'd been planning to go into New York. I thought of dressing the body, putting it in his car, and then wrecking the car somewhere down the line."

"You said, 'for one thing.' What other thing?"

"He had evidence of what he was holding over me. Certain documents—and I thought he might have made a tape in case anything happened to him. I told Emerson to look for those items and to burn them if he found them."

"And did he do what you asked?"

"Yes. He found the evidence and he burned it in the incinerator in the cellar. Bob and I went out to deal with the body. We were too late. My daughter and Palmer had already discovered it."

"So you decided to frame one or both of them and you called me and you fed me a large wad of malarkey," Zack said, his voice angry.

"I had to throw you off the trail. If Laura and Johnny really got cornered I'd have come forward," T.J. said.

"You say!" Zack said, his voice rising. "But you and your sons were ready to kill again when you found Palmer nosing around the incinerator."

"Let me make one thing clear to you," T.J. said grimly. "If Emerson botched the burning of that evidence and Palmer found it I had the same situation on my hands all over again."

"And your sons were willing to help you kill Palmer?"

"To get back the evidence. To make certain," T.J. said.

"It must have been quite a thing that Julian Traynor found out about you," Zack said. He turned to Emerson. "What exactly was it you burned, Mr. Gibney?"

Emerson moistened his lips. "Some—some papers and—and a tape," he said.

"Did Palmer have parts of those papers and that tape when you found him in the basement?"

"We—we thought he must have," Emerson said.

Zack turned to me. "What *did* you find, Palmer?"

T.J. and his two sons were staring at me. I had the feeling they were silently pleading with me not to speak. I didn't feel kindly toward them, to make the understatement of the year. I reached in my pocket and took out the small piece of charred toweling.

"*That's* what you found?" Zack asked, his eyes widening.

"That's all there was," I said. "The rest was ashes."

"And they tried to kill you for *that*?"

There was a kind of choking sound. I turned my head and I saw that it had come from Lydia. She had risen from her chair, her hands locked, her knuckles white.

"I'm sorry to have caused you so much trouble and the loss of so much time," she said in an oddly reasonable voice.

"Lydia, stop it!" T.J. bellowed at her.

Bob and Emerson were on their feet. "Forget it, Mother," Bob said. "There's a way to ride this out. Trust us."

Lydia ignored the men in her family. "That little piece of cloth, Mr. Zack, is the remains of a terrycloth coat of mine. It was rather horribly bloodstained, which is why the boys burned it. You see, I killed Julian Traynor."

T.J. lowered his head onto his clenched fists resting on the desk. His big shoulders heaved. We all watched, hypnotized, as Lydia moved to him and put one of her hands on his shoulder.

"I'm sorry, my darling," Lydia said gently. She made an unexpected gesture. She rolled up the sleeve of her sweater and held out her arm toward Zack. "As you can see, Mr. Zack, I have been a narcotics addict for some time."

"Oh, God," Bob Gibney said, and turned toward Sheila. There were tears in his eyes and I saw Sheila hold out her hand to him.

"I would prefer, in a more private moment, to give you the details—if you must have them, Mr. Zack," Lydia said. "I have had problems in my life—with alcohol and—and with other things." Her hand tightened on T.J.'s shoulder. "When Julian came to live here while he worked on the Gibney book I liked him. He seemed such a kindly, warm, understanding young man, full of gentle humor. I—I found myself thrown with him a great deal, and of course he had many questions to ask me about T.J.—all quite natural. I was almost old enough to be his mother, you understand.

"Then one day he discovered my secret—a secret I thought I'd managed to keep from my family. I expected, if anything, help and sympathy from him. Instead he became a kind of monster. He found a way to control my supply." Her mouth trembled. "He forced me to become his creature. I must come to his room whenever he said so. I must meet him in New York whenever he said so. I—I became his slave. I—I have been quietly going out of my mind.

"I said he had found a way to control my supply of heroin. Last night, before the party, I needed it desperately. He held out on me. He said he would give it to me when the party was over. I was to meet him at the pool where we could be alone. He implied there would be new demands—money demands. I knew he would ask for more than I could give him without T.J.'s finding out the truth. I could not bear to have that happen."

She touched T.J.'s bearded cheek with her fingers. "T.J. would have believed I could stop by sheer will power. It meant cold turkey. You know what that means, Mr. Zack?

"I guess I went a little out of my mind. I decided I couldn't stand another day of Julian—not another hour of him. So I decided, quite unhysterically, to kill him. After the party I changed into some garden clothes and my terrycloth coat. It was quite cool just before morning. I went to the tool shed and got a pair of gloves and the shears and then went to the pool to wait for him.

"Julian wasn't surprised to see the shears and the garden gloves. I often did work in my garden in the dawn hours. I—I don't sleep well." She took a deep breath, then went on, "He told me what his new demands were—the money— and how it was to be delivered to him. And I sat there beside him, listening, and I told myself I would—I would count to ten and then I would kill him. So I began to count, slowly, to myself. And—and when I came to ten I—I plunged the shears into his body.

"He—he tumbled backwards into the pool, but as he fell—well, blood spurted out of him and all over my terrycloth coat. I dropped the shears and threw away the gloves. And then—"

She suddenly lifted her hands and covered her face, her whole body shaking as though she'd had some kind of seizure. But she controlled it. "And then somebody started screaming and I looked up the bank toward the house, and there was Laura. I cried out to her and she turned away from me. I—I started up after her and when I got to the top of the bank T.J. came running out of the house and then Bob and Emerson were there. And I told them.

"They got me into the house and Emerson took my bloodstained coat and T.J. kept telling me he'd protect me and the truth need never come out and that surely Laura could be persuaded to keep silent when she knew the truth. But—but when they found Laura, Johnny was with her and Laura had gone into shock, and there was no way of telling what would happen when she came out of it. We could only wait and see.

"I've sometimes thought T.J.'s way of handling things was—was evil. But in all honesty I hoped he would be successful this time. I—I have no regrets about killing Julian Traynor. He was—he was monstrous." She drew another deep breath. "And that's the way it was, Mr. Zack."

No one spoke. No one moved for a few moments, and then T.J. got up from his chair and put an arm around his wife.

"I would have protected you from this, any way on earth, Lydia," he said. He looked over the top of her head at us. "She was driven beyond endurance by that blackguard!" he said. "There must be a way we can help her." He looked at me. "Johnny, I'm sorry. We've all gone a little out of our heads, I guess. When you found that piece of cloth we knew that sooner or later it would be traced to my wife. We were all ready to do anything on earth to save her. I would have smashed you or anyone else in the world to save her."

He meant it. He would have taken the rap for her if she had let him.

"I won't complicate your situation, Mr. Gibney, by bringing charges against you and your sons—on one condition," I said.

"What condition?"

"I'd like to wait in Laura's room till she wakes up," I said. "I'd like to be with her then. If she wakes up remembering, it's going to be a very bad time for her."

Lydia looked at me, and two large tears were running down under the rims of her black glasses. "She may never want to lay eyes on me again, Johnny. Be kind to her. Please, be kind to her."

"I promise," I said.

My Brother's Keeper

I have a theory that when identical twins are born, the one born second must be the one who lacks originality. This, I believe, was certainly true in the case of my brother Joseph and myself. He lacked originality, I think, even in his criminal turn of mind. Thus, when he proposed that we be partners in crime—that one twin would commit the crime and the other would have himself "seen" in another city so as to establish an alibi "proving" that the perpetrator actually must have been somewhere else—all he was doing, in truth, was reacting to a newspaper story he had read back in the 1950's, describing two identical twins who were on the F.B.I.'s wanted list. They were jewel thieves. One would stick up a store in San Francisco while the other was in Chicago, living a normal and extremely public life.

"It's foolproof, Eddie," Joe said to me.

"It isn't foolproof, Joe," I said to him. "If it was, the F.B.I. wouldn't know about it."

We looked alike, we walked alike, we talked alike—but we thought quite differently. Our only real physical difference was that for some strange reason—again, I believe, the result of my having been born first—Joe's feet were bigger than mine, nearly two sizes larger. This, in my judgment, was a compensation—nature's way, if you like, of giving him more feet to make up for less head.

By "less head" I mean, if you please, less brains. One does not like to talk this way about his own identical twin, but the truth is the truth.

I say these things, too, more in sorrow than anger, for I was not only Joe's brother but his lawyer as well, and when he went to jail for embezzlement, Miss Bates and I were the only visitors he ever had. Miss Bates is my secretary. We used to visit Joe together at the State Prison. Because I was his lawyer we were entitled to visit with him not in the large Visitors' Room, where a glass-and-wire barrier separates you from the prisoner, but in the so-called "lawyer's room," which was a private cubicle. This is standard procedure in most prisons, but it fascinated my brother Joe.

"You could slip a knife to me," he suggested.

"I could," I said, "but I won't. All it would result in would be more trouble for you and me."

"So I rot in jail," he said.

"You do not rot in jail," I said. "I'm arranging for your parole."

"Nobody would ever know about the knife," he said. "They're very loose about things around here."

"Less loose than you think," I told him.

"What about Miss Bates coming here?" he said.

"What about her?"

"She signs your signature in the Visitors' Book," he said, "and nobody ever notices."

"What difference does that make?"

"She can imitate your signature close enough to fool them," he said.

"So what?" I said. "She's from my office and she's with me. All she does is sign my name. Imitating my signature doesn't have anything to do with it."

"But she *can*," he said. "Can't you, Miss Bates?"

"Yes," Miss Bates said. "When I was in college I worked in the office of the lieutenant governor, signing his name to letters and proclamations. I am very good at imitating signatures."

"You see?" Joe said to me.

"I do not see," I said.

"What do you need to get away with forgery?" Joe said. "You need somebody who can imitate somebody else's handwriting. With Miss Bates here, we have it ready-made. She can imitate any signature she sees. The three of us together could—"

And he was off again, sitting there in jail, outlining a new career in crime— and one just as unoriginal as the one that had put him behind bars. After a while Fat Louis, the prison guard, rapped on the door and said, "Time's up." I was never so happy to see anyone in my life.

In due course Joe's parole came through. We got him a job in a foundry and turned him toward a gainful life; but always in the back of his mind, I knew, was one of those silly schemes of his, and when he started dating Miss Bates I reacted badly.

"He doesn't want you for yourself," I warned Miss Bates. "He wants you for your penmanship."

"No," she said. "It is a physical thing."

"He wants to make a criminal out of you," I insisted.

"No," she said. "He wants to make a fallen woman out of me."

"Has he succeeded?"

"No."

"Well," I said. "He has a job and a car. He is a member of society once again. He's entitled to a sex life, I suppose. But not with you, Miss Bates. I have designs on you myself."

"So I noticed," she said.

"Then why do you keep seeing him?"

"For exactly the opposite reason that you suppose," she said. "In my own way I'm trying to rehabilitate him. Not join him in crime, as you seem to believe."

"But you're not attracted to him?"

"No."

"Then you shouldn't lead him on," I said.

"If you don't want me to I won't," she said.

This conversation, occurring as it did in my bachelor apartment at six o'clock in the morning, was the first inkling I had that Miss Bates was willing to be not just my woman, but my only woman. It was at that precise point that I proposed marriage to her, and she accepted. It was at approximately half a minute past that precise point that I realized how clever a woman can be: by playing up to Joe she had forced a proposal from me, which was exactly what she had wanted.

And the pleasant thing was that I was completely happy about it.

I began to tell her how happy I was. As I did so, the doorbell rang. I went to answer it in my pajamas, and it was Joe standing there.

"Let me in," he said. "I think I did something wrong."

I let him into the living room. "What do you mean, you did something wrong?"

"Violated my parole," he said.

"How?"

"Went out of the state. To Las Vegas. Gambled. Won $2000."

"Oh, for God's sake," I said.

"You'll have to cover up for me," he said.

"Did anybody see you there?"

"I think so. I signed some checks."

"That was smart."

"It occurred to me," he said, "if I could marry Miss Bates—"

"If you could *what*?"

"If I could marry Miss Bates," he said, "then everything might be all right. I could say I won the $2000 as a wedding present. It would be a human-interest thing. The parole people would understand."

"The parole people would not—"

"You don't understand," he said to me. "They'd like the idea I've been keeping company with such a nice girl. It's part of my becoming a good citizen again."

"Ah," I said. "I do understand."

"I knew you would," he said.

"What I understand," I said, "is that this is another one of your worthless, unoriginal ideas."

"But I love her."

"That's not enough. You'd be better off if you just cool it. Don't tell anybody anything. Maybe you won't be reported. Maybe they won't examine your canceled checks."

"But this way—"

"This way," I said, "all you do is call attention to yourself, and all that will do is make trouble. You know what it means when you violate parole? It's back in the can for good. I'm your lawyer, but I won't be able to help you. This time there's no bail, no trial, not even an arraignment. They just take you, cart you off, slap you back in the cell, and forget you."

He was thinking. "Maybe you're right," he said. "But then, what do I do with the money?"

"The money?"

"The $2000 I won."

"I don't know. Whatever you do, don't spend it. And don't carry it around with you."

"Can I leave it here?"

"I'd rather you didn't."

"But you're my brother," he said.

"I know I'm your brother."

"Besides," he said, "there's the gun."

"The gun?"

He took a pistol out of his pants pocket.

"Where'd you get that?" I said.

"It was one of those things," he said.

Stupid Joe. My twin brother Joe.

"The more I think about it, the more I guess you're right," he said. "I'll have to leave it here. At least for the time being."

"The money?"

"The money and the gun both."

"I don't want them here."

"It won't be a problem," he said. "There must be a place. At least till you think of a better somewhere—"

"No—" I began, but it was too late. He was off into the bedroom, with me following, and there was Miss Bates.

When I got in there, Joe turned and pointed the gun at me.

"Get your pants on," he said. "And a shirt. You and I are going to take a ride in my car."

"Joe," I said. "Calm down."

"This is what I get," he said. "My whole life was wrapped up in this woman."

"It wasn't what you thought," I said. "Miss Bates and I are going to be married."

His jaw tightened. "That makes it worse," he said. "To think. My own brother." He waved the gun. "I mean it. Get dressed. Fast! Don't worry about taking your wallet and your keys. Where you're going, you won't need them."

Once again he had not thought things through. It was dangerous for him to leave Miss Bates here alone. Suppose she called the police? But it was nothing I could mention to him, for if I did he'd have taken her along too.

So: "Cool it," I said to Miss Bates, and she knew what I meant. I had talked Joe out of things before, and would again.

Meanwhile, I got into my clothes and went downstairs with him to his car. He drove to an isolated place outside of town where they had once done some steam mining, stopped the car, and again pointed the gun at me.

I said to him, "Give me that thing."

"No," he said. "I'm going to kill you."

"Give me the gun," I said.

"No."

"The gun, Joe!"

All of a sudden a meekness came over him. He realized what he was doing and handed me the gun.

I shot him with it. Six times. To make sure, and also to get rid of all the bullets. Then I took his money, his wallet, his ring, and his watch.

I guess the truth of it was I didn't want him pestering Miss Bates any more. After all, if a woman likes one identical twin, she might also like the other.

Part of the steam mine was an open crater, where they had capped a runaway flow, and into this crater I dumped Joe's body and watched it disappear from view. Then I got back in the car and returned to my place. I would have to abandon the car somewhere else, later in the day.

But they were waiting for me when I drove up—two policemen and the parole officer.

"Hello, Joe," the officer said.

I started to say, "I'm not Joe, I'm Eddie"—but then what would I say next? Here I was in possession of his car, his keys, his wallet, his ring, his money, his watch. And as for Joe himself, I had just finished—

"All right," I said. "I'll go quietly."

"You want to give us the gun and the money, Joe?"

I turned over the gun and the $2000, and I got in the back of the police car.

Halfway to State Prison I said, "Can I make a phone call?"

"To who?"

"My brother."

"No."

"He's also my lawyer."

"That's right," the parole officer said. "Okay. Once we get to the prison you can make that one call."

We got to the prison—I noticed that Fat Louis, the guard, was happy to see me—and they let me go into a booth to make one call.

I called Miss Bates, who was still in my apartment.

"How did things come out?" she said.

"Joe's back in jail," I said. "They were waiting for him. As for me, I've got to be out of town for a few days. Meanwhile, I want you to go visit Joe on Tuesday—first visitors' day."

"But you won't be with me?"

"No. This time you don't sign me in as his lawyer. Just sign yourself in, and you can see him in the regular Visitors' Room. I'll be back on Thursday."

"All right," she said. "I love you, Eddie."

"I love you, too," I said and hung up.

"Ready, Joe?" Fat Louis called out.

"Ready," I said, and went along with him to my cell.

On Tuesday, Miss Bates came to see me. We viewed each other through the grillework. "My God," she said. "You're not Joe. You're Eddie."

"You're the only person in the world who knows it," I said. "Now, here is what you must do, in addition to keeping your voice down while we talk. Come back on Thursday, sign my name as my lawyer—the way you've always done before. Understand? You put down *my* signature."

"So I can see you in the private room," she said.

"No," I said. "Just sign the book and mingle with the other visitors. Hang around for ten or fifteen minutes. Then leave. Don't try to see me."

"I don't understand," she said.

"You will," I said. "Meanwhile, trust me and keep your mouth absolutely shut. Officially, I'm out of town on business. This has all been a terrible mistake."

"But—"

"No buts," I said. "Just do what I told you."

She did exactly what I told her. On Thursday morning Fat Louis came and opened the cell door and said, "Joe, your brother Eddie's here to see you. In the lawyer's room."

"Let's go," I said.

I followed him downstairs, and when we got into the little corridor just outside the "lawyer's room," I turned and hit Fat Louis as hard as I have ever hit anybody in my life.

He turned, bleeding from the mouth, and I hit him again. Then he grabbed me and we wrestled. He's a big guy, Fat Louis, and I didn't last long.

"Straight to the Warden with you, Joe," he said.

We went straight to the Warden.

"Joe," the Warden said, "what is this?"

"What this is," I said, "is that I'm not Joe. I'm his lawyer, his brother, his identical twin. My name is Eddie, not Joe."

"He's crazy," Fat Louis said, and told the Warden what had happened.

"No," I said. "It wasn't quite that way. What happened was that I went in the lawyer's room and Fat Louis here brought Joe down to see me, and as soon as the door closed, Joe pulled a knife on me."

"Where'd he get the knife?" the Warden said.

"How do I know?" I said. "Why don't you ask Fat Louis here, so he can add something to that crazy story he's already given you about how I suddenly tried to beat him up in the hall? Anyway, Joe forced me to change clothes with him— put his prisoner's clothes on me—and then left me screaming and yelling. Fat Louis came in and of course I struggled with him. Tried to explain what happened. He wouldn't believe me, that's all."

"You mean Joe forced you to switch places with him and then—"

"Of course!" I said. "I'm Eddie! Sure, I look like Joe, but if you want to check, check it. Check my fingerprints. Check my signature in the Visitors' Book. Check my shoes, for God's sake! Look at these shoes—two sizes bigger than my feet! How do you think that happened?"

"Then there's been a jail break," the Warden said.

"That's your problem," I said.

"And the guard here—"

"Fat Louis?" I said. "He's your problem too. If you want to think my brother had help from the inside, I can't stop you."

To this day I have not told Miss Bates, who is now my wife, the whole story, even though a wife may not testify against her husband. She thinks that I sacrificed myself by going to jail in Joe's place, then employed this clever ruse to get out, all in order to protect my brother. What she does not know is that he was dead at the time.

They found his body the other day. A new gush of steam had pushed it back to the surface of the crater. The body was badly decomposed, but they identified him through his dental charts. I don't know how carefully they're looking for his murderer. They reason, perhaps, that anyone with his record, who could stage a prison break like that just after violating parole, was bound to come to a violent end. Unimaginative people often do.

P.D. JAMES

Murder, 1986

The girl lay naked on the bed with a knife through her heart. That was the one simple and inescapable fact. No, not simple. It was a fact horrible in its complications. Sergeant Dolby, fighting nausea, steadied his shaking thighs against the foot of the bed and forced his mind into coherence—arranging his thoughts in order, like a child piling brick on colored brick and holding its breath against inevitable tumble into chaos. He mustn't panic. He must take things slowly. There was a proper procedure laid down for this kind of crisis. There was a procedure laid down for everything.

Dead. That, at least, was certain. Despite the heat of the June morning the slim girlish body was quite cold, the rigor mortis already well advanced in face and arms. What had they taught him in Detective School about the onset of rigor mortis, that inexorable if erratic stiffening of the muscles, the body's last protest against disintegration and decay? He couldn't remember. He had never been any good at the more academic studies. He had been lucky to be accepted for the Criminal Investigation Department; they had made that clear enough to him at the time. They had never ceased to make it clear. A lost car; a small breaking and entering; a purse snatch. Send Dolby. He had never rated anything more interesting or important than the petty crimes of inadequate men. If it was something no one else wanted to be bothered with, send Dolby. If it was something the C.I.D. would rather not be told about, send Dolby.

And that was exactly how this death would rate. He would have to report it, of course. But it wouldn't be popular news at Headquarters. They were over-worked already, depleted in strength, inadequately equipped, forced even to employ him six years after his normal retirement age. No, they wouldn't exactly welcome this spot of trouble. And the reason, as if he didn't know it, was fixed there on the wall for him to read. The statutory notice was pasted precisely over the head of her bed.

He wondered why she had chosen that spot. There was no rule about where it had to be displayed. Why, he wondered, had she chosen to sleep under it as people once slept under a Crucifix. An affirmation? But the wording was the same as he would find on the notice in the downstairs hall, in the elevator, on every corridor wall, in every room in the Colony. The Act to which it referred was already two years old.

PRESERVATION OF THE RACE ACT—1984
Control of Interplanetary Disease Infection Carriers

All registered carriers of the Disease, whether or not they are yet manifesting symptoms, are required under Section 2 of the above Act to conform to the following regulations . . .

He didn't need to read further. He knew the regulations by heart—the rules by which the Ipdics lived, if you could call it living. The desperate defense of the few healthy against the menace of the many condemned. The small injustices which might prevent the greatest injustice of all, the extinction of man. The stigmata of the Diseased: the registered number tattooed on the left forearm; the regulation Ipdic suit of yellow cotton in summer, blue serge in winter; the compulsory sterilization, since an Ipdic bred only monsters; the rule prohibiting marriage or any close contact with a Normal; the few manual jobs they were permitted to do; the registered Colonies where they were allowed to live.

He knew what they would say at Headquarters. If Dolby had to discover a murder, it would have to be of an Ipdic. And trust him to be fool enough to report it.

But there was no hurry. He could wait until he was calmer, until he could face with confidence whomever they chose to send. And there were things they would expect him to have noticed. He had better make an examination of the scene before he reported. Then, even if they came at once, he would have something sensible to say.

He forced himself to look again at the body. She was lying on her back, eyes closed as if asleep, light brown hair streaming over the pillow. Her arms were crossed over her chest as if in a last innocent gesture of modesty. Below the left breast the handle of a knife stuck out like an obscene horn.

He bent low to examine it. An ordinary handle, probably an ordinary knife. A short-bladed kitchen knife of the kind used to peel vegetables. Her right palm was curved around it, but not touching it, as if about to pluck it out. On her left forearm the registered Ipdic number glowed almost luminous against the delicate skin.

She was neatly covered by a single sheet pulled smooth and taut so that it looked as if the body had been ritually prepared for examination—an intensification of the horror. He did not believe that this childish hand could have driven in the blade with such precision or that, in her last spasms, she had drawn the sheet so tidily over her nakedness. The linen was only a shade whiter than her skin. There had been two months now of almost continuous sunshine. But this body had been muffled in the high-necked tunic and baggy trousers of an Ipdic suit. Only her face had been open to the sun. It was a delicate nut-brown and there was a faint spatter of freckles across the forehead.

He walked slowly around the room. It was sparsely furnished but pleasant enough. The world had no shortage of living space, even for Ipdics. They could live in comfort, even in some opulence, until the electricity, the television, the domestic computer, the micro-oven broke down. Then these things remained broken. The precious skills of electricians and engineers were not wasted on Ipdics. And it was extraordinary how quickly squalor could replace luxury.

A breakdown of electricity in a building like this could mean no hot food, no light, no heating. He had known Ipdics who had frozen or starved to death in apartments which, back in 1980, only six years ago, must have cost a fortune to rent. Somehow the will to survive died quickly in them. It was easier to wrap themselves in blankets and reach for that small white capsule so thoughtfully provided by the Government, the simple painless way out which the whole healthy community was willing for them to take.

But this girl, this female Ipdic PXN 07926431, wasn't living in squalor. The apartment was clean and almost obsessively neat. The micro-oven was out of order, but there was an old-fashioned electric cooker in the kitchen and when he turned it on the hot plate glowed red. There were even a few personal possessions—a little clutch of seashells carefully arranged on the window ledge, a Staffordshire porcelain figurine of a shepherdess, a child's tea service on a papier-mâché tray.

Her yellow Ipdic suit was neatly folded over the back of a chair. He took it up and saw that she had altered it to fit her. The darts under the breasts had been taken in, the side seams carefully shaped. The hand stitching was neat and regular, an affirmation of individuality, of self-respect. A proud girl. A girl undemoralized by hopelessness. He turned the harsh cotton over and over in his hands and felt the tears stinging the back of his eyes.

He knew that this strange and half-remembered sweetness was pity. He let himself feel it, willing himself not to shrink from the pain. Just so, in his boyhood, he had tentatively placed his full weight on an injured leg after football, relishing the pain in the knowledge that he could bear it, that he was still essentially whole.

But he must waste no more time. Turning on his pocket radio he made his report.

"Sergeant Dolby here. I'm speaking from Ipdic Colony 865. Female Ipdic PXN 07926431 found dead. Room 18. Looks like murder."

It was received as he had expected.

"Oh, God! Are you sure? All right. Hang around. Someone will be over."

While he waited he gave his attention to the flowers. They had struck his senses as soon as he opened the door of the room, but the first sight of the dead girl had driven them from his mind. Now he let their gentle presence drift back into his consciousness. She had died amid such beauty.

The apartment was a bower of wild flowers, their delicate sweetness permeating the warm air so that every breath was an intimation of childhood summers, an evocation of the old innocent days. Wild flowers were his hobby. The slow brain corrected itself, patiently, mechanically: wild flowers had been his hobby. But that was before the Sickness, when the words "flower" and "beauty" seemed to have meaning. He hadn't looked at a flower with any joy since 1980.

1980. The year of the Disease. The year with the hottest summer for 21 years. That summer when the sheer weight of people had pressed against the concrete bastions of the city like an intolerable force, had thronged its burning pavements, had almost brought its transport system to a stop, had sprawled in checkered ranks across its parks until the sweet grass was pressed into pale straw.

1980. The year when there were too many people. Too many happy, busy, healthy human beings. The year when his wife had been alive; when his daughter Tessa had been alive. The year when brave men, traveling far beyond the moon, had brought back to earth the Sickness—the Sickness which had decimated mankind on every continent of the globe. The Sickness which had robbed him, Arthur Dolby, of his wife and daughter.

Tessa. She had been only 14 that spring. It was a wonderful age for a daughter, the sweetest daughter in the world. And Tessa had been intelligent as well as sweet. Both women in his life, his wife and daughter, had been cleverer than Dolby. He had known it, but it hadn't worried him or made him feel inadequate. They had loved him so unreservedly, had relied so much on his manhood, been so satisfied with what little he could provide. They had seen in him qualities he could never discern in himself, virtues which he knew he no longer possessed. His flame of life was meager; it had needed their warm breaths to keep it burning bright. He wondered what they would think of him now. Arthur Dolby in 1986, looking once more at wild flowers.

He moved among them as if in a dream, like a man recognizing with wonder a treasure given up for lost. There had been no attempt at formal arrangement. She had obviously made use of any suitable container in the apartment and had bunched the plants together naturally and simply, each with its own kind. He could still identify them. There were brown earthenware jars of Herb Robert, the rose-pink flowers set delicately on their reddish stems. There were cracked teacups holding bunches of red clover, meadow buttercups, and long-stemmed daisies; jam jars of white campion and cuckoo flowers; egg cups of birdsfoot trefoil—"eggs and bacon," Tessa used to call it—and even smaller jars of rueleaved saxifrage and the soft pink spurs of haresfoot. But, above all, there were the tall vases of cow-parsley, huge bunches of strong hollow-grooved stems supporting their umbels of white flowers, delicate as bridal lace, yet pungent and strong, shedding a white dust on the table, bed, and floor.

And then, in the last jar of all, the only one which held a posy of mixed flowers, he saw the Lady Orchid. It took his breath away. There it stood, alien and exotic, lifting its sumptuous head proudly among the common flowers of the roadside, the white clover, campion, and sweet wild roses. The Lady Orchid. *Orchis Purpurea.*

He stood very still and gazed at it. The decorative spike rose from its shining foliage, elegant and distinctive, seeming to know its rarity. The divisions of the helmet were wine-red, delicately veined and spotted with purple, their somber tint setting off the clear white beauty of the lip. The Lady Orchid. Dolby knew of only one spot, the fringe of a wood in old Kent County in the Southeast Province, where this flower grew wild. The Sickness had changed the whole of human life. But he doubted if it had changed that.

It was then that he heard the roar of the helicopter. He went to the window. The red machine, like a huge angry insect, was just bouncing down onto the roof landing pad. He watched, puzzled. Why should they send a chopper? Then he understood. The tall figure in the all-white uniform with its gleaming braid swung himself down from the cockpit and was lost to view behind the parapet of the roof. But Dolby recognized at once that helmet of black hair, the confident poise of the head. C. J. Kalvert. The Commissioner of the Home Security Force in person.

He told himself that it couldn't be true—that Kalvert wouldn't concern himself with the death of an Ipdic, that he must have some other business in the Colony. But what business? Dolby waited in fear, his hands clenched so that the nails pierced his palms, waited in an agony of hope that it might not be true. But it was true. A minute later he heard the strong footsteps advancing along the corridor. The door opened. The Commissioner had arrived.

He nodded an acknowledgement to Dolby and, without speaking, went over to the bed. For a moment he stood in silence, looking down at the girl. Then he said, "How did you get in, Sergeant?"

The accent was on the third word.

"The door was unlocked, sir."

"Naturally. Ipdics are forbidden to lock their doors. I was asking what you were doing here."

"I was making a search, sir."

That at least was true. He had been making a private search.

"And you discovered that one more female Ipdic had taken the sensible way out of her troubles. Why didn't you call the Sanitary Squad? It's unwise to leave a body longer than necessary in this weather. Haven't we all had enough of the stench of decay?"

"I think she was murdered, sir."

"Do you indeed, Sergeant. And why?"

Dolby moistened his dry lips and made his cramped fingers relax. He mustn't let himself be intimidated, mustn't permit himself to get flustered. The important thing was to stick to the facts and present them cogently.

"It's the knife, sir. If she were going to stab herself, I think she would have fallen on the blade, letting her weight drive it in. Then the body would have been found face downwards. That way, the blade would have done all the work. I don't think she would have had the strength or the skill to pierce her heart lying in that position. It looks almost surgical. It's too neat. The man who drove that knife in knew what he was doing. And then there's the sheet. She couldn't have placed it over herself so neatly."

"A valid point, Sergeant. But the fact that someone considerately tidied her up after death doesn't necessarily mean that he killed her. Anything else?"

He was walking restlessly about the room as he talked, touching nothing, his hands clasped behind his back. Dolby wished that he would stand still. He said, "But why use a knife at all, sir? She must have been issued her euthanasia capsule."

"Not a very dramatic way to go, Dolby. The commonest door for an Ipdic to let life out. She may have exercised a feminine preference for a more individual-istic death. Look around this room, Sergeant. Does she strike you as having been an ordinary girl?"

No, she hadn't struck Dolby as ordinary. But this was ground he dare not tread. He said doggedly, "And why should she be naked, sir? Why take all her clothes off to kill herself?"

"Why, indeed. That shocks you, does it, Dolby? It implies an unpleasant touch of exhibitionism. It offends your modesty. But perhaps she was an exhibitionist. The flowers would suggest it. She made her room into a bower of fragrance and beauty. Then, naked, as unencumbered as the flowers, she stretched herself out like a sacrifice, and drove the knife through her heart. Can you, Sergeant, with your limited imagination, understand that a woman might wish to die like that?"

Kalvert swung round and strode over to him. The fierce black eyes burned into Dolby's. The Sergeant felt frightened, at a loss. The conversation was bizarre. He felt they were playing some private game, but that only one of them knew the rules.

What did Kalvert want of him? In a normal world, in the world before the Sickness when the old police force was at full strength, the Commissioner wouldn't even have known that Dolby existed. Yet here they both were, engaged, it seemed, in some private animus, sparring over the body of an unimportant dead Ipdic.

It was very hot in the room now and the scent of the flowers had been growing stronger. Dolby could feel the beads of sweat on his brow. Whatever happened he must hold onto the facts. He said, "The flowers needn't be funeral flowers. Perhaps they were for a celebration."

"That would suggest the presence of more than one person. Even Ipdics don't celebrate alone. Have you found any evidence that someone was with her when she died?"

He wanted to reply, "Only the knife in her breast." But he was silent. Kalvert was pacing the room again. Suddenly he stopped and glanced at his watch. Then, without speaking, he turned on the television. Dolby remembered. Of course. The Leader was due to speak after the midday news. It was already 12:32. He would be almost finished.

The screen flickered and the too familiar face appeared. The Leader looked very tired. Even the makeup artist hadn't been able to disguise the heavy shadows under the eyes or the hollows beneath the cheekbones. With that beard and the melancholy, pain-filled face, he looked like an ascetic prophet. But he always had. His face hadn't changed much since the days of his student protest. People said that, even then, he had only really been interested in personal power. Well, he was still under thirty, but he had it now. All the power he could possibly want.

"And so we must find our own solution. We have a tradition in this country of humanity and justice. But how far can we let tradition hamper us in the great task of preserving our race? We know what is happening in other countries, the organized and ceremonial mass suicides of thousands of Ipdics at a time, the humane Disposal Squads, the compulsory matings between computer-selected Normals. Some compulsory measures against the Ipdics we must now take. As far as possible we have relied on gentle and voluntary methods. But can we afford to fall behind while other less scrupulous nations are breeding faster and more selectively, disposing of their Ipdics, re-establishing their technology, looking with covetous eyes at the great denuded spaces of the world? One day they will be repopulated. It is our duty to take part in this great process. The world needs our race. The time has come for every one of us, particularly our Ipdics, to ask ourselves with every breath we draw: have I the right to be alive?"

Kalvert turned off the set.

"I think we can forego the pleasure of seeing once again Mrs. Sartori nursing her fifth healthy daughter. Odd to think that the most valuable human being in the world is a healthy fecund female. But you got the message, I hope, Sergeant. This Ipdic had the wisdom to take her own way out while she still had the choice. And if somebody helped her, who are we to quibble?"

"It was still murder, sir. I know that killing an Ipdic isn't a capital crime. But the Law hasn't been altered yet. It's still a felony to kill any human being."

"Ah, yes. A felony. And you, of course, are dedicated to the detection and punishment of felonies. The first duty of a policeman is to prevent crime; the second is to detect and punish the criminal. You learned all that when you were in Detective School, didn't you? Learned it all by heart. I remember reading the first report on you, Dolby. It was almost identical with the last. 'Lacking in initiative. Deficient in imagination. Tends to make errors of judgment. Should make a reliable subordinate. Lacks self-confidence.' But it did admit that, when you manage to get an idea into your head, it sticks there. And you have an idea in your head. Murder. And murder is a felony. Well, what do you propose to do about it?"

"In cases of murder the body is first examined by the forensic pathologist."

"Not this body, Dolby. Do you know how many pathologists this country now has? We have other uses for them than to cut up dead Ipdics. She was a young female. She was not pregnant. She was stabbed through the heart. What more do we need to know?"

"Whether or not a man was with her before she died."

"I think you can take it there was. Male Ipdics are not yet being sterilized. So we add another fact. She probably had a lover. What else do you want to know?"

"Whether or not there are prints on the knife, sir, and, if so, whose they are."

Kalvert laughed aloud. "We were short of forensic scientists before the Sickness. How many do you suppose we have now? There was another case of capital murder reported this morning. An Ipdic has killed his former wife because she obeyed the Law and kept away from him. We can't afford to lose a single healthy woman, can we, Dolby? There's the rumor of armed bands of Ipdics roaming the Southeast Province. There's the case of the atomic scientist with the back of his skull smashed in. A scientist, Dolby! Now, do you really want to bother the lab with this petty trouble?"

Dolby said obstinately, "I know that someone was with her when she picked the flowers. That must have been yesterday—they're still fresh even in this heat, and wild flowers fade quickly. I think he probably came back here with her and was with her when she died."

"Then find him, Sergeant, if you must. But don't ask for help I can't give."

He walked over to the door without another glance at the room or at the dead girl, as if neither of them held any further interest for him. Then he turned: "You aren't on the official list of men encouraged to breed daughters in the interest of the race, are you, Sergeant?"

Dolby wanted to reply that he'd once had a daughter. She was dead and he wanted no other.

"No, sir. They thought I was too old. And then there was the adverse psychologist's report."

"A pity. One would have thought that the brave new world could have made room for just one or two people who were unintelligent, lacking in imagination, unambitious, inclined to errors of judgment. People will persist in going their own obstinate way. Goodbye, Dolby. Report to me personally on this case, will you? I shall be interested to hear how you progress. Who knows, you may reveal unsuspected talents."

He was gone. Dolby waited for a minute as if to cleanse his mind of that disturbing presence. As the confident footsteps died away, even the room seemed to settle itself into peace. Then Dolby began the few tasks which still remained.

They weren't many. First, he took the dead girl's fingerprints. He worked with infinite care, murmuring to her as he gently pressed the pad against each fingertip, like a doctor reassuring a child. It would be pointless, he thought, to compare them with the prints on any of the ordinary objects in the room. That would prove nothing except that another person had been there. The only prints of importance would be those on the knife. But there were no prints on the knife—only an amorphous smudge of whorls and composites as if someone had attempted to fold her hand around the shaft but had lacked the courage to press the fingers firm.

But the best clue was still there—the Lady Orchid, splendid in its purity and beauty, the flower which told him where she had spent the previous day, the flower which might lead him to the man who had been with her. And there was another clue, something he had noticed when he had first examined the body closely. He had said nothing to Kalvert. Perhaps Kalvert hadn't noticed it or hadn't recognized its significance. Perhaps he had been cleverer than Kalvert. He told himself that he wasn't really as stupid as people sometimes thought. It was just that his mind was so easily flustered into incoherence when stronger men bullied or taunted him. Only his wife and daughter had really understood that, had given him the confidence to fight it.

It was time to get started. They might deny him the services of the pathologist and the laboratory, but they still permitted him the use of his car. It would be little more than an hour's drive.

But, before leaving, he bent once more over the body. The Disposal Squad would soon be here for it. He would never see it again. So he studied the clue for the last time—the faint, almost imperceptible circle of paler skin round the third finger of her left hand. The finger that could have worn a ring through the whole of a hot summer day . . .

He drove through the wide streets and sun-filled squares, through the deserted suburbs, until the tentacles of the city fell away and he was in open country. The roads were pitted and unmended, the hedges high and unkempt, the fields a turbulent sea of vegetation threatening to engulf the unpeopled farmlands. But the sun was pleasant on his face. He could almost persuade himself that this was one of the old happy jaunts into the familiar and well-loved countryside of Old Kent.

He had crossed the boundary into the Southeast Province and was already looking for the remembered landmarks of hillside and church spire when it happened. There was an explosion, a crack like a pistol shot, and the windshield shattered in his face. He felt splinters of glass stinging his cheeks. Instinctively he guarded his face with his arms. The car swerved out of control and lurched onto the grass verge. He felt for the ignition key and turned off the engine. Then he tentatively opened his eyes. They were uninjured. And it was then he saw the Ipdics.

They came out of the opposite ditch and moved toward him, with stones still in their hands. There were half a dozen of them. One, the tallest, seemed to be their leader. The others shuffled at his heels, lumpy figures in their ill-fitting yellow suits, their feet brown and bare, their hair matted like animals', their greedy eyes fixed on the car. They stood still, looking at him. And then the leader drew his right hand from behind his back, and Dolby saw that it held a gun.

His heart missed a beat. So it was true! Somehow the Ipdics were getting hold of weapons. He got out of the car, trying to recall the exact instructions of such an emergency. Never show fear. Keep calm. Exert authority. Remember that they are inferior, unorganized, easily cowed. Never drop your eyes. But his voice, even to him, sounded feeble, pitched unnaturally high.

"The possession of a weapon by an Ipdic is a capital crime. The punishment is death. Give me that gun."

The voice that replied was quiet, authoritative, the kind of voice one used to call educated.

"No. First you give me the keys to the car. Then I give you something in return. A cartridge in your belly!"

His followers cackled their appreciation. It was one of the most horrible sounds in the world—the laughter of an Ipdic.

The Ipdic pointed the gun at Dolby, moving it slowly from side to side as if selecting his precise target. He was enjoying his power, drunk with elation and triumph. But he waited a second too long. Suddenly his arm jerked upward, the gun leaped from his grasp, and he gave one high desolate scream, falling into the dust of the road. He was in the first spasm of an Ipdic fit. His body writhed and twisted, arched and contracted, until the bones could be heard snapping.

Dolby looked on impassively. There was nothing he could do. He had seen it thousands of times before. It had happened to his wife, to Tessa, to all those who had died of the Disease. It happened in the end to every Ipdic. It would have happened to that girl on the bed, at peace now with a knife in her heart.

The attack would leave this Ipdic broken and exhausted. If he survived, he would be a mindless idiot, probably for months. And then the fits would come more frequently. It was this feature of the Disease which made the Ipdics so impossible to train or employ, even for the simplest of jobs.

Dolby walked up to the writhing figure and kicked away the gun, then picked it up. It was a revolver, a Smith and Wesson .38, old but in good condition. He saw that it was loaded. After a second's thought he slipped it into the pocket of his jacket.

The remaining Ipdics had disappeared, scrambling back into the hedges with cries of anguish and fear. The whole incident was over so quickly that it already seemed like a dream. Only the tortured figure in the dust and the cold metal in his pocket were witnesses to its reality. He should report it at once, of course. The suppression of armed Ipdics was the first duty of the Home Security Force.

He backed the car onto the road. Then, on an impulse, he got out again and went over to the Ipdic. He bent to drag the writhing figure off the road and into the shade of the hedge. But it was no good. Revolted, he drew back. He couldn't bear to touch him. Perhaps the Ipdic's friends would creep back later to carry him away and tend to him. Perhaps. But he, Dolby, had his own problem. He had a murder to solve.

Fifteen minutes later he drove slowly through the village. The main street was deserted but he could glimpse, through the open cottage doors, the garish yellow of an Ipdic suit moving in the dim interior and he could see other yellow-clad figures bending at work in the gardens and fields. None of them looked up as he passed. He guessed that this was one of the settlements which had grown up in the country, where groups of Ipdics attempted to support themselves and each other, growing their own food, nursing their sick, burying their dead. Since they made no demands on the Normals they were usually left in peace. But it couldn't last long. There was no real hope for them.

As more and more of them were overtaken by the last inevitable symptoms, the burden on those left grew intolerable. Soon they too would be helpless and mad. Then the Security Force, the Health Authorities, and the Sanitary Squads would move in, and another colony of the dispossessed would be cleaned up. And it was a question of cleaning up. Dolby had taken part in one such operation. He knew what the final horror would be. But now in the heat of this sun-scented afternoon, he might be driving through the village as he had known it in the days before the Sickness, prosperous, peaceful, sleepy, with the men still busy on the farms.

He left the car at the churchyard gate and, slipping the strap of his murder bag over his shoulder, walked up the dappled avenue of elms to the south entrance. The heavy oak door with its carved panels, its massive hinges of hammered iron, creaked open at his touch. He stepped into the cool dimness and smelled again the familiar scent of flowers, musty hymn books, and wood polish, saw once again the medieval pillars soaring high to the hammer beams of the roof, and, straining his eyes through the dimness, he glimpsed the carving on the rood screen and the far gleam of the sanctuary lamp.

The church was full of wild flowers. They were the same flowers as those in the dead girl's apartment but here their frail delicacy was almost lost against the massive pillars and the richly carved oak. But the huge vases of cow-parsley set on each side of the chancel steps made a brave show, floating like twin clouds of whiteness in the dim air. It was a church decked for a bride.

He saw a female Ipdic polishing the brass lectern. He made his way up the aisle toward her and she beamed a gentle welcome as if his appearance were the most ordinary event in the world. Her baggy Ipdic suit was stained with polish and she wore a pair of old sandals, the soles peeling away from the uppers. Her graying hair was drawn back into a loose bun from which wisps of hair had escaped to frame the anxious, sun-stained face.

She reminded him of someone. He let his mind probe once again, painfully, into the past. Then he remembered. Of course. Miss Caroline Martin, his Sunday School superintendent. It wasn't she, of course. Miss Martin would have been over 70 at the time of the Sickness. No one as old as that had survived, except those few Tasmanian aborigines who so interested the scientists. Miss Martin, standing beside the old piano as her younger sister thumped out the opening hymn and beating time with her gloved hand as if hearing some private and quite different music. Afterward, the students had gone to their different classes and had sat in a circle around their teachers. Miss Martin had taught the older children, himself among them. Some of the boys had been unruly, but never Arthur Dolby. Even in those days he had been obedient, law-abiding. The good boy. Not particularly bright, but well behaved. Good, dull, ineffectual. Teacher's pet.

And when she spoke it was with a voice like Miss Martin's.

"Can I help you? If you've come for Evensong services, I'm afraid it isn't until five thirty today. If you're looking for Father Reeves, he's at the Rectory. But perhaps you're just a visitor. It's a lovely church, isn't it? Have you seen our sixteenth-century reredos?"

"I hoped I would be in time for the wedding."

She gave a little girlish cry of laughter.

"Dear me, you are late! I'm afraid that was yesterday! But I thought no one was supposed to know about it. Father Reeves said that it was to be quite secret really. But I am afraid I was very naughty. I did so want to see the bride. After all, we haven't had a wedding here since—"

"Since the Act?"

She corrected him gently, like Miss Martin rebuking the good boy of the class.

"Since 1980. So yesterday was quite an occasion for us. And I did want to see what the bride looked like in Emma's veil."

"In what?"

"A bride has to have a veil, you know." She spoke with gentle reproof, taking pity on his masculine ignorance. "Emma was my niece. I lost her and her parents in 1981. Emma was the last bride to be married here. That was on April 28, 1980. I've always kept her veil and headdress. She was such a lovely bride."

Dolby asked with sudden harshness the irrelevant but necessary question.

"What happened to her bridegroom?"

"Oh, John was one of the lucky ones. I believe he has married again and has three daughters. Just one daughter more and they'll be allowed to have a son. We don't see him, of course. It wasn't to be expected. After all, it is the Law."

How despicable it was, this need to be reassured that there were other traitors.

"Yes," he said. "It is the Law."

She began polishing the already burnished lectern, chatting to him as she worked.

"But I've kept Emma's veil and headdress. So I thought I'd just place them on a chair beside the font so that this new bride would see them when she came into church. Just in case she wanted to borrow them, you know. And she did. I was so glad. The bridegroom placed the veil over her head and fixed the headdress for her himself, and she walked up the aisle looking so beautiful."

"Yes," said Dolby. "She would have looked very beautiful."

"I watched them from behind this pillar. Neither of them noticed me. But it was right for me to be here. There ought to be someone in the church. It says in the prayer book, 'In the sight of God and of this congregation.' She had a small bouquet of wild flowers, just a simple mixed bunch but very charming. I think they must have picked it together."

"She carried a Lady Orchid," said Dolby. "A Lady Orchid picked by her bridegroom and surrounded by daisies, clover, white campion, and wild roses."

"How clever of you to guess! Are you a friend, perhaps?"

"No," said Dolby. "Not a friend. Can you describe the bridegroom?"

"I thought that you must know him. Very tall, very dark. He wore a plain white suit. Oh, they were such a handsome couple! I wished Father Reeves could have seen them."

"I thought he married them."

"So he did. But Father Reeves, poor man, is blind."

So that was why he risked it, thought Dolby. But what a risk!

."Which prayer book did he use?"

She gazed at him, the milky eyes perplexed. "Father Reeves?" she asked.

"No, the bridegroom. He did handle a prayer book, I suppose?"

"Oh, yes. I put one out for each of them. Father Reeves asked me to get things ready. It was I who decorated the church. Poor dears, it wasn't as if they could have the usual printed service sheets. Emma's were so pretty, her initials intertwined with the bridegroom's. But yesterday they had to use ordinary prayer books. I chose them specially from the pews and put them on the two prayer stools. I found a very pretty white one for the bride and this splendid old book with the brass clasp for the bridegroom. It looked masculine, I thought."

It lay on the book ledge of the front pew. She made a move to pick it up, but he shot out his hand. Then he dropped his handkerchief over the book and lifted it by the sharp edges of the binding. Brass and leather. Good for a print. And this man's palm would be moist, clammy, perhaps, with perspiration and fear. A hot day; an illegal ceremony; his mind on murder. To love and to cherish until death us do part. Yes, this bridegroom would have been nervous. But Dolby had one more question.

"How did they get here? Do you know?"

"They came by foot. At least, they walked up to the church together. I think they had walked quite a long way. They were quite hot and dusty when they arrived. But I know how they really came."

She nodded her unkempt head and gave a little conspiratorial nod.

"I've got very good ears, you know. They came by helicopter. I heard it."

A helicopter. He knew almost without thinking exactly who was permitted the use of a helicopter. Members of the Central Committee of Government; high ranking scientists and technicians; doctors; the Commissioner of the Home Security Force, and his Deputy. That was all.

He took the prayer book out into the sun and sat on one of the flat-topped gravestones. He set up the prayer book on its end, then unzipped his murder bag. His hands shook so that he could hardly manage the brush and some of the gray powder was spilt and blew away in the breeze. He willed himself to keep calm, to take his time. Carefully, like a child with a new toy, he dusted the book and clasp with powder, gently blowing off the surplus with a small rubber nozzle. It was an old procedure, first practiced when he was a young Detective Constable. But it still worked. It always would. The arches, whorls, and composites came clearly into view.

He was right. It was a beautiful print. The man had made no effort to wipe it clean. Why should he? How could he imagine that this particular book would ever be identified among the many scattered around the church? How could he suspect that he would ever be traced to this despised and unregarded place? Dolby took out his camera and photographed the print. There must be continuity of evidence. He must leave no room for doubt. Then he classified its characteristics, ready for checking.

There was a little delay at the National Identification Computer Center when he phoned, and he had to wait his turn. When it came he gave his name, rank, secret code, and the classification of the print. There was a moment's silence. Then a surprised voice asked, "Is that you, Dolby? Will you confirm your code."

He did so. Another silence.

"Okay. But what on earth are you up to? Are you sure of your print classification?"

"Yes. I want the identification for elimination purposes."

"Then you can eliminate, all right. That's the Commissioner. Kalvert, C. J. Hard luck, Dolby! Better start again."

He switched off the receiver and sat in silence. He had known it, of course. But for how long? Perhaps from the beginning. Kalvert. Kalvert, who had an excuse for visiting an Ipdic Colony. Kalvert, who had the use of a helicopter. Kalvert, who had known without asking that the television set in her room was in working order. Kalvert, who had been too sure of himself to take the most elementary precautions against discovery, because he knew that it didn't matter, because he knew no one would dare touch him. Kalvert, one of the four most powerful men in the country. And it was he, the despised Sergeant Dolby, who had solved the case.

He heard the angry purr of the approaching helicopter without surprise. He had reported the armed attack by the Ipdics. It was certain that Headquarters would have immediately summoned a Squad from the nearest station to hunt them down. But Kalvert would know about the message. He had no doubt that the Commissioner was keeping a watch on him. He would know which way Dolby was heading, would realize that he was dangerously close to the truth. The armed Squad would be here in time. But Kalvert would arrive first.

He waited for five minutes, still sitting quietly on the gravestone. The air was sweet with the smell of grasses and vibrating with the high-treble midsummer chant of blackbird and thrush. He shut his eyes for a moment, breathing in the beauty, taking courage from its peace. Then he got to his feet and stood at the head of the avenue of elms to wait for Kalvert.

The gold braid on the all-white uniform gleamed in the sun. The tall figure, arrogant with confidence and power, walked unhesitatingly toward him, unsmiling, making no sign. When they were three feet apart, Kalvert stopped. They stood confronting each other. It was Dolby who spoke first. His voice was little more than a whisper.

"You killed her."

He could not meet Kalvert's eyes. But he heard his reply.

"Yes, I killed her. Shall I tell you about it, Sergeant? You seem to have shown some initiative. You deserve to know part of the truth. I was her friend. That is prohibited by Regulation. She became my mistress. That is against the Law. We decided to get married. That is a serious crime. I killed her. That, as you earlier explained, is a felony. And what are you going to do about it?"

Dolby couldn't speak. Suddenly he took out the revolver. It seemed ridiculous to point it at Kalvert. He wasn't even sure that he would be able to fire it. But he held it close to his side and the curved stock fitted comfortably to his palm, giving him courage. He made himself meet Kalvert's eyes, and heard the Commissioner laugh.

"To kill a Normal is also against the Law. But it's something more. Capital murder, Dolby. Is that what you have in mind?"

Dolby spoke out of cracked lips, "But why? *Why?*"

"I don't have to explain to you. But I'll try. Have you the imagination to understand that we might have loved each other, that I might have married her because it seemed a small risk for me and would give her pleasure, that I might have promised to kill her when her last symptoms began? Can you, Sergeant Dolby, enter into the mind of a girl like that? She was an Ipdic. And she was more alive in her condemned cell than you have ever been in your life. Female Ipdic PXN 07926431 found dead. Looks like murder. Remember how you reported it? A felony. Something to be investigated. Against the Law. That's all it meant, isn't it?"

He had taken out his own revolver now. He held it easily, like a man casually dangling a familiar toy. He stood there, magnificent in the sunshine, the breeze lifting his black hair. He said quietly, "Do you think I'd let any Law on earth keep me from the woman I loved?"

Dolby wanted to cry out that it hadn't been like that at all. That Kalvert didn't understand. That he, Dolby, had cared about the girl. But the contempt in those cold black eyes kept him silent. There was nothing they could say to each other. Nothing. And Kalvert would kill him.

The Squad would be here soon. Kalvert couldn't let him live to tell his story. He gazed with fascinated horror at the revolver held so easily in the Commissioner's hand. And he tightened the grip on his own, feeling with a shaking finger for the trigger.

The armored car roared up to the churchyard gate. The Squad were here. Kalvert lifted his revolver to replace it in the holster. Dolby, misunderstanding the gesture, whipped up his own gun and, closing his eyes, fired until the last cartridge was spent. Numbed by misery and panic, he didn't hear the shots or the thud of Kalvert's fall. The first sound to pierce his consciousness was a wild screaming and beating of wings as the terrified birds flew high. Then he was aware of an unnatural silence, and of an acrid smell tainting the summer air.

His right hand ached. It felt empty, slippery with sweat. He saw that he had dropped the gun. There was a long mournful cry of distress. It came from behind him. He turned and glimpsed the yellow-clad figure of the female Ipdic, hand to her mouth, watching him from the shadow of the church. Then she faded into the dark.

He dropped on his knees beside Kalvert. The torn arteries were pumping their blood onto the white tunic. The crimson stain burst open like a flower. Dolby took off his jacket with shaking hands and thrust it under Kalvert's head. He wanted to say that he was sorry, to cry out like a child that he hadn't really meant it, that it was all a mistake.

Kalvert looked at him. Was there really pity in those dulling eyes? "Poor Dolby! Your final error of judgment."

The last word was hiccupped in a gush of blood. Kalvert turned his head away from Dolby and drew up his knees as if easing himself into sleep. And Dolby knew that it was too late to explain now, that there was no one there to hear him.

He stood up. The Squad were very close now, three of them, walking abreast, guns at hip, moving inexorably forward in the pool of their own shadows. And so he waited, all fear past, with Kalvert's body at his feet. And he thought for the last time of his daughter. Tessa, whom he had allowed to hide from him because that was the Law. Tessa, whom he had deserted and betrayed. Tessa, whom he had sought at last, but had found too late. Tessa, who had led him unwittingly to her lover and murderer. Tessa who would never have picked that Lady Orchid. Hadn't he taught her when she was a child that if you pick a wild orchid it can never bloom again?

HENRY T. PARRY

Season's Greetings

Dec. 14

Dear Friends:

This year I've decided to write one of those blanket letters that are getting so popular and wish everybody a Merry Christmas and tell them all the news at the same time.

As most of you already know we moved to Florida last February right after Charley retired and we bought a place in Del Sol, just three blocks in from the Coastal Waterway. All on one floor, which is new for us. But even though the house was fairly new it must have been lived in by someone who had retired from being the caretaker of a town garbage dump. You know that I had a reputation back in Ridgevale of being a fussy housekeeper. Well, I couldn't stand this place, it was that dirty.

I scrubbed and polished and dusted and scraped and painted and waxed and oiled and everything else for three solid weeks just to get that house to the point where you wouldn't be ashamed to keep pigs in it. During that time we lived on frozen food and soda pop that Charley brought in. Charley said it was one of the most prolonged cleaning fits I had ever had. I told him it was nothing of the kind, just any normal person's desire to have cleanliness and order in their house.

Charley said all right but did I really have to wash out the fireplace chimney as far up as I could reach just to be orderly? I might add that I cleaned a bird's nest out of that chimney Charley was so sarcastic about. Gives you an idea of how dirty this place was when we moved in.

Even though I had gotten the house in some kind of order—not to where it ought to be—I kept having the feeling that I hadn't settled down to Florida living yet. Something kept bothering me. There was something out of place and irregular in the way of living down here.

At first I thought it might be the warmer climate or the new breed of insects. Or it might have been the people except I took good care not to have anything to do with the neighbors and I told Charley he'd have to do the same and not pick up with just any old Tom or Dick just because they might have had something in common up North. Then I decided what was bothering me. It was the lot next door.

The lot had about 100 foot frontage and was about 75 feet deep. It was vacant if you call anything vacant that was knee-deep in weeds and had a young forest of scrub oak and pine growing in it. I walked through it and, as I suspected, there was trash hidden in the weeds—a couple of tires, a refrigerator, and about a ton of miscellaneous debris.

Charley told me I was crazy walking through the scrub like that because it wasn't very long ago that this area had been undeveloped and everyone said a pocket of rattlers could have been living there since rattlers were common around here. The neighbors had also been dumping garden trash in the lot but I noticed that nobody ever walked very far in from the street to do it so there might have been something to what Charley said about rattlers.

But the untidy lush growth, the junk that I knew was lying hidden in the brush, and the weeds getting higher each week just bothered me so that I knew I was never going to feel settled until I set that lot to rights.

"Charley," I said, "go down to the real estate office and find out who owns that lot and buy it from them."

Well, Charley let on that it might be a good investment at that but didn't I realize that our income was half of what it used to be before he retired?—and so on and so on.

"Charley," I said, "that lot is driving me out of my mind. I will not live another day next to a transplanted section of the Everglades."

So Charley went down to the real estate office and I got out an ax, a rake, and some weed spray, and set to work. Even if Charley couldn't buy the lot I was determined to clean it up and bring some order to the place. He got the lot all right but he grumbled about having to pay a thousand dollars more than it was worth but I said it was a good investment and even if it wasn't I was willing to spend a thousand dollars just to remove an eyesore from my view.

It's a good thing I'm 15 years younger than Charley or I couldn't have worked the way I did, especially in that hot sun. I would start at seven in the morning and plug away until before I knew it Charley would be standing there telling me lunch was ready. I was so taken up with what I was doing that it used to give me quite a start sometimes to find Charley standing there.

Anyway, I poisoned every bush, weed, leaf, shrub, and every other green thing that grew on that lot. Then I went in with my ax and I chopped and grubbed everything out of the ground until Charley said the lot looked like a graveyard where the help has suddenly gone on strike.

Charley came out to get me for lunch one day and as he stepped into the clearing where I was working he jumped.

"Holy smoke! Look at that!"

He pointed down at a snake, a rattler, with its head chopped neatly off and its tail still squirming. I was frightened because I didn't remember even seeing it, let alone chopping its head off but I must have hit it when I was hacking at the roots of a scrub oak. I didn't let on to Charley.

"What's there to get excited about? Back in the country a ways I bet the natives kill them all the time. I told you there wasn't anything to worry about as long as you're careful."

Charley looked at me as though I was off my rocker but he didn't say anything, just got out of there, putting his feet down as carefully as a ballet dancer.

It took me nearly six weeks but I got that lot cleaned up and some grass started in it. It gave me a great deal of satisfaction to see it so neat and clean although the neighbors did give me some strange looks when they would drive by and see me chopping away in the hot sun.

Well, I was all right for a month after that but then the feeling came back of something being out of the normal pattern and routine that I was accustomed to. The house was shined up and the lot was coming along but I still felt that the days were not running as smoothly as they had before we moved down here. Then I realized what it was. It was Charley.

After you have had your house to yourself from eight to six every day for 25 or more years, it's upsetting to have someone hanging around the house all day and getting in your way. I encouraged Charley to try fishing, thinking it would keep him out of the house for long periods, but he said the people he met when he tried it just sat around in expensive boats with expensive equipment and exchanged nonsensical talk about what fish liked to eat and what they didn't, as if anyone knew. When I suggested golf to Charley he said he'd just as soon hire himself out to the post office and get paid for walking around in the hot sun pushing a cart.

I'd have been glad to see him get a job in the post office or anywhere just to get him out of the house. To see somebody come into your kitchen and tramp with muddy shoes across a floor you have just waxed or to always have to be after someone to move their chair so you can vacuum where they're sitting. Once I asked him when he was going to start on the three volumes of "The Decline and Fall of the Roman Empire" as he always intended. He said that he had let it go too long and that now he wouldn't have the patience to start it, let alone finish it. This was just as well because after I suggested it I realized if he took up reading he'd *always* be around the house.

I made the same mistake again when I asked him why he didn't start writing that book he'd been talking about for so many years, especially when he had a drink or two before dinner, the one exposing the company he worked for and telling about the intrigues that went on. He could never decide whether he would call it "Of Rats and Men" or "Phonies I Have Known." He just gave me a sour look and mumbled maybe they weren't such a bad lot after all.

Then when I mentioned that he might go down to Waterfront Park—this was when I had run out of errands to send him on—and talk to some of the retired men who hung around there I thought he would split a vein in his forehead. He said he'd be a so-and-so before he would sit around in the park with a lot of old coots talking about the jobs they had retired from and waiting to die. Just as soon rent a bench in front of the funeral home so he'd be ready when the call came. Might even stretch out on the bench while waiting and really be ready.

I was about at my wit's end to find something that would keep Charley away from home all day when one day here comes Charley home with one of those green and white folders put out by a pump company. He'd picked it up at the garden center—they don't say seed store any more—and it said: "Make your own fountain. Dig a hole. Put in a fiberglass pool. Drop in one of our recirculating pumps and you're in for many hours of quiet pleasure."

"Just what do you think you're going to do with that?" I asked.

"I thought maybe since I have so much time on my hands I might dig up at the back property line of the new lot, put in a little pool and one of these little pumps and have a fountain. Or maybe even pile up some rocks and have a waterfall. And instead of one of these fiberglass pools they advertise I thought for the basin part I might make it out of concrete. It would be simple to mix up a batch of cement and sand—"

"Cement and sand! You out of your mind? What is messier than cement? Remember the time we had the plasterer I didn't get the house clean for a month? And digging up the new lot just after I worked like a slave to set it to rights? Charley, I just won't hear of it. You must be getting senile to want to start on a messy project like that. I suppose you'll want to have one of those tin flamingos wading in your pool."

Generally when I put my foot down Charley just sighs and gives in to what's right. This time he didn't say anything, just clamped his mouth shut in that stubborn disappointed way he has and went off. He hadn't given up the idea completely though because when I was straightening up his desk a few days later—and what a mess it was—I found some sketches for the pool. In each one the size of the pool kept getting bigger—first four feet, then six, then eight, and the number of bags of cement and sand he figured he'd need got higher and higher. I tore up the sketches and threw them away.

Charley brought up the subject just once more.

"About that pool, not only would it be kind of a pretty thing but the birds might come there to drink and we could get some of those bird-watching books and keep a list of the various kinds of birds we identified."

"Charley, you are getting senile. Birds! The dirtiest things there are except maybe dogs. And what do you want to be cluttering up the house with books for? I thought we agreed that when we sold your books before coming down here we weren't going to litter up the new place with a lot of dust-catching books."

Charley left me the next day.

I had driven over to the next town where I heard there was a place you could stock up on cleaning supplies and get a good discount. I was held up coming home because I stopped to watch a demonstration of a new kind of floor waxer and I got into an argument with the man who was showing it.

When I pulled into the driveway I saw Charley at the back property line of the new lot, standing in a hole and shoveling dirt onto a big pile. The hole was already knee-deep. Charley was soaked with sweat and I could see that he probably had been working steadily ever since my back was turned. My neat, orderly lot that I worked on in the hot sun was being disfigured by that hole for Charley's pool.

I felt the return of my need to get things clean and orderly again. So I grabbed the shovel from Charley and just as he was about to explain I said: "Shut up. Get out of there and let me get this place cleaned up again."

I pitched into that pile of earth and threw it back into the hole and whacked it down good and hard because I didn't want any ugly mound of raw earth left over. I worked at top speed without paying any attention to how hot it was, the insects, or anything else and almost before I knew it I had that hole refilled, packed down hard and I even reseeded it. It wasn't as neat as before, a raw patch in the new grass, but it was orderly. I was so absorbed in what I was doing I didn't notice when Charley left.

When he didn't show up for dinner that evening I tried to call the marina where he hangs out sometimes but our phone wasn't working. I went to the next house up the street and asked to use the phone but they said it hadn't been working since the morning. Same story at the house beyond that one. Pretty fishy, I thought, that three houses in a row should all have their telephones out of order. They probably didn't want to let me see what sloppy housekeepers they were.

Charley hadn't returned by the time I went to bed. I went early because I was very tired from the strain of restoring order to the lot. When he hadn't come home by the next morning I was quite upset and drove down to report it to the county police, the phone still being out of order. They were helpful and asked like did he carry much money around with him, were any of his clothes missing, and did he have a girl friend (imagine, Charley!).

I answered "No" to all this and they said they would put out a "Missing Persons." They did but they never heard anything from it.

I must close because the lights go out in five minutes. A Merry Christmas and a Happy New Year to everyone.

All the best,
Frieda

P.S.: It seems Charley didn't run out on me after all. The telephone company tested out the buried cable that feeds our block and located a break where Charley had been putting in the pool. When they dug down to repair the cable, they found Charley. Someone had hit him with a shovel.

Nobody believed me when I said I didn't know anything about it. However, it's not so bad here as you might think. Everything is clean and orderly and already I've been put on a cleaning detail. Please write. The address is Florida State Prison, Tallacoola.

JOYCE PORTER

Dover Tangles with High Finance

The directors of Sewell & Vallotton Company, Limited, together with the upper echelons of management, enjoyed a rare privilege in their London offices. They had their own private entrance hall and over the years a great deal of care and company money had been lavished on it. Delicate works of art and exquisite antiques were dotted about the vast expanse of the hall with a tastefulness which was always being photographed by the glossier monthly magazines. Whatever economies might be made elsewhere, nobody begrudged the extravagant luxuries here, and even the doormen had their uniforms made in Savile Row.

Not that the doorman on duty at the moment was looking particularly happy as he lurked behind an expensive sculpture by Henry Moore and waited for the next batch of policemen to arrive.

He brooded resentfully about the lot he already had upstairs, trampling round in their great boots and upsetting everything. He realized, of course, that when one of your directors gets himself murdered in his own boardroom there's bound to be a bit of disturbance; but, the doorman reminded himself, there's moderation in all things. He'd been watching directors come and go for the last 25 years and he was blowed if he could see that one more or less made that much difference.

He looked at his watch. Half-past eleven! Blimey, how much longer were they going to be? You could walk it from Scotland Yard in ten minutes! He'd been hanging about here for nearly an hour already and had missed his coffee break in the bargain.

A big black car drew up in the private driveway. The doorman smoothed down his jacket and peered through the holes which Mr. Moore might have placed there for just such a purpose. Two of the occupants of the car appeared to be trying to extricate a third from the confines of the rear seat. The doorman sniffed contemptuously. Yes, well, if it hadn't been for the murder, that fat one coming out of the car like a tight cork out of a bottle wouldn't have got his foot over the threshold! What a lout! A filthy bowler hat and a disgusting old overcoat—*not* the sartorial standards you expected in the Sewell & Vallotton directors' private entrance hall!

The fat man was now laboring up the short flight of marble steps with a younger, thinner fellow chasing athletically after him. The doorman stood his ground. He'd long ago given up falling over himself to welcome anybody, never mind a couple of peasants like these.

The plate-glass doors, untouched by human hand, swung noiselessly open and the two new arrivals moved forward to receive a blast of warm scented air on the top of their heads. Another step and—

"'Strewth!" exploded Detective Chief Inspector Wilfred Dover.

There was a fastidious shiver from the glass in the chandelier but the attention of "Fattie of the Yard" was riveted on the floor. Eyes popping, he watched in astonishment as his boots sank up to the ankles in the thick pile of the carpet. For one who had spent his life wallowing in lower-middle-class squalor it was an intriguing, if unnerving, experience.

The younger, thinner man—Detective Sergeant MacGregor—went a bright pink as he always did when his superior made an exhibition of himself in public. The sergeant was just as impressed with the opulence of his surroundings as Dover was, but he would have died rather than show it.

The doorman adjusted his sneer and came forward, casually skirting the five-foot-high T'ang vase and arriving just in time to stop the fat man getting his paws on a charming little Fabergé clock which was standing defenseless on one of Sheraton's finer tables.

"H'are you the—er—gentlemen from Scotland Yard?"

Poor Sergeant MacGregor was cut to the quick by the doorman's hesitation, but if you wanted to insult Dover you had to use a sledge-hammer. In any case Dover was far too busy gawping enviously round to pay much attention to the doorman. This lot must have cost somebody a pretty penny or he was a Dutchman! What about that picture? Looked as though it had been done by a two-year-old kid with its feet but they wouldn't have stuck it in a posh frame like that if it weren't valuable. And that dirty great mirror over there? Dover swung round suddenly on the doorman.

"Here—you got all this junk properly insured?"

That took the wind right out of the doorman's sails and without another word he led the two detectives over to the directors' own personal elevator, ushered them in, showed MacGregor which button to press, and thankfully watched them slowly disappear from sight.

The directors' own personal elevator was worth a king's ransom on its own account. The wrought-iron gates were Fifteenth Century Florentine work and the two carved clusters of fruit on the side walls had been confidently attributed to Grinling Gibbons; but it was the icon on the rear wall that caught Dover's eye. Not that Dover was exactly a connoisseur of early Novgorod religious painting but he found the gold and jewels with which this particular example was covered well-nigh irresistible.

"Do you reckon those rubies are real?" he demanded as the elevator wended its way gently upward.

"Oh, I should think so, sir," said MacGregor, noting with relief that the icon seemed to be securely bolted to the wall. "They wouldn't have any imitation stuff here."

Dover's hand was already moving towards his trouser pocket. "I'll bet you could prize 'em out easy as pie with a penknife," he observed as though challenging his sergeant to say that you couldn't.

But MacGregor was quick to scotch any bright ideas in that direction. "I don't advise you to try, sir. Sewell and Vallotton's collection of antiques is very well-known and you can be quite sure they've taken all the necessary precautions against theft. I imagine this place is absolutely crawling with burglar alarms. Closed-circuit television cameras, too, I shouldn't wonder."

"Oh." Dover continued to stare wistfully at the rubies while MacGregor hoped fervently that Sewell & Vallotton had indeed got everything portable well nailed down. "I didn't know they were second-hand furniture dealers."

"Sir?"

"This dump. I thought it was some sort of an office building we were coming to."

"It is, sir. It's the head office of Sewell and Vallotton. You know"—MacGregor, who was more than a bit of a snob, looked down his nose—"they make soap."

"Soap?"

"Well, detergents now, I suppose, but they started off making soap. They're one of the biggest firms in that line in the country. Blanchett, Squishy-Washy, Alabas, Sparkle-Spume, Blua—they market all that and a dozen others besides."

"Well, what's all this stuff then?" Dover jerked an inquiring thumb at the icon.

MacGregor shrugged. "It's just their gimmick, sir. Some firms sponsor golf matches or horse shows; Sewell and Vallotton buy and display works of art. They make a specialty of saving national treasures from going abroad. It brings them millions of pounds' worth of free publicity and I suppose the antiques themselves are a pretty gilt-edged investment."

"Seems a funny way of going on," sniffed Dover.

"Sewell and Vallotton can more than afford to indulge their whimsies, sir."

Eventually the elevator reached the top floor, and Dover and MacGregor emerged to find themselves in what was known as the Directors' Suite. Here, too, money had been splashed around with a most liberal hand, as witness the fine Aubusson tapestry which covered the whole of the facing wall.

As MacGregor was closing the elevator gates they heard the creaking of regulation boots and a second later a young chubby-faced policeman came tiptoeing toward them, his cap tucked underneath his arm.

"Chief Inspector Dover, sir?" he inquired in a respectful whisper.

"Who are you?"

"Police Constable Saunderson, sir. C Division. Me and my mate answered the original 999 call and we've sort of been holding the fort ever since." In his innocence P.C. Saunderson considered himself entitled to administer a mild rebuke. "We thought you was never coming, sir."

Dover's face went black but MacGregor stepped in with a ready lie. "We were held up by the traffic," he explained quickly. "Now, what's going on here?"

"Well, nothing really at the moment, Sarge," replied P.C. Saunderson who was proving to be a rather complacent sort of lad. "I think you might say that me and my mate have got the situation well under control." He started to get his notebook out of his tunic pocket. "You've missed all the excitement—see?—what with you being held up by the traffic and everything. Now"—he flicked the pages of his notebook over—"me and Stokes—he's my mate—we got the 999 call relayed to us at ten seventeen precisely.

"A sudden death in suspicious circumstances was the message and we arrived downstairs at ten twenty-one. A nippy bit of driving that but, of course, the streets are pretty quiet round here in the middle of the morning. Or, at least, that's been my experience. Right—well, by ten twenty-three approximately we was up here and I conducted a preliminary examination of the deceased. Strictly between you and me, old Stokes is a bit of a dead loss when it comes to First Aid.

"Now, at ten twenty-five I turned to Stokes and said,"—P.C. Saunderson solemnly consulted his notebook—" 'I reckon this is a blooming murder, Jack, or' "—he turned over a page—" 'or maybe he croaked hisself.' "

"For God's sake," snarled Dover, his feet giving him hell as usual, "do we have to stand here all day listening to this twaddle?"

P.C. Saunderson, whose romantic ideas about Scotland Yard's glamorous murder squad were about to take quite a beating, was disconcerted by the violence of the interruption. "Did you want to see the body, sir?" he stammered.

"Not likely!" came Dover's indignant retort. "If I'd wanted to spend my life looking at corpses I'd have joined a blooming mortuary! Isn't there somewhere we can go and sit down?"

"Oh, yes, sir! As a matter of fact I've already requisitioned the secretary's office for your use."

"And where's the secretary?" demanded MacGregor sharply, because somebody had to keep a check on these things.

"Having hysterics in the ladies' cloaks, I shouldn't wonder," chuckled P.C. Saunderson as he led the way down a corridor devoted exclusively to masters of the Seventeenth Century Dutch school. "Funny how it takes some people, isn't it?"

"Good God, man!" shouted MacGregor. "You don't mean to say you've let her out of your—"

"Now, now, Sarge," said P.C. Saunderson soothingly, "give us credit for a bit of the old common or garden. She's in the clear. Never went in the boardroom after the bottle of sherry was opened. Everybody agrees about that. And she didn't have any contact with the suspects after the old fellow snuffed it either, so she can't be an accomplice. Ah"—he opened a door—"here we are! Think you can pig it in here?"

The secretary's room was startlingly elegant but the furnishings were merely expensive and not priceless. Dover didn't care. He homed to a comfortable-looking chair behind the desk and flopped into it with a sigh of relief. MacGregor propped himself up against a filing cabinet and got his own notebook out.

P.C. Saunderson decided not to push his luck and remained standing by the door.

"Sherry?" prompted Dover, ever hopeful.

The constable twinkled roguishly at him. "The murder weapon, sir."

"The murder weapon? Do you mean the victim was hit over the head with a bottle?"

"Oh, no, sir." It was P.C. Saunderson's turn to register surprise. "He was poisoned. Didn't they tell you?"

"Nobody ever tells me anything," grumbled Dover, with considerable justification. "And that goes for you too, laddie, so you can wipe that stupid grin off your face! I don't know what you young coppers are coming to, straight I don't! Why, when I was your age I'd have had the bloomin' case solved by now."

"Give us another half hour, sir, and I'll have it all tied up for you," responded P.C. Saunderson eagerly and watched with some trepidation as Dover's usually pasty face turned dark crimson.

The trouble with Chief Inspector Wilfred Dover was that he had a rather dog-in-the-manger attitude to work. He didn't want to do it himself, but he got exceedingly nasty if anybody else tried, too obviously, to relieve him of the burden. MacGregor, who had more experience than anybody else in the delicate art of handling the old fool, stepped in once more to smooth things over.

"Just give us the facts, Constable," he said, "and leave the detective work to us."

And, sulkily hoping that everybody realized how hurt his feelings were, P.C. Saunderson did just that.

The crime had occurred just as the monthly board meeting of the Sewell & Vallotton directors was about to start. Only five directors had been present and they had eventually divided themselves up neatly into one victim and four suspects.

"And the name of the dead man?" asked MacGregor.

"Sir Holman Hobart." P.C. Saunderson dutifully waited while MacGregor wrote it down. "He was chairman of the Board. Chap in his early sixties, I should think."

MacGregor nodded and the story continued.

The five directors had all arrrived for their meeting at about ten o'clock. According to Mrs. Doris Vick, the secretary who had welcomed them and taken their hats and coats, they had behaved quite normally and gone straight into the boardroom. When everybody had arrived she had closed the door and left them to their weighty deliberations.

MacGregor looked up. "That's a bit odd, isn't it? Doesn't the secretary usually sit with the Board and take down the minutes or something?"

"I believe that is the accepted procedure, Sarge, but from what I've been able to ascertain that lot in there"—P.C. Saunderson inclined his head toward the beautifully inlaid double doors in the wall directly opposite the secretary's desk—"are a bit of a law unto themselves." The constable lowered his voice.

"Seems they prefer to have all their argy-bargies in private and *then* call Mrs. Vick in and dictate an expurgated version of what happened. She says they're real gentlemen and they don't like cussing and swearing in front of a lady."

"What the hell," demanded Dover, temporarily abandoning his search for some decent writing paper that wasn't defaced by Sewell & Vallotton's engraved letterhead, "are you whispering for?"

"Well," said P.C. Saunderson defensively, "we don't want them to hear us talking about them, do we, sir?"

"No skin off my nose," grunted Dover and opened another drawer.

MacGregor, however, was blessed with a more inquiring mind. He pointed his pencil at the double doors. "That's the boardroom, is it?"

"Right, Sarge."

"And the dead body?"

"Oh, that's in there too, Sarge." P.C. Saunderson drew himself up proudly. "The doc wanted to take it away with him but I said no, not until you'd had a chance to look at it."

"The police surgeon's been and gone?" asked MacGregor, shooting an anxious glance at Dover.

"Said he couldn't hang about any longer, Sarge. Still, I made him give me his preliminary report. He can't tell us anything more until he's done the post-mortem."

"But I don't get this," persisted MacGregor. "You mean that all the surviving members of the Board are sitting in there with the corpse?"

"It's nicely covered up with a sheet, Sarge, and they insisted. Of course, I've got my mate, Stokes, in there too, keeping an eye on them. I told you they was a queer lot, didn't I? Not one of 'em has so much as set foot outside that room since the old boy dropped down dead."

MacGregor took a deep breath to steady himself. "Yes, well, let's get back to that, shall we? You can explain these peculiar goings on when we come to them. Now, we'd got as far as the five of them having their board meeting."

But P.C. Saunderson was a stickler for accuracy. The board meeting, he ponderously pointed out, had not actually started. There was, it seems, a rather charming tradition at Sewell & Vallotton according to which the directors, before settling down to their meeting, refreshed themselves with a glass or two of choice sherry. Poured, added the constable, looking meaningly at MacGregor, from an unopened bottle.

Dover, who had been quietly resting his eyes, opened them and smacked his lips.

"You're sure of that?" asked MacGregor.

"Quite sure, Sarge. I got it from that commissionaire chap downstairs. It's his job to supply two bottles of sherry for each board meeting. Anything the directors don't consume is his perks. He bought the bottles on his way to work this morning from an off-license in Pewter Street and he'll take his oath that they hadn't been tampered with when he left 'em on the table in the boardroom.

Anyhow, we don't need to worry too much about what happened to the sherry at this stage. If the poison had been put in the bottle, the whole lot of 'em would have died, wouldn't they?"

MacGregor chewed the end of his pencil and admitted somewhat helplessly that this would appear to be so.

P.C. Saunderson looked pleased; then, sucking in his second wind, he continued inexorably. One of the directors, the Marquis of Arnfield, had opened the sherry and poured it out, but the tray of glasses had been handed round by another director, the Honorable Gisbert Fittsarthur. Presumably either nobleman could have surreptitiously slipped in the fatal dose, but it was a little difficult to see how they could have insured that Sir Holman took the right glass. As Chairman he had been served first out of courtesy and had had the choice of five more or less identical goblets.

"You can hold a tray so that a man will probably take a particular glass," MacGregor pointed out doubtfully. "Still, it's pretty risky. What happened next?"

Nothing, really. The directors had stood around, sipping their drinks and chatting. After about ten minutes Sir Holman had called them to order and suggested that they might as well make a start. Everybody was just beginning to sit down when Sir Holman, standing at the head of the table, had gasped, clutched his throat, choked, retched, doubled up in obvious agony, and dropped down dead.

"And the funny thing is, Sarge," P.C. Saunderson went on with a wondering shake of the head, "that none of 'em seems to have doubted for a minute that he'd been poisoned. And not accidental, neither. They spotted straight off that they'd all be under suspicion, so they called the secretary on the intercom and told her to get the police. After that they just sat tight, watching each other. Until me and Stokes arrived nobody was allowed to enter or leave the boardroom. What do you think of that, eh?"

MacGregor shrugged.

"If you ask me, Sarge, it's a conspiracy."

"Well, nobody is asking you, laddie, so shut up!" Dover, having delivered himself of this pleasantry, crooked a finger at his sergeant. MacGregor hurried over to the desk. "Sling him out!" Dover ordered.

"Sir?"

"You heard me! Cocky young smart aleck—get rid of him!"

P.C. Saunderson might have had his faults but being stone-deaf wasn't one of them. "I haven't quite finished my report yet, sir," he said and went so far as to produce a friendly man-to-man smile.

Dover's habitual scowl deepened. "You were finished ten minutes ago, laddie," he growled ominously. "Take my word for it."

MacGregor moved in smartly before the situation could degenerate any further. He caught the constable by the arm and began to lead him over to the door. "Well, come on!" he urged impatiently. "What else is there? And for God's sake keep it short!"

"It's just that me and Stokes searched all the suspects, Sarge."

"And?"

"I thought that whoever brought the poison into the room must have carried it in something—see?—and they might still have the container on their person."

MacGregor gave the arm he was grasping a warning shake. "Did you find anything?"

"Well, not exactly. I haven't had time, have I? But I confiscated everything they had in their pockets. I've got all the stuff locked up in that filing cabinet and I'd just finished making a list when you arrived." P.C. Saunderson risked a sideways glance in the direction of the desk. "I hope I did the right thing."

MacGregor opened the door with one hand and held out the other. "Give me the key. Now"—he dropped his voice and spoke more kindly—"take my advice and stay out of sight for a bit. No, better still, see if you can't rustle up some coffee for him, and a few biscuits. He's generally a bit more amenable when he's been fed."

With the door open and escape in sight, P.C. Saunderson threw the discipline of years to the winds. "What's his favorite food, Sarge?" he demanded in an aggrieved whisper. "Babies?"

Dover watched in gloomy silence as MacGregor unlocked the filing cabinet and brought out five small cardboard boxes, all neatly labeled with names. It was only when the boxes had been deposited on the desk in front of him and he caught sight of the contents that he sat up and began to take notice.

"Blimey!" he squealed. "Get an eyeful of all that!"

"Oh, sir, I don't think—"

MacGregor was too late. Chief Inspector Dover had already got at the loot and was dribbling gold watches, silver cigar cutters, platinum ballpoint pens, and plump soft leather wallets through the stickiest fingers in the Metropolitan Police. MacGregor scrabbled desperately, trying to return each avidly snatched-up goodie to its own box.

"Who are they, for God's sake?" gasped Dover, flicking away unsuccessfully at a diamond-studded lighter before abandoning it for another in opalescent strawberry enamel. "Bleeding millionaires?"

MacGregor caught the diamond-studded lighter just before it hit the desk. "As near as makes no difference, I believe, sir. Now, which box did this come from? Oh, sir, please, we shall get them all muddled up and—"

"It's downright unfair!" whined Dover, grabbing for an alligator-skin wallet. "Nobody ought to be this rich! 'Strewth, look at this!" He opened the wallet to reveal a thick wad of five-pound notes. "I'll bet he doesn't even know how much he's bleeding well got!"

"He may not, sir," said MacGregor, literally pulling the wallet out of Dover's stubby fingers, "but P.C. Saunderson certainly does. He's made a complete inventory of everything."

"He would!" Dover looked around for a consolation prize. A heavy gold cigarette case caught his eye and by the time MacGregor had returned the wallet to its box Dover was already lighting a fat white cigarette with the enameled lighter.

"Oh, *sir*!" said MacGregor.

Dover ignored the reproach and went through the routine of hacking, coughing, and spluttering which, more often than not, accompanied his first puff.

"Don't you think we'd better start questioning the people concerned, sir? They must be getting very impatient at having to wait so long."

Dover mopped his eyes and regarded his purloined cigarette with disgust. "Talk about sweaty socks!" he observed disparagingly. "What did you say? Oh, I suppose we might as well. Wheel the first one in."

In some bewilderment MacGregor examined the names, titles, and decorations which P.C. Saunderson had painstakingly written on the little boxes. How was one with only a scanty acquaintance of the beau monde to sort out the precedence in this bunch? Of course Sir Holman Hobart Bt., K.C.V.O., C.B., D.S.O., M.C. (the deceased), could be ignored; but that still left the Marquis of Arnfield, M.V.O., M.B.E., T.D.; Dr. Benjamin Zlatt, O.B.B., Q.C., M.Sc., LL.D., F.R.I.C.; Vice-Admiral T. R. Jonkett-Brown, C.B.E., D.S.O., D.S.C., R.N. (ret); and the Honorable Gisbert Fittsarthur, B.A., F.R.G.S.

"Alphabetical order!" grunted Dover, cutting the Gordian knot.

As a matter of fact, almost any sequence would have served, as there was a remarkable similarity in the appearance of the surviving Sewell & Vallotton directors. Dover, indeed, never really did get round to telling t'other from which. It was almost as if all four of them had been cast from the same mold and only as an afterthought had a few superficial details been added to distinguish one from the other. Each was vaguely middle-aged, agressively well-nourished, beautifully groomed and suited by a tailor who knew, where necessary, how to conceal an incipient paunch.

The Marquis of Arnfield, as befitted a peer of the realm, played it very aloof and distant. He waited with only the merest hint of impatience as MacGregor placed a chair for him in front of the desk.

Dover was busy examining a packet of picture postcards which he had found tucked away in Admiral Jonkett-Brown's possessions, but the Marquis appeared not to notice the snickers and grins which ensued. He had condescended to make a statement to the police but that was going to be the limit of his social contact with them.

"I think I should say right at the beginning," drawled the Marquis, gazing at a delightful little Gainsborough which hung on the wall over Dover's right shoulder, "that I did not murder Sir Holman Hobart."

"Disgusting!" chuckled Dover under his breath. "They bloomin' well want running in for having muck like—oh, crikey!" And then, just to show that his mind really was on his work, he swung round suddenly on the Marquis. "You seem damned sure it's murder."

"Accident would appear to be extremely unlikely and Sir Holman was the last man in the world to commit suicide, especially in public."

"Might have been a heart attack or something," said Dover, wondering why he hadn't thought of that lovely labor-saving idea before.

The Marquis continued to feast his eyes on the Gainsborough. Most people, finding themselves face to face with Dover, would have done the same. "Your police doctor didn't think so."

Dover sighed and shuffled through his picture postcards. "Who are you putting your money on?"

The Marquis didn't bother pretending not to understand. "I'm afraid I haven't the faintest idea. They say poison is a woman's weapon, don't they? Perhaps you ought to arrest our faithful Mrs. Vick."

"The secretary? But I thought she—"

The Marquis deigned to look straight at Dover. "I was being facetious," he murmured. "But, since we are on the subject of poisoning, perhaps I ought to mention that Dr. Zlatt is a qualified chemist."

"Is he now?" said Dover, pushing the picture postcards to one side.

"And a very distinguished one. Sewell and Vallotton often employ him as a consultant and so do several other firms. He must have unrestricted access to a number of industrial research laboratories."

"Fancy." Dover looked up hopefully. "You didn't happen to see him slipping anything in Sir What's-his-name's drink?"

The Marquis squinted down his nose. "Of course not."

Dover sighed again and dragged some sheets of typing paper over in front of him. "You'd better tell us what happened in there, I suppose," he grumbled and began hunting through the boxes in front of him. Eventually he selected an old-fashioned fountain pen belonging to the Honorable Gisbert Fittsarthur and unscrewed the top. "You're the one who poured the sherry, aren't you?"

"Yes. I always do. I filled the five glasses on the tray, took my own, then old Gissie Fittsarthur handed the others round. He loves appearing generous when somebody else is footing the bill."

There was a strong rumor circulating round Scotland Yard that Chief Inspector Wilfred Dover couldn't even write his own name. Judging from the way he was futilely scratching with the borrowed fountain pen, the rumor was probably true. MacGregor watched him jabbing the nib irritably into the paper and decided that he had better carry on with the questioning until Dover had less important problems on his mind.

"Did you speak to Sir Holman, sir, after you poured out the sherry and before he died?"

The Marquis acknowledged MacGregor's presence by a languid quarter turn of his head. "Naturally. I went over to have a word with him as soon as I'd finished pouring the sherry. I suppose we stood chatting over by the window for several minutes."

By judicious use of his teeth Dover managed to restore the fourteen-carat gold nib to something approaching its original condition. MacGregor hurried on with his next question.

"What happened after that, sir?"

The Marquis withdrew a fine linen handkerchief from his cuff and waved it negligently across his nose. The scent of lavender filled the air. "After that? Well, Sir Holman was called away by Dr. Zlatt. Zlatt had a great sheaf of papers in his hand and the pair of them stood looking at them. I joined Gissie Fittsarthur and the Admiral by the sherry table. Gissie was knocking back as much free drink as he could get his hands on, of course. Then Sir Holman started walking to the head of the table to call the meeting to order and Admiral Jonkett-Brown muttered something about wanting a quick word with him. He caught him about halfway up the table and they had a brief chat. After that Sir Holman suggested that we should all take our seats."

Dover chucked the fountain pen back in its box and scowled disagreeably at the Marquis of Arnfield. "So the whole bang shoot of you talked to Sir What's-his-name while he was guzzling his sherry?"

An expression of acute distaste passed over the Marquis' countenance. "Not exactly. Gissie Fittsarthur didn't speak to him, as far as I can remember."

Dover grunted and returned to an examination of the little boxes.

The Marquis wafted his handkerchief over his face again. "Is that all?" he asked MacGregor faintly.

"Well, just another question or two, if you don't mind, sir." MacGregor cringed visibly as Dover emerged triumphant with a carved ivory toothpick. "When Sir Holman left you to go and talk to Dr. Zlatt, can you remember how much sherry he still had left in his glass?"

"Yes."

"I beg your pardon, sir?"

The Marquis closed his eyes in a slow blink of martyrdom. "I said, yes, I do remember how much sherry he still had in his glass. He had it all left."

"All, sir?"

The Marquis directed a bleak stare at MacGregor. "Are you having difficulty in hearing me, my good man?"

MacGregor blushed. "No, sir."

"I am glad to hear it. I rather pride myself on the clarity of my enunciation. Now, as I was saying, when Sir Holman left me to talk to Zlatt he hadn't touched his sherry. There was nothing unusual about this. Sir Holman was a whiskey man and didn't care much for sherry. However, it is the tradition at Sewell and Vallotton to serve sherry before each board meeting, so there was nothing Sir Holman could do about it. He just used to carry his glass around until he was ready to open the meeting. Then he went to the head of the table, tossed the whole glassful down at one go, and called us to order. Like," added the Marquis with a very aristocratic sneer, "someone drinking cough mixture."

"That's very interesting, sir," said MacGregor and shot a glance at Dover to see if this vital piece of information had penetrated the solid ivory. Was there a momentary hesitation in the delicate exploration, with the borrowed toothpick, of the Chief Inspector's left ear? It was difficult to tell. MacGregor turned back to the Marquis. "I suppose everybody in the boardroom knew that Sir Holman usually drank his sherry like that?"

"Of course." The Marquis flourished his handkerchief with studied grace. "It was no secret. He did it for years."

MacGregor tried to hide his excitement. "No doubt that's why he never noticed the poison."

"No doubt. Is there anything else?"

"Er—just one more point, sir." MacGregor turned back a page or two in his notebook. "Ah, yes. Could you tell me what you and Sir Holman were talking about, sir?"

The Marquis looked annoyed. "I fail to see what damned business it is of yours," he snapped, "but, if you must know, we were discussing my re-election to the board. I am due to retire in a couple of months under our rules and I wanted to be quite sure that our chairman knew that I was intending to stand again."

"There was no quarrel or disagreement, sir?"

"None. Sir Holman assured me of his full support." The Marquis stood up and glared icily at Dover who was now engaged in trying to get the top off the Marquis' own pocket flask. "No doubt you will be returning my personal possessions in due course. I would prefer to have them in an undamaged condition, if that is possible . . ."

The Honorable Gisbert Fittsarthur was a watery-eyed, shriveled old chap who was clearly keen to get on pally terms with two real-life detectives.

"Always been a great one for mystery stories," he confided as he hitched his chair nearer to the desk. "Started as a nipper with those Sherlock Holmes ones and never looked back since, hm? Borrow 'em from the library, don't you know. Can't afford to buy books with surtax the rate it is. So—you've me to thank that there was no tampering with the evidence in there, hm? Knew there was something pretty fishy about the way old Holman keeled over. Fit as a fiddle, he was. 'Don't touch anything!' I told 'em. 'And nobody's to leave the room, either!' I knew exactly what to do, hm?"

Dover scowled resentfully and pulled the Honorable Gisbert's box in front of him. The old-fashioned fountain pen, a rather shabby wallet, four pieces of string, three bus tickets, a large sheet of hastily folded blotting paper—the Honorable Gisbert's personal possessions were not up to the high standards Dover had come to expect. He opened up the sheet of blotting paper and glowered at its virgin whiteness.

The Honorable Gisbert grinned sheepishly. "Always stock up on a bit of stationery, hm? Well, Sewell and Vallotton won't miss it, will they?"

Dover pushed the box away and got down to business. "You were the one who handed the sherry round?"

"Ah! Yes, well, I can explain that. Innocent as a newborn babe, hm? Sherry glasses all laid out on a heavy silver tray. Lord Arnfield pours the sherry out. I pick up the tray. Both hands, see? Takes both my hands to lift the damned thing. Couldn't possibly have held it in one hand while I popped the poison in. Besides, how did I know which glass poor Holman was going to take?"

"You served him first," Dover pointed out through an enormous yawn.

"Who told you that? Oh, Arnfield, of course! Well, if it's a suspect you're after, have a good look at our noble Marquis, hm? *Cui bono*, that's what I always say."

MacGregor knew it was no use waiting for Dover to respond to a Latin phrase, however well-known. "Are you suggesting that the Marquis of Arnfield benefits from Sir Holman's death?" he asked.

The Honorable Gisbert bared his yellow teeth in what could have been a smile. "Five thousand a year. What I'd call a substantial motive, hm?"

"He stands to inherit that, sir?"

"No, not inherit! Keep. That's what he gets for serving on the board, don't you know. Arnfield's term of office coming to an end. No re-election for him without poor Holman's backing. Ergo, five thousand a year gone up the spout and Arnfield's got some very expensive hobbies to keep up."

"And Sir Holman was not going to support him, sir?"

The Honorable Gisbert winked, tapped the side of his nose, and leered knowingly. "Little bird!" he sniggered. "Little bird, hm? Holman wanted the seat for his nephew. Everybody knows that."

"You accusing this Marquis of Who's-your-father of murder?" demanded Dover who could occasionally get to the point with amazing speed.

The Honorable Gisbert squirmed uncomfortably. "Hey, steady on!" he whinnied. "Arnfield and I belong to the same club. Not that I'll be able to keep my dues up much longer with the way—"

"Well, who do you fancy then?" demanded Dover.

"I'd give you six to four on Zlatt," responded the Honorable Gisbert maliciously. "Well, you can't call poisoning an Englishman's crime, can you?"

Dover had found himself an ebony comb in a chased silver case. "That all you've got to go on? That Zlatt's not an Englishman?"

"No. He's got a motive, too."

"So has this Marquis fellow."

"Zlatt's is bigger," said the Honorable Gisbert. "*Cui bono*—told you that before." He paused in wonder as Dover slowly drew the comb through his meager tufts of hair. "I say, that's a bit unhygienic, isn't it?"

"Why?" asked Dover, continuing his combing unperturbed. "Zlatt's not got dandruff, has he?"

"That's Zlatt's comb?"

"In his box," said Dover, idly running his thumbnail along the teeth.

The Honorable Gisbert whickered like a senile horse. "Bald as a coot!" he tittered. "What's he want a comb for?"

"Maybe it's a reminder of happier days," chuckled Dover and warmed to the Honorable Gisbert as this shaft of wit was greeted by flattering guffaws.

MacGregor, who had lost his sense of humor the day after he was appointed Dover's assistant, cleared his throat. "You were telling us about Dr. Zlatt's motive, sir."

"Ah!" The Honorable Gisbert pulled himself together. "Next chairman of Sewell and Vallotton. No doubt about it. Ten thousand a year plus perks." The yellow teeth were revealed once more. "Might be tempted to commit murder myself for that, hm? And he had the opportunity. While he was showing poor Holman those papers. Quickness of the hand, hm? Juggling about like that he could easily have dropped something in Holman's sherry."

Police Constable Saunderson brought in the coffee.

Dover welcomed the refreshments with his usual charm and grace. "Coffee? 'Strewth, it's a square meal I want, laddie!" He grabbed the stickiest-looking cake. "This muck wouldn't keep a fly going."

"Maybe I can get you some sandwiches, sir," said P.C. Saunderson as another cake plunged down the Chief Inspector's gullet.

"Sandwiches? With my stomach, laddie?" Dover shook his head and his face assumed a suitably solemn expression. "I've got to be careful, I have. Doctor's orders: I've got a very delicate stomach, you see, and—"

But MacGregor had no intention of letting Dover get started on the subject of his stomach. "I do think, sir, that we ought to finish off these interviews before lunch. We've kept these people waiting long enough already and they are pretty important men, you know. We don't want them to be making complaints."

"Let 'em try!" blustered Dover with the bravado of one who'd had more complaints made against him than most of us have had hot dinners. "We're dealing with murder, not some bloomin' parking violation."

"That's what makes speed in the initial stages so important, isn't it, sir?"

Dover, after a pause for thought, decided that MacGregor hadn't the guts to try being cheeky. He helped himself to another cake.

"Er—have you got any theories yet, sir?"

Dover wiped a blob of cream off his lapel and slowly licked his finger. "Didn't care much for the look of that Marquis fellow," he admitted grudgingly. "Or the other one, come to that."

"The Honorable Gisbert, sir? No, he wasn't very impressive, was he? This Dr. Zlatt looks as though he might be a good possibility." Dover nodded, his mouth full again.

"Actually, sir"—MacGregor broached the subject with considerable care because Dover had a habit of reacting unfavorably to other people's ideas—"I was wondering about the Marquis of Arnfield myself. It's this business of Sir Holman not liking sherry, you see. Now, presented with a tray of glasses, wouldn't he be likely to take the one that was *least* full? The Marquis could have poisoned one glass and then only half filled it—"

"You don't have to spell it out in words of one syllable!" snapped Dover, indicating that he was ready for his second cup of coffee by shoving the saucer noisily across the desk.

"It was just a suggestion, sir."

"And a damned stupid one!" snarled Dover as he stuffed the last cake in his mouth. "Anyhow, I thought of it myself hours ago."

"Yes, sir," sighed MacGregor.

Dover dropped six lumps of sugar in his cup and started stirring it with a silver swizzle stick that he'd come across in the Marquis of Arnfield's box. The gentle exercise appeared to give him pleasure and for some minutes he swizzled away. MacGregor and P.C. Saunderson stood in bemused silence until the Chief Inspector at last raised his head. "Well, what are you waiting for? Bring the next one in!"

Vice-Admiral Jonkett-Brown had bright blue mariner's eyes, a red face, and a nasty temper. In spite of this he very nearly became Dover's friend for life when he stormed in declaring that he would make no statement and answer no questions without the professional advice of his solicitor.

"Very wise!" approved Dover, most of whose attention was currently devoted to thumbing through a little address book he'd found. "Pity there aren't a few more like you. Get the next one, MacGregor!"

The Admiral was a little taken aback. "It's not that I want to obstruct your inquiries," he explained awkwardly.

"Of course not," agreed Dover, delicately moistening a finger before he turned over the next page.

"But you must admit we've all been placed in a deuced sticky position."

Dover's face was beginning to ache with the effort of sustaining an encouraging smile. "You can't be too careful," he mumbled.

"Not that I've anything to hide," the Admiral went on. "Damn it, I only exchanged a couple of words with Holman before he went down as though he'd been felled with a marlinespike." Without thinking he sat down in the chair and the last traces of benevolence faded from Dover's countenance. "So, you see, I couldn't have killed him, even if I'd wanted to. Poor old devil! what a rotten way to go, eh? Still, one of us four must have done it. There's no getting away from that. Well, luckily I'm not the sort of man who flinches in the face of unpleasant facts. Now, let's have a look at the rest of the field, shall we? What about the Marquis of Arnfield for a start? I daresay you've formed a few opinions of your own about him but I'd just like you to listen to a little theory of mine."

Dover reached for a watch from the Honorable Gisbert's box, wound it up, and placed it ostentatiously on the desk.

The Admiral beamed. "Good! I'm glad to see you're a man after my own heart. Be brief and keep to the point—that's what I used to tell my young officers. I can't tolerate chaps who ramble on and on without ever saying anything. I've been accused of being a trifle too blunt in my time, but nobody's ever called me a shilly-shallier. Thirty years in the Navy's taught me a thing or two—and keeping my eyes open is one of them. And using the old brain. I haven't been wasting my time sitting out there, you know. I've been thinking and in my opinion the Marquis of Arnfield might well be your man. And I can give you a lead as to how he did it, too."

To Dover's patent dismay the Admiral settled back comfortably in his chair and crossed one immaculately trousered leg over the other. "As soon as he'd poured out the sherry, Arnfield dashed across the room and caught poor Holman over by the window. They were talking together for quite a while, discussing Arnfield's chances of being re-elected to the board, I shouldn't wonder. Still, that doesn't matter at the moment. What does matter is that Arnfield is congenitally incapable of speaking to any of us members of the lower orders without waving that damned handkerchief of his about like a distress signal. You must have noticed him. It's a damned dirty habit, if you ask me, and dashed distracting, too. With that flapping about in your face you could have a ton of bricks dropped in your sherry and never even notice."

MacGregor caught Dover's eye and correctly interpreted the finger being drawn grimly across the Chief Inspector's throat as an indication that somebody's patience was becoming exhausted. Vice-Admiral Jonkett-Brown, however, was not a man who let himself be interrupted lightly and MacGregor's half-hearted attempts were sunk without a qualm.

"Mind you, the Marquis of Arnfield isn't the only one you ought to be keeping your eye on. There's our Herr Doktor Zlatt, too. I've always thought he was a deuced sight too clever by half. Ambitious, you know. Sort of blighter who'd stop at nothing. Well, now"—the Admiral uncrossed his legs and glanced expectantly up at Dover—"there's a couple of pointers for you to follow up."

Dover's eyes had been closed for some time and they didn't open.

The Admiral, his ears already beginning to steam a little, turned brusquely to MacGregor in search of enlightenment. "The fellow's not gone to sleep, has he?" he demanded.

"Of course not, sir!" MacGregor's attempt to pass off a tricky situation with a gay laugh was not helped by the faint bubbling sound which started to come from Dover's lips. "Er—what about the Honorable Gisbert Fittsarthur, sir?"

"He happens to be a very old friend of mine," said the Admiral coldly, as though that settled the matter.

"But that doesn't mean that he isn't capable of murder."

"It makes it dashed unlikely!"

"He did hand the sherry round, sir."

"True." The Admiral pursed his lips. "But we were all watching him very closely. He dropped the tray last month. He's beginning to show his age, you know. Getting doddery and more than a bit potty, too. He's got this bee in his bonnet about how poor he is. Well"—the Admiral's red face creased in a frown as he tried to be fair—"I don't suppose he's worth a penny more than half a million these days but that's no excuse for some of the things he does. I mean, we've all got to tighten our belts a bit but there's no need to go writing your letters on the blank pages torn out of library books, is there?"

"I suppose not, sir," said MacGregor.

"And the way he goes on at these board meetings! It's a positive disgrace for a fellow of his breeding. Filling his fountain pen out of the chairman's inkwell, purloining pencils and sheets of paper, downing as much free sherry as he can get his hands on! I've warned him about it. 'Never you mind about finishing up in a pauper's grave,' I told him. 'It's the loony bin you're heading for.' I might as well have saved my breath because he went through the whole rigmarole just the same this morning. Jolly poor show, you know, with people like Zlatt looking on. Gives 'em an entirely false impression of British aristocracy."

* * * *

By the time Dr. Benjamin Zlatt settled himself with bland composure in the suspects' chair, Dover had had more than enough. His stomach was rumbling like a jumbo jet at takeoff. Dr. Zlatt suddenly found himself at the tail end of Dover's fury.

"I'm thinking of charging you with the murder!" snarled Dover.

Dr. Zlatt didn't turn a hair. "In that case, my dear sir, I can only advise you to think again."

"You have access to poison!" roared Dover, determined now to make some-body pay for all the trouble he was being put to. "You'll be the next chairman of this bloomin' board and you could have slipped the poison into Sir What's-his-name's sherry when you were showing him those papers."

"Ah!" Dr. Zlatt nodded his head wisely. "Means, motive, and opportunity! Luckily I can demolish your hypothesis without much difficulty."

"Oh, can you? Well, take it from me, mate, if there's any demolishing to be done round here I'll do it!" Dover, suiting his actions to his words, raised his fists and clenched them threateningly. It would have been more impressive if they hadn't looked like a couple of rather dirty, pink, overstuffed cushions.

Dr. Zlatt merely smiled. "May I be permitted to deal with your accusations one at a time? First, the question of the poison. I agree—nobody in that boardroom could have got hold of whatever poison may have been used more easily than I. But, please, give me credit for some intelligence. Should I ever contemplate committing murder, poison is the last means I should choose. It would point the finger of suspicion at me immediately."

"It's the old double bluff," said Dover. "You used poison because you thought I'd think you'd be too clever to use poison."

There were thirty seconds of respectful silence while everybody, including Dover, dissected the cunning logic of this statement.

"And then," Dr. Zlatt continued calmly, "we come to my presumed motive. No doubt the chairmanship of the Sewell and Vallotton board will be offered to me but that doesn't mean that I shall accept it. In fact, I shall not. I am an extremely rich man, my dear sir, and my time is already fully occupied with much work. You will have to take my word for it, but I can assure you that I simply am not interested in becoming Sir Holman's successor."

Dover was now regarding Dr. Zlatt with the utmost loathing. "You'd have to say that!"

"I turned down the chairmanship of another company only last week and the fees were nearly double what I would get here."

Dover turned green with envy and fished out his last ace. "You were the only one with the opportunity to poison the sherry."

Dr. Zlatt trumped the ace. "Now that, my dear sir, is just not true. All the others were in the near vicinity of Sir Holman and had just as much chance as I did. Even more, I would imagine."

"They weren't waving papers all over to distract his attention."

Dr. Zlatt leaned back rather gracefully in his chair. "I'm afraid you have been slightly misinformed. I did talk to Sir Holman for several minutes and I did wave papers about. I was showing him the plans for a new research laboratory which Sewell and Vallotton are thinking of building. However, at that time, Sir Holman's glass of sherry was not in his hand."

Collapse of stout party. "Wadder y'mean?" gabbled Dover.

"Before looking at the plans Sir Holman quite naturally put his glass down so that he could have both his hands free. He stepped across to the boardroom table and left his glass by the things in front of his chair. You know about his habit of draining his glass at one gulp just before he opened the meeting?"

"Oh, damn and blast!" said Dover and retired from the interrogation in a sulk.

Dr. Zlatt proved that he could manage quite well without him. "I wonder if you would permit me to offer you a small suggestion, Sergeant?" he said, turning to MacGregor. "It's this problem of motive. Sir Holman wasn't the sort of man who had murderous enemies, certainly not among his fellow directors. On the other hand we are all of us interested in money. Now, as soon as the stock market gets wind of Sir Holman's death, Sewell and Vallotton shares will drop like a plummet of lead. Somebody with prior knowledge could, if you will excuse the expression, make a killing."

MacGregor looked up from his notebook. "You mean buying up shares in the hope they'll rise later, sir?"

"That's one possibility, but I was thinking of another manipulation. Selling short. A man contracts to sell at some future date shares which he doesn't yet possess. He hopes, of course, to be able to buy the shares meanwhile at a lower price and thus make a profit."

"Ah"—MacGregor had recently bought himself a paperback on the art of investing and reckoned he knew his way around the corridors of high finance— "you mean a bull, sir?"

"Well," said Dr. Zlatt kindly, "it's a bear, actually, but you've got the right idea."

Dover sniggered and got a reproving glance from Dr. Zlatt.

"We'll have to look into this, sir," said MacGregor thoughtfully.

"I should get your Fraud Squad people on to it. They know their way around the City. You see, if somebody in that boardroom did deliberately kill Sir Holman so that the Sewell and Vallotton shares would drop, he certainly wouldn't have used his own name in his financial dealings. You'll probably need an expert to unravel all the complications."

"And what," asked Dover, removing a fat cigar from Vice-Admiral Jonkett-Brown's pigskin case, "do you think you're doing?"

MacGregor paused in mid-dialing. "I was calling the Yard, sir."

"Wafor?"

"I thought we should follow up Dr. Zlatt's suggestion, sir, and see if anybody has been playing the market with Sewell and Vallotton shares."

" 'Strewth!" said Dover, his piggy little eyes gleaming contemptuously through a cloud of richly aromatic smoke. "You don't half like to do things the hard way."

MacGregor dropped the telephone back onto its stand. "Well," he said with as much patience as he could muster, "I really don't see what other line we can pursue at the moment, sir." He glanced in some despair at his notebook. "Our questioning of the four obvious suspects doesn't seem to have got us very far, does it? We can't do much about checking up where the poison came from until we know exactly what it was and it may be hours before the lab comes up with the answer. And as far as I can see from the rather muddled picture we've got of what happened immediately prior to the murder, any one of the four men could have put the poison in Sir Holman's glass of sherry."

MacGregor waited politely while Dover draped himself over the edge of the desk and coughed his heart up. "Actually I was wondering, sir, if perhaps we oughtn't to try staging a reconstruction of the crime. I don't know about you, sir, by I don't feel I've got a very clear idea of what people's movements really were. Of course," added MacGregor rather bitterly, "it would perhaps have helped if we'd examined the boardroom first."

Dover, strangely enough, was no longer coughing. He was laughing. Uproariously, triumphantly, and quite obviously at MacGregor's expense.

MacGregor, his jaw locked, counted up to ten. "Sir?"

"Reconstruction of the crime!" spluttered Dover. " 'Strewth, you'll be the death of me yet!"

MacGregor hoped so from the bottom of his heart, but he was inhibited by police discipline from voicing his desire aloud.

"We'll make the arrest after lunch," said Dover, rubbing it in.

"Arrest, sir? But—who are you going to arrest?"

Dover picked up his bowler hat and screwed it on his head. "What's-his-name—that Australian fellow."

Australian fellow? MacGregor almost sagged with relief. The old fool had gone clean off his rocker at last. Or did he mean Austrian? "Dr. Zlatt, sir?"

"No, not Zlatt, you damned fool! He wasn't Australian, was he?" Dover dragged himself to his feet and tapped the ash off his cigar onto the lush carpet. "The one who kept saying 'cooee.' What's his name?" He looked at the labels on the little boxes. "Fittsarthur. The Honorable Gisbert."

"The Honorable Gisbert Fittsarthur, sir?" echoed MacGregor incredulously. "But you can't arrest him!"

"Oh, can't I?" scowled Dover. "You just wait and see, laddie!"

MacGregor wrung his hands and tried an appeal to reason and common sense. "Sir, you can't just charge a man with murder because you don't like the look of him. You have to have *evidence*. You can't run in a man of his standing as though he was just some smelly old tramp. He'll kick up the most frightful shindy, sir, and you'll be—"

"I've got evidence," Dover broke in crossly. "What do you think I am? An idiot?"

It was not a question that MacGregor dared to answer. "You've got evidence that the Honorable Gisbert Fittsarthur murdered Sir Holman, sir?"

"As good as," muttered Dover, showing a belated sense of caution. "All it wants is a bit of checking. Motive and the like."

"A bit of checking? I see, sir. Well, would it be asking too much to inquire of what it consists?"

The ironic tone was not lost on Dover. His face twisted up into a scowl. "Don't you start coming the old sarcastic with me, laddie!" he snarled. "I was solving crimes when you were still in diapers and don't you forget it! Here"—he grabbed the old-fashioned fountain pen out of the Honorable Gisbert's box and chucked it at MacGregor—"there's your blooming evidence!"

MacGregor turned the fountain pen over doubtfully in his hands and tried to fathom out where it could possibly fit into the murder. Of course, the Chief Inspector was probably as far off the beam as he usually was but you could never be sure. Once in a blue moon the bumbling old idiot did manage to make two and two add up to four and, when he did, MacGregor was never allowed to forget it.

Luckily Dover wasn't prepared to postpone his lunch one second longer than was absolutely necessary. "That's what he carried the poison in, nitwit!"

Light dawned and MacGregor could have kicked himself. Of course! Oh why, oh why hadn't he spotted it first? It was so childishly obvious when you knew. "The Honorable Gisbert filling his fountain pen from the chairman's inkwell!" he gasped.

Dover gave a withering sniff. "My God, it's taken you long enough to see it! You're that busy scribbling down every blooming word in your little book that you miss what's sticking right up under your nose. When this Gisbert joker went to fill his fountain pen with ink, Sir What's-his-name's glass of sherry was next to the inkwell on the boardroom table, wasn't it?"

MacGregor agreed eagerly that it was. "Dr. Zlatt told us that Sir Holman had put his glass down there—"

"And somebody else mentioned Gisbert filling his fountain pen."

"Vice-Admiral Jonkett-Brown."

"But when I tried to use the pen there was no bloomin' ink in it! I couldn't get the damned thing to write at all."

MacGregor, prompted by the most unworthy of motives, clutched at a final straw. He unscrewed the cap of the fountain pen and tried it. It didn't write. He wiggled the little lever on the side hopefully, but it was no good: the fountain pen was empty.

"Of course, sir," MacGregor said, "this doesn't *prove* that the Honorable Gisbert squirted poison into Sir Holman's glass of sherry while pretending to fill his fountain pen from the inkwell."

"'Strewth!" roared Dover, heading for the door and his lunch. "You want it with jam on, you do. I've told you what happened, laddie. I've done my bit. The rest is up to you."

WILLIAM ARDEN

The Bizarre Case Expert

In our city before a case ends up in the Unsolved File it comes to the Central Squad, Inspector Frank Stockton in command. Most of the jobs at Central are big touchy cases like rackets, narcotics rings, bank holdups, counterfeiting, and the like. But not all.

Central gets anything that stumps the precinct squads—what we call the "circus cases." Or, to be more exact, I get them: Detective Sergeant Joseph Marx, the one-man Circus Case Squad.

This one began in the Tenth Precinct on Diamond Hill, one of our richer sections. I got it at 4:10 P.M. on a Monday. The Inspector gave me the word himself.

"What's their problem?" I asked warily.

"Well," the Inspector said solemnly, "it seems that they don't exactly know. Maybe it's a locked room or a perfect alibi or a vanished weapon. What I do know is, it's two days old."

"Two days? And they still don't know what the problem is?"

"They know they're in a hole. So go dig them out. Fast."

"I'll be back tonight."

I wasn't. It was the start of a long haul, but I didn't know that then. What I knew was, I was getting a reputation that wasn't good for me—The Circus Case Man. It could ruin me with my colleagues; they don't like hot-shots.

It didn't seem as if Lieutenant George Mastro thought I was a hot-shot. The Chief of the Tenth's Detective Squad looked as if he were sorry for me.

"We're stumped on this one, and so is Homicide," Mastro said bluntly. "How do you want to start?"

"I'll read the reports, if that's okay with you."

"Fine. Maybe you can spot something we've missed."

The first report was by Patrolman Sid Lewis in the tortured style of a man who agonized over paperwork. At 12:22 A.M. Saturday night Lewis and his partner, Patrolman Ed Lincoln, went to investigate a complaint of noise.

They found 1415 Laguna Terrace to be a new apartment house with a well-lighted lobby and a doorman. In the lobby they met the manager, the doorman, and two female tenants. The two women were irate over the noise being made by "that tramp in 6-B."

The manager had a different view, and said, in Lewis' stilted words, "Mrs. Sally Tower is an excellent tenant. She is a well-known interior decorator, and a lady. Her only visitors, so far as I know, are her business associates, her fiancé Mr. Tolliver, and her ex-husband. She is not a giver of noisy parties."

The ladies, according to Lewis who wrote down every detail he could remember whether it seemed important or not, had more to say about Mrs. Tower, including: "Crazy way she dresses!"—"That sick apartment!"—"Arty egghead with no morals!" Lewis put it all down, apparently on the way up to 6-B. When he got there all was quiet in 6-B.

With the ladies and the manager in tow, Lewis knocked on the door. There was no response; no sounds at all.

"She's in there all right," said a lady, later identified as Mrs. Kuzco. "I've been watching her door. Yelling and shouting something awful!"

Lewis asked the manager to use his passkey. The manager did, but it turned out that the door was chained on the inside. Suspicious of the total silence, Lewis and Lincoln managed to kick the door in.

At that point Lewis and Lincoln were busy for a few minutes. The ladies screamed. The manager actually fainted. People poured out of the other apartments to stare at the carnage.

The reason for the silence in 6-B was now clear: murder . . .

Lewis officially reported the scene: "After restoring order I crossed a large foyer into a living room. The room was in great disorder from some violent struggle.

"A female Caucasian, aged about 30 years, lay on the floor near a bedroom door. There was considerable blood, all fresh. I ascertained her condition, bloodying my person and uniform, and found her to be dead.

"A male Caucasian, aged about 40, lay some feet away, near a dining table. He was unconscious, bloody, breathing in a shallow manner, but was not dead.

"I observed that the window to the fire escape was open. The manager having revived, I asked him to identify the body, and sent Patrolman Lincoln to examine the area beneath the fire escape. The manager, having examined the female body, identified her as Mrs. Sally Tower. He identified the injured man as Mr. Paul Tower, her ex-husband. I then called the precinct and reported. The time was 12:32 A.M. I remained in the apartment until the arrival of detectives."

Patrolman Lincoln's report added only that he had found nothing in the yard or basement, that the yard was all concrete, that the other buildings were close and had similar yards. I turned to the report of the Medical Examiner.

Mrs. Sally Tower, 32, had died of multiple blows to her head by a blunt instrument. Her left arm was broken, and her head had four distinct skull fractures. She had died between 12:00 midnight and 12:45 A.M. Since the patrolmen had arrived at 12:28, and the noise had ceased about 12:20, the time of murder was fixed in those eight minutes.

Paul Tower, 40, had suffered concussion, a hairline skull fracture, and a broken nose, all from two blows to the head. According to the M.E., Tower had been unconscious about thirty minutes when the M.E. arrived at 12:50 A.M. The one blow on the cranium, in the M.E.'s opinion, had rendered Tower instantly unconscious. The M.E. had revived Tower who was now in good condition in the hospital.

Paul Tower's own statement came in two parts. The first statement, unsigned, had been given at 12:57 A.M. when he had regained consciousness: "A man, tall, masked—came in window, didn't see—too late. He hit me. I fell. Sally? Where's Sally? . . ."

Tower's formal statement had been taken at 10:00 A.M. Sunday morning in the hospital:

"I called on my ex-wife, Mrs. Sally Tower, at 10:00 P.M. Saturday night. I went to ask her what plans she had to marry Max Tolliver. She informed me that she was seriously considering remarriage, which was good news. We had a few drinks on it and became a little intoxicated. Yes, we made considerable noise.

"Shortly after midnight I became aware of a man in the room, wearing work clothes. I challenged him. Sally screamed—more than once, I'm sure. I attempted to defend us, but he hit me with a small statue. I fell and must have struck my head. I remember nothing more until I was revived by the police."

I sat back and stared at the reports. I didn't read any more, but went to find Lieutenant Mastro.

"What is this?" I said. "Looks like a routine killing by a prowler, that's all."

"Yeah," Mastro said, and stood up. "Except that it isn't routine and it wasn't a prowler."

In the back seat of the squad car on our way to 1415 Laguna Terrace, Mastro told me, "We too were sure at first. Even after we found that nothing was disturbed in any other room, and nothing was missing. We figured the intruder panicked and ran right after killing. So we started the normal routine.

"We found no evidence of an intruder anywhere. Nothing that didn't belong in the place, and no fingerprints except Mrs. Tower's, Paul Tower's, some of her business friends', and the apartment-house manager's.

"The killer must have worn gloves and was careful. Obviously Tower didn't notice the gloves."

Mastro shrugged and went on, "A panicky prowler usually leaves *some* evidence, but okay, let's say he was lucky. So we started on the neighbors. That's when the roof fell in. You remember Mrs. Kuzco in Lewis' report? She was watching the front door of 6-B and swears no one came out after midnight.

"Anyway, the front door of 6-B was chained on the inside. So was the back door. There're no other doors. All the windows are sheer drops, and besides, they were locked on the inside. Except the open fire-escape window.

"A Mrs. Miller in Apartment 1-B stated she'd been sitting at her window directly under the fire escape all evening. She's an invalid. She likes to look out of that window. She saw no one go up or come down the fire escape all night. Everyone else with a window facing the fire escape was home, and no prowler entered their apartments.

"A Mr. Bugatti, in the building directly behind our 6-B, had been attracted by the noise in 6-B, so he too was watching the fire-escape window. He saw no one go in or out. He saw no one go down the fire escape to the yard, or up the fire escape to the roof.

"In other words, Marx, there's no way anyone could have left 6-B except by the fire-escape window—and no one went through that window."

I sat and let it sink in. The classical locked room. Only there isn't any such thing. There's *always* an explanation. Except in this case I couldn't see one. Unless I could find some flaw in what Mastro had told me.

The lobby of the building was bright and bare. The only way out was past the doorman. The door of 6-B opened into the apartment foyer that Patrolman Lewis had described.

The foyer hit me hard. I saw why the ladies of 1415 Laguna Terrace hadn't taken to Mrs. Tower. She had been a very "arty" interior decorator, all right.

The foyer walls were purple. The rug had purple and white stripes. The ancient, upright-style telephone was painted lavender and had a rhinestone-encrusted dial in a lavender marble base. The phone stood on a side table made from a Colonial washstand—complete with chamber pot. A grotesque hat tree was topped with a boar's head. There was a beautifully simple, genuine 17th Century bench next to a sideboard in fake marble that was the cheapest modern.

Mrs. Tower had been in the thick of the latest fad for odd decoration and old-fashioned ugliness, and the living room was a lot more of the same. It was a chaos of ugly Victorian, clean 17th Century, and ultramodern—mixed with things like rotted old fire bellows when there wasn't even a fireplace.

Mastro pointed to the spots where the bodies had been found. The marble statue used on Tower was on the floor near a heavy table. There was blood on the statue, and a gash on a table leg.

I checked every way out I could think of—even from inside the closets. There were only the two doors and the fire-escape window. Modern apartments don't have secret panels.

"Okay," I said, "so there's no way out. I don't believe in magic, so it has to be Tower himself. They fought, maybe she hit him with the statue and broke his nose, he went crazy and hammered her to death. In the struggle he fell and hit his head and was knocked out. She may even have died after he became unconscious."

Mastro nodded. "The M.E. thinks she did. He thinks she was alive when he was knocked out, which fits his story."

"But he has to be lying. No one could have come into this room."

"He's got the motive," Mastro agreed. "He was paying big alimony, and he wanted to marry a Dolores Finch, but he couldn't afford to marry again unless the alimony stopped. That could happen only if Mrs. Tower married again, and her fiancé, Tolliver, said she wouldn't set a definite date. She had Tower in a bind."

"They brawled about it, she hit him, and he went berserk. It's the kind of motive that makes a man go crazy. He had to beg, and she probably laughed at him."

"Sounds fine," Mastro agreed.

That was when I got the uneasy feeling. Mastro was agreeing too easily—and besides, they hadn't arrested Tower.

"Okay," I said, "what's the kicker this time?"

Mastro shrugged. "We can't find the weapon that killed Mrs. Tower. It isn't in the room."

No weapon? In a room that no one had left?

"Impossible," I said.

"Sure," Mastro said, "but the M.E. and the lab insist that nothing we found could have killed her. The M.E. says the weapon was solid and sort of circular and narrow. It had to be pretty long to hit so deep. The statue doesn't fit. There are two pokers, but they don't fit. We found a hammer, but that doesn't fit. Two paperweights are all wrong in size and shape.

"Most of the lamps would fit the wounds, but none of them had any blood, hair or bone on them, or Tower's prints. Nothing we gave the lab had blood, hair, skin or bone on it, and nothing had Tower's prints. Her prints were on the statue that she hit Tower with, but she sure didn't hit herself."

"Tower got rid of it."

"We searched the whole place, every square inch, and outside the windows for at least two hundred feet. No holes, no water, nothing in the trees, no drainpipes, and nothing hanging. Anyway, he *couldn't* have gotten rid of it."

"How do you figure that?"

"The M.E. said that Tower was knocked out the instant he got that blow on the cranium. There's no way a man can hit his own head hard enough to knock himself out for that long, or make that bad a wound, except by running full speed into a wall."

I nodded. "In other words Tower had to fall violently to hit his head that hard."

"That's it," Mastro said. "If he battled with his wife she somehow knocked him out before she collapsed herself. And if he was knocked out *during* the brawl, or just as it ended, he couldn't have gotten a weapon out of the room. So it has to be here."

I looked around the garish room. I looked at everything Mastro hadn't taken away to be examined. There was nothing that fitted the requirements. The vases were too light. The pitchers, jugs, ashtrays were too small. Nothing movable was shaped right or hard enough.

"Of course," Mastro said, "if Tower *is* telling the truth, then it fits fine. The prowler carried off the weapon."

"Okay," I said, "then the witnesses made some mistake."

"That puts you right on our schedule," Mastro said. He was not being sarcastic. He was serious. "That's what we decided, and that's when the Captain figured a new man could help."

"I've been a big help," I said.

"You're helping. Do we try the witnesses again?"

"We try," I said. "One thing. I'd rule out a prowler or burglar. I've been thinking—a prowler wouldn't go into a lighted room where two people were partying out loud. I think it had to be someone who knew them, or at least her."

"That's good, I didn't think of that," Mastro said; "but I did check all the men in her life. They all have alibis."

"How good?"

"Airtight. For instance, the boyfriend, Max Tolliver, was in Los Angeles giving a talk until 11:00 P.M. No doubt."

"What about the women? Tower's lady friend, Dolores Finch, for instance? He wanted to marry her, and the wife was preventing it."

"She doesn't have much of an alibi. Says she was home alone. But Tower says it was a man, a tall man."

"What if Tower and Dolores Finch were in it together? He's lying to give her an alibi."

"Damn!" Mastro said. "Maybe you've got it!"

The Lieutenant was excited. The idea of a plot between Tower and another person could hold the key to how the killer got in and out. Mastro decided to see if he could locate anyone who had seen Dolores Finch leave her apartment Saturday night. I went to talk with the witnesses.

If I was right and Tower had used an accomplice, there still had to be some way the accomplice had got in and out.

This time I was excited, too. It was a good feeling. It didn't last long. The three witnesses were adamant.

"No, I never left the door," Mrs. Kuzco said. "No telephone call. I got no baby, and I wasn't cooking. I tell you, no one came out."

Mrs. Miller said, "I need help to move, Sergeant. I didn't doze and I saw no one at all. No one."

I pressed. "Maybe it was someone you saw but didn't really notice? The manager? A handyman? A woman acting casual?"

"No one, Sergeant, I'm positive."

Mr. Bugatti across the yard admitted, "I sort of like to watch that window, see? She was a good-looking woman. Saturday I watched real good 'cause she was partying. I didn't see no one near that window. Just talking, shouting, banging around."

"Was there movement inside the window after the noise stopped?"

"Nope, not even a shadow. Just awful quiet."

I had to give up. I went back to the Tenth's squadroom. I was still trying to think it out when Mastro came back. He looked as discouraged as I was when he dropped into a chair.

"No one saw the Finch woman leave her place. I checked all the women Mrs. Tower worked with. They're clean. If it was an intruder, Joe, it's going into the Unsolved File. That's it."

There are a lot of cases in the Unsolved File: every cop has at least one, and no cop likes it. Those are the cases you dream about ten years later. You know you missed something, and they still rankle even on the day you retire.

* * * *

I wouldn't give up. "Let's say the witnesses are right. So let's go back to Tower himself. I've been thinking about his story. It was fast, pat, and the only decent story he could tell. And it absolutely depends on the weapon being missing.

"He couldn't have hidden the weapon, and if he was knocked out in the brawl it doesn't stand to reason he had the story ready before he blacked out. He couldn't have invented the yarn while he was unconscious."

Mastro agreed, "So when did he do it?"

"He had to invent it after he woke up. Say that he actually revived a few minutes before anyone noticed. You were all busy, so you might have missed it."

"Go on," Mastro said.

"He saw something in the apartment that gave him the idea you would miss the weapon. He heard you talking in a way that showed you suspected some prowler. You did think that at the time, right?"

"Yeah. I was sending men out to find witnesses."

"So he heard you, and he saw that maybe you'd miss the weapon. He had nothing to lose by telling a desperate story."

Mastro stood up. "Damn it, let's find that weapon!"

We returned to Apartment 6-B and searched again. We turned that living room upside down. I even tried every table leg to see if it was loose. There just wasn't anything.

"No weapon," Mastro said.

We sat down in that clutter of gaudy and grotesque objects from half a hundred periods of human artifacts. We were grim and bitter.

"You can't win 'em all," Mastro said.

I didn't answer. I was sitting where I could see all the way across the room into the foyer. Then I saw it.

"Mastro," I said. "Right in front of our eyes!"

He whirled, looked into the foyer. "Where? What?"

"There! The telephone!"

I hurried into the foyer and looked at that purple telephone. An old-fashioned, antique telephone! Upright like a club, made of hard rubber and with a heavy marble base. It fitted the description of the wound, and it had a long, thirty-foot extension cord that would easily reach to where the body of Mrs. Tower had been found.

"So obvious," I said, "that we overlooked it every time! Right in front of our noses, but so familiar we didn't see it. A modern telephone wouldn't be heavy enough, but this one is. It even has blood on it!"

"Yeah," Mastro said. I heard a sad, weary tone in his voice.

I stared at him. "Something wrong?"

Mastro sighed. "I got excited too. But look where it is, Joe."

I looked. It was on the foyer side table where it was obviously supposed to be since the wall connection was there.

"It's twenty feet or more from where the body was," Mastro said. "We know

Tower couldn't have gotten any weapon out of the living room before he passed out, right? He couldn't have hit her with the phone, then carried it out to the foyer."

"The blood on it?" I said weakly, feeling my inspiration fading.

"Lewis used it to call in, Joe. Remember, he had a lot of blood on him from examining Mrs. Tower."

After that there was nothing to do but go back downtown and brood. Mastro had other work to do, and so did I. How long could we work on one impossible case?

I went back to my regular assignments. Up in the Tenth, Mastro continued to comb Diamond Hill for any reports of a prowler. He continued to hammer at the alibis but nothing developed, and Tower had to be released when he left the hospital.

But I couldn't get the case out of my mind. I went over and over it lying awake at night, or on stakeouts in other cases. Twice, on my own time, I went up to Diamond Hill and searched the whole ground again. Then after giving it a week's rest I decided to start once more from the beginning.

I began with Patrolman Lewis' report.

And that's when I spotted it.

Mastro had Lewis and the rest of his men who had worked on the case in his office when I arrived at the Tenth. I started right in on Patrolman Lewis.

"Lewis," I asked, "where was the telephone in the Tower apartment when you used it to call in to precinct?"

"Well," Lewis began, frowning in thought.

"Think, man! Where were you standing when you called?"

Lewis brightened. "Sure, I remember. I was right near the body. Let's see, yeah, the telephone was in the living room on a coffee table near the body."

Mastro blinked at Lewis. "Not in the foyer, Lewis?"

"No, sir," Lewis said firmly. "I remember I was looking down at Mrs. Tower while I talked to you."

I said, "Was it lying on its side? Knocked over?"

"No, Sergeant, it was just standing there regular like."

"You're sure it wasn't on the floor near the body?"

Lewis was shocked. "I wouldn't have touched anything that was on the floor near the body, Sergeant!"

Mastro roared, "But it's in the foyer now! How did it get *there*?"

I said, "After you called in, Lewis, where did you put the telephone?"

"Right back where it was," Lewis said, and then he stopped. His eyes blinked. "No, I think maybe I set it out of the way some. Yeah, I remember now. That long cord was tangling up the room, so I set it over on an end table near the wall."

Mastro looked a little stunned. "You moved it? How far?"

"Well, maybe three or four feet, sir. Just across the room."

"So how did it get into the foyer?" Mastro demanded.

Mastro's men fidgeted, stammered, and slowly the whole story came out. One after the other, Mastro's men told the saga of that telephone. I listened, fascinated.

One detective had called Homicide. He remembered that the telephone had been on an end table in the living room. He moved it to a chest because the long cord was always getting in the way.

Another detective had called the laboratory. He put the telephone on a table near the door to the foyer.

A third officer recalled that the ambulance men had used the telephone. He didn't remember where they put it down.

Someone thought that the M.E. had used the telephone. And he was pretty sure the M.E. had been in the foyer when he used it.

I listened in a kind of dream. I could almost see the progress of the telephone across the living room and into the foyer. Each police pair of hands moved it another few feet, all innocent, and all oblivious of what they were doing. The peripatetic phone.

Mastro groaned. "I think I even used it myself once."

No one actually recalled wiping the phone, but Lewis said he might have, and the others admitted they might have. Later it turned out that the M.E. had also wiped it when he'd used it in the foyer.

Mastro sent them all out with a snarl. Then he glared at me.

"Okay, that's how it got to the foyer, but how did it get on that coffee table near Sally Tower's body? I mean, Tower was knocked out in the fight. He couldn't have set it upright on that coffee table. Are you saying it just *happened* to fall from his hands after he clobbered her and land upright on the table?"

"Maybe," I said, "but I don't think so."

I went to the door of Mastro's office. I told them to bring in the manager of Laguna Terrace whom I'd called to come down and wait. The manager entered nervously.

"When you went into Mrs. Tower's apartment with the officers," I asked him, "where was the telephone?"

"The telephone? You mean that purple one?" the manager said.

"That purple one," I said.

"Well, let me see," the manager said, thinking. "I fainted, you know—the shock and all. Well, when I revived, the officer asked me to identify the body. I went to the body, yes, and—wait, I remember! The officer was busy for a moment with the other officer and I had to wait. I was standing over poor Mrs. Tower—"

The manager stopped, closed his eyes. "Yes, I was just standing there and waiting. The telephone was lying on the floor near poor Mrs. Tower. The telephone was knocked over and the cord was all tangled up. Very messy. I picked it up, straightened out the cord, and put it on the coffee table."

"You put it on the nearest table," I said softly. "You sort of cleaned up a bit?"

The manager nodded. "Yes, that's it. I'm rather neat about my rooms. One does it automatically, you see? I mean, after a time when you run an apartment house you sort of have a reflex to keep the place neat."

"Automatic," I said. "You see a telephone knocked over, so you just automatically pick it up and put it on a table."

The manager beamed. "Exactly. I hate mess."

After the manager left, Mastro and I just sat there.

"That's what Tower saw when he revived," I said. "He saw the telephone standing all tidy on a table quite a distance from the body. He heard you and your men talking about a prowler. He realized you'd probably never think of the telephone. He didn't know how or why it had been removed from where it had fallen after he used it to beat Mrs. Tower, but he saw a chance and invented a prowler."

Mastro looked sick. "He had an accomplice after all—an unconscious, automatic accomplice."

In the end the lab examined that purple telephone with a microscope. It had been wiped pretty good, but it still had traces of fingerprints on it; but more important, they found tiny fragments of bone and hair, and with no other possible killer in that room the jury didn't take long to find Tower guilty.

Inspector Stockton was pleased with me in the end, and up in the Tenth the boys pulled a lot of extra duty for a while. And the Chief issued a loud blast to all precincts—never touch *anything* on the scene of a murder. Nothing! Ever!

EDWARD D. HOCH

The Spy at the Crime Writers Congress

They'd held the retirement party for Jeffery Rand on the previous Friday night, but he was still around the office four days later, clearing out a decade's accumulation of trifles and trinkets from his desk at Double-C. Though he was not yet 50, a number of factors had converged in recent months to convince him that retirement from British Intelligence was the proper course for him to follow.

For one thing, there was his forthcoming marriage to Leila Gaad, who'd shared his adventures in Egypt before moving to England to be near him. The wedding date was only a month away, and Leila deserved a husband who wouldn't be up half of the night trying to crack an intercepted cipher, or worse yet, programming a computer to crack it.

Then, too, there'd been the death of Taz. His Russian archrival had come out of retirement to handle one more Kremlin assignment—only to meet a grisly death on a street in Switzerland. Rand didn't want to end up that way.

So he was going off with Leila and leaving the Department of Concealed Communications in the hands of Parkinson and the others—men more skilled than himself in the new technology of code-breaking. Only one assignment remained for that afternoon, something wished on him by Hastings in the month prior to his retirement.

"You're retiring, Rand. You're the perfect one for it," Hastings had insisted.

Rand was dubious. "Talk to a roomful of crime writers about ciphers?"

"That's what they want. They're having an International Congress for three days at the Piccadilly Hotel, and they asked to hear a talk on codes and ciphers. They've already lined up Scotland Yard men, locksmiths, crime reporters, and firearms experts, in addition to a good many authors."

"I'm no speaker," Rand insisted.

"That's no problem. Your segment of the program will be chaired by Chancy O'Higgins, the mystery writer and television host. If you should falter he'll get you going with the proper questions."

Along with most other Britons, Rand had watched O'Higgins on Weekend television, seated with an hourglass and a flickering candle while he spun ghost stories, interviewed witches, and created an eerie atmosphere that was uniquely his own. The prospect of sharing the program with O'Higgins persuaded Rand to accept.

And so on this Tuesday afternoon in early October, Rand journeyed up to the Piccadilly Hotel. He remembered with some amusement Leila's comment when he'd told her about it. "A good thing! You'll meet some publishers and they'll ask you to do a book about your experiences. We must live on something after you retire."

Oddly enough, the first person he met in the hotel lobby turned out to be a publisher. Rand approached him when he saw the silver sheriff's badge that identified him as a member of the Organizing Committee. "Pardon me, are you with the Crime Writers?"

"I certainly am. Don't have my name tag on, but I'm George Bellows. I do some writing, but mainly I'm with Bellows Brothers, the publisher."

"Jeffery Rand. I'm one of the afternoon's speakers."

"Rand of Double-C! Of course we've all heard of you. Anxious to hear your talk. Come along—this way." He led Rand to the elevator, pausing on the way to introduce him to Edgar Wallace's daughter, Penelope Wallace, the Congress Director. "She's done a fine job," Bellows said when they had squeezed in among the others on the elevator. "And so has Jean Bowden, our Chairman. Jean was out to Heathrow Saturday morning to meet the American delegation. The opening sessions have gone very well."

"Are many here from America?"

"Over a hundred. They're the ones with white name tags. The British and Canadians have red tags, the Scandinavians yellow—you'll see a great many of those—and the other Europeans are blue."

Rand turned to a white-haired woman crowded into his corner of the elevator. "You must be American," he said, glancing at her name tag. The name on it was Gretta Frazer.

"That I am, from Chicago and Washington. I write paperback Gothics. It may not be literature, but it's fun and it pays the bills." The elevator jolted to a stop and they found themselves deposited in a reception area adjoining the conference rooms. A bar ran along one wall and many of the delegates had a drink in hand. "I hope we can chat more later," Gretta Frazer said before she was swept away by a couple of friends.

"That's Pat McGerr," Bellows said, "another writer from Washington. And the fellow with the black beard is H. R. F. Keating. Perhaps you've read some of his books."

Bellows steered him expertly through the crowd, aiming toward a large familiar figure who was the center of attention near the bar. He recognized Chancy O'Higgins at once from his weekly appearances on the television screen. He was not quite so fat as he appeared on camera, but he'd still be hard to miss. His sandy hair flew off in all directions like some latter-day Dylan Thomas, and his jacket didn't quite come together across his bulging abdomen.

"Rand!" he thundered in his familiar television voice. "I was just telling Michael Gilbert I hope we can start the session promptly at two. The publishers sponsored a cruise on the Thames this morning and people are just getting back from it. But I think we'll have enough to begin. Anyway, it's good to meet you. I think we'll have a lively session."

Rand followed him into a large meeting room, past rows of chairs to the speaker's table. Already placed on it were the twin props from the O'Higgins television show, the hourglass and the candle. The bulky author eyed his watch until the hands showed exactly two o'clock, then he upturned the hourglass so that the sand would start its descent. "Come on, everyone!" he boomed out. "Take your seats, please."

He lit the candle, as he did at the beginning of each TV show, and opened with a glowing recitation of Rand's accomplishments during his years with Double-C. Rand saw the American woman, Gretta Frazer, slip in and take a seat next to Penelope Wallace. George Bellows was down front in the first row.

O'Higgins concluded his opening by turning to Rand. "Now then, Mr. Rand, what can you tell an assembly of crime writers about codes and ciphers that we don't already know?"

Rand stood up, gazing out at the sea of expectant faces. "Thank you for your kind introduction, Mr. O'Higgins. It's indeed a pleasure to meet you and the other crime writers assembled here from all over the world. Your work, of course, is what keeps people interested in my work. In truth, communications today between governments or agents of a government are more likely to be concealed by electronic technology than by the traditional book codes or Vigenere ciphers. I want to go into some of these things in detail—though naturally I won't be telling you anything that hasn't already been hinted at in the public press."

He paused for a sip of water, then continued. "Sometimes communications are concealed merely by the geography of the situation. For example, staff cars and limousines in the Moscow area have long communicated with the Kremlin and each other by radiotelephone. The Americans had a secret spy satellite with an antenna system so highly sophisticated it could listen in on those conversations as the satellite passed slowly over Moscow."

He went on like this a bit longer, then switched to an account of his own experiences, ending with the story of Taz's recent death in Switzerland. A few in the audience headed for the doors then, but most remained for a brief question-and-answer period.

Finally, as the last of the sand trickled through the hourglass, Chancy O'Higgins rose to end the session. Rand glanced at his watch and saw that it was exactly three o'clock. "Accurate hourglass you have there."

O'Higgins smiled. "It has to be, for television."

He bent to blow out the candle as the audience streamed toward the doors. At that instant, as if by some bizarre cause-and-effect relationship, a muffled boom shook the building.

George Bellows came instantly alert. "That was a bomb—in the hotel!"

"Damned I.R.A.!" someone else muttered. The bombings of London hotels and restaurants, apparently the work of an Irish Republican Army splinter group, had grown to epidemic proportions that autumn. Barely a week passed without some new outrage and a new list of casualties.

Bellows and some others ran to the stairs, and Rand was left standing with

O'Higgins and Gretta Frazer. "It was a fine, interesting talk," she complimented him. "This is my first meeting with a real spy."

"I'm hardly that," Rand protested.

They were still chatting and moving toward the door when George Bellows returned. "Terrible thing!" he told O'Higgins. "It was a bomb, all right, and it killed Tom Wager."

O'Higgins was shocked. "Not Tom!" He turned to Rand. "Did you know him? He was a journalist who turned to writing spy thrillers."

"Afraid I don't read much in the field. But where did the bomb go off?"

"Down in the lobby. Couple of other people were injured. I suppose Tom was on his way up here when it happened."

"I'd better go right down," O'Higgins said. They started for the stairs and Rand trailed along, though he noticed the American woman stayed behind. Perhaps she was squeamish.

When they reached the lobby it was a scene of turmoil. Firemen, police, and Scotland Yard men mingled with doctors and ambulance attendants. The blast seemed to have gone off near the center of the small lobby, leaving a large scorched spot in the carpeting. Every window and glass partition in sight was shattered.

Rand sidestepped a uniformed bobby trying to clear the lobby and found his old friend Inspector Stephens standing with two bomb-squad experts. "Hello, Rand. What are you doing here?"

"Speaking to the Crime Writers International Congress. I'd just finished when we heard the blast."

"It was one of their chaps who got killed. Fellow named Wager."

"More Irish terrorists?"

Inspector Stephens hesitated. "Probably. Who else sets off bombs in hotel lobbies these days?"

"But you're not sure?"

"Too soon to tell."

Rand could sense that something was wrong. "What's the rub?"

"Bomb wasn't planted in the lobby. It was in the briefcase Wager was carrying."

"You think he was bringing it in to plant it?"

"Doubtful. He must have known all the hotels run spot searches these days. More likely it was planted without his knowledge."

"That makes it premeditated murder," Rand said.

"It's a possibility," Stephens admitted.

Rand had expected to leave the hotel at once, letting Scotland Yard deal with the bombing, but that was not to be. George Bellows caught him at the door and urged him back. "You can do us a great service, Mr. Rand, if you'll talk to Tom Wager's widow."

"That's a bit out of my line. Perhaps a clergyman—"

"She heard you speak upstairs. She won't talk to anyone else."

A bit puzzled, Rand followed the publisher to a room just off the lobby. A tall slim woman, a bit younger than he'd expected, awaited him with dry eyes. "You're Mr. Rand. I'm Joyce Wager, Tom's wife."

"A terrible thing about your husband," he said, taking her hand.

"Tom was fated to die violently. He often said so himself. I've no tears to shed for him."

Rand made no comment.

"But that doesn't mean I intend to let his killer go unpunished. He was a good man, for all his faults."

"I don't see how I fit in," Rand said. "I'm not with the police, and I've just retired from British Intelligence."

"Tom's new book is a factual one—about a writer who worked with the Germans during the war, writing propaganda for them while serving as a correspondent in Switzerland. The truth about the man never came out after the war, and he's had a successful writing career since that time."

"The man's name?"

"Tom's manuscript, to be published next month, only identifies him by the code name of Lucky."

"He never told you who Lucky was?"

She shook her head. "That's what I want you to find out. I think Tom was killed by this man Lucky. Tom told me he met someone for lunch while I was on the boat ride this morning, and that he was meeting him again in the lobby at five minutes after three."

"Who's publishing the book?" Rand asked, glancing at Bellows.

"Not me, old chap. Red Lion is his publisher."

"Will you help?" Joyce Wager asked Rand.

"I'll ask a few questions. I can't do more than that."

Inspector Stephens entered the room and indicated that Mrs. Wager was needed. When she'd left, Rand said, "The woman's composure astounds me. Her husband hasn't been dead a half hour."

"They were not terribly close," the publisher admitted.

Wager's body had been removed and a crew was busy cleaning up the lobby. Rand and Bellows crossed to the hotel lounge with its shattered windows and found a number of the delegates talking in hushed tones about the tragedy. He was getting quite skilled at reading name tags now, and he identified Michael Gilbert standing with Nigel Morland and Josephine Bell. A number of American writers, including Robert L. Fish and Stanley Ellin, were seated at a table close to the door. Hillary Waugh and Franklin Bandy stood nearby, looking serious.

Chancy O'Higgins was holding court at a round center table, his booming voice only slightly softened by the tragedy. He motioned Rand to join them and said, "I've often thought crime writers would make the perfect murderers. What do you say, Rand?"

"Do you think one of the crime writers killed Tom Wager?"

"It's a possibility, isn't it? Just as likely as the I.R.A., heaven knows!"

"You're only saying that because you're Irish," the American woman, Gretta Frazer, said.

"I'm a Scotsman and there's quite a difference," O'Higgins corrected her with a smile. "But really, wouldn't we make the perfect murderers?"

George Bellows joined them with a drink from the bar. "We'd be forever killing our victims with icicles in locked rooms."

After another round of drinks and some comments by Christianna Brand and Desmond Bagley, Rand excused himself and went outside for a taxi. As he glanced in both directions, a familiar black limousine glided to the curb. "This is an honor," Rand said, climbing into the back seat with Hastings.

"Part of the service for retired personnel. How was your talk?"

"Seemed well-received. Until the bombing, that is."

"Ah, yes. Poor Tom Wager."

Rand smiled. "I gather you have an interest in him."

"We have an interest in a book he's written."

"You know about that?"

"It's no secret. His publisher issued a press release a month ago. We asked to see galley proofs as a matter of routine."

"What do you think?"

Hastings shrugged. "It reads like fiction but it could be fact. If so, it could be dangerous for someone trying to live down his past. The bombing just doesn't feel like an I.R.A. job."

"I'm retired, remember? Where do I fit in?"

Hastings snorted. "You'll never really retire, Rand. This business is in your blood."

"All right, what do you want?"

"If this Lucky—the fellow in the book—did kill him, it was because he feared Wager would start naming names. I want you to go back to tomorrow's sessions and see what you can find out."

The limousine passed Rand's apartment and circled the block. "I can do that," Rand admitted. "But I might not find Lucky. He might be pure fiction, or he might have been Wager himself. Did anyone ever call him Lucky Wager?"

"Not that I know of. But he *was* in Switzerland during the war."

"There's no doubt the dead man is really Wager?"

"His wife identified him."

"Could she have killed him for his book royalties?"

"That's highly unlikely as a murder motive. He'd only received a small advance from his publisher."

This time around the block Rand signaled the driver to stop. "All right," he said, getting out. "I'll be in touch."

Rand took the elevator to his apartment and unlocked the door. It was nearly dark, and only the last of the twilight filtered through his mesh curtains. But when he saw the curtains closed he knew he had a visitor. "Leila?" he called.

A light by the sofa snapped on, and then he saw her.

It was Gretta Frazer and she was pointing a gun at him.

"Sit down," she said, lowering the weapon. "I won't shoot you."

"Getting in the mood for one of your Gothics?" he asked the American woman.

"Not exactly."

"I thought I left you back at the hotel."

"You did. You must have taken the long way home."

"I was chatting with a friend. What's the gun for?"

"I didn't know how you might react to finding me here. I'm a bit old for a housebreaker."

"What are you, usually?"

The white-haired woman opened the purse and tossed him her wallet. "Inside pocket, under the calendar."

He found an ID card and recognized it at once. "National Security Agency in Washington. I'd like to read one of your Gothics someday."

"The novels are a sideline. I've worked in N.S.A.'s Communications Section for the past twenty years."

"Then my talk this afternoon was nothing new to you."

"I've heard it all before, if not in so public a forum. The information about our spy satellites was especially distressing."

"It's all been in print."

"Nevertheless, we don't like that sort of information turning up in every other spy novel."

Rand smiled. "I understand N.S.A. is even more computerized than we are. Is it true you have a machine programmed to read every cablegram sent to or from the country, and to print out any messages containing key words like 'oil' or 'Mideast' or 'Russia'?"

"We have something like that," she conceded. "I'll give you a tour next time you're in Washington."

"What do you want of me now?"

"I came to talk about Tom Wager's death."

"It seems to be a popular subject today."

"His book is popular at N.S.A. I drew the assignment of coming here because my writing gives me a perfect cover at an International Convention like this. My mission was to contact Wager and offer him money to reveal the identity of Lucky."

Rand nodded thoughtfully. "You may have supplied the motive I've been searching for. If Wager went to Lucky and demanded more money than you offered, it could have got him killed."

"We think that's what happened, and that's why I'm here. We need someone familiar with operations during the Second World War, and I understand you were in intelligence work back then."

"As a *very* young man," Rand assured her. "But I'll do what I can for you."

And for Hastings, *and* for Joyce Wager, he added silently. He'd never been so much in demand when he was head of Double-C.

He just wondered how he was going to satisfy any one of them, let alone all.

Rand spent much of Wednesday morning at his old office, looking through microfilmed records of the war years. Tom Wager certainly had been a correspondent in Switzerland for a time, but there was no hint he'd committed any of the acts he had ascribed to Lucky. Working from a list of delegates to the Crime Writers International Congress, Rand attempted to pin down any sort of trail leading back to the war years.

But there was nothing.

The closest he came was a cross-indexed note on publisher George Bellows, who'd served as a P.O.W. interrogator for Army Intelligence. There was nothing on Chancy O'Higgins. When he struck out with the other names as well, he began to wonder about different nationalities—but he decided the task was fruitless. He had no real evidence that the mysterious Lucky was a crime writer.

A little before noon he went back to the hotel.

The first person he saw in the lobby was an American novelist, Richard Martin Stern, who directed him to a downstairs meeting room where a panel discussion on mystery writing was about to begin. Stern himself was on the panel, along with Eric Ambler, Gavin Lyall, and Stanley Ellin. Rand stood near the back of the room listening to the introductory remarks offered by moderator Dick Francis, then walked over to where Gretta Frazer was standing. "Hello," she greeted him. "I understand we missed a very good demonstration by the Police Dog Squad yesterday afternoon. The dogs sniffed out hidden drugs."

"Dogs that could sniff out explosives would be more to the point."

"The police have those too."

Chancy O'Higgins appeared, along with Mrs. Wager, and Rand drifted over to catch their conversation. "I can't put you on the show to talk about spies and your husband's murder," the wild-haired writer was saying, "much as I'd like to. I tell ghost stories. The public—my public—doesn't want reality. There are enough talk shows on the BBC for that."

Joyce Wager turned to Rand for help. "Can't you convince him? I need all the help and publicity I can get to bring Tom's killer to justice."

"We're all doing the best we can," Rand assured her.

When she walked away to join a group of Swedish writers, O'Higgins muttered, "Damn woman's trying to promote his book on my show."

They listened to the rest of the discussion, and when it broke up the writers scattered about the room in small groups, chatting informally while photographers snapped pictures. Rand watched Gretta Frazer deep in conversation with Ruth Rendell and Celia Fremlin. Then, as she moved away toward the door, a uniformed bellman appeared. He was paging someone, and Gretta Frazer motioned to him. He handed her an envelope and moved on.

". . . and I did line up a few people for my show," O'Higgins was saying. "C.P.

Snow was here for our opening dinner Sunday night, and Kingsley Amis was on the boat ride yesterday. Both of them have written mysteries, you know, and I thought—"

Gretta Frazer tore open the flap of the envelope.

There was a flash and roar of an explosion.

Rand leaped forward, but it was too late.

Inspector Stephens was unhappy. "Letter bomb," he told Rand. "A favorite terrorist weapon, though fortunately one that isn't used too often. A flat piece of plastic explosive with a detonator that went off when the envelope was opened."

"How many injuries in all?"

"Gretta Frazer was killed almost instantly, and three people near her were taken to the hospital. A few others have minor cuts. We're lucky there weren't more."

"Gretta Frazer wasn't lucky," Rand said. "Have you traced the letter?"

"It was left at the desk upstairs, with a note to deliver it down here after the discussion. The clerk didn't see who left it." Stephens shook his head. "I can't see any reason for singling out this American woman."

"There may have been a reason," Rand confided. "She worked for N. S. A. in Washington. She was sent here to buy information from Tom Wager."

"So the same killer disposed of them both?"

"Looks like it. He may not have been sure how much Wager told her before he died."

Rand left Stephens and moved among the others, aware of the shock etched deep on their faces. Though they wrote about murder, this was the closest most of them had ever been to one. He spotted O'Higgins talking with the American writer William P. McGivern, and when they separated Rand cornered the Scotsman and asked, "Are you staying here at the hotel?"

The stout man nodded. "I live in Cambridge and each night after the TV show I enjoy a late drink with fellow writers who live more than an hour's train journey away. I'm here till tomorrow."

"I'd like to talk to you about these killings. Could I come up to your room?"

"Certainly, old man. Room 334. I'll be there in half an hour." He glanced around at the others. "The closing dinner tonight will be more like a wake, I'm afraid. And the press isn't helping any. They seem to think mystery writers can solve crimes as well as write about them."

Rand found Joyce Wager trying to comfort some of the dead woman's American friends. Once more he was amazed at her calm in a crisis. When she was alone he asked her, "Was your husband ever called Lucky?"

"You mean like in his book? Certainly not, Mr. Rand. Tom wasn't writing about himself."

"But he was in Switzerland at the time he described."

"So was Lucky. That was how Tom learned about him."

"Why would he wait thirty years to tell about it?"

"I have no idea." She stared at the knot of policemen clustered around the spot where Gretta Frazer had died. "Do you know who did it yet? Who killed Tom and that woman?"

"I think I do," Rand told her. "Even if I have no evidence, I can't risk waiting for another bomb and another death."

Chancy O'Higgins greeted him at the door and showed him to an overstuffed chair, adjusting the cushion as Rand sat down. His ubiquitous hourglass and candle stood on the low coffee table between them, though the candle was unlit.

O'Higgins turned over the hourglass as he sat down opposite Rand. "Have to keep track of the time. In an hour I must start dressing for tonight's dinner."

"I heard there was some talk of canceling it."

"Just talk. If the bombs are the work of the I. R. A. we can't buckle under that easily. We went through the blitz, after all, so I guess we can survive a few bombs."

"The bombs aren't the work of the I. R. A.," Rand said. "They're the work of this man named Lucky, a ghost from thirty years ago."

Chancy O'Higgins frowned. "Have you discovered who he is?"

"I think it's you, O'Higgins. I think you killed Tom Wager and Gretta Frazer."

"Oh, come now!"

"His wife is certain Lucky exists."

"His wife! Have you considered the possibility that *she* killed him?"

"I'm sure she'd have put on a more grief-stricken act if she were the murderer. And she'd have had no motive for killing Gretta Frazer, who'd hardly be interested in the Wagers' marital problems. No, I'm betting on you, O'Higgins."

The stout man remained calm, tapping the tips of his fingers together. "Even if Joyce Wager didn't kill her husband, she might have lied about the identity of the dead man. Wager could still be alive, and behind the whole thing himself."

"I considered that too, but it doesn't hold up. The bomb went off in the lobby of a hotel where scores of people who knew Wager were attending a convention. Anyone might have caught a glimpse of him just before the explosion. Anyone might have said, 'No, the dead man isn't Tom Wager.' Hardly the sort of risk a clever murderer would take. The victim had to be Wager, and it's highly unlikely his wife was involved. After all, wives can find far less risky ways to kill their husbands."

O'Higgins was still frowning. "So we're back to me as Lucky—correct?"

"Correct. You see, Wager was supposed to meet his killer in the lobby at 3:05. The meeting was necessarily in the lobby to make certain Wager didn't wander into the session where I was talking and endanger so many people—or if he did enter the session room, that he'd leave before the bomb went off. It also had to be in the lobby because you hoped the explosion would be blamed on the I. R. A. Now I asked myself, why was the time set at 3:05 instead of three o'clock? Since the killer didn't intend to keep his appointment anyway, what difference could five minutes make?

"But if Wager knew Lucky had to be somewhere else until three, the odd timing is explained. Where did Lucky have to be? At my talk, of course. But not as a spectator, because any of them could have left early. Only one person besides myself *had* to stay until three o'clock, and that was you. To convince Wager you really meant to meet him, you had to set the time for a few minutes *after* three."

"What sort of proof is that?" O'Higgins scoffed. "If Wager was meeting me, he would have come upstairs where he knew I was."

"I'm sure you persuaded him against it. According to his wife he'd already had a luncheon meeting with Lucky—when I suppose you managed to hide the bomb in his briefcase—and the later meeting could only have been arranged so you'd pay him the money he demanded. You could easily have convinced him that the money shouldn't be passed upstairs, in view of hundreds of delegates who knew you both. You no doubt suggested meeting in the lobby and then strolling up Piccadilly."

"Anything else?"

"Oh, yes. Wager's book exposed a man he named Lucky. Your name, Chancy, is the Scottish word for Lucky, isn't it?"

Chancy O'Higgins was still smiling, but now—in a movement too fast for Rand to follow—his right hand held a small Beretta automatic. "Keep talking, Rand. You have until the sand runs through this hourglass, and then you will die."

"Oh?"

"You are seated on the last of my little infernal machines. When I adjusted the cushion for you, I tripped the timer so it would explode in one hour. Watch the sand. It is your life draining away."

Rand shifted uneasily. He was certain the man was serious. "Do you intend to remain here until it explodes?"

"Of course. My bombs are carefully made. It will destroy you and the chair. I will shield my face and body and suffer a few minor burns at worst. Just enough to place me above suspicion."

The sand was already a quarter of the way through the glass. "Why don't you light your candle too," Rand suggested, "and really set the scene?"

O'Higgins flicked a lighter with his left hand and leaned over to touch the wick. "I'll do just that. It pleases me that you're not afraid to die."

"Forty-five minutes is a long time."

"No one will rescue you, if that's what you're thinking. I used the hour timer to give you a chance for your life. If you hadn't accused me you could have walked out of here alive without ever knowing about the bomb in the chair."

Rand reached out and pushed the candle close to the hourglass.

"*Don't touch that*! Another movement and I'll shoot you! The bomb will easily hide the traces of a bullet wound."

"Sorry. I just wanted a little more light on my life slipping away. While we're waiting you can tell me about Gretta Frazer. I understand that you killed Wager to silence him, but why did you kill the American woman?"

"Because Wager told me of her money offer, and I couldn't be sure I'd killed him before he talked. When she left the lounge immediately after you yesterday,

I followed her to your apartment. I knew you were both after me then, and I couldn't risk leaving her alive. The letter bomb was carefully made to kill only her."

The sand was now halfway through the hourglass, and Rand imagined he could feel the outline of the bomb under his cushion. "Well—thirty minutes to live, more or less. What shall we talk about? Your years in Switzerland?"

O'Higgins sighed. "I was a young man then, too young for the assignment, I suppose. Reporting the war from a neutral country like Switzerland was a bore at best. I fell in with some people from the German Embassy and it was the first excitement I'd had. I imagined writing a book about it later, but of course I never did. Tom Wager wrote the book."

"He waited thirty years."

"He waited until I was a successful author and television personality. Then he came to me for money. When I refused him, he threatened me with the book. My only mistake was in not killing him at once. I waited, and too many people became interested in the book—people like you and Gretta Frazer."

He fell silent for a moment, and Rand focused his eyes on the hourglass. Only a quarter of the sand remained in the upper part now. He watched the candle flame flickering next to it and asked, "But why use bombs? Why injure innocent people?"

"The Germans got me interested in explosives and bombmaking while I was writing propaganda for them. Later I kept it up, as a hobby. On weekends I'd go off to the fields outside Cambridge and set off little bombs. If I say so myself, I'm now quite an expert on the technique. I've never had a bomb that failed."

"If I die you'll never get away with it, O'Higgins. Too many people know what I'm working on."

Chancy O'Higgins shook his head. "Nobody knows. People in your line of work are secretive."

Rand's eyes were on the sand. "You can't kill me like this!"

"You're retired, Rand. Your life is over anyway."

"At forty-nine?"

"It's you or me." He raised the pistol an inch. "Don't move and don't try kicking the table."

They sat in silence, facing each other, as the last of the sand trickled away. Still holding the gun steady, the stout man rose and stepped behind his chair, shielding his lower face with his arm.

Rand watched the sand.

Just a few grains more, and then—

The sand was finished. The hour was up.

Nothing happened.

"Your bomb is a bit late," Rand remarked.

"It *couldn't* be late! The timer is foolproof!" He glanced at his watch but that did him no good, since he hadn't checked it at the beginning of the hour.

They waited another minute. Rand could feel the sweat running down his back.

Nothing happened.

"It's not going to explode," Rand said. "It's a dud."

O'Higgins motioned with his gun. "Get out of the chair and stand facing the wall! No tricks!"

Rand did as he was told and the stout man moved forward, clawing at the cushion with his left hand.

That was when the bomb went off.

Hastings found Rand in the emergency ward at the hospital, having some lacerations on his back treated by a young nurse. "Wait till Leila hears of this!"

Rand smiled through a lip he'd cut when his face hit the wall. "I hope you won't tell her. Is O'Higgins dead?"

Hastings nodded. "Dead on arrival. So he was our bomber?"

"*And* the mysterious Lucky. I'll tell you all about it."

"Stephens already told me you were sitting on a bomb. How'd you turn the tables?"

"He was timing it with his hourglass. When it didn't go off on schedule he had to have a look. Said he'd never had one fail. But I'd gotten him to light his damned candle, and I shoved it up right next to the glass. Among Sixteenth Century seamen it was called 'Warming the glass.' To shorten their watch they put the hourglass near a lantern or lamp. The glass expanded from the heat and the sand ran through faster. It was a flogging offense on most ships."

"So the hour wasn't really up when O'Higgins thought it was."

"Luckily for me! I didn't really know if my hourglass stunt would work, but it was the only chance I could think of."

"He should have known better than to go examining an unexploded bomb."

"He had too much pride. He couldn't believe it when it didn't explode on schedule."

"By God, Rand, you can't retire! What will we do without you?"

Rand turned over as the nurse finished dressing his wounds. "You'll get by. There'll be others a good deal better than me."

"I'm betting you'll be back within six months," Hastings said.

Rand remembered what had happened to the Russian, Taz, when he came out of retirement. That had been a bomb too, only Taz hadn't been as lucky as Rand.

"No," he told Hastings, "don't bet on it."

VICTOR CANNING

Baskets of Apples
and Roses

The Department of Patterns is known to only a very few people in France, and the inside of its offices on the Quai d'Orsay to even fewer. Young men—and sometimes young women—are transferred to it from the security services and the police for periods of training and research. If at the end of two years you come out of it with the rating *Assez bien* from its chief, Papa Grand, you have done well—very well indeed.

Apart from training, the Department specializes in solving old cases which have been abandoned by the police, or in originating cases which arise from its own study of the patterns of crime. Most of the time you sit sifting through masses of data, official records, newspaper reports, and files, hoping that by arrangement and analysis some pattern of significance will emerge. Sometimes, however, you get a pattern handed to you on a plate.

This is what happened to me at the end of my first year in the Department. It had been a good year for me because, of all the other new members, I was the only one without a black mark, and I felt very pleased with myself.

I was called into Papa Grand's office one morning and found him with the head of the Sûreté's political branch, Monsieur Arbroy. Papa Grand had his feet up on his desk, his back to the little window that looked out over the Seine, and he was smoking a pipe. Papa Grand is Monsieur Alphonse Grand. He could be tough and he could be jovial—a big, fleshy, white-haired man of about 60 with bright blue eyes and a strong Norman accent still distinguishable in his voice.

Papa Grand introduced me to Monsieur Arbroy, then passed a file across to me and said, "My dear Mascaux, the Sûreté's political branch is snowed under at the moment with all this O.A.S. stuff and the Algerian trouble, so as our brightest first-year student, consider yourself attached to them until further notice. I want your comments on the contents of that file in twenty-four hours."

He paused, then rubbed the bowl of his pipe against his nose, smiled slyly and said, "I'm not sure about this, but I think I'm right in giving this assignment to you because of all my young men I think you are the least politically minded."

I saw Monsieur Arbroy give a little frown, make a move as though to say something, and then change his mind. And I knew why he had changed his mind. He had once been in the Department and he knew Papa Grand. And I must say, something in Papa Grand's manner made me momentarily uneasy.

I took the file back to my room and went through it. It consisted of police reports on a series of bomb outrages which had occurred over the last twelve months. There had been four of them, all in Paris.

The first had occurred the previous January. An ornamental basketful of roses and apples had been delivered to the house of a Paris editor at six o'clock in the evening. About three o'clock that night an explosion had occurred in the basket which had been left on the sideboard in the dining room, and the editor's house had been almost gutted by the subsequent fire. No lives had been lost. The bomb had been established as a phosphorus incendiary bomb, and it was thought that it had been in the form of an artificial apple.

A card with the gift had indicated that it had come from a personal friend of the editor. This friend, it developed, had denied sending the gift, and the maid who had received it had said that it had been delivered by an elderly man, shabbily dressed, but who spoke with a good accent.

In March a similar basket of flowers and fruit had been delivered to a topflight journalist on another Paris paper, and during the night his house had been badly damaged by the same kind of explosion and fire. In his case there had also been a card from a friend, and once again the same shabbily dressed man had delivered it.

In June another journalist on another Paris paper had been similarly treated.

And in August the editor of still another Paris paper had received the same kind of destructive gift—always roses and apples with the phosphorus bomb concealed in the basket. Sûreté inquiries had established without doubt that the signatures on all four cards with the baskets had been forged.

There it was—a consistent pattern of roses and apples and incendiary bombs, and always the victim had been a newspaperman. So far, happily, there had been no loss of life, but there had been a great deal of damage.

I went to work on it, checking the existing police detail, interviewing the victims, and spending some time reading back copies of the newspapers involved. I knew perfectly well that, although Papa Grand had handed this to me as a straight assignment, he had also given it to me as a test. I'd done well in the Department so far. Papa Grand would know that I was pleased with myself— might even think that I was too pleased with myself—and, so, had picked out something extra-special for me.

I knew, too, that Papa Grand had not idly said he had picked me because I was not politically minded. All the papers and men concerned could, from their records, have been the objects of political revenge of one kind or another.

I checked with all the well-known florists in Paris to see if they had made up fruit and floral baskets on the days in question. None of them had. By the time I was ready to go and see Papa Grand, I had a feeling that although I could sense the kind of picture these crimes had made, I was missing the central character in them. That didn't make me very happy as I went into the Old Man's room.

Papa Grand was in a mellow mood. He poured a glass of Calvados for me, took one himself, drank it as he read my report, and then tipped backward in his chair and for a while stared at the ceiling.

Then he said, "All right, Mascaux, you've got it all there. All you need now is to find this shabbily dressed man. He's educated, elderly, clever with his hands, and he probably collects and repairs clocks and watches; also, of course, he knows more than most people about chemistry. A strong character, almost to the point of fanaticism—which, of course, is always based on love. Distorted love, perhaps, but none the less love. You agree?"

"Yes, *Patron*. There's a clear revenge motive. I also think that the dates of the outrages must have some significance. Probably anniversaries of events that mean a great deal to him. But I don't think it's a political revenge pattern."

"Why?" Papa Grand filled his glass but ignored mine. He had to be very mellow indeed to offer you two glasses.

"Because the editors and journalists concerned are not all of the same political convictions. Some are of the right, one of the left, and one is a liberal. So far as I can see, they only have one thing in common."

"Which is?"

I told him. They all acted as dramatic critics for their papers, but because of their standing they only covered the important productions.

"So," said Papa Grand, "we have a revenge motive associated with the theatre. An explosive mixture." He smiled. "You agree?"

"I do, *Patron*."

"I see that it is clearly established that the bombs went off around three o'clock at night. Do you agree with me that probably the exact time was three minutes past three?"

I looked blank.

Papa Grand chuckled. "What an actor you are, Mascaux. You want to keep everything to yourself. Very good. Then I shall ask you some more questions and see how blank you can manage to look. The basket of roses and apples— why roses and apples?"

"Because, *Patron*, they are an integral part of the pattern in this man's mind, somehow associated with whatever it is he is compelled to vindicate or revenge."

"True. But specifically, why roses and apples?"

I knew that I was being tested hard, and I knew Papa Grand well enough to know that not one word he spoke now was without significance. He could be helpful, but he never handed out anything openly. I looked stupid again.

Papa Grand made a rumbling noise in his throat and then said, "You stand there acting as innocent as an angel, Mascaux. But I know how deep you are. You want to keep all the credit for yourself. And you shall. Find this man. He will be gentle and make no trouble when you do. He's in love, Mascaux—a rare and dangerous love which some men have for some women. You know her name, of course. Yes, of course, you do. Dorothea. It has to be that, doesn't it?" He smiled, nodded his head at my silence, and said, "I'm glad you agree."

I left the room feeling as limp as a rag and wondering what had ever made me think that I was worthy of being in the Department of Patterns. Just then I knew that I couldn't even hold down a job as a village policeman. And what is more, I knew that Papa Grand had just given me "the treatment"—not humiliation, but a lesson in humility. Somewhere along the line he had spotted that I was getting too cocky, too self-assured about my progress. He was just correcting the balance.

I sat down at my desk, opened the file, checked everything in it, read my own report, and then went back in my mind over every word Papa Grand had used during our interview. It didn't get me very far. According to Papa Grand, this man was presumably revenging an actress named Dorothea. How the devil did he know that? Apples, roses—and Dorothea. It didn't make any sense to me.

The next morning I went back to the newspaper offices, to the files of back copies. I made a list of the female members in the casts of all the plays which had been reviewed by the four men concerned. There wasn't a Dorothea among them.

If it hadn't been for my Department training I might have stopped there—but one of Papa Grand's maxims was that things and people are seldom labeled clearly. You must dig deep for the truth. I dug very deep, consulting theatrical agents on the telephone, and poring over reference books—and suddenly Dorothea appeared.

After that it was fairly easy. At five o'clock that afternoon I was admitted into the house of Mlle. Delabre. It was a modest little villa in Passy where she had lived all her life. Mlle. Delabre was a fragile, vague-minded woman of about 50, with gray hair; she wore a large cameo brooch at the tight neck of her black dress.

I said that I was a journalist and wished to have some details of her sister's career for a history of the French theatre which I contemplated writing. She was very happy to help me. Her sister had been the great Clea Delabre who had made her reputation before the war and then, some time after the war, had left the stage.

"She thought she was leaving it for good," said her sister. "But the pull of the theatre was too much for her. We had a little money, but somehow it went. All of it. So, two years ago she decided to return to the stage. Somehow we found help from backers, and then there was the problem of the play. Poor Clea, she liked nothing that was shown to her. In the end—unwisely now, I see—she put on a play of her own writing."

Mlle. Delabre smiled gently. "She was a great actress, monsieur, but not a great playwright. The play was very bad and the critics were very unkind—yes, very unkind. I must confess that dear Clea went to pieces—even the greatest actresses, you know, can give bad performances."

"So it was a failure?"

"Yes. It lasted only one week—one week in January, two years ago. Clea collapsed. She was older than me. She died the following March, literally from a broken heart."

January, I thought, the month of the play's failure, of the scathing notices which I had read in the newspaper files.

Then March, the month of her death, the month also of the second bomb outrage.

"Was June a significant month for your sister?" I asked.

"She was born in June, monsieur."

"And August?"

"That was the month in which she made her first great success, long before the war—the month Paris acclaimed her."

"She was never married?"

"No. She was once very much in love—but he was killed during the war."

"Clea Delabre—the great Delabre," I said. "But her full name was Dorothea Clea Delabre, was it not?"

'Yes. But Clea—that was how the public knew her. In the family she was always Dorothea."

"Who is there left in the family who loved her as much as you do?"

"Only myself and my brother, Arnaud. He was devoted to her. He could tell you much more about her theatrical life than I could. He was her manager. Would you like to see him?"

"If I may."

She took me out of the room and led me across the hall to a study door. She knocked gently, called, "Arnaud," and we went in.

The walls of the room were crowded with books. There was a desk littered with papers, and a work bench under a far window. I was aware of the ticking of innumerable clocks. They were everywhere—on the walls, on the shelves, on brackets, and the bench was littered with an accumulation of clocks to be repaired.

"I'm sorry, he's not here," said Mlle. Delabre. "I remember now—he went out just before you came in. Really, my memory—"

"Where did he go?"

"I think I saw him carrying a basket of roses and apples. He loves giving them to his special friends."

"Apples and roses!"

"Why, yes, monsieur. What is the trouble?"

"I must know where he's gone!"

With a vague gesture of her hand she said, "Well, you could wait and ask him when he comes back. But he is very absent-minded. It sometimes worries me. Often he stays away all night. Then again he might be back in half an hour."

If he stayed away all night, the basket would be sitting in someone's house waiting to go off. I had to do something about it at once.

Vigorously, I said, "Mademoiselle, think! Does this particular day or month have any significance in your sister's life or in her theatrical career?"

To my surprise she nodded her head and said, "Why, of course it does. But why are you so upset, monsieur?"

"Please, just tell me."

"Well, this is the day Dorothea was confirmed. It is also her saint's day, monsieur. Maybe that is where Arnaud has gone—to the little church around the corner where she was confirmed. I remember now—he usually makes the curé a gift on this day. Dear, dear, how forgetful of me."

But I wasn't waiting to hear any more. I ran out of the house and into my car. Arnaud must be completely mad if he was now turning his attention to innocent people who had once been connected to Dorothea. ·

I caught him as he was coming down the steps of the curé's house, which was next door to the church. A woman was just closing the door and I saw in her hand a golden wickerwork basket piled with apples and roses.

I ran up the steps and held on to Arnaud. He was an elderly, grayhaired man with a long, drawn, tired face and a pair of gentle brown eyes.

I said, "Monsieur Delabre, I am from the police. I must ask you to wait while I get that basket back from—"

"The police?" he interrupted me mildly. "I see." Then he shook his head. "You do not need the basket, monsieur. It will harm no one. They are real apples and roses. You wish me to come with you?"

I nodded. I took him back to Papa Grand, and a man was sent to the curé's house to check the basket. It was harmless, as Arnaud had said.

Papa Grand was very courtequs to him. "You loved your sister very much, monsieur?"

"Very much," said Monsieur Delabre. "She was a saint."

"Saint Dorothea." Papa Grand looked at me. "You understand, Mascaux?" I shook my head.

Papa Grand turned to Monsieur Delabre. "Perhaps you would tell this young man, monsieur, the story of the real Saint Dorothea."

"But, of course," he said meekly.

And he did—the story of Saint Dorothea who was martyred in the year 303 at exactly three minutes past three—what a fund of knowledge there was in Papa Grand! As Dorothea went out from her sentence, the judge's secretary, Theophilus, had said mockingly, "Send me some apples and roses when you get to Paradise." That night as Theophilus roistered with his companions at dinner, an angel appeared to him bearing a basket of roses and apples; the angel said, "From Dorothea, in Paradise," and then vanished.

JOYCE HARRINGTON

The Couple Next Door

The new couple next door was young and the girl was pregnant. It rained the day they moved in, a fine gentle mist, and as the girl trudged in and out of the building she raised her face to the wetness, her round eyes blinking and her blonde hair lank and straggling. Her husband dashed back and forth with his head lowered and his shoulders hunched, carrying chairs and boxes. They carried the large rolled mattress for the double bed between them.

The rented truck was soon emptied—they had few possessions—and the young husband drove it away. Carmela left the window and listened to the bumping and scraping sounds that came clearly through the shared walls.

"That's all I need," she complained into the telephone. "An infant screaming all night long. I'm on my feet all day and I need my sleep at night. And I'm sure I saw them bring in a hi-fi. I hope you told them not to play it after ten o'clock. I can't think why you rented to them in the first place. They look unreliable."

The landlord gave Carmela no satisfaction. "They paid cash—a month's rent and two months' security. Anything else, Miss Jade?"

Carmela slammed down the phone and began to dial again.

"Their furniture looks like thrift shop junk. He has long hair and a beard. She was walking around in the rain as if she were dreaming or doped or something. I tell you, I feel sorry for that baby. But what can I do?"

"You have a good heart, Carmela," her friend said. "Listen. I can't talk right now. Got to do some shopping. See you at work on Monday."

Carmela went into the bathroom and under the fluorescent light probed the roots of her glossy black hair. Were there more gray hairs than last time? She put on an old stained smock and a pair of rubber gloves. She mixed the dye in a plastic bottle with a long spout and began applying it to the gray roots.

While she worked, she heard the shower in the next-door bathroom start running. The bathrooms were back to back. She heard splashing and laughter, a high squealing laugh and a deeper more resonant chuckle. There were words, too, but the intervening wall and the sound of the rushing water robbed the words of sense. Carmela listened closely but could make out nothing of what was being said.

In the mirror her face under the muddy cap of black dye looked bare and strained. As a girl, her black hair, blue eyes, and pale skin had made her proud and demanding. She had dreamed of a handsome professional man, a doctor or lawyer, who would carry her away. None of her local suitors had quite filled the bill, and one by one they had married other less-demanding girls.

Carmela told herself she had no regrets. She was still as slender as a girl, but sometimes her shoulders sagged. The pale skin around her blue eyes was loose and puffy; tiny creases surrounded her lips, and the skin of her neck, under close scrutiny, was reddish and crêpy. She gazed into the mirror and listened to the laughing and splashing from next door.

"Disgusting," she said.

She went into the kitchenette and lit the oven. While she waited for the hair dye to do its work, she began making an applesauce cake.

The girl, breathless and rosy, turned the shower off.

"Dry my back, Dougie," she said.

"You look like you swallowed a watermelon."

"He's kicking. Put your hand right here."

"You must think I love you or something. Crazy broad!"

"Isn't it nice to have a shower? When I think of that crummy old bathtub! I like this place, Dougie. And the washing machines in the basement. No more launderette. And the little room for the baby. Oh, it's going to be perfect!"

"Well, put some clothes on, Big Mama. We still have work to do."

"Slave driver!"

"We have to put the bed together."

"One-track mind!" She climbed into a baggy pair of jeans and put on one of his old shirts. "Oh, Dougie, did you notice the lady watching us from the window? All the time we were unloading the truck, she stood there watching us. She looked like a witch. Right next door. Did you see her?"

"Nope. Come on. Let's get crackin'. I have to go out tonight."

"On, Dougie!" Disappointment dragged at her voice. "Tonight?"

"Yeah. And see if you can find my gun. I put it in one of those boxes."

Together they fumbled the bed frame into position. It occupied most of the bedroom. There was room for the dresser and an old high-backed rocking chair. Somewhere, in one of the boxes, was a cushion for the chair, a patchwork cushion the girl had bought at an Appalachian crafts festival because it reminded her of stories her mother had told her of the old days. She would have bought a quilt for the bed, but there wasn't enough money. There was never enough money. Together they heaved spring and mattress onto the frame.

The girl sat panting on the edge of the mattress. Her face was broad, round, and flattish, with a short upturned nose. Across this nose and the wide cheekbones a band of freckles stood out, glowing against her sudden pallor. She laid a hand on top of the mound of her stomach and took cautious sips of air, as if she were listening intently to some inner happening and was afraid of disturbing it with normal breathing.

"You okay, Karen?"

"Yes, I think I am." She answered tentatively, waiting for the true answer to be revealed. "Yes, I think everything is okay."

"You've had a rough day, Big Mama. Why don't you lie down for a while?" He sat beside her and stroked her long blonde hair, tucking damp strands of it behind her ears.

She laid her head back and his arm tightened around her. She sighed deeply, her breath warm and moist against his neck.

"I'm all right, Dougie. I was just a little out of breath. Everything's really all right." As if to confirm this, color flooded back into her cheeks, and she kissed him lightly, reassuringly. "If you're going out, I'd better fix something to eat."

"Oh, hey, listen. Don't do that. I can get something on the way."

"Well, I'm hungry, too. And I really have to unpack that kitchen stuff."

She went to the door and looked back at the room—the bare mattress, the battered suitcases and heap of cartons in the corner, the uncurtained window. And her husband sat on the bed, watching her. Soon, she thought, soon I'll have it fixed up. I'll get new curtains and a soft fleecy rug for the floor. Soon we'll have enough money to get some nice things. Especially for the baby.

"I'd feel terrible if I let you go out tonight without any supper," she said. "Suppose something happens to you."

"Nothing's going to happen. I'm always careful. I've got to get ready. Frank's picking me up at seven thirty."

In the kitchen Karen unpacked a frying pan and a couple of plates. She found some bacon, eggs, and a loaf of bread. There was no milk; they would have to drink their instant coffee black. Tomorrow she would go shopping. While the bacon sizzled, she went into the living room and rummaged through the boxes there.

The early evening sunlight broke through the gray drizzle, sending a final golden shaft through the window, then faded into purple twilight. Karen plugged in a table lamp and set it on top of one of the hi-fi speakers. The hi-fi was new, a present from Doug. To keep her company, he said, when he was out late and she waited up for him. She had a growing collection of country-Western records. But she wouldn't have its company tonight. She didn't know where to put the hi-fi in this new room, and Dougie probably wouldn't have time to hook it up until tomorrow. Well, she could plug in the television in the bedroom and lie in bed watching it until he came home.

In the third box Karen opened she found the gun. It lay nestled in a neatly folded stack of new baby clothes, its hard blue-black contours shockingly bold against the soft whiteness of the little gowns and shirts. When Karen picked it up, it left its impression on the fabric beneath. Somehow it hurt to see the baby's clothes bearing that harsh imprint. She felt a vague sense of spoiled innocence and wanted to ask Doug why he had put the gun into that particular box.

But the bacon was now sputtering and smelled strongly of hot grease. She put the gun down on top of one of the boxes where she knew he would see it, then hurried into the kitchen.

They ate fried egg sandwiches and crisp bacon—she'd saved it just in time— and drank black coffee. They spoke of the chores they would have to do tomorrow, settling into the new apartment. Karen always avoided thinking and speaking of what Doug did when he went out at night. By tacit agreement he never spoke of his nocturnal activities. At first he had tried to assure her that he was hardly ever in danger. But she refused to believe this, so he found it best not to speak of it at all. So far he had always come home safely.

The doorbell rang just as they were finishing their coffee. Doug looked at his watch.

"Must be Frank. He's a little early."

While Doug went to answer the door, Karen cleared away the few dishes. She was surprised to hear him call her.

"Karen, we have a visitor."

She dried her hands on her jeans—the towels had not yet been unpacked—and went, wondering, to the door.

"Oh," she said, "hello."

"Hello," said the woman in the doorway. "I'm your next-door neighbor, Carmela Jade. I hope you won't think I'm being pushy or nosy. I happened to notice you were moving in today, and I knew you wouldn't have time to do much cooking. So I brought you this cake. Just being a good neighbor."

Karen's eyes flitted from the cake on its cut-glass plate, to the woman's face, to Doug lurking behind the door and frankly grinning through his beard.

"Of course I would like to have the cake plate back," the woman went on. "But take your time about it. I'm right next door, apartment 2B. Been there for fifteen years. This has always been a quiet building. I hope you enjoy living here. Anything I can do to help you, just let me know. I believe in being a good neighbor."

"Thank you, Mrs. Jade." Karen was very conscious of the woman's sharp blue eyes searching past her into the apartment. "It's a beautiful cake."

"It's Miss, but you can call me Carmela. I hope we'll be friends. The last people who lived in this apartment were very good friends of mine. A nice quiet couple, no children." The woman's eyes rested on Karen's bulging middle. "What did you say your name was?"

"I'm Karen. And my husband is Doug. Fletcher." As Karen stepped forward to take the cake from Carmela Jade's outstretched hands, the woman gave an involuntary shudder, blinked rapidly, and backed off a few paces into the hallway.

"I'd ask you to come in for a cup of coffee," Karen said, "but we're still in such a mess."

"Some other time," the woman stammered. She shoved the cake into Karen's hands and fled down the hall to her own apartment. "Nice meeting you," she called over her shoulder. The door slammed behind her, and Doug and Karen could clearly hear the ramming home of several locks.

"What was that all about?" Karen wondered. "Did I say something scary?"

"Beats me. Is she the one you saw watching us from the window?"

Karen nodded. "Um-mmm. Oh, Dougie, did you dig that hairdo? And about a ton of makeup. She looked like an aging geisha girl. But I wonder what made her take off like that."

"Be kind, Big Mama. Not everybody's as naturally beautiful as you. Are you gonna cut that cake or just admire it? I've just got time for a piece of cake before I meet Frank downstairs."

He picked up the gun from the top of the box. Karen went into the kitchen with the cake. She heard the sharp clicking sounds that meant he was checking out the gun, loading it from the handful of cartridges he always kept in the pocket of his old Army jacket. She turned on the water to drown the sounds. It was decent of him to meet Frank downstairs. Frank made her nervous. She was intimidated by his huge greasy bulk and his beady suspicious eyes, even though Doug had told her that Frank was a good man to be with in this night work, street-wise and cunning, never taking unnecessary risks. Frank wasn't married, and he made her feel like excess baggage.

When she came out of the kitchen with two slices of cake, the gun had disappeared. She knew it was in the bulging right-hand pocket of the fatigue jacket. She put the knowledge from her mind and munched the applesauce cake. It was spicy and full of raisins.

"Good cake," said Doug. "You'll have to get her recipe."

"If I don't scare her to death. I wish I knew what made her run off like that."

"Got to go now. You get some rest. I made the bed for you."

"Thanks. I guess I'll do some unpacking first."

"Don't work too hard. And lock the door behind me. Can't be too careful these days.". . .

"But I *can't* come over now, Carmela. I'm in the middle of getting dressed. I have a date with Walter. What are you so nervous about, anyway?"

Carmela Jade whispered into the phone. "It's my new neighbors. They're crooks, drug addicts. I'm sure of it. She's a shifty-eyed little tramp. Pretending to be married, but I doubt it. And he was grinning at me like a wolf through that awful beard. There's something very wrong about them."

"Carmela. Stop imagining things. You're making something out of nothing."

"I am *not* imagining things. They have a gun. I saw it. Scared me half to death. And now he's gone out. He met this terrible-looking thug in front of the building and they went off together. Probably to murder innocent people in their beds and rob them of everything they own."

"Well, if he's gone off to murder someone else, he isn't going to be bothering you. Relax, Carmela, have a drink, watch television, get out your knitting. Anything, just get your mind off them. I've got to go now. Walter'll be along any minute."

"I never drink. I don't watch television, and I wouldn't be caught dead knitting. And I don't know why you go out with that Walter. He's nothing, a shoe salesman. You can do better than that."

"No, I can't. And neither can you. At least I get out once in a while and have a little fun. I don't sit home inventing murderers. Do you want to come out with us? Walter has a friend. We can pick you up."

"Thanks, but no thanks. Any friend of Walter's couldn't possibly be worth my time. And if I don't show up at work on Monday, you'll know it's because I've been murdered in my own apartment by those freaks next door."

"Stop exaggerating, Carmela! Just lock the door. I've got to go now."

"It is locked. Yale lock, chain lock, and police lock."

"Goodbye, Carmela. Have a nice night."

"Wait. Don't go yet—" Her voice was slammed back at her by the empty line.

She looked around her apartment. Reclining lounge chair to soothe her aching legs and feet after the long days at the department store, days that seemed to get longer as the years went by; the three-piece suite, carefully saved for and scarcely used; coffee table with magazines precisely arranged to display their titles; shelves with knick-knacks; her collection of china dogs of nearly every breed. A real dog would make messes and have to be walked. It was all perfect, just the way she wanted it, and perfectly neat. Visitors seldom came, and there were no relatives with noisy dirty children. For no apparent reason Carmela felt like crying.

She walked purposefully into the kitchenette. No chores to be done there. The mixing bowl, cake pan, and the remains of her own small supper had long since been tidied up. With an almost absentminded air she opened a cupboard. Her hand, with its long, strong, red-painted fingernails, snaked its way unerringly to the space behind the oatmeal carton.

The bottle was about half full. Years ago, how many she did not care to dwell on, she had been in the habit of mixing the vodka with tomato juice. She had long forgotten who had introduced her to Bloody Marys—one of that unending stream of unsuitable suitors, no doubt. The stream had dried up; only the habit remained. But all that tomato juice had given her heartburn. The vodka on its own merits was much nicer. And quicker.

She poured half a tumblerful and dropped in two ice cubes. The oily liquid gleamed invitingly in the glass, purer than water and far more quenching to the parched and thirsty soul. But before Carmela would allow herself even one sip, she stowed the bottle away in its dark hiding place and wiped the counter clean of any possible spots.

She carried the glass into the living room, settled into her reclining chair, and with the remote control switch in one hand, the glass in the other, took her first sip while tuning the television to any program that would engage her interest and take her mind off the problem of the couple next door. Occasionally, in the quieter moments between car chases, shootouts, and commercial breaks, she heard thumps and patterings from the apartment next door. Probably stowing away a whole arsenal, she thought—rifles, hand grenades, Molotov cocktails. What if they were members of some lunatic liberation army? The whole building might go up in one earthshaking blast. It could happen!

Carmela groaned and eased herself out of the recliner. Might as well go to bed for all the comfort she got from television. She refilled her glass, then meticulously performed the bedtime ritual she had never once neglected in all her adult life. She creamed her face, brushed her teeth, wrapped her head in a satin turban to protect her hairdo. She massaged lotion into her hands, then put on a pair of white cotton gloves to keep the lotion working all night.

All this done, she shook into one gloved hand a single red and blue capsule. The vial was almost empty. The capsule looked so cheery, bright blue and vibrant red, and electric violet where the two ends overlapped. She must remember to get the prescription refilled. It wouldn't do to get caught some night without a cheery pill to blot out the long uneventful day. Carmela popped it into her mouth and washed it down with a mouthful of vodka.

Propped against two ruffled pillows, Carmela flipped the pages of a magazine while waiting for sleep to free her mind of the probable past and future iniquities of the brazen couple next door. The magazine, usually much concerned with 101 ways to cook hamburger and the problems of a certain movie-star princess and her teen-aged daughter, featured an article on how, or indeed whether, to protect yourself against rape. Carmela sipped her vodka and read of knees applied with a swift upward motion, of biting, gouging, scratching, of heels or heavy wooden wedgies ground into insteps, and finally, of the probability of winding up either victorious or dead if you tried it at all. She hadn't considered the neighboring threat in this light at all, but anything was possible with that kind.

At last she felt the approach of the lovely gray fog. Her eyelids grew heavy and her jangled nerves relaxed. The words on the page ceased to make sense and she dropped the magazine to the floor and switched off the bedside lamp. For a moment all was silent in the darkened room. Carmela drifted . . .

Then a burst of sound through the intervening wall jolted her wide-awake. What on earth was going on next door? Scarcely moved in and having a wild party already? Carmela envisioned unspeakable activities just beyond her bedroom wall. But when she sat up to rearrange her pillows, she recognized the sound for what it was. The television in the next apartment was blaring forth the eleven o'clock news.

She raised her gloved fist to thump a reprimand on the wall. But then, fearing reprisal, she drew back her hand. The landlord would certainly hear about this in the morning! Let him deal with it. That was his job. He was responsible for renting the apartment to dangerous young criminal types. If anybody was going to get shot at, let it be him. No telling what those two would do if they were crossed.

But in the meantime what was *she* to do? Her head ached and her eyes burned, but the droning of the television kept her just on the edge, would not let her fall asleep. Another pill? Maybe that would do it. She staggered into the bathroom, shook another cheery pill into her white glove, and downed it with a mouthful of water from the tap. Then back to bed. In twenty minutes or so Carmela slept, mouth open, her satin turban slightly askew, her gloved hands clenched beneath the coverlet.

Beyond the wall the television murmured of love and intrigue and other late-late movie subjects . . .

* * * *

A brazen gong rang and the gun in Carmela's hand went off with a thud, thud, thud.

"You're doing it wrong. Do it again."

Once more the gong. And the gun went off, but Carmela couldn't get her finger on the trigger. If she could only find the trigger, she could make it stop. Her hand felt numb.

"Again, Miss Jade. Again, again, again, Miss Jade."

A disembodied male voice issued commands and she had to obey.

The gong echoed and the gun kept firing. It was firing at a store mannequin and hitting it every time. The mannequin's head fell off.

"Miss Jade! Miss Jade!"

Thud, thud, thud.

Carmela opened her eyes on blackness. Someone was calling her name and banging on her door. The doorbell pealed. The luminous hands of the alarm clock dazzled and swam so that she could not tell what time it was.

"Coming . . . I'm coming . . . just a minute."

She groped for the bedside lamp, while the knocking and shouting continued. Her gloved hands fumbled with the switch, and all her movements seemed sluggish and clumsy. At last she managed to light the lamp. She blinked away the last vestige of sleep and looked again at the clock.

Three thirty! In the morning! Who could be knocking at the door and calling her name? What would the neighbors think? Oh, the neighbors! She remembered who her new neighbors were, and her lips pressed thin against each other.

"Be quiet!" she muttered. "I'm coming."

She crawled out of bed and found her robe. Knotting the belt, she lurched through the darkened living room to the door.

"Who is it?" she whispered to the closed and thrice-locked door.

"Miss Jade? It's me. Doug Fletcher. I need your help. It's Karen."

"At this hour of the morning?"

"Miss Jade, please. I'm sorry to wake you up," came the shaking voice from the other side of the door. "I need to use your telephone. We don't have one yet."

Carmela paused with her hand on the police lock. It could be a trick to get into the apartment. Once she let him in, she'd be alone and defenseless while he had a gun and could do what he liked with her. She could tell him to leave his gun at home, but then he'd know that she knew. No! That would never do.

"Miss Jade? Are you there?"

"There's a bar down the street. Don't they have a phone?"

"I've already been there. It's closed. Miss Jade, I think Karen's going to have the baby. Please let me use your phone."

"Just a minute."

Carmela hurriedly made a circuit of the living room, turning on every lamp, even the overhead fixture she never used because of its glare. She returned to the door, took a deep breath, and unlocked the police lock. She slid its long steel bar out of the groove and held it in her hand while she unlocked the Yale lock. She left the chain lock in place and opened the door the few inches it allowed. She peered through the slit at the distraught figure in the dimly lit hall.

Doug Fletcher was not a reassuring sight. His eyes were red-rimmed and he sagged with fatigue. Or drug-induced lethargy—Carmela could not be sure which. He wore a disreputable Army jacket and faded jeans. He supported himself with one hand pressed against the door jamb, and Carmela was very much aware of the strength and menace that could be lurking in his square blunt fingers. Why, he could strangle her before she could make a sound. Every day the newspapers told of women being beaten, stabbed, strangled for a few dollars or for no reason at all.

"Why don't you ask the landlord? He's got a phone."

"I tried. He doesn't answer the door. You're the only other person I know here. Please, Miss Jade! I just need to call the doctor and a taxi. Karen—she's— I think she overdid it today. The baby's not due for another month, but she's having—pains."

"Well. All right. Just a minute."

Carmela closed the door again and unlocked the chain lock. She swung the door wide to allow the young man to pass.

"Leave the door open," she said. "The phone's over there." She indicated a low table and small chair against the wall.

"Thanks, Miss Jade. I'm really sorry to wake you up in the middle of the night. Now where's that phone number?" He began groping in his pockets as he shambled across the room.

Carmela remained by the door, watching him closely. Maybe she had misjudged him. Babies often did come in the middle of the night, at least in the magazine stories she read. And young husbands were always ten times more upset than the brave young wives.

Carmela's imagination leaped to the days ahead when she would offer her mature advice to the inexperienced young parents. Perhaps with a baby to set an example for, Karen and Doug could be induced to improve their own appearance. Carmela felt like a benign conspirator in the shaping of three lives. Her fears had been foolish. Her new neighbors were just young and ignorant. She prepared her face to smile and offer to sit with Karen until the taxi arrived.

At the telephone table Doug began unloading his pockets.

"I know it was here," he muttered. Carmela was about to point out the telephone directory when she saw the gun in his right hand. In an instant she felt the terrible wrench of betrayal. She had been right all along! He was here to threaten and rob her! Maybe even to kill her!

His back was still turned to her. Quickly, before he could turn around, before the gun was pointed at her, she had to protect herself. Fear, rage, and self-vindication lent her strength.

She rushed forward with the steel bar of the police lock clutched in both white-gloved hands. She brought it down on the back of his head with more force than she thought she could muster. He crumpled silently to the floor.

She picked up the phone and, after several fumbling attempts at dialing, managed to get connected with the police.

"I have just apprehended an armed robber," she stated. She responded calmly to the unemotional voice at the other end of the line, giving her name, address, and the particulars of her adventure.

It wasn't until she put down the phone that reaction set in. Her legs felt queer and her stomach fluttered wildly. She sank into the recliner and pressed both hands over her eyes. She wanted desperately to know if the young man lying on the floor was dead or alive, but she couldn't bear to look at him let alone touch him. She was still in the recliner when sirens wailed and tall men in uniform began to fill her living room.

Several of them clustered around the body on the floor, hiding it from view, while another sat beside Carmela and questioned her. Earnestly Carmela told of her suspicions, of the trick played on her to gain access to her apartment, of the gun being drawn and her instant stroke of self-defense. She felt calm and heroic. She would be written up in the newspapers.

Out of the whispered consultation over the body one man raised his head and addressed her questioner.

"Hey, know who this is?"

"A known criminal, I have no doubt," said Carmela.

"Not exactly, lady." He read from an open wallet in his hand. "Douglas Martin Fletcher. Badge Number 17582. Narco Squad."

The man who had been questioning her turned and looked at her with stony eyes. Carmela felt bewildered.

"A policeman?" she quavered. "Is he—?"

"You guessed it, lady. Nice going."

More men arrived—men in rumpled suits and in the white jackets of ambulance attendants. Carmela lay ignored in her recliner while their voices rumbled over her head. In a sudden hush she followed their eyes to the door. A small voice pierced the stillness.

"I heard the siren. Did Dougie call an ambulance? I don't think I can wait much longer."

Carmela had just a momentary view of the pale freckled face, intense and anxious in the doorway, before Karen was surrounded by a protective phalanx of broad blue shoulders and swept away.

Her questioner returned.

"Better get dressed, lady. You'll have to come with us."

"Yes. Of course. May I make a phone call first?"

"Okay. But make it fast."

Carmela went to the extension phone in the bedroom. She stripped off her white gloves and dialed the familiar number. The phone buzzed many times before she heard the answering click.

"Hello?" the voice was blurred with sleep.

"I won't be in the store on Monday. Something has come up."

"You had to call me *now*? Carmela, you're really crazy."

"Maybe I am. Read the newspaper if you want to know why."

"What happened? What's going on?"

Carmela replaced the receiver. She felt an odd lightness, a sense of walking on a strange new path. Maybe she would never have to go back to the store again. From her closet she took her best black dress. She sat at her dressing table and began making up her face. Good thing she'd done her hair today. There might be photographers.

The Palindrome Syndrome

Geore Potter sighed at the cruel fate that compelled him to go through life burdened with a nocturnal affliction. Rays from the streetlight, filtering through a gap in the curtain, caught the lampshade and threw a shadow on the ceiling. George stared at the shadow and tried to make it represent something new. But it refused to resemble anything except a black bear. While he watched, the black bear faded slowly into a dirty polar bear, then disappeared altogether as night tipped over into dawn.

He sighed again, a sigh that went unheard because of the jangle of the alarm. Ethel stopped in mid-breath, slapped the clock to silence, yawned, stretched, and jumped out of bed. She wrapped her short plump figure in a fuzzy pink garment. "Good morning, George. It's time to get up." Her blue eyes were clear and bright.

George moaned and rubbed his gritty, bloodshot, brown ones. Once he was up he had great difficulty with things like toothpaste and shoelaces. Later, at his office, he had trouble distinguishing the debits from the credits. In the drug store at noon he was yawning into his vegetable soup when Henry Williamson slid onto the stool next to him.

George didn't care much for Henry. Henry was a round-faced beaming man who still had all his hair even if it was gray. But today George was so demoralized that his troubles came spilling out. George admitted he had a severe problem.

He suffered from insomnia. All too often he stumbled to bed at 11:30 after fighting to keep awake until the end of the news, only to find that once in bed his heavy eyelids recoiled as though held by a tight spring and released a flurry of night thoughts like pigeons from a coop.

He tried everything from warm milk and hot baths to counting sheep and picturing the word *sleep* on a blackboard, written with each inhalation and erased with each exhalation. He tried taking his age, 55, and counting backward. He even doubled it and counted back from 110. He supposed he could count the gray hairs on his head, but as there were less of them each night that would be more depressing than somniferous.

Months ago he had learned that none of these devices produced the desired effect. Driven by the circumstances, he worked out a careful pattern. Night after night, feeling he was the only person awake in a world of the sleeping, he would get out of bed, don robe and slippers, and shuffle out to the kitchen leaving Ethel, breathing gently, alone in the bed. Ethel slept like the goldmining stocks he had once bought from a friend.

He fixed himself a pot of hot chocolate and settled in his overstuffed chair in the living room. For exactly one hour he worked crossword puzzles in the stack of magazines on the bottom shelf of the bookcase.

Then George moved on to the jigsaw puzzle and for precisely one hour he fitted pieces together. He studied the shape and color of each particular piece before picking it up. He prided himself on his ability to choose the correct piece before touching it with his fingers. A certain number of pieces fitted in this manner was a good omen. But if he made too many errors, if the pieces he chose didn't slip into the allotted spots, it meant sleep would be more elusive than ever that night.

Leaving the jigsaw puzzle, he moved back to his chair and selected a book from the row of current bestsellers on the second shelf of the bookcase. He read for exactly 30 minutes. Often this was a slow and gentle soporific, bringing on a yawn by the end of the first chapter and drowsiness by the end of the third.

The top shelf of the bookcase held his last and most desperate measure. Here he kept publications of the latest political activities, and he read these for 45 minutes.

He must follow this routine meticulously. If he deviated by so much as one minute, then all was lost. But if he followed his schedule exactly, then sometimes—oh, sometimes!—he was rewarded with a few hours of blessed sleep. Indeed sometimes, so deadly dull were the politicians' statements that he stumbled toward the bedroom, removing robe and slippers on the way, and reached the bed just in time to flop comatose across it.

If occasionally he was tricked into staying in bed by thinking that sleep was just a few minutes away, his adversity was compounded. He was then beguiled by the flock of thoughts fluttering around his head and he would pluck one from its fellows and examine it until an hour or two before he had to get up. Too many nights of insufficient sleep were making him old before his time, causing his hands to tremble and dulling his keen mind.

"Is that all that's bothering you?" Henry said, slathering ketchup on French fries and piling onions and pickles on a hamburger. "Don't give it another thought. I know just the thing to solve your problem." He paused to balance a slice of tomato on top of the heap, then said, "Palindromes." He smiled like a man with eight solid hours of sleep behind him.

"Palindromes?"

"Sure. You know, words that read the same backwards or forwards."

"I don't think I understand," George said, already sorry he had confided in Henry.

"My boy, you really are in bad shape, aren't you? Good thing you ran into me today. Your troubles are over, believe me. Palindromes are the answer. Words like *madam*. The same backwards or forwards. Surely, you know the famous one about Napoleon: *Able was I ere I saw Elba*. Spelled the same each way. A-b-l—"

"Yes, but how is that going to help me to get to sleep? Am I supposed to say it over and over?"

"Oh, no, no. You don't get the idea at all." Henry washed a mouthful of hamburger down with a gulp of coffee. "You have to make up your own. You start out small with single words like *dog god*. You see? Then you work up to sentences like the *Able Elba* one. Whenever I can't sleep, out come the old words and in fifteen minutes I'm sleeping like a night watchman. Never fails. I've been working on one for weeks. Starts out *Enid Star* and ends up with *rats dine*. But I always fall asleep before I get the middle part worked out."

George had no faith in anything Henry might suggest, but that same night when George had gone from the crossword puzzles to the politicians and was still awake at 4:30, he felt he had nothing to lose. He got *level* right off. A few minutes later he had *snip pins*, a revolutionary new sewing gadget. He was working on *ten net* when sleep swarmed over him.

The next night with something very near panic he abandoned his carefully worked-out schedule—the crosswords, jigsaws, bestsellers, and politicians that had served him long if not faithfully. With nervous trepidation he hesitantly embraced this new endeavor. He reviewed the previous night's crop, then produced *reel leer* and *devil lived* and *snap pans*. The last one was a special kind of cookware, he thought, floating on clouds of sleep. From then on there was no stopping him.

He was ecstatic. He was getting six or seven hours of sleep where before he only got one or two, sometimes none. It wasn't long before he was doing sentences. *Warts level straw* was his first. After that came *Pat repaid a diaper tap*. He was rather proud of that one. No more single words—grander creations were ahead.

In his delirium of joy there was something George failed to notice. Any addict could have pointed it out to him, but George went along happily building up his palindromic power without realizing that it was taking stronger and stronger doses each time before he drifted off to sleep. The night he finished Henry's *Enid Star* he was back to a mere two hours. But he couldn't wait to tell Henry what he had created. *Enid Star lived ere devil rats dine*.

One morning two months later, after no sleep at all, he sat down at the breakfast table and blurted out to Ethel, "*Mort's war on time did emit no raw storm*." He was too groggy from lack of sleep to catch the error in the first and last words.

Ethel stopped dishing out scrambled eggs to stare at him.

"Well, there's this guy Mort," George said, "who was extremely angry about buying all these products on the time-payment plan, so he—"

"You're sick, George," she said, dumping eggs on his plate. "You better see a doctor."

"*Rot cod?*" George pooh-poohed that idea. He wasn't sick. Far from it. At work his mind seemed to clack away like a well-oiled computer. True, he felt a little tired now and then and his boss was becoming a mite unreasonable about George's nonchalance in the matter of debits and credits; but other than that, George never felt better.

His excitement with the game became so high that like all fanatics he wished to share the enchantment and bring in converts. He took to waking up Ethel when he had worked out a particularly intricate treasure.

The first time, Ethel responded with *dam mad* and George soared to dizzying heights of happiness. He could see it all now—he and Ethel lying side by side through endless nights of palindromes. She would be the *Anna* to his *Otto*, and *edit* to his *tide*, the *loop* to his *pool*, the *smart* to his *trams*, the—

But alas, this sweet dream did not come to pass, because when he woke her on a subsequent occasion she threw the pillow at him, yelling she had to go to work in the morning. Reluctantly he was forced to the conclusion that her first response represented the state of her mind and that she had not grasped the delights of the game.

But George wasn't discouraged. Periodically he would wake her to share a new find and each time he hoped she would lovingly join him in palindroming through the long dark hours.

Not only was Ethel stupidly uninterested in the palindromes, but he noticed she was beginning to behave oddly. She seemed to get thinner, and there were black smudges under her eyes. Any unexpected noise sent her flying apart like a startled cat. Sometimes she stared blankly into space or just sat and whimpered. She definitely wasn't her usual self.

Perhaps it's her age, George thought. He renewed his efforts to arouse her interest in his game. Almost every night he would wake her to astound her with a new discovery. He would have been willing to do it more often but the time came when she refused to speak to him after being awakened.

One evening, six months after it all began, George felt he was ready. He intended to compose the greatest palindrome of all time. He was so eager to get started that he could hardly wait until the news was over before he rushed off to bed. He plumped his pillow, lay on his back staring at the black bear on the ceiling, and flexed his mental fingers. This was it. He was ready and confident. All his rigorous training had led up to this supreme moment.

While Ethel tossed around making herself comfortable he did a few warmup exercises. *Civic. Sagas. Solos.* By the time he completed these simple scales, Ethel was sleeping.

Midnight. Time to begin. Adrenalin coursed through his body and his heart jumped with the thrill of challenge, this greatest of all challenges.

George wiped his sweaty palms on the blanket and took a few deep breaths. With talent such as his there was no need to be nervous. In a short time he had selected his beginning words. *Pat. Let.*

At one o'clock he could see that he'd have to make notes. His was the caliber of champions. This creation would be much too long to figure out without writing it down. He switched on the lamp and rummaged through the drawer to find pencil and paper.

Ethel opened one bleary blue eye and glared at him. "George, what are you doing?"

"It's okay," he said. "It's coming along fine."

She put the pillow over her head.

George scribbled hastily for moments at a time, then chewed on the end of the pencil while his brain worked at lightning speed. All went well until three o'clock. At three o'clock he was stuck. At 3:30 he was still stuck. He howled in frustration and pounded the bed with his fist.

Ethel reared up in bed, looking around in confusion. "What?"

"A little bit of a problem. But don't worry. I'm not going to quit."

Ethel mumbled something that sounded like never-get-any-sleep, but George was too involved in his words to hear clearly. She punched her pillow and turned her back on him.

A half hour later he was still stuck. He placed his hands on the mound next to him and shook it. "Ethel?"

"Mmm?"

"Ethel!"

She sat up and shook her head groggily. "What is it?"

"Ethel, tell me a word that ends in r-e-m."

"What? You woke me up at four o'clock in the morning to ask me for a word that ends in r-e-m? You're crazy, George. That's what you are. Crazy." Her face got dangerously red and she started to vibrate like a rocket about to take off.

George waited tensely, hoping the vibrations meant her mind was working on r-e-m. But after a few moments she flopped back down and flung the blanket up over her quivering cheeks.

At first George was hurt, but then he understood. Of course. Ethel was quite right. He must solve the problem by himself. Otherwise it wouldn't count. He had almost ruined his night's work by asking for help. He sighed and rested briefly, letting relief at his narrow escape cool his sweaty brow.

Then he went back to it. It was, indeed, a knotty problem. *Theorem* seemed to be the only word in the English language that ended in r-e-m. And that word was totally useless to him. He strained and suffered in agony while his brain toiled on. Then at last he had it. "*Oh ho*," he shouted, then repeated it backward. "*Oh ho.*"

The mound under the blankets muttered.

"*Harem*," George told the mound joyfully.

He worked brilliantly and steadily until five o'clock when he began to get drowsy. He got up, not bothering with the robe and slippers, and made a pot of strong black coffee. He put this, along with a cup and saucer, on a tray and carried it back to the bedroom. The empty cup tended to rattle just a little.

As he was placing the tray on the bedside table, Ethel leaped out of bed, ripped off the blankets, and dragged them out of the room.

George stared in puzzlement until she disappeared into the dark of the living room. Then he poured a cup of coffee and went back to his creation.

At 6:30 he finished the coffee and the last word at the same time.

Masterful! He held the paper at arm's length and read it, then clasped it to his chest. Magnificent!

"Ethel," he shouted jubilantly as he ran into the living room. "Ethel, I've done it! I'm finished!"

Ethel, wrapped in blankets, was lying on the couch. He grabbed her shoulder and jerked it back and forth. "I'm going to read it to you," he said. "But first let me explain that it's a note from this boss to his secretary. The boss is planning a lecture series for small towns and the secretary knows of several local men who want to give lectures. One wants to talk about a nomad. You understand? It starts out *Pat*. That's the name of the secretary. *Pat, Let—*"

"*Red rum!*" Ethel yelled, erupting from the blankets and racing to the kitchen.

George paled. "No, no," he whispered.

"On, on," Ethel replied, returning with a knife. Waving it above her head she ran toward him shrieking, "*Bats! Bats! Bats!*" and she plunged the knife into his chest.

"*Enog esoog*," George gasped as he crumpled to the floor.

Ethel dropped the knife and staggered wearily to the bed.

In the afternoon when she got up she found the paper lying next to the body. It was covered with rusty brown spots, but she was still able to read it.

Pat,

Let one rustic at a time yammer. "A hag, nomad, evil madam lived among a harem" may emit a tacit, sure note.

L. Tap

When she showed it to the psychiatrist he said it was definitely the product of a disturbed mind.

At her trial the judge was very sympathetic. He said that owing to the extreme provocation of the conditions leading up to this tragic event her action was understandable and under the circumstances was "*no evil, Madam. Live on.*"

F As in Frame-Up

Lieutenant William Decker, Chief of Homicide, was a tall girder of a man with gray hair and gray eyes that were widely spaced. After 30 years of police work, one of the few illusions left to him was the quaint superstition that tough cases always started before breakfast. So when the dispatcher phoned just after Decker had finished his second cup of coffee, he told himself this would be an easy one; and what the dispatcher said reassured him.

There had been a robbery in the exclusive Short Hills section. The address was 59 Burroughs Lane, the name of the party was Welland, and some jewels had disappeared. It was the type of case in which regulations specified that Homicide had to be notified and had to send a man to assist, but which the local precinct usually handled thereafter. Because Decker had nothing pressing on his desk and because, for a change of pace, he hankered after expensive houses and well-bred people, he said he'd go there himself.

The house was brick, Georgian and semi-palatial, and an affable, easy-going man wearing a Shetland sports jacket opened the door. He was in his early thirties and he introduced himself as Alec Welland.

"Sorry about making all this fuss," he said. "People ought to learn to take care of their property. They shouldn't let themselves get robbed."

Lieutenant Decker agreed, and strode past him to get a report from the precinct detective who was carrying the case. His name was Quinn, and he looked as if he'd gone to college and majored in physical education. He was obviously surprised at finding the head of the Homicide Squad here; he took the Lieutenant into a spacious living room and motioned him to a corner. Decker sensed that Quinn saw a chance to impress him and maybe land himself a job on the Homicide Squad next time there was a vacancy.

"Here's the story," Quinn said, lowering his voice confidentially. "The Wellands went away for the weekend, down to Scofield. They both agree that the necklace, which was insured for forty grand, was in Mrs. Welland's bureau drawer late yesterday afternoon, when they left. She says she always kept it there loose, as if it was junk, because that was safer than locking it up in a jewelry box."

"I guess she found out how safe it was," Decker remarked.

"That's what I told her," Quinn said forcefully. He glanced at the door as if to make sure nobody was eavesdropping. "Well, about midnight the maid, Felicia, called them to say that the necklace was gone and they'd better come back, which they did. Felicia, incidentally, is no ordinary maid. Comes from Lithuania, she's a refugee, and only escaped a few months ago; but she's well educated and more a friend of the family than a servant. There are other servants, but they don't sleep in."

"What made Felicia wake up and discover the robbery?" Decker asked.

"She had a reason," Quinn said. "She's taking courses in adult education at the local high school, and she met a man there called George. She doesn't know his last name, but he apparently fell for her and came over last night to take her to the movies. When he made a pass at her, she refused to go. Then, to sort of make up, they had a drink together. He must have drugged hers, because that's all she remembers until she woke up with a king-size headache."

"When did she find out about the necklace?"

"Right away. She says she realized she'd been had, and so she looked around the house and saw that Mrs. Welland's bureau had been searched and one of the drawers turned upside down. The necklace was gone. She phoned the Wellands and—" Quinn consulted his pad—"they got back around two a.m. Mrs. Welland was upset, Felicia was still sick, and the two of them had minor hysterics. Mr. Welland says he couldn't stand it. He slammed out of the house and went driving in his big Chrysler. He got back about six and they all had breakfast, and then he called us. I think that covers it."

"It sure as hell does," Decker said. "You're trying to locate this George, of course."

"Yes, sir. We're checking up at the school, but what I'm wondering about is who told George where the necklace was. With nothing touched except that one bureau drawer, it looks like a put-up job." Decker nodded. Quinn had made a competent, orderly investigation. They'd find George and he'd probably deny the robbery and the drugging, and the maid might or might not turn out to be an accomplice. But there was plenty on George, and everything shaped up as a run-of-the-mill case. Still, it might be a good idea for Decker to see the two women.

He met Isabel Welland in the dining room, over a cup of coffee. She was blonde and lovely, and her eyes were blue and clear and intelligent. When she smiled, she brightened the lot of the poor and gave comfort to mankind. She was a lady, endowed with beauty and trained to carry it gracefully.

Felicia, who brought the coffee, was something else again, and Decker studied her with respect. She was young and attractive, with dark hair and deep, liquid eyes. It was hard to realize that she was one of those remarkable people who had begged, fought, and forced their way from behind the Iron Curtain through sheer force of will and at the risk of their lives. She spoke English with a barely noticeable accent.

On the surface she was soft and pliable, gleaming with innocence, and the sight of her went right through Lieutenant Decker. Forty years dropped off him in a breath, and he almost popped out of his chair. He was glad he didn't have to interrogate her, because all he wanted to do was protect her.

"I understand you had a tough time of it," he remarked to her.

"It was a nothing," she said. "It is over." Then the phone rang and she answered it.

"For the Lieutenant Decker," she said, turning toward him and addressing him as if he were royalty.

With that phone call, the fun was over. There was a homicide over in the slum section, near the river. A man named George McCoster had been shot.

Decker blinked. "George," he said thoughtfully. "George."

He looked squarely at Felicia, and she stared straight back at him as if she'd heard every word over the phone and had guessed every thought that had gone through Decker's mind.

The facts surrounding the murder of George were as clear as plastic. George McCoster had been a known jewel thief. His body was lying just inside the door of his shabby, furnished room, and a reconstruction of the crime indicated that he'd been shot twice without warning, from a distance of about a foot. Time of death was set around 4:00 a.m., and the bullets had probably been fired from a .32 Smith & Wesson. The gun was not found, nor was there any trace of the Welland necklace.

Later in the day, after the dull, grim work of examining the body and after Decker had put the squad to work trying to find witnesses and trying to pump information out of them, he sent for Felicia. She came, escorted by a uniformed cop, and she gazed without a tremor at the dead face and said confidently, "He is the man who visited me."

Since the robbery tied in with a homicide, the whole business was now dumped in Decker's lap. Like it or not, he had Felicia as a prime suspect, and he questioned her in the privacy of his pint-sized office that contained his desk and three chairs, a stuffed crocodile, and stacks of unfiled and unread police journals.

"Felicia," he said, "you're in trouble. You realize that, don't you?"

She smiled, as if *he* were in trouble and she felt sorry for him.

"Every piece of evidence points right at you," Decker continued, "so tell me what you did with the necklace."

"I did not take it," she said quietly. "Mrs. Welland is my so good friend. I could not steal from her."

"Maybe not," Decker said. Her eyes, limpid and trusting, haunted him, and instead of blasting away with his usual dynamite, he fumbled like an Assistant D.A. on his first assignment. "Maybe," he said, "but how could you meet this George in school when he wasn't even enrolled?"

"He was in the corridor. He saw me, he spoke."

"A guy like him—you figured him for a student? It was written all over him that he was a thug."

"I do not know the types here in America. Or the customs."

"You don't have to," Decker said. "You're a woman—you know when a guy's genuine or not. And you typed him fast enough after he came to the house."

"I asked him to go," she said with dignity, as if her obvious virtue ought to answer all the Lieutenant's questions.

Decker glowered and waited for the sparks to fly between them, but she merely studied him with a sorrowful, pitying look. Then, in the grip of one of his wild, extravagant hunches, he asked a question that had no apparent reason behind it.

"Felicia," he said, "did Mr. Welland ever make a pass at you?"

She frowned, not understanding the expression, and Decker had to explain. "Did he ever try to make love to you?"

"But certainly. I am so nice."

"And you let him?"

"No. I am very strong, Mr. Lieutenant, and I do not let anybody do that."

"So he tried, and you sent him packing, and I suppose you told Mrs. Welland about it."

"Oh, yes. We discussed it often."

"I see," Decker said meekly. "Now tell me exactly what you did and what you and Mrs. Welland talked about between two and six in the morning."

She told him, and later on, when Isabel Welland confirmed every detail, Decker crossed Felicia off the list. Not that the two women couldn't have cooked up that alibi, with their mutual understanding that almost amounted to telepathy, but because he believed in Felicia.

With a growing sense that he was up against something unusual, Decker analyzed the problem. He reasoned that McCoster must have been killed because of the missing necklace, and that only three people knew McCoster had taken it—namely Felicia and the two Wellands. Therefore, if neither Felicia nor Isabel had gone to McCoster's house, then Alec Welland had.

Before questioning Alec, however, Decker ordered a full-scale investigation of Alec's background, of his purchase of the necklace, and of his relationship with Isabel.

The reports were dismal enough. Isabel, the heiress to a substantial fortune, had married Alec when she was only 17. She'd fallen for his charm and his easy-going assurance, and she'd let him manage her affairs and gradually transferred all her assets to his name. Today she had practically nothing in her own name.

Alec was a gambler. He'd played the horses and he'd lost; he'd gone to Las Vegas and he'd lost; and he'd bet on all the wrong numbers in the private roulette clubs—until he'd run out of Isabel's cash.

Money poured through his fingers like a handful of water, and he spent it by the gallon. He signed checks without regard to his bank balance, borrowed money in a casual, offhand way, and if he ever found any loose currency around, he simply took it. He was a wastrel and an unfaithful husband, and everybody agreed that Isabel was a saint and that any other woman would have left him long ago.

Once Alec was divested of his posture of the wealthy squire, Decker brought him into the Squad Room, and with Bankhart and Charlie Small assisting, the Lieutenant blazed away.

"You bought the necklace for twenty thousand," Decker said, tapping a copy of the bill of sale, "and you insured it for forty. Right?"

"Right," Alec said. "Smart of me, wasn't it?"

"Where'd you get the money to buy the necklace?"

"I refuse to answer on the grounds that—"

"We know where you got it," Decker said. "You had a lucky night in a dice game. You paid five grand in cash and talked the jeweler into giving you credit for the rest."

"If you know all about it," Alec said, "why ask me?"

"What did you buy it for?"

"For my wife's birthday."

"Her birthday's in January. This is October."

Alec shrugged. "I thought you sent for me to get some information. But instead—"

"Instead—what?" Decker asked sharply.

"Instead, you're accusing me."

"Of what?"

"I'll tell you," Alec said grandiosely. "You think I planned on an insurance fraud. Maybe I did. I'd be stupid if the idea never crossed my mind, but that's as far as it went. This McCoster solved my problem. He stole the necklace, probably in cahoots with Felicia. That girl's capable of anything."

"You own a gun," Decker said. "You have a license for a Smith and Wesson 'thirty-two.' Where's the gun?"

"Funny thing," Alec said, "but I don't know. It disappeared."

"Under what circumstances?"

"Well, I always kept it in the night table next to my bed, and it was there when we left for the weekend. Do you think McCoster took it?"

"When was the first time you met him?" Decker asked.

Alec didn't fall into the trap. "Met him?" he said. "I never even heard of him until he turned up dead after Felicia brought him into the house."

"Do you deny knowing him?" Decker asked.

"Never saw him in my life."

"You hired him to steal the necklace," Decker said grimly. "You figured you had a wingding of an idea—he keeps the necklace and sells it for whatever he can get, and you collect the insurance."

"Did *he* tell you that?" Alec asked, grinning.

Bankhart slapped a big paw on Alec's shoulder and spun him around in his chair. "Better not kid around," Bankhart said.

Alec stopped grinning. "I don't know what this is all about," he said, swallowing nervously.

Decker, reasonably confident that he'd guessed Alec's scheme, switched the line of questioning. "Just tell us," Decker said, "where you were from two a.m. when you left your house until six a.m. when you returned."

"I went driving," Alec said. "I headed north—I don't remember exactly where I went. But I like speed and I had a good fast car, and I wanted to get away from those women. You don't know them. They're together all the time. They hate me, they'd like to see me dead. They put on a scene about the necklace and they accused me of the same thing you did—hiring this George to steal the necklace."

"They were right about it," Decker said.

"No. I'm telling you—I didn't know McCoster, I had nothing to do with him."

The next day four members of the Homicide Squad spent a total of 28 hours trying to disprove Alec's statement. They came up with the information that Alec had seen McCoster twice. The first time they'd had a drink together in a bar and the waitress had overheard them talking about a necklace; and a day later Alec had parked his big gray car in front of McCoster's and had been seen entering the house.

Decker reviewed the situation at the regular morning session of the Homicide Squad.

"We're beginning to see the peep of daylight," he said. "Alec practically admitted the insurance fraud. He saw McCoster and discussed necklaces; and somebody must have told McCoster where to find Felicia, what she looked like, where the necklace was, and on what night the Wellands would be away from home. Can anyone except Alec fit the role?"

"So what?" Bankhart said. "That adds up to an insurance fraud, but where's the evidence of a homicide?"

"You hit it on the pimple," Decker said. "We're playing ring-around-the-rosie with him, and the guy knows it. Until we can nail him to the scene, or else find that gun—"

"I'll tell you where it is," Balenky said. "It's buried under a tree or else lying in a junk heap, and it's maybe fifty miles away. The guy was driving for a couple of hours, so how do we dream up where he hid the gun? And maybe the necklace, too."

"Check," Decker said, "but somebody saw Welland around four a.m. Somebody heard the shot. Somebody saw the car. Go find the guy."

With that, Decker broke up the meeting, and the squad went out grumbling. It was the sort of slow, dogged, dull work that they hated, but they knew Decker wouldn't let up. He'd decided there was a witness and that they'd find him.

Charlie Small came back late in the day, and with an unexpected answer. Nobody had seen Alec's big gray Chrysler, but a couple of bums had seen a small green, foreign car parked in front of McCoster's at about 4:00 a.m. and one of the bums had leaned over the fender and been sick.

Decker let out a whoop and sent for the Wellands' second car, which was a small green, foreign one. Jub Freeman, looking like an overgrown cherub, studied the stains and made scrapings and said that their analysis was a job for the pathologist, over in the Medical Examiner's office. Mitch Taylor took charge of the samples and brought them over, and a few hours later the verdict came in. Somebody had been sick all right, and on the right rear fender, after drinking too much cheap whiskey and eating too many peanuts.

That finding was the big break in the case. It put the Wellands' second car at the scene of the crime, and all Decker had to do was to show that Alec had been in it. He decided that Mrs. Welland was his best witness for that, and he sent for her early the next morning.

She came willingly. She was pure and radiant and serene, and she answered his questions with an air of frankness and composure. Nevertheless she defended her husband with all her strength.

"You said you'd heard Alec drive off," Decker said. "You heard the sound of the motor, didn't you?"

"Yes, of course."

"And you can tell the difference between the roar of your big Chrysler and the squeak of that little foreign bug of yours, can't you?"

Isabel Welland seemed to search her soul to find an honest answer. "Is there a difference?" she said archly.

"Never mind," Decker said. "Did you see which car he took?"

"You're trying to prove that Alec committed murder," she said, "but he couldn't have killed this man because Alec didn't have his gun."

"How do you know?" Decker asked.

"It was in his night table when we left for the weekend. I saw it there. And when we got home it was gone. I looked."

"What made you look?"

Isabel shrugged off the question. "I just did. Intuition, perhaps. So how could Alec have shot this man?"

"Mrs. Welland, you didn't get along very well with your husband. Why didn't you divorce him?"

"Divorce Alec?" she said in surprise. "Oh, no, and for the most sordid of reasons. He's not a very steady provider, but he does manage. And besides, he has all my money."

"The court would give you a pretty good settlement."

"That wouldn't help me," she said. "Can you conceive of Alec actually paying up? Lieutenant, I wouldn't let myself in for that."

Which, Decker reflected, was a strange answer. Because, if she wanted to divorce her husband and couldn't, what was sweeter than framing him for a murder? And her very defense of him was suspicious. The loyal, virtuous wife lying to defend her husband? Any jury would see through that, and she knew it. So if she wanted to fry Alec, she was going about it the right way.

The implications obsessed Decker, and he locked himself up in his tiny office and communed with the small stuffed crocodile on top of his bookcase. He told himself that he'd lost his objectivity in this case. He'd gone soft on Felicia and believed every word she'd told him, and as a result had concentrated on Alec. But now Decker reviewed the case from scratch.

The small foreign car pointed to a woman, and Decker had two women and they both hated Alec. He recalled Felicia's quiet admission that Alec had tried to make time with her and that she'd even discussed the matter with Isabel. So— here were two women, overly close to each other, and both of them had motive to destroy Alec. All they needed to accomplish it was to cook up an alibi for the two of them, and then stick to it. The murder of McCoster would merely be the means.

Decker put himself in the position of a woman who had just killed somebody and had a gun and a necklace to dispose of, and who was all alone in a car at four o'clock in the morning. She'd be frantic with the fear that Alec would get back to the house before she did. Whatever else, she had to act fast and get rid of the incriminating evidence in a hurry.

Decker sent for a city map, put an X on it where McCoster had lived, and another X at the Welland residence. He traced out three probable routes that Isabel or Felicia would have taken. Then he got in his car and, driving slowly, he followed the routes and looked for a place where she might have discarded a gun and a necklace.

On his second trip he passed two open lots and a junk pile of old cars. He couldn't find any sign of recent digging in the lots, and he spent an hour looking for the needle in the haystack of old cars. He was mildly pleased with the metaphor, but otherwise discouraged.

He returned to headquarters in a black mood, went over the day's reports, and sifted out assignments for tomorrow. He decided he could spare four men for the search.

Instead of the usual bull session the next morning, he blasted off and orbited himself into space. "Forget Welland," he said. "The little point that we skipped is that either of those two women could have killed McCoster, because they both had motive. That means one of them dumped the gun and the necklace somewhere after leaving McCoster's, and it's got to be in a junk yard or an open lot, and here are the locations."

He slapped the city map down on the table in front of him. "Taylor, Bankhart, Balenky, Small—you're going out there with shovels and pickaxes, so get your tools from the Supply Room. And if anybody has any questions, I don't want to hear them." And Decker swung around and stalked off to his office, where he sweated out the day and burned himself out with waiting.

At five o'clock the four men came back from the junk heap, and they had the gun and the necklace. The necklace, made up of three large diamonds and more smaller ones than Decker bothered to count, was wrapped up in a piece of cleaning tissue, and the gun was jammed with the sand and dirt in which it had been buried. Somebody had shoved it under one of the wrecked cars and covered it lightly with earth.

"Brother!" Decker exclaimed. "Start figuring out when you want to take a couple of days off. You earned 'em."

Seething with suppressed excitement, and at the same time scared that there would be a hitch somewhere, the Lieutenant brought the gun and necklace up to the lab.

"Got 'em!" he said triumphantly to Jub. "Let's see what you can make out of them."

The examination of the gun was simple. Two bullets had been fired, and the serial numbers identified the gun as Alec's.

"I'll clean it up later on and fire some test shots," Jub said. "There's not much doubt about its being the murder weapon. Now, let's have a look at the necklace."

He bent over it, studying the settings under a lens and removing bits of dirt and foreign matter with a small pair of tweezers. "No blood," he muttered. "With all the filigree work and these sharp edges I thought I might find—"

He broke off. "That's funny," he said. "This—"

"What?" Decker demanded.

"Dunno, yet." Jub, holding a fragment of something in the tweezers, brought it over to a microscope. He gazed through the eyepiece, adjusted it, then straightened up. "Somebody broke a fingernail," he announced, "and the piece got dropped in the tissue and has nail polish on it."

"Brother!" Decker exclaimed. "So all we need is to locate a woman with a broken fingernail, and then match up her nail polish." His face lit up. "Want to come out to the Welland house with me?"

Jub's grin dimpled up both cheeks. "A pleasure," he said.

They drove off with high hopes. The case stacked up as a classic of modern scientific analysis. Isabel or Felicia, in grabbing the necklace after she'd shot McCoster, had ripped her nail and lopped off a sliver, and it had dropped into the cleaning tissue in which she'd wrapped the necklace. And, as Decker observed wryly, she'd hang by her fingernail.

Briefly, in his mind, Decker reviewed the case against each of the women. Motive and opportunity were clear. Both of them had had access to the gun, and either of them could have committed the murder in the expectation that Alec would be held responsible. As long as they backed each other up, they were safe.

Until the fingernail showed up.

Isabel, smiling and gracious, answered the bell when Decker rang it. "Lieutenant," she said, "whatever do you want?"

"To see your hands," he said.

She held them out proudly—patrician hands with slender, tapering fingers and polished, manicured nails. All the nails were intact, and Decker said curtly, "Could we see Felicia for a moment?"

"Why, of course," Isabel said.

Felicia arrived a minute later and Decker, shaking hands with her, glanced down. The polish on her nails was worn and cracked, and several of the ends were broken off.

Decker indicated them. "How come?" he asked.

She pulled her hand away in distaste. "It is always so," she said. "With the work I do, I cannot have beautiful nails. It matters?"

"It matters," Decker said, and explained precisely why. "So that's the end of your mutual alibi. One of you drove over to McCoster's, and all I have to do now is match up the nail polish."

"It would seem so," Isabel said. She hesitated and exchanged a look with Felicia. Decker, keyed up and watching like a hawk, sensed the quick passage of some critical issue between them, followed by a tacit renewal of their loyalty.

"It would seem so," Isabel repeated, "except that I broke my nail a couple of days ago, on the hood button of the car. I had to file my nail down and repair it with a plastic strip. This one." She extended one hand. "It's quite apparent if you look closely."

Obediently, Jub stepped over to examine Isabel's finger. He bent down over it, then lifted his head and nodded. As for Decker, Isabel's statement left him high and dry, and he wondered why she'd made that admission. To protect Felicia? Or to head Felicia off from an accusation fatal to Isabel?

Hood button? The green foreign car had one too, and Felicia—

Suddenly Decker's mind clicked.

He turned to Felicia and said casually, with apparent innocence, "Can you drive?"

"No, I—" She broke off, aghast.

Isabel, stunned, furious, unable to believe she'd heard correctly, froze up in sheer shock.

Decker cleared his throat. "That's what I thought," he said. "Not many cars in Lithuania, not many people there learn to drive. And Felicia never did learn . . . Mrs. Welland, will you come with us?"

EDITORS' NOTE: Here is an interesting footnote to Lawrence Treat's story: according to the 18th Decennial Census taken in April 1960, there are more motor vehicles in the United States than in the entire rest of the world. In metropolitan Los Angeles alone, there are more cars than in Greece, Ireland, Holland, Norway, Poland, and Denmark combined. So Lieutenant Decker's deduction was not mere "hunch"—it was based on fact—the essence of procedural detection.

The Great Bread Swindle

onday was the first of the month. On Tuesday the figures for the previous month were released. And on Wednesday Harry Carlson got his usual call from the district manager.

"You know why I'm calling, Harry," Budney said. "You saw the figures and you saw where we stood. And all because we've taking a dead loss on your operation. And you know how I feel about that, Harry."

"Mr. Budney," Harry said, "I keep telling you. There are reasons."

"And I keep telling you, Harry, I don't want reasons. I want results." Budney's voice softened. "I had a lot of high hopes for you, Harry," he said. "You remember how we talked when I put you in there about what the future could hold for a bright ambitious young man at Honeyloaf?"

"Yes, sir," Harry said despondently.

"Well, just remember this too, Harry. People who don't live up to their promise don't have any future at all. So if you know what's good for you, you'll get off your duff and get that store showing a profit. Or, by George, I'll get somebody in there who can."

Harry winced as the phone on the other end was banged down. Sighing, he replaced his own receiver with a great deal more care, then got up, left the cubicle that served as his office, and went out into the store proper.

It was empty except for Marcie Fleming at her post behind the cash register. She looked at Harry sympathetically. "More trouble, Harry?" she said.

Harry shook his head. "No," he said. "Just the same old one. We're not showing a profit—which makes Budney unhappy. And when he's unhappy, everybody's unhappy."

"That's not fair," Marcie said fiercely. She was a pert blonde, 23 years old and 115 pounds soaking wet. She'd been Harry's assistant six months now and had been hopelessly in love with him since the second day. To her satisfaction, things had progressed to where they had an "understanding." To her disappointment, it was becoming increasingly clear they'd never get beyond that.

Harry shrugged, sighed, and looked around the store. It was a small, rather plain place, crowded with display racks which in turn were piled high with loaves of Honeyloaf bread. Suspended from the ceiling above the racks were large handlettered signs reading uniformly: 20 CENTS EACH—SIX LOAVES

FOR A DOLLAR. Other racks were stocked with Honeycakes, Honeypies, Honeycookies, and other Honey-goodies, all at prices substantially below those normally charged for first-class bakery goods at any respectable supermarket.

Not that the Honey line wasn't first class or Harry's store respectable—in its fashion. The reason for the bargain prices was simply that these particular items were "day-old"—which, of course, is an industry euphemism for "not fresh." By whatever term, though, it was stuff that hadn't sold in its alloted time and the regular deliverymen would pick it up on schedule as they restocked the stores on their routes, then turn it over to Harry to sell at discount. Or try to anyway.

Actually it wasn't a bad idea as ideas go. The bread might be a little drier than when fresh baked but by any other standard it was just as good and by selling it at any price the company got at least some return on what otherwise would be a total loss. The problem was, though, that the *place* to sell it was in the inner city or out in one of the low- or middle-income suburbs, not here in affluent North Shore.

Placing the store here had been Budney's idea. Budney wanted to be Manager of the Year. And you didn't get there, he was fond of pointing out, by letting money you could be making yourself go out of the district. Budney, Harry decided for the umpteenth time, was a fool.

It was a satisfying thought, but now Marcie called him back to the less-satisfying present. "Harry," she said, "you can't just shrug this off."

"I know," Harry said. The only thing that bothered him about Marcie was that at times she sounded very much like his mother. She went on sounding that way.

"So what are you going to do?"

"Well," Harry said, "the way I see it, I can either stay here and brood. Or I can go for coffee and brood." He picked a package of doughnuts off a nearby rack. "I think I'll go out for coffee," he said.

And with that he did go out, leaving an exasperated Marcie behind.

That evening, as he did every Wednesday, Harry had dinner at his mother's. As usual the evening started out with a cross-examination.

"You don't look happy, Harry," Mrs. Carlson said. "You and Marcie have a fight or something?"

"No," Harry said, "of course not, Mom."

"That's good." Mrs. Carlson finished setting the table and sat down opposite her son. "You know, Harry," she said, passing him the meat platter, "I can't help but worry about you. Twenty-seven years old and still not settled down. When are you and Marcie going to name the day?"

"When it's time, Mom," Harry said. He speared a pork chop from the platter.

"Sure," Mrs. Carlson said. She frowned as Harry started to put the platter down. "Take another one, Harry. You have to eat if you're going to keep up your strength."

"I eat all right, Mom," Harry said.

"Sure you do," Mrs. Carlson said. "Once a week." She watched until Harry dutifully took a second chop. Then she took the platter back and passed him a large bowl of mashed potatoes. "And speaking of eating," she said, "next time you come bring some of that bread you sell. You know, the twenty-cent kind."

Harry paused with the serving spoon half raised. "I thought you said you only liked bread if it was fresh?"

"That was before it went to fifty-three cents," Mrs. Carlson said. "Honest to God, Harry, I bought a loaf at the supermarket the other day and by the time I got around to using it there wasn't that much difference from that stuff of yours. Not thirty-three cents' worth anyway. Bring some for Mrs. Evans too."

"I will," Harry said. He was so impressed he took a larger helping of mashed potatoes than he'd intended.

The impression lasted, and the next morning he mentioned the incident twice, first to Marcie, then later to Murphy the deliveryman when he brought the day's quota of leftover bread and cakes. "It's inflation," Harry said as he helped Murphy unload his truck, "finally catching up with North Shore. First the older people, then the housewives."

"You think so, Harry?" Murphy said.

Harry shrugged. "I don't know," he said. "Maybe two swallows don't make a summer, but I sure hope so."

Murphy looked at him pityingly. "Did you ever stop to think why all the regular drivers passed up this—uh—promotion of yours, Harry? It was because they were all smart enough to realize that you couldn't win here no matter what happened. So maybe people do start buying from you. All that means is they're buying less at retail. And what do you think our ever-loving district manager will do when that happens? Take three guesses."

Harry needed only one, and his face showed it. Because one of the main considerations in locating the store here was that there were no retailers handling Honeyloaf in the immediate neighborhood.

Murphy clapped him commiseratingly on the shoulder. "If you're smart," he said, "you'll quit before they fire you. It looks better on the record."

Left to his own decision, Harry would have probably done just that. But before he could make up his mind, fate or luck, or maybe pure blind chance handed him a reprieve. Of a sort, that is. Because two days later Harry slipped on a wet spot on his kitchen floor, tried to catch himself as he fell, and as a result was laid up for weeks with a badly wrenched back.

When he finally got back to work it was the first of the month again. For some reason, though, the day came and went without the usual phone call from Budney. At first Harry thought it was consideration for his recent accident. But then he got a look at the profit-and-loss figures and learned better.

For the first time the store had begun to show a profit. A small one, it was true, but black ink just the same. Better still, there was no matching drop-off in the district's retail sales.

"I don't know what you did," he said to Marcie, "but if you promise to keep it up I'll promise to take off more often."

Marcie started to sniffle.

"Hey," Harry said, "there's no reason to cry."

"I'b nod crying," Marcie said. "I hab a code."

"That's awful," Harry said. "You ought to be home in bed. I mean it. Take the rest of the day off."

Marcie started to refuse, but then a sneeze interrupted, and in the end she agreed and left for the day.

Which is why Harry happened to be tending the cash register when Chestnut came in.

Not that Harry knew he was Chestnut at the time. All he saw was a small furtive-looking man in a leather jacket and cloth cap glancing apprehensively around the store.

"Where's Marcie?" the man said at last.

"Miss Fleming's sick," Harry said.

"Oh? Who are you then?"

"I'm the manager," Harry said. "Now, look—"

"Oh," the small man said again, but in a completely different tone of voice. "You must be Harry. Yeah, Marcie talked about you a lot." He pointed to himself. "I'm Chestnut," he said. "I came for the order."

Harry looked at him blankly.

"I got a standing order. Didn't Marcie tell you?"

"No," Harry said, "she didn't."

"Don't tell me you're sold out?"

Harry shook his head.

"Whew," Chestnut said. "You had me worried there for a minute. Once before I was a little late getting in and Marcie had to short me twenty-five loaves. You can guess what a sweat that was. Anyway, that's when I went to the standing order. Safer."

"Much," Harry agreed dubiously. "Uh, just how much do you want?"

"A hundred loaves white," Chestnut said, suddenly crisp and businesslike. "And forty-five rye. You got any pumpernickel?"

"Some."

Gimme twenty of those then. No, better make it fifteen."

Harry nodded, still not sure what he was agreeing to, but agreeing anyway. Then he went off to fill the small man's order.

It took more than several trips to the stockroom but finally Harry had it all together, ringing up the sale and then helping Chestnut carry the bread out to his car, a three-year-old station wagon with no identifying marks or signs.

When Harry went back into the store, a second man in a leather jacket almost identical to Chestnut's stood by the cash register. "Where's Marcie?" the stranger said.

"Marcie," Harry said, "for God's sake, who *are* these men?"

It was two days later. Marcie was back on the job but still sniffling. She touched a crumpled tissue to her nose. "What men?" she said.

"Little men in leather jackets," Harry said. "A steady stream of them regular as streetcars, and they all know you by name."

"Oh," Marcie said. "Those men." She shrugged. "They aren't anybody, Harry. They're just men who buy bread here, that's all."

"That's all!" Harry said. "Marcie, those men cleaned us out yesterday. And the day before that too. They'll probably clean us out again today."

"Of course they will," Marcie said. "But that's what we're in business for, isn't it? To sell bread." She gave Harry a long curious look. When he had no comeback she touched the tissue to her nose again as if to say that as far as she was concerned that was the end of that.

Harry probably wouldn't have left it there because he didn't like puzzles. But right after that Marcie's men—as he'd come to think of them—started coming in and he got so involved taking care of them that he never got back to it. In fact, it wasn't until he was closing up for the night that he remembered it was Wednesday and that he'd forgotten to set aside any bread for his mother.

The bread shelves were empty now, but fortunately Saul Dubrow's convenience food store across the street was still open and rather than show up empty-handed Harry crossed over to the small grocery and picked up a couple of loaves of Honeyloaf.

Saul's youngest daughter-in-law was tending the cash register. She looked at Harry curiously as he plumped the two loaves down on the checkout counter. "Talk about coals to Newcastle," she said.

"Just checking the competition." Harry accepted his change—a dime and four one-dollar bills from a five—declined a bag and left with his purchases.

He was halfway to his mother's before it hit him.

The next morning Harry waited until he saw the bread delivery truck leave. Then he crossed over again to the small grocery. As he had hoped, this time Saul himself was in the store.

Harry came straight to the point. "Since when did you start carrying Honeyloaf, Saul?"

Saul shrugged. He was a tall spare man in his mid-60's with a lugubrious face and thin graying hair. "A couple of weeks now," he said. "Ever since one of your drivers stopped by and made me an offer I couldn't refuse."

"You're sure it was one of our drivers?"

"He said he was," Saul said. "Should I have questioned him?"

"Maybe you should have, Saul," Harry said. "Because it must have been quite a bargain he offered you if it lets you resell eight cents cheaper than the supermarkets. Didn't that make you suspicious at all?"

"Of course it did," Saul said. "I wasn't born yesterday and I haven't beaten a supermarket price since they invented them. But he had an explanation. Something to do with expanded production and lower unit costs."

"And you believed it?"

"Frankly, Harry," Saul said, "no. I figured the real gimmick was to get me hooked and then raise the price. But I thought why not? When he talks higher price I can always say, 'No, thanks, but it's been nice knowin' you.'" The older man shrugged again. "I have to admit, though, so far he hasn't even mentioned a higher price."

"And he won't either," Harry said. "Because what's happening, Saul, is you're being taken. A bunch of sharpies are buying my discount bread and then reselling it to people like you as fresh."

"That's crazy, Harry," Saul said, "You don't think after all these years in the business I wouldn't know if somebody was passing stale bread off on me? Particularly, as you say, somebody who was offering me a bargain?"

"As a matter of fact," Harry said, "you probably wouldn't. Because you can't tell any more just by squeezing, not with all the preservatives they pump into everything. But there is a way if you know where to look."

He picked up a loaf from the display counter. "They put a little colored mark on all the wrappers as a freshness code. It's how the deliverymen know when to replace. And if you look right here it tells you—" Harry's voice trailed off.

Saul raised an eyebrow. "Tells you what, Harry?" he said.

"It's today's bread," Harry said slowly. "It's fresh bread."

"Don't give up so easily, Harry," Saul said. "Maybe they're counterfeiting wrappers as well."

Harry shook his head absently. "They couldn't," he said. "It would be too expensive."

"So where's the crime then, Mr. Detective?"

Harry shook his head again. "I'm damned if I know," he said.

But now he was more determined than ever to find out, and on Friday he called Marcie at the store to tell her he wouldn't be in. A doctor's appointment, he said, to have his back checked—an appointment he'd forgotten to mention earlier. He didn't like lying to Marcie, but he wanted her to behave normally when her customers started coming in, and he didn't think she'd be able to if she knew what he really had in mind. Which was to drive down to the store, pick a spot about half a block away, park, wait.

Luckily he didn't have to wait long. Less than half an hour after he'd settled himself in, Chestnut's familiar station wagon pulled up in front of the store. When it pulled out again, laden with its usual stock of bread, Harry followed.

It was the first time Harry had ever tried to tail a car without the other driver knowing it. But luckily again there wasn't much traffic and the small man drove with almost singleminded directness, turning twice and then pulling into a large double garage set well back on a side street.

Harry drove past slowly. Chestnut was already out of the station wagon and closing the garage doors, which prevented Harry from seeing anything inside. But the small man gave no sign he'd recognized Harry. So Harry went on down to the end of the street, made a tight, illegal U-turn, and settled down to wait once more.

Twenty minutes later he was rewarded. The garage doors opened and a truck drove out.

"It was like a bad dream," Harry said. "I followed that truck from store to store until we'd covered every supermarket in that part of town." It was later in the day and Harry was back at the store, sitting at his desk and talking to Marcie who leaned sober-faced against the doorjamb.

"Why a *bad* dream, Harry?" she said.

"Don't you understand?" Harry said. "That was a Honeyloaf truck I followed. Those men who 'buy bread' here. They're company deliverymen, every one of them. And they've got a beautiful little swindle worked out. They pick up their bread at the bakery every morning, just like they're supposed to. But instead of delivering it where they're supposed to, they sell it to small-store owners like Saul. Then they come here and buy our bread to use on their regular routes.

"And it works, because they're so well known there that everybody just takes them for granted. You know, you see your regular route man restocking the store and you just naturally assume he's putting in fresh and taking out old because that's what he's always done. But this time he isn't. He's just substituting one batch of old bread for another. And it's foolproof. Or almost foolproof," he amended grimly, reaching for the phone.

Marcie sighed. "I was afraid you'd take this attitude, Harry. That's why I didn't tell you."

Harry's hand stopped short of the receiver. "What do you mean," he said, "you didn't tell me before? Marcie! Did you know about this?"

The girl nodded. "Actually," she said, "I'm afraid it was even sort of my idea. Mr. Murphy was helping me one day while you were out and, well, one thing just led to another."

"Oh, God!" Harry said, "Marcie, it's *dishonest*."

"Is it really, Harry? I mean, *really*? Oh, I know, we profit and so do the drivers. But who's hurt? Not the company for sure. They're selling more bread and making more money than ever—although admittedly they don't understand quite why. Not Saul or any of the other small-store owners either. And the supermarkets haven't complained, Harry. Neither have any of their customers. So they can't be hurting too badly if they don't even know it's happening to them."

Harry just shook his head. Marcie looked at him earnestly. "Listen, Harry," she said, "I had to do something! Otherwise we'd have had an 'understanding' for the rest of our lives."

"Marcie—" Harry began. He took a deep breath. "Marcie," he began again. The phone rang, and Harry picked it up quickly, glad of the interruption. "We'll talk about this later," he said to Marcie, who turned and ran from the room. Harry sighed and put the receiver to his ear. "Hello," he said.

"Harry," Budney said. The district manager was fairly bubbling. "You'll never guess what happened, Harry. J.K.—the big man himself—asked me into his office for an advance look at this month's figures. Because we're Number One, Harry. And you know why."

"I have an idea," Harry said carefully.

"Even J.K. commented on it, Harry," Budney said. "A remarkable turnaround, he called it. You didn't let me down, Harry, and I'm not going to let you down either. There's going to be a little something extra in that pay envelope from now on. No, don't thank me, Harry. Just keep that profit showing—and growing."

"Mr. Budney," Harry said, "about that profit . . ."

"Yes, Harry? What about it?"

"Well," Harry said. "Well, you know, things aren't always what they seem—"

"Look, Harry," Budney said, and now he had changed back to the old, familiar Budney again, "they had better be what they seem or—well, let me put it this way. You just keep on doing what you're doing and everything's going to be just fine. But if you mess me up now—if you lose me Manager of the Year— well, we've talked about that before, haven't we, Harry, and I don't have to tell you what would happen then, do I? So what's it going to be, Harry?"

Harry looked up. Marcie had come back to lean against the doorjamb again. She was smiling and Harry had the distinct impression she'd been listening on the store extension. "Well, Harry?" she said. "What's it going to be?"

Harry turned back to the phone. "Whatever you say, Mr. Budney."

Raffles on the Riviera

The formal opening of the Oceanographic Museum built to house the trophies collected by the Prince of Monaco, famous yachtsman and ichthyologist, was a unique social occasion.

Among the beautifully dressed ladies and grey-toppered gentlemen who had the honour of paying their respects to the genial Prince and his gracious Princess, and of inspecting the exhibits, were A. J. Raffles, his young sister Dinah, and myself, Bunny Manders.

With us, as we sauntered under the outrigger canoes, harpoons, strangely shaped nets, and great fishes suspended from the lofty ceiling of the museum, was Raffles' friend Oppie, a fellow member of a respected London club to which Raffles belonged. It was thanks to Oppie, an influential Riviera resident, that we were present at this remarkable occasion, and he identified for us now some of the celebrities in the fashionable throng.

"There, for instance," he said, "is Mr. Joseph Pulitzer, the great newspaper magnate. And there's Sir Hiram Maxim, inventor of the automatic gun. The dapper gentleman he's talking to is Signor Guglielmo Marconi, joint winner last year of the Nobel Prize for Physics."

"No novelist, Dinah," said Raffles, "knows more about this Principality and the mysteries, intrigues, and hidden passions of the cosmopolitan society of the Riviera coast than good old Oppie."

"Oh, I know," said Dinah to Oppie. "Your novels are my favourites, because you set your plots in such beautiful, worldly places."

The novelist smiled at her. Urbane and experienced, he was an epicure of life's graces, and Dinah, with her fair hair and grey eyes, her lacy dress, becoming little hat, and the pretty parasol and small gold-mesh purse she carried, was a creditable young sister for Raffles to have.

"I'm sure your brother takes too good care of you, Miss Dinah," said Oppie, "for *you* ever to figure in the kind of plot I conjure from the air of this delectable coast. But if you'll excuse me, I must have a word with Sir Hiram Maxim. He's published a small book on the mathematics of roulette, and there's a point in it I'd like to take up with him. I'll be on the look-out for you at the Casino this evening."

As Oppie left us, Raffles drew the attention of Dinah and myself to the glass-topped specimen-case beside which we were standing. The case displayed, on a bed of sand, various shells and lumps of amber, together with starfish, coral, and oysters.

"You see, Dinah?" Raffles said. "Each of these oysters reveals a different stage in the process by which an intrusive grain of sand is transformed into a worthwhile end result."

"What a lovely end result!" Dinah exclaimed. "A beautiful big pearl! D'you think it's a real one?"

"That's a good question," said Raffles.

Immaculate, his keen face tanned, he was about to subject the exhibit to a more searching scrutiny when we were approached by a footman in the princely Grimaldi livery.

"Oh, look!" said Dinah, as we accepted glasses of champagne from the footman's proffered tray. "There's a notice over the doorway there saying: *To the Turtles.* Shall we go and see if they're live ones?"

"Why not?" said Raffles.

Taking our champagne with us, we passed through a low doorway, went down some narrow steps cut in rock, and found ourselves in a cavern. From iron-barred window apertures sun shone in onto a pool in the rock floor of the cavern. Four large turtles were swimming around in the pool, but their splashings were drowned by an intermittent surging sound which filled the cavern with hollow echoes.

The surging came from a round hole in a corner of the floor. A waist-high rail surrounded the hole and, when we looked down into it, it was like looking down a well with sea and sunshine at the bottom of it.

"A natural rock-shaft," said Raffles, "a sea blowhole."

Impelled by some ground-swell, the sea quenched the sunshine, deep down there, and came seething about halfway up the hole, then sank down to admit sunshine again into the sea-filled cavern.

"I'd hate to fall down there," said Dinah.

"Your arrival in the Grimaldi Deep, mademoiselle," said a voice from behind us, "would make the mermaids jealous."

We turned. A man was standing there. In tailcoat and grey topper, a glass of champagne in one hand, the other hand behind his back, he was strikingly handsome, in his early thirties. And he was drunk.

Swaying slightly on his feet, he totally ignored Raffles and me.

"Have you not yet missed, mademoiselle," he said, his heavy-lidded dark eyes on Dinah, "something you put down on a specimen-case upstairs, the better to accept a glass of champagne?"

He took his hand from behind his back.

"Oh!" Dinah exclaimed. "My purse! Thank you very much."

She would have taken the purse, but he did not let go of it.

"Captain Boris Enani," he said, still holding the purse. And Dinah, too, was holding it, and she looked a little startled as Captain Enani, faintly smiling at her, sipped his champagne, clearly with no intention of releasing the purse until he got a response to his introduction of himself.

But, in Raffles' eyes, his sister Dinah was taboo to men who approached her when they were drunk and who looked at her as admiringly as this Captain Boris Enani was looking at her.

"Thank you," Raffles said. "I will take the purse."

He took it, firmly, from both of them. He handed the purse to Dinah, took her arm, and, turning his back and hers on Captain Enani, moved away with her towards the steps up from the cavern.

"So?" said Enani, deprived of introductions. He gulped the rest of his champagne. "*So!*" he said, with an ugly look at me, and he hurled his glass into the turtles' pool.

I ignored him and followed Raffles and Dinah to the steps, where a man standing a little way up moved aside courteously to let us pass on up and re-enter the museum.

Finding that the Prince and Princess were now gone and that the guests were leaving, we went on out into the blaze of sunshine, where Dinah opened her pretty parasol. On tall flagstaffs, pink-striped white banners bearing the golden Grimaldi blazon shimmered in the heat-currents, and glossy carriages were jingling away with the cream of Riviera society.

We ourselves had not far to go, for Raffles had obtained, from a rich acquaintance in England, the loan of a house—with its resident domestic staff— called the Villa Sappho. It was one of a number of pleasant villas dotted about, amid date-palms and massed blossoms, on the slope that dropped away steeply before us to the blue water of the harbour, where many fine yachts lay spotlessly white at their moorings. On its eminence at the far side of the harbour stood the elaborate white casino.

As, with Dinah between Raffles and myself, we strolled down the path to the Villa Sappho, Dinah said, "What a strange man, that Captain Enani!"

Raffles said nothing.

"Didn't *you* think so, Bunny?" Dinah asked me.

"A most curious man, Dinah," I concurred.

"Dear Bunny, what an agreeable person you are!" said Dinah, and she tucked her arm in mine.

But Raffles said nothing.

That evening, as we dined, just the three of us, at a candlelit table on the terrace of the Villa Sappho, I sensed a certain reserve between Raffles and Dinah. It made me a bit uneasy, for really they knew very little about each other.

They had grown up separately, owing to their parents' early demise, and had quite lost touch with each other—until Dinah suddenly had taken it into her head to leave the shelter of her guardian's roof and join her brother in London.

"What a problem, Bunny!" Raffles had said to me, at the time. "I shall have to do something for her, of course. I'm her only relative. But, good God, I'm a dangerous brother for a girl to have! I may have Scotland Yard on my track any day. I'm currently England's cricket captain and, if I should be exposed as a criminal, there'll be an appalling scandal. It could affect Dinah's chances in life. The best thing I can do for her is take her abroad and amass a dowry for her, so that I can get her safely married into some European family of sound social and financial standing—while the going's still good!"

Accordingly, he had borrowed the Villa Sappho—where, as we sat now at dinner, we were waited on by the discreet, white-jacketed houseman, Latouche. He, his wife Marie-Claire, who cooked admirably, and their daughter Fanchon, the parlourmaid, constituted the resident domestic staff of the villa.

Because of the slight strain I sensed in the atmosphere between Raffles and Dinah, I was rather relieved when, Latouche having brought us our coffee and liqueurs and gone back in through the French windows, Dinah said she thought she would not come with us to the Casino, but would have an early night.

"Sleep well, my dear Dinah," said Raffles.

It was a warm night, the sky splendid with stars, as he and I walked together, in evening-dress but hatless, past the harbour where the yacht-lights twinkled, towards the brilliantly illumined Casino.

"The question is, Bunny," Raffles said abruptly, "did Dinah leave her purse on that specimen-case by mere oversight? Or had she noticed that fellow Enani staring at her? Was she intrigued by him? Did she leave her purse behind deliberately—to give him an excuse to make her acquaintance?"

"Raffles," I said, startled, "that hadn't occurred to me!"

"For the simple reason," Raffles said, "that you know no more about the character of my sister Dinah than I do."

I knew this much—that I was in love with her. But I dared not let Raffles suspect it. If one day he should stand in the dock at the Old Bailey, it was odds on that I should be standing there beside him. So I was far from being the kind of suitor he was seeking for Dinah, and I had to watch my step.

I pointed out to him now that, if he knew little about his own sister, she knew as little about him.

"In fact, Raffles," I said. "I think she's been wondering about all the expensive clothes and things you've bought her. Anyway, she asked me something, the other day, that I don't think she quite likes to ask you personally."

"What did she ask you, Bunny?"

"She asked me where your money came from."

"Did she, by God! What did you tell her?"

"Oh, I fobbed her off, Raffles. I told her it was difficult for a girl to understand a gentleman's financial arrangements—especially if he's England's cricket captain—and I advised her not to bother her head about such tedious matters."

"What did she say?"

"She said she wouldn't."

"Well done, Bunny," Raffles said. "But if she feels some sort of attraction to this Captain Boris Enani, I want to know something about the fellow—and if anybody can give us chapter and verse on Riviera characters, it's my fellow clubman Oppie, who said he'd be at the Casino this evening."

But the first person we saw, when we entered the Casino's spacious foyer, all glittering chandeliers, red plush banquettes, and gilt-rich walls, was not Oppie. It was Captain Boris Enani.

"Over there, at the *vestiaire* counter," Raffles murmured to me. "If he sees us, pay no attention to him."

Out of the corner of my eye, as we collected our *cartes d'entrée* from the three liveried functionaries at the high desk, I saw Enani on the far side of the foyer. His back was to us. In evening-dress, hatless, his hair ash-blond, he was collecting a white silk scarf from the *vestiaire*. People were going to and fro, passing in and out.

Enani turned, putting his scarf on carelessly. He was swaying slightly, drunk again. But he saw us. I felt him staring after us as, paying no attention to him, we crossed to the arch of the atrium, where a man stood aside courteously to let us pass through to the roulette tables.

"Enani's gone, Bunny," Raffles murmured, casting a quick glance back over his shoulder as he offered me a Sullivan from his cigarette-case.

"He's drunk again," I remarked.

"Yes," Raffles said thoughtfully. "Very. Keep an eye open for Oppie."

Throngs four deep surrounded the roulette tables in the atrium. Jewels glittered, starched shirtfronts gleamed. Through the restrained hum of voices sounded the ritual chanting of the croupiers as their ebony rakes slid towers of gold louis and stacks of banknotes to and fro across the green cloths, watched over by the *chefs-de-partie* on their high rostrums at each table. Here and there, against the panelled walls, lurked keen-eyed men in evening-dress.

"Oppie country," Raffles murmured to me, "the most discreetly policed Casino in the world."

We wandered from table to table, trying a stake here and there, but it was not our night, and I was glad when Oppie joined us. We had a drink with him in a small bar off the foyer, and Raffles asked him if he knew anything about a Captain Boris Enani. The novelist nodded.

"I've been watching the baccarat in the *salles privées*," he said, "the shrine of the Golden Goat. Enani was in there just now, playing against the Greek Syndicate's bank. He left, about an hour ago, with a pocketful of their money."

"Did he now," Raffles said softly. "Tell me, Oppie, is it true that the Casino has a big winner shadowed to make sure he reaches safely wherever he's going?"

"Yes, that's true of a big winner, Raffles. But Enani's win, the equivalent of about three thousand pounds—bank-notes—wasn't enough to warrant that service." The author lighted a cigar, his shrewd eyes, under strongly marked black brows, studying Raffles. "What's your interest in Enani?"

"His interest," Raffles said, "in my young sister Dinah. And hers—possibly—in him."

"Ah! Then your question has merit, Raffles. Women are Boris Enani's—hobby. Women and cards. He's believed to be the by-blow, the illegitimate son of a Balkan king, and to receive a handsome allowance so long as he stays out of his own country and involves himself in no political plots against his royal sire."

"An Oppie character, in fact," Raffles said.

"Yes," said the novelist, "I must hatch a plot I can use him in, one of these days. 'Lucky at cards,' they say, 'unlucky in love.' That doesn't seem to be true of Boris Enani. He wins both ways. Several Riviera ladies of previously unblemished repute are rumoured to have succumbed to his slumbrous charm. One wonders if the lucky Lothario has some extra card up his sleeve—when he plays games with the fair sex."

"Oppie," Raffles said, "many thanks for this information."

"From one clubman to another," said Oppie. "I'm going back to the *salles privées*. Are you and Manders coming?"

But Raffles excused us, and, as the novelist left us, gave me a hard look. "An extra card, Bunny?" Raffles said. "I wonder. If Enani took a quick look into Dinah's purse this morning, he'd have found cards in it—visiting-cards that I had printed for her, with the address of the Villa Sappho. When he saw us here at the Casino—*without* Dinah—can he have thought it, drunk as he was, a good opportunity to pay a private call on her?" He stood up abruptly. "Let's go back to the villa."

As we walked briskly down the sloping road from the Casino, with the harbour lights reflected in the water on our left, a *fiacre* was coming up the slope. I heard the passenger call to the cabbie to stop. The horse jingled to a standstill level with us. Dinah, in an evening cloak, the hood thrown back, her hair fair in the light from the white globe of the streetlamp, looked out at us.

"I'm so glad I've found you!" she said.

Raffles told the cabbie to take us to the Villa Sappho. We got into the *fiacre* with Dinah, and Raffles asked her if Enani had come to the villa, and she said that he had—about half an hour after we had left.

"So he lost no time," Raffles said, "after he saw us in the Casino, Bunny. Dinah, did you let Latouche admit him?"

"The Latouches weren't there," she said. "Their other daughter, Fanchon's married sister, was having a birthday party, so I told them they could go to it."

Over the clip-clop of the horse's hoofs and the harness jingle, the cabbie on his box, his back to us, could not possibly hear her voice as Dinah told us that, when the Latouches had left, she had gone into her bedroom. She had opened the curtains and stepped out to the balcony.

"It was all so pretty," she told us, "the stars, and the lights in the harbour and over in the Casino. I could hear the crickets in our garden and music in the distance."

After a few minutes she had gone back into her bedroom, leaving the French windows ajar, but closing the curtains. As she started to get ready for bed, she had heard a sound on the balcony. The curtains had parted. Captain Enani had stepped in.

"I told him to leave at once," Dinah said, "or my brother would kill him."

I knew that was true, for I knew Raffles, and though he said not a word, the hair stirred on my scalp.

"But you can't kill him now," Dinah said, and she drew in her breath, deeply, with a tremor in it. "He's dead."

Hoofs clopped, harness jingled. Dinah told us that Enani had seized her hands, covered them with kisses. She had told him he was mad or drunk or both, and had wrenched her hands free.

"And then?" Raffles said, very softly.

My heart thumped. How could Dinah have killed the man? With what weapon? Pistol? Scissors? But no, she told us that Enani had taken from the pocket of his white waistcoat a small phial of pills. Poison, he had said. One kiss from her lips, he had said, or he would kill himself in her bedroom and the scandal would ruin her.

"And then?" said Raffles.

"I told him he was mad and a coward," Dinah said, "and would never do it. But—he did! He swallowed one of the pills. He had—a sort of seizure. He contorted. He fell back across my bed. I couldn't believe it! I ran out and came to find you."

Raffles took her hand.

"Dinah," he said, "those pills, of course, were about as lethal as sugar candy. If, from fear of scandal, you'd paid that man his ransom of a kiss, he wouldn't have stopped at that. But you called his bluff. I'm surprised he bothered to go through with his charade. Don't worry, Dinah. When we get to the villa, we'll find him gone—but he'll have to go a long, long way before he escapes settlement of this little account I have with him."

He laughed, without mirth.

"You see, Bunny?" he said to me. "We're in a Principality where scandal is inadmissible. It means, for those involved, whether innocent or guilty, polite expulsion. If it becomes rumoured that one is *persona non grata* in the Principality of Monaco and Monte Carlo, one is no longer received anywhere in good society. So we now know the extra card up Boris Enani's sleeve in his games with women—the ugly card of scandal. For fear of it, women yield to him—and afterwards, from the same fear, keep silent."

The *fiacre* pulled up at the gate of the Villa Sappho. Raffles paid off the cabbie. In the house the lights were on. The Latouches were not yet back. All was still.

"To put your mind at rest, Dinah," Raffles said, "I'll just take a look into your bedroom. Wait here in the salon."

He went upstairs to Dinah's room. I followed him. Her bedroom door stood wide open. The lights were on. Raffles stopped dead on the threshold. Over his shoulder I saw Enani. He lay sprawled on his back across Dinah's bed. Raffles moved forward, into the room. I followed, staring, unbelieving.

Enani's hands were clamped on the bed coverlet, his face was congested and mottled, his jaw fallen; his bulging eyes gleamed blindly in the light.

Raffles stooped over the bed, slid a hand under the breast of Enani's dinner-coat, sniffed the man's mouth.

"Close those curtains, Bunny."

The window-curtains were slightly parted. I closed the gap and turned. Raffles was picking up from the carpet a small phial of pills and its cork. He corked the phial, pocketed it, and went back downstairs. I followed.

Dinah was standing in the salon, an intent question in her eyes.

"Dinah," Raffles said, "Bunny and I have a little job to do before the Latouches get back. We won't be long. Sit down. Don't worry. Bunny, give her a brandy."

While I poured Dinah the drink, Raffles crossed to the *escritoire* and let down the flap. He wrapped his handkerchief round his hand, took from the pigeon-holes some sheets of notepaper, held them up to the light, then pocketed them. He took from a pigeonhole a small pot of gum with the brush-handle protruding through the top. He pocketed the pot of gum, then tucked his handkerchief back into the breast-pocket of his dinner-coat.

He ran back upstairs. I followed. He went into his own bedroom, returned in a moment, pocketing a pair of black kid gloves. He handed me a pair, told me to put them in my pocket, and went back into Dinah's room. I followed.

"What do you intend to do?" I said. I could hardly breathe.

"I intend to do the only thing that can prevent a scandal that would ruin my plans for Dinah's future," Raffles said. "I intend an act of oblivion. Come on, up with him!"

We lugged Enani up off the bed and, each taking one of his arms around our shoulders, carried him, facing forward between us, his head lolling on his shirtfront, the ends of his white silk scarf dangling, his feet dragging like a comatose inebriate's down the stairs and out to the garden gate.

"A warm night, a starry night," Raffles said, "and not much past eleven o'clock. There'll be people strolling by the sea or sitting at the sidewalk tables of the seafront cafés. So every access to the briny is useless to us, Bunny—except, let's hope, just one."

I knew now where we were going as we bore Enani up the sloping path which we had followed, both up it and down it, that very morning. Here and there, among the date-palms on either side of the path, shone the white globes of lamp-standards. Crickets chirred tranquilly amid the blossoms. We saw nobody. We had not far to go before the Oceanographic Museum loomed up before us, its lofty windows reflecting starshine.

The building stood on a slope, so the rear windows were more accessible than those in front; and at the rear of the building we laid Enani down.

"There may or may not be a watchman in the building," Raffles murmured, as we put on our gloves. "We've got to risk it."

He held a sheet of notepaper to the glass of the window before which we stood. He brushed gum over the paper, reversed it, and pressed the paper to the glass. This was not the first time I had seen him use the little implement he carried, which had a diamond cutting-edge. It squeaked slightly as he etched it around the paper.

He gave a corner of the paper a sharp tap with the implement. A fragment of glass fell inward, scarcely audible. He inserted the implement into the hole and levered the square of glass gently outward. It came, adhering to the paper, with a slight cracking sound. He laid the glass on the ground and reached in to the window-latch. The window opened inward, and Raffles went in, soundless, over the sill.

I heaved Enani up and, between us, we lifted him inside.

"Hold him," Raffles whispered, and was gone.

Starshine glimmered down through the skylights of the lofty ceiling. Here and there, from the glass-topped specimen-cases, gleamed points of phosphorescence, as of glow-worms. From a dark doorway to my right sounded faint splashes and an intermittent surging sound. A shadow moved. Raffles was back.

"When the broken window's found, Bunny," he whispered, "the police will wonder what the intruder was after. It's advisable to give them a reason, so I've picked the lock of the oyster-case and taken the exhibit 'pearl.' The police will think, let's hope, that the intruder was gullible enough to think it a *real* pearl. It should give them a laugh. Now, let's do what we're really here for."

Between us we carried Enani through the dark doorway, down the narrow steps, into the turtles' cavern. In the faint starlight from the iron-barred window-apertures facing seaward, the turtles splashed restlessly in their pool. The intermittent surge of the sea in the blowhole filled the cavern with hollow echoes.

"Lay him down for a minute," Raffles said. "There's something I want from him."

"Of course!" Belatedly, the thought flashed upon me as we laid Enani down on the rock-floor and Raffles dropped on one knee beside him. "His baccarat winnings!" I said.

"Bunny," Raffles said, his hand busy at Enani's collar, "when I felt for his heartbeat, back there in Dinah's room, I felt also for his bank-notes. He had neither the one nor the other."

He stood up. I glimpsed in his hand Enani's white silk scarf.

"Now, come on," Raffles said. "Up with him!"

He pocketed the scarf. Together we lifted Enani over the waist-high rail surrounding the blowhole. For a moment we held him, by his ankles, suspended over eternity. Then we let him go, and I heard the sea surge up the dark shaft to receive him.

"And this false pearl can follow him," Raffles said.

He tossed the exhibit down the shaft, and we stole back up the rock steps and left the cavern to the restless Grimaldi turtles.

But what had happened to Boris Enani's baccarat winnings? And why had Raffles taken Enani's white silk scarf?

There were questions in my head, and forebodings, when I went down in the morning to breakfast on the terrace of the Villa Sappho.

Sleek in his white jacket, Latouche was setting down on the table a tray bearing crisp croissants and fragrant coffee.

"*Mademoiselle et messieurs sont servi*," he said, and with his discreet smile and a slight bow went back in through the French windows.

The sky was blue. Monaco lay spread before us, with its fine buildings and harbourful of yachts, a haven of riches, tranquil in the opaline glory of the Mediterranean morning.

I noticed faint, violet shadows under Dinah's grey eyes as she poured the coffee, but Raffles, in a light suit, a pearl in his cravat, seemed his usual easy-going self.

He suggested that we lunch at the Café de Paris, opposite the Casino.

"One sees such interesting people going to and fro past that corner," he said. "It is to Monaco as the corner of the Rue de la Paix is to Paris—everyone passes it sooner or later."

At a table under a sun-umbrella on the café terrace, thronged with the usual gay, fashionable crowd, we lingered long over lunch, watching the comings and goings of the Principality's citizens and visitors.

Dinah grew restless. "Why don't we go somewhere else?" she asked.

"Personally," said Raffles, "I like this corner. But, Bunny, why don't you take Dinah to see the *Jardin Exotique*? It's said to have a thousand varieties of cactus."

To my surprise Dinah fell in with this suggestion, and I understood why, a little later. For, as we strolled together, Dinah with her pretty parasol raised, along a path through that high-up, prickly garden of rust-red and yellow blossoms, she asked me a question.

She said, "Bunny, what became—last night—of Captain Enani?"

"Dinah," I said, "your brother would like you to put Captain Enani out of your mind. He won't be bothering you again."

She was silent for a while, as we wandered on, then she said, "I believe my brother thinks I left my purse on that specimen-case in the museum *deliberately*. But, Bunny, I didn't."

"I'm glad, Dinah," I said. "Thank you for telling me that."

"It's strange," she said. "Sometimes I think I love my brother. But sometimes—I'm not sure."

"That, Dinah," I explained, "is because you don't yet know him as well as I do."

"What a loyal person you are, Bunny!" she said, with a smile, and she linked her arm with mine.

It was a way she had, but I wished she would not do it to me, for her touch set up a cardiac turbulence in me, and in Raffles' eyes she was no less taboo to me than she had been to the late Boris Enani. In the circumstances, as I did not trust myself when alone with Dinah, I thought it prudent to suggest that it was time we rejoined her brother.

But Raffles was gone from the café opposite the Casino. Nor did we find him at the Villa Sappho when we returned there. So I was alone with Dinah, willy-nilly, all through dinner, which we had at the candlelit table on the villa terrace.

I found it so hard to keep my eyes off Dinah that, as the hour grew late, I was relieved when she decided to retire. I saw her light come on, in a window upstairs. She was not now using the bedroom in which Boris Enani had played out his tragic farce. I watched her window. Once or twice, across the curtains, I saw her shadow pass. Taboo!

Crickets chirred in the garden. The lights of Monaco twinkled. I must have drowsed. Suddenly a hand fell on my shoulder and I sprang to my feet.

"It's all right, Bunny," Raffles said. "Come inside. Bring the brandy."

I followed him into the salon. He closed the French windows, drew the curtains together, crossed to the door, opened it, listened for a moment, then shut the door. He poured himself a brandy.

"Bunny," he said, "d'you remember the courteous gentleman who stood aside for us to pass through the atrium arch to the roulette tables in the Casino?"

"Vaguely," I said. "I hardly noticed him."

"D'you remember," Raffles said, sitting down in an easy-chair, "that when Oppie told us Enani had about three thousand pounds in baccarat winnings on him, I asked if the Casino had a big winner followed—for his own safety?"

"Yes. But Oppie said Enani wasn't a big enough winner for that."

"So," said Raffles, "the courteous gentleman, who gave me a distinct impression that he was following Enani when Enani left the Casino, wasn't a Casino agent. But I had a feeling I'd seen that courteous gentleman before. And I remembered where. He was the same man who stood politely aside for us on the steps up from the turtles' cavern after that little scene in the morning, when Enani returned Dinah's gold-mesh purse."

Raffles drank his brandy, lighted a Sullivan.

"You see, Bunny?" Raffles said. "If the courteous gentleman was keeping an eye on Enani in the morning, when he had no baccarat winnings on him, it wasn't for the money that Enani was followed out of the Casino in the evening. So what was the courteous gentleman following Enani for?"

"Raffles," I breathed, "I can't imagine!"

"Neither could I," Raffles said wryly. "But I was certain that the courteous gentleman *did* follow Enani from the Casino. And Enani came straight here to the Villa Sappho. Dinah was on her balcony—like Juliet. So the courteous gentleman saw Enani, that evil Romeo, watching Dinah from the garden. And saw him pull himself up on to the balcony and enter her room. And the courteous gentleman himself climbed to the balcony. Through the gap in the curtains he watched the scene between Enani and Dinah. He saw Enani collapse on the bed—and Dinah run out of the room."

Raffles took a small phial of pills from his pocket.

"Am I giving you a headache, Bunny? Try one of Enani's pills. I've tried one myself. They're aspirin."

"But Enani was *dead* on Dinah's bed!"

"Yes, Bunny," Raffles said. "But it was pretty evident, from his face, that he hadn't died of poison. There was never the slightest chance that Enani would have swallowed one of those pills if they'd been poison. No, Bunny, when Enani played out his ugly farce and 'collapsed,' and Dinah ran out, Enani started drunkenly to get up off the bed—but the courteous gentleman came at him through the curtains. Bunny, Enani died of strangulation."

Raffles poured himself another brandy.

"I'm much obliged to the courteous gentleman, Bunny. But I wanted to see him again. So I watched for him from the terrace of the Café de Paris on that corner everyone in Monaco must pass sooner or later. And he passed by about an hour after you took Dinah to the *Jardin Exotique*."

"You followed him?" I said, my throat dry.

"To a street called the Rue des Oliviers," Raffles said. "The courteous gentleman has a small office there. He stayed in it rather a long time. When he left, I went in—with the aid of the little picklock I carry. In the office was a metal filing-cabinet—locked. I got it open. I found a thick file in it—carbon copies of reports, in French, on Boris Enani, over the past eighteen months."

"Reports?" I said.

"Addressed," said Raffles, "to a postbox number in a Balkan capital. The reports told all, Bunny. Enani *is* the by-blow of a royal person—who's had him watched, got tired of his doings and the expense of his fat allowance, and ordered the royal agent, that courteous gentleman, to remove the nuisance. And the courteous gentleman saw his opportunity when he witnessed the scene in Dinah's room."

Raffles looked at me with a dancing vivacity in his eyes.

"Incidentally, Bunny," he said, "the courteous gentleman treated himself to a bonus. It was locked in his metal filing-cabinet. Catch!"

He tossed me a thick sheaf of bank-notes held together by a paper band.

"Enani's baccarat winnings," he said, "and a good start for amassing a dowry for Dinah, after you've taken your share."

"No," I said, twisting the arrow in my own heart. "All for Dinah's dowry."

I handed him back the bank-notes. He gave me a strange look.

"All right, Bunny," he said quietly. "I shall remember." His tone changed. "Anyway, I left a receipt in the courteous gentleman's filing-cabinet. It seemed only right that he should have a receipt for this three thousand pounds. So I left him the thing he strangled Enani with. I left him," said Raffles, with a wicked look, "Enani's white silk scarf."

The door handle turned. My heart stopped. The bank-notes vanished into Raffles' pocket. The door opened and Dinah was standing there. She came in. She was in *negligée*, her fair hair in two braids, her grey eyes, so like his own, on Raffles.

"I couldn't fall asleep till I knew you were back," she said to him. "Then I heard you talking in here."

"And did you," said Raffles gently, taking a Sullivan from his cigarette case, "hear what we were talking about?"

"Why, no," said Dinah. "What was it?"

"We were talking," Raffles said, "about the kind of plot of mystery, intrigue, and passion that your favourite novelist conjures from the air of this delectable Principality. I ran into him an hour ago. He was coming out of the Casino, so we had a nightcap together. He's invited you and Bunny and me to tea to-morrow—or, rather, today—on his yacht."

"On his yacht? Oh, how exciting!" Dinah exclaimed. "I've never had tea on a yacht before. What d'you think I should wear?"

Her brother smiled.

"That's a good question, Dinah. Your favourite author knows all the best people, so you'll probably meet some of them on board. In the circumstances, and I'm sure Bunny will agree with me, there'll be no danger of our breaking the bank if we take you shopping in the morning for something especially attractive for you to wear," said A. J. Raffles, "at the tea-party with Oppie—with Mr. E. Phillips Oppenheim."

RICHARD MATHESON

Needle in the Heart

A *pril 23*: At last I have found a way to kill Therese. I am so happy I could cry. To end that vile dominion after all these years! What is the phrase?—"'tis a consummation devoutly to be wish'd." Well, I have wished it long enough. Now it is time to act. I will destroy Therese and regain my peace of mind. I will!

What distresses me is that the book has been here in our library all these years. Why, I could have done it ages ago!—avoiding all the agonies and cruel humiliations I have borne. Still, I must not think like that. I must be grateful I found it at all. *And* amused—how droll it really is!—that Therese was actually in the library with me when I came across the book.

She, of course, was poring avidly over one of the many volumes of pornography left by Father. I shall burn them all after I have killed Therese. Thank God our mother died before he started to collect them. Vile man that he was. Therese loved him to the end, of course. She is just like him really—brutish, carnal, and disgusting. Oh, I will sing for joy the day she dies.

Yes, there she was, below, darkly flushed with sensuality while I, attempting to avoid the sight of her, moved about on the balcony where the older volumes were kept. And there I found it on an upper shelf, a film of gray dust on its pages. *Voodoo: An Authentic Study* by Dr. William Moriarity. It had been printed privately. The Lord only knows where or when Father acquired it.

The astounding thing: I perused it, bored, then actually put it back in place! It was not until I had walked away from it and glanced through many other books that, suddenly, it came to me.

I could kill Therese by use of voodoo!

April 25: My hand is trembling as I write this. I have almost completed the doll which represents Therese—yes, almost completed it. I have made it from the cloth of one of her old dresses which I found in the attic. I have used two tiny jeweled buttons for its eyes. There is more to do, of course, but the project is at last under way.

I am amused to consider what Dr. Ramsay would say if he discovered my plans. What would his initial reaction be? That I am foolish to believe in voodoo? Or that I must learn to live with Therese if not to love her. Love that *pig*? Never! How I despise her! If I could—believe me—I would happily surrender my half of Father's estate if it would mean that I would never have to see her dissipated face again, never have to listen to her drunken swearing, to her tales of lewd adventuring.

But that is quite impossible. She will not leave me be. I have but one course left me—to destroy her. And I shall. I *shall*.

Therese has only one more day to live.

April 26: I have it all now—all! Therese took a bath before she left tonight—to Lord knows what debaucheries. After the bath she cut her nails. And now I have them fastened to the doll with thread. And I have made the doll a head of hair from the strands I laboriously combed from Therese's brush. Now the doll truly *is* Therese. That is the beauty of voodoo. I hold Therese's life in my hands, free to choose, for myself, the moment of her destruction. I will wait and savor that delicious freedom.

What will Dr. Ramsay say when Therese is dead? What *can* he say? That I am mad to think voodoo had killed her? (Not that I will ever tell him.) But it will! I will not lay a hand on her—as much as I would like to do it personally, crushing the breath from her throat. But no. I will survive. That is the joy of it—to kill Therese willfully and yet to live! That is the utter ecstasy of it!

Tomorrow night. Let her enjoy her last adventure. No more will she stagger in, her breath a reeking fume of whiskey, to regale me in lurid detail with the foul obscenities she had committed and enjoyed. No more will she—oh, I cannot wait! I shall thrust a needle deep into the doll's heart, rid myself of her forever. Damn Therese, *damn* her!

I shall kill her now!

From the notebook of John H. Ramsay, M.D.

April 27: Poor Millicent is dead. Her housekeeper found her crumpled on the floor of her bedroom this morning, clutching at her heart, a look of shock and agony frozen on her face. A heart attack, no doubt. No marks on her. Beside her, on the floor, was a tiny cloth doll with a needle piercing it. Poor Millicent. Had she some brainsick notion of destroying me with voodoo? I had hoped she trusted me. Still, why should she have? I could never have helped her really. Hers was a hopeless situation. Millicent Therese Marlow suffered from the most advanced case of multiple personality it has ever been my misfortune to observe . . .

JAMES HOLDING

The Mutilated Scholar

I was standing in the rear of a crowded bus when I caught sight of the stolen library book.

It was the wildest coincidence, the sheerest accident. For I don't ride a bus even twice a year. And normally I can't tell one copy of a particular library book from another.

I craned my neck to get a clearer view past the fellow hanging onto a bus strap beside me. And I knew immediately that I wasn't making any mistake. That library book tucked under the arm of the neatly dressed girl a few seats forward was, without a doubt, one of the 52 library books which had been in the trunk of my old car when it was stolen six weeks before. The police had recovered my car three days later. The books, however, were missing—until I spotted this one on the bus.

Maybe I'd better explain how I recognized it.

As a library cop, I run down overdue and stolen books for the Public Library. I'd been collecting overdues that day, and about eleven in the morning I'd got back a bunch of books from a wealthy old lady who'd borrowed them from the library to read on a round-the-world cruise. She couldn't have cared less when I told her how much money in fines she owed the library after ten weeks' delinquency. And she couldn't have cared less, either, when I taxed her with defacing one of the books.

It was a novel called THE SCHOLAR, and she'd deliberately—in an idle moment on the cruise, no doubt—made three separate burns on the cover with the end of her cigarette, to form two eyes and a nose inside the O of the word SCHOLAR. I was pretty irritated with her, because that sort of thing is in the same class with drawing mustaches on subway-poster faces, so I charged her two bucks for defacing the book in addition to the fine for overdue. You can see why I'd remember that particular copy of THE SCHOLAR.

I scrutinized the girl now holding it under her arm on the bus. She certainly didn't look like the kind of girl who goes around stealing old cars and Public Library books. She was maybe 30 years old, well-dressed in a casual way, with a pretty, high-cheekboned face and taffy-colored (dyed?) hair, stylishly coiffured.

A crowded bus wasn't exactly the best place to brace her about the book. Nevertheless I began to squeeze my way toward her between the jammed passengers.

I wanted to know about that book because I still winced every time I recalled the mirth of Lieutenant Randall of the Police Department when I called him that first day to report the theft of my car and books. First he had choked with honest laughter, then he accused me of stealing my own library books so I could make myself look good by finding them again, and finally he offered to bet I had sunk my car in the river somewhere so I could collect the insurance on it. The idea of a book detective being robbed of his own books sent him into paroxysms. It was understandable. I used to work for him and he's always needled me about quitting the police to become a "sissy" library cop.

The girl with the book was seated near the center doors of the bus. I managed to maneuver my way to a standing position in front of her, leaned over, and in a friendly voice said, "Excuse me, Miss. Would you mind telling me where you got that library book you're holding?"

Her head tilted back and she looked up at me, startled. "What?" she said in a surprised contralto.

"That book," I said, pointing to THE SCHOLAR. "My name is Hal Johnson and I'm from the Public Library and I wonder if you'd mind telling me where—"

That was as far as I got. She glanced out the window, pulled the cord to inform the bus driver of her desire to get off, and as she squeezed by me toward the center doors of the bus she said, "Excuse me, this is my stop. This book is just one I got in the usual—"

The rest of what she said was lost in the sound of the bus doors swishing open. The girl went lithely down the two steps to the sidewalk and made off at a brisk pace. I was too late to follow her out of the bus before the doors closed, but I prevailed on the driver to reopen them with some choice abuse about poor citizens who were carried blocks beyond their stops by insensitive bus drivers who didn't keep the doors open long enough for a fast cat to slip through them.

While I carried on my dispute with the bus driver, I'd kept my eye on the hurrying figure of the girl with THE SCHOLAR under her arm. So when I gained the sidewalk at last, I started out at a rapid trot in the direction she'd gone.

Being considerably longer-legged than she was, I was right behind her when she approached the revolving doors to Perry's Department Store. Whether or not she realized I was following her I didn't know. As she waited for an empty slot in the revolving door, a middle-aged, red-haired woman came out. She caught sight of my quarry and said in a hearty tone, loud enough for me to hear quite plainly, "Why, hello, Gloria! You here for the dress sale too?"

Gloria mumbled something and was whisked into the store by the revolving door. I hesitated a moment, then stepped in front of the red-haired woman and said politely, "That girl you just spoke to—the one you called Gloria—I'm sure I know her from somewhere—"

The red-haired woman grinned at me. "I doubt it, buster," she said, "unless you get your hair styled at Heloise's Beauty Salon on the South Side. That's where Gloria works. She does my hair every Tuesday afternoon at three."

"Oh," I said. "What's her last name, do you know?"

"I've no idea." She sailed by me and breasted the waves of pedestrian traffic flowing past the store entrance. I went through the revolving door into Perry's and looked around anxiously. Gloria, the hairdresser, was nowhere in sight.

After a moment's survey of the five o'clock crowd jamming the store's aisles, I turned away. I was due to meet Susan for drinks and dinner at The Chanticleer in half an hour. And I figured Susan, whom I hoped to lure away from the checkout desk at the Public Library into marriage with me, was more important than a stolen copy of THE SCHOLAR. Especially since I now knew where to find Gloria and the stolen book.

Some of my pickups next morning were on the South Side, so it wasn't out of my way to stop at Heloise's Beauty Salon. I went in, and letting my eyes rove uneasily about the shop, feeling self-conscious, I asked at the reception counter if I could speak to Gloria.

"Gloria Dexter?" said the pretty black receptionist. "I'm afraid you can't. She's not here this morning."

"Her day off?"

"No. Yesterday was her day off."

"How come she's not here today?"

"We don't know. She just didn't show up. She usually calls in if she can't make it, but this morning she didn't."

"Did you try telephoning her?" I asked.

She nodded. "No answer."

"Well," I said, "maybe I can stop by her home. All I wanted to ask her about was a library book that's overdue. Where's she live?"

After I'd shown her my ID card, the receptionist told me Gloria Dexter's address. I thanked her and left.

The address wasn't fifteen minutes away. It turned out to be a single efficiency apartment perched on top of what used to be a small gatehouse to a private estate. The private estate was now two fourteen-story highrises set back from the street in shaded grounds. The only way up to Gloria's apartment was by a rusty outside stairway rather like a fire escape.

I was just starting up it when somebody behind me yelled, "Hey!"

I stopped and turned around. The hail had come from a burly man in dirty slacks and a T-shirt, who was clipping a hedge behind the gatehouse. "No use going up there, Mister," he informed me, strolling over to the foot of Gloria's staircase. "Miss Dexter isn't there."

I'd been expecting that. I said, "Do you know where she is?"

"At Memorial Hospital probably," he replied, "or the morgue. They took her off in an ambulance a couple of hours ago. I was the one who found her."

I hadn't been expecting that. "Did she have an accident or something?"

"She sure did. Fell all the way down that iron staircase you're standing on. Caved in her skull, it looked like to me."

I assimilated this news in silence. Then, "You found her at the bottom of this staircase?"

"Yep. Like a ragdoll."

"What time?"

"Eight thirty this morning when I came to work. I'm the yardman here. The ambulance boys said she'd been dead for quite a while, so she musta taken her tumble last night sometime."

Remembering the pretty receptionist at Heloise's Beauty Salon, I said, "I stopped at the beauty shop where she works before I came here. They're worrying about her because she didn't show this morning. Maybe you ought to let them know."

"Never thought of that. Who'd you say you were, Mister?"

I showed him my ID card. "I wanted to see Miss Dexter about an overdue library book," I said. "Say, could I go up and get the book out of her place now? It'll save the library a lot of bother later on."

"Go ahead," the yardman said. "On second thought, I'll come with you, to see you don't take nothing but your library book." He grinned, exposing stained teeth. "Besides, you can't get in her place 'less I let you in. It's locked."

We climbed the rusty iron steps together. He unlocked the door at the top and we went into the Dexter apartment. It was as simple, pretty, and tasteful as Gloria herself. A daybed with a nubby red-and-gold coverlet stood against one wall, and over the bed there was a single hanging shelf filled with books.

I went straight to the bookshelf. "The book I want should be here some-where," I said to the yardman. My eyes went down the row of spines. THE SCHOLAR wasn't there. Neither were any of the other 51 library books that had been stolen with my car.

"Take a look in her kitchenette and bathroom," the yardman advised me. "People read books in funny places."

A quick search failed to turn up THE SCHOLAR anywhere in the apartment.

The yardman was becoming impatient. "Tough luck," he said. "I guess you'll have to wait for the book and get it the hard way." He looked at the telephone on a dropleaf table near the kitchenette door. "I'll call her beauty shop from here," he said. "It'll be handier." He opened the telephone book, then hesitated. "What's the name of the place, anyhow?" he asked me. "Some fancy French name I can't remember."

"I'll look it up for you," I said. "Heloise's Beauty Salon is what it's called. With an H." I riffled through the telephone book and found the number for him. Another number on the same page was underlined in red. The yardman thanked me and I thanked him, and as I left, he was dialing the beauty shop.

My car was stifling when I climbed back into it. I rolled down the windows and sat for a couple of minutes, trying to figure out what to do next. Finally I drove downtown, left my car in the parking lot behind Perry's Department Store, and went inside.

At the Lost and Found counter I asked the girl, "Has a Public Library book been turned in recently?"

She gave me a funny look and said, "Yes, the clean-up crew found one in a trash basket."

"Mine," I said with relief. "May I have it, please?"

"Can you describe it?" she said.

"Sure. The title is THE SCHOLAR. There are three cigarette burns inside the O on the cover. Like eyes and a nose." When she looked prim I added, "Somebody else put them there, not me."

She was suddenly businesslike. "That's the book, all right. But we don't have it here. You'll have to claim it at the Security Office." She dropped her eyes. "I turned it over to them a few minutes ago."

"What did you do that for?" I asked curiously.

"Ask Security," she said. "Mr. Helmut."

"I will. Mr. Helmut. Where can I find him?"

She pointed toward the balcony that ran along one side of Perry's street floor. "Up there. Behind the partitions."

I mounted to the balcony and pushed open an opaque glass door with the words *Security Office* stenciled on it. An unattractive girl with dull eyes behind horn-rimmed glasses was sitting at a desk inside the door, typing. She asked me what I wanted in a no-nonsense voice that didn't go with her bitten fingernails.

"You the Security Chief?" I asked, giving her my best smile.

"Don't be silly!" she answered sharply. "Mr. Helmut is our Security Chief."

"Then I'd like to see him for a minute, please."

"He's out in the store making his morning round. Maybe I can help you?"

"Your Lost and Found desk sent me up here to ask about a book from the Public Library that was found in the store last night."

She gave me a blank look. "I'm sorry. I don't know anything about any library book. Mr. Helmut ought to be back soon if you'd care to wait." She waved at one of those form-fitting chairs for which I understand the Swedes are responsible. I sat down on it.

Ten minutes later a burly black-browed man with long sideburns pushed open the Security door and came in. He paused abruptly when he saw me. He had my stolen copy of THE SCHOLAR in his hand.

"Mr. Helmut," his secretary fluted, "this gentleman is waiting to see you about a library book."

He shot me a sharp glance out of quick intelligent brown eyes and said, "Okay. Come on in." He held the door to his private office open and I preceded him inside. He motioned me to a straight chair and sat down behind a desk bearing a small metal sign that read C. B. HELMUT. He put my library book on the desk top and raised his black eyebrows at me. "A library book?" he inquired. "This one?" He pointed at THE SCHOLAR.

I nodded. "That's the one. It was stolen from me some time ago, Mr. Helmut. The reason I'm here is that yesterday, on a bus, I saw a girl carrying it under her arm. I recognized it by those burns on the cover. When I tried to ask the girl about it, she ducked into your store—maybe to brush me off in the crowd of shoppers, or maybe to get rid of the stolen book before anybody caught her with it."

"The clean-up crew found it in a trash basket here last night," Helmut said.

"So your Lost and Found girl told me. She also told me the book was turned over to her first. Then she turned it over to you. Mind telling me why?"

"Routine security measure, that's all." Helmut ran a thick finger over the cigarette burns on the cover of THE SCHOLAR. He was enjoying himself, acting the important executive.

"Security measure?" I said. "How does store security come into it?"

Idly he opened the cover of THE SCHOLAR and leafed through the first 20 pages or so in a leisurely manner, wetting his fingertip to turn the pages. Then suddenly he said, "Look here, Mr. Johnson," and held out the opened book for my inspection.

THE SCHOLAR was a 400-page book, more than two inches thick. The copy Helmut held out to me was only a dummy book. The insides had been cut out to within half an inch of each page, so that the book was now, in effect, an empty box, its covers and the few pages left intact at front and back concealing a cavity about seven inches long, four wide, and an inch and a half deep.

I said, "So that's it."

"That's it," Helmut echoed me. "A shoplifting gimmick. You see how it works? Shoplifter comes into the store, puts down her library book on the counter while she examines merchandise, and when our salesclerk isn't looking, the shoplifter merely opens the book and pops in a wrist watch or a diamond pin or a couple of lipsticks or whatever and walks out with them, cool as you please."

Helmut shook his head in reluctant admiration. "Can you imagine a more innocent-looking hiding place for stolen goods than a Public Library book? Why, it even lends class to the shoplifter, gives her literary respectability."

"Shoplifting!" was all I could think of to say.

"Pilferage ran almost a million bucks in this store last year," Helmut went on. "Most of it shoplifting. So we're pretty well onto the usual dodges—shopping bags with false bottoms, loose coats with big inside pockets, girls leaving fitting rooms with three or four sweaters under the one they wore going in, and so on. But this library-book trick is a new one on me. And it's a beaut!"

It was a beaut all right. I said, "You better watch out for more of the same, Mr. Helmut. Because that girl stole fifty-one other library books when she stole this one. Out of my car."

"Ouch!" he said. Then, "You're from the Public Library?"

I nodded and showed him my card.

"Well," said Helmut, "since you scared her yesterday, let's hope she'll think twice about using the library-book method again."

"Let's hope so. Can I have the book now?"

"Sure," he said. He handed me the book.

"I wish I hadn't lost the girl last evening," I said. "I might have got my other books back too."

"Wouldn't do you much good if she's gutted them all like that one," Helmut said as I went out.

At two o'clock I was sitting across his scarred desk from Lieutenant Randall, my old boss. I'd just related to him in detail my adventures in recovering THE SCHOLAR, now considerably the worse for wear.

The book lay on his desk between us.

Randall put his cat-yellow eyes on me and said, "I'm very happy for you, Hal, that you managed to recover a stolen book for your little old library. Naturally. But why tell me about it? Petty book theft just doesn't interest me." He was bland.

I gave him a grin and said, "How about first-degree murder, Lieutenant? Could you work up any interest in that?"

He sat forward in his chair. It creaked under his weight. "You mean the Dexter woman?"

I nodded. "I think she was killed because I spotted her with my stolen book."

"She fell downstairs and fractured her skull. You just said so."

"She fell downstairs, all right. But I think she was pushed. After somebody had caved in her skull in her apartment."

"Nuts," Randall said. "You're dreaming."

"Call the coroner," I suggested. "If the dent in her head was made by hitting one of those rusty iron steps, there could be some rust flakes in the wound. But I'll bet there aren't any."

"Jake hasn't looked at her yet. She only came in this morning. I've seen the preliminary report—fatal accident, no suspicion of foul play."

"Ask him to take a look at her now, then."

"Not until you give me something more to go on than rust flakes." He laced his voice with acid. "You're a showoff, Hal. So you probably think you know who killed her, right? *If* she was killed."

"Mr. C. B. Helmut," I said. "The Security Chief at Perry's Department Store. That's who killed her."

Randall's unblinking yellow stare didn't shift. "What makes you think it was Helmut?"

"Three pieces of what I consider solid evidence."

"Such as?"

"Number One: when I looked up the phone number of Heloise's Beauty Salon for the yardman in Gloria Dexter's phone book, there was another number on the same page underlined in red ink."

Randall frowned. "Helmut's?"

"C. B. Helmut."

"If she was a shoplifter," Randall said, "why the hell did she want to know the phone number of Perry's Security Chief?"

"Especially," I said, "since the underlined phone number was Helmut's *home* number, not the extension for Security at Perry's Department Store."

Randall's knuckles cracked as he curled his hands into fists. "What's evidence Number Two?" he asked in a neutral tone.

"Helmut called me by name, although I was a perfect stranger to him and he to me."

Randall said, "Why not? You showed him your ID card."

"He called me Mr. Johnson before he saw my ID card."

"The Lost and Found girl or his secretary told him who you were."

"I didn't tell either one of them my name."

"Well." Randall stared past my shoulder in deep thought. "He knew who you were and what your job was before you told him, then?"

"Yes. And there can be only one explanation for that."

"Don't tell me. Let me guess. You think he stole your car and your books."

"Right. I'm sure he recognized me the minute he saw me today."

"I don't see what the hell that has to do with Dexter's murder."

"Dexter was in cahoots with Helmut," I said. "She told him I followed her and chased her into the store."

"Wait a minute," Randall said. "You've lost me."

I laid it out for him. "The girl was scared when I braced her about the library book. She ducks into Perry's to lose me, but has the bad luck to meet one of her hairdressing customers at the entrance. From inside the door she looks back and sees that I have stopped her customer and am obviously asking about her, about Dexter. So she panics. She steps into one of the store telephone booths, gets Helmut on the phone, tells him a Hal Johnson from the Public Library is hot on her trail and by now probably knows who she is on account of the hairdressing customer. What should she do?

"Helmut tells her not to come near the Security Office, just throw the library book into a trash basket and go on home. And deny she ever had the book if anybody asks her again about it. Helmut hopes the book will be burned in the store incinerator with the other trash, of course. But the book is turned in to the Lost and Found desk this morning, so Helmut's stuck with it. And I show up before he can dispose of it."

"You should have been a detective," Randall said, deadpan. "I still don't see how that gets Dexter murdered."

"Helmut knows I'll get to Dexter sooner or later, now that I know who she is. He knows I'll apply pressure about the stolen book and eventually go to the police. So he figures she'll blow the whole sweet setup he's got going for him, unless he takes her out of the picture completely."

"What setup?"

"Don't you get it? The guy's a modern Fagan," I said. "He's got a bunch of girls like Dexter shoplifting for him all over town! Using scooped-out library books—the books he stole from me—as containers. And reporting to him by telephone at home."

Randall took that without blinking. "Well, well," he murmured. He contemplated his folded hands on the desk top. "You said something about a third piece of evidence?"

I gave him a sheepish look. "I hesitate to tell you about that one. It's slightly illegal."

"So is your friend Helmut, you think. So tell me."

"I talked my way past Helmut's super and got into his apartment at Highland Towers—"

Randall blinked at last.

"And—?" he said.

"I found twenty-seven of my stolen library books at the back of his clothes closet."

"Scooped out?"

I shook my head. "No, perfectly normal."

"So." Lieutenant Randall leaned back and put his hands behind his head, his elbows spread. "Twenty-seven, you said? You think he's got people using the other twenty-four books in shoplifting for him?"

I nodded.

"That he's recruited a gang of otherwise respectable people like Dexter to turn shoplifter for him?"

I nodded again.

Randall ruminated aloud. "He's store Security Chief. In the course of his job he runs into a lot of people who are *already* shoplifters, is that what you mean? So he blackmails some of them into working for him by threatening them with the police?"

"It could be, couldn't it?"

Randall looked at me with the air of a man who suspects his son of cheating on a geography exam. "Hal," he said, "you recently remarked, and I quote: 'The guy's a modern Fagan. He's got a bunch of girls shoplifting' et cetera." He tapped his desk top with a finger like a sausage. "How do you know they're all *girls*? You holding out something else?"

"I found a list of girls' names in one of the stolen library books in Helmut's place. Here's a copy." I tossed an old envelope on his desk.

He made no move to touch it. "That isn't evidence, Hal. It could be a list of his daughter's friends. Members of his wife's bridge club. Anything."

I said, "I *know* one of the girls on that list, Lieutenant. Ramona Gomez—she works in the library cafeteria. Couldn't you go and ask her in a friendly way if she's been blackmailed into shoplifting for Helmut? With what you know now, it shouldn't be hard to make her talk."

Randall stood up. "Yeah," he grunted, "I guess I could do that much, Hal. And a couple of other things too. Leave the book, will you?"

"Let me know how you make out," I said, "because the books in Helmut's closet still belong to the library, you know."

I was at home having a lonely shot of Scotch after my delicious TV dinner when Lieutenant Randall phoned. Seven hours. He was a fast worker. "How's the stolen library-book business?" he asked by way of greeting.

"Booming," I replied. "And how's it with the brave boys of Homicide?"

"Also," he said. "We've got your pal Helmut."

"For Murder One?"

"What else? That print we turned up under the dash of your stolen car, remember? It's Helmut's."

"Good," I said. "Does it match anything else?"

"Strange you should ask," said Randall. "It matches a thumbprint on the metal buckle of Dexter's dress. I guess Helmut dragged her to the iron stairway by the belt after he conked her."

"No rust flakes in her head wound?"

"None."

"What'd he conk her with?"

"Swedish ashtray. Glass. Hers. Weighs about two pounds. A perfect blunt instrument. His prints are on that too."

"Careless, wasn't he?"

"You might say so. He failed to reckon with the brilliance of the police is how I'd put it."

"You talked to Ramona Gomez?"

"Yep. We couldn't turn her off when we hinted that Helmut had knocked off Dexter. She spilled everything. Helmut caught her shoplifting at Perry's and blackmailed her into working for him, just as you figured. Same with the other girls."

"Poor Ramona," I said. "You're not going to take any action against her, are you?"

"Immunity," said Randall wryly, "in exchange for her memoirs about Helmut. Same with all the girls on the list."

I sipped my whiskey and asked, "Did Ramona say anything about fingering me to Helmut?"

"Yeah. She admitted telling Helmut he could get a whole load of books from the Public Library without any chance of their being traced if he just swiped your car when you had the trunk filled with overdues." Randall chuckled. "Your Ramona pointed you out to Helmut as a prime source for library books when he got his big idea about using them for shoplifting."

"That wasn't nice of Ramona," I said. "Maybe you better charge her with conspiracy or something, after all."

"We only picked up Helmut half an hour ago," Randall said. "He was taking a briefcase full of stolen goodies to the fence he's been using. We trailed him to the fence before we jumped him, and got the fence too. Isn't that clever?"

"Brilliant," I said. "Who's the fence? Anybody I know?"

"None of your business. You're a book detective, remember? Fences are for adult cops, my boy."

"As a book detective, then, I'm interested in whether any more of the library's books will turn up as shoplifters' tools," I said. "Bad for the library's image— you can understand that, Lieutenant."

"Don't fret yourself, Hal. Helmut called all his girls last night after killing Dexter and instructed them to discontinue using library books in their work. At least, that's what all the girls have told us."

"That means the library's lost twenty-five books, Lieutenant. Who wants to read a scooped-out novel, even for free? But you got the other twenty-seven for me, didn't you, out of Helmut's closet?"

"Evidence," said Randall. "You'll get them back after Helmut's trial."

"What!" I yelled. "That'll be months, maybe years!"

Randall sounded hurt. "You've got nobody but yourself to thank for that," he said. "If you're going to solve my murders, you can't blame me for collecting your library books."

Never To Be Lost Again

Today is the first time the sun shone all this week. That's why I'm sitting here in the window seat. The view from this side of the house is still beautiful. It used to be nice from all the windows before Da sold the back garden. He sold it to property developers, as they are laughingly called, who took simply ages to build that great useless pile of brick and glass. They paid Da a good price for the property, but when it had been ours it had given us flowers and vegetables and birdsong each year. Now the brick monstrosity stands unrented, collecting dead leaves and broken windows.

Ron, the only son of the next-door neighbors, was a squatter before he came home this last time. Oh, not in the building out back, but somewhere right in the middle of town. The only reason he returned at all was because the house he shared with the rest of his commune was raided by the police and condemned as a health hazard. Da is very upset at having Ron living next door again and he'd do something about it if he could, but Da is helpless. Ron's father owns the house next door, so the boy has a perfect right to stay there.

I'm glad Da can't chase him away, though. Ron always waves and smiles when he passes my window. And I don't really care if he was or is a mainliner; he's kind to me and I love him for it. I suppose you could sort of say it is a Romeo and Juliet romance—really! Guess what my name is? It's Julie—Julie Benson. My father, Da, is Terence Benson, an author and former Ambassador to various African countries.

Anyway, to get back to Ron. He is tall and slender, like a dancer. That's what I want to be, too. I want my legs wound with ribbons, my feet clasped in tiny pink-toed shoes, a tutu swirling around my flying limbs. Some day you'll see me on television floating featherlike across the screen just like the ballet dancer I saw last night. I won't mind the hard work or the practising. Ron and I can be together that way.

We'll get married and keep right on dancing until we become as famous a ballet team as Rudolf Nureyev and Margot Fonteyn. Our clamoring public will throng the stage door each time we give a performance, and like the Red Sea they'll part for us to pass, their hands reaching out just to touch the air we've moved through. A long elegant Rolls-Royce will whisk us home to our "squat" in the building that has usurped Da's back garden.

I suppose you doubt the truth of the things I have been telling you. You should. Sunshine after rain always makes me daydream. I'm not a dancer and Ron is not my boyfriend. Seriously though, I'm going to be a nurse. I became interested in nursing when Da was Ambassador to Mali. My ambition is to go where Dr. Schweitzer was—they need people there who are brave and strong like me.

Mother won't hear of it because I want to nurse in Black Africa. She's racist, as you can see. So, unless something drastic happens to make Mother change her mind, I suppose nursing as a career will have to be forgotten, even though Da has no objections. But what else can I do? I wouldn't like to be a secretary or a salesgirl in a boutique, and I must make up my mind. Time is growing short. I'll be 22 years old next month.

The sun has gone away, darkening the sky. Soon the clouds will shed large tears—tears almost as large as the ones locked inside my heart where even Da can't find them.

The rain will ruin Da's *Times* again because he won't carry an umbrella, ever. He says it makes him look like a comedy Englishman. He never wears a hat either, just uses the *Times* to protect him from the rain. Mother hates him to get the paper wet, and says he looks like an old washerwoman with it clutched over his head. She doesn't really appreciate Da. Or me, for that matter.

But then, you see, she didn't really want me. Oh, there was nothing personal. Mother just didn't want children. She had neglected to tell Da of her aversion to childbearing prior to the wedding, but the dear man had been so smitten by her raven-haired beauty, I suppose he would have married her if she had confessed to being Dracula's daughter.

Theoretically I should have two siblings: I was the last of three pregnancies Da hoped through. The first two were terminated by Mother. Number one, a scant year after the marriage, she was the victim of a fall down the stairs. The second had been lost when Mother had ridden to hounds against Da's explicit wishes. When she miscarried for the second time, Da was heartbroken. More than anything he wanted a family. His brothers and sisters had 27 children between them. Mother had come from a long line of single children, and she had decided the line would stop with her.

Years later, when she found herself pregnant for the third time, Mother was off again, dancing, riding—she even took up trampolining. Nothing helped; I stayed the course. After I was born, Da gave up trying for a big family, deciding to quit while he was ahead, I suppose.

I am sure it will come as no surprise if I tell you that Mother and I are not friends. I wouldn't care two cents if she dropped dead tomorrow. All my love is for Da. He is my idol. When I think that maybe someday I'll be without him, my heart almost shatters with the pain. If anything happened to him, I think I'd die too, I love him so much.

There goes the front doorbell. You hear that ugly clumping? That's Mother tripping daintily in her new platform shoes. She looks simply ridiculous stumping along. She always has embarrassed my dear dignified Da with her way-out dress. From beatnik to hippie, she has been "with it" for years. If it were the Twenties, Mother would be dripping fringe and champagne-warped slippers all over pianos in the wee hours of the night; but I shouldn't be unkind. She wasn't always foolish. I've seen pictures of her before my birth and, I must admit, she was beautiful. But no longer, with her bleached piled-up hairdo and platforms worn to dazzle her latest protégé.

The new boy is sallow and acne'd and teaching her Ancient Greek. I wonder if she finds Greek very much different from the modern French or modern Italian she studied in past lessons.

How brazen she is about these grotty little affairs! She flaunts them in my face, knowing I'd never tell Da, that I'd rather die than see him hurt. I try to make it up to him as best I can. He knows how much I love him. But it's difficult when one is grown up. A barrier seems to grow. No longer can I sit clasped tight in his arms, so tight that all feeling of lostness is cradled away. I'm too big for that now.

I remember once, long ago when I was quite small, he took me on a merry-go-round. Mother objected, making some malicious remarks that I recall to this day. I can still hear the cruelty of them and feel the terrible hurt. Da didn't say a word and finally she went away. We stayed on the merry-go-round and the horse went up and down, round and round. Lights flashed, cymbals crashed, music blared, and Da's arms held me so tight I could hardly breathe as he insisted over and over, "It's not your fault, little love. It's not your fault."

Soon after that Da put up the rear garden for sale. Those few months, while it was still ours, were the last happy times Da and I had together. I was on the brink of growing beyond lap size but he could still hold most of me snuggled in his arms. Every evening that long lovely summer he held me close and told me of the "Jumblies" and "The Duck and the Kangaroo." How I wished to be the Duck! To wear socks to keep my feet dry so the kangaroo would take me around the world on his tail, never to be lost or alone again.

If only I could have stayed little, never have grown up. The happy memories are all from those days so long ago when I was a child. Like the Sundays we spent at the beach before the terrible thing happened and we never went again. That last Sunday was just like all the others until Da said he'd go for ice cream. As soon as he was out of sight, Mother took me into the sea and swam swiftly out to the breakers. For a minute or so she held me, riding the waves. Then Mother disappeared.

After the momentary terror of being left alone had passed, I felt quite happy. Gentle waves led me down into a shimmering fairy tale where I'd find playmates—the Little Mermaid, the Water Babies, and other storybook friends. Yearnings would be fulfilled, everything would be as it should be. I was home at last.

Then strong arms snatched away the dream, and I was back to being me again. The sand felt warm and dry, and there was a pleasant hum of voices. Someone was rubbing my hands—Da, of course. He was the first person I saw when I opened my eyes. For a moment I thought he was wearing a wreath, then I saw it was a wreath of faces, that haloed his head.

Curious bathers were murmuring concern and nodding encouragement on seeing that the half-drowned little girl was going to be all right. Everyone was glad, every one of them, except one—Mother. She returned my gaze with eyes so filled with hostility, with such naked hatred, that all at once I understood. I had defied her once more by unreasonably clinging to life.

There goes the bell again. I wish she'd answer the door. I get nervous listening to it ring while the person outside is getting cold and wet. It's only the doctor, of course, but he's human and should be let in. He comes every Tuesday and Friday at this time, regular as clockwork. Supposedly he's Da's friend, but that doesn't keep him from having a bit of fun with Spring.

Spring is Mother's name. Ridiculous, isn't it? Spring, at her age! I do wish she'd answer, but she won't until she's finished primping. Fluff, fluff, long red claws combing through her recently bleached hair. I don't have to see her to know every move she makes. The flap of the puff against her nose, the wipe of lipstick, the fingers tracing the fine webbing of wrinkles that creep like mildew, blurring the fineness of her cheek.

She wants to go to Switzerland to have her face lifted, but she can't because Da doesn't have the money. She wants a new mink coat, too, for all the good that will do her. Everything has gone on doctor bills. Just this morning, Da was on the phone to a real-estate agent. The man didn't seem too hopeful—nobody really wants a Georgian white elephant of a house as large and cold as ours is. So Mother will have to grow older and uglier, colder and poorer. There is no way now for her to avoid the misery that old age will bring to her.

Ah, at last that horrid ringing has stopped and the wet Dr. Madison has finally been admitted. And here they come, straight as arrows into this room. Oh, oh, look who's slinking in their wake. The little Greek protégé. This could be interesting.

I wonder if she has any idea how unwelcome she is, and the doctor, not to mention the Greek. Mother comes near and dabs in my direction with her handkerchief. Dr. Madison glances at me briefly before settling himself by the fire. The Greek boy sulks in the shadows.

An ear-shattering crash of thunder startles the handkerchief from Mother's hand. The storm shades the room with false night. Mother moves toward the light switch, then changing her mind, she borrows the doctor's lighter. Soon the room springs to life again with the cheerful glow of candles. That's Mother for you, always the poseur.

But in her zeal she makes one unbelievable mistake. She lights the candle that stands on the taboret in front of my window. She's sitting over there beside the doctor, smoking and chattering like a schoolgirl. The Greek boy is watching them, but nobody is paying the least attention to me. Here, at last, is the chance that I have been waiting for all these years, since that Sunday on the beach.

With one bold stroke I will solve all Da's problems. He'll have money from insurance policies, and then maybe he'll marry some lovely young woman who will give him the family he's always wanted.

If only I can knock over the candle without being seen. Oh, please God, help me now to free Da. I hit the candle—it's rocking. Oh no! The wrong way! Get away from the curtains! Oh, God, what will I do, what will I—

But look! A breeze has fluttered the curtain across the tiny guttering flame, and the curtain has caught fire. Oh, see the hungry fire, the lovely hungry fire! Goodbye, Mother! Goodbye, Dr. Faithless Friend Madison! Goodbye, Foolish Greek Boy! Oh, Da, be happy!

Flames leaped up to welcome the falling roof. Water arched into the gutted shell of the once-beautiful house. Just a moment before, a man had stood black against the flames, and in one sudden thrust shoved a wheelchair out of the inferno to safety. Then he was gone, swallowed in a burst of flame that enveloped the old house.

A patrolman stood talking to a tired fireman lit by the nickelodeon flicker of the fire.

"How'd it start?" asked the cop.

"Crippled kid, Julie Benson, knocked over a candle," answered the fireman.

"Any casualties?"

"One. The crippled kid's father. He got home just in the nick of time to save the girl. Julie's mother was too hysterical to do anything but scream. Two men saved from the fire, too—a foreign kid and a man who says he's a doctor. They're in pretty bad shape." The fireman's voice was hoarse.

"Some kind of dame to run out and leave her kid even if she was hysterical." The cop took off his hat and wiped the sweatband with a handkerchief.

"Yeah, some dame! But she sure has all the luck. She's just become a very wealthy widow. The house was insured for over a hundred thousand, and her husband carried a life policy twice that big so that the kid, Julie, would never have to worry! If it's a double indemnity, that woman certainly will be well-heeled. But I wonder what will happen to the girl . . ."

The fireman looked over at the blanketed figures being helped into the ambulance.

"She'll have the best care money can buy, I suppose. What luck! And all because that poor helpless kid accidentally knocked over a candle."

The cop put back his hat and started on his beat once more.

FRANCIS M. NEVINS, JR.

Leap Day

Whenever Harry E. Hokinson reflected that he had nothing to show for his 37 years but a house-painting business and a side enterprise of selling combat knives by mail, he tended to voice pessimistic sentiments, even though no one could hear them but himself. The glum outlook fitted well with Harry's face, which with its beady panda eyes, bulgy nose, plump jowls, and floppy earlobes was at the best of times a study in mournfulness.

"It's a rotten world," Harry confided to himself.

"You said a snootful, pal," he agreed.

The cocktail party had turned out to be a noisy gathering of dull and stupid people—that is, people whom Harry couldn't talk into getting a house painted or buying a combat knife. Having downed several free Scotches and satisfied himself that no business prospects were in sight, he was about to take off when he found himself boxed in a corner with a decrepit retired attorney named Gideon Prendergast.

The old man accompanied his nonstop monologue with such freely swinging gesticulations of both his snack-filled hands that Harry couldn't edge out of the corner without having an assortment of pretzel crumbs dusting his new sports jacket. After three attempts Harry shut his eyes and resigned himself.

"Yessir, as I was saying, my job for the widow was nowhere near done when the cops got the confession out of the brother that he'd killed Dr. Trout. To make sure Mrs. Trout got the whole of the doc's estate we had to make certain the brother was convicted of Murder One—of Murder One and nothing short of Murder One. For the statute of our sister state east of the river is very clear on that, y'see. I can give you the exact words if you'd like—"

"You don't have to—" Harry tried to interrupt.

"—which have been graven on my memory to this very day, twenty-seven years later," declaimed Prendergast, jabbing a pretzel stick under Harry's bulbous nose. "'A surviving heir, spouse or devisee who is convicted of feloniously and with premeditation killing the decedent is not entitled to any benefits under the will of the decedent nor under the laws of intestacy, and the decedent's estate shall descend and be distributed as if the said convictee had predeceased the decedent.'

"Y'see, my boy, property is paramount in our American system of justice, and the law doesn't divest a man of his property except in the rarest of cases. Many many years ago the Supreme Court of our sister state east of the river handed down a landmark decision called *Kunkle v. Gucci* which ruled that nothing short of a conviction for murder in the first degree can trigger the operation of the divestment statute. So of course to protect the property rights of Mrs. Trout we had to make sure brother Sylvanus Trout received the full extent of his deserts for his dastardly act of fratricide. Heh heh—let me tell you how the widow and I fixed the estate funds so he couldn't hire himself a lawyer to defend him."

It took Harry another twenty minutes before he broke free on the excuse of a raging headache and scrambled out of the smoke-filled reception room as if the devil were two paces behind him. But seven weeks later, after Delbert Coombes had smashed the bronze bust of Gandhi against Mrs. Coombes's skull, Harry became rather grateful that he'd been buttonholed by the old legal shark.

When Delbert committed his crime he had not the least idea of the juridical can of worms he was opening. The legal ramifications were surely the last thing on his mind that sunny September afternoon when he came home early from tramping the woods of his wife's estate and found the young and sportive Mrs. Coombes intertwined indiscreetly with the gardener.

Felicia Detweiler Coombes was ecstatically contrasting the gardener's repertoire with Delbert's as Delbert entered the bedroom. He had been a life-long believer in nonviolence but the bloody underside of his nature took command for the few moments needed to smash the Mahatma into Felicia's cranium. The gardener would have been next but before Delbert could reach him he dived off the balcony into the rosebushes and scurried away like a large naked jackrabbit. When Delbert saw what he had done he wept, and called the police.

It was a sordid, intellectually uninspiring murder, the kind with which the police blotters of the world are glutted. A spoiled young heiress, an unwise marriage to a gentle unworldly professor many years her senior, a cycle of extramarital romps, and then the payoff. The world would leer but otherwise couldn't care less. Felicia was the last of her line, leaving no relatives to mourn her. Delbert knew of no relatives he had living, and would not have expected help from them had he known of any. Newspapers and wire services carried the story across Middle America.

It was the Wauwau *Argus* that brought the murder from the sister state east of the river into the home of Harry E. Hokinson, who had not thought of Delbert Coombes for years. Certainly he had had no idea that his second cousin once removed had married money. Had he known of Delbert's good fortune he would have long ago introduced himself and wangled a contract to repaint every building on the Coombes grounds.

But the story in the *Argus* gave Harry even bigger ideas. It was a very complete story, giving readers not only a judicious estimate of the extent of the Detweiler holdings but also the information that by her will Felicia Detweiler Coombes had left all these holdings after taxes to her beloved husband, Delbert Coombes.

Harry E. Hokinson began to think. Three nights later, after he had prepared the parcels of combat knives that would go out in the morning mail, he picked up the evening's *Argus* and noticed two items in the follow-up story on the Coombes murder case that made him think even harder.

Item One: The District Attorney had announced at a press conference that he would seek against Delbert Coombes a verdict of murder in the first degree.

Item Two: Murder being a bailable offense in the sister state east of the river, Delbert had been released on $250,000 bond and on condition that he remain in the city. He had stated that he would move into the Coombes penthouse apartment at 454 West Boulevard pending further legal steps.

Harry E. Hokinson's general knowledge of law was limited to what he had picked up from watching Perry Mason reruns and painting the Wauwau County Courthouse two years before, but the details of Gideon Prendergast's monologue had stuck to his memory like wet paint to a wall, and their application to his own desires was a matter of plain common sense—a quality which every house painter is forced to develop on penalty of painting himself daily into a corner.

Point A: If Delbert should be convicted of first-degree murder, he would be divested of all the property left to him under his late wife's will. That was the rule in *Kunkle v. Gucci.*

Point B: If he should be convicted only of a lesser offense, like second-degree murder or manslaughter, he would keep all the property. That was the point of old Prendergast's yammerings.

Point C followed as naturally as it followed from the nature of paint and the nature of water that one does not paint the exterior of a building in a rainstorm. If cousin Delbert should happen to suffer a fatal accident *before* he went to trial, while he was out on bail, then as Delbert's closest living relative Harry E. Hokinson would take by intestacy every cent of the fortune Delbert had inherited from Felicia.

"It's as simple as Q.E.D.," Harry assured himself.

"Wait a minute, pal," he cautioned himself. "Suppose Delbie just happens to have made a will leaving everything to someone besides you. Unless he dies without a will you get nothing."

"No one makes a will in our family," he reminded himself. "It's been taboo ever since a passing horsecar cut Great-Grandpa Lasswitz in two the very day he had signed his last will and testament."

"Well then, suppose Delbie has relatives you don't know about who are closer than you? Then you'd be disposing of him just to fatten someone else's pockets."

"Uh uh. Delbert and I are the only ones left, and even we haven't met face to face. No, wait. I think there may be one other twelfth cousin or something, but I seem to recall he's in graduate school somewhere out west. Probably one of these long-haired radical punks that sets fire to ROTC buildings. Even if I have to share with the kid, half the Detweiler estate is worth it."

"Right," he agreed. "And after all, it's not really murder to execute a self-confessed wife killer. But just remember you have to make it look like suicide or an accident. If the cops should ever suspect you, that law Prendergast quoted might keep you from inheriting from Delbie."

"Don't worry," Harry E. Hokinson replied to himself. "I thought up the perfect plan tonight when I read that he's staying in a penthouse. It's going to be a long drop to the ground for cousin Delbert."

And as Harry let a long swallow of the evening's fourth beer plummet from gullet to gut he belched with self-satisfaction.

It took patience to wait for the right moment, but patience like common sense is the house painter's stock in trade. It wouldn't do for Harry to close up shop and be suspiciously out of Wauwau at the precise time Delbert took his leap— unless, of course, Harry scheduled Leap Day for a time when all the businesses would be closed and many townspeople were away, such as the four-day Thanksgiving weekend.

So Harry E. Hokinson continued to slap paint on moldering exteriors by day and prepare parcels of combat knives for his mail-order clients by night. On Election Day he voted a straight Law-and-Order ticket.

At quitting time the day before Thanksgiving, Harry went home, carefully cleaned the paint from under his nails, showered, changed to turtleneck, slacks, and sports jacket, strapped one of his combat knives to an ankle sheath in case of emergency, packed an unmonogrammed suitcase, threw it into the well of his second-hand BMW, and headed east through the purple twilight. During the six-hour drive on the Interstate to the far end of the next state he reviewed each step of his plan and found the whole flawless. He reached the outskirts of the city just before midnight, checked into a chain motel as Roger Smyth, and slept like a baby, serene in the knowledge that he was about to achieve his version of the American Dream.

On Thanksgiving Day he rose early and breakfasted, then drove north into the wooded foothills to take his first view of the property that would shortly be his. For half an hour he circled the sprawling grounds, carpeted in bronze with crisply drying leaves. He could glimpse the big house from a distance but decided it was too risky to drive nearer for a closer look.

"God, it's rich," he sighed to himself. "Too good for an egghead like Delbert."

"But just right for an average Joe like Harry Hokinson," he replied.

He made one last swing around the property, then headed back toward the city. Downtown was all but deserted, but Harry had noted an inconspicuous place where he could park. He drove around the vicinity of the 29-story highrise at 454 West Boulevard until he located a classy-looking restaurant whose adjacent parking lot had just begun to fill with the early-afternoon Thanksgiving trade.

He pulled into a slot surrounded by other cars, locked up, sauntered out of the lot, and began the eight-block crosstown walk back to his destination. Except for a few customers in front of Sampson's MiniSuperMart, Open Seven Days a Week, he passed no one.

He strolled casually past the glassed-in vestibule of the highrise and saw that the doorman more or less on duty was a frail and wizened gnome of about 90 who slouched in a chair to one side of the inner door. Harry approached the entrance and made loud rattling and jangling noises with his keyring while pretending to fit a key into the outer door's lock. The dodge worked. The doorman got up, shambled over, and opened up for him.

"How goes it, old buddy?" Harry greeted him, as if he'd been coming in and out of the building for years.

"Oh, fine, fine, Mr. Gwumpf," the old man replied.

Harry walked past him confidently, marveling at how often the doormen in these highrises were too old and feeble to recognize who belonged and who didn't but would eat live coals rather than admit they were failing. He punched the elevator's Up button and a waiting cage lifted him.

As he ascended he went over his plan again. One: Be casual but touch nothing in the apartment. Two: Get Delbert out to the rooftop and push. Three: Take the elevator down to the basement garage, walk up the ramp to the street, mingle with the crowd around Delbert's remains for a few minutes, then slip away, walk back to the restaurant, drive to the motel, check out, then return to Wauwau.

The elevator door whispered open at 29 and Harry strode past the line of closed apartment doors and mounted the flight of azure-carpeted spiral stairs at the end of the corridor. At the top of the flight he knocked on the massive door. After a half minute's wait it opened and there stood his quarry, framed in a coffin of light.

Delbert Coombes, egghead, wife killer, and sudden millionaire, looked like a man at the edge of his nerves. His bloodshot eyes were ringed by grimy circles of sleeplessness. He was unshaved, his shirt was rumpled, and he walked in a listless shuffle.

"Mr. Coombes? My name is Percy Cranbrook. I'm a novelist. You may have heard of me?" It would have staggered Harry if his cousin had nodded yes, since the name had been made up on the crosstown walk; but Delbert said nothing. "I write psychological crime novels," Harry went on glibly. "I happened to be visiting friends here for the holiday and wondered if I could impose on you to talk with me for a few minutes about—uh—"

"You're not from the newspapers or TV?" Delbert demanded in a quavering voice.

"Absolutely not. The media giving you a hard time? Thought so. I can tell just from looking at you that this mess has hit you where you live. No one in your corner, everybody kicking you when you're down. Well, maybe I can help. I'll bet you haven't eaten a square meal for a week! Suppose I take you out for a full-course Thanksgiving dinner?"

It was a simple adaptation of Harry's technique of persuading little old ladies on Social Security that they needed their places painted, a technique he had honed to perfection over the years. Watching Delbert's face, he could see the soft sell working.

"That's kind of you, Mr. Cranbrook, but even if I managed to get anything down, I couldn't hold it. I had the delivery boy from Sampson's drop off some groceries a few days ago but I can't eat any of it. I'm living on booze and instant coffee and cigarettes. Could I offer you something?" He led the way into a magnificent but unused-looking kitchen. "I've got some fresh fruit that'll go bad in a few days if you don't have some."

"Well, thanks very much," said Harry, reaching into the fruit bowl on a formica counter and helping himself to a plump orange with the thought that disposing of the peel and pits would give him an excuse later for walking around and getting the layout of the place. They passed through the foyer into a forty-foot living room, with oak rafters supporting an inverted V-shaped ceiling, inch-deep azure carpeting, and enough chairs and sofas in elegantly subdued blues and grays to seat a small convention. A haze of stale tobacco smoke hung in the air and the ashtrays on the occasional tables were overflowing. Between bites of the orange Harry began to draw Delbert out.

"It's a terrible thing to see yourself in all your hideous nakedness," Delbert said after about ten minutes of disjointed reminiscences. "All my adult life I've thought of myself as an enlightened, liberal, tolerant guy. I worked hard to get the junior college where I teach—taught—to set up a special admissions program for black students. I rang doorbells for McCarthy in '68 and for McGovern last year. And yet when I saw Felicia in bed with that—that gardener—I coldbloodedly murdered her, and if the man hadn't jumped off the balcony I would have killed him, too."

"But, Mr. Coombes, you were driven beyond human endurance," Harry said. "I just can't see how that stupid prosecutor can insist on charging you with murder in the first degree."

"Mr. Cranbrook, the Detweiler family virtually founded this city. They're an institution here, and Felicia was the last of the line. Now she's not only dead at the age of twenty-eight but publicly shamed. There's an old American tradition that whoever reveals the truth about an honored institution will be made to suffer for it. That's why they're going for first degree. But, hell, I deserve it.

"When I made my statement to the police I told them the same things I'm telling you. I stopped and, God help me, I thought about it before I killed her. That's premeditation. I'm guilty. My lawyer wants me to plead temporary insanity but I'm going to plead guilty and take whatever punishment they give me. It won't be anything compared with how I'm punishing myself."

Harry thought he knew what Delbert wanted to be told and decided it was good tactics to accommodate him. "Mr. Coombes, you're too good a man to destroy yourself this way," he insisted with all the solemnity he could muster. "Uhhh—where can I throw this orange peel? No, sit still, I remember where the kitchen is."

Slowly and full of thought he walked past the French door opening onto the balcony. He didn't think it would take him more than a few minutes now to persuade Delbert that the balcony would be a more comfortable spot to continue his ruminations. Then a quick blow to the solar plexus, a hearty heave over the railing, and it would be done—and this penthouse and the country mansion and whatever else had been in the Detweiler family would be his, all his, and money beyond measure would pour down on him like green paint from up-turned cans.

He made his move on his return from the kitchen wastebasket. "It's, uh, a little stuffy in here, wouldn't you say? All this smoke—I was born with weak lungs, you know. Do you mind if I let in some air from the balcony?" He didn't wait for permission but strode to the nearest French door and tugged on the knob with a handkerchief-wrapped hand, concealed from Delbert's sight by the bulk of his body. "Hey," he said after a few seconds, "this door seems to be stuck or something."

Delbert rose and walked over to him, causing Harry to cram the handkerchief hastily up his coatsleeve. "Not stuck," Delbert explained. "Sealed. As soon as I moved in here I realized how simple it would be to jump off and end this nightmare. I can't let myself off the hook that easily. I had workmen come in and seal this door. There's no way out to the balcony. That's why the place smells so stuffy."

"Oh," said Harry E. Hokinson.

Inwardly he was more loquacious and far more eloquent. He turned away so that Delbert couldn't see the frustration that mottled Harry's face. Every obscene imprecation he had heard in his life poured soundlessly from his tight lips. To be so near the climax and then to have his whole beautiful plan ripped to shreds by this masochistic social-conscious creep!

Harry thought furiously. He had to devise a substitute plan, and fast. He looked up to the stout overhead oak beams as if for inspiration, and suddenly he had it. Beams—rope—despondent wife killer hangs himself. The train of thought formed itself in an instant.

But he needed a rope. And he had no reason to believe there would be one in this plush penthouse. He would have to find an open hardware store and pay a return visit to Delbert tomorrow.

Pleading his lung weakness, Harry made a diplomatic departure and prom-ised faithfully that he would look in on Delbert the same time next day. Delbert almost smiled when they said goodbye but it was like the grin on the face of a corpse. Self-delight put a spring into Harry's step as he went down the spiral stairs, and during the 29-floor elevator descent he perfected the details of his revised plan.

Hadn't there been a sign Visit Our Garden Shed in the window of that MiniSuperMart? Garden Shed probably meant he could buy a good stout rope in Sampson's. He swung blithely through the mirrored lobby and as he let himself out he said, "Working hard, old-timer?" "Not bad, Mr. Grlugg," the ancient doorman replied.

He had been standing for five minutes waiting his turn in the long line of shoppers in front of Sampson's checkout counter, a length of rope coiled around his forearm, when suddenly a young man weaving through the aisles strode full-tilt into him and knocked him halfway to the floor. The young man looked about 20, with long sandy hair curling over his ears, and he wore a stained white workjacket with the store's name stitched over the breast pocket. "Oh, gosh, I'm sorry, sir," he apologized. "Here, let me help you with that rope."

As they bent together over the task the young man said, in a whisper inaudible to anyone else above the noise of cash registers and chattering customers, "Happy holiday, cousin Harry. You haven't killed him yet, have you?"

Harry's eyes ballooned in consternation and fright. He froze in his hunkered position and tried to think of something nonincriminating to reply.

"I'll be in the dirty chartreuse Toyota in the back lot," the young man whispered. "Meet me." He handed the coil of rope back to Harry and walked toward the rear of the store.

A few minutes later the youth reached across the stick shift of his car and offered a diffident Harry his hand. "Let me introduce myself. Clyde Bream. You may call me Clyde. I'm your third cousin four times removed or something. Yours and Delbert's."

"My name is Smyth, Roger Smyth—" Harry began feebly.

"Oh, come off it, cuz. My dear sainted mother was a genealogy nut. She made me memorize our entire family tree and the physical characteristics of each branch. Man, with those beady panda eyes and that W. C. Fields nose and those flabby jowls and floppy earlobes you are a Hokinson if ever there was one! And the last time I looked there was only one in that branch of the family left alive, and that must be you, cousin."

Harry tried desperately to change the subject. "What are you doing working in a grocery three blocks from Delbert Coombes?" he demanded.

"Oh, the same thing you're doing, I imagine, only I've been at it longer. Did you kill him, by the way? No, you wouldn't be in need of that rope if you'd just made yourself a millionaire. Look, I think we'd better coordinate our operations, as we used to say in the Army, before we foul each other up. What say we form a partnership? Even-steven split."

Harry saw certain advantages in a temporary alliance. "All right, Clyde, you're on, buddy. Shake on it." They gripped each other's hands like comrades in a noble cause. "I punched out on the time clock just now, only have to work half a day today," Clyde went on. "Let's drive while we talk."

He gunned the Toyota out of the lot and along West Boulevard across the near-empty city and out into the wooded countryside, filling Harry in on his recent history while he drove. "So after I bagged my share of gooks in Nam, I got out and started law school up in the Northwest on my GI Bill. I took a course in Wills and Administration and learned about a famous case they have in this state called *Kunkle v. Gucci.*

"And then when cousin Delbert's mess hit the headlines I saw that with a little American initiative I wouldn't have to waste my life as an overworked legal hack. So I took a leave of absence for a semester and moved here, found out where Delbert ordered his groceries, got myself a delivery-boy job, and waited for the right moment. And it came, cuz, it came!"

"You've, uh, got a plan?"

"Had one."

"Uh, how are you going to work it?"

"Naughty, naughty. I plead the Fifth. Well, okay, I'll give you one hint. Did you see the city dump we passed a few miles back?" Harry nodded. "I went out there a few nights ago to throw away a set of works. You know what a set of works is?" Harry shook his head. "Narcotics paraphernalia. And I've never shot up in my life, not even in Nam. That's for misfits with no goal in life. There's your clue. Now you tell me what you've been doing."

Harry could make nothing of Clyde's hint but saw no alternative to unburdening himself and proceeded to do so while the Toyota sped along the deserted two-lane highway through the low hills. At the end of Harry's recital Clyde Bream grinned boyishly at him. "Good planning, cuz, quick thinking on your feet. You might have made a good lawyer. But I don't think you're going to need that rope."

"Why not?" Harry demanded peevishly.

"Did I tell you I was a pharmacy major in college before they drafted me? Thought I could talk them into making me a prescription clerk in a PX but they put me into a helicopter gunship outfit. Hey, cuz, what's wrong with you? You look kind of sick all of a sudden."

"Ugh—stop the car—need air." Clyde braked and pulled onto the gravel shoulder of the deserted road. Harry was bent double, his head between his knees, groaning. Clyde leaned over to help him.

Clyde never straightened up. Harry E. Hokinson whipped the combat knife from his ankle sheath and plunged it deep, thrusting upward in the approved commando style. After five stabs he was certain his young cousin was dead. Bloody flecks dribbled from his mouth and his eyes were glazed and wide-open. "Greedy little jerk," Harry grunted, his pig eyes gleaming. "Who needs you? The partnership's over."

He pushed the body away before it could bleed on his clothing. When the body was slumped over the wheel to Harry's satisfaction he manipulated the passenger door handle with his coat sleeve and squeezed himself out, being very careful not to touch anything inside the car. He basked in the glow of his own professionalism, like a young Green Beret back from his first dangerous mission. Just before he kneed the door shut he remembered to retrieve the coil of rope from the back seat.

The next item of business was to put as much distance as possible between himself and the chartreuse Toyota, just in case a patrol car should stop to investigate the vehicle parked on the shoulder. He had a long walk ahead of him but he decided that his new status as Delbert Coombes's sole surviving relative was worth the investment of sweat.

He struck out for the wooded hills and tramped through the autumn countryside for half an hour until he felt safe, then slowed his pace. He was sweating freely despite the crisp coolness of the day, and his stomach had begun to bother him. "You're out of shape, pal," he told himself, and resolved to get back in condition by jogging daily through the grounds of the Detweiler estate once it had legally become the Hokinson estate.

His walk slowed to almost a crawl and his stomach ached fiercely now. He hoped that the pain was not a reaction to the act of justifiable life-taking because it would suggest he might not have the guts to hang Delbert from the oak rafter. "But if I bug out now," he told himself, "I'll be a house painter the rest of my life."

That specter gave him the courage to go on. He resolved to carry out his plan, but tomorrow, after a good long rest tonight. God, how he needed rest! He trudged on through the gold-brown woods. His head buzzed. The forest seemed to be whirling. He had to stop and catch his breath every few minutes. His stomach was doubling him up.

He stumbled to the ground and propped himself against a thick spruce, using the rope coil as a pillow. He rubbed his unbearably aching belly and gasped for breath.

And suddenly four sentences came alive in his mind with the clarity of a noonday sun.

Delbert Coombes: "I had the delivery boy from Sampson's drop off some groceries a few days ago."

Clyde Bream: "I found out where Delbert ordered his groceries, got myself a delivery-boy job."

Clyde again: "A few nights ago I threw away a set of works. Narcotics paraphernalia."

And Clyde again: "I was a pharmacy major in college."

"Oh, my God!" screamed Harry E. Hokinson into the forest. "Oh, God, no! He injected poison into the fruit he delivered to Delbert! The orange!"

An unbiased observer might have pointed out that Clyde's scheme had failed to take into account the necessity to make Delbert's death seem an accident or a suicide and hence was far less professional than Harry's plan. But there were no observers in the vast autumnal loveliness of the forest and Harry died alone, badly.

And since both Clyde and Harry had carried on the family tradition of dying intestate, Delbert Coombes shortly found himself the owner of a set of law-books, a dirty chartreuse Toyota with blood-smeared seat covers, a secondhand BMW, a storeful of house paint, and a gross of combat knives. A week later Delbert scrawled a holographic will leaving all he possessed to The Flat Earth Society, smashed a table through the sealed French door of his penthouse, and stepped off the roof into nothingness.

Miss Phipps Discovers America

Wat first put you on to me?" asked the murderer.

"It was a matter of literary history," said Miss Phipps. She explained.

"I get your point, and I'm sorry," began the murderer, "because as it is—"

"That's the trouble, you see," said Miss Phipps sorrowfully, shaking her head. "One murder so often leads to another. I felt some sympathy for you about the first. I must warn you that I'm wearing a life-jacket," she added hastily.

"That won't help you any after a hard crack on the head with this paddle."

"A dangerous drifting log? I see. But my body will float."

"Not after my well-meant but futile attempts at rescue."

Miss Phipps plucked a whistle from her capacious bosom and blew three loud blasts . . .

On Wednesday morning Miss Phipps had wakened with a start. Whether it was the reflection of the lake water moving in silvery ripples across the bedroom ceiling, or whether it was some sound which had broken her slumber, Miss Phipps was not sure.

Her sleep had been heavy, for she had flown from London to New York the night before, then traveled by another plane, a car, and at last her host's new speedboat, to join her friends, the Stones, in their summer camp in the Adirondacks.

Waldo Stone—short, dark, square, hairy, and friendly—the editor of one of those glossy American magazines which pay such delightfully fabulous sums for serials and short stories, and his small blonde wife Louella, who wrote some of the stories, had been friends of Miss Phipps's ever since a tale of hers had first appeared in Waldo's "book." When Waldo and Louella had married a few years ago, after previous matrimonial misadventures, Miss Phipps had rejoiced greatly.

Now some kind of mixup had arisen about her new serial for Waldo and its television rights, and Louella had cabled her: WHY NOT COME OVER AND TAKE CARE OF IT AND PLAY ON OUR LAKE—and here she was. So far the Adirondack scenery was all that had been claimed for it. The mountains, the lakes, the huge pines, the chalk-white birches, the graceful spruce . . . Miss Phipps slipped out of bed, put on her spectacles, and went to the window.

The landscape visible from the Stones' handsome "camp"—this was the proper word, Miss Phipps had discovered, though she tended to think of these lakeside summer houses as wooden chalets—had been lovely in hot sunshine yesterday afternoon, when the lake waters were deep blue and the unbroken slopes of surrounding trees deep green; it had been lovely last night when a moonlight path lay across the black lake; it was lovely again now, in still another different guise.

The hour was very early, not quite full dawn, and as Miss Phipps watched a gleam of sun cut a narrow swathe of light across the lake through one of the stretches which divided the Erwins' pine-covered island from the mainland, wreaths of mist still swirled and brooded over the calm silver water. The Stones' wooden boat-dock lay full in this ray of light, but dark patches of moisture—footprints pointing to the shore—still remained on it here and there, undried.

Even as Miss Phipps gazed, however, the mist curled in on itself and grace-fully withdrew. Across the water, to the left, on the point of their long private island, the Erwins' smartly painted white camp gleamed in the sunshine. Then suddenly the green of the trees brightened, and the lake water took on a delicate tinge of blue.

"Heavenly!" exclaimed Miss Phipps.

She slid back into bed and fell asleep.

It seemed only a moment—though in reality it was some three hours—before she was wakened again, this time by shouts of "Phippsy!"—for this was the name by which she went in the Stone household. "Coming for a swim, Phippsy?" called Louella, putting her head round the bedroom door.

With some reluctance Miss Phipps heaved herself from the warm bed, squeezed her curves into a sea-blue swim suit, and went down to the boat dock, where Louella (in smart white) and Waldo (in scanty red) were already waiting.

"Hurry up, Randall!" cried Louella to the young man who, in a dark blue bathing suit sporting the white insignia of an athletic club, was neater than Miss Phipps had expected from his tousled appearance the night before. The young man was coming through the trees.

"Don't wait for me!" he called out.

There was more urgency in his tone than the occasion seemed to require, and Miss Phipps looked at him with some interest as he approached. He was tall, dark, and very thin, with a haggard aquiline face, a mass of tumbled black hair, and brilliant brown eyes. It had emerged last night that Waldo regarded him as one of the new young poets of whom America might hope one day to be very proud.

Louella had known Randall's mother at school, so they were both glad to invite him up to the camp for a month and had bedded him in one of their outlying cabins where he could be alone and work to his heart's content. He had felt like working last night soon after Miss Phipps's arrival—so that she had been able to settle the serial and television matter with Waldo at her ease, and had seen little of her fellow guest.

Now as he scrambled down the uneven bank she perceived that Martin

Randall limped, and she remembered that Waldo had told her of the childhood riding accident which had crushed the bones of his left foot.

At this point Waldo, looking owlish without his glasses, splashed into the lake in a flat but vigorous dive. Louella lowered herself carefully down the vertical ladder from the dock into the lake, gave a girlish scream at the water's low temperature, and then floundered off in a somewhat spasmodic breast stroke. Miss Phipps followed with a similar scream and stroke, for the water was cold and deep. Randall, she observed, came down the ladder too; possibly his leg injury made it difficult for him to dive.

The day's program proved entirely delightful. After a quick dip, they sipped hot coffee beside a crackling log fire, ate an ample breakfast, dressed at their leisure, then began to make plans. Waldo and Louella decided to invite their lakeside friends for cocktails the next afternoon.

As they had no telephone, the invitations must be given in person, and the quickest route was not by the distant and winding road, but by water.

Louella and her two guests went down to the boathouse and stood around while Waldo discussed which of the families who had camps around the lake were in residence with Ben Hunter, the guide employed by Waldo. With his lean height, long curly gray hair and beard, and rather impish blue eyes, he appeared to Miss Phipps the image of James Fenimore Cooper's Natty Bumppo in old age, and she listened to his calm ironic drawl with much enjoyment.

"Are the Erwins in, Ben?" inquired Louella.

"I wouldn't know anything about the Erwins, Mrs. Stone," said Ben. "But I've heard they came two days ago."

"Their flag isn't up," objected Waldo.

A gleam of amusement crossed Ben's blue eyes.

"I did hear as how Mr. Erwin was rather mad about that, Mr. Stone. Seems his flagstaff broke in a blow last winter. He ordered a new one from town, but they haven't delivered it yet. Seems he didn't pay his last bill there in full. Had an argument about an item, or something."

Miss Phipps gave a sympathetic murmur.

"Don't waste any sympathy on John Clayton Erwin, the third, Phippsy," said Louella tartly. "He's a rich playboy who never did a stroke of work in his life. Isn't that so, Ben?"

"I never heard of his working any," drawled Ben. "Course, my testimony ain't impartial, ma'am," he added, turning to Miss Phipps.

"Ben worked for the Erwins at one time," explained Louella. "But they didn't see eye to eye on various matters, did you, Ben?"

"It was chiefly deer, Mrs. Stone," murmured Ben.

"Clay shot more deer than his license entitled him to," said Louella. "He was fined heavily and his license revoked—after Ben left him."

Ben gazed across the lake—possibly, thought Miss Phipps, to hide the spark of satisfaction which brightened his elderly eyes. "He's not what you'd call a good shot, Mrs. Stone," he murmured.

"We shall have to ask the Erwins all the same, Louella," said Waldo testily.

"That might spoil the party for your other guests, Mr. Stone," said Ben. "Professor Firbaum and those young Normans, it seems they don't feel very neighborly to Mr. Erwin."

"Why not?"

"I couldn't say, I'm sure," said Ben. "Will that be all, Mr. Stone?"

"Yes, Ben," said Waldo.

"He's a native of these parts and knows everything about everyone," Waldo added to Miss Phipps as Ben disappeared among the trees.

"So I gathered," said Miss Phipps.

A considerable discussion followed as to who should fetch the mail, who should give the invitations, and which boats should be used for these errands. It seemed that Waldo and Louella were both proficient paddlers, and Randall a promising pupil; Miss Phipps declined to attempt a paddle, but was eager to ride in a canoe. So one was drawn down from its rack and launched by Waldo with some noise and splash, but then rejected by Louella as too slow.

Miss Phipps was content to listen idly to the talk, lounging in the now blazing sunshine, and gazing out over the rippling blue lake. From time to time a boat or two passed in the distance; in the mountain peace every sound carried far and accurately across the water.

All at once a loud bang nearby caused Miss Phipps to jump in alarm.

"A squirrel, Mr. Stone," said Ben, appearing with a long gun in one hand and a limp gray form in the other.

"Good," said Waldo.

"Why do you shoot squirrels?" asked Miss Phipps, her voice full of distaste.

"They eat the birds' eggs, ma'am," said Ben, disappearing again among the trees.

Miss Phipps sighed. She was familiar with the anomaly by which some people adored horses and dogs but hunted foxes; to love deer and birds and hate squirrels was part of the same perplexing paradox. But then all life was perplexing, mused Miss Phipps, since all animals, in order to sustain life, must destroy other life. Man, however, had imposed laws on this ruthless scheme—at least, to some extent.

"Dreaming up a plot, Phippsy?" shouted Waldo in her ear. "Your royal barge awaits you."

They all climbed into the speedboat and roared off down the lake.

Miss Phipps studied the customs of the lake with great interest. One slowed the speedboat when approaching canoes or persons fishing. One shouted, "Hi, there!" or waved, to every boat or person one passed. It was permissible to blow a whistle to attract attention, and Waldo explained, without demonstrating, the arrangement of long and short blasts which meant a call for help.

They swerved, turning toward the Erwins' handsome boathouse.

"Clay and Virgie are there—I see them," said Waldo.

"Virgie's wearing a hat and a town suit. They must be going somewhere. Perhaps they won't be able to come for cocktails," said Louella—it seemed to Miss Phipps that she spoke with relief.

"Erwin isn't wearing town clothes," observed Randall.

The contrast between the dress of the Erwin pair was certainly marked. Clayton was wearing the typical lake uniform of shorts and a T-shirt—of the very finest quality, Miss Phipps observed—while Virginia had a suit of gray corded silk and a little hat to match which, though of the most expensive simplicity, certainly belonged to town.

The Stone speedboat drew up jerkily alongside the dock, for dear Waldo was not the most expert of navigators, thought Miss Phipps; he had not been born to inherited wealth, but had achieved a lake camp recently, the hard way. Miss Phipps saw a look of contempt cross the fair, well-chiseled features of the handsome young Clayton Erwin, and she disliked him on sight.

"Hi, Clay! Hi, Virgie!" cried Waldo, beaming.

"Hi, Waldo," replied Erwin. The deliberate calm and level cadence of these two words had an effect of mockery, and Miss Phipps disliked him even more.

"We came to ask you up for cocktails tomorrow," said Waldo.

"Virginia can't. Her father's ill again," said Erwin.

His slight emphasis on *again* indicated that in his view the health of his wife's father was an unmitigated bore.

"We're just off to see if I can get a seat on the afternoon plane," said Virginia.

Miss Phipps heard in her voice that she was anxious to leave at once. But to show her anxiety to her husband is a mistake, she thought.

Sure enough, Erwin said promptly, "Oh, there's plenty of time. Come up and have a drink, Waldo—Louella. Oh—and you, Randall." His glance raked Miss Phipps, who had never felt plumper and plainer in her life. The introduction was effected. "I'm afraid I haven't read any of your books," said Erwin with a cold smile.

"I don't believe we've time, Clayton," said Louella, with a glance to Miss Phipps to call her attention to Virginia's unease.

"Oh, come, Louella!" urged Erwin. "Virgie will think she's been inhospitable if you don't stay a while."

The speedboat party disembarked and trailed unhappily up the rocky woodland path to the white camp. Miss Phipps took it slowly for Randall's sake, and Virginia hung back with Miss Phipps.

"Clayton won't have a telephone when he's on vacation, you see," explained Virginia. "We received the telegram about father's illness only yesterday afternoon when we fetched the mail. It was no use trying for a place on the morning plane, Clay thought."

Her voice was wistful. Poor child, thought Miss Phipps, she's a sweet, simple person—she really believes she's been inhospitable. She believes all her husband's gibes. She's desperately unhappy. And very beautiful, added Miss Phipps, surveying the wings of dark hair, the lovely gray eyes, the clear fine skin, the delicate profile.

"As a matter of fact," lied Miss Phipps in a loud cheerful voice so as to be overheard by the three in front, "we really mustn't stay long. Both Mr. Randall and myself have manuscripts which must be posted in time to catch the plane. Isn't that so, Mr. Randall?"

"It certainly is," lied the poet promptly.

A faint color tinged Virginia's cheek. She turned. "Hi, Martin," she said.

"Virginia and I are old schoolmates," said Randall quickly. "She and I and Louella come from the same home town."

Oh, lord, he's in love with her and the riding accident was in some way her fault and he was too proud to take advantage of it and she feels guilty, diagnosed Miss Phipps rapidly.

"The Stones' camp used to be my father's, you see," said Virginia. "Waldo and Louella bought it after—"

"Virginia!" called her husband imperiously.

Virginia hurried meekly ahead.

Louella and Miss Phipps sat on a log outside the neat little white wooden building, in a grassy clearing framed by pines, which to Miss Phipps's delight had proved to be the nearest U.S. Post Office. Randall, who did not relish the mile walk from the foot of the lake down the road, had remained in the speedboat, and Waldo was inside the Post Office. A huge salmon-pink car flashed by; Virginia Erwin waved, her husband lifted a disdainful finger, in greeting.

"Horrid man!" exclaimed Miss Phipps with emphasis.

"You don't have to tell me," agreed Louella.

"Possessive. Wants his wife at his beck and call every moment. I wonder he allows her to go home alone," said Miss Phipps.

"That's how he holds her. They've no children. Through her father's comfort, I mean. Her mother died some time ago. Her father took a financial tumble, and Clayton rescued him—more or less."

"Less rather than more, I should think. Keeps both of them on the end of a chain. Emotional blackmail, I'd call it. Don't let him blackmail you, Louella."

"What makes you think he does?" said Louella quickly, flushing.

"Oh, just a vague indication here and there—it's surprising what an intonation or pause can suggest . . ."

"Waldo has always said how keen your observation is, Phippsy," said Louella drily. She hesitated. "It's really too absurd," she said. "After all, I'm almost old enough to be Clayton's mother."

"But still handsome, Louella," murmured Miss Phipps, glancing admiringly at the charming petite figure and thick blonde curls.

"It was a party at our camp. I was getting some more liquor from the closet, when Clayton came up behind me and kissed my neck."

"But did that matter so much?" marveled Miss Phipps. "Everyone kisses and calls darling nowadays."

"No, of course it didn't matter," said Louella angrily. "I disliked it because I dislike Clayton Erwin, but I never thought of it again until he began hinting about it, referring to the incident as if it were something important between us."

"Ah, I see," said Miss Phipps thoughtfully. "You didn't tell Waldo."

"Why on earth should I? It wasn't worth telling."

"But with the lapse of time and these continual hints—"

"Waldo," said Louella, busily lighting a cigarette, "in spite of his editorial airs, is basically not very self-confident. He always tends to think of himself as poor and plain."

"Louella," said Miss Phipps earnestly, "tell Waldo tonight."

"No, I won't!" said Louella. "It's too late."

"You're running a foolish and unnecessary risk, Louella."

"On your way, girls," cried Waldo, emerging from the Post Office with a handful of mail. "We've three invitations to deliver before lunch."

The speedboat swerved, straightened, ceased to roar, and drew up rather neatly beside the boat dock of Colonel Merriam, retired. Waldo climbed out and Randall quickly followed.

Instantly pandemonium reigned. Six small children, clad in six life preservers of varied colors, mingled with six golden retrievers, rushed out on the dock. Waldo and Randall almost disappeared in a confusion of yapping and barking, of screaming and laughing, of a flourishing of tails and paws, a waving of small bare arms and a tossing of curly heads.

Suddenly a voice from above boomed out a word of command, unrecognizable by Miss Phipps, but completely efficacious, for the noise ceased at once. Louella and Miss Phipps, somewhat impeded by several friendly dogs who wished to lick their faces, were at length hauled out of the boat and followed Waldo up the path to the camp, Randall trailing behind. The Colonel, tall, broad, gray-haired, neat in slacks and shirt of becomingly pale khaki, met them halfway. Miss Phipps and Randall were introduced.

"Grandchildren," said the Colonel, indicating them with a wave of the hand. "Come for a month. My sons won't be here again till the week-end and my daughters-in-law have gone marketing with my wife. So I'm in charge. Always put 'em all into life preservers right away—safer, you know. Only two of these dogs are mine, but my sons have two each. Boo-ya!" he shouted—or at least it sounded like that to Miss Phipps.

The dogs and children sat down at once, and Miss Phipps marveled at the similarity of Colonels of all nations. Drinks began to be administered and invitations issued.

"Glad you've dropped by, Waldo," said the Colonel seriously. "Here's Fritz and Ruth come with an awkward problem. Professor and Mrs. Firbaum, Miss Phipps—lake neighbors."

Professor Firbaum (white-haired, fresh-complexioned, probably a Hitler refugee) and his wife (university lecturer, younger, with a spark in the brown eyes behind her spectacles) reminded Miss Phipps strongly of Professor Baer and Jo March in that childhood classic of Louisa Alcott's, *Little Women Wedded*. As these two characters had always been favorites of Miss Phipps's—indeed, the youthful literary efforts of Jo had helped to confirm Miss Phipps's own ambitions—she listened with great sympathy to their account of their troubles.

The details were somewhat too dependent on local topography for Miss Phipps to grasp completely, but she understood the general problem well enough. Clayton Erwin wished to "buy in" part of the Firbaums' land, which faced his own on the mainland on the opposite side of the lake from the

Stones—to protect his view, Erwin said. The Firbaums did not wish to sell any of their small holdings. Erwin therefore was causing trouble by throwing doubt on their title to their land. Surveyors had been summoned, and lawyers called in.

"But why protect his view? We do not threaten his view. Our camp can scarcely be seen from his windows. We do not even go often on the lake in a boat. We are not good with the boat," explained the Professor, turning to Miss Phipps.

It occurred to Miss Phipps, and she could see that the thought was present in the minds of the others, that the explosions and roarings involved in the inefficient starting and conduct of an outboard motor boat might well disturb a neighboring island's peace. But what arrogant selfishness on Clayton Erwin's part—to be unable to tolerate an infrequent noise! Just like him, however, thought Miss Phipps.

"Fellow's a damned little dictator," boomed the Colonel. "Thinks he rules the earth because he owns a few bonds. Like to have him under my orders for a day or two. Why don't you and I go into town with Fritz, Waldo, and tell the surveyors' office a few things, hey?"

"Be glad to," said Waldo. "All the same it would be better to tackle Clayton privately and try to get him to call it off. Bound to cost Fritz a lot of money if he has to go to court to establish his title."

"I certainly wish I hadn't asked the Erwins for tomorrow," said Louella in distress.

"Might be a good opportunity—I might say a few words to him on Fritz's behalf," said the Colonel, a gleam of battle in his eye.

"He might turn nasty," object Louella.

"Wouldn't frighten me," boomed the Colonel with obvious enjoyment.

It was agreed to await the result of the Colonel's "few words" before taking any public action.

"We must go—it's late—we still have to call on the Normans," said Louella.

The Normans' camp pleased Miss Phipps greatly, because it was so neat and so obviously homemade. The small house looked exactly like the illustration of the log cabin in the book *From Log Cabin to White House* which Miss Phipps had enjoyed in her teens. A small patch of grass in front was green and well kept. The boat dock, where a canoe and an outboard motorboat were tied up, was clean and new. What Miss Phipps called a nice normal young man, American married-postwar type, was sawing a log by hand on a sawhorse, watched by a healthy-looking ten-year-old boy.

"Hi, Les!" called Waldo.

"Hi, Waldo," replied Leslie Norman. "Come on in."

He put down the saw carefully and came toward the dock. Miss Phipps noted that his tone, though friendly, seemed subdued. Waldo and Louella evidently noted it too, for they spoke together, with the same intent.

"Sorry—no time," said Waldo. "Just dropped by to ask you and Fran to come in for a drink tomorrow about five."

"Is anything wrong, Les? Where's Frances?" said Louella.

"You haven't heard, then? Tom and Ed here were nearly drowned yesterday morning. Canoe overturned."

The four in the speedboat exclaimed their concern.

"Sure were. 'Course they can both swim, and I went after them pretty quick when Ed blew his whistle—he kept his head and blew it fast, I'll say that for him," said Ed's father, ruffling his son's already tangled hair with a proud hand. "But Tom being younger got a bit of a fright, and he isn't feeling so good this morning. So Fran's kept him in bed and she's staying near him."

"Very wise," said Miss Phipps.

Leslie seemed to find this sympathy agreeable, for he relaxed and said, "But come on in," in a more energetic tone.

"But how did it happen, Les?" said Waldo. "I thought your kids were too well trained on the water to turn over a canoe."

"It was that blasted Clayton Erwin!" growled Leslie, suddenly crimson. "He came past the kids in his speedboat, far too close and far too fast, and naturally the waves of his boat's wake upset their canoe. Of course," said Leslie, swallowing and clearly making a great effort to be fair, "I don't say he saw it happen. He'd be round the point before the wake reached them. But all the same, I'd like to tell Mr. John Clayton Erwin the third just what I think of him."

"You ought to report it to Colonel Merriam as chairman of the Lake Association," suggested Louella.

"Yes, that's the thing to do," urged Waldo. "It was a clear violation of our lake-navigation laws."

"Well," said Leslie doubtfully, "that's what Fran says. But for myself, I'd rather take a poke at that arrogant, condescending—"

"No sense in putting yourself in the wrong, Les," warned Waldo. "Frankly, as an up-and-coming young architect in this neighborhood, you can't afford to make enemies."

"And think of Fran," urged Louella.

"Come round tomorrow and we'll talk it over," said Waldo. "Bring the kids, of course. 'Bye, now!"

"'Bye now," echoed the young father.

As their boat left the shore Miss Phipps observed that Norman stood looking after them for some time.

"Just tell me, Waldo Stone, what we shall do with Clayton Erwin if he turns up at five tomorrow evening," said Louella.

"We'll turn him over to Phippsy," said Waldo, grinning.

Miss Phipps groaned . . .

A swim, a nap, and a short stroll through the woods filled the afternoon very pleasantly.

"'*This is the forest primeval. The murmuring pines and the hemlocks,*'" quoted Miss Phipps, gazing up at the towering trees.

"Longfellow!" snorted Randall with derision, while Waldo murmured deprecatingly that the trees were not in fact primeval, but second or third growth.

"Why jeer at Longfellow?" said Miss Phipps. She knew several answers to her question, but wanted to make the young man talk. "Arnold Bennett called him the chief minor poet of the English language."

"What did he know about poetry?" scoffed Randall.

"What do you think of modern English poetry, Mr. Randall?"

"There haven't been any English poets worth mentioning since Shelley and Keats," said Randall, his eyes sparking as he threw out this challenge.

"Wouldn't you include Lord Byron?"

Randall muttered something that Miss Phipps could not make out. The young man was obviously annoyed.

"Tell me about modern American poetry," said Miss Phipps encouragingly.

At first sulky, Randall presently recovered his spirits and talked enthusiastically.

But the best part of the day proved to be the evening, when in two canoes—Louella and Randall in one, Waldo and Miss Phipps in the other—the party set off to remoter stretches of the lake in search of deer. The canoes glided silently through the calm water in which the huge trees were mirrored with astonishing exactness; in the twilight hush came a sudden *swish-swish* noise, and a red deer bounded suddenly away into a thicket.

The purpose of the excursion being thus achieved, the canoes turned homeward. They had quite a long way to go, and the moon was silvering the black water before they rounded a point of land and saw the lights of the Stones' camp in the distance.

"This is the Erwins' island," said Miss Phipps, proud of the local knowledge she had acquired in only one day. "Oh, no, it can't be," she added, disappointed. "There are *two* lighted houses."

"It's the Erwins' all right," said Waldo. "The other building is where their butler and cook live. In the old days when Clay's father was alive, they had scads of guests and scads of servants, four or five big guest cabins and huge servants' quarters. Even Erwin can't do that nowadays—he just has a married couple. They've a lot of cabins still on the island, though."

"Don't talk to me about that young man," said Miss Phipps. "He spoils the view."

On Thursday morning Miss Phipps woke late and happy, feeling that she had her new environment well in hand. She was now well acquainted with canoes, speedboats, inboard and outboard motors, boat docks, squirrels, deer, gunshots, beaver, chipmunks, trees, drifting logs, guides, camps, and navigation laws. The day began with the agreeable routine which now seemed familiar. After breakfast Randall decided to work and retired to his cabin; Louella entered into consultation with her elderly housekeeper; Waldo and Miss Phipps were sent down the lake to the nearest small town, to fetch additional liquor for the party.

"That's Les Norman ahead with our local doctor," said Waldo. He put on speed and overtook the Norman outboard, in which an elderly man in more formal clothes than those usually worn by the lake dwellers was sitting rather stiffly. "Hi there, Les! Isn't young Tom feeling well this morning?"

"He's had a very restless night—so Fran wanted the doctor here to have a look at him," said Leslie.

"He has been in shock, and has a cold," said the doctor in a professional tone. "But all he needs is slight sedation and the comfort of his mother's presence. Nothing seriously wrong."

"Glad to hear that," said Waldo, roaring away.

On their way back from town Waldo and Miss Phipps called at the little Post Office to collect the mail.

"I was just wondering, Mr. Stone," said the neat young postmistress, "if you would be so kind as to deliver a telegram to Mr. Erwin. He hasn't been in this morning . . . and . . . as it *is* a telegram . . . it might be important."

She blushed; it was clear that, of course, the contents of the telegram were known to her.

"I'll be glad to," said Waldo.

"I suppose Virginia's father has died," said Miss Phipps.

"I guess so. Clay will need to catch the afternoon plane," said Waldo soberly.

"Shall I stay in the boat?" suggested Miss Phipps a little later, as they tied up at the Erwin dock.

"Certainly not," said Waldo. "Clay is a good character-study for you, and as your editor I insist that you give him the full treatment."

Miss Phipps climbed meekly up the path behind him. At the top they were met by a dignified butler, bald, lined, and adipose, who led them into the large airy living room of the Erwin camp.

"Good morning, Pearson," said Waldo.

"Good morning, sir. I regret that Mr. Clayton is not up yet," said Pearson in an accent which revealed his origin.

"You're English—a fellow-countryman," said Miss Phipps.

"Yes, madam," said Pearson, bowing. "I encountered the late Mr. John Clayton Erwin in France in the First World War and have been butler in the family ever since. My wife too is English."

"I hate to interrupt you two at your old-home week," said Waldo, "but I have an urgent telegram for Mr. Erwin."

The butler hesitated. "It is beyond my instructions to waken Mr. Clayton before he summons me," he said.

("He's accustomed to his master lying blotto with a hangover," decided Miss Phipps with malice.)

Waldo exclaimed impatiently and strode toward an inner door.

"Would you care for a little refreshment, madam? A cup of coffee? A pot of tea? My wife would be happy to prepare it," said Pearson.

Miss Phipps was about to decline when she was interrupted by a loud shout from Waldo, who came rushing out to them in obvious terror, his face white.

"Clayton's dead!" he cried.

"Oh, no, sir," said Pearson calmly. "Mr. Clayton often appears somewhat lifeless after a little overindulgence the previous night. Last night, Mrs. Clayton being absent, he was a trifle—under the weather, shall I say—when I took him another bottle of whiskey about eleven o'clock."

"Don't be a fool, man," panted Waldo. "His brains are strewn all over the pillow."

The butler, his face a mask of horror, rushed into the bedroom. Miss Phipps followed. Both soon withdrew; the facts were as Waldo had stated them. It was an unpleasant sight.

"He's been murdered!" gasped Pearson.

"What makes you think of murder?" demanded Waldo roughly.

"Mr. Clayton would never kill himself, sir—he likes himself too well. It might have been an accident, perhaps?"

"I don't see how you can have an accident with a deer rifle, while lying horizontally in bed in silk pajamas," said Waldo. "The gun's on the floor at the foot of his bed. Was it his own gun, I wonder? Yes, probably it was," he answered himself, pointing to an empty place in the rack beside the hearth. "Did you hear any shot during the night, Pearson?"

"Not to distinguish from other shots in the woods, sir," stammered Pearson. "There will be fingerprints on the gun, perhaps?"

"I doubt it," said Waldo. "I must ask you, Pearson, to stay here on the island, with your wife, while I go down the lake and notify the police. I shall lock the bedroom door and take the key with me. Don't touch anything."

"Certainly not, sir," said Pearson.

"This dock is under observation, clear if distant, from my camp," continued Waldo, "so any attempt to leave would be instantly noticed."

"I have no desire to leave, sir," said Pearson with dignity.

"Were you attached to your master, Pearson?" asked Miss Phipps.

The butler hesitated. "Mr. Clayton was very charming as a little boy," he said. "After his father died and he inherited so much wealth, he became spoiled. Of late years my wife and I would, I own, have been glad to leave his service, but we should have found it difficult to obtain fresh suitable posts at our age. We are very fond of Mrs. Clayton," he added wistfully.

"I feel this is all wrong, Phippsy," said Waldo as they hurried down the path. "I oughtn't to leave the body, I oughtn't to leave the Pearsons alone. But you can't drive the boat, so I can't stay there myself, and I don't fancy leaving you there alone with the Pearsons. Suppose one of them is the murderer? Not that I think it likely—what the old chap said about the difficulty of finding a new place at his age is true enough, so why should he kill off his present employer?"

"How old is his wife?" inquired Miss Phipps.

"Every month as old as he is," said Waldo, casting off, "and plainer if possible. Erwin hasn't been playing round with her, if that's in your mind. Now if their daughter had been living here—but she hasn't; she married years ago and went to California. And their son is in England—married and stayed there after the war. No, I can't see either of the Pearsons firing a bullet into Erwin's head. But who else could it have been? This is an island, you know—a murderer can't just drop in and out . . . I think I'd better take you back to our camp, Phippsy, before I go for the police—I may be hours with them."

The roaring of the engine made further conversation difficult.

"How far is your camp from Erwin's, Waldo?" shouted Miss Phipps.

"About two miles," shouted Waldo.

When they approached the Stone camp, they saw Louella at the window, with Randall at her side, both waving to them cheerfully. Waldo cut off the engine.

"This is going to be a very unpleasant affair, Phippsy," said Waldo. "So many people round the lake have reason to dislike Clayton Erwin. The police will ferret everything out. It will be a mess."

"Still, as you say, the Erwins' camp is on an island," said Miss Phipps.

Waldo glanced at her sharply. "If you have any bright ideas about solving the murder, Phippsy," he said, "produce them—and fast!"

"I think I know who the murderer is," said Miss Phipps thoughtfully.

"What!" barked Waldo.

"Only there are one or two details I should like to check first."

She outlined her plan.

"Well, okay, why not?" said Waldo. "What do we have to lose?"

Miss Phipps, leaning forward, surreptitiously took possession of the whistle which lay in the dashboard compartment.

The murderer paddled the canoe toward the Erwin camp.

"Though I don't see what we're going to do when we get there."

"Neither do I," said Miss Phipps thoughtfully. "I don't think the Pearsons murdered Clayton Erwin, do you? No motive."

"They had a strong motive *not* to do so," said the murderer emphatically. "Besides, to point a gun at a man's head from a yard away, and fire, takes more nerve than an old fellow like Pearson is likely to have."

("The usual pathological conceit of the criminal showing its ugly head," thought Miss Phipps. "He means: 'Pearson couldn't but *I* could.'")

Aloud she said, "He was a soldier once."

"Forty years ago."

"We acquit the Pearsons then, do we? Although they did have the best opportunity . . . Perhaps it would be well to consider all the suspects under the headings of motive and opportunity?"

"It would be better," said the murderer, "to leave it all to the police."

"I'm hoping to clear up the case before the police arrive," said Miss Phipps. The murderer gave her a sudden grim look, and she continued rather nervously, "The people with motives are Louella, the Firbaums, the Normans, Randall, old Ben. Of these, the motives of the Normans and Ben belong to the past; the murder, if committed by them, would spring from revenge for wrongs already inflicted. Now old Ben, I think, has had his revenge: I think it was he who reported Clayton Erwin to the authorities, resulting in the hunting license having been revoked."

"Your analysis so far is excellent," said the murderer. "I agree."

"As for Leslie Norman, it's true he expressed a desire for revenge on Erwin. But he had no opportunity, I think. The boy Tom had a restless night—a statement confirmed by the doctor who had heard the child's own account—so the Normans must have been up several times during the night to comfort him. Therefore, Leslie Norman could not have slipped away to murder Erwin without his departure being noticed. Of course the whole question of opportunity is a very difficult one," said Miss Phipps. "The Erwins' camp being an island, you know."

"You are omitting Colonel Merriam from consideration?" said the murderer.

"I acquit Colonel Merriam on grounds of character, and his sons because they were absent," she said. "His wife and daughters-in-law of course I haven't met. But I acquit the whole family from lack of opportunity. Imagine any murderer trying to slip away quietly in the night from that camp! Those dogs! Whoever tried to leave or return, at least four of them would bark their heads off! The Colonel's command to stop them is a pretty loud bark too."

"True," said the murderer.

"As for Louella," began Miss Phipps.

"Louella surely has no motive."

"I'm afraid she has," said Miss Phipps soberly. "But, I am glad to say, no opportunity. If she had tried to start a motor at our camp, we should all have been wakened by the noise. As for a canoe—the two canoes are on stands and they make a grating noise when pulled across the dock. I doubt, too, if Louella has the strength to launch one. Yes, it is this question of transport which is decisive," she continued. "Consider the Firbaums, for example. Their motive is clear. But they are 'not good with the boat,' you remember? Can you imagine either of them making their way *quietly* across the lake in the dark? Their motive rests on Erwin's objection to the noise they make when they attempt to boat. Yes, the question of transport is, I repeat, decisive."

"How did the murderer reach the Erwins' island then?"

"He swam. I woke up early on Wednesday morning and saw damp footprints, pointing inwards to the camp, on the Stones' dock. The sun had not yet risen to dry them."

"But Erwin was alive later that Wednesday morning—we all saw him."

"Quite. Wednesday's swimming performance was your *rehearsal*. For some date when you hoped Virginia would be safely absent—for you love Virginia, don't you? I didn't realize the significance of the footprints on the dock at the time, of course."

"What first put you on to me?" asked the murderer.

"It was a matter of literary history, my dear Randall," said Miss Phipps. "You were so sensitive about Lord Byron yesterday afternoon. Byron was a poet, like you, and lame, like you. Because other sports were closed to him he made himself into an exceptionally strong swimmer. So did you—I noticed when I first saw you at the dock that your bathing suit bore the insignia of an athletic club. Byron swam the Hellespont, you remember—the strait between Asia Minor and Europe, the one Leander swam in classical times to see his girl— about four miles."

"I get your point, and I'm sorry," began Randall, "because as it is—"

"That's the trouble, you see," said Miss Phipps sorrowfully, shaking her head.

"One murder so often leads to another. I felt some sympathy for you about the first. I must warn you that I'm wearing a lifejacket," she added hastily.

"That won't help you any after a hard crack on the head with this paddle."

"A dangerous drifting log? I see. But my body will float."

"Not after my well-meant but futile attempts at rescue."

Miss Phipps plucked the whistle from her capacious bosom and blew three loud blasts. At the Stones' dock the speedboat started with a roar.

Randall was silent, then he said with surprising calm, "You win, Miss Phipps." He sprang up, tilting the canoe, and threw himself into the lake. "Give my love to Virginia," he said.

He disappeared from view and did not rise again.

The Strong and the Weak

Their parents named them May and June because their birthdays occurred in those months. A third sister, an April child, had been christened Avril but she had died. May was like the time of year in which she had been born, changeable, chilly and warm by turns, sullen and yet to know and show a loveliness which could not last.

In the 1930s, when May was in her twenties, it was still important to get one's daughters well married, and though Mrs. Thrace had no anxieties on that score for sunny June, she was less sanguine about May. Her older daughter was neither pretty nor graceful nor clever, and no man had ever looked at her twice. June, of course, had a string of admirers.

Then May met a young lawyer at a *thé dansant*. His name was Walter Cheney, he was extremely good-looking, his father was wealthy and made him a generous allowance, and there was no doubt he belonged in a higher social class than that of the Thraces. May fell passionately in love with him, but no one was more surprised than she when he asked her to marry him.

The intensity of May's passion frightened Mrs. Thrace. It wasn't quite "nice." The expression on May's face while she awaited the coming of her fiancé, her ardor when she greeted him, the hunger in her eyes—that sort of thing was all very well in the cinema, but unsuitable for a customs officer's daughter in a genteel suburb.

For a brief period she had become almost beautiful. "I'm going to marry him," she said when cautioned. "He wants me to love him, doesn't he? He loves me. Why shouldn't I show my love?"

June, who was clever as well as pretty, was away at college, training to be a schoolteacher. It had been considered wiser, long before Walter Cheney had appeared, to keep May at home. She had no particular aptitude for anything, and she was useful to her mother about the house. Now, of course, it turned out that she had an aptitude for catching a rich, handsome, and successful husband. Then, a month before the wedding, June came home for the summer holidays.

It was all very unfortunate, Mrs. Thrace said over and over again. If Walter Cheney had jilted May for some other girl, they would have been bitterly indignant, enraged even, and Mr. Thrace would have felt old-fashioned longings to apply a horsewhip. But what could anyone say or do when Walter transferred his affections from the older daughter to the younger?

May screamed and sobbed and tried to attack June with a knife. "We're all terribly sorry for you, my darling," said Mrs. Thrace, "but what can we do? You wouldn't marry a man who doesn't love you, would you?"

"He does love me, he does! It's just because she's pretty. She's cast a spell on him. I wish she was dead and then he'd love me again."

"You mustn't say that, May. It's all very cruel to you, but you have to face the fact that he's changed his mind. Isn't it better to find out now than later?"

"I would have had him," insisted May.

Mrs. Thrace blushed. She was shocked to the core.

"I shall never marry now," said May. "She's ruined my life and I shall never have anything ever again."

Walter and June were married, and Walter's father bought them a house in Surrey. May stayed at home, being useful to her mother. The war came. Walter went straight into the army, became a captain, then a major, finally a colonel. May also went into the army, where she remained a private for five years, working in some catering department. After that there was nothing for her to do except to go home to her parents once more . . .

May never forgave her sister.

"She stole my husband," she would remind her mother.

"He wasn't your husband, May."

"As good as. You wouldn't forgive a thief who came into your house and stole the most precious thing you had or were likely to have."

"We're told to forgive those who trespass against us, as we hope to be forgiven."

"I'm not religious," said May, and on those occasions when the Cheneys came to the Thrace home she took care to be absent. But she knew all about them—all, that is, except one thing.

Mr. and Mrs. Thrace were most careful never to speak of June in May's presence, so May listened outside the door, and she secretly read all June's letters to her mother. Whenever Walter's name was mentioned in a letter, or spoken, she winced and shivered with the pain of it. She knew that they had moved to a larger house, that they were building up a collection of fine furniture and valuable paintings. She knew where they went for their holidays and what friends they entertained. But what she was never able to discover was how Walter felt about June.

Had he ever really loved her? Had he repented of his choice? May thought that perhaps, after the first flush of infatuation was over, he had come to long for May as much as she longed for him. Since she never saw them, she could never know, for, however he might feel, Walter couldn't leave June. When you have done what he had done—what June had made him do—you can't change again. You have to stick it out till death.

It comforted May—it was perhaps the only thing that kept her going—to convince herself that Walter regretted his bargain. If there had been children— what the Victorians called pledges of love . . . Sometimes, after a letter had come from June, May would see her mother looking particularly pleased and satisfied. And then, shaking with dread, May would read the letter, terrified to learn that June was pregnant. But Mrs. Thrace's pleasure and satisfaction must have come from some other source, from some account of Walter's latest *coup* in court or June's latest party, for no children came and now June was past 40.

Trained for nothing, May worked as a canteen supervisor in a women's hostel. She continued to live at home until her parents died. Their deaths took place within six months, Mrs. Thrace dying in March and her widower in August. And that was how it happened that May saw Walter again.

At the time of her mother's cremation, May was ill in bed with a virus infection and unable to attend. But she had no way of avoiding her father's funeral. When she saw Walter come into the church, a faintness seized her and she pushed against the pew rail, trembling. She covered her face with her hands to make it seem as if she were praying, and when at last she took them away Walter was beside her.

He took her hand and looked into her face. May's eyes met his, which were as blue and compelling as ever, and she saw with anguish that he had lost none of his good looks, but had become only more distinguished-looking. She would have liked to die then, holding his hand and gazing into his face.

"Won't you come and speak to your sister, May?" said Walter in the rich deep voice which charmed juries, struck terror into the hearts of witnesses, and won women. "Shall we let bygones be bygones on this very sad day?"

May shivered. She withdrew her hand and marched to the back of the church. She placed herself as far away from June as she could, but not too far to observe that it was June who took Walter's arm as they left and not Walter who took June's; that it was June who looked up at Walter for comfort while his face remained grave and still; that it was June who clung to him while he merely permitted the clinging. It couldn't be that he was behaving like that because she, May, was there. He must hate and despise June, as May, with all her heart, still hated and despised her sister.

But it was at a funeral that they were reconciled.

May learned of Walter's death by reading an announcement of it in a newspaper. And the pain of it was as great as the one she had suffered when her mother had told her he wanted to marry June. She sent flowers, an enormous wreath of snow-white roses that cost her half a week's wages. And of course she would go to the funeral, whether June wanted her there or not.

Apparently June did want her. Perhaps she thought the roses were for the living bereaved and not for the dead. She came up to May and put her arms around her, laying her head against her sister's shoulder in misery and despair.

May broke their long silence. "Now you know what it's like to lose him."

"Oh, May, May, don't be cruel to me now! Don't hold that against me now. Be kind to me now, I've nothing left."

So May sat beside June, and after the funeral she went back to the house where June had lived with Walter. In saying she had nothing left, June had presumably been referring to emotional rather than material things. Apart from certain stately homes she had visited on tours, May had never seen anything like the interior of that house.

"I'm going to retire next month," May remarked, "and then I'll be living in what they call a flatlet—one room and a kitchen."

Two days later a letter came from June:

"Dearest May: Don't be angry with me for calling you that. You have always been one of my dearest, in spite of what I did and in spite of your hatred of me. I can't be sorry for what I did because so much happiness came of it for me, but I am truly, deeply sorry that you were the one who suffered. And now, dear May, I want to try to make up to you for what I did, though I know I can never really do that, not now, not after so long.

"You said you were going to retire and wouldn't be living very comfortably. Will you come and live with me? You can have as many rooms in this house as you want—you are welcome to share everything with me. You will know what I mean when I say I feel that would be just. Please make me happy by saying you forgive me and will come. Always your loving sister, June."

What did the trick was June saying it would be just. Yes, it would be justice if May could now have some of those good things which were hers by right and which June had stolen from her along with her man. She waited a week and then she wrote:

"Dear June: What you suggest seems a good idea. I have thought about it and I will make my home with you. I have very little personal property, so moving will not be a great bother. Let me know when you want me to come. It is raining again here and very cold. Yours, May."

There was nothing, however, in the letter about forgiveness.

And yet, May, sharing June's house, was almost prepared to forgive. For she was learning at last what June's married life had been.

"You can talk about him if you want to," May had said hungrily on their first evening together. "If it's going to relieve your feelings, I don't mind."

"What is there to say except that we were married for forty years and now he's dead?"

"You could show me some of the things he gave you." May picked up ornament after ornament, gazed at paintings. "Did he give you that? What about this?"

"They weren't presents. I bought them or he did."

May couldn't help getting excited. "I wonder you're not afraid of burglars. This is a proper Aladdin's Cave. Have you got lots of jewelry too?"

"Not much," said June uncomfortably.

May's eyes were on June's engagement ring, a poor thing of diamond chips in nine-carat gold, far less expensive than the ring Walter had given his first love. Of course she had kept hers, and Walter, though well off even then, hadn't been rich enough to buy a second magnificent ring within six months of the first—not with all the expenses of furnishing a new home. But later, surely . . . ?

"I should have thought you'd have an eternity ring."

"Marriage doesn't last for eternity," said June.

May could tell June didn't like talking about it. June even avoided mention-ing Walter's name, and soon she put away the photographs of him which had stood on the piano and on the drawing-room mantelpiece. May wondered if Walter had ever written any letters to his wife. They had seldom been parted, of course, but it would be strange if June hadn't received a single letter from him in 40 years.

So the first time June went out alone, May tried to open her desk. It was locked. The drawers of June's dressing table disclosed a couple of birthday cards with *Love from Walter* scrawled hastily on them, and the only other written message from her husband June had considered worth keeping May found tucked into a cookbook in the kitchen. It was a note written on the back of a bill, and it read: *Baker called. I ordered a large white bread for Saturday.*

That night May reread the two letters she had received from Walter during their engagement. Each began "Dearest May." She hadn't looked at them for 40 years—she hadn't dared—but now she read them with calm satisfaction.

"Dearest May: This is the first love letter I have ever written. If it isn't much good you must put it down to lack of practice. I miss you a lot and rather wish I hadn't told my parents I would visit them on this holiday . . ."

And "Dearest May: Thanks for both your letters. Sorry I've taken so long to reply, but I feel a bit nervous that my letters don't match up to yours. Still, with luck, we soon shan't have to write to each other because we shan't be separated. I wish you were here with me . . ."

Poor Walter had been reticent and shy, unable to express his feelings on paper or by word of mouth. But at least he had written love letters to *her* and not notes about loaves of bread. May decided to start wearing her engagement ring again—on her little finger, of course, because she could no longer get it over the knuckle of her ring finger. If June noticed, she didn't comment on it.

"Was it you or Walter who didn't want children?" May asked one day.

"Children just didn't come."

"Walter *must* have wanted them. When he was engaged to me we talked of having three."

June looked upset, but May could have talked of Walter all day long. "He was only sixty-five," she said. "That's young to die these days. You never told me what he died of."

"He needed an operation," said June, "and never regained consciousness."

"Just like mother," said May. Suppose June had had an incurable disease and had died—what would have happened then? Remembering Walter's tender look and strong handclasp at her father's funeral, May thought he would have married her. She twisted the ring on her little finger. "You were almost like a second wife, weren't you? It must have been a difficult position."

"I'd much rather not talk about it," said June, and with her handkerchief to her eyes, she left the room.

May was happy. For the first time in 40 years she was happy. She busied herself about the house, caring for June's things, dusting and polishing, pausing to look at a painting and reflecting that Walter must have often paused to look at it too. Sometimes she imagined him sitting in this chair or standing by that window, his heart full of regret for what he might have had with May. And she thought how, while he had been longing for her, she, far away, had been crying for him. She never cried now, though June did, often.

"I'm an old fool. I can't help giving way," June sobbed. "You're strong, May, but I'm weak and I miss him so."

"Didn't I miss him?"

"He was always fond of you. It upset him a lot to think you were unhappy. He often talked about you." June looked at her piteously. "You *have* forgiven me, have't you, May?"

"As a matter of fact, I have," said May. She was a little surprised at herself. But, yes, she had forgiven June. "I think you've been punished for what you did." A loveless marriage, a husband who talked constantly of another woman . . .

"I've been punished," said June, and she put her arms around May's neck.

The strong and the weak. May recalled that when a movement downstairs woke her in the middle of one night. She heard footsteps and a wrenching sound as of a door being forced. It was the burglar she had always feared and had warned June about, but June would be cowering in her room now, terrified, incapable of taking any action.

May put on her dressing gown and went down the passage to June's room. The bed was empty. She looked out of the window, and the moonlight showed her a car parked on the gravel driveway that led to the lane. A yellower, stronger light streamed from the drawing-room window. A shiver of fear went through her, but she knew she must be strong.

Before she reached the head of the stairs she heard a violent crash as of something heavy yet brittle hurled against a wall. There was a cry from below, then footsteps running. May got to the stairs in time to see a slight figure rush across the hall and slam the front door behind him. The car started up.

In his wake he had left a thin trail of blood. May followed the blood trail into the drawing room. June stood by her desk which had been torn open and all its contents scattered onto the table. She was trembling, tearful, and laughing with shaky hysteria, pointing to the shards of cut glass that lay everywhere.

"I threw the decanter at him. I hit him and cut his head and he ran."

May went up to her. "Are you all right?"

"He didn't touch me. He pointed that gun at me when I came in, but I didn't care. I couldn't bear to see him searching my desk, getting at all my private things. Wasn't I brave? He didn't get away with anything but a few pieces of silver. I hit him and then he heard you coming and he panicked. Wasn't I brave, May?"

But May wasn't listening. She was reading the letter which lay open and exposed on top of the papers that the burglar had pulled out of the desk. Walter's handwriting leaped at her, weakened though it was, enfeebled by his last illness. "My darling love: It is only a minute since you walked out of the hospital room, nevertheless I must write to you. I can't resist an impulse to write now and tell you how happy you have made me in all the beautiful years we have been together. If the worst comes to the worst, my darling, and I don't survive the operation, I want you to know you are the only woman I ever loved . . ."

"I wouldn't have thought I'd have had the courage," said June, "but perhaps the gun wasn't loaded. He was only a boy. Would you call the police, please, May?"

"Yes," said May. She picked up the gun.

The police arrived within 15 minutes. They brought a doctor with them, but June was already dead, shot through the heart at close range.

"We'll get him, Miss Thrace, don't you worry," said the Inspector. "It was a pity you touched the gun, though. Did it without thinking, I suppose?"

"It was the shock," said May. "I've never had a shock like that, not in the last forty years."

THOMAS WALSH

The Dead Past

But never once was it a dead past, not even years later, for Ned McKestin. After it happened he told Kate and Uncle Gerry the whole story, being that honest with them, but no one else. He had done it, after all. Therefore it was right that he, and he alone, should bear the burden of it. And so he did. He bore it silently, never once able to completely force it out of his mind, not even after three or four years had gone by, and then five, and then six.

He carried it by himself all that time, and his sole comfort was a feeling that he now understood the big secret of human life. To be a straight decent man one simply established straight decent habits. There it was, as simple as that. Then why did he go on worrying and worrying about it?

Yet he did. Occasionally at night, when he found himself tossing restlessly hour after hour; now and again during work hours at the store with Uncle Gerry; but here and there, every so often, he would sense that the dead past was beginning to darken and close in around him, biding its time. Very stupid. How long were the odds now that he would ever see Preston Ruby or Dandy Jack O'Hara again? Yet still . . .

Still. "What's the matter?" Kate sometimes would demand of him. "You seem awfully quiet tonight, Ned. What's wrong?"

"No, no," Ned would insist, managing to slip a reassuring arm around her shoulders. "Nothing at all, Kate. I'm just the original quiet man, maybe. I feel fine."

Because his shadow was not her problem. It was Ned's, and Ned deserved it, and could only do the best he could to live with it. Why was it impossible, however, to feel that the dead past was over and done with for him? Why did he have to have the silly idea that somehow, somewhere, even now, it still waited for him? At 24 he knew at last what really mattered to him, and what did not. The important thing was to concentrate on his new life.

And in the year 1975 the new life became more wonderful than ever. Uncle Gerry retired to the Florida Keys with Aunt Mamie and his fishing tackle and left Ned in complete charge at G. G. McKestin & Company, as a third partner.

"I've got enough," Uncle Gerry said to him that night, "and you've earned what I'm giving you, Ned. You've done better than I ever expected up here. You've settled down, thank God, and there won't be a worry in the world for me with you running things. I'm depending on you. You're the best man I ever had in the store."

And Ned was. He had great manual ability at driving a car, and as a handyman at odd jobs around the house, and at fixing almost anything in the electrical line. So by the time Uncle Gerry retired, the firm of G. G. McKestin, TV Sales and Service, 36 Main Street, was one of the biggest and best of its kind in the whole North Country. For 30 years Uncle Gerry had worked day and night to give it the most trustworthy reputation possible, and in the spring of 1975 Ned's one-third interest meant all clear sailing ahead. He and Kate had it made.

"Oh, golly," Kate said, after hugging Uncle Gerry half breathless. "I never had any desire to be rich, Ned. All I ever wanted was to have you and maybe three or four kids. There's only one thing I'd like. Do you suppose we could have our own house now?"

Because Kate had always been a great one for their own house. Until then they had lived in a small apartment over the store, where Ned had often caught her sighing wistfully at night at pictures in home magazines of the newest and most modern in kitchen equipment, or the latest fashion in bathroom fixtures. So that year they got their own house, building it in the woods out of town near the lower lake, with a spectacular view of Whiteface Mountain in back, and he and Kate had never been so happy.

They had a wonderful summer—almost every week there were cookouts or picnics with friends, or swimming and boating off their own dock—and after Christmas, Kate discovered radiantly that she was pregnant. But there were a few complications about a blood factor, and in the end, on the local doctor's advice, Ned took her down to Albany Medical Center when her time came. A few days later she had a fine healthy boy, no problems at all, and driving home to Martinsville that night, 150 miles north, Ned felt wonderfully exuberant.

He got back about ten o'clock and, still too excited to sleep, mixed a mild Scotch for himself in the kitchen. Just as he was taking his first sip the front doorbell rang. That time, when it turned out to be the dead past in brute fact, there was no premonition of any kind. A neighbor, Ned thought, wanting to hear how Kate had made out down in Albany; and with the drink in his hand and a huge happy grin on his lips, Ned walked out to the front door.

But it was not a neighbor who had seen his kitchen light on and had stopped off to hear the good news. Instead, dapper as ever, it was Dandy Jack O'Hara.

Ned stood frozen, his grin dead on his lips, and Dandy Jack allowed himself a moment of maliciously covert triumph.

"Well, what do you know?" Dandy Jack drawled, studying with his foxily wizened face and cunningly observant gray eyes the front hall behind Ned. "Sure enough. Nobody but the kid himself. Long time no see, kid. How you been?"

And he did not wait for Ned to ask him inside. He came in, at once establishing the authority between them, removed a dark green Borsalino hat with a negligent sweep of his right arm and tossed it onto the hall table.

"And you know something else?" he went on, glancing at the antique wall mirror with the gold eagle on it, at the soft green carpeting, and at the beautifully waxed old drum table with the big porcelain bowl of fresh flowers. "What a great layout you got, kid. Everything you'd ever want, eh? Guess you did all right for yourself. But how long has it been, anyway? Five or six years, ain't it?"

Ned closed the front door. He closed it numbly, one breathless catch of the heart in him, and with his ears ringing. But Dandy Jack, elegant gold sweater with a knitted white scarf at the throat, red-and-brown houndstooth slacks, and highly polished English brogues, paid no attention at all to the lack of welcome for him.

"Funny how things happen," he remarked, slipping a cigarette out of his monogrammed gold case. "Like tonight. I'm in a taproom downtown just to kill a little time, and a guy on the next stool asks the bartender if he heard how Ned McKestin's wife was getting along down in Albany. Now that's kind of an exceptional name, kid—Ned McKestin. But you know me. I start asking a question here and there to see if you're the same guy I once knew. And what do you know? You turn out to be the same Ned McKestin, all right. The kid himself. You know Preston and me often wondered what the hell ever happened to you."

Ned had to clear his throat. It felt dry as desert sand.

"Nothing much," he got out. "I did what you and Ruby did, that's all. I got out as fast and far as I could, Dandy. I bummed rides up here to an uncle I have."

"Yeah, who wouldn't?" Dandy Jack said, still studying Ned with his mockingly observant gray eyes. "Matter of fact, Preston and me got to hell and gone all the way out to the coast. No sense hanging around for trouble, the way we saw it. Got another drink in the house?"

"In the kitchen," Ned told him. "This way, Dandy."

But he was still numb, although with a slight pressing pain making itself felt at the back of his skull. Yet maybe there was nothing at all to worry about, he tried to convince himself. Why should there be? A couple of old friends meeting unexpectedly and exchanging the news with each other. No need to push the panic button. Best that he take this meeting between them just as casually as Dandy Jack was taking it.

"But it looks," Dandy Jack said, noting with approval the glistening new stove and refrigerator in the kitchen, and the alcove near the back door with the new washer and dryer, "you've done a lot better for yourself than me and Preston. We've had to scamper. I mean, a layout like this, and you married and settled down and all. What's wrong with your wife, kid?"

Ned told him, pouring out his drink.

"Well, well, well," Dandy Jack murmured. "How sweet it is. A real family man, eh? Great. But how about showing me around the house now? Like to see how you did for yourself. Come on, kid. Give me the grand tour."

So Ned showed him the whole place, upstairs and down—the basement clubroom, the basement garage with the automatic electric door. But the very odd feeling he had while doing so was that it was not Ned and Kate McKestin's new house any more. Something had happened. Something had moved in. It seemed that it was Dandy Jack's house now, and Preston Ruby's.

Back in the kitchen again, Dandy Jack settled himself comfortably and began talking about old times. It was half an hour later before he got up and reached for the Borsalino hat.

"Seem kind of nervous," he remarked casually, "but don't be. Way out in the woods here, who the hell ever saw me come in? See what I mean, kid? Mum's the word. I'm just up here for a couple of days on a little scouting trip, as you might call it. Leaving first thing tomorrow morning."

Ned followed him out to the hall, the pressure noticeably tightening around the back of his skull. He attempted to make his next question very casual.

"Oh? A little scouting trip, Dandy?"

"Well, yeah," Dandy Jack said, daintily wiping off his fingers with an immaculate linen handkerchief. "Only looking around, that's all. Just in case. But of course there's no telling when lightning could strike. You keeping clean?"

"Ever since," Ned told him tightly, to get everything clearly understood between them. "The straight and narrow, Dandy. My first and last experience. Never again."

"Atta boy," Dandy told him, with another slyly covert grin on his lips. "Nothing like it, they tell me. Still, though—we were all damned lucky to get out of it that time, weren't we? Or all of us but Rod Connihan. He's the one bought it, eh?"

Ned had opened the door, but without putting on the porch light. It was a clear frosty night with a lot of stars, but very dark off in the woods. And suddenly, against the dark, like a confused movie montage, Ned could see himself six years ago at the steering wheel of a big Buick, with Preston Ruby and Dandy Jack darting out to him from the bank entrance. Behind them, crawling and scrambling horribly, was Rod Connihan, blood all over one leg of his gray trousers.

Then more shots had rung out in the blazing stillness that seemed to have frozen all around Ned, and Connihan had sprawled full length on the pavement, at the same time dropping the bag in his hands. "Don't," Ned could hear again, and in the most breathless and anguished tones he had ever heard, "Wait a minute. Give me a hand, fellow! Don't leave me!"

But there was one more shot from inside the bank door, with Connihan jerking forward at it, and then lying rigidly still. It was only Ned who attempted to get out of the car to him, but Preston Ruby had knocked him back with a savage thrust of his right arm. "Get out of here!" Dandy Jack had begun yelling. "They got him, you damned fool. Start driving the car!"

Six years ago—and Ned was only 18.

But now Dandy Jack, out on the porch steps, turned for one more moment.

"Well, all the best," he said. "Sincere good wishes, kid—like all the postcards have it. I'll only tell Preston I saw you, but that's all. And you know what? I kind of got an idea he's going to be pretty damned glad to hear."

Alone then in the front hall, Ned leaned back against it with his eyes closed and his hands behind him. He remembered himself at 18, all alone on the city streets after his parents had died, and how that Ned had thought Connihan and Dandy Jack were just about the greatest guys in the world. They fed him, gave him a few dollars now and again, took him around—and in return he had fixed up cars for them, a lot of cars that he never inquired about, and had run their errands.

"Might have a driving job for you tomorrow," Connihan had told him one night. "You're some jockey, kid. Just love the way you can cut around a corner slick as a whistle at seventy or seventy-five. How about it?"

"Well, sure," young Ned had replied earnestly. "Of course, Rod. Where are we going to go?"

"Let you know," Rod had told him, winking brightly. "Couple of things to arrange first. Just bring the car around here right after breakfast, that's all. I got the idea it's going to go easy as pie for us."

But it had not gone easy as pie, or not for dead Rod. And alone in the hall now, still with the ugly nausea in him, Ned once more had that bad feeling in him. Somehow not his own house any more; and most likely, if he could be useful in any way to Preston Ruby, not even his own life any more.

Later on, sitting on the edge of his bed and staring off into the dark woods, Ned kept thinking about the last remark that Dandy Jack had made to him. "Pretty damned glad to hear," Ned remembered. "I'll tell Preston. I'll tell Preston, kid. I'll tell Preston."

Two days later Ned went down to Albany again, to see Kate and the baby, who were just fine although the doctor wanted her to stay on a few more days for another couple of tests. Ned did not tell her anything about Dandy Jack, however; his problem. Instead he was very cheerful with her, forcing himself; but he went out of her room finally a bit paler than usual, and with his heart heavy in him.

The thing would happen, Ned felt, just as he had always known it would happen. He had too much now, and had got it too easily. He would have to pay. When? How? Those were the only questions. For six years he had not known in what way it would happen, but he had known it would. The dead past was closing in. Preston Ruby had found him.

And that conviction was perfectly correct. It happened that night. It happened in the slight drizzle down in the parking lot, when he saw two men waiting by the car for him. The one in the trench coat and the dapperly slanted Borsalino was Dandy Jack. The one beside him was Preston Ruby.

"Thought we might run into you here," Dandy Jack began affably. "Even waited around till ten o'clock last night, Ned. Look. Preston and I thought you might like to give us a ride with you back to Martinsville. Seems like we got a little unfinished business up there. How about it?"

Ruby said nothing. He did not even bother to say hello. But then he always stuck to the bare essentials in conversation, as Ned knew. Dark hat and overcoat; dark glasses; undersized, very quick body, quick as light when required; calm and narrow white face.

"Well, I don't know," Ned began painfully. "The car's not running too hot. I'd hate it if—"

It was time for the essentials, apparently. Ruby reached over for the car door, opened it and gestured.

"Not asking you," Ruby said. "Telling you. Get in."

And Ned got in. Nothing else for it. Dandy Jack sat in front with him, and Ruby behind. When he spoke again, Ned's voice was a lot weaker and jumpier than he wanted it to be.

"What do you want to go back to Martinsville for?" he asked them. "What's the business?"

"Wait'll you hear," Dandy Jack said, in the same cheerfully persuasive manner of Rod Connihan six years ago. "Easiest thing in the world, kid. Just like old times for all three of us. Preston and I decided that maybe we'd like to board with you for a few days. Little company, see—you being alone in the house and all. Feed us real good and we might even throw you a couple of grand when it's all over. Fair enough?"

Ned took the Northway turn without answering, but it seemed to be time for essentials there too. Ruby stirred.

"Keep it right at fifty," he ordered. "We don't want no trouble with the cops."

"Yeah," Dandy Jack agreed. "We wouldn't like to get stopped by one of them troopers, kid. Your interests, understand? This way nobody's going to know we're in the car with you, just as nobody's going to know when you get us back to Martinsville tonight, either. So there ain't a thing for you to worry about, not a thing. You're all covered. All anyone knows but you, me and Preston could be up on the moon."

"Covered on what?" Ned asked grimly, discovering that his hands had become clammy. There was not only Ned McKestin to think about now. There were Kate and the baby. It was necessary to get hold of himself. The thing had happened.

"On the favor we want you to do for us," Dandy Jack said. "It's this way, see? I hear tell a lot of prominent people live in those big camps off in the woods in your neighborhood, all around the upper lake. Saw some of them the other day when I took a ride. Biggest and best one you can't even see from the road—too private. Forest Ridge, it's called. Mrs. James Devereux Murchison."

Ruby said nothing at all in the back seat—not time yet.

"And that old biddy," Dandy Jack murmured almost reverently, "has just about everything there is, the way I get it. Place in Palm Beach, in New York, in Paris, France, in Washington, and the swellest summer camp in the whole country just about a mile and a half from where you live. Paced it off the other afternoon, just to be sure. She invites people and they get flied in there on her private plane. Land on the lake, then go up the mountain on her own private elevator. Built right into it—saw it myself that afternoon, the whole thing. And three chefs, Preston, did I tell you? Meat chef, salad chef, pastry chef. Maybe thirty or thirty-five in help, but only one watchman. Only one watchman, kid. Kind of careless, huh?"

Fifty miles steady on the speedometer, Ned saw; just as ordered. A bad sign? He struggled to rouse himself.

"Yes, I've heard about it," he said. "Never saw it, though. Quite a place, eh?"

"Just lemme tell you," Dandy Jack said, pressing the most companionable of hands on Ned's right knee and squeezing in gently. "You wouldn't believe, kid. A big main house where they all go for their meals, the old biddy and her friends, and then a lot of little guest cottages all over the grounds, so everybody can be in his own place when he wants to be. Met a fellow down in New York who worked there a couple of years ago, and what he says is that the old lady herself lives in one of them guest cottages, of course the nicest one, when she's in residence, which I found out she is now. You can see her cottage right at the edge of the mountain overlooking the lake. Wonderful view from there. That's where she sleeps. Nobody else in her cottage, either. Not even a maid.

"So this guy brings her breakfast in bed one morning when her personal maid is sick, and just as he walks in with the tray she's opening a big wall safe back of some hangings. Holy smoke, he says. Like a damn jewelry store. Rings and necklaces and brooches, and whatever the hell else you can think of. Dough, even—nice fresh packets of it right from the bank.

"I see this guy around for three or four days maybe, treating him like he's the greatest guy in the world, and little by little coaxing the whole story out of him, and then I come up here to check it out for myself. Of course I never tell him my right name and after the three or four days he never sees me again. So don't worry about that part—no connection at all the way I foxed that dumb jerk. You following all this?"

Ned said nothing. Ruby said nothing. Dandy Jack inched forward and tightened his affectionate pressure on Ned's knee.

"So there it is, understand? Why keep all that dough in one pocketbook, kid? Why not spread it around? Who the hell is she to have a setup like that all to herself? Only one thing—how to get away afterwards. Damned easy to block off all the roads up in this part of the state, and to check every car that tries to get in or out for the next week. That was what Preston and me really had to figure out. But of course when I met you, and saw the kind of setup you had established for us—"

"Perfect," Ruby cut in, his dark glasses dangling wearily from his right hand, as if he had become just a little impatient with all this talk. "We don't have to try to get away afterwards. You put us up. When we get back tonight, you drive into your cellar garage before we even get out of the car, so who sees anything? Who can even guess we're inside with you? After the caper we make sure we've got a clean hour or so to get back to your place, to that basement clubroom of yours Jack told me about. We're quiet as mice in there, we pull down the shades, you don't invite anybody out to your house—and nobody ever knows a damned thing about it. How can they? So what's your complaint, McKestin?"

"Oh, he's in with us," Dandy Jack said. "He ain't a damned dummy, Preston. The kid's all right. When they stop watching the roads, which he can find out easy for us, he drives his pickup truck down to Albany on business, with a couple of big busted television sets in back—just the cabinets, though, and you and I squeezed inside them all the way down. It's like a dream, I tell you. It's all there right in our hands, kid. Don't you see?"

"G. G. McKestin and Company," Ruby murmured, swinging the dark glasses in his hand—almost happily for Preston Ruby. "Thirty-six Main Street, Sales and Service. I think it's all there, Jack. What else could we want?"

Ned took one hand off the steering wheel and wiped his mouth.

"But maybe she won't tell you how to open the safe," was all he could think of saying. "And you couldn't blow it, not with thirty or forty servants around. If you even tried—"

"Kid, kid," Dandy Jack said, with the foxy little smile on his lips. "She'll tell Preston. In about ten seconds she'll be damned glad to tell him. I give you my word."

Yes, very probably, Ned had to admit. Mrs. James Devereux Murchison, who looked like a nice ordinary old lady, absolutely no side to her. Once or twice he had seen her on the Martinsville streets, and once she had bought three television sets for the servants from G. G. McKestin. She had a nasal but rather pleasant New England twang, and had looked just like an old farmwife to Ned.

But what would she look like in that isolated cottage of hers when Ruby and Dandy Jack got through? Ned found himself wincing, not wanting even to think of it. Suppose she tried to scream or to make a fight of it? He felt the whole top of his scalp crawling.

"No," he heard himself get out breathlessly. "I don't care how easy it is. I won't do it for you! I was only a kid with Rod Connihan that time, and he didn't even explain first what you were going to do. I told Dandy the other night. I'm through with that business. I've got a wife and a child now. I won't do it!"

In the back seat Ruby whistled *Night and Day* very softly to himself. Dandy Jack chuckled.

"Look," he said. "Look, kid, with what we know about you, you figure you got any kind of a choice? Then figure again. Use your head. We're including you in."

And that night, trying uselessly to think of a way out, with Ruby and Dandy Jack quiet as quiet down in the basement clubroom, Ned realized he was in beyond question. It was not necessary for Preston Ruby even to threaten him. Why waste words? Ned was intelligent enough to see for himself. He had a wife and a child now and a new life—so he had a lot to protect. And Ruby was not a man to be moved by any consideration if you got in his way or spoiled his plans. That attempted bank robbery down in New York City might be still unsolved, but of course the police had the case still open. And just one anonymous phone call identifying the man who had driven the getaway car that day . . .

No, they had him. And he did not have them. He had been foolish enough, not knowing until too late what he was in for, to leave his fingerprints all over the steering wheel of that abandoned Buick; but they had not left a print. He could still be identified through the fingerprints, identified beyond question. But they could not. And the testimony of an accomplice in crime, Ned had read somewhere, would not be accepted in court without corroborating evidence.

No, Ruby had thought out that part too. There was not a hole anywhere, and Ned had no choice. He would do exactly as they ordered or Ruby and Dandy Jack would turn him in. And then what? Five or ten years in jail probably; G. G. McKestin & Company, after all Uncle Gerry had done for him, would never be trusted or patronized again; and Kate and the baby would be left to fend for themselves. The dead past . . .

He heard, smoking silently, two o'clock chime out from the Town Hall belfry; three o'clock; four. It was no use—nothing came to him, nothing at all. The dead past was back again, blacker and more ominous than ever. He had to accept it. Ned McKestin was caught.

Next morning he was making early coffee for himself in the kitchen when the basement door opened and dark glasses and a narrow calm face—Ruby had always been troubled with bad eyes—looked out at him.

"Think it all out yet?" Ruby inquired softly. "Made up your mind, McKestin?"

Ned, his jaws clamped, kept his two hands on the coffee pot. That was advisable. He wanted to use them at this moment more than he ever had in his life.

"Not yet," he muttered. "Not decided yet, Ruby."

"No?" Ruby said, a faint chilly smile on his lips, so obviously knowing better; just pushing the pin. "Then take your time. Go to the store today, do what you always do, and watch your step. Now bring down some coffee for Jack and me, and don't forget to lock everything up here tight as a drum when you leave. We wouldn't like any visitors, McKestin. We want things just as they are."

All that day, Ned sat numbly in his small cubbyhole of an office at G. G. McKestin's, but late in the afternoon, again with set jaws, he took Uncle Gerry's big old .38 revolver out of his desk. There was even more than Ned McKestin and his family to worry about. There was the safety of that one watchman out at Forest Ridge and the physical well-being of a nice old lady named Mrs. James Devereux Murchison. Nobody knew who was in the house with Ned now, in view of the care with which Preston had thought out the whole business. Good.

There was a spade in the basement and a lot of dark empty woods back of the house. Ned McKestin did not want to do anything like that. But if Ruby and Dandy Jack forced him to the last step . . .

But could he actually bring himself to do it? To shoot down two men, even men like Ruby and Dandy Jack, shoot them like caged rats? No, that would mean the dark past would be with him forever. Impossible. What else then? How to manage it?

Nothing came to him until he was closing the store and saw old Charlie Burger walking past on the other side of the street. Ned stopped off at the supermarket for a carton of cigarettes, then made one brief call in the pay-phone booth. It was not even necessary to disguise his voice. It seemed to him that he would never have recognized it himself. "But who's this?" Charlie Burger demanded. "And how do I know that you're not just—"

Ned hung up. He wiped his mouth shakily, the .38 still heavy in his coat pocket, and drove home. But it was a silent meal down in the basement clubroom that night, just bread and butter, hot dogs and baked beans. Then, with television on, Ruby sat there. Ned sat there. Dandy Jack sat there. Yet undoubtedly there built up a certain tension in the air: zero hour. Which meant tonight, Ned told himself, and probably late tonight, without even the least warning to him. Much better that way, Ruby would have decided. Then early tomorrow they would confront him with the *fait accompli*. And what could Ned McKestin do about it? Nothing at all. Just go back to the dead past.

About ten o'clock he went up to bed, making a bit of noise in the bathroom, then slamming the bedroom door to let them hear; but after that, very quietly in stockinged feet, he tiptoed down. He was still sitting motionless in his dark kitchen, the .38 out in plain view on his knee, when the basement door opened noiselessly and Ruby and Dandy Jack came out. It was three o'clock then, and Ned deliberately raised the .38 so that they could see it. Preston Ruby stopped dead, and behind him Dandy Jack gawked.

"Now I'm going to tell you what to do," Ned gritted. "Tell you exactly. You're going to take my car and drive down to Albany tonight without a care in the world. I've got something to say. You're not going on with this thing. You can't. Because I've—"

"Now, kid," Dandy Jack said, wetting his lips. "Don't start to act up, will you? Preston and I might be willing to cut you in for a full third, say. Could be a hundred grand right in your pocket. What the hell's the matter with you? Why can't you see the thing?"

Ruby said nothing at all; thinking it out, Ned understood, in the Ruby manner. What Ned forgot momentarily, however, was how quick Ruby could be when he once decided to act. Now his head jerked around and he jumped back, as if in blind panic, for the basement door.

"Who's that?" Ruby cried out. "What are you trying to do here, McKestin? Who's out in your back porch?"

And Ned turned to look. It was altogether instinctive, and of course altogether stupid. Behind him there came the impression that something whizzed in the air, whizzed fast and venomously, and he turned back just in time to get the kitchen hammer, the one Kate always hung up on the basement door, across the top of his head. When he fell under it, Ruby was quick as light once more, and Dandy Jack moved in savagely from the other side.

"No, wait," Ned wanted to say. "You don't understand, Ruby. I'm trying to warn you! I called the town police chief this afternoon and he's waiting for you out at Forest Ridge right now. If you show up there, his men will shoot you down like a couple of mad dogs. Listen to me!"

But it came out in a confused shout, and Ruby, getting hold of the .38, slashed down calmly but grimly with it. The last thing Ned remembered was Ruby's face over him and the .38 smashing . . .

When he came to, he was lying face down on the coolness of the linoleum floor, and the illuminated kitchen clock showed him that a half hour had passed. For some reason, Ned understood, it was a very important half hour. But why?

He lay dazedly, trying to think. At last he managed to push himself up, shaking his head, then realized that half an hour was long enough to cut through the empty woods and run over the little bridge on Conklin Creek to the Murchison place. Dandy Jack and Preston Ruby could be out there by now.

They might already have knocked out the night watchman, or killed him. But wait—wait a minute! If Chief of Police Burger had paid attention to Ned's anonymous phone call this afternoon—

Distantly, in the direction of Forest Ridge, there was a flurry of gunshots. The last few sounded deliberate, final. Ned whispered a few low words, rested against Kate's kitchen stove, and closed his eyes.

There were no more shots. But presently, from the direction of Forest Ridge once more, he could dimly hear men shouting . . .

"But I guess they never counted on somebody like Old Charlie," little Jack Holleran exulted shrilly the next morning. He was the stock boy at G. G. McKestin's, and now he danced around Ned excitedly. "Two guys, Ned. Seems like they kept shooting and shooting when he tried to warn them, and the one little guy, quick as a cat, winged Harry Johansson in the right shoulder. But Old Charlie had his rifle out and they say he can knock the spots off a playing card at a hundred yards. You hear anything yet?"

Ned, a strange pale smile on his lips, nodded. All night he had been waiting motionless in the shadows of his dark kitchen for Old Charlie to ring his front doorbell. He had not known what the delay meant. He could not imagine.

"So he caught them, Jack? Where are they now?"

"Walter Engstrom's funeral parlor," Jack crowed. "I just stole a peek at them in the back room. After they shot Harry, they both got it smack through the head, the damned fools. Dead as doornails, both of 'em!"

Ned went into his cubbyhole and sat down numbly. He had thought that when he told them about Chief Burger they would have no other recourse but to do as he said—to get out of town right away. He had tried to warn them, but they had not let him. So now . . .

He covered his eyes with both hands. But after a few moments, steady as rock now, he took three deep breaths, reached out for his desk telephone, and called Kate. At long last the past was dead.

BARBARA CALLAHAN

Don't Cry, Sally Shy

The puppets have been misbehaving lately. They refuse to speak their lines correctly. They miss cues. They sing their songs too loudly. And I've lost my best accompanist because of them.

I tried to explain to him that it was the puppets' fault, not mine. His face grew redder when I told him that. His words still sting whenever I think of them.

"If the puppets are out of control, Miss Jenkins, it is because you, the puppeteer, are out of control. You have crossed the border into fantasyland, Miss Jenkins. You attribute life and will to puppets which have neither. You had better see a doctor, and quickly."

As if to convince him that the puppets reacted on their own, the puppet Bobby Bold who had been lying limply in my hand suddenly became rigid and parroted his words: "You had better see a doctor, and quickly." As I tried to shush the naughty puppet, Bobby added, "*You* see a doctor quickly, you broken-down pulverizer of piano keys."

The accompanist's voice trembled as he told me never to call him again for a performance. He rushed toward the exit of the hall without giving me the opportunity to apologize for Bobby's brazenness. He covered his ears as I shouted that I had nothing to do with Bobby's outburst.

Bobby laughed as I shoved him into the suitcase that houses him and his companions—Grandmother Good, Sally Shy, and Fox Trot. I knew that Grandmother Good would soundly scold him after I closed the suitcase. She never tells me what happens inside their home but I can guess. Sally Shy would cry—Bobby's brashness always frightens her. Fox Trot, that sly old pet, would grin when Grandmother chastised Bobby—Fox Trot enjoys Bobby's transgressions. I believe that tricky fox encourages Bobby in his mischief.

The puppets, even Bobby, used to be quite docile, but since the automobile accident they have been maliciously asserting themselves. I know the accident disturbed them. Although they were safely cushioned in their suitcase, they were informed of all the details by Grandmother Good. I had taken Grandmother into the hospital with me when the police officer drove me there for x-rays.

I needed the sweet consolation that Grandmother Good always provided. That's why I insisted on holding her in my hand throughout the ordeal. The hospital personnel thought the puppet's presence was an indication that I had suffered a concussion when my head bumped against the windshield. It was too difficult to explain to them how soothing Grandmother is, so I didn't try.

After the x-rays I fell asleep on the gurney. When I awoke, Grandmother repeated to me the words I thought I had dreamed: "The little boy, Jack, is dead. He was killed instantly by the impact of your car."

The boy's parents visited me at my apartment. In their grief they told me they held nothing against me. They knew their son Jack, only five years old, frequently dashed across the street without looking out for cars. I brought Grandmother Good out of the suitcase and permitted her to tell the parents how I would re-dedicate my talents as a puppeteer to bringing joy to the lives of children. I sent all the fees from my next three performances to the boy's parents.

It was during the fourth performance after the accident that Bobby began interrupting the nursery rhymes that Sally Shy was reciting. It was so mean of Bobby to disturb her. My audiences always love it when Sally finally speaks. For most of every performance she hides behind Grandmother's skirt. When she grows weary of the taunts of Bobby and Fox Trot, she triumphs by shaming them with her superb memory and diction. The children cheer when Sally recites. So many of the children must identify with her shyness.

She had begun with the rhyme "Jack, be nimble, Jack, be quick" when Bobby pushed her aside and chanted, "Jack can't be nimble, Jack can't be quick, Jack's a broken candlestick." The children, thinking Bobby's rudeness was part of the act, laughed and laughed. Sally cried onstage because she knew that Jack was the dead boy's name.

Fox Trot saved the day by doing the special dance in which he prances around the stage while whisking away Bobby's ball and Grandmother's mixing spoon with his bushy tail. I can always depend on Fox Trot to improvise when it's necessary.

When those awful telephone calls came in the middle of the night, I slipped Fox Trot on my hand to let him answer. I was sure he'd know how to thwart the caller. He is so shrewd that he had only to listen to four of the calls before he knew who was making them. He determined that those terrible words, "If you had stopped sooner, the boy would still be alive," came from a rival puppeteer who desperately wanted all the engagements I was receiving.

"I'll call the cops on you, Mary Reedy," he shouted. "I know it's you making these calls. It's the kind of lowdown trick a fox like me can spot right away."

Mary Reedy was so startled that she dropped the phone on a table before hanging up. She never called again.

"She's just trying to ruin your nerves, kiddo, so she can get your jobs. But amateurs can't shake up real pros like us, can they, kiddo?" Fox Trot cackled.

"No, they can't shake us up, dear pet," I told him. To prove it, I spent the rest of the evening sewing new outfits for the entire puppet family. Sally loved her dress, Grandmother was pleased with her apron, and Fox Trot strutted happily in his new feathered hat. But Bobby, vicious Bobby Bold, how he loves to torment me! He deliberately ruined the sweatshirt I had so painstakingly made for him. I had lettered the number 3 on it. When I inspected my handiwork the next morning, I saw what he had done. He had put the number 5 next to the 3. His shirt read 35. When I saw that number, I collapsed on a chair. The last time I had seen 35 was on the bloodstained sweatshirt worn by Jack, the little boy I had hit.

His cruel prank upset me so much that I could not fulfill the engagement I had at the Hill School. I could only sit sobbing in a chair. Grandmother Good clamored to be let out of the suitcase. She wanted so much to comfort me. I could hear Sally Shy crying and Fox Trot yelling, "Don't let him get you down, kiddo," but I could not move from the chair.

When the doorbell rang, I forced myself to answer it. The detective who had been so kind to me on the day of the accident was standing in the hall. I hated for him to see me looking so forlorn, so I ran into my bedroom and shut the door. I heard him walk into the kitchen. In a few minutes he knocked on my door.

When I didn't open it, he entered the room carrying a cup of tea. "My mother always told me that tea is an excellent remedy for whatever ails a person," he said.

I took the cup from him and we went into the living room. He didn't seem to hear all the noises coming from the suitcase.

"I had some time off this morning," he said, "and I thought I'd like to see you perform. I knew you were going to be at the Hill School, so I went to the auditorium. The children were very disappointed when you didn't come. I thought perhaps you were sick, so I decided to drop by."

"I'm glad you came," I told him after a few sips of tea.

When I had finished it, he handed me my coat.

"Let's go," he said.

The puppets abruptly stopped arguing in the suitcase to listen to him. I heard nothing but my heart beating.

"Go where?" I asked.

"To a restaurant."

"Restaurant?"

"Yes, I know a fine place. You need some lunch."

As I put on my coat, I heard Fox Trot whispering advice. "Charm him, kiddo, charm him. It's good to have a cop for a friend."

I picked up the suitcase and headed for the door.

"Why are you taking that?" the detective asked.

"The puppets are in it. I take them everywhere. They'll be upset if I leave them here."

He laughed, but didn't attempt to dissuade me. He carried the suitcase to his car.

As we drove to the restaurant, I tried so often to ask him something, but I was too embarrassed. I had to bring out Sally Shy to ask him for me.

"You name, nice man, is Clark?" she asked.

"No, it's Mark," he said, "Mark Evans. And your name is?"

"Sally Shy," I answered.

Sally cringed when he reached over and lifted her off my hand.

"She's cute," he said, "but I like *you* better, Miss Jenkins."

"You may call me Alice," I told him softly.

I gently tucked Sally into the suitcase. Grandmother Good would take care of her.

It wasn't until dessert that Mark discussed the accident. He said I might be suffering from a delayed reaction to the shock. He told me the best cure would be to keep busy. "Above all," he advised, "don't cancel performances the way you did today."

I nodded in agreement. I was touched by his concern and wanted to tell him that. But I couldn't until we had a glass of wine after lunch. And before I knew it I was telling him all my troubles about the puppets misbehaving.

He didn't laugh as I expected, nor did he become angry with me as the accompanist had. He simply said, "You'll have to be more firm with the puppets. Remember, you're in the driver's seat."

I must have blanched at the expression "driver's seat" because he patted my hand. He asked me to forgive him for his poor choice of words.

We took a long walk after lunch, the first of many walks we took in the course of our dating. It would have been awkward to carry the suitcase with the puppets during the walks, so I just put Grandmother Good into my pocketbook. Whenever I felt nervous, I would slide my hand into Grandmother's arms and she would give me a reassuring squeeze.

Although I am 30, I had never dated anyone more than twice. Somehow I could never feel relaxed in a dating situation. Mark seemed to sense this. He never forced himself on me. He was patient, oh, so patient. For the three weeks we saw each other every day, I had never been happier.

Aside from Grandmother Good, the puppets hated to see me so contented. They performed well but they resented not going out with Mark and me. One night after we had come home from a marvelous concert, Mark sat very close to me on the sofa. I was delighted and rested my head on his shoulder.

Suddenly I heard the muffled voice of Bobby Bold coming from the suitcase. He sounded so distressed that I had to release him. Mark seemed annoyed when I jumped up from the sofa to get the vicious puppet. I apologized and told him that Bobby would have to have his say or he would give me no peace.

I asked Bobby what was bothering him. He turned to Mark and yelled, "If you're thinking of marrying sweet little Alice Jenkins, flatfoot, come see me, I could tell you some things about her that would curl your hair."

I heard Grandmother Good gasp and Sally begin to cry and Fox Trot cackle. Bobby had gone so far out of bounds that there was only one thing to do. I slapped him. I slapped him so hard that he flew off my hand. I went to pick him up to hit him again, but Mark restrained me.

"He's a monster," I sobbed, "a vicious monster."

Mark made me tea and sat with me until I fell asleep. When I awoke, I felt cold and numb. I opened the suitcase and saw Bobby sleeping peacefully, not at all affected by what he had said. I reached for Grandmother, but Fox Trot climbed onto my hand.

"Pull yourself together, kiddo. Don't let the little brat get you down. Play your cards right. Be foxy and you'll have that guy eating out of your hand."

"But how?" I asked. "After Bobby's outburst Mark will never want to see me again."

"Fret not. Call him up at the office and tell him how unnerved you've been. Tell him you haven't been able to sleep at night since the accident."

"But I do sleep, Fox Trot."

"Yeah, we know that. You sleep like the dead."

"Don't say 'dead,' you horrible beast."

"Okay, okay, but you do go out like a light."

"Shut up, shut up, I tell you."

"All right, kiddo. But just do what I told you. Call that guy and cry a lot on the phone. He's a pushover for the dependent type. I know. Tell him you need him and he'll be back in a flash. And be sure to cry a lot."

"I can't pretend to cry," I told him.

"Then get Sally Sob to cry for you. It's what she does best."

I gave Fox Trot a big kiss. I knew he liked it. He acts hardboiled, but underneath his sly exterior he's as soft as kitten fur.

The next morning, after I had dialed the phone, I put Sally on my hand. I started the conversation but let Sally talk after I detected a coldness in Mark's voice.

Sally was superb. She never cried better.

She was so good that Mark promised to take me for a drive right after work.

I spent the afternoon soaking in a bubble bath, doing my nails, and setting my hair in a long flowing style. The red dress that I had thought too provocative after I'd bought it seemed to be the perfect selection for my afternoon date.

Mark whistled appreciatively when he saw me. He took my yellow coat from the living-room closet, but I didn't think it blended well with my dress, so I went into the bedroom to get my fur jacket. When I returned, Mark handed me the puppets' suitcase.

"Aren't you going to bring your friends?" he asked.

"No, Mark, I don't need them any more."

"Great," he smiled.

We had a beautiful ride, through the River Drive, out into the country, and back toward town for dinner at our favorite restaurant. I slid close to Mark in his car and rested my head on his shoulder. I was so happy and relaxed that I closed my eyes to visualize him pouring the wine out of the little carafe at the restaurant.

I was jolted out of my reverie by the sudden slamming of brakes. I opened my eyes and screamed.

"It's nothing," Mark said. "A cat crossed in front of me."

I quickly looked toward the pavement. I didn't see a cat, but I did see Jack's house. We had stopped at the exact spot where I had hit the little boy. The house was not on the way to the restaurant.

"Why are we here, Mark?" I cried.

"Somebody wants to talk to me," he answered.

"The boy's parents?"

"No," he said, "a young lady."

He reached into his pocket. When he showed me what he held, I started to tremble. He had Sally Shy in his hand. He must have taken her out of the suitcase when I went in the bedroom to get my jacket. He slipped Sally onto my hand. Each time I pulled Sally off, he pushed her back on.

"She has nothing to tell you," I said.

"I think she does," he said quietly.

"I do, I do," sobbed Sally.

"Don't say anything," I begged her.

But the poor distraught puppet didn't listen to me. She blurted out those terrible words.

"She was drunk," Sally choked. "Drunk. She had been drinking just the way she always does before a performance. When the little boy ran out into the street, she didn't even see him."

Then Sally cried as I had never heard her cry before. Mark leaned over and removed her from my hand.

"Don't cry, Sally Shy," he told me. "I'm sorry I had to do this, but I hate sloppy work. The procedure in an accident such as yours wasn't followed through. You didn't have a blood test at the hospital, so the thought occurred to me that you could have been drunk when you hit that boy. I had to find out."

On the way to the police station I tried to explain to Mark that I had wanted to tell the truth as soon as it happened, but Fox Trot wouldn't let me. The sly fox told me, "Act like you bumped your head on the windshield. They'll have to take x-rays of you at a hospital. When the x-rays are finished, they'll let you lie down and rest. If they don't, carry on, act hysterical. They'll give you a needle to make you sleep and then forget to give you a blood test. Fake them out, kiddo, fake them out."

Mark drove the rest of the way in silence. I needed someone to talk to me. So I listened very hard and soon I heard Grandmother Good calling to me from my apartment. She told me that everything would be all right. Bobby Bold said that I got what I deserved, so I ignored him. As usual Fox Trot voiced what was in my mind.

"That Mark's a sly one," he said. "I'll tell you something, kiddo, not all foxes are puppets."

WILLIAM BRITTAIN

The Second Reason

Keach flicked a blob of wet cement onto the base of the cinder block, slathered it with his trowel, then hoisted the block laboriously into place. As he snugged the block home with taps from the handle of his trowel, a bead of sweat dribbled from his chin to the ground. It disappeared almost at once, half evaporating into the dry desert air and half soaking into the baked, hard-packed earth.

Damn it all, it was hot! But then, he hadn't expected a picnic. Not at $200 for a single day's work at a time when nearly everybody in the building trades was screaming for something—anything—in the way of jobs.

Keach wiped sweat from his forehead with the back of his hand and looked about at the landscape. Flat, except for the hills away off to the north. A *playa*, the bed of a lake long since dried up in the blasting heat of the desert sun. Little cracks in the flatness where the parched earth, bullet-hard, had shrunk in on itself. Hell must be something like this, Keach figured—hell or the far side of the moon.

Oh, there were some things to break the monotony of the land. His flatbed truck with the piles of cinder blocks and the drums of water. The three men taking their ease in folding chairs under the shade of a canvas fly, with their fancy new car parked nearby. And off to his left there was even a mound of rock that looked for all the world like a deck of cards with one card in the middle sticking out a little way. I bet it's an ace, thought Keach, and the dealer's about to hand it to himself.

He shook his head angrily, calling himself all kinds of a fool for seeing a card game in a hunk of rock. But the emptiness was getting to him. The truck and the car. The men sitting there with their iced drinks. Himself. That was all there was.

Except for the wall.

Ten feet long and eight feet high, except for the one corner he hadn't finished yet. It ran almost due north and south with its flat eastern face on a line between holes, each about three inches in diameter, that had been drilled into the earth twelve feet apart. The holes were at least a foot deep—Keach had stuck the handle of his trowel into one without reaching bottom.

Oh, the wall was a good one, all right. One of the best walls Keach had ever built. Two cinder blocks thick, and dead plumb from top to bottom. Why, that wall would stop a charging rhinoceros dead in its tracks, or even a bull elephant. There wasn't anything that could bring down the wall. Except—

Except what was it for?

Walls were supposed to keep things out, or in. Or sometimes they were made to enclose an area, but that required corners or curves. They could even provide beauty, as in a garden or around a public building.

But this wall just didn't qualify for anything Keach could think of. There it stood in the middle of the dry lake like some monument erected by a prehistoric tribe. A man could walk clear around it in a few seconds, and the dreary view on one side was exactly like that on the other. Keach remembered a movie he'd seen in which beings from outer space had erected a monolith in the middle of a tribe of apes. The thing had resembled an enormous slab of black marble, its shape not unlike his own wall.

Could the thing he was building be some kind of landmark or signal for creatures from another planet? The dry lake would be an ideal place for a flying saucer to land—remote, perfectly flat. Besides, when the three men had come to ask about his services and give their specifications, they'd been especially interested in how much he watched TV. When he said he didn't own one and only watched at a friend's house once a month or so, they'd obviously been happy, and the deal was closed on the spot.

Things from outer space. In his mind's eye Keach imagined monstrous beings with leathery green skin and reptilian eyes plodding across the lake bed toward the distant hills. He turned around suddenly, half expecting the shapes of the men behind him to waver and begin to change.

But they hadn't changed. The fat one sat with his belly almost out to his knees, drinking deeply from a glass beaded with moisture. The tall thin one was next to him, leaning forward and conversing in a low hum of words. And the shortest one was lounging in a folding deck chair, probably asleep, with his hat over his eyes.

Mr. Fat, Mr. Tall, and Mr. Short. The names were as good as any since Keach didn't know their real ones. They'd just walked in off the street, asked a few questions, and bang!—Keach had a $200 deal just for a long night's drive, followed by a single day's work building the wall. What did he care whether they came from California as their license plate indicated, or from the moon? And it wasn't as if he was doing something wrong. There was no law against building a wall in the desert, was there?

But what's it for, Keach? his brain demanded.

Annoyed with himself, he stomped off toward his truck. First he took a canteen from the shade behind one wheel and drank deeply. He'd had more than a gallon, and here it was just shy of noon. That desert sun did suck the moisture out of a man. Then from under the flat bed he drew out a metal trough, dented and layered with scales of hardened cement.

"Got to mix up a new batch," he said to Mr. Fat, who waved in reply. He dug cement from an open bag with a shovel and followed that with sand from a pile on a tarp near the cab. As he scooped out his first bucket of water from the one drum which hadn't been emptied, he realized that the low hum of speech from the shade under the canvas fly was coming to him clearly through the dry desert air.

"Are you sure this is going to work?" Mr. Tall was asking Mr. Fat. "Isn't he going to notice—"

"Notice what?" Fat answered. "You don't think our big hero will all of a sudden get ambitious and come out here ahead of time, do you? Hell, he always leaves the scut work to us. And when he finally is ready, the light won't exactly be in his favor. Say, you aren't having any second thoughts about this, are you?"

"No, of course not," Mr. Tall pouted. "First time we get to do something where there's a decent amount of money involved, he decides to get rid of us and bring in his own crew. It isn't fair."

"Right. And his yapping about how he's going to tell the chief just because we called him a damn no-good— It's not going to be easy for us to get work after that."

Keach caught himself holding the mixing hoe motionless and staring at the men. With a start he began stirring the slithery liquid concrete which was gray ooze around the blade of the hoe as it sloshed in the trough.

Mr. Short had joined the other two men by this time. Mr. Fat held him by the shoulder with one hand, while with the other he pointed to a spot some 20 yards from the wall.

"I'll be right there, grinding away," he said. "You two will be up in the chopper, same as always. Everything nice and natural."

"Bu-bu-bu-but won't they know it wa-wa-was us?" stuttered Mr. Short.

"How're they going to know?" asked Mr. Fat. "So long as we keep our stories straight, that is. We just say we figured it was something special that some other crew rigged up without telling us. How were we to know it wasn't a phony?"

"Y-yeah, I suppose," said Mr. Short dubiously.

"C'mon, it can't miss." Mr. Fat gestured toward the wall. "There it is. It's real, and everything's going to happen just the way we planned. And nobody's going to catch on ahead of time because we're the only three who are dumb enough to come out here."

"And him?" Mr. Short nodded in Keach's direction.

"He's not only dumber than us," said Mr. Fat. "He's yellow too. I'll put the fear in his bones, don't you worry."

Mr. Tall gave a harsh dry laugh. "Big hero came through the first reason and picked up more loot than we see in a year. So now that he's making it big, he tries to drop us after all the things we showed him about the business. But I think he's going to have some rough sledding with the second reason."

"Gentlemen," said Mr. Fat, raising his glass, "I give you—the second reason."

"Y-yeah, man!" giggled Mr. Short. "The se-se-second reason. BaLOOM!"

The little area where the men sat was swept by a wave of laughter. And then the laughing was cut short as Mr. Fat raised his hand. His gaze locked ominously with that of Keach.

"Just finish the wall, Mr. Keach," said Mr. Fat in a low growl.

Less than an hour later the wall was complete. As Mr. Fat doled out the $200 in tens and twenties into Keach's gritty palm, he spoke in a patronizing manner, as if addressing a small child.

"Your work, Mr. Keach, is A-one. And now that you're finished you should keep in mind that we know a lot about you—where you live and work and all—while you don't know anything about us. So maybe you'd just better forget about what you did here today and look on the two hundred as found money."

"Forget? But—"

"Forget, Mr. Keach." The voice was cold, without emotion. "Too good a memory can be a dangerous thing." Mr. Fat's eyes were as grim and menacing as the dry flatness of the desert.

With the money wadded into a ball in his pocket, Keach climbed into the cab of the truck, slammed it into gear, and roared off across the lake bed. The air streaming through the truck's open windows was hot and acrid, but he felt goosebumps rise on his shoulders, and a cold shiver ran up his spine.

Late that night back in town, with the truck put away and his body cleansed by a hot shower, Keach decided to use a part of his $200 to get drunk. He'd earned every nickel of the money, and now he needed the soothing effect of whiskey.

The bar was dark, quiet, with only a few midweek customers. On a stool at one end of the mahogany strip, Keach downed a pair of shots—one, two, just like that. He knew this was going to be a bad drunk. During the good drunks—when a big construction project was in the offing or a new labor contract had been negotiated—he sipped his whiskey slow and easy. But when times were bad, when he was angry or scared or worried, he gulped.

He looked at his image in the mirror and seemed to see Mr. Fat's eyes boring into his.

Why in hell would anyone build a wall out in the middle of the desert?

The aproned bartender switched on the TV at the other end of the narrow room.

". . . and now for some scenes from next week's adventure of Barney Kalso, Private Eye."

Two men, pummeling each other. Than a close-up of a hand holding a pistol. The pistol roared twice, and there was a high-pitched scream from off camera. Finally a car plunging in flames from a bridge.

"Too damn much violence," said a boozy voice from a booth. "See if you can find the boxing, huh, Vic?"

"Leave it there," said a powerfully built kid wearing a leather jacket and motorcycle boots. "I wanna see the movie coming up. It's got Cesar Romero and Betty Grable."

The bartender shrugged and moved away from the set as the show's final credits rolled. Prefacing the station break, a filmed commercial began on the screen.

"The Cheetah!" The announcer might have been broadcasting the end of the world, his voice was so deep and serious and compelling. "America's newest small car."

No music. Complete silence as the camera made a half circle about some dimly lit place. Then the camera lifted and there was a bright yellow semicircle on the screen. A blare of trumpets on the sound track.

"Sunrise," the announcer went on. "Time to get up and go—with Cheetah!"

A small dark spot appeared directly in front of the rising sun. Gradually it grew bigger and became an automobile.

"The Cheetah. America's move to economy. Tested at thirty-two miles per gallon on the open road . . ."

The car was nearer now, cruising along a shaft of sunlight, a tiny green insect getting larger every second.

". . . and twenty-four miles per gallon in city driving."

The cameraman had switched to a wide-angle lens, and the objects in the foreground of the picture jumped into sharp focus at the same time.

Keach shook his head. It was amazing what those TV cameramen could do. And then he froze.

The drink in his hand sloshed onto the bar. No. Yes, there it was. Off to the side of the screen.

That rock—the one that looked like a deck of cards. He's spent the whole day right at the spot where the film of the car had been taken.

An overhead view of the Cheetah, now traveling along the ray of light across the cracked surface of the lake bed.

"Fuel economy. Your first reason to buy the exciting new Cheetah!"

A huge sheet of paper stretched between upright posts occupied the whole TV screen. Splashed across the paper in large red letters:

Reason #1
Fuel Economy
Buy CHEETAH

And then the car, doing at least 70, tore through the sign with a growl of power, tearing the paper to shreds. The driver skidded to a halt a hundred yards beyond.

Keach's mind screamed with things remembered.

The deck-of-cards rock.

The three-inch-wide holes.

The wall, with its solid cinder-block surface facing due east—toward the rising sun.

The announcer continued: "You've seen our film of Reason Number One for buying the new Cheetah. Next week on this same channel we will show you Reason Number Two. Be sure to watch."

Keach visualized the driver—whose name he didn't even know—smashing unsuspectingly into the paper sign, expecting thin air behind it.

But he, Keach, had built a wall—a solid wall in the middle of the desert.

And if he said anything? If he could warn the unknown driver before the second reason was filmed? What would Mr. Fat do then?

As Keach leaned across the bar, he could feel the raw whiskey churning in his stomach and burning his throat. His groan of outrage, shame, fear, became a high keening in the small barroom.

And from the TV came the announcer's voice in a final message:

"Buy Cheetah. It's a hit!"

ELLERY QUEEN

Murder Dept.: Half a Clue

M orning. When the doctor left, Ellery ran down to the corner drug store.

"The doctor wants dad to start on the antibiotic as soon as possible, Henry," Ellery said to the owner of the pharmacy. "Can you fill this while I wait?"

"Sure, these come all made up," said Henry Brubuck. "Albert, fill this for Mr. Queen right away, will you?"

The twins, Albert and Alice, who like their stepfather were registered pharmacists, were busy behind the high partition of the Prescription Department. Albert took Inspector Queen's prescription and greeted Ellery heartily; but Alice, whose eyes were on the red side, merely gave him a wan smile. "Sorry your father's sick, Ellery."

"It's some virus or other."

"The neighborhood's full of viruses. And that reminds me." The old pharmacist went over to his soda fountain and drew some water. "Forgot to take my own antibiotic dose this morning."

Henry Brubuck dipped into his gray store jacket for a little white box. It had some yellow-and-green capsules in it; he swallowed one and returned the box to his pocket. "Druggist, heal thyself, eh, Ellery?" he chuckled. "My doctor says I'm the worst patient he has."

"I live with an old coot, Henry, who'll give you cards and spades," said Ellery dolefully. "Thanks, Albert. Charge it, will you?" And he hurried out.

The moment Ellery was gone, Alice set the bottle of cough mixture down on the prescription counter and said tensely, "Dad, I've got to talk to you. *Please?*"

"All right, honey," sighed Henry Brubuck; he knew what was coming. "Take over, Albert. We won't be long."

"Good luck, sis," said Albert in a low voice. But his twin was already running up the stairs that led from the back room to the Brubuck apartment over the store.

Her stepfather followed patiently. A man did his best to bring up his dead wife's children, he thought, but somehow he always seemed to do the wrong thing. The twins were one problem after another; and he rarely saw his other stepson, Alvin, who was a used-car salesman, since Alvin's marriage.

"It's about Ernie again?" the old man asked his stepdaughter.

"Yes, daddy," said Alice passionately. "And please don't put me off any longer. I tell you I love Ernie. I want to marry him—"

"—but he won't marry you unless $10,000 goes along with you," her stepfather said dryly. "Some romantic! Honey, what kind of fellow is it who makes a package deal out of a marriage proposal? What kind of life would you have with a loafer who's even been in trouble with the police?"

Alice burst into heartbroken tears. "You think I'm Elizabeth Taylor or something? I know what I look like, daddy. If you don't give Ernie that money, he'll marry Sadie Rausch. I'll *die* if he does—I'll do something—something *desperate.*"

Old Brubuck put his arm around the sobbing girl. "Don't talk like that, baby. Believe me, you're better off without him."

Alice raised her swollen eyes. "Then you won't give me the money? That's final?"

"It's for your own good, honey. You'll meet some nice boy—"

Alice grew very quiet. Then, just as quietly, she went back downstairs. Henry Brubuck stood where he was, appalled. There had been a look on his stepdaughter's face . . .

Noon. Old Brubuck was jarred out of his after-lunch nap by the eruption of the extension phone. Half asleep, he reached over from the bed and picked up the receiver just as the phone was answered in the Prescription Department downstairs.

"Brubuck's Pharmacy," he heard Albert say.

The old man was about to hang up when a heavy voice said, "Gimme Albert Brubuck. This is the book store."

Book store? thought Henry Brubuck, suddenly alert. Albert hadn't been inside a book store since leaving college. Had he been secretly playing the horses again? The pharmacist listened. He was right; it was Albert's bookie.

"Listen, welsher," the bookie said. "You think I'm gonna carry you forever? You're into me for eight grand, Pill Boy, and I want my dough. *Now.*"

"Wait, wait," Albert said; his stepfather could tell that the boy was badly frightened. "So you'll have your goons work me over, Joe. How will that get you your money? Give me just another few days, Joe. What do you say?"

"Is this another one of your runarounds?"

"Joe, I swear, I'm working on the old man." Henry Brubuck could almost hear Albert sweat. "A few days more and I've got it made. How about it? All right, Joe?"

"Okay. But I don't get my eight grand by Friday night, kid, you start praying."

The pharmacist waited until his stepson hung up before replacing the bedroom receiver. So he's working on me, is he? thought the old man. Poor Albert. He wasn't a bad boy—except for the horses. Henry Brubuck had settled a great many of his younger stepson's gambling debts before putting his foot down; he had had to put a stop to it.

Then what had Albert meant . . . ?

Evening. The old pharmacist trudged upstairs from his drug store and stopped in his kitchen to have a look at the roast that Alice had in the oven. He could hear his other stepson, Alvin, and Alvin's wife talking in the living room. Alvin had phoned with a rather ashamed, "Hiya, pop!" to invite himself and Gloria to dinner. The old man wondered what Alvin's wife was after this time.

He found out immediately—Gloria had a penetrating voice.

"Well, then you just ask that old miser *again*, Alvin! I'm not letting you pass up this chance to buy into the car agency for a measly $15,000!"

"But pop thinks they're in trouble and are out to take me," Alvin said feebly.

"Pop thinks! What does he know about it? Are you going back on your promise to me, Alvin Brubuck?"

"No, Gloria," said Alvin in a harassed way. "I told you I'd ask pop again, and I will. Do you have to keep hacking away at me?"

"And you remind him that most of the money he's got is really yours and the twins'. You *make* him give you your share, or else!"

"All right, all right!" shouted Henry Brubuck's other stepson. "I'll do whatever you want! Just stop hounding me!"

The Following Night. "I don't quite get what's bothering you, Henry," Inspector Queen said. He was in pajamas and bathrobe, still nursing his virus, but Ellery had long since given up trying to keep him in bed. "Okay, you won't buy Alice this crumbum the poor kid's set on marrying; you won't pay off any more of Albert's gambling debts—and don't worry about that bookie's threats, I'll take care of *him*; you won't finance the partnership Alvin's wife wants because you're convinced it's a bad deal. Seems to me you're acting like a responsible parent. What's the problem?"

"The problem, I think, dad," said Ellery, frowning, "is that Henry is afraid for his life."

The Inspector stared. "You're kidding, Henry."

The pharmacist shook his head. "I wish I were, Inspector."

"But *murder*? All right, they're not your children. But the twins aren't delinquents, and no matter what a shrew Alvin's wife is, Alvin himself is a hardworking boy—"

"If you're right about this, Henry," Ellery said, "there's a simple way to discourage murder for profit. I take it you have a will, and that Alice, Albert, and Alvin get everything?"

"Of course."

"Then simply write a new will cutting them out. No profit, no danger, period."

Old Brubuck shook his head. "I can't do that, Ellery. I promised their mother on her deathbed that they'd inherit. Most of what I have she left me. Her children are entitled to it when I die."

"Drat it, Henry," the Inspector said testily, "if you're so sure they're out to kill you, give them the money now."

"I can't. It would bankrupt me. I'd even lose my drug store." Brubuck laughed bitterly. "I'm losing my mind, too! I clean forgot to take my last dose of antibiotic. Ellery, could I have a little water?"

While Ellery went for some, the Inspector said, "Blast it all, Henry, I'm afraid there's nothing I can do *before* a crime is committed. That's the law."

"Besides which, Henry, you're holding something back," Ellery said as he returned with a glass of water. "I know you wouldn't dream up a murder plot merely on what you've told us. There's something more definite, isn't there?"

"I can't believe it yet," Brubuck nodded miserably. He fished a yellow-and-red capsule out of his little white box without even looking at it, and swallowed it with a sip of water. "But the fact is, some poison's been taken from a pharmaceutical cabinet in my back room."

The druggist named the poison, and the Queens exchanged grave glances; it was lethal in very small quantities, and it brought death on the gallop.

"I know it was stolen some time during the past thirty-six hours," Brubuck continued. "I even know which one of my stepchildren stole it, though I can't prove it."

"Why didn't you tell us this before?" the Inspector exploded. "Which one of them stole it?"

The pharmacist said with sudden difficulty, "It . . . was . . . Al—" and stopped with a gasp.

He began to choke and claw the air. An inhuman change came over his face. His body convulsed. His knees collapsed. Then, incredibly, he was spread out on the Queens' floor like a bludgeoned beef.

"*Dead.*" The Inspector, ghastly pale, looked up from the pharmacist's corpse. "Murdered in front of our eyes. Do you smell the poison, son?"

"It was in that capsule he just swallowed." Ellery snatched the white box from the quiet hand and opened it. It was empty. "It was his last dose, all right," he said wildly. "Why didn't I realize—?"

"Killed him as soon as the capsule dissolved." Inspector Queen was still dazed. "One of the three filled an empty capsule with the poison and managed to substitute it for the last antibiotic capsule in Henry's box. If he'd only lived long enough to finish the name . . ."

"Maybe," Ellery said suddenly, "it doesn't matter."

"But son, all he got to say was 'Al—'. He could have meant Al*ice* or Al*bert* or Al*vin*. That's only half a clue—the useless half!"

"Half a clue, dad, is better than no clue."

The Inspector shot erect. "Ellery Queen, do you mean to stand here and say that Henry Brubuck drops dead at our feet, and practically as he hits the floor you know who killed him?"

Ellery said, "Yes."

CHALLENGE TO THE READER
Which of his three stepchildren murdered Henry Brubuck? And how did Ellery know?

Ellery explained that while he had been in the dead man's pharmacy the previous morning, waiting for the Inspector's prescription to be filled, he had witnessed Henry Brubuck take one of his own antibiotic capsules from the box—a yellow-and-*green* capsule.

"Just now," Ellery went on, "we both saw him swallow a yellow-and-*red* capsule from the box. Too bad Henry didn't bother to look at it—he knew there was only one left, or he'd certainly have noticed the discrepancy in color. And it all happened so fast I didn't have time to recall it.

"The question is, then: Which of Brubuck's stepchildren—he stated as a fact that he knew it was one of them—substituted a home-made yellow-and-red capsule containing poison for the last of the yellow-and-green manufactured capsules containing the antibiotic.

"Well, would a pharmacist, with a professional's knowledge of standard antibiotic preparations, have used *a different-colored capsule* when the object was to trick the victim, himself a pharmacist, into swallowing it? Hardly. Only a *non*-pharmacist could be guilty of such ignorance of oversight.

"So the poisoner can't be either of the twins, A*lice* or A*lbert*, because both are registered pharmacists. Therefore it has to be the car salesman, A*lvin* . . . at the instigation, I'm afraid, of that virago he's married to!"

GERALD TOMLINSON

The K-Bar-D Murders

Robert Ollinger, the syndicated columnist, swept into the reception area of his K Street office like a dreadnought under full steam. A hulking, combative man of 54, one of the most powerful journalists in Washington, his column *Capitol Hot Line* ran in 112 newspapers from Maine to California. Ollinger dredged up news, molded news, insinuated news, and made news.

In 25 years of investigative reporting he had left a host of enemies in his wake. "The terrible price of telling the truth," he explained to David Susskind on late-night television. "I'm America's witness at large, David. The Diogenes of the Potomac." After his 1959 exposé of TV's soap-opera scandals, a wave of angry mail had nearly swamped his office, but Ollinger survived the deluge. His twelve staff members called their K Street office "The House of Storm."

Over the years a dozen foes had thrown punches at him. A critic from San Francisco had tried to run him through with a sword. An unidentified woman from Albuquerque had mailed him a plastic bomb. A slight, soft-spoken hairdresser from Indianapolis had sprayed .25-caliber bullets in his direction. Each time he had escaped without serious injury.

But his enemies were everywhere. So were his paid informants and his electronic bugs. "An investigative reporter," *Time* quoted him as saying, "needs the eyes of Argus, the ears of Panasonic, and the cold playback capability of Memorex." He had many secret sources of information. "More secret sources than the Nile," his fourth wife Cleo was fond of burbling at Georgetown dinner parties.

Ollinger had just returned from a meeting in the basement of an abandoned warehouse in Bethesda, Maryland, where he had talked secretly with Vice-Presidential press secretary Wayne Davidson. Ollinger had given Davidson the code name of "Batman." A brash, spiteful fellow with narrow shoulders and bulging eyes, Davidson was trying to link Steven M. Arcato, the wealthy Hyattsville attorney, to a local Satanism ring, after having failed to wring Arcato dry in an extortion squeeze.

The phone in Ollinger's reception area jangled. Sally Pickerel, his secretary, reached for it, but the columnist grabbed it from under her darting fingers.

"Ollinger here."

An operator answered. "I have a collect call for Mr. Robert Ollinger from"—

she paused for an instant, then finished the sentence flatly, with no change in her voice—"from Mr. Napoleon Bonaparte in Honotassa, New Mexico. Will you accept the charges?"

Ollinger had no source with the code name "Napoleon Bonaparte" and no regular contacts in Honotassa. His nearest secret source was "Chief Thundercloud" in Santa Fe. But he did have a policy of taking unexpected phone calls. He took them because one such call early in his career had led him to a small but newsworthy scandal in the Department of Health, Education, and Welfare.

"Put the man on."

Ollinger nodded curtly to his secretary, retired to his soundproof inner office, and lifted the receiver.

The man from Honotassa spoke in a pleasant Western drawl. "*Merci, monsieur. Bonjour.*"

"Talk English," Ollinger snapped. "My French is terrible."

"Mine too," the man said. "I never could get the accent right. Corsica, you know. Douglas County. Cold, cold, cold up there, especially this time of year. A hundred and sixty miles from Pierre as the crow flies."

"What's on your mind, Emperor?"

A sigh. "Field Marshal Kutuzov. Moscow winters."

"That does it, Bony. So long." Ollinger started to hang up.

"No, wait." Napoleon's voice rose imploringly from the earpiece. "Listen to me, Mr. Ollinger. Your life is in danger."

Ollinger grunted. "So what else is new?"

"I mean it. I'm not kidding. This Poindexter is bad news. I mean he's *really* bad news."

"Poindexter?—got that, Sally? Poindexter. Yes?"

"He's already killed Baker and Grant—"

"Spell it out, Corporal. No riddles. Baker. Grant. Who?"

"—Beckwith, Hindman. He shot Baker down right here in New Mexico. Over in Roswell. It was terrible. When I say bad news, Mr. Ollinger, I mean *bad* news."

"Come again?"

"The K-Bar-D murders. The big ones. The branding-iron jobs. Don't you read the newspapers?"

"I've got two assistants to do that."

"You're kidding."

"I'm not kidding. I never kid. Okay, I've heard of the K-Bar-D murders. Vaguely. But fill me in."

"Four murders in two months. Frank Baker over in Roswell. He was a plumber, I think. Joseph Grant in St. Louis. Robert Beckwith—where? I forget. George Hindman out East. Pittsburgh. Bad news, eh?"

"I'll check it out."

"Check it out? There's no need to check it out. It's in all the papers. And I'm telling you, the kid's going to kill you too. He's going to kill Robert Ollinger somewhere, sometime."

"Why?"

"Why? You get to be a big-shot Washington columnist and that's all you know? You're *Robert Ollinger*. You're not Dick Brewer or J. H. Tunstall. Do you think I'm a pal of the Duke of Wellington? Do you think John Dillinger still likes the Lady in Red? You see what I mean?"

"No."

"Poindexter shot Hindman a week ago in Pittsburgh. Hindman. Pittsburgh. Get it? It means he's moving east. Toward you. And you're so well-known I just can't see him going through a dozen phone books to find some *other* Robert Ollinger. Can you?"

"This Poindexter—what's his first name?"

"I don't know. But be careful, Mr. Ollinger. I'm giving you fair warning. Don't take chances. Remember Waterloo. That was a bad day in *my* life, I'll tell you. If only Marshal Grouchy—"

"I'll check it out, Bonaparte. Thanks for calling."

Ollinger lowered the receiver to its cradle, leaned back in his swivel chair, and studied the Mondrian canvases on his far wall. Their pure geometry, he thought, contrasted nicely with the formlessness and chaos of modern life. Madmen. Murderers. Scandals. Scoundrels. A soft-spoken Napoleon Bonaparte out in Honotassa, New Mexico, worried that Bob Ollinger, hard-nosed Washington columnist, might be gunned down by a kid named Poindexter. Crazy? Sure. Almost as crazy as some of the happenings on the Hill.

He leaned forward and punched a button on his desk. "Sally, ask our high-rise cage king to come in here. That means Bell."

Mort Bell, a former college basketball star, six-feet-four-inches, with sleepy brown eyes and a black handlebar mustache, had joined the Ollinger investigative team three months before, hired on the rebound from routine reporting. A motorcycle enthusiast, he craved excitement, the open road, the whiff of diesel oil. His work had offered nothing of the sort. For a couple of months after college he had idled away his time on the police beat of a Baltimore daily, a job he found as dreary as the drunk tank and as boring as the police blotter.

One rainy morning in November Bell had shouted, "I quit!" at precisely the instant his managing editor had screamed, "You're fired!" They sealed it with a fight in which Bell lost his Sigma Delta Chi key and two front teeth. Nothing daunted, he jumped on his Yamaha and barreled through the Harbor Tunnel, bound for glory.

"Mort," said Ollinger as Bell strolled into his office, "grab a seat. What's on the front burner?"

Bell dropped into a chrome-and-cowhide sofa and scowled. "Payoffs in the Jersey legislature," he said. Glory was still around the corner.

"Give it to Armstrong. Jersey's his bag—graft and corruption in Trenton—he's handled it for years. I've got a new job for you. A hot one. I want you to dig up everything you can on the K-Bar-D murders."

Bell looked startled. An embarrassed grin widened beneath the handlebars.

"As a matter of fact, Chief," he said, "I've been writing a five-thousand-word article on the K-Bar-D case for *Smashing True Detective*. As a free-lance."

Ollinger stared hard at him, his cold eyes pitiless as a time clock.

"In my spare time," Bell added lamely.

"In your spare time," Ollinger echoed, lighting a perfecto and exhaling a cloud of smoke. "Sure. Well, at least you're in the right ballpark for once." He leaned forward. "What about these K-Bar-D murders?"

Mort Bell crossed his long legs and took a sip of coffee from the styrofoam cup he had brought in with him.

"It's short and simple, Chief. The killer, whoever he is, is as crazy as the Mad Hatter. A trigger-happy psychopath. He shoots his victims with an old-fashioned .41-caliber revolver, usually in their living rooms. Then he brands their foreheads—"

"Hold on, Mort. He does *what*?"

"So help me, he brands their foreheads with a branding iron. From the K-Bar-D Ranch. Just like out West, only he uses a hibachi to heat the branding iron. When he's finished, he leaves the hibachi and takes the branding iron with him."

Ollinger whistled. "Not exactly the man next door. Not your usual domestic squabble: a hasty wedding, bang-bang. Where's the K-Bar-D Ranch?"

"There isn't one. There never has been. It's his own private brand."

"Who are the victims? What are their names?"

"Let me think. They all have common names. Grant is one, I think—yes, Joseph Grant, a stockbroker. Let's see. There's a Beckwith. A Baker."

"Okay, Mort. That's the Mad Hatter I'm after. What's the link between the victims? What's the pattern? What's the motive? Why the K-Bar-D Ranch brand?"

"It's a four-star mystery, Chief. There's no motive. No robbery. No violence except the bullet hole and the brand. No sex angle. One man's been murdered in New Mexico, one in Missouri, one in Indiana, the latest one in Pennsylvania. Four altogether. And the victims don't have a thing in common. Nothing. They didn't all serve on the same jury, or fight in the same platoon in World War Two, or take the same plane from Dulles to O'Hare, or receive the same coded message from Hong Kong. It's as if the guy is killing names, not people."

"But why those particular names?"

"Nobody knows. Or nobody's talking. If the police have come up with any link between them, they haven't said so. And I couldn't find any."

"Do they expect the killer to try again?"

"Sure."

"Why?"

"I told you, he's nuts."

Ollinger adjusted his steel-rimmed aviator glasses, ran his fingers through a dark and expensive hairpiece. "The killer's name is Poindexter, Mort. And I think we'd better find him pronto. In time to prevent another man's murder. Maybe mine."

Bell studied his boss through sleepy eyes. "We're reporters, Chief. We're not private eyes. This is a job for the police, isn't it? Or the F.B.I.?"

"This is a job for you," Ollinger said evenly, pointing his finger for emphasis. "It's your assignment as of this minute. I want you to work on it night and day.

No more moonlighting. I want you to run scared this time, Mort. I want you to find the K-Bar-D killer or else find yourself another job."

"You're kidding."

Ollinger never kidded. He made his ultimatums, carried them out, and ignored whatever human debris he created. "I never look back," he once informed Mike Wallace in a TV retrospective on his career.

Mort Bell accepted the assignment, aware that gumshoeing netted more than unemployment insurance. No man missing could be a greater menace than Robert Ollinger threatening. Bell headed for the privacy of his cubicle and the dubious solace of his telephone.

Concentrating once again on his Mondrians, Ollinger began putting together the next *Hot Line* column in his head. It concerned a prominent politician's wife suffocated in her Miami hospital bed by a nurse with anarchist leanings. "While the patient slept, death stole softly into Room 18—" the column began. Ollinger intended to make it poignant. "Tears that smear the newsprint," he often advised his staff, "grow cabbage that pays the rent."

Before the final line of *Capitol Hot Line* was fixed in his mind, Mort Bell burst back into Ollinger's office, bypassing Sally Pickerel like a Harley on a shunpike.

"How about that, Chief? An hour and ten minutes on the case and I've found out what K-Bar-D means."

"Let's have it." Ollinger punched a button on his tape recorder.

Bell's voice hummed with excitement. "Well, a few days ago the police in St. Louis—that's where Grant was killed—turned up a cocktail waitress named—you're not going to believe this, Chief—Kay Bardee. Perfect, no? It must take a kook to catch a kook. Who would think of going through the local phone book to find a person named Kay Bardee? Sergeant Vickers of the St. Louis P.D., that's who. He did, and there she was. Kay Bardee, 317 Hunting's End Road. Sergeant Vickers' triumph."

"I doubt it."

"You're right. But the police checked into Miss Bardee like the Warren Commission checking into Lee Harvey Oswald. They learned so much about her private life that they've booked her on charges of petty larceny, loitering, possession of a controlled dangerous substance, and impairing the morals of a minor."

"But not on the K-Bar-D murders."

"No. She's innocent of those. She had no connection with the murders. She was loitering with her boy friend in Jefferson City at the time Grant was being killed in St. Louis."

Ollinger waved his hand in irritation. "So all you've really found out is that K-Bar-D doesn't mean Kay Bardee."

"No, there's more. During the Kay Bardee publicity a professor of American History at Dahlgren University wrote a letter to the St. Louis *Chronicle*, telling them that the cattle brand they'd been showing on the front page wasn't a K-Bar-D brand at all."

"What do you mean?"

"The bar in the K-Bar-D brand was a Roswell police lieutenant's mistake. Everybody else followed his lead. What was being called a bar is actually, in the heraldry of the range—that's what the professor called it—a sideways *I*. A 'Lazy *I*.' So the brand is K-Lazy I-D. K-I-D. Get it?"

"I'm beginning to. Back to work, Mort. Hunt with the hounds."

Bell left for his cubicle, and Ollinger, after handing Sally Pickerel the tape for transcription, began putting in a series of phone calls, picking up a brief liberal education in Western Americana. His first two calls went to the Library of Congress and the Smithsonian Institution. His last call went to the Melora Valley Sanitorium, near Honotassa, New Mexico. After some insistence on his honored status in American journalism he got through to an assistant director, Dr. Mervyn Keller. "Dr. Keller," Ollinger said, "do you have a Napoleon Bonaparte there?"

The doctor chuckled. "You're in luck, Mr. Ollinger. We have two Napoleons. One is from Arizona, the other from South Dakota. They're splendid fellows, sharp as tacks. Most of the time they're as rational as we are. But they do have their one little delusion. And how they fight about that delusion—about who's the real Napoleon and who's the fake."

Dr. Keller cleared his throat as if to annul his chuckle and his commentary. In a businesslike voice he concluded, "We also have a Winston Churchill, a Madame Curie, and a Joan of Arc."

"Do you have a Billy the Kid?"

There was a telltale silence. "I'd rather not talk about the patients who have left us, Mr. Ollinger. I prefer to speak no evil of the departed. You realize that we are a private institution. Many of our patients have, or their families have, a great deal of money—enough money to hire psychiatrists, nurses, guards, companions, and the like. Sometimes we release patients who are still quite disturbed, knowing these patients will receive excellent care at home."

"In other words, you once had a Billy the Kid. You set him loose while he was still trying to figure out where you'd hidden his sixguns."

A sigh. "At various times in the past," the psychiatrist said, "we have had Jesse James, Annie Oakley, Billy the Kid, John Dillinger, and Judas Iscariot. Jesse James, I might add, is now a prominent dentist in Albuquerque. John Dillinger is an estate planner in Kansas City. There's no predicting how these things will turn out."

"Thank you, Doctor."

So that was the answer, the crux of the case. Billy the Kid, resurrected in the addled brain of a man named Poindexter, was roaming the countryside, reliving a legendary past, killing innocent plumbers, stockbrokers, and others who happened to have the same names as Billy the Kid's old victims. The branding iron was a bizarre touch, but one that gave the crimes a cachet.

Napoleon Bonaparte, the informant of the Honotassa Bonapartes, had been right. Poindexter was big news, bad news.

Ollinger dialed the number of Mort Bell's cubicle. No answer. He slammed down the receiver. If that lazy jock had left for the day . . .

At six o'clock, as dusk was settling over the city, Ollinger, according to custom, was switching from black coffee to straight Scotch, partly to unwind from the day, partly to escape the night.

He tried Bell's extension again. Still no answer.

He stalked across the room and threw open the door. Sally Pickerel, who worked the same exhausting hours as her boss, thrust a paperback book hastily into a top drawer. "What's up?"

"Where's Bell?"

"I don't know. He left the office about five hours ago. I asked where he was going, but all he would tell me was that he was bound for glory."

"He's bound for the unemployment line," Ollinger grated, heading for Bell's cubicle.

The light had been dimmed for the night in the large room that held twelve pea-green cubicles topped by frosted glass. No one was there. To Ollinger the silence was offensive and oppressive. Offensive because he felt that at least one of his assistants should work through the night; Ollinger had provided a metal cot for the purpose, but it stood unused at the far end of the room. Oppressive because he knew his life really was in danger.

He walked toward Bell's cubicle near the cot. As he did so, he heard a slight sound behind him. Not usually a nervous man, he whirled at the noise and yelled, "Who's there?"

In the dim light he saw a tall figure approaching, a cowboy hat pulled low over his brow. The man wore a plaid shirt and blue levis. A gun glinted in his hand.

The figure approached without speaking, as Ollinger backed up to the cot, stood there, his legs trembling, his mind racing. He often carried a tear-gas pencil on the street, but he never did in the office.

As the figure swaggered closer, Ollinger caught sight of a handlebar mustache and—a grin.

"Hi, Chief," Mort Bell said. "In the immortal words of Wilt Chamberlain, 'Relax.'"

Bell turned without replying and sauntered past Sally into the inner office. He flopped down on the cowhide sofa, lit a perfecto, pointed his finger at Ollinger, and said, "Chief, you're safe. Billy the Kid is in the hands of the F.B.I."

"You're kidding."

"I never kid. You gave me an assignment, I carried it out. I took Poindexter into custody myself."

"How did you find him?"

"It took some time. About four hours on the phone, as a matter of fact. I started with the name you gave me: Poindexter. I also tried William Bonney, which was the Kid's real name. Four hours later, bingo. The jackpot. Alvin Poindexter, an eighteen-year-old kid with an Adam's apple the size of his big delusion, was in the Washington area, registered under the name of William Bonney.

"Registered where?"

"At the El Rancho Rio Motel in Arlington. I tried thirty or forty hotels and motels, asking for either Poindexter or Bonney, before I found him. He still had seven thousand dollars in his wallet when I picked him up. The Poindexters of Corsica, South Dakota, are very rich, you know."

"I didn't know. Did Poindexter have a gun?"

"A .41-caliber Double Action Colt with enough ammo to fight the Lincoln County War. Also a branding iron, five hibachis, and a spiral notebook with a list of names."

"My name was on the list?"

"It sure was, Chief. Right at the top. It seems you were once a deputy marshal in southern New Mexico. The Kid killed you back in April, 1881."

"How did you capture him?"

"By craft and low cunning."

Ollinger looked respectful. "That's the way to do it. Did you go to his motel?"

"About an hour ago. I'm about the right height and weight for the role." He paused.

"The role?"

Bell winked. "The role I had to play. Mort Bell, lawman. I've got a black handlebar mustache. But I had to change into these blue levis and a plaid shirt. Then I went out and bought a ten-gallon hat—"

"I get it!"

"—borrowed an antique .44 revolver from a friend of mine, and took off for the motel. I knocked on Bonney-Poindexter's door. When he opened it, I ambled in, leveled the .44 at him, and told him I was—"

"Sheriff Pat Garrett!"

"Right."

"Great Scott! And it worked?"

Bell puffed his perfecto coolly. "It worked. The kid was scared to death. He knew, he just *knew* I was going to gun him down. After all, I'd killed him once, back in 1881. He cried. He begged and pleaded. He offered me his money and his hibachis."

"Son of a gun," Ollinger muttered.

"Right on. I won his confidence by telling him we'd call him 'a youthful blue-eyed killer' in the column. Finally I talked him into coming with me. About ten minutes ago I dropped him off at the J. Edgar Hoover Building."

Ollinger slammed a congratulatory fist on his rosewood desk. "Good work, Mort. And to think I figured you for the office clinker. Using that Pat Garrett trick was an inspiration. Worthy of Bob Ollinger himself in his younger days."

Mort Bell grinned. "I'm glad I used somebody else's name, though. Two of the other men on Poindexter's list were William Morton of Syracuse and James Bell of Boston. I don't know whether I would have survived with my own name."

"You'd have survived, Mort. You've got class. You're still wet behind the ears, you've got no top-level sources, but you've got potential. Let's talk bonus."

Before they could settle on an amount, Sally Pickerel poked her head inside the office. She smiled at the sheriff and spoke briskly to the columnist. "There's a 'Captain Hook' on the line, Mr. Ollinger. Would you like to take the call?"

"I'll take it," Ollinger snapped. "But I already know what it's about." He pointed a triumphant finger at his junior assistant. "The Captain is my secret source in the F.B.I., Mort. He'll want to tell me they've solved the K-Bar-D murders."

The Final Twist

There are three things that need to be said about the killing of Murphy Stevenson. First, he deserved to die. Second, he died quickly where some might have said he deserved to suffer. Third, he *did* experience at the end a few seconds of exquisite mental anguish because of a simple action performed by Eloise Knott. She could not resist giving him the final twist, the final cruel shock. I don't think I would have thought of it, but then Eloise is a woman. And Murphy had made her furious.

I remember how she sounded off to me after Stevenson had played his dirty trick on her. "That man has stepped on my toes," she said, sounding like a heavy in a spaghetti Western. Eloise is "one of the boys" and sometimes speaks with very little lip movement. She rolls her own cigarettes, yet she is female all the same. "I don't like it," she emphasized, "when they step on my toes."

"Hell hath no fury," I ventured, "like a woman's corns."

She let it pass and we got on with planning Murphy Stevenson's leap to death which was to be witnessed by the man in the top-floor office of the high-rise building across the alley. We made sure that he saw Stevenson alone on the roof, saw him position himself on the parapet and take his final dive. That's what made the coroner's verdict a clear case of suicide. That is how we got away with murder.

Let me emphasize right here that I, Brendan Tilford, am not in favor of people committing murder and getting off scot-free. On the other hand, I believe that extermination is a legitimate activity and should be pursued with efficiency whether the object is a nest of cockroaches under a kitchen floor or the sadistic head of a small advertising agency.

It would be hard to imagine an ad agency more compact than Murphy Stevenson Associates or a man more cruelly sadistic than our president, good old Murph. A couple of examples from his long and nasty record should establish our case against him.

Take the Christmas Bonus Deception which was perpetrated last year. We were accustomed to receiving a bonus of two weeks' salary on December 15th. We depended on it to buy our presents and our holiday booze. But it had been a bad year in the business community; the economy was on the rocks, profits were down the drain, and most firms had let it be known there would be no melon to slice this time around.

So we went to see the boss one afternoon late in November, Eloise and myself and Farley Dixon who made up the entire staff, and we put the question to him. If there was no money, we wanted to know now.

Stevenson hung that big face in front of us, gnarled and russety like the last apple in the barrel. "You get your bonuses, that I promise you." He raised his arm and we could see a salty circle in the armpit of his pin-stripe jacket. "Have I ever lied to you?"

We went about our business then, I writing copy, Eloise designing the layouts, and Farley Dixon looking after everything else—typesetting, engravings, shipping of material to publications. When December 15th came and went and we received only our regular paychecks, a tremor of angst ran through the office. But Stevenson strode about with a smug grin on one side of his face, humming *Santa Claus Is Coming to Town*. So we waited.

Then on the afternoon before Christmas Day he came round to our offices, delivered sealed envelopes, and said in his loudest client voice, "Glad tidings of comfort and joy!"—and stepped into a descending express elevator. We opened our envelopes and each of us found a $5 bill wrapped in a typewritten note which said:

"As you know, it has been a bad year for this and every other agency. But Stevenson maintains his unbroken record of always awarding a bonus, even though this time it has to be only a token payment. The spirit is there, if not the substance.

Merry Christmas,

Murphy K. Stevenson."

We drank up our bonuses quickly in the bar downstairs and I think the plot to get rid of Mr. Stevenson was hatched then and there. Not the details but the idea—the wish to see it done. Never underestimate the power of such a wish. Because of a determination no more sincere than ours, today there are man's footprints on the moon.

You may be wondering why we did not simply hand in our resignations while telling Murphy K. Stevenson to stick his five-dollar bills into his checking account. Well, to begin with, the economy was indeed slow. Jobs in advertising agencies were scarce as subway seats at rush hour, and when you had one, you sat on it.

Besides, we were a picturesque group of misfits not ideally suited to job interviews. I am a former high-school English teacher with a drinking problem. It shows in my nose. Eloise is a good designer but she is also a hysteric and a compulsive talker. I have seen people crawl out of her meetings, stunned like blast victims. As for Farley Dixon, he had suffered from some sort of obscure illness when he was a teen-ager. He still has a full deck to play with, but his eyes don't focus too well and his speech contains a lot of air and bubbles.

So we slave on for wages, putting up with Stevenson because he puts up with us. Why, then, make plans to eliminate the man? Would that not be, so to speak, killing the lizard that lays the golden eggs?

Not at all. If Stevenson cashed in his chips, the firm would go on. Our clients would still need their ad campaigns and we three were the team who wrote, designed, and produced them. Without old Murph, the client contact, we would simply do our jobs while arrangements were made for new leadership. Most likely some larger agency would absorb us into their operation.

Perhaps the crucial example of Stevenson's inhumanity was his treatment of Eloise Knott. This happened shortly before I joined the company and was told to me by Farley Dixon over beer in the bar. It seems my copywriting predecessor was a youth named Skippy Schiff. He was handsome, a competent writer, and because he was young and single and simple, Stevenson was able to pay him peanuts.

Anyway, Eloise and Skippy began having lunch together and one day they realized they were in love. Since this was a new experience in Skippy's young life and a rare phenomenon in Eloise's older one, they made no secret of it. They had got it, so they flaunted it. Naturally Murphy Stevenson became aware of what was going on.

Then he did three things. He began courting Eloise Knott with great energy, wining and dining her every night, whipping her away for weekends in Vermont, walking her significantly past windows where diamond rings were on display. When she succumbed to the seriousness of his approach and told Skippy it was finished between them, Stevenson fired the copywriter, gave him two weeks' pay, and sent him packing. Then he let one more week go by before ending his courtship of Eloise Knott. He never took her out again.

A shaken Eloise went looking for Skippy, but the boy had climbed aboard a boat for South America. Gone on the tide.

"Why do you suppose the boss did a rotten thing like that?" I asked Farley.

"He looks on all of us as his property," Farley said. "He resented the boy coming in and taking over his art director."

"Crafty guy," I said. "If he'd just fired Skippy straight away, she'd have quit and followed him. Right?"

"Right." Farley's eyes looked two different ways, his mouth ajar with beaded bubbles winking at the brim. "She almost left anyway, but I asked her what would happen to me, so she stayed on."

This loyalty of Eloise Knott's turned out to be Stevenson's tough luck. Because the plan to do him in originated with her—the "hell hath no fury" thing. I remember sitting in her office one afternoon as she doodled on her pad and started the idea rolling. The premise was preposterous, but we kept the monster alive for a couple of days and it put on weight and developed a sort of zany credibility. If you have ever worked in advertising, you'd realize this sort of thing can happen.

So we talked and dreamed and drank in the evenings and made lists of what props we'd need. We went up on the roof which was just two floors above us and looked down 23 stories to the alley below. From the roof Eloise noted the line of sight into the office of the man in the next building who always worked late and would become our eyewitness. We observed that he could see the rooftop but that a ledge blocked his view of the alley below. Perfect. Then we got down to the details.

I was sent to the hardware store to buy a gallon of flat white exterior paint and a brush. Farley organized a slide projector and a tape recorder and I helped him dub the required sounds on tape. Eloise herself went round to the publicity department of the Municipal Fire Department and borrowed the required photograph which she converted into a color slide.

Then it only remained to choose our evening and set the plan in motion. We were under no pressure; if something went wrong, we could abort at any stage and postpone our retribution to a more suitable night.

But nothing went wrong.

On the afternoon of the appointed day I went into the alley and painted a large area of the pavement flat white. There was no vehicular traffic in this narrow lane; the most the surface might acquire would be a few dusty footprints.

Farley Dixon then tested the slide projector. He took it into the washroom near his office and extended it through the window on the wooden frame he had built, aiming it down at my white patch on the alley and switching it on. The image was pale, but after dark it would be fine.

Then, at a quarter to five, Eloise set up Murphy Stevenson. She went into his office and said, "Mr. Stevenson, we are having a little drink in the Creative Department."

Our peerless leader glanced at his watch. "Not for another fifteen minutes, I hope."

"Of course not. And we'd like you to come and join us."

"Why me?" he probed.

"Why not?" she countered.

So in he came, pausing in the doorway, observing the gin, ice, mixer, and polished glasses, his shifty eyes darting here and there. Back in the days when he was a despised schoolboy, good old Murph must have been the butt of many a practical joke and he could sense the setup here. But he could not put his finger on it. He sniffed his empty glass before I poured the gin, he let us drink first, then he sipped tentatively. And immediately his own physical condition betrayed him. He became drunk quickly, and from then on it was easy.

We let him do most of the talking, arrogant and abusive and then incoherent, while I kept on pouring and Eloise raised her glass occasionally to the man in the office across the alley. Then, as darkness fell over the city, we moved our plan ahead. First, Farley Dixon excused himself and I knew he was organizing his slide projector and his tape recorder. When he came back, Eloise went out and set the fire. She did a good job. Within minutes of her return the smell of smoke reached us from the hall.

"Hey," I said, "the place is on fire!"

"What do we do?" Eloise asked.

"Stay away from elevators and stairwells. They're death traps in these tall buildings."

"What, then?"

"The only safe place is the roof." I took Stevenson's arm and dragged him into the hall. Farley and Eloise followed, closing my office door to keep the smoke, which was thick out here, from becoming visible to the man across the way.

Stevenson's eyes got big when he saw the smoke. He was moving erratically under his load of booze and I had to guide him up the two flights of stairs to the roof. There I snapped on the tape recorder Farley had planted behind a ventilator. Below us I knew Eloise was using soda water to extinguish the fires in the wastebaskets before the smoke alarmed the building staff.

I went to the parapet overlooking the main street and looked down. At the same moment Farley's tape-recorded fire sirens began to sound through a mix of traffic noises, the sirens distant at first, then drawing nearer.

"Do you see the fire engine?" Stevenson was hanging back from the edge.

"They're heading around to the alley side. Traffic is too thick over here."

My boss confronted me, his dazed eyes full of panic. "Listen, they don't have ladders this tall. How do we get off?"

"They have safety nets," I said. "Just like jumping into a feather bed."

The sirens stopped. It was not in the plan for me to be seen on the roof, so I said, "Take a look over the alley side. See if the net is up."

Stevenson went and looked over. "That was fast," he said. "There's a ring of firemen down there holding a net." He rubbed his gin-dimmed, smoke-bleared eyes.

"Don't think about it then, Murph. The longer you hestitate, the harder it will be. Just jump."

And he did.

I was surprised, really, that he went for it. I was also surprised that as soon as he disappeared over the edge, he screamed all the way down. Men jumping into safety nets don't scream; they probably hold their breath.

I asked Eloise and Farley about that when we had tidied up the premises and the police ambulance had come and gone, taking away Murphy Stevenson's body. Their report was terse and I noticed a wary tension between the two of them.

"The slide looked beautiful on the white paint," Farley said. "Just like on a screen. The firemen looking up and the big net held between them—very realistic."

"As soon as you were on the roof," Eloise said. "I telephoned the man across the way. I said my boss had run out of the place and we were worried. Could he see him on the roof? That got him to the window looking up."

"Fine," I said. "There's our eyewitness if needed. Stevenson was alone, he jumped, therefore suicide." Then I asked the question that was on my mind. "I wonder why he screamed like that on the way down? As far as he knew, he was jumping into a safety net."

Farley Dixon threw as much of a critical glance at Eloise as he could manage. "It was her," he said, and I could hear disapproval in his halting voice. "As soon as Murph stepped over the edge of the roof, she turned off the projector."

EDGAR WALLACE

A More-or-Less Crime

I t's a strange thing," said Superintendent Minter, "that when I explain to outsiders the method and system of criminal investigation as practiced by the well-known academy of arts at Scotland Yard, they always seem a bit disappointed.

"I've shown a lot of people over the building, and they all want to see the room where the scientific detectives are looking at mud stains through microscopes, or putting cigar ash in test tubes, or deducting or deducing—I don't know which is the right word—from a bit of glue found in the keyhole that the burglar was a tall dark man who drove a gray touring car and had been crossed in love.

"I believe there are detectives like that. I've read about 'em. When you walk into their room or bureau or boudoir, as the case may be, they give you a sharp penetrating look from their cold gray eyes and they say, 'You came up Oxford Street in a motorbus; I can smell it. You had an argument with your wife this morning; I can see the place where the plate hit you. You're going on a long journey across water; beware of a blue-eyed waitress—she bites.'

"I believe that the best way to detect a man who's committed a crime is to see him do it. It isn't necessary even to see him do it. In nine cases out of ten the right man will come along sooner or later and tell you he did it, and what he did it with.

"Most criminals catch themselves. And I'll tell you why. Not nine out of ten, but ninety-nine out of every hundred of these birds of paradise don't know where to stop, and as they don't know where to stop they stop halfway. I've never met a crook who was a whole hogger and could carry any job he started to a clean and tidy finish. There never was a burglar who didn't leave something valuable behind, but that's understandable, for burglars are the most nervous criminals in the world. They lose heart halfway through and there's a lot of people like 'em. As Mr. Rudyard Kipling, the well-known poet, says: 'All along of doing things/Rather more or less.'

"The most interesting more-or-less crime I ever saw was the Bidderley Hall affair. Bidderley Hall is a country house in the Metropolitan Police area—right on the edge of T division near Staines. It was an old Queen Anne house—it's been pulled down lately—standing in a ten-acre park, and it was owned by a gentleman named Costino—Mr. Charles Costino. He was a rich man, having inherited about half a million from his brother Peter.

"In the beginning Peter was rich and Charles was poor. Peter boozed but Charles never got happy on anything stronger than barley water. Charles was artistic and knew a lot about the Old Masters; he never bought any but he knew about 'em. His brother Peter knew nothing except that two pints made a quart and two quarts made you so that you weren't responsible for your actions.

"As a matter of fact, he was a bit of a bad egg, Peter was—gave funny parties at his home in Eastbourne and was pinched once or twice for being tight when in charge of a motorcar.

"One morning the coast guard found Peter's car at the foot of a two-hundred-foot cliff, smashed to blazes. They never found Peter. The tide was pretty high when his car went over—about three in the morning, according to a revenue boat that saw the lights; and after a time Charles got leave to presume Peter's death and took over all that Peter had left of a million.

"I saw Peter once. He was one of those blue-faced soakers who keep insurance companies awake at night.

"It was a grand bit of luck for Charles, who had this old house on his hands and found it a bit difficult to pay the taxes.

"When he came into money, Charles didn't live much better than when he was poor. The only time he broke out was when he took in a man-of-all-work, who was butler, footman, valet, and fed the chickens. In a way it was not a good break, as I could have told him if I had only known him at the time.

"Mr. Costino, it seems, had had an old lady looking after him—I forget her name, but anyway it doesn't matter. She'd been in the family for four generations, and she either left to better herself or died. Whatever she did she bettered herself.

"Anyway, Mr. Charles Costino was without a servant. He only lived in four rooms of the house since he came into the money and there wasn't much cleaning to be done, but he did have a bit of silver to clean, and there were the chickens to look after. The silver used to be locked up in a cupboard in the dining room and was pretty valuable, as I happen to know.

"Now, the new man he employed was named Simon. He's no relation to anybody you know, and I very much doubt whether that was his real name at all. He was a graduate of the University of Dartmoor where he had spent three happy years at the taxpayers' expense. I knew him as well as the back of my right hand.

"One day, by accident, I was passing through the Minories and I saw Simon come out of a shop that buys a bit of other people's silver now and again, so I pulled him up. According to his story, he had been to this pawnbroker's shop to buy a ring for his young lady, but they didn't have one to fit. I know most of the young ladies Simon has promised to marry—they've all been through my hands at one time or another—but I've never met one that he bought anything for, except a bit of sticking plaster. So I took him back to the shop, and the fence blew it and showed the silver Mr. Simon had parted with.

"It was not in my division at all and perhaps I had no right to interfere. To tell you the truth, the Divisional Inspector was a bit nasty about it afterwards, but what made it all right for me was when Simon said it was a cop and volunteered to come back with me to Staines.

"He didn't want any trouble and he told me he was tired of working for Mr. Costino and would be glad to get back amongst the boys at the dear old college. He said he had sold four pieces and had six hidden in the house ready to bring away.

"'Costino wouldn't notice them going,' he said. 'He's soused half the time and the other half he's in delirium tremens.'

"It was news to me, because I didn't know that Costino drank.

"We drove from the station to the house in a cab and on the way there Simon told me how slick he'd had to be to get the stuff out of the house at all. Apparently he slept in a room over a stable, some distance from the house but on the grounds. Nobody slept in the house but Charles Costino.

"We drove up to the Hall—and a miserable-looking building it was. I think I told you it was a Queen Anne house. Queen Anne is dead and this house was ready to pop off at any minute. None of the windows was clean, except a couple on the ground floor. It took us a quarter of an hour to wake up Costino and even then he only opened the door on the chain and wouldn't have let us in, but he recognized me.

"I have never seen such a change in a man. The last time I saw him he was a quiet sober feller and his idea of a happy evening was to drink lemonade and listen to the radio. Now he was the color of a bad lobster. He stared at Simon, and when I told him what the man had told me, Charles sat down in a chair and turned gray—well, it wasn't gray, but a sort of putty color.

"After a bit he said, 'I'd like to speak to this man. I think I can persuade him to tell me the truth.'

"I don't like people coming between me and my lawful prey, but I humored him, and he took Simon into the other corner of the room and talked to him for a long time in an undertone.

"When he finished he said, 'I think this man has made a mistake. There are only four pieces of silver stolen, and those are the four pieces he has sold. I can tell you in a minute.'

"With that he unlocked the door of a high cupboard. It was so crowded with silver that it was impossible for any man to count the stuff that was in it. But he only looked at it for a minute and then he said, 'Quite right. Only four pieces missing.'

"So far as I was concerned it didn't matter to me whether it was four or ten, so long as he gave me enough for a conviction. It was not my business to argue the point. I took Simon down to the cooler and I could tell something had happened, because he was not his normal bright and cheery self. Usually when you take an old con to the station he is either telling you what he's going to do when he comes out to your heart, lungs and important blood vessels, or else he's all friendly and jolly. But Simon said nothing and sort of looked dazed and surprised. He was hardly recovered the next morning when I met him at the police court and got my remand.

"It was a very simple case. It came at the Sessions, and Mr. Costino went into the box and said Simon was one of the best servants that had ever blown into a country house. You expect perjury at the Assizes but not that kind of perjury. But that was his business.

"Anyway, Costino made such a scene about what a grand fellow Simon was, how he fed the chickens so regular that they followed him down the street, that Simon got off with six months, and that, so far as I was concerned, was the end of it till it came my turn to take him in again.

"About seven months after this I was on duty on the Great West Road, watching for a stolen motorcar. It was one of those typical English summer days you read about—raining cats and dogs, with a cold north wind blowing—and I was getting a bit fed up with waiting when I saw a car coming along following a course that a yachtsman takes when he is tacking into the breeze.

"The last tack was against an iron lamp standard, which smashed the radiator and most of the glass, but it didn't apparently kill the driver, for he opened the door and staggered out. I had only to look at him to see that he had about twenty-five over the eight.

"My first inclination was to hand him over to my sergeant on a charge of being drunk while driving. It would mean a lot of bother, because if he had plenty of money he'd produce three Harley Street doctors and fourteen independent witnesses to prove that the only thing he'd drunk since yesterday morning was a small glass of cider diluted with tonic water.

"I was deciding whether or not to pinch him when I recognized him. It was Simon.

"'Hello!' I said. 'How long is it since *you* came out of the home for dirty dogs?'

"He didn't know me at first, and I oughtn't to have known him at all, because he was beautifully dressed, with a green tie and a brown hat, and a bunch of forget-me-nots in his buttonhole, not that anybody who had ever put their lamps on this dial would ever forget him. I asked him if it was his car, and he admitted it was.

"While I was talking to him one of my men came up and told me that they had stopped the stolen car about a hundred yards down the road, so I was able to devote myself to my little friend.

"We helped him along and got him into the substation round the corner. He was, so to speak, flush with wine. He got over his shock and began to talk big, flash his money about, and gradually, as he recognized the old familiar surroundings—the sergeant's desk and the notice on the wall telling people not to spit on the floor—he saw he was in the presence of law and order and it gradually dawned on him that I was me.

"'What bank have you been robbing?' says I.

"He laughed in my face. 'Costino gave it all to me for saying that I only pinched four bits of silver.'

"He started to laugh again and stopped. I have an idea that in the thing he called his mind he realized he had said too much. Anyway, he wouldn't say any more. We took his money away from him, counted it, and put him in a nice clean cell.

"Now I am not a man who is easily puzzled. Things in life are too straightforward for anybody to have anything to puzzle about, but this certainly got me thinking. Costino must have given him the best part of a thousand pounds to admit that he had stolen only four pieces of silver. Now why did he do that?

"I thought it out. At about eleven o'clock that night I said to my sergeant, 'Let's go and do a real bit of detective work.'

"I drove him down in my car to the road in front of Bidderley Hall. We parked the car in the drive, just inside the old gates, and walked up to the house. The rain was pelting down. I don't remember a worse night. The wind howled through the trees and gave me one of those bogey feelings I haven't had since I was a boy.

"When we got up to the house, we made a sort of reconnaissance. All the windows were dark; there was no sign of life; if there had been any sound we couldn't have heard it anyway. We went all round trying to find a way in, and just as we got back to the front of the house one of the worst thunderstorms I can remember started up without any warning.

"My sergeant was all for knocking up Mr. Costino and putting the matter to him plump and plain, but I saw all sorts of difficulties and my scheme was to pretend that we found a window open and being good policemen and not being able to make Costino hear, we had got in through the window and had a look round. There was only one place possible, we decided, and that was a window on a small balcony at the back of the house.

"We searched round and found a ladder, and put it against the balcony. I went up first and I had just put my leg over the parapet and was facing the window when there came a blinding flash of lightening that made my head spin. It was one of those flashes of lightening that seem to last two or three seconds, and in the light of it, as plain as day, I saw right in front of me, staring through the window, a horribly white face with a long untidy beard.

"I was so startled I nearly dropped back. I called my sergeant up the ladder. I wasn't afraid, but I wanted somebody with me. I don't know whether you have ever had that feeling. Two can be frightened to death better than one.

"I told him just what I had seen, and then I got my pocket lamp and flashed it into the room. As far as I could see through the dirty window the room was empty. Between the window and the room was a set of iron bars. They weren't very thick; they looked like the kind put up in West End houses so that children can't escape from a nursery when the room catches fire.

"We got the window open. The sergeant and I not only bent the bars, but we bent the whole frame. It was not very securely fastened—a bit of carpentry work done by a plumber.

"There was no furniture in the room. It was thick with dust. On the wall was a picture hanging cockeyed. The door was open and we went on and found a landing and a narrow flight of stairs leading down. But the curious thing about those stairs was that they didn't stop on the ground floor. In fact, there was no door opening until we got to the basement. There had been a door on the ground floor, but it had been bricked up.

"We were going down the last flight of steps when we heard a door bang and the sound of a bolt being shot. When we got to the basement level we found a door. It was shut, and we couldn't move it. I could find nothing on the stairs in the light of my lamp except evidence that somebody was in the habit of going up and down.

"When I went back up to the room with the balcony and examined the bars we had bent, I made rather an interesting discovery. Three of the screws on the lower left-hand corner had been taken out, and they had been taken out with a jagged top of a sardine tin. We found the 'opener' lying on the floor. It must have taken a long time to loosen those screws, for one of the screwholes was quite dark, and must have been exposed for months.

"There were two courses left to us: one was to come the next day with an official search warrant, which no magistrate would grant on the information we had; and the other was to go round and wake up Costino and ask him to let us go through the house. But there was a good reason for not doing that.

"I took off my shoes and went down the stairs in my stockinged feet, with my sergeant behind me. We crept up to the door and listened. For a little time I heard nothing, partly because the thunder was still turning the house into a drum, and partly because we could not quite tune in. But after a while I heard a man breathing very quickly, like somebody who had been running.

"We waited for a quarter of an hour and then another quarter of an hour. It seemed like a week. And then we heard the bolt being very gently pushed back. A man on the other side of the door opened it an inch. In another second I was through. He ran like the wind along the cellar and was just reaching another door when I grabbed him. He fought like six men, but we got him down.

"And then he said, 'Don't kill me, Charles. I'll give you half of the money.'

"And that was all I wanted to know.

"We pulled him up and sat him on an old box, and I explained that we were just innocent police officers, that we very seldom kill anybody except under the greatest provocation, and after a while we got Mr. Peter Costino calm, and he told us how his brother had come down to Eastbourne to see him and borrow some money, and how Charles got him drunk and intended driving him and the car over the cliff.

"Peter wouldn't have known this but his brother told him afterwards. Charles had lost heart and let the car go over by itself, then brought Peter back to Bidderley Hall, and shut him up in the cellar. Peter didn't know very much about it till he woke up the next morning and found himself a prisoner, and after two years of this kind of life he got more or less reconciled, especially as he was allowed to go up to the room with the balcony. It was the only bit of the world he was allowed to see, and then only at nights.

"That's the trouble with criminals—they never go the whole hog. Charles didn't have the nerve to kill his brother. He just locked him up. He got the house and half a million pounds, but he got about two million worries. Those two years made Peter a sober man and turned Charles into a drunkard. Peter might have eventually died in this cellar if Mr. Charles Costino hadn't given Simon a thousand quid to keep his mouth shut about the silver he had stolen and hidden in the house. Charles was in mortal terror that we would search the house for the missing silver, and if we had searched the house we'd have found Peter.

"Charles is in Dartmoor now. So is Simon. He got a lagging for a big smash-and-grab raid, and drew five years. From what I've heard, he and Charles are quite good friends. The last I heard of Charles he was painting angels in the prison chapel. As I say, he was always a bit artistic."

DAVID BRADT

A Kind of Madness

Maybe it wasn't right, her Jim dead and buried only a year and all, to sit here by his grave in the clearing back of the house and fret over the Sheriff arresting Wayne Chandler today. But the glade was quiet and peaceful when the still summer days retreated before the warm dark nights, and Sarah seemed to always end up here when something was troubling her mind.

Just a couple of months before she'd been leaning against this same sturdy little pine, letting her loneliness and her fears melt into the June night, when she'd first heard Wayne call. He'd ventured up the road, tired and looking for a bed and maybe a bite to eat, insisting he'd pay her husband or help with the morning chores for his night's keep.

When Sarah told him her Jim had passed on, Wayne flushed and wrung his hands together for no reason and said he'd be off now and was sorry to have bothered her. But the hired man hadn't shown for two days and she'd heard he was drinking his paycheck again, so she told Wayne she surely could use some honest work around the place as the chores were piling up faster than she could get to them.

She'd fed him supper that night, she remembered as she sat in the clearing watching the moon rise just above the treetops. And after supper she'd boiled up a pot of coffee and they got to conversing until before she knew it dawn spilled over the hills and the rooster was crowing. When she laughed at his jokes or near cried when he described some of the pretty places he'd seen, the lonely ache inside her disappeared for the first time in a year.

Recollecting the first evening with Wayne made her cry for what seemed the hundredth time today. She got to her feet and tried to think of the crops and the harvest coming up soon. But when she shut her eyes she saw Wayne just as plainly as if he were standing in front of her. She knew she couldn't visualize Jim so clearly any more without pulling out one of the photographs she'd hidden away in the bureau drawer shortly after Wayne had moved in. But she supposed what with time passing and a new man on her mind this was natural.

Then this morning, when Wayne was working out in the barn and she was scrubbing the last of the breakfast dishes, everything had gone bad again. Sheriff Tucker and his deputy, Charlie Weber, they'd come and taken him away.

Sarah opened her eyes. The moon was big and round and she wondered if Wayne could see it from the jailhouse. And she wondered crazy things, like if they'd fed him a proper supper and if he was thinking about her as much as she was thinking about him. Seemed this was a worse fit of loneliness than when Jim went and got killed in the fields.

The noise of a car bouncing up the rut-filled road broke the solemn tranquility of the moment. Sarah sprinted from the clearing. Could be the Sheriff was bringing Wayne back. It was all a mistake and now they'd forget it ever happened and return to things just as they were.

She raced around the corner of the house and saw the Sheriff's black and white jeep approaching. And it did seem that two people were riding in the front seat. Straining her eyes, wishing she could turn up the moon's brightness like a lamp, she waited nervously on the porch.

Her heart plummeted like a bird shot on the wing. It was Charlie Weber who rode next to the Sheriff. A flash of disgust went through her. She suspected Charlie was just as happy to see Wayne Chandler in jail as she knew he'd been when her Jim had died.

"Evening, Sarah," Sheriff Tucker called too loudly, braking to a halt in front of the porch. She watched the two men closely but did not acknowledge the greeting. Charlie Weber jumped out the far door and strode around the car. He looked at her the way he always did, real calculating and cold, like he was sizing her up in a way she didn't appreciate.

"Evening, Sarah," he said slowly, a strange half smile cracking his face.

She dropped her gaze for an instant and when she raised her head again it was the Sheriff she watched.

"What do you want, Sheriff?"

"We got a few facts about Wayne Chandler I think you ought to know. I figured I best tell you right away and maybe it would ease your mind some." He glanced over at Charlie Weber before continuing. "This information came over the wire today. Just like we thought, Chandler's a wanted man. We've got enough on him to send him up for a right long stretch, it appears to me. It's all on paper, Sarah." He pulled a folded piece of paper from his shirt pocket, stepped onto the porch, and handed it to her.

"It's all right there on the paper," Charlie Weber said from below. He struck a match and lit a cigarette. The acrid smell of the sulphur and the thick smoke he blew her way nearly turned Sarah's stomach. She snatched the paper from the Sheriff and tossed it onto the wooden planks of the porch.

"I don't need to read those lies. I know my Wayne."

The Sheriff shrugged and bent down to pick up the paper. "I'm just trying to make it easier for you."

Sure he was, she thought. Ever since her Jim died folks had tried their darnedest to make it easier for poor Sarah. Trouble was, their sympathy seemed to come not from their hearts, but from some sense of obligation, as if it was a duty they had to perform. Sarah knew the womenfolk didn't like her because she was young and pretty, and when she watched them as they brought their baskets of food and listened to their idle chatter, she thought she sensed in them a secret relish for the tragedy of others.

If the women weren't bad enough themselves, they sent subdued young men around after a proper mourning period, who sat quietly watching her and not sure how to act. Worse yet were the heartless fellows like Charlie Weber, who barely concealed their intentions when they came calling and saying they could make her forget all about her Jim.

Jim had been a good man, more decent than any of the folks who gathered in the clearing the day he was buried, standing uncomfortably under the hot sun in their dark suits and heavy dresses. Never had she regretted marrying him. And when he died there was an emptiness that all the vistors could no more fill than could the few farm animals she had kept.

Then Wayne had burst into her life and swept away her sorrow even that first night when they'd talked until dawn, opening to her an enchanting and joyous way of life she'd never experienced before.

Theirs was a love she never had dreamed possible. While her relationship with Jim had developed slowly, maturing only after marriage, steady and sure as the seasons, with Wayne it was as if a winter storm had exploded or spring rains were falling or the fall winds were blowing so hard you could hardly walk against them. A kind of madness she had never before felt. It was as if they were made of the same dreams and desires, sorrows and sadnesses. When he held her at night she had to be the happiest woman on earth.

"Let me tell you somethin', Sarah," Charlie Weber drawled. "If that boy were free to go he'd hightail it to the stateline so fast a fellow wouldn't even see him go by. No way that joker'd come back to you after we've exposed him for what he is."

"He would too. I know Wayne. He don't have anything to be ashamed of."

Exasperated, the Sheriff shook his head. He peered down the road into the darkness and then spun quickly around toward Sarah. Too bad she'd gotten mixed up with Chandler. He felt sorry for her. She was a sweet good-looking woman, and if he could convince her of what a lowdown character Chandler was she'd be making one of the local boys a fine wife in no time. He approached her and placed his hands firmly on her shoulders.

"Listen, Sarah. Men like Wayne Chandler just prey on women like you. They have ways of finding out you collected that big policy when Jim died. They know you're gonna be lonely. Chandler would talk you out of every cent you own and the farm too, give him half a chance. Now why in the devil can't you understand that?"

Her arms shot up from her sides and slapped Sheriff Tucker's hands off her shoulders. "Then why didn't he try?" she said, wheeling around and stalking to the far end of the porch. From this side of the house you could see around the corner just enough to view where Jim was buried. She stood with her arms crossed and her back to the men, and tried to catch the peaceful feeling a quiet night in the clearing brought her. She felt the rough boards under her bare feet.

A wisp of warm wind, sluggish as the river in late summer, blew through her dress.

The Sheriff eyed her apprehensively, then sighed loudly and walked down the steps to the jeep. "Just thought you ought to know, Sarah," he said. "Sorry you had to find out this way. Let's go, Charlie."

She heard the car start and the engine rumble when the Sheriff gunned it a couple times, and then the crackle of the gravel crunching under the tires as the jeep pulled away. Suddenly, desperately, she bolted down the steps, ran across the sharp gravel, and dashed down the dusty road.

"Wait!" she cried.

The jeep halted, but she ran until she reached Sheriff Tucker's open window.

"What is it, Sarah?"

"Can you take me to see him? Right now?"

"What for?"

"I've got to tell him I'll wait. He needs me now. I know it."

"Needs a good lawyer, is what he needs," Charlie Weber laughed from the far side of the jeep.

"Charlie's right," Sheriff Tucker said. "And dammit, girl, I spelled it out for you plain as day. Wayne Chandler was after your money. I can't make it any clearer than that."

Sarah didn't answer, but stared at the Sheriff so intently that he turned his head and studied the dashboard, as if some wisdom were lurking in its gauges. "Tomorrow morning," he said finally. "Come down tomorrow morning. By then we'll probably have a rap sheet on this guy long enough to paper your bedroom walls with."

"You gonna tell her what he said?" Charlie Weber asked the Sheriff.

The Sheriff's head snapped to the side as if it had been slapped. "You tell her since you had to go and bring it up," he snarled.

Charlie leaned low so he could see Sarah through the window. "You want to hear somethin' kind of humorous considering all we've told you, Sarah? That boy wanted us to let you know that he loves you. Imagine him saying he loves you." He laughed harshly and sat up straight as soon as he saw the pain in her eyes. "Let's get goin', Sheriff."

Sheriff Tucker shifted into first gear and the jeep lurched down the road. Standing still as a tree on a near-windless night, Sarah watched until the red taillights vanished in the distance. The moon wrapped her in its somber light and made her tears glisten faintly.

Early the next morning Sarah awoke from an uneasy sleep. She grabbed the cotton dress off the foot of the bed and stepped through the waning darkness to the bathroom, where she switched on the lamp. Every movement she made, it seemed, she'd rehearsed during the restless night. She bathed and pulled her dress on and brushed her hair until it sparkled like rich golden grain when the sun washes over it at dawn. Each stroke with her brush seemed to add more luster.

Looking serious in the mirror, she combed her bangs just the way Wayne liked them, pulled to one side and drooping close over her eye. What a joy it would be to see him. If she could just hold him for a minute, hear his whisper in her ear, then everything would be fine again.

Already the day was warm, the air heavy, she noticed as she hurried down the eroded driveway to the dirt country road, and then, after a mile or so, onto the paved highway to town. She was regretting that she hadn't listened to Jim and learned to drive the truck, when she heard an approaching car behind her. She twirled around and waved. An old pickup loaded with produce for the town market skidded to a halt on the dusty shoulder.

She climbed in unhesitatingly and listened as well as her concentration allowed while the driver complained of the dry weather and how it was going to ruin his season unless a bit of rain fell soon. He was still carrying on when he let her off at the jailhouse, and never did inquire as to what business she had there.

She ran up the concrete walkway and flew expectantly through the door, as if she thought Wayne would be standing there all set to go free.

The Sheriff and Charlie Weber, though, were alone in the office, and she was disappointed to discover that the cells weren't visible except through a small window on a massive gray door. The Sheriff mumbled a greeting and turned away. Charlie, sitting with his feet propped on his desk, smiled, but didn't rise.

"Can I see him now?" she asked breathlessly.

The Sheriff spoke, and she could barely hear him. "That's not possible."

"But you said I could," she pleaded. "I have to!"

He didn't answer right away, and when he started to speak no words followed the first few.

"Sheriff seems a bit tongue-tied," Charlie Weber said. "Don't know why. Every jail has to deal with an escapee now and then."

Sheriff Tucker glanced forlornly at his deputy, breathed deeply, then walked up to Sarah. She'd gone pale and her hands were trembling. "Wayne Chandler escaped last night, Sarah," he said rapidly. "Don't know how, but a trustee or somebody got hold of the office key. We usually keep it pretty well hidden. We finally caught up with him and when we called and he didn't stop we had to fire."

Sarah stood still as the words settled into her mind, looking into his face but not really seeing it. Suddenly she sprang toward Charlie Weber. "You killed him!" she screamed. "*You* killed him!"

Charlie fended off her small fists and the Sheriff grabbed her shoulders and twisted her around. "I did," he whispered, eyes inches from her own. "I had to."

Her body went limp and the Sheriff tightened his grip on her, fearing she would fall if he let go. Then she slowly stiffened, as if coming back to life. Without looking at either man she walked to the door. "I'm sorry," the Sheriff said.

She opened the door and stepped outside. "What surprised me," she heard Charlie Weber say purposefully loud enough for her to hear before she shut the door, "was where we caught up to him. Hell, I would've sworn he'd go for the stateline. But you had to shoot him, Sheriff. He didn't give you a choice. No tellin' what he had in mind for poor Sarah if he'd actually made it to her place, like he was tryin'."

But the Sheriff was thinking about the key. There was no sure way of knowing who got it to Chandler. He looked at Charlie sitting with his feet on the desk and smiling like he hadn't really seen a man die last night. There was no sure way of knowing.

Sarah closed the door. The street glared brightly in the morning sun. But it was still too early for people to be up and about much, and the only sound she heard was the whisper of a loneliness like she had never known before.

JACK RITCHIE

Beauty Is As Beauty Does

When I noticed the lavender envelope protruding from under the door of my suite, I picked it up. Inside I found a single typewritten sheet of paper.

Dear Mr. Walker: If I am not selected Miss Fifty States in the finals tomorrow, I promise that I will kill you. I mean this quite seriously. My entire life would be ruined and so I might just as well murder you. I think I would even enjoy it.

I showed the note to Stubbins and McGee.

McGee rubbed his jaw. "Now that's peculiar."

I regarded him coldly. "That is clearly the understatement of the year. It is a threat to murder me."

"I mean that the note isn't *signed*. How are you supposed to know which girl to vote for?"

I read the note again. "Hmm. You are quite right, McGee. I didn't notice it at first. Then what the hell is the point of sending me the note in the first place?"

McGee gave it thought. "Possibly she just forgot to sign her name."

McGee, Stubbins, and I are the three judges of the Miss Fifty States Beauty Contest. However, since I am the senior judge and McGee and Stubbins were likely to defer to any decision I might make, I was obviously the person to influence if someone wanted to win the contest.

"You *do* want to find out who wrote that note, don't you?" Stubbins asked.

"Of course. But there are *ten* finalists."

Stubbins quickly paged through the files of the contestants, apparently searching for one item in particular. He put three folders aside. "There we are."

I had been looking over his shoulder. "There we are what?"

"You will notice that the note is typed," Stubbins said. "There is not a single typing error and the entire message is nicely centered on the sheet of paper. In other words, the typist is obviously not a novice at the machine." He indicated the folders. "These three girls are the only finalists who can type—Miss Wisconsin, Miss New York, and Miss South Carolina."

I frowned. "I still can't figure out that lack of a signature. Could she actually have forgotten?"

McGee brightened. "Maybe she first wanted to see how you would *react* to a threat, even if it was anonymous. If you are frightened and intimidated, she will press home the advantage and make herself known."

"She will be disappointed," I said. "I am neither frightened nor intimidated."

"Ah, yes," McGee said. "But suppose you *pretend* that you are?"

I saw his point. "Very well, summon the three girls here."

McGee and Stubbins accomplished the errand and brought back the girls and their chaperones. I had the latter remain in an anteroom while we spoke to the girls and showed them the note.

Gretchen—Miss Wisconsin—handed it back to me and smiled sweetly. "Why isn't it signed?"

"I don't know. Perhaps the writer forgot?" I gazed at the three of them and got innocent silence.

Olivia—Miss New York—could smile sweetly too. "Why pick on us three? There are *ten* finalists."

Stubbins beamed his information. "You three are the only ones who can type."

I allowed my hands to tremble slightly as I folded the note and returned it to my pocket. "I don't see why anybody wants to kill me just because of this contest. I have been nice to all of you, haven't I?"

"Of course, Mr. Walker," Melissa—Miss South Carolina—said. "You've been a dear, sweet, intelligent man."

I nodded. "It's quite a difficult job to judge a beauty contest. All I'm trying to do is be fair." I used my handkerchief to wipe my forehead. "Now I want whoever wrote this note to think it over carefully. You wouldn't *really* want to kill me, now would you?"

Behind them, McGee lifted a book a foot above the table top and raised a questioning eyebrow.

I read his message and nodded almost imperceptibly.

He dropped the book and it made a loud bang.

I leaped wildly. "What was that?"

McGee apologized. "I'm sorry, Mr. Walker. The book just slipped."

I laughed nervously. "That sounded rather like a pistol shot." I wiped my face again. "Now, girls, I just want you to remember that I am your friend. Honestly and truly your friend. I'm here to help you in any way I can. If there is anything troubling you, I would be only too happy—yes, *eager*—to do whatever I can."

It was nearly nine o'clock that evening and I was alone when there came a knock on my door.

I found a huge young man with a look of determination in his eyes. "Are you Mr. Walker? One of the judges of the Miss Fifty States Beauty Contest?"

I nodded cautiously.

"This has got to stop," he announced firmly.

"What has got to stop?"

"I am not going to let you crown Gretchen Miss Fifty States."

"And why not?"

"Because I intend to marry her."

I sighed. "Come in and sit down."

He found a chair. "I just can't have her gawked at."

"She has been gawked at from Sheboygan to Milwaukee."

"I know. But this time it will be on nation-wide television. Can't you just imagine what all those millions of men will be *thinking* when they see her in that skimpy bikini?" He brushed sandy-colored hair from his forehead. "Gretchen and I grew up together. We went to the same grade school, the same high school. We took Biology together."

"You were that close?"

He breathed heavily. "I shouldn't have let it go on and on. First it was the Montmorency Cherry Queen, then the Sebago Potato Princess, and on to the McIntosh Apple Darling. I thought that would finally satisfy her, but it all just went to her head."

He seemed quite desperate. "Do you realize what will happen to her if she wins this contest? She'll be famous and meet all kinds of rich men and celebrities and get married a half a dozen times before she's through. And she'll be dieting all the time and that isn't healthy. When she weighed a hundred and forty she was always cheerful and light-hearted. Have you come to a decision yet about who's going to be Miss Fifty States?"

"I am still giving it thought."

He rose and hovered over me. "Mr. Walker, if you pick Gretchen, I swear I'll kill you. I won't have any reason for going on anyway." He paused at the door. "The last time I went trap-shooting, I got ninety-nine out of one hundred."

I took optimistic comfort in that he had missed at least one.

When he was gone, I decided I needed a drink. I was making it when there was another knock on the door.

It was Olivia.

I glanced past her. "Where's your chaperone?"

She shrugged. "I got some sleeping pills from the hotel doctor and accidentally spiked her milk." She closed the door behind her and a moment later I was a bit astonished to find that we were sitting side by side on the sofa. Her raven-black hair seemed to exude an aggressive fragrance.

She showed the whitest of teeth. "Mr. Walker, I can see that a man of your educated type likes a woman with brains and a lot of culture. How did you like my painting?"

As her contribution to the talent segment of our contest, Olivia had entered one o her paintings of what was very possibly a bridge in the moonlight entitled *Spanscape*.

She leaned closer. "You've been so nice to all of us, and I, for one, am very appreciative."

I cleared my throat. "Appreciative is an adjective."

Her fingers crawled about the back of my neck. "I could be ever so grateful for any little favor you might do for me tomorrow, Mr. Walker. So very grateful." Her eyes were close. Her lips were close. As a matter of fact, all of her was close.

The memory of my Puritan ancestors pulled me to my feet. "Young woman," I said sternly, "that won't do you a bit of good."

She studied me for a few seconds and then shrugged. "All right, then I'll play it straight. I was the one who wrote you that note and I meant every word of it."

I moved to the phone. "I am going to call the police."

She smiled. "Go ahead if you want to. But I'll just deny that I said anything at all. It will be your word against mine." She put a gleam into her eyes. "You're as good as dead if I'm not Miss Fifty States by this time tomorrow."

She swept out of the door.

Fifteen minutes later I had finished my drink and was working on the second when I had to answer the door again.

It was Melissa.

She carried what appeared to be a liquor bottle gift-wrapped. "Just a token for all the nice things you've done for little old helpless me. It's really good bourbon."

"Where is your chaperone?" I asked routinely.

"The dear thing's fast asleep. Just drank her milk and conked out." She put the bottle on the table. "We won't drink any of this now. I know the rules and I wouldn't want to be accused of trying to influence you in any way. So we'll just save the bottle for a *private* victory celebration tomorrow in case I somehow *happen* to become Miss Fifty States."

Her green eyes looked into mine. "You know, you look so distinguished and educated and all that you remind me of my Uncle David who writes poetry and has it published in the *Tuskachee Clarion*. Right on the editorial page."

Her fingertips began a Braille exploration of my lapels.

"Young woman," I said stiffly, and perhaps a little tardily, "I will not be swayed by any blandishments, present or promised. My judging integrity remains unshaken."

There were some seconds of silence. Then she smiled coldly. "I didn't think there was any harm in trying sugar first. All right then, buster, have it your way. I'm the one who wrote that note. And killing runs in my family because my great Aunt Phoebe once shot a Yankee captain who had the gall to walk into her drawing room wearing spurs."

She went to the door, turned, and decided to restore some of the warmth to her smile. "Keep the bottle and think it over. We could get to be such *good* friends tomorrow night."

She was gone less than ten minutes when I was called to the door again. Frankly, I expected to find Gretchen, but it was a tall young man with untamed red hair.

"Ha," I said, "I suppose you want to kill me too?"

He blinked. "I wouldn't kill anybody. I'm a pacifist. Except in time of war, of course."

"You are refreshing. What can I do for you?"

"If you could get my painting back, I'd be very appreciative."

"What painting are you talking about?"

"*Spanscape.*"

"You own the picture?"

"I also painted it. Then I lent it to Olivia, but that was before I knew that it was worth anything."

"Let me get this straight. Olivia did *not* paint the picture?"

"No. I did. And I just got a five hundred dollar offer from somebody who saw it in my studio last week and you simply can't pass up something like that. But Olivia says that she's going to keep it for a year while she's Miss Fifty States and after that she doesn't give a damn who knows or doesn't know that she didn't paint the picture."

"Does she know that you came to me?"

"No. She said she'd kill me if I did, but five hundred bucks is five hundred bucks." He looked a bit worried though. "You don't suppose she actually would kill me?"

"Cross your fingers," I said. "I'll see what can be done."

When he left I locked the door and I had no intention of answering it again that night, even if Gretchen didn't miss her turn.

The next evening at eight, Stubbins, McGee and I were seated at the judges' table on the stage of the arena as the finals of the Miss Fifty States Beauty Contest began.

As I watched the ten girls, it seemed to me that Gretchen, Olivia and Melissa were clearly a notch above the seven others. Perhaps that was just coincidence, perhaps it had something to do with learning how to type, or perhaps it was just because I'd seen more of them than I had the other girls.

I sighed. Two of the girls had threatened to kill me, but which one of them was actually responsible for the note?

Olivia?

She had verbally threatened to kill me, but had she written the note too or was she just taking advantage of a trend?

And there was the matter of *Spanscape*. She had not painted the entry herself and that automatically disqualified her from consideration in the contest.

Yes, Olivia was definitely out.

That left Gretchen and Melissa.

Gretchen had not come to visit me last night, but was that because she was not the letter writer, or was it because she could not get her chaperone to drink spiked milk?

And Melissa?

Had her Aunt Phoebe pleaded self-defense and been freed by a sympathetic jury or had she been sent to prison?

It was nearly ten o'clock when Stubbins, McGee and I went into a huddle to make our decision and found that our choice was unanimous.

I stepped to the microphone and announced to the waiting world that the new Miss Fifty States was none other than Melissa—Miss South Carolina.

The usual pandemonium, of course, ensued.

Melissa broke into tears of joy. Gretchen and Olivia instantly followed suit. Gretchen hugged Melissa and *sincerely* congratulated her. Olivia hugged Melissa and said that she knew all along that Melissa really *deserved* to win the contest. And finally Olivia and Gretchen hugged each other and wept over their sheer happiness at Melissa's good fortune.

It was past eleven before I managed to get back to my suite.

There was a knock on my door.

Damn, I said, but I opened it.

Melissa stood in the doorway and she appeared to be somewhat breathless.

I blinked. Had she really meant it last night when she said that we would have a cozy little celebration?

My eyes went to the gift-wrapped bottle still on the table. I felt a bit warm. Melissa's offer hadn't influenced my decision in the slightest, but now that the contest was over—

I smiled.

"You've been *so* considerate," she said. "But I'm afraid that I really won't have time for our little old victory celebration tonight. A Miss Fifty States is *so* busy, you know. You *do* understand, don't you?"

I sighed at the vanish of a dream. "Never mind. I'll drink the whole bottle myself."

Her lashes fluttered over innocent blue eyes. "That's just it and I'm *so* glad I got here in time. If I were you I wouldn't touch one teensy-weensy drop of that bourbon. Because if you do, you'll get an awful, awful tummy ache. If you know what I mean?"

When she was gone, I emptied the bourbon bottle down the drain and poured myself a full tumbler of my own safe brandy.

ROSALIND ASHE

The Long Glass Man

I take it we all agree on the fact of A Supernatural, and that so-called ghosts that most of us accept as the supernatural take form only for a select few. But the idea of a *harmful* ghost is to me simply ridiculous."

We had finished dessert and adjourned to the smaller common room at the top of the staircase, a move that tended to sort the men from the boys. Only the hard-drinking, hard-talking brigade usually made the final assault up the spiral staircase, headed by the bachelors, natural climbers with nothing to lose, closely followed by the long-married—those who knew that, by this late hour, their North Oxford home fires would be banked down with tea leaves for the night, and the only voice in the house would be a note of instructions on the kitchen table concerning cats and dustbins.

Here the firelight glowed through one's malt whiskey, and the deep leather chairs were difficult to get out of. But Littlemount did not sit; he was in good voice and needed props and space to make his points: three strides to the sideboard and back, tap out pipe, eat a Chocolate Oliver from the silver biscuit box especially stocked for him—and never once a pause in his flow. He was summing up an argument that had started at his end of the long table. I had asked someone quite casually, "Are you afraid of the dark?" and it had all stemmed from that.

"So we must conclude," said Littlemount, "that the only harm a ghost can do is to drive us into self-inflicted harm, mental or physical: we can die of fright; or flee, and fall downstairs and break our necks; or allow our shaking candle to set the bed curtains alight; but we cannot be stabbed or strangled by an immaterial being. How could it hold a knife? Or press insubstantial thumbs on our windpipe? They would pass right through, would they not, and meet ineffectually on the other side. Admit, sir, ghosts do not have the molecular structure to commit murder."

The target of his punch line was a stranger, presumably someone's guest. He too was on his feet; he stood very tall and saturnine, observing Littlemount's restless terrier-like scuttling. Only his eyes moved, bright under heavy brows. "In that case, we must take care not to alter that molecular structure," he said.

"Oh, come now, Littlemount—" Stacey, one of the younger dons, was busy with bottles at the sideboard and seemed not to notice the hush of confrontation, all eyes on the tall guest. "Surely ghosts must have *some* sort of structure or, according to your theory, they would simply sink through the floor."

It was the stranger who answered him.

"It seems that apparitions run along well-defined tracks, the grooves carved out by the horrific circumstances of their own peculiar tragedy. Extreme suffering or guilt, or both, appear to be the commonest causes. The happy ghost that haunts its favorite spot is as surely a cosy Victorian invention. The strongest motive for a ghost to return is that of completion—something unfinished, something still to do, whether it's revenge or the expiation of guilt. Hidden treasure? Aye, sir, but usually come by foul play. True love? But unrequited, unsatisfied: 'I will hang my heart on the weeping willow tree—'

"'So that the nun who wrings her hands—'

"'And the horseman who rides over the cobbles and up to the door—'

"'The baby in the guest wing that crouches by the grate—'

"Yes, they are all endlessly replaying their tragic moment, fixed in their groove. And that, gentlemen, is some people's idea of hell."

"Certainly, certainly—" Littlemount clearly felt it was time to gather up the reins again. "We are not disputing that ghosts are attached to one place; no well-documented apparition *follows* folk to haunt them, or materializes anywhere but in its proper lair. But that is not to say that a ghost, even an armed ghost, like Hamlet's father, could inflict an injury—"

"You mean if, even briefly, it could have assumed some sort of corporeal solidity."

"Ah, by possession of a living person—that is an altogether different matter, my good fellow, if you will forgive the pun."

"Very well, we shall agree to keep Possession out of this, or we will get bogged down in Demonism and have to resort to the Power of the Church. There is an example of materialization in its full sense of which I could tell you, if you have the patience to hear. It is a disturbing documentary but sufficiently rare to amount to a curiosity rather than a threat to your peace of mind."

Littlemount himself recharged the stranger's glass and installed him in what was habitually the Master's chair. Another log was thrown on the fire, and someone even suggested turning down the lights.

"No," said our storyteller, "they will do very well. Let us approach this in the spirit of the well-illuminated scientific inquiry—for that is just the way it started.

"It was nearly thirty years ago, just after the war, in this university; the college we can ignore, and for the individuals we shall invent names. Many undergraduates were older then, coming back from the front. Black, let us call him, had served in Burma and returned to finish his degree, changing from mathematics to philosophy.

"Now, Black was psychic—abnormally so. Early in his country childhood he had shown what is commonly called 'second sight,' in everything from party games to the revelation of distant disasters. His adolescence had been troubled by poltergeists; in the army he learned to conceal his powers both from his commanding officers—it does morale no good to have a clairvoyant in the lines—and from his fellows, for whom he confined it to light betting; he was never short of cigarettes.

"In Burma he made contact with the mystic sect of a religious order who accepted him as a gifted seer, and opened their sacred books to him. So, equipped with a full appreciation of his powers, and the discipline to disguise them, he returned to Oxford. His purpose was research, but not quite on the lines laid down by his tutors.

"Our other protagonist is an American, a Fulbright scholar who amply merited the hopeful title. White, we shall call him, was a child prodigy, a so-called 'Whiz kid,' who had been 'discovered' early and overexposed on wireless and television in the United States. His had been a childhood of tutors and business managers, of hotels, taxis, the bright lights. He had a nervous break-down in his teens, after being accused of cheating—a resounding scandal in that deeply puritan nation, and the occasion for extended editorial heartsearching. He took the only other way out; he cut loose from his family, changed his name, and buried himself in a small midwestern college. There he covered himself with honors, *summa cum laude*, and won a scholarship to Oxford, England.

"White knew he was psychic, but had never fully exploited his powers; he was afraid of them. Now, like a reformed alcoholic, he refused even to touch the charmed bottle—he did not know what sort of djinn he might release. But, like the reformed alcoholic, he grew confident, and halfway through his first term he decided to test himself. He saw an ESP Meeting advertised on the Junior Common Room notice board, and dared to attend.

"He found it disappointing. It seemed chiefly concerned with the phenomenon of coincidence. In the darkened church hall fuzzy slides of drawings that approximated each other, produced by subjects in isolated cubicles, were flashed onto a screen; lists of numerals were analyzed and hummed over. All so much Wincarnis to the alcoholic. He left early, and was followed and joined by a fellow deserter. They walked back toward College together.

"Now, Black had already marked down the young American as a fellow psychic; seeing him at the ESP gathering had simply determined him to make a move. White was flattered by the attentiveness, indeed the concentration, with which his cautious observations were treated by his senior. He had found his fellow freshmen generally hearty and callow, straight from school, unlike the war heroes now in their second and third years. They, he felt, had lived; he, who had already been through so much, longed to be accepted by them—and especially by Black, the loner in his army greatcoat, for whom he sensed a peculiar affinity.

"So the acquaintanceship flourished; they visited each other's rooms, went to concerts together, walked on Otmore, and at the end of term Black invited the American home for Christmas. Before they left, they made arrangements for White to move to his friend's staircase; the freshman who had the small attic room there was only too glad to agree to the exchange, though at the time White did not understand the reason for this eagerness.

"Up to this point the two young men had discussed the supernatural only because they had discussed everything. White had told his new friend of his prodigious childhood and the traumatic denouement that ended it. Black had spoken of the monks and their teachings, but both had avoided the subject of the extrasensory powers of which they were increasingly aware.

"In White this was fear; in Black, the patient taming of that fear. Full revelation Black left to the vacation, and to his possessive mother—a simple woman who had been cheated of her maternal rights by Black's violent independence. As he foresaw, she took the young American under her wing and used him at once as a second son and confidant. To him, late one evening, she unburdened her worries about her dark lamb—so clever, but so unstable; and the mess the poltergeists used to make; and how he had known when a favorite cousin in Inverness was killed rock climbing.

"The American spent the night in heartsearching; but he knew he could not deny this supernatural gift now summoned by one of even greater strength. The reformed alcoholic reached for the bottle.

"I have dwelt on this relationship to show how emphatically young Black was the prime mover; it also helps to explain the load of guilt he carried ever after.

"But at the time it felt more the shedding of a load. It was Christmas morning; they celebrated their new partnership with juvenile high spirits; on the way to Church they predicted the hymn numbers. Both hit on the same numerals, in the same order, and the board beside the pulpit simply confirmed the result. Without a word they abandoned the family and service, turned their backs—symbolically?—on the Church, and walked and talked on the moors till dark and dinnertime.

"Now for the first time in his life Black opened his whole mind to another individual. From their original encounter they had found themselves anticipating each other's thoughts, answering unspoken questions, meeting without arranging time or place. Now, in a few hours, the older told the younger all he knew, all the monks had taught him, all he planned to do. For his great experiment was with the supernatural, his goal to effect a true materialization, and he needed a more powerful 'current' than he alone could supply. He explained his deliberate choice of rooms in college: they were said to be haunted.

"Back at Oxford, term had not yet started, and they had the staircase to themselves. It was in the corner of the inner quadrangle; White's was only a small fusty garret, but he spent most of his time in his friend's rooms below. Even here the large study was dark, set in the angle of the two high walls, but there was always a bright fire in the opulently carved fireplace, for Black had a well-trained and devoted scout. Bunce had been with the college all his life and was held to be the authority on the staircase ghost; he could remember it all being told when he was a lad and considered too young to listen to such things.

"It seems that Black's rooms had been the scene of a Victorian scandal, when the rooms were occupied by an aging and eccentric theologian in holy orders, as most dons still were. It was said that he had been the cause of driving a pupil mad, to the point of suicide. Soon after, the don himself had died of causes unknown—had been discovered lying by that same ornate chimney-piece; and it was he who apparently haunted the staircase—footsteps on the creaking treads, sometimes the frantic rustling of pages. Once he had been seen, a tall gaunt figure standing motionless with his hands on the mantel shelf.

"Fifty years later these were still the hardest rooms in college to fill; none of the Fellows wanted them—too dark, they said. So when Black volunteered, on condition he could have the whole suite to himself, the Bursar had agreed. In this way Black acquired an inner sanctum, the dressing room, which he kept locked, even to his cleaner. There his precious books were safe from curious eyes, and he could meditate without interruption.

"Moreover, he covered the window with blackout material and developed photographs in the basin. He told White how for many nights he had set up a camera with its shutter open, focused to take in the whole of the fireplace, in an attempt to capture an impression of the ghostly theologian. One of the prints was quite interesting.

"In it there appeared to be two things hanging from the mantel shelf, barely discernible among the carved swags and curlicues—they might have been a pair of socks put there to dry. He let White pore over it, then produced his master-piece, a blowup of one of the 'socks'; now one could guess that it was not furry, or gauzy, as it had seemed at first sight, but that it had moved. And the upper edge, pale against the back wall, was corrugated, bumpy, like a row of knuckles.

"'I believe that is where it stands,' said Black. 'Why only its hands appear I don't yet know. But I propose to stand in just that place—hence the importance of this photograph—and concentrate on putting out as much current as I can summon. If I feel anything—well, that is where you come in. For then we will need to boost the output. According to my theory, my batteries would be drained before our aim is achieved—a theory that explains many of the disas-trous attempts at materialization in the past. But between us we may have enough psychic 'juice' to bring this thing about. And if one of us should suffer, or worse, there is a helper at hand, someone to give first aid, and—more important in my eyes—to be a witness.'

"Out of term college retires early. By eleven only a few dim squares of light showed where the midnight oil burned, and by twelve our psychic investigators decided there was no further fear of interruption. They locked the door, built up the fire, and turned out all except one small reading lamp. Then, while White stood where the camera had been and directed him from the photograph, Black positioned himself with his hands on the mantelpiece.

"At first Black gazed down at the fire, but it distracted him. He closed his eyes and summoned up all his concentration into a single fierce imperative: 'Come.' Fifteen minutes passed by White's watch, and still his friend hung, his head fallen forward, crucified against the high carved fireplace.

"Suddenly he gave a low moan. 'It's *cold*,' he whispered, and turned his head towards his left hand. White could see nothing. 'My hand is so cold.' As they watched, a mistiness appeared over the fist that clung to the shelf. Slowly a line of light emerged along the translucent blur, defining its upper edge: a long delicate bony hand apparently fashioned out of cloudy glass—for the whiteness of the knuckles was still visible through it.

"Then with a sharp cry Black twisted his head the other way, his eyes staring. 'Quick, help me! It's got both my hands—' His friend was beside him. 'Take over its left hand with your right,' Black whispered, 'palm to palm, remember. I will concentrate on this one—oh, the cold is creeping through me—'

"White moved warily round him; whatever might be standing there, he had no wish to pass through it. He stood close to the two left hands, felt the chill radiating from them, and saw the horrible perfection of the 'glass' one, engraved with the outline of nails and a fine mesh of wrinkles. It was only the desperate, voiceless appeal in his friend's face as he twisted round for a moment that gave White the strength to put his right hand forward. He slid it, palm upward, under the transparent hand, as Black gently removed his.

"The penetrating cold struck into White; it seemed to paralyze everything but the memory of Black's reiterated command: 'When it comes, do not flinch. Think, this is what we have worked toward; it is in our grasp. And give it all your strength.'

"Concentrating on that, White slowly raised his frozen hand; the glass one rose with it, and he could feel the answering pressure, as of something living, through the clinging tackiness of something dead.

"Black flexed his free hand, held it briefly to the fire's warmth, then placed it, palm up, under the icy mist that was gathering over his right. He reached out to White, and their grip completed the circuit. Now they stood with their backs to the fire, and grateful for it, pressing against a force they could not see, passing their vital strength to it, willing it with all their combined psychic powers to take form. There appeared before them a cloudy shape; next, the glassy outline, high and narrow. They felt their strength fading as it grew more solid, like a sketch being colored in, obscuring the room behind it, and even casting a flickering shadow across the carpet.

"It was a villainous old man, tall and stooping, in a crumpled dog collar and a long rusty academic gown. It nodded sharply and withdrew its hands from theirs. 'Thank you, dear boys—that will suffice.' The voice was a harsh whisper carried on foul carrion breath. It grinned wolfishly. 'Your part is over for the present. It will be interesting to see, will it not, how long your little experiment holds shape.' It stalked to the door. 'I will be back again when I have need of you.'

"White took a step forward and crumpled up in a dead faint. Black had fallen to his knees, his senses weak and whirling. He tried to crawl forward, and caught at the creature's gown, but he heard the key turn, the door slam, and it was gone. His fading thought was: Lord, what have we done?

"The scout found them still unconscious beside the dead fire. The room was icy cold. He called the cleaner from the next staircase, and she covered them with blankets while he brewed coffee and built up a roaring blaze in the grate.

"'Such goings on all in one night!' Black heard them from a great distance, clucking together as they set the room to rights—and was suddenly wide-awake. He kept his eyes closed and listened.

"'I don't surmise, Mrs. Hart, that the two happenings could be in any way connected. I observe no signs of violence here—overindulgence, perhaps—but nothing like the state of the Lodge. Poor Mr. Cartwright—porter for twenty-two years—and then to be bludgeoned to his death like a dog by some interloper!'

"'So you don't think it can have been anyone from College, Mr. Bunce?'

"'No, Mrs. Hart. Mr. Cartwright was, I imagine, persuaded to open the night door to this stranger, tried to ring the police when he was attacked—and there's the switchboard mangled, the door left open—'

"Black groaned and sat up. 'Ah, you're better, sir. What happened to you and Mr. White? Nothing odd was it, sir? Can you remember?'

"Black felt extraordinarily weak, and needed time to disentangle the events of the night. He pleaded a hangover, and dismissed the raised eyebrows and pursed lips with a boyish appeal for lots of ham and eggs. 'It must have been some gin one of the medical students pressed on us to try,' he said; 'tasted more like methylated spirits—' Murmuring indulgently, they went off to the kitchen.

"Then Black tried to wake his friend who still lay, breathing stertorously, wrapped in a blanket on the floor. He carried him to his own bed, tried to rouse him with brandy, and placed wet towels on his forehead, but without success. He closed the door on him when his scout carried up the breakfast, and was forced to hear out, and react suitably to, the awful tale of the murdered porter.

"'I'll bring you up the *Mail* when it arrives, sir. Terrible thing. The police will want to question everyone who was in College last night, I understand, sir.' And at any moment White might stagger through the door saying, 'Where did it go? What has it done?'

"At last Black was alone again. He put his friend's breakfast on a trivet by the fire and went into the bedroom. White was lying with his eyes open, dazed and feeble; he let himself be helped into the study, and sat hunched, sipping his coffee, while he heard about the disastrous results of their experiment. Neither of them was in any doubt that the spirit they had summoned and given corporeal being was the porter's killer.

"'It will not get far,' Black said over and over again; 'not enough current. No, it will just disappear, and revert to its proper place. And that is where we shall leave it.'

"'But a *double* tragedy! To have indirectly caused a murder, and, worse still—for the interests of science—to have succeeded so triumphantly and have no proof. For now we are forced to remain silent, and we cannot, we must not, call it back.'

"Bunce arrived with the newspaper, from which he read aloud the full account of the Lodge murder and the findings so far. The murder weapon was identified as a heavy shovel that was kept in the Lodge in winter for clearing snow from the doors; and a policeman on his beat in the High Street had seen a tall bent man in a cloak or gown hurrying towards Magdalen. He followed, but found only a drunk drowsing on one of the benches along the bridge, babbling of a 'long glass man.' 'Must have seen a deal too many long glasses already that evening, I don't doubt,' commented Bunce. 'And please, sirs, to come down to the Bursary. The police want fingerprints of everyone in College.'

"Black and White answered a few questions put to them by the detective inspector. They knew that the glass man must have disappeared, and that their story was too incredible to put forward; so they felt their implication in the affair was best forgotten. Let it be another unsolved murder—for now there was no murderer.

"No, they said, they had heard nothing, seen nothing; they had drunk too much and slept heavily and late. Their fingerprints were taken—and, abruptly, the whole situation changed. When the sets of imprints were compared with those the police had found, it became clear that those of Black's left hand and White's right hand *were the same as those on the shaft of the shovel*; and again, among others, on the handle of the night door and its key.

"Every whorl and twist was there, crisply reproduced, totally incriminating, even down to the cut on the cushion of Black's thumb from testing the keenness of the Christmas carving knife two weeks before. The law gathered round, holding the glass slides of ink imprints up to the light, and comparing them with the photographs taken of the marks on the handle of the shovel. It was an open-and-shut case.

"The accused men were white and dumfounded. 'But we didn't do it!' stammered Black. 'I mean, how could we *both* have held the shovel—'

"'Perhaps you will tell me,' said the inspector; 'but you both seem to be in pretty bad shape. I suggest that it was simply a matter of neither of you being strong enough to manage the wretched business alone.'

"'Please, sir—' It was the young policeman who had been on the beat. 'There's something funny about these here prints. We've been holding them the wrong way round.'

"'Nonsense, Constable. See here—exact!'

"'Yes, sir, but the ink is on the other side of the glass. Look, sir, they're the right imprints but the wrong way round—mirror images like, sir—'

"White leaped to his feet and was pressed down by heavy hands.

"'But that's what happened!' he cried. 'Don't you *see*?' He turned to Black. 'We gave it *our* fingerprints. It had no form: its hands took shape against ours—like ectoplasm, like putty—'

"'Yes, and during the time it was drawing on our strength its hands were against ours, your right, my left. The rest of it grew solid in its own form—but it kept the mark of its first contact, the prints we passed on to it.'

"Then there was nothing for it but to tell the law all that had happened—all about their precious, closely guarded experiments, their extrasensory powers, the materialization. The police took it all down, as they were bound to do. But they did not believe a word of it.

"'But don't you see? *There is no murderer!*'

"'Just because he has not been found? How can you prove your story? I suggest rather that you have worked yourselves—through this tampering with the so-called occult—into a sort of irresponsible, indeed vicious, stupor—drugs may have been involved. And in attempting to leave College after midnight you encountered opposition from the porter and, together, killed him. You may plead temporary insanity—but *only your prints* are on that shovel.'

"'But *reversed*! How were they reversed? Give us a chance to show you what happened—' Black pleaded.

"'Oh, no!' said White. 'Not that way—'

"'It's all we can do, you fool! Let them be at hand and arrest It if they can, fingerprint It, put It behind bars. And I wish them joy of It.'

"The mystery of the mirror-image fingerprints would not, as they well knew, stand up in court; so the police agreed to give them one night to prove their case. They were kept under strict surveillance in Black's rooms, and at midnight the detective inspector and the constable went out and waited on the landing.

"The two policemen were weary and skeptical, and as the hour they had granted crawled by, only the cold and their hard upright chairs kept them awake. Beyond the door all seemed quiet; once they tried it and found it had been locked on the inside. For a moment they suspected an attempted escape, but then were reassured by the low murmuring of two voices.

"At a quarter to two there was a terrible moan, a piercing cry, a crash. They hurled themselves against the stout oak door but barely shook it. All at once they heard the sound of the key turning, and stood back. A hinge creaked, and in the doorway was a tall gaunt figure in a gown, outlined by the firelight beyond. The two men tackled it but it shook them off with a terrible strength, and rushed past them and down the staircase like some monstrous evil-smelling bat.

"The stalwart band of policemen in the quadrangle overpowered and hand-cuffed the wild creature, and locked it, still fighting and howling obscure obscenities, in the back of the Black Maria.

"On the floor of the study by the fireplace lay two huddled figures. First aid was brought, a doctor was called, but adrenalin injections did not rouse them. White died without coming out of coma: it was as if his soul had been sucked out of him. Black's faint pulse continued, and soon after dawn he opened his eyes. 'It was too soon. No time to recharge,' was all he said.

"And inside the police van? The commotion ceased suddenly on the way to the station. The constable in the passenger seat looked through the grille and saw what he described afterwards as a 'gray man' slumped on the bench—'gray and shiny like dirty glass, sir. We pulled in to the side of the road and opened up the back, and all there was were the handcuffs. They were still locked, sir.'"

In the common room there was a general letting go of breath.

"Excellent," said Littlemount, rising and stretching. "It illustrates your tenets very well—and I promise solemnly not to tamper with the molecular structure of ghosts, should I ever get the opportunity to do so."

Nervous laughter and movement and the drawing back of curtains on the pale first light. Thank-yous and goodbyes were said, and soon the common room was empty—except for myself and the teller of tales. "And you are Black," I said.

"Yes. I guessed you knew. I have come to revisit my old rooms. The College has very kindly agreed to my writing up the materialization theory for *Mind*.

Needless to say, I changed my name long ago; they have no idea I was involved in the case, which was hushed up, of course."

"Are you really going to try to bring White back?"

"Yes, indeed. It is the least I can do in an attempt to expiate my guilt—and the only way I can ask his forgiveness."

"And you know he will be there—'something unfinished,' I think you said, 'something still to do.'"

"Yes, he will be there. It is for him I shall call, and hope it is he who comes. Of course, I may achieve nothing alone, in spite of the years between I have spent in developing my 'current'—"

I heard myself offering assistance. "My gift is not much," I said, "but at least I can help bear the strain, help complete the circuit."

He has accepted, although reluctantly. We shall attempt the materialization tonight. I hope we succeed in raising poor young White, and not the old Victorian bat. I set this down more to kill the hours of waiting than as any form of testament. Now it seems a little melodramatic; it will no doubt be an embarrassment to me when I reread it tomorrow morning.

The whole idea is mad, and so is "Black" himself; and I shall seal this lest anyone read it in my absence; I would never hear the last of it! But I am superstitious enough to write: *To be opened in the event of my demise.* I believe one calls it hedging one's bets.

E. X. FERRARS

The Rose Murders

It was on the day that Mrs. Holroyd refused Mr. Pocock's offer of marriage that he first thought of murdering her.

The rejection, so gently and kindly put but so utterly unexpected, filled him first with astonishment, so that he felt as if he had tripped over something uneven in his path and fallen flat on his face, and then with a searing rage.

For a wild moment he wanted to clasp his hands around her slender neck and squeeze the life out of her. But after that flare of hatred came intense fear. He had made up his mind, after his last murder, never to kill again.

On that occasion he had escaped arrest only by the skin of his teeth and he knew that the police still believed he was guilty, although they had never had enough evidence to bring a charge against him. That had been largely because of Lucille's passion for cleanliness. She had polished and washed and scrubbed everything in her little flat at least twice a week, so that the police, in their investigation, had not been able to find a single one of Mr. Pocock's fingerprints.

Dear Lucille. He remembered her still with a kind of affection, partly because she had cooperated so beautifully in her own death. Except, of course, for that business of the roses. It was the love she had had for roses and the pleasure it had given him to bring them to her from his own little garden that had almost destroyed him.

There had been no complications like that about his first murder. Almost no drama either. He had nearly forgotten why he had committed it. Alice had been a very dull woman. He could hardly recollect her features. However, it had happened one day that she told him in her flat positive way that she did not believe a word he had told her about his past life, that she was sure he had never been an intelligence officer during the war, that he had never been parachuted into occupied France, that he had never been a prisoner of the Nazis and survived hideous tortures at their hands—in all of which she had been perfectly correct; and really the matter had been of very little importance, but her refusal to share his fantasies had seemed to him such a gross insult that for a few minutes it had felt impossible to allow her to go on living.

Afterward he had walked quietly out of the house, and it had turned out that no one had seen him come or go, and her death had become one of the unsolved mysteries in the police files. There had been a certain flatness about it, almost of disappointment.

But in Lucille's case it had been quite different. For one thing, he had been rather fond of her. She had been an easy-going woman, comfortable to be with, and she had never expected gifts other than the flowers he brought her. But one day when he had happened to say how much he wished she could see them growing in his glowing flowerbeds, but that the anxious eye of his invalid wife, who would suffer intensely if she even knew of Lucille's existence, made this impossible, she had gone into fits of laughter.

She had told him there was no need for him to tell a yarn like that to her of all people, and he had realized all of a sudden that she had never believed in the existence of any frail, lovely, dependent wife to whom he offered up the treasure of his loyalty.

The dangerous rage that had possessed him only a few times in his life had exploded like fireworks in his brain. It had seemed to him that she was mocking him not merely for having told her lies that had never deceived her, but for having tried to convince her that any woman, even a poor invalid, could ever love him enough to marry him. His hands, made strong by his gardening, although they were small and white, had closed on her neck, and when he left her she had been dead.

By chance he had left no fingerprints in her flat that day. But he had been seen arriving by the woman who lived in the flat below Lucille's. Meeting on the stairs on his way up, he and the woman, an elderly person in spectacles, had even exchanged remarks about the weather, and it turned out that she had taken particular notice of the bunch of exquisite Kronenbourgs he had been carrying.

The rich velvety crimson of the blooms and the soft gold of the undersides of the petals and their delicious fragrance had riveted her attention, a fact which at first he had thought would mean disaster for him, but which actually had been extraordinarily fortunate. For afterward she had been able to describe the roses minutely, but had given a most inaccurate description of the man who had been carrying them, and in the lineup in which he had been compelled to take part when the police had been led to him by a telephone number scrawled on a pad in Lucille's flat, the woman had picked out the wrong man.

So the police had had no evidence against him except for the telephone number and the rose bush in his garden. But half a dozen of his neighbors, who had imitated him when they had seen the beauty of that particular variety of rose, had Kronenbourgs in their gardens too, and so Lucille's murder, like Alice's, had remained an unsolved mystery.

Yet not to the police. Mr. Pocock was sure of that and sometimes the thought that he might somehow betray himself to them, even now after two years, that he might drop some word or perform some thoughtless action, though heaven knew what could do him any damage after all this time, made terror stab like a knife into his nerves. He would never kill again, of that he was certain.

But that was before Mrs. Holroyd refused to marry him.

It had taken him a long time to convince himself that marriage to her would be a sound idea, even though he was certain she had been pursuing him ever since she had come to live in the little house next door to his. She was a widow and she believed him to be a widower, and she often spoke to him of her loneliness since her husband's sudden death and sympathized with Mr. Pocock because of his own solitary state.

She admired his garden and took his advice about how to lay out her own, was delighted with the gifts of flowers he brought her, and when he was ill with influenza she did his shopping for him, cooked him tempting meals, and changed his books at the library. And she had let him know, without overstressing it, that her income was ample.

"I'm not a rich woman," she had said, "but thanks to the thoughtfulness of my dear husband, I have no financial worries."

So it seemed clear to Mr. Pocock that Mrs. Holroyd's feelings were not in doubt and that it was only his own which it was necessary for him to consider. Did he want marriage? Would he be able to endure the continual company of another person after all his years of comfortable solitude? Would not the effort of adapting his habits to fit those of someone else be an extreme irritation?

Against all that, he was aging and that bout of influenza had shown him how necessary it was to have someone to look after him. And marrying Mrs. Holroyd might actually be financially advantageous instead of very expensive, as it would be to employ a fulltime housekeeper. She was a good-looking woman too, for her age, and an excellent cook. If he wanted a wife, he could hardly do better.

Of course, she had certain little ways which he found hard to tolerate. She liked to sing when she was doing her housework. If he had to listen to it in his own house, instead of softened by distance, it would drive him mad. She chatted to all the neighbors, instead of maintaining a courteous aloofness, as he did. And she had a passion for plastic flowers. Every vase in her house was filled with them, with a total disregard for the seasons, her tulips and daffodils blooming in September and her chrysanthemums in May.

She always thanked him with a charming lighting up of her face for the flowers he brought her, but he was not really convinced she could distinguish the living ones from the lifeless imitations. But no doubt with tact he would be able to correct these small flaws in her. On a bright evening in June he asked her to marry him.

She answered, "Oh, dear Mr. Pocock, how can I possibly tell you what I feel, I am so touched, so very honored! But I could never marry again. It would not be fair to you if I did, for I could never give my heart to anyone but my poor Harold. And our friendship, just as it is, is so very precious to me. I think we are wonderfully fortunate, at our age, to have found such a friendship. To change anything about it might only spoil it. So let us treasure what we have, won't that be wisest? What could we possibly give to each other more than we already do?"

He took it with dignity and accepted a glass of sherry from her. What made the occasion peculiarly excruciating for him was his certainty that she had known he was going to propose marriage and had her little speech already rehearsed. It disgusted him to discover that all her little kindnesses to him had simply been little kindnesses that had come from the warmth of her heart and not from desire to take possession of him.

Looking at her, with her excellent sherry tasting like acid in his mouth, he was suddenly aware of the terrible rage and hatred that he had not felt for so long. However, he managed to pat her on the shoulder, say that of course nothing between them need be altered, and go quietly home.

The most important thing for the moment, it seemed clear to him, was not to let her guess what her refusal had done to him. She must never be allowed to know what power she had to hurt him. Everything must appear to be as it had been in the past. In fact their relationship was poisoned forever, but to save his pride this must be utterly hidden from her. Two days later he appeared on her doorstep, smiling, and with a beautiful bunch of Kronenbourgs for her.

She exclaimed over them with extra-special gladness and there was a tenderness on her face that he had never seen there before. She was so happy, he thought, to have humiliated him at apparently so little cost to herself. Tipping some plastic irises and sprays of forsythia out of one of the vases in her sitting room, she went out to the kitchen to fill the vase with water, brought it back, and began to arrange the roses in it.

Up to that moment he had not really intended to murder her. He would find some way of making her suffer as she was making him suffer, but when his hands went out to grasp her neck and he saw at first the blank astonishment on her face before it changed to terror, he was almost as surprised and terror-stricken as she was. When she fell to the floor at his feet in a limp heap and he fled to the door, he was shaking all over.

But then he remembered something. The Kronenbourgs. Once before they had almost destroyed him. This time he would not forget them and leave them behind. Turning back into the room, he snatched the roses from the vase, jammed the plastic flowers back into it, and only pausing for a moment at the front door to make sure the street was empty, made for his own house.

Inside, he threw the roses from him as if they carried some horrible contagion and for some time left them lying where they had fallen, unable to make himself touch them. How mad he had been to take them to the woman, how easily fatal to him they could have been.

He drank some whiskey and smoked several cigarettes before he could force himself to pick the roses up and put them in a silver bowl which he placed on a bookcase in his sitting room. They looked quite normal there, not in the least like witnesses against him. It was very important that everything should look normal.

The next morning, when two policemen called on him, he was of course prepared for them and felt sure that his own behavior was quite normal. But he was worried by a feeling that he had met one of them before. The man was an inspector who now told Mr. Pocock that the body of his neighbor had been discovered by her daily woman, then went on to ask him when he had seen the dead woman last and where he had spent the previous evening.

He supposed that such questions were inevitable, but he did not like the way, almost mocking, that the man looked at him. But standing there, looking at the roses in the silver bowl, the inspector remarked admiringly, "Lovely! Kronen-bourgs, aren't they?"

"Yes," Mr. Pocock said, "from my garden."

"I've got some in my own garden," the inspector said. "There's nothing to compare with a nice rose, is there? Now your neighbor doesn't seem to have cared for real flowers. She stuck to the plastic kind. Less trouble, of course. But a funny thing about her, d'you know, she kept some of them in water? Some irises and forsythia, they were in a vase full of water, just as if they were real. That's carrying pretense a bit far, wouldn't you say, Mr. Pocock?"

"Unless there'd been some real flowers there first like, say, your roses. You'd a way of giving her flowers, hadn't you, Mr. Pocock? That's something she told the neighbors. But really you ought to have learned better by now than to take them with you when you're going out to do murder."

LAWRENCE BLOCK

Gentlemen's Agreement

The burglar, a slender and clean-cut chap just past 30, was rifling a drawer in the bedside table when Archer Trebizond slipped into the bedroom. Trebizond's approach was as catfooted as if he himself were the burglar, a situation which was manifestly not the case. The burglar never did hear Trebizond, absorbed as he was in his perusal of the drawer's contents, and at length he sensed the other man's presence as a jungle beast senses the presence of a predator.

The analogy, let it be said, is scarcely accidental.

When the burglar turned his eyes on Archer Trebizond his heart fluttered and fluttered again, first at the mere fact of discovery, then at his own discovery of the gleaming revolver in Trebizond's hand. The revolver was pointed in his direction, and this the burglar found upsetting.

"Darn it all," said the burglar, approximately, "I could have sworn there was nobody home. I phoned, I rang the bell—"

"I just got here," Trebizond said.

"Just my luck. The whole week's been like that. I dented a fender on Tuesday afternoon, overturned my fish tank the night before last. An unbelievable mess all over the carpet, and I lost a mated pair of African mouthbreeders so rare they don't have a Latin name yet. I'd hate to tell you what I paid for them."

"Hard luck," Trebizond said.

"And just yesterday I was putting away a plate of fettucine and I bit the inside of my mouth. You ever done that? It's murder, and the worst part is you feel so stupid about it. And then you keep biting it over and over again because it sticks out while it's healing. At least I do." The burglar gulped a breath and ran a moist hand over a moister forehead. "And now this," he said.

"This could turn out to be worse then fenders and fish tanks," Trebizond said.

"Don't I know it. You know what I should have done? I should have spent the entire week in bed. I happen to know a safecracker who consults an astrologer before each and every job he pulls. If Jupiter's in the wrong place or Mars is squared with Uranus or something he won't go in. It sounds ridiculous, doesn't it? And yet it's eight years now since anybody put a handcuff on that man. Now who do you know who's gone eight years without getting arrested?"

"I've never been arrested," Trebizond said.

"Well, you're not a crook."

"I'm a businessman."

The burglar thought of something but let it pass. "I'm going to get the name of his astrologer," he said. "That's just what I'm going to do. Just as soon as I get out of here."

"If you get out of here," Trebizond said. "Alive," Trebizond said.

The burglar's jaw trembled just the slightest bit. Trebizond smiled, and from the burglar's point of view Trebizond's smile seemed to enlarge the black hole in the muzzle of the revolver.

"I wish you'd point that thing somewhere else," he said nervously.

"There's nothing else I want to shoot."

"You don't want to shoot me."

"Oh?"

"You don't even want to call the cops," the burglar went on. "It's really not necessary. I'm sure we can work things out between us, two civilized men coming to a civilized agreement. I've some money on me. I'm an openhanded sort and would be pleased to make a small contribution to your favorite charity, whatever it might be. We don't need policemen to intrude into the private affairs of gentlemen."

The burglar studied Trebizond carefully. This little speech had always gone over rather well in the past, especially with men of substance. It was hard to tell how it was going over now, or if it was going over at all. "In any event," he ended somewhat lamely, "you certainly don't want to shoot me."

"Why not?"

"Oh, blood on the carpet, for a starter. Messy, wouldn't you say? Your wife would be upset. Just ask her and she'll tell you shooting me would be a ghastly idea."

"She's not at home. She'll be out for the next hour or so."

"All the same, you might consider her point of view. And shooting me would be illegal, you know. Not to mention immoral."

"Not illegal," Trebizond remarked.

"I beg your pardon?"

"You're a burglar," Trebizond reminded him. "An unlawful intruder on my property. You have broken and entered. You have invaded the sanctity of my home. I can shoot you where you stand and not get so much as a parking ticket for my trouble."

"Of course you can shoot me in self-defense—"

"Are we on *Candid Camera*?"

"No, but—"

"Is Allen Funt lurking in the shadows?"

"No, but I—"

"In your back pocket. That metal thing. What is it?"

"Just a pry bar."

"Take it out," Trebizond said. "Hand it over. Indeed. A weapon if I ever saw one. I'd state that you attacked me with it and I fired in self-defense. It would be my word against yours, and yours would remain unvoiced since you would be dead. Whom do you suppose the police would believe?"

The burglar said nothing. Trebizond smiled a satisfied smile and put the pry bar in his own pocket. It was a piece of nicely shaped steel and it had a nice heft to it. Trebizond rather liked it.

"Why would you want to kill me?"

"Perhaps I've never killed anyone. Perhaps I'd like to satisfy my curiosity. Or perhaps I got to enjoy killing in the war and have been yearning for another crack at it. There are endless possibilities."

"But—"

"The point is," said Trebizond, "you might be useful to me in that manner. As it is, you're not useful to me at all. And stop hinting about my favorite charity or other euphemisms. I don't want your money. Look about you. I've ample money of my own—that should be obvious. If I were a poor man you wouldn't have breached my threshold. How much money are you talking about, anyway? A couple of hundred dollars?"

"Five hundred," the burglar said.

"A pittance."

"I suppose. There's more at home but you'd just call that a pittance too, wouldn't you?"

"Undoubtedly." Trebizond shifted the gun to his other hand. "I told you I was a businessman," he said. "Now if there were any way in which you could be more useful to me alive than dead—"

"You're a businessman and I'm a burglar," the burglar said, brightening.

"Indeed."

"So I could steal something for you. A painting? A competitor's trade secrets? I'm really very good at what I do, as a matter of fact, although you wouldn't guess it by my performance tonight. I'm not saying I could whisk the Mona Lisa out of the Louvre, but I'm pretty good at your basic hole-and-corner job of everyday burglary. Just give me an assignment and let me show my stuff."

"Hmmmm," said Archer Trebizond.

"Name it and I'll swipe it."

"Hmmmm."

"A car, a mink coat, a diamond bracelet, a Persian carpet, a first edition, bearer bonds, incriminating evidence, eighteen and a half minutes of tape—"

"What was that last?"

"Just my little joke," said the burglar. "A coin collection, a stamp collection, psychiatric records, phonograph records, police records—"

"I get the point."

"I tend to prattle when I'm nervous."

"I've noticed."

"If you could point that thing elsewhere—"

Trebizond looked down at the gun in his hand. The gun continued to point at the burglar.

"No," Trebizond said, with evident sadness. "No, I'm afraid it won't work."

"Why not?"

"In the first place, there's nothing I really need or want. Could you steal me a woman's heart? Hardly. And more to the point, how could I trust you?"

"You could trust me," the burglar said. "You have my word on that."

"My point exactly. I'd have to take your word that your word is good, and where does that lead us? Up the proverbial garden path, I'm afraid. No, once I let you out from under my roof I've lost my advantage. Even if I have a gun trained on you, once you're in the open I can't shoot you with impunity. So I'm afraid—"

"No!"

Trebizond shrugged. "Well, really," he said. "What use are you? What are you good for besides being killed? Can you do anything besides steal, sir?"

"I can make license plates."

"Hardly a valuable talent."

"I know," said the burglar sadly. "I've often wondered why the state bothered to teach me such a pointless trade. There's not even much call for counterfeit license plates, and they've got a monopoly on making the legitimate ones. What else can I do? I must be able to do something. I could shine your shoes, I could polish your car—"

"What do you do when you're not stealing?"

"Hang around," said the burglar. "Go out with ladies. Feed my fish, when they're not all over my rug. Drive my car when I'm not mangling its fenders. Play a few games of chess, drink a can or two of beer, make myself a sandwich—"

"Are you any good?"

"At making sandwiches?"

"At chess."

"I'm not bad."

"I'm serious about this."

"I believe you are," the burglar said. "I'm not your average woodpusher, if that's what you want to know. I know the openings and I have a good sense of space. I don't have the patience for tournament play, but at the chess club downtown I win more games than I lose."

"You play at the club downtown?"

"Of course. I can't burgle seven nights a week, you know. Who could stand the pressure?"

"Then you *can* be of use to me," Trebizond said.

"You want to learn the game?"

"I know the game. I want you to play chess with me for an hour until my wife gets home. I'm bored, there's nothing in the house to read, I've never cared much for television, and it's hard for me to find an interesting opponent at the chess table."

"So you'll spare my life in order to play chess with me."

"That's right."

"Let me get this straight," the burglar said. "There's no catch to this, is there? I don't get shot if I lose the game or anything tricky like that, I hope."

"Certainly not. Chess is a game that ought to be above gimmickry."

"I couldn't agree more," said the burglar. He sighed a long sigh. "If I didn't play chess," he said, "you wouldn't have shot me, would you?"

"It's a question that occupies the mind, isn't it?"

"It is," said the burglar.

They played in the front room. The burglar drew the white pieces in the first game, opened king's pawn, and played what turned out to be a reasonably imaginative version of the Ruy Lopez. At the sixteenth move Trebizond forced the exchange of knight for rook, and not too long afterward the burglar resigned.

In the second game the burglar played the black pieces and offered the Sicilian Defense. He played a variation that Trebizond wasn't familiar with. The game stayed remarkably even until in the end game the burglar succeeded in developing a passed pawn. When it was clear that he would be able to queen it, Trebizond tipped over his king, resigning.

"Nice game," the burglar offered.

"You play well."

"Thank you."

"Seem's a pity that—"

His voice trailed off. The burglar shot him an inquiring look. "That I'm wasting myself as a common criminal? Is that what you were going to say?"

"Let it go," Trebizond said. "It doesn't matter."

They began setting up the pieces for the third game when a key slipped into a lock. The lock turned, the door opened, and Melissa Trebizond stepped into the foyer and through it to the living room.

Both men got to their feet. Mrs. Trebizond advanced, a vacant smile on her pretty face. "You found a new friend to play chess with. I'm happy for you."

Trebizond set his jaw. From his back pocket he drew the burglar's pry bar. It had an even nicer heft than he had thought. "Melissa," he said. "I've no need to waste time with a recital of your sins. No doubt you know precisely why you deserve this."

She stared at him, obviously not having understood a word he had said to her, whereupon Archer Trebizond brought the pry bar down on the top of her skull. The first blow sent her to her knees. Quickly he struck her three more times, wielding the metal bar with all his strength, then turned to look into the wide eyes of the burglar.

"You've killed her," the burglar said.

"Nonsense," said Trebizond, taking the bright revolver from his pocket once again.

"Isn't she dead?"

"I hope and pray she is," Trebizond said, "but I haven't killed her. *You've* killed her."

"I don't understand."

"The police will understand," Trebizond said, and shot the burglar in the shoulder. Then he fired again, more satisfactorily this time, and the burglar sank to the floor with a hole in his heart.

Trebizond scooped the chess pieces into their box, swept up the board, and set about the business of arranging things. He suppressed an urge to whistle. He was, he decided, quite pleased with himself. Nothing was ever entirely useless, not to a man of resources. If fate sent you a lemon you made lemonade.

ROBERT EDWARD ECKELS

Bread Upon The Waters

Criminal: MAJOR HENRY T. MCDONLEVY

The first time I met the Major I was in jail, serving out a $100 fine for disturbing the peace at the time-honored rate of $1 a day. I understand inflation has played havoc with that as it has with all things these days, and the judges now trade the time you have for the money you haven't at the rate of $3 or even $4 a day. But be that as it may, it was $1 a day then. And by my reckoning I still had 72 days to go when the turnkey lumbered down the corridor, unlocked my cell, and jerked his thumb up to motion me to my feet.

"Vacation's over," he said. "It's back to the cold cruel world for you."

"Now?" I said. "Just when the chef is learning to make the hash the way I like it?"

The turnkey gave me a sour look. "You want to lay there and crack wise," he said, "or do you want to get out?"

I really didn't have to give that much thought. "I want to get out," I said.

I was curious, though, and at the entrance to the cell block I asked the bored clerk who passed over the envelope containing my meager personal possessions, "How come I'm being sprung?"

"Ask the man at the front desk," he said without looking up.

Which I did. "Your fine's been paid," he said. "by your friend over there," he added, nodding his head to indicate a short barrel-chested man with a square ruddy face, full gray mustache, and close-cropped hair of the same gray color. The man was standing near the door.

His face lit up as soon as he caught me looking at him curiously, and he advanced with his hand outstretched to grasp mine. "Ah, James," he said. "Thought I recognized you from your picture. Sorry not to have got here sooner, but I only just learned your whereabouts this morning. Still, better late than never, eh?"

"If you say so," I said, "although—"

"I have the advantage of you, eh? Of course. But let me rectify that." He drew himself to his full five-foot-five and thrust out his chest even farther. "Major Henry T. McDonlevy, late U.S. Army. And the world's greatest adjutant until some bureaucratic mixup got me passed over for promotion and forced my retirement. Still," he added cheerfully, "the Army's loss is your gain. Because if I hadn't retired I wouldn't have been your fellow lodger at Mrs. Peters' and therefore wouldn't have heard about your plight."

"Yes," I said, "that's all very interesting. But—"

"But you don't want to hang around a jailhouse discussing it. Of course not." He took my arm and guided me out through the double doors. "On a beautiful day like this," he went on, "a young man—and even an old one—can find better things to do."

I let him take me a couple of steps down the street. Then I carefully disengaged my arm. "I don't want to appear ungrateful," I said, "but I can't help wondering just why you'd plunk down $100 for a total stranger, fellow lodger or not."

The Major's face sobered and he nodded thoughtfully. "Yes," he said, "I suppose it does seem a little odd. But," he continued, taking my arm again and pulling me with him down the street, "you see, my boy, I try to guide my life by the Good Book."

"You mean 'Do unto others' and that sort of thing?" I asked.

"No," the Major said, dragging the word out. "As a matter of fact, I had a different text in mind. Ecclesiastes ten, twenty: 'Cast thy bread upon the waters.'"

"Now," I said, "I do see. But if you're looking for a thousandfold return from me, I'm afraid you're in for a disappointment. If I had any money, Major, or any prospects of getting any, I'd have paid that fine myself."

"I think you'll find the exact text is 'for thou shalt find it after many days,'" the Major said unperturbed. "Although I must admit most people would have it your way and I myself have found that my investments generally result in a tidy profit.

"As for your prospects. Well"—he coughed delicately into his cupped hand— "I'm afraid I overstated the case somewhat when I said we were fellow lodgers. Actually, I rented your room after you—ah—vacated it. Apparently, however, the postman wasn't aware of the change and this morning he delivered this."

He took an envelope from his breast pocket and handed it to me. "I'm afraid I opened it—inadvertently, of course—before I noticed the name of the addressee."

"Of course," I said drily, opening the letter. It was three months old, having kicked around a bit before catching up with me, and it was clearly addressed to Thomas James.

"Dear Mr. James (it read), I regret to inform you that your great-uncle Arthur Wallace passed away on the 15th of last month, naming you his sole heir. If you will call at my office with proper proof of identity I will arrange transfer to you of his estate, said estate consisting of 750 acres in the heart of Michigan's vacationland."

It was signed Byron Swope, Administrator of the Estate of Arthur Wallace, Appleby, Michigan.

I glanced up from reading and as my eyes met the Major's he smiled brightly. "I took the liberty of doing a little research on your behalf," he said. "And the area *is* blooming, summer cottages being a big thing right at the moment."

I refolded the letter and stuck it in my pocket. "All right, Major," I said. "Fair's fair. I'll see you get your money back plus a reasonable profit."

"Fine," the Major said. He puffed out his chest and strutted along beside me. "We can discuss what constitutes 'reasonable' later, after the extent of my services has been determined. For now, though, let's concentrate on getting you to Michigan. And since one should never undertake a journey of that magnitude alone, I'll just trot along—if you don't mind."

Actually, whether I minded was something of a moot question. If I was going to get to Michigan at all, somebody was going to have to pay for the trip. And the Major was as good a prospect as any.

I'd never been to Appleby, Michigan, but I had a pretty good idea of what the town was like from my mother's description of her childhood—a wide spot on the road somewhere between Tawas and Traverse City. As far as I could tell from my admittedly limited knowledge, about the only thing that had been added since her day was a sign at the edge of town proclaiming it "The Heart of Michigan's Vacationland."

I remarked as much to the Major as we drove past in the car we'd rented when we'd found that the only public transportation north from Saginaw was a bus.

"Tush, tush, my boy," he said. "Nobody's asking you to live here. We simply realize our profit and move on to greener pastures, as agreed."

"And the sooner the better," I said, surveying the weathering storefronts that made up Main Street. The area might be booming as the Major had said, but the town certainly wasn't being ostentatious about it.

Swope's office turned out to be a narrow book-and-paper-cluttered cubicle on the second floor above the town's only restaurant. And Swope himself was a tall spare individual in his mid to late sixties with small glittering eyes in a long narrow face and a tight, almost lipless mouth.

"Well," he said, as the Major and I presented ourselves, "this *is* something of a surprise. After all these months I'd just about decided you didn't intend to claim your inheritance."

That should have alerted me. What I mean is, people just don't *not* claim inheritances. Unless, of course, there's some reason not to. But to tell the truth, in the last several days I'd sort of got used to letting the Major make the decisions. So I just stood there and let him take charge now.

"No mystery," he said bluffly. "The lad had simply moved and I didn't manage to track him down with the news until just recently."

Swope favored the Major with a long cool glance, then turned back to me. "I suppose you've brought your birth certificate," he said.

"I did," I said and passed it over.

Swope examined it briefly, then nodded. "Seems to be in order," he said. "Now all we have to do is transfer the land formally to you. Let's see now. I've got one of those forms around here somewhere." He rummaged through his desk and the cabinets surrounding it, finally coming up with a legal-sized document which he began to fill in with a ballpoint pen, the only modern touch as far as I could see in the entire office.

"I should warn you, though," Swope said, "that this is going to cost you some money."

"I knew it," I said. I took hold of the Major's arm. "Come on, Major, let's go."

But McDonlevy held back. "Not so fast," he said. "First let's find out how much."

"Well," Swope said, scratching behind his ear with the click button end of the ballpoint, "as I recollect, the taxes are paid through the end of this year, and there was enough in Arthur's bank account to cover my fee as administrator." His face brightened. "So all you have to pay is the standard recorder's fee of $20."

"Well," the Major said heartily, "I think we can afford that." He took two $10 bills from his wallet. "I assume we pay this to you," he said to Swope.

"That's right," Swope said, deftly lifting the bills from the Major's hand and stuffing them into his own pocket. "Among other things I'm deputy clerk of the court here and the recorder."

Swope set about finishing filling in the form, stamped it with an official-looking seal, and handed it to the Major who passed it on to me. I looked at it briefly, then folded it and put it in my coat pocket.

"Now that that's out of the way," the Major said, "my young friend and I would like to see the property. You can tell us how to find it, I assume."

"Sure," Swope said. "It's about five miles northeast of town. You can't miss it. It's the only slue land anywhere close by."

The Major looked blank. "I don't think I'm familiar with the term," he said. "Slue land?"

"I am," I said. I looked hard at Swope. "Do you mean to tell me that what I've traveled so far to inherit is nothing but a swamp?"

"Well," Swope said. " 'swamp' is probably too strong a word. But it is wet. Except in the winter, of course, when it freezes."

"Sure, though, man," the Major said, "it must be worth something?"

"It would be," Swope admitted, "if you could find a buyer. Which isn't too likely, I'm afraid, unless you can figure out how to drain it. About eight, ten years ago Arthur had some engineers up from Bay City. They said it wasn't 'feasible.' That means you can do it, but it'd cost more than the land's worth."

"I know what it means," I said. "Tell me, though, if the land's so worthless why did you bother to write me in the first place?"

"Had to," Swope said. "The law says the heir has to be notified." He smiled tightly. "I suppose I could have told you before you paid the transfer fee. But it never occurred to me."

"I'll bet," I said and left, followed by the Major.

"Sorry," I said to him outside, "but it looks as if you cast your bread on the wrong waters this time."

"Perhaps," he said. "But if I may mix metaphors—no battle's lost until the last shot's been fired."

"And just what shots do you plan to fire in this particular battle?"

"Who knows?" he said cheerfully. "But surely it wouldn't hurt to spend one night in the hostelry here, would it?"

I agreed it probably wouldn't. But I wasn't so sure when I saw the room they gave me. Still, I'd learned in jail that you can sleep anywhere and on anything when you're tired enough. And that's just what I was preparing to do—sleep— when the Major popped in. "Come, come, my boy," he said, "moping alone is no good. Let's be out where the action is."

"Action?" I said. "In Appleby, Michigan?"

"There's action everywhere, my boy," the Major said. "All it requires is a nose to ferret it out."

The particular action the Major's nose had ferreted out this time was a poker game at—of all places—Swope's bachelor quarters. Besides Swope there were two others present—a frail-looking, much younger man named Forbus who taught English at the local high school and a stolid hulk of a man named Mitchell whom I took to be a farmer.

"Good of you to help us out, Major," Swope said. "The man who usually fills in the fourth chair had to go out of town and we don't like to play three-handed."

"My pleasure," the Major said, settling into the fourth chair.

Swope picked up the deck and began to shuffle. "Seven-card stud all right with everybody?" he said.

Forbus and Mitchell nodded, and so did the Major after a moment. "I'm more partial to draw," he said. "But when in Rome, you know."

Swope gave the Major another of his long cool looks. "Yes, of course," he said, finished shuffling and began to deal.

Everybody seemed to take it for granted that I was just there to kibbitz. Which was fine with me, because seven-card stud is a game I try to avoid even when I'm flush. On the surface, it's a deceptively simple game. You're dealt two cards face down, then four more face up and another face down in rotation. Best poker hand based on any five cards wins. The kicker is that you bet after *every* card except the first two. In other words, there are five bets (six if there's a raise along the way) to be met on each hand. Compared with regular draw poker, stud is a real plunger's game where you can lose a lot of money in a very short time if you're not careful. Sometimes even if you are.

Partial to the game or not, the Major knew his way around a card table, and it soon became apparent—at least to me—that he and Swope were the only real poker players present. Forbus was the eternal optimist, always hoping for a miracle and consequently always staying with a hand too long. Mitchell, on the other hand, was an out-and-out bluffer who hadn't learned that bluffing works only when it's the exception to the rule.

Poker isn't entirely a game of skill, though. Luck enters into it as it does in everything else, and the other two couldn't help but win a pot now and then. And since both the Major and Swope played especially tight games, dropping out unless the third or fourth card showed strength, that wasn't as infrequent as you might expect.

So it began to look like the Major's "action" was just what it appeared to be on the surface—a friendly, not too exciting game in which not enough money was going to change hands to make or break anybody. Until 11:30, that is.

At 11:30 Forbus glanced nervously up at the clock on the mantlepiece as he passed his cards back to the dealer—Swope again—at the end of a hand. "Half an hour to go," he said.

"So it is," Swope said mildly. "We always make it a rule," he explained to the Major as he shuffled and reshuffled the cards, "to quit exactly at twelve. Saves argument and embarrassment. But," he added, "for that last half hour we pull out all the stops and play no limit. We find it makes a more interesting evening."

"I'm sure it does," the Major murmured. He straightened in his chair and put his hands flat on the table before him.

Something flickered momentarily behind Swope's eyes. Then he finished shuffling and began to deal the cards. The Major's first face-up card was an ace. Swope showed a king, Forbus a three, and Mitchell an eight. "Your bet, Major," Swope said.

The Major sat quietly for a moment, his fingers toying with a stack of white chips. "When a man says 'no limit'," he said at last, "I have to assume he means just that." He pushed the stack of chips forward into the pot. "Fifty dollars," he said.

That was exactly twenty-five times the highest bet made up to that moment, and it effectively served to separate the men from the boys. Forbus and Mitchell pushed their hands in and for all practical purposes joined the kibbitzers' circle, leaving the game to the Major and Swope.

With only two hands to deal, the game went faster than before. And by the time the large and small hands on the clock met at twelve, the Major owed Swope slightly over $900.

"I assume you'll accept my check," the Major said, reaching inside his jacket for his check book.

Swope's eyes went bleaker than usual.

"And," the Major added, "give me a chance to win it back before I leave town."

Swope's eyes brightened. "Planning on staying around for a while, are you, Major?" he said. "In that case, I'll be glad to take your check *and* honor your request."

He accepted the check the Major dashed off and, holding it loosely in his hand, walked with us to the door. "Same time tomorrow night then?" he said.

"Looking forward to it," the Major said.

I waited until we were about half a block away from the house. Then I said, "Operating on the assumption that the check is going to bounce back faster than a tennis ball, I suggest we just keep on going and not even bother stopping at the hotel. That Swope looks like a mean enemy and this is his town, not ours."

"Nonsense, my boy," the Major said. "All I did tonight was cast a little more bread on the waters and it would be foolish to leave before we found it again. But if it bothers you, reflect on this: it will be Monday morning—two days from now—before friend Swope can present that check at any bank and several days more before it clears to the bank it's drawn on. Surely that should give us ample grace period to do what we have to do and leave—even if, as you assume, the check is no good."

"Well, maybe," I admitted.

The Major slapped my shoulder heartily. "Of course it does," he said. "Now have a good sleep. Things will look better in the morning."

Actually, they looked worse. Because when I stopped by the Major's room on my way to breakfast, he was gone and his bed hadn't been slept in.

It took about a minute for the realization to sink in. Then I spent another minute swearing silently at him before settling down to figure out what to do. Instinct told me to cut out, too. Because even if technically only the Major stood to fall on the bad-check charge, small town justice has the regrettable tendency to overlook technicalities and settle for the bird in hand. And if they wanted a peg to hang a case on, there was the small matter of a hotel bill I couldn't pay.

Unfortunately, getting out of town wasn't going to be that easy. The Major had taken the car and hitchhiking meant at least a ten-mile walk down to the main highway since rural drivers are understandably skittish about picking up strangers in city clothes.

Of course, there are worse things than walking ten miles, and going to jail is one of them. But I felt I still had some grace period left. And when some unobtrusive checking around revealed that there was a bus at four that afternoon I opted for it, figuring I could slip on board just before it pulled out and be on my way before anybody realized what had happened.

What I failed to take into account, though, was just how fast and efficiently news spreads in small towns. Swope and Mitchell cornered me a half hour before the bus was due to leave. Mitchell had changed into his working clothes. And despite his farmerish appearance and willingness to break the laws against gambling, it turned out he was a deputy sheriff.

"Haven't seen much of your friend, the Major, today," Swope said conversationally.

"As a matter of fact," Mitchell put in more bluntly, "we haven't seen him at all."

"I'm not surprised," I said. "He said he was tired and was going to stick pretty close to his room."

"Now that's strange," Swope said, "because he isn't there now. And the chambermaid told the desk clerk the room looked as if not a thing had been touched."

"Well," I said searching for something to say, "you know how it is with these military types. They spend so much time getting ready for inspection they forget how not to be neat."

"Perhaps," Swope said, "But his—shall we say, unavailability—does raise some questions. Particularly since I had our local banker call a banker friend of his in Detroit and neither one of them had ever heard of the bank your friend's check is drawn on."

"Now, look," I said. "That check is a matter strictly between you and the Major."

"It certainly is," a familiar clipped voice said, bringing all heads swiveling around.

The Major glowered from the doorway, hands locked behind his back and his barrel chest thrust out. "What's this all about, Swope?" he said.

"Just a little misunderstanding, Major," Swope said coolly.

"Hmph," the Major sniffed. "It seems to me that gentlemen don't misunderstand each other this way."

"Perhaps not," Swope agreed. "But then how would either of us know?" He moved to the door, followed by Mitchell. "Same time tonight?"

"Of course," the Major said stiffly, stepping aside to let them pass. "Cheeky buzzards," he added in a mild, almost disinterested voice after they had disappeared down the hall.

"Maybe I'm one, too," I said. "Because I sure would like to know where you disappeared to today."

The Major's face brightened into a smile. "Just following the Good Book again, my boy," he said. "And now if you'll excuse me I'd better get some rest if I'm to be at my best tonight."

The same players as before were waiting for us at Swope's house that evening. No one made any reference to the events of that afternoon. But, whether for effect, or not, Mitchell had left on his deputy sheriff's uniform. The only thing lacking was for him to place his gun meaningfully on the table beside his cards.

"Seven-card stud still all right, Major?" Swope said as the Major took his seat.

"It's your game," the Major said. "I do have one suggestion, though. Since I'm the big loser, how about giving me a chance to catch up by extending the no-limit period to an hour or two? Or even," he added a shade too casually, "to the whole game?"

Forbus and Mitchell both looked at Swope, who let the moment drag out before shaking his head. "No," he said. "A rule's a rule. And as you said yourself, 'When in Rome—'"

"Do as the Romans," the Major finished. "Of course."

But it was apparent from the way he fidgeted in his seat and slapped his cards down that he was straining at the leash, impatient for the real game to begin. It wasn't long before Forbus began to fidget, too, and even Mitchell began to show signs of nervousness. Only Swope appeared unaffected, accepting his cards and playing them as unperturbedly as ever.

As for myself—well, I'd thought time had passed slowly in jail. But those days were sprints compared with tonight. And it was with a real sense of relief that I heard Swope announce: "Well, Major, half an hour to go. Now's your chance to get even—if you can."

As before, the game narrowed down immediately to Swope and the Major, and the cards and chips passed back and forth between them with such rapidity that it was impossible to keep track of who was winning. Still, when the dust settled at midnight, the Major was ahead.

"$800, I make it," he said, tallying his chips.

"So do I," Swope said equably, "and since you said you wanted a chance to win your check back, I saved it for you." He reached in his pocket and threw the now folded and crumpled check on the table between them. "I'll take my change in cash if you don't mind," he said. "$125, *I* make that."

He permitted himself a sly smile, and Forbus and Mitchell both grinned openly. The Major looked at them blankly for a moment. Then he smiled, although a bit wryly. "I have to hand it to you, Swope," he said. "You're a hard man to get the better of."

"I try to be," Swope said drily. He flicked his thumb rapidly over his fingers. "Now I'll take my money, please."

"Of course," the Major said. He counted $125 out of his wallet, passed it over to Swope, then picked up the deck of cards and regarded it with the wry expression still on his face. "Perhaps from now on I should stick to parlor tricks." He grinned suddenly, fanned the deck, and offered it to Swope. "Go ahead," he said, "Pick a card."

Swope hesitated, then selected a card, showed it to Forbus, Mitchell and me, and put it back in the deck for the Major. The Major cut and recut swiftly, then began dealing cards, laying them out in neat rows. When he'd got about halfway through the deck, he stopped, his thumb just flicking up the edge of the top remaining card. "One last fling, Swope," he said. "My next half-year's income against your next half-year's fees of office that the next card I turn over is yours."

I started to open my mouth, because Swope's card—the four of Spades—lay about a third of the way back in the rows of cards already face up! But a heavy look from Mitchell killed whatever I had planned to say.

Swope's face was as impassive as ever. "You have a bet," he said.

Smiling faintly, the Major reached out and turned the four of Spades face down!

There was a moment of silence. Then Mitchell guffawed and slapped Swope hard across the shoulders. "By God, Byron, he took you that time," he said.

"So he did," Swope said mildly. His eyes came up to the Major's. "That was clever," he said. "Deliberately going past the card you knew was mine. It lured me into overlooking the first rule of gambling—never bet on another man's game.

"Still, maybe you haven't won as much as you thought. I make my living from law and real estate. I only took that job as deputy clerk and recorder for the political weight it carries. That $20 I got from you was the first fee I've collected in six months and the last I'm likely to collect in as many—unless, of course, you manage to find someone foolish enough to buy that worthless land your friend

James inherited, in which case you'll be more than welcome to the $20 that sale will bring." And with that he laughed nastily. So did Forbus and Mitchell. They were still laughing when the Major and I let ourselves out.

"Satisfied now, Major?" I said after the door had closed behind us.

"Very much so," he said.

"Then let's get out of this town while we still have money to buy gas."

"Nonsense, my boy," the Major said. "It would be foolish to leave now when we're just about to find again the bread we've cast upon the waters." He took my arm and marched me along beside him. "Old Swope was right about one thing," he said. "You *can't* sell that land of yours. But you *can* give it away. Which, as your agent, is just what I proceeded to arrange for this afternoon.

"First thing Monday morning a reliable direct-mail firm in Detroit will begin releasing letters notifying the lucky 3000—selected at random from the telephone directories maintained at the excellent public library there—that they have each won a quarter of acre of land 'in the heart of Michigan's vacationland.' All that's required to confirm the price is that the lucky winner record the deed and pay the standard $20 fee before the end of the month.

"Naturally, I wouldn't expect too many to be able to come up and do that in person. So a convenient return envelope will be enclosed. And all we have to do as the letters come in is simply extract the money and pass the work on to Swope." He smiled benignly. "If experience is any guide, we can expect about fifty percent to respond, giving us a gross of $20 times 1500, or $30,000. Which isn't a bad return at all."

EDWARD D. HOCH

The Spy Who Didn't Remember

Melbourne left the cab at Leicester Square and headed up Coventry Street toward Piccadilly. He walked quickly, with eyes straight ahead, altering his pace only to avoid the occasional knots of theater-goers who crowded the sidewalk. The time was 7:21, and in less than ten minutes he would give the signal that would bring Saffron out of hiding for the rendezvous.

It was a cool April evening in London, and Melbourne breathed deeply of the crisp air as he walked. He passed the Prince of Wales Theatre, where something called *Catch My Soul* was playing in its third month, then a small brightly lit bookshop that displayed the latest American bestseller in its window. Ahead, the flashing signs of Piccadilly drew him on and he felt a springy certainty in his walk. Once contact had been established with Saffron the rest would be easy.

He thought of Gilda, waiting for him back in the room, but only for a moment. There would be time for her later, after the evening's business was attended to—after the man named Saffron had closed the deal and sold out his country. A slight smile played along Melbourne's lips as he considered the evening's mission, and he wondered what these crowds of dull, chattering theater-goers would think if they knew. He could give them a better show than any of those on stage, and it would be played out right here, in the very center of London.

Melbourne paused for a moment on the curb, and then started across Piccadilly Circus. There was a sudden jostling behind him, and he turned his head, irritated, to utter some sharp words of complaint.

That was the last thing he remembered.

Rand met Hastings in the lobby of the hospital and he could see the lines of worry on the older man's face even before he reached him. Hastings didn't often look like that, so he knew the news was not good.

"How is he?"

"Bad, Rand. Very bad. Bad for us, that is. The doctors think he'll pull through, but there may be some brain damage."

Rand caught his breath, remembering the cheerful greetings he had always exchanged with Melbourne, the grin on the man's ruddy face as he told a funny story or listened to one. "What sort of brain damage?"

"Partial amnesia. It may be only temporary, but at this stage of things they just don't know."

"All right. Let's go see him."

George Melbourne was in a private room on the fifth floor, his head swathed in bandages and a blank staring look on his face. Rand dropped into a chair at the bedside and spoke softly. "Hello, George. How are you feeling?"

The head tilted slightly to look at him. "Who—who are you?"

"Rand, from Concealed Communications. Surely you remember me?"

"I don't—"

Hastings spoke from Rand's side. "George, we have to know about your meeting with Saffron."

"No—I don't—" And Melbourne's voice faded.

Rand stood up and moved to the window. After a few moments Hastings joined him and said, "I'm afraid it's hopeless for now."

"Just what happened to him last night?"

"He'd gone to Piccadilly to meet Saffron. I gather he'd worked out some elaborate signal to bring Saffron into the open for the meeting. Anyway, he was crossing Piccadilly just before 7:30 when he was hit by a bus."

"Accident?"

Hastings glanced back at the bed and shrugged. "He may have been pushed from behind, before the bus struck him. Perhaps someone didn't want the meeting to take place."

"Do we have any other leads to Saffron?"

"None." Hastings looked again at Melbourne's bandaged head and said, "Let's go back to my office. There's nothing more we can do here."

An hour later, seated in Hastings' cramped and cluttered office overlooking the Thames, Rand lit one of his American cigarettes and asked, "Just how important was Melbourne to the success of the mission?"

"Damn it, Rand, he *was* the mission! He laid all the groundwork with Saffron and arranged for the man's defection. It was to take place last evening, right in Piccadilly. Melbourne was to signal him in some manner and Saffron would make himself known."

"Just how important is Saffron?"

"Only the top Russian agent in all Britain," Hastings told him, his voice and expression a study of frustration. "He wants to come over to our side, bringing with him a full list of other Red agents operating here, along with code books and planning directives. He telephoned Melbourne at home one night about a month ago. We've been carefully reeling him in since then, but his only contact has been with Melbourne. The actual defection was set for last evening."

"Perhaps Saffron will make contact with someone else if he's that anxious to come over."

"And perhaps not. If Melbourne was pushed in front of that bus it was by someone who knew about the intended defection. That might be enough to scare Saffron off."

Rand leaned back in his chair. "You think this is something for Double-C?"

"It is, if you want those code books. There's a secret message here, all right—the message Melbourne meant for Saffron. But it's not written on any piece of paper. It's locked somewhere in George Melbourne's brain."

Rand nodded. "Where it might be beyond the reaches even of Double-C."

The girl's name was Gilda Bancroft, and Rand remembered meeting her once in Melbourne's company. She was a striking blonde, quite young, with the pouting face and wide lips one often saw in the cheaper London dance halls. When she opened the door to Rand she seemed to know at once why he'd come.

"George is dead, isn't he?"

"No, he's not. In fact, the doctor thinks he's coming along. I just wanted to ask you some questions. My name is—"

"Rand. I remember you. I remember faces."

She stood aside and allowed him to enter. Her apartment was little more than a sparsely furnished loft—a long narrow room with wide windows looking out on a dreary street scene. The room had been partitioned into sleeping and eating quarters by the addition of a folding screen of some vague oriental design.

Gilda directed him to a couch in what was meant to be the living-room section of the apartment. The furniture there seemed fairly expensive, and he suspected that Melbourne had bought it for her.

"I saw him this morning," Rand said. "He's going to pull through."

She eyed him uncertainly. "Then what do you want from me?"

"We know he's been seeing a great deal of you lately, Gilda."

"Yes," she admitted. "What's wrong with that? He's divorced from that bitch he was married to."

"Nothing's wrong." Rand tried to soothe her. "George was working on an assignment and we're trying to piece it together. We thought you might be able to help us."

"He didn't talk much about his work," she murmured.

"Did he tell you who he was meeting in Piccadilly? Did he ever mention a man named Saffron?"

She didn't answer immediately, but sat there regarding him with a calculating uncertainty. Finally she said, "I don't know how much I should tell you. I don't want to get George in trouble."

"Believe me, you'll be helping him. Anything you can tell us—"

"He went there to meet Saffron. He was quite excited about it, really. He talked of nothing else ever since this Saffron began calling and writing him."

"There were letters?" Rand asked. He didn't remember Hastings saying anything about letters.

"Yes. He showed them to me. They're with his things."

Rand's heart beat faster. "May I see them, Gilda?"

She retreated into a pout. "I don't think he'd like that. They're here in his brief case, but he wouldn't like me going through it."

"I can assure you it's all in the national interest. The man named Saffron is a Russian agent—an important agent. He wants to come over to our side."

"I know. That's why George went to meet him."

"Get the letters, please."

She hesitated a moment longer and then stood up. He watched her disappear behind the screen, then return in a moment with two envelopes. "Here, I do hope it's all right."

Rand glanced at the postmarks and opened the first envelope. The letter was neatly typed, brief and to the point: *I am writing as I promised. The offer to come over to your side is a real one, and I will be in Piccadilly Circus every evening at 7:30, waiting for your signal. I long to flee the Russian yoke, and live with the freedom of one of your English blackbirds.*

There was no signature.

"He received that one about two weeks ago," Gilda Bancroft said. "The second one just came last week."

Rand opened it and read: *I have been waiting in Piccadilly Circus, even though I know it is too soon for your signal. I long to come over, but I know I must be careful. When you light up the sky with the numbers I give you, I know it will be safe, and I can live out my days in London like a good fat hen.*

Again there was no signature.

"This is all?" he asked the girl.

"All he showed me."

"Let me take these. It'll be all right. I'll give you a receipt for them, and when Melbourne is back on his feet I'll make it right with him. You won't get into any trouble."

"I hope not."

He rose to leave. "Is there anything else you can remember?"

"No."

"I'll be going, then."

She saw him to the door. "It's hell."

"What is?"

"Having a spy for a lover. . ."

Hastings looked at the letters and read them over carefully.

"They seem authentic," he said at last, "though there's really no way of knowing for certain. Mailed a week apart, here in London."

"It seems to me that Saffron is being unusually cautious. Why not simply arrange the meeting and then do it? Why all this playing with telephone calls and letters?"

Hastings leaned back, swiveling his chair around toward the window. "Saffron is a spy, Rand, the same as George Melbourne, the same as you and I. They can call us by all the fancy names they want, but we're still simply spies. Or counterspies—spying on the spies. After a time I think it begins to affect one's mind. Just look around you—Colonel Nelson forced into retirement with a nervous breakdown, Melbourne in the hospital with amnesia—"

"You can't blame Melbourne's condition on his work."

Hastings shrugged. "The doctor's not so certain. The bump on the head really shouldn't have caused all that damage. They think now it may simply have triggered a pent-up anxiety caused by overwork. Speeded up some sort of breakdown that was coming on anyway."

"And Saffron?"

"Why should the other side be any different from ours? Saffron may have become obsessed with passwords and secret messages. Then, too, he may want time to be certain he could trust Melbourne." He picked up the second letter. "*Light up the sky with the numbers I give you*—what do you make of that, Rand?"

"The signal was to be in the form of numbers. When Melbourne showed them in some way, Saffron would know he was safe to identify himself."

"Numbers in the sky? What could it mean?"

"I think I'll go over to Piccadilly this evening and try to find out."

Standing in the center of the famed intersection Rand imagined himself feeling much as George Melbourne must have on the previous evening. He glanced around at the colorful signs, occasionally allowing his eyes to wander down to street level, taking in the crowds of theater-goers and diners.

It was just 7:30, and if Saffron's letter had told the truth the Russian agent was somewhere in Piccadilly Circus at this very moment, waiting for the numbered signal that would light up the sky for him. Rand stared hard at the sky, but there were no numbers up there—only the inky blue of approaching night. He read the news bulletins on the moving electric sign along the south side of the intersection, but there was nothing for him there. He turned north, toward the line of movie theaters with their twinkling marquees, but all he saw were more people.

"Well! Mr. Rand!"

He turned, startled, and saw that the speaker was a bearded man named Max Stroyer, a sometime police informer whom Rand had dealt with on occasion. "How are you, Max?"

"What brings you to Piccadilly, my friend? Looking for a woman?"

"Hardly."

"I didn't think so." He stepped a bit closer, lowering his voice. "Then you must be on assignment. Looking for spies and codes?"

Rand gazed at the bearded man, whose sharp brown eyes were on a level with his shoulder. "Let me buy you a beer, Max," he said suddenly. "There's a pub across the street."

"You think old Max can help you, eh?"

"Maybe."

Stroyer drank his beer while Rand was still waiting for the head on his to settle. "Now what do you want to know?"

"About a man named Saffron. Ever hear of him?"

Stroyer screwed up his face. "You're on to big things, ain't you?"

"Then you do know him."

"Not really. But I've heard the name. They say he delivers the information when it's needed."

"To the Russians?"

"Sure. Who else?" He finished the dregs of the beer. "I think you guys are all in a dying occupation. Nobody wants spies any more. Hell, they don't die spouting patriotic slogans these days. They just get old and curl up and blow away in the wind."

"Yes," Rand agreed. "I suppose you're right."

"You know I'm right. Don't let it happen to you, Rand."

"Max, where can I find Saffron?"

"Maybe he's right here, listening to us now. Remember those old war warnings? *Even the walls have ears!*"

"If you see him, Max, tell him I want to help him. Tell him he can reach me at this phone number."

"Hell, I won't see him."

"If you do, Max."

"All right. Sure."

In the morning Hastings came into Rand's office in the Department of Concealed Communications. "The doctor phoned to say that George is much better. His memory seems to be returning."

Rand sighed with relief. "Thank God! I was beginning to think we were at a dead end."

"There's something else, too."

Rand saw the envelope in his hand. "What is it?"

"I sent a man over to George's apartment last night, since he lives alone. This was in the mail. Looks like another letter from Saffron."

Rand studied the postmark. "Mailed the day of George's accident."

He ripped it open and read the familiar typed sentences: *This is my last letter. I look forward to meeting you soon, beneath the lights of Piccadilly Circus. I am ready to come over. I have the codes and the lists you want. I will end my days sitting in the park, watching the swimming swans.*

Rand put the letter in his pocket with the other two. "Come on. Let's go see Melbourne."

They found him sitting up in bed, a good color in his face and a tentative smile on his lips. "I say, don't I know you two? Let's see . . . Rand. Is that it? Rand!"

Rand smiled and shook his hand. "Glad to have you back with us. We were worried."

Melbourne touched his bandaged head. "It's all coming back to me, slowly. But I don't remember everything yet." He turned his head slowly toward Hastings. "I'm afraid I don't remember you, sir."

Hastings cleared his throat and identified himself. "That's all right, George. Think nothing of it."

"Do you remember anything about Saffron?" Rand pressed.

"Saffron . . . Saffron . . . I don't . . . The name seems familiar, though."

"Numbers. Piccadilly Circus."

"No . . . I was there, though, wasn't I? That's where it happened. The accident."

"Why were you there, George?"

He looked blank. "I don't remember."

The following morning Rand found Hastings working at the main information computer bank. "Any word on Melbourne today?" he asked.

"Still coming along, but it's slow progress. Damn it, Rand, I hate to think of Saffron standing in Piccadilly Circus every night just waiting for the signal to defect, and we can't give the signal."

"You don't hate it half as much as I do. Perhaps we should simply put up a sign there and run a newspaper ad."

"And have him killed before he could do anything? Someone almost killed Melbourne, remember."

"I've been thinking about that," Rand said, watching the older man as he selected a reel of computer tape. "Are we really so sure that's the way it happened?"

"What do you mean?"

"Perhaps somebody lured Melbourne there to kill him for private gain, for some personal motive unconnected with Saffron."

Hastings shook his head. "You don't lure someone to the busiest spot in London to kill him, Rand." He punched a series of buttons on the machine and watched the reel begin to spin. "What about the letters? Any luck?"

"Not a thing. If they're concealing the number to be used as a signal, it could be done in any one of a hundred ways. Count the words, count the letters, substitute numbers for the first letter of each line, or the last letter. Add the dates shown on the postmarks, or subtract them. Everything is numbers, Hastings."

"Any idea what we should do?"

"Just wait for his memory to return. And hope Saffron will wait, too."

Rand went back to the hospital that afternoon and found George Melbourne with a visitor. She was a sad-faced middle-aged woman named Clare, who proved to Melbourne's ex-wife. After the introductions she stared hard at Rand across the bed and finally said, "I hope you're pleased with what you've done to him."

"I didn't do it to him, Mrs. Melbourne."

"Don't call me that! It's not my name any more!"

"Sorry."

"Your foolish little children's games, your spying behind trees! The world doesn't need you any longer, Mr. Rand."

"So I've been told."

"You see what you've done to his mind?"

The man in the bed stirred uneasily. "Clare . . ."

She had worked herself close to tears. "Why did I even come to see you? Go back to that tramp you spend the nights with. Go back to your spy games!" She turned and left the room.

"I'm sorry," Rand said. "I'm afraid that was my fault."

"Not at all," Melbourne reassured him. "She was always that way."

Rand pulled up a chair. "How's the memory coming along?"

"Good, good."

"Saffron?"

"Yes. It's vague, but I'm beginning to remember. A Russian agent, here in London. He telephoned me at my apartment and offered to come over to our side. I . . ." He put his hand to his head.

"That's all right, George. Take it easy." Rand drew the letters from his pocket. "After the phone calls he sent you these letters. The third one arrived after your accident."

Melbourne read over the letters with growing excitement. "Yes, yes! I remember these first two—it's coming back to me now. He wanted some sort of signal, so he'd know he was surrendering to me and not to someone else. He said he knew of me, trusted me. We agreed that I would flash a number over Piccadilly Circus at 7:30 in the evening. Then he would walk to the center island where I'd be waiting, and identify himself."

"He gave you the number over the phone?"

"No," Melbourne answered slowly. "He said he'd sent it to me, in case his phone was tapped. He said he'd sent it in three letters, because the chances of all three falling into the wrong hands were slim."

"Who did he fear so much?"

"The Russians, I suppose. He was bringing valuable data with him. If they knew his plan to defect, they would have killed him to keep the data out of our hands."

"Tell me about this number. How were you going to signal him? What does he mean in this letter about lighting up the sky?"

But the dazed look had returned to Melbourne's eyes. "I can't . . . it's there but I can't quite grasp it, Rand. Perhaps tomorrow more of it will come back to me." He smiled pathetically. "I'm trying. I really am."

"I know you are, George."

Rand went back to Piccadilly that evening and watched the crowds at 7:30. They were only faces to him, and he saw no one he knew except the bearded Max Stroyer, who was lounging in a pub doorway. Rand felt frustration running deep within him as he watched the people passing, fully realizing that any one of them might be the person he was seeking—any one of these men or—

He found the nearest coin telephone and called Hastings at home. "I'm in Piccadilly," Rand explained. "Something just occurred to me."

"What?" Hastings asked.

"Could Saffron be a woman?"

"A woman? We never considered that possibility. Why?"

"In the second letter there's something about *living out my days in London like a good fat hen*. Well, a hen is female, right?"

"I can't deny that."

"Why would a man use the phrase?"

"No idea," Hastings admitted.

"All right," Rand sighed. "It was just a thought." He hung up and went back to watching faces.

Two days later Rand took Gilda Bancroft with him to the hospital. Melbourne was sitting up and the bandage was gone from his head, revealing only a bump and some irregular stitches across his forehead. He remembered Gilda and rose unsteadily to greet her.

"I wondered if you'd ever come," he told her.

"Mr. Rand brought me. It's so far on the bus."

He turned to Rand. "I'm coming along fine. They say I can go home in another few days."

"That's good."

"I've been thinking about Saffron. We really do have to get to him somehow."

"Any suggestions?" Rand asked.

Melbourne sat down again. "It's a number. I know it is. A number in three parts."

"Three digits?"

"Perhaps more. I can't be sure."

"And where were you going to put the number?"

Melbourne frowned out the window, searching the sky. "High up somewhere. On a sign. On a moving sign."

"Yes," Rand said, remembering the moving news bulletins. That was where it had to be, the number in the sky that would lure Saffron out of hiding. "And the number was hidden in those three letters."

Melbourne nodded. "I just can't remember the details, though."

"What about the accident? Can you remember how it happened?"

"There was a jostling behind me. I started to turn—"

"He needs his rest," Gilda Bancroft interrupted. "You can't go on questioning him like this."

"No," Rand sighed. "You're right, of course. Take it easy, George. I hope you're out of here the next time I see you."

He waited in the hall for Gilda and she joined him in a few minutes. "He's better than I expected," she said.

"Yes, he's coming along."

"What about you? Any luck with your investigation?"

"Some. Mainly we're waiting for George's memory to come back."

"The man he was going to meet that night—Saffron—will he wait?"

"We can only hope so."

They walked outside, into the blinding April sunlight, and headed back toward Rand's little car. "When he's better I hope he quits this business," she said.

"Everybody wants us to quit. Two people told me the same thing in recent days. Nobody wants spies any more. Nobody wants war."

"George said his ex-wife came to see him."

"Yes."

"I met her only once. She's a bitch."

"She probably feels the same about you."

Rand climbed the worn stairs to the second floor of the office building overlooking Piccadilly Circus. The man he'd phoned was waiting for him and showed him into a narrow, crowded room dominated by a large desk with a typewriter-like keyboard.

"This is where we do it, Mr. Rand," the man explained. His name was Hawkins, and he was an employee of the London newspaper which ran the electric sign with its moving news flashes. "The message is punched onto tape by this machine, and the tape is then fed through here. The tape can be made into an endless loop to repeat the same news bulletins, or new messages can be added. Occasionally we might send through some random letters or numbers just to test the system, or to see if all the thousands of individual light bulbs out there are working properly."

"And, George Melbourne asked you to flash some numbers for him?"

The man nodded. "Mr. Melbourne came to me about two weeks ago. He identified himself and explained that it was a national security matter. He said that on a given night he would supply me with a number which I would run once on the news bulletin at exactly 7:30. It was a simple enough request, so I agreed to it."

"And the night was to be—?"

"He phoned last Tuesday—the day you say he was hit by the bus. He gave me the number and said to run it that night. I did as he said, but never heard any more about it. I never even knew he was injured until you told me today."

"He actually gave you the number?"

"Yes. I have it written down here. Do you want it?"

Rand picked up a pencil and jotted down six digits. "Was this it?"

"Yes. How did you know? Did Mr. Melbourne tell you?"

Rand shook his head. "A man named Saffron told me."

Two days later George Melbourne was released from the hospital. Rand and Hastings were waiting for him and they drove to his apartment while Rand outlined the plan. "I have the number, George. I figured it out from the three letters. You don't have to remember it now."

Melbourne looked relieved. "That's good. That was the one thing I still couldn't come up with."

"We can flash it on the sign, George, but we need you there. Saffron knows you and trusts you. The night you were injured, the number flashed on, but he didn't reveal himself—simply because you weren't there. I want you to come to Piccadilly with us tonight, George, and stand on that island in the center."

"Mightn't it be dangerous?" Hastings objected. "He was almost killed the last time."

"We'll be there," Rand assured him. "One of us on each side."

They arrived in Piccadilly shortly after seven, when the sky was still bright with the memory of the spring day, and the usual theater and dinner crowds were filling the sidewalks on all sides of the circle. Standing there on the center island, facing the moving sign above them, Rand could almost imagine what Saffron must have felt on all those nights. He only hoped it wasn't too late.

"You said you knew the number," Hastings prompted him.

Rand nodded. His eyes were scanning the crowds on the opposite sidewalk for a familiar face. "The part about the hen, in the second letter. It really didn't make sense, until I realized that each of Saffron's three letters ended with some reference to an animal. The first letter had blackbirds, the second had the hen, and the third had swans. If there was a number concealed in the letters, it was most probably concealed there. Now, are there any numbers connected with these three animals? Yes, there are—*four and twenty blackbirds*, from the famous nursery rhyme, gives us the number 24."

"But what about that good fat hen?"

"Another nursery rhyme, Hastings. *One, two, buckle my shoe*, and *nine, ten, a good fat hen*. Which makes our number so far read 24910." Rand's eyes were on the moving sign above them. It was almost 7:30. His eyes scanned the crowd once more. If he was wrong all three of them could be in deadly peril. If he was right—

"The last part of the number?"

"Those swimming swans. *Seven swans a'swimming*, from *The Twelve Days of Christmas*."

At his side Rand saw Melbourne tense. It was exactly 7:30 and the ribbon of light bulbs had gone suddenly blank. Rand continued talking, his voice a bit louder than he'd planned. "Making the full number 249107—the number that will bring Saffron out of hiding. The number that—"

And there it was, above them, starting its bright lonely journey down the track of light. 249107.

At his side George Melbourne turned and said, very quietly, "My name is Saffron. I am a Russian agent. I want to defect."

It was morning before Rand could talk about it, and he sat again in Hastings' office overlooking the muddy Thames and thought about the labyrinthine ways of the human mind.

"You mean you knew it all the time?" Hastings asked, incredulous.

"Not all the time, no." Rand was feeling very old. Once, long ago, George Melbourne had been a friend. "And even at the end I wasn't absolutely certain—not till he spoke. But I had to get him there to see the number on the sign. I knew if Melbourne and Saffron were two parts of the same person, the number would trigger Saffron's defection."

"It's like something out of Jekyll and Hyde!"

Rand nodded.

"Or Freud and Jung. Melbourne was a double agent in the truest sense. I think he began as any other double spy, simply playing both sides, but something happened along the line. Saffron gradually became an entirely separate personality—so much so that when he decided to come over to the British side he insisted on surrendering only to Melbourne. That's when the letter writing began, and the imaginary phone calls.

"And the accident?"

"It really was an accident, a jostling by the crowd. Of course Melbourne must have been under tremendous mental pressure that night, and the slightest damage to his head brought on the temporary amnesia. Remember, the doctor told you he suspected some pre-existing mental condition that was merely triggered by the accident. That was the only danger last evening. If I was wrong, and someone had tried to kill him, our lives might have been in jeopardy standing out there. But I was almost certain I was right."

"How could you have known, though, Rand? I never suspected such a thing."

"The number. It was all in the number. Melbourne went to meet Saffron last Tuesday night *knowing the complete number*. In fact, he'd even phoned the sign man that day and told him the number to flash on the screen of light bulbs. But remember, the third and final letter did not arrive at Melbourne's apartment till the following day, the day after his accident. On Tuesday he could not possibly have known that 7 was the final digit of the number. He could not have even guessed at it, because the first two letters contained two-digit and three-digit numbers, both from nursery rhymes. The final letter contained a one-digit number from a Christmas song. Melbourne could not possibly have anticipated that final number—he could have known it only if he had originated it, only if he had written the letters himself. Only if, in short, he was Saffron."

"What will happen to him now?" Hastings wondered.

"That's for the doctors to say. In my opinion he's pretty far gone on this split personality."

"And the codes and lists he was to deliver?"

"I think he'll tell us about them. If he doesn't, I have an idea where they might be found—in that brief case of his at Gilda Bancroft's apartment."

Hastings nodded, stirring uneasily behind his desk. "What was it that did it to him, Rand? Overwork? His wife? What pushed him over the line?"

There was no simple answer. Rand stood up and walked to the window. The river seemed darker than usual this day. "He was on the road to madness, Hastings, and the games we play were too much for his mind. Sometimes, when I think about it, I wonder if we're not all on the road to madness—the spies and the generals and even the politicians who pay us. We're in a world that doesn't want us any more, and maybe Melbourne knew it."

"I think he did," Hastings said quietly. "I think we all know it. But we keep on with it anyway."

CHRISTIANNA BRAND

Clever and Quick

Y ou had to keep up appearances; so the apartment was very showy, everything phony right down to the massive brass fender in front of the electric fire. But keeping up appearances was one thing and keeping up the payments was another; and with the theater as it was these days, both of them had
been "resting" for a long, long time. So the fact was that they really ought to let
Trudi go.

Trudi was the *au pair* girl and for different reasons neither one wanted her
to go.

They were having a row about it now, standing in front of the fireplace. They
had a row on an average of once an hour these days—nag, nag, bloody nag.
Colette was driving Raymond out of his mind. And now this thing about Trudi.
If he secretly (somehow) made up Trudi's pay? He suggested, "Try offering her a
bit less for the work."

"*You* try offering her a bit less—for the pleasure," said Colette. It touched him
as ever on the raw. "Are you suggesting—?"

"Raymond, that girl thinks of nothing but money and you know it."

Yes, he knew it, and with the knowledge his heart grew chill. If a time came
when he could no longer give Trudi presents— He was mad about her—a little
sharp-eyed, shrew-faced mittel-European—and yet here he was, caught, crazy
for her, helpless in the grip of her greedy little claws. He, Raymond Gray, who
all his life had been, on stage and off, irresistible to women, now caught in the
toils of a woman himself. If I were slipping a bit, he said to himself, if my profile
were going, if my hair and my teeth weren't so perfect as once they were—but he
was wearing marvelously well. Why, even that drooling old monster in the
opposite apartment—

She was not a monster, though she was a big woman and, having once been
something of an athlete, now found all the fine muscle running to flabby white
fat. But drooling? She was disgusting, she thought, out of her mind—a fat, ugly,
aging widow, sitting here drooling over a has-been matinee idol not much more
than half my age.

But, as he was caught and helpless, so was she—caught and helpless, sitting
there like a silly schoolgirl, yearning only to pop out to her balcony and see if,
through his window, she could catch a glimpse of him. From her room she could

not see into his; the apartments were not in fact opposite each other but across a corner, at the same level.

But she dared not venture forth. The plane trees in the street just below were in full pollination and if she so much as poked out her nose, her allergy would blow up sky high. And even just passing in the corridor, going up and down the elevator, he mustn't see her with streaming red eyes and nose.

She spent a good deal of time in the corridors and the elevator. "Oh, Raymond," she would cry, "fancy running into you again!" She had long ago scraped up an acquaintance and it was Raymond, Colette, and Rosa between them now. They were not unwilling—her place was rich in champagne cocktails and dry martinis, with lots of caviar on little triangles of toast. She was loaded.

Colette said so now "Can't you wangle something out of the old bitch over there? She's loaded, and if you'd so much as kiss her hand she'd chop it off and give it to you, diamond rings and all."

Her hand was like a frog's back, all speckled with the greeny-brown patches of aging skin. "All the same, I'll tell you something," he said. "If you were out of the way, damn nagging so-and-so that you are, she'd make me a ruddy millionaire, I swear she would."

"Yes and where would your precious Trudi be then? Because," said Colette nastily, "I don't think dear Rosa would put up with very much of *that* little load of fancy tripe."

"Don't you call Trudi names!" he shouted.

'I'll call her what she is. I'm entitled to that much, surely?"

She had a vile mind, a vile mind and a foul mouth to express what was in it. It flashed across him in a moment of hazy light, red-streaked, that once he had loved her—never dreaming that behind the façade lay this creature of venom and dirt, never dreaming that one day he would stand here with upraised hand, would lunge forward and strike out at her, would have it in his mind to silence her forever.

But his hand did not touch her. She stepped back and away from him, tripped over the rug on the polished floor before the fireplace, fell heavily, almost violently throwing herself back and out of his reach. A brief shriek, arms flailing, a sickening scrunch as the base of her skull hit the rounded knob of the heavy brass fender. And suddenly—stillness.

He knew she was dead.

Trudi stood in the doorway, then moved forward to him slowly. She said, "Is all right. I saw. You did not touch her." And she fumbled for the English word. "Was—accident?" She came close beside him, staring down. "But she is dead," she said.

She was dead. He had not touched her, it had been an accident. But she was dead—and he was free.

It took him a little while to accept that Trudi was not going to tie up her life with an out-of-work, has-been actor, free or not free. "But, darrleeng, you know that your money is all gone, soon I must anyway leave. Mrs. Gray she has told me so." And since Mrs. Gray was lying there dead on the floor and could not contradict, she improvised a hurried tally of the debts already owing to her. "And this I must have, Raymond, soon I go home if I have no more a job here."

To be free—to be free to marry her and now to lose her! He pleaded, "Don't you love me at all?"

"But of course! Only how can we marry, darrleeng, if you have no money to live? So this money I must have, to go home."

"You can't go yet, anyway. You'll have to stand by me about—her." He had almost forgotten the poor dead thing lying there, ungainly, at their feet. "You'll have to give evidence for me."

She shrugged. "Of course. Was accident. But then I go home."

"Leaving me here like this? Trudi, I have no wife now, no money—"

The little shrug again, so endearing to his infatuated heart, half comic, half rueful; the wag of the pretty little head toward the window across the corner. "As to wife, as to money—over there, plenty both."

He said quickly, "Then I should be rich. So you and I—?"

But she said, as a few minutes earlier Colette had said, "I don't think Mrs. Rosa Fox puts up with nonsense. I think she suddenly pulls the moneybags—tight."

Did the idea come to him all in a flash as it seemed at the time?—or was there an interval while he thought?—while he stood over his wife's dead body and carefully, deliberately, thought it all through to the end? All he knew afterward was that suddenly he had Trudi by the arm, was talking to her urgently, pulling her to kneel down beside as, very delicately, he scraped from the round brass knob of the fender a fleck of the blood so rapidly congealing there, smearing it over the round brass knob of the poker, the knob identical in size, covering the smears with his own hand. And finally he threw the poker back into the fireplace.

"Now, Trudi, slip out, don't let anyone see you. Buy something somewhere. Come back right away and this time let the porter see you."

He did not look back, as he scrambled to his feet, at the still sprawled body—he had not even that moment to spend on the past. The future was now ahead of him. Only, he prayed, as he furtively slid out into the corridor, let Rosa be in! And let her be alone!

She was in and alone. She was always in and alone these days, flopped in an armchair, dreaming like an adolescent girl of her hopeless, her helpless, love. "A woman of my age," she thought, "sitting here mooning over another woman's husband." But she'd been quite a gal in her day and widowed a long, long time. Now she said, "Raymond—how lovely!" And at once, "But what's the matter, my dear? Are you ill?"

"Rosa," he said, "You must help me!" And he fell on his knees before her, grabbing at her skirt with shuddering hands—really, with all that talent it was quite extraordinary that he couldn't get more work! He threw a hoarse quaver into his voice. "I've killed her," he said.

She stepped back and away from him. "Killed her?"

"Colette. I've killed her. She went on and on. She said horrible things about—about you, Rosa. She thinks you—she always said that you—Rosa, I know you've liked me—"

"I love you," she said simply; but she took a deep, deep breath while the future spread out before her—as earlier his own had opened out to him. His wife was dead and he was free.

He pretended amazement at her answer—amazement and gratitude; but he was too clever to claim immediately a return of her feeling. He came at last to the point. "Then, even more, Rosa, may I dare to ask you what I was going to. I am throwing myself on your mercy, just praying that out of friendship you will help me. And now, if you really mean that you—"

And he went with her to the sofa and sat there gripping her hands and poured it all out to her. "She was being so vile. She had—well, she's dead, but Colette had a filthy mind, Rosa. She'd been going on like this for weeks and suddenly I couldn't stand it any more. I saw red. I—I picked up the poker. I didn't mean to harm her—honestly, I swear it—just to frighten her. But when I came to myself again—" And he prayed, "Oh, my God, please try to understand!"

"You did this because she was saying foul things about *me*?"

"You've always been so nice to us, Rosa; it just made me sick, her talking like that, sneering and jeering." And he poured it all out again, living through the scene, only substituting her name for Trudi's. Her big plain face went first white, then scarlet, then white again. She held tightly to his hand. "What do you want me to do?"

"Rosa, I thought very quickly—I do think quickly when I'm in a spot. It seems awful now, her lying there dead and me just thinking of myself, trying to fight my way out of it. But that's what I did. And then I knelt down and—well, there are two brass knobs on the fender exactly like the one on the poker and I—I moved her head so that it looked as though she'd hit it against one of the fender knobs, and then I cleaned all the—the blood and stuff off the poker—"

She was a clever woman—quick and clever. The body might have slowed down, the body that once had been so strong and under control, but the mind was still clever and quick. "An accident," she said.

"Yes, but—people knew we were always quarreling. Trudi must have known it, of course. They could say I'd pushed her, given her a shove." He gave her a sick look that was not too difficult to assume. "At the least—manslaughter," he said.

Clever and quick. "You want me to say that I *saw* what happened? That you didn't hit her?"

"My God," he said, "you're marvelous! Yes. You could say you saw it all through the window, saw me standing there talking to her, say frankly that we seemed to be arguing, make it look as though you're not too much on my side, just a casual neighbor. And then—there's a rug there, you know it, very silky and slippery—you skidded on it once yourself, remember? Perfectly possible for her to have taken a backward step, slipped and fallen backward; and of course that would be all you'd know—you can't see down to the floor of our room, even from your balcony."

"But I'd have to say I was out *on* the balcony. I can't see your window from in here."

He had thought that out too. "Your balcony's only overlooked by two flats, and all those people will have been out; I know them. No one could say that you *weren't* there."

"All right," she said.

"You'll do it for me?"

"Of course. But what about that girl, that little trollop, whatever her name is—the *au pair?*"

He could hardly keep the stiffness from his voice but he controlled himself. "Out shopping, thank God!" And thank God, also, that Rosa couldn't in fact have been on the balcony, looking in, seeing Trudi there in the room with him. He knew all about the allergy, and one glance at her face confirmed it—Rosa hadn't been out.

"Well, go back now. You must call a doctor quick. And say nothing about me. Just tell your story, don't seem even to think of bringing me into it. They'll be round here soon enough, asking if I saw anything. Now, time's passing, you really must go."

He started for the door but suddenly he paused. "Rosa!" He had assumed a look of shame but over the shame a flush of exultancy. "Rosa, it's awful to have even thought of it, but suddenly it's come to me. A trial for murder! You know how things are in the theatrical business, you know how things have been with me lately. But if I were suddenly in the news! Accused of murder—standing there at the Old Bailey, headlines in all the papers, a *cause celebre*! And then— the dramatic intervention, the witness who'd seen it all, the last-minute evidence." He stood before her, half shame-faced, half pleading. "Rosa?"

"Why didn't I give evidence before? They'd never even have charged you if I'd spoken at once."

"Well, that's the point. I *must* get myself arrested and tried. You'd have to say you hadn't realized, you didn't want to get mixed up in it. But then of course the moment you heard I was accused—"

"Even so you wouldn't get further than the first hearing, whatever it's called. No publicity in that."

"You couldn't—just be abroad for a little while, out of touch?"

She opened her mouth to say that none of it mattered, he'd never need to work again. But she held her peace. He was an actor, actors needed to work, they had to express themselves. "Leave it all to me. I'll handle it," she said.

The earlier headlines were not too bad though hardly sensational and then came the long dull period before the trial opened. However, at last—the day. Himself in the dock, very pale, very handsome. The police in the witness box.

"Accused stated—" A flipped-over page in a notebook. "Accused stated, 'Oh, my God, this is awful, I must have hit out at her, I must have had a blackout, she was nag nag nag at me the whole bloody time because I wasn't getting work, but I never meant to harm her, I swear I did not.'"

And the forensic evidence. "On the head of the poker I found a small smear of blood." The smear had been consistent with the blood of the dead woman, with having come there at the time of her death. Tests showed that the accused had handled the poker after the blood came there. Yes, consistent with his having attempted to remove marks of blood with the palm of his hand, missing the one small smear. The blade of the poker appeared to have been wiped—it showed no fingerprints.

In reply to defense counsel: Yes, it was true that the blade of a poker would not be much handled in the ordinary way and the wiping might well have been simply the previous routine cleaning. The doctor testified that the woman had been dead between half an hour and an hour when he saw her.

Trudi in the box for the defense: shrewd and cool. Had arrived back from the shoppings to find Mr. Grray on his knees beside the body; had had almost to lift him to his feet. Yes, he might very well have touched the poker with his hand, made bloody by his examination of the wound; his arms were all over the place as she hauled him up. She had trried to get him calm; wanted to call a doctor but did not know the number of him, and Mr. Grray seemed so dazed she could get no sense from him. And anyway, what was the hurry, said Trudi with one of her shrugs. Anybody could see that Madame was dead.

And so at last to Rosa Fox. She had with extraordinary dedication deliberately shed all aids to such doubtful charms as she possessed—stripped off the jewelry, dressed herself drably, sacrificed the cosmetics which ordinarily, to some extent at least, disguised the ravages of her age. Not for one moment could anyone suspect that here stood a woman with whom the prisoner could ever have had the slightest rapport.

Into the agreed routine. The casual acquaintance, the occasional drink together. The question of the police directly after the—accident. Agreed she had previously insisted she had seen nothing. She had been unwell, under great private tensions, wanted only to get abroad to a health spa where she had been ever since. She hadn't wished to become involved. Never dreamed, of course, that there could possibly be any charge against Mr. Gray, knowing as she did with absolute certainty that the thing had been entirely an accident. Because in fact she had actually seen it happen.

"From my balcony you can look straight into their room. I glanced over and saw them standing there. They seemed to be having an argument. He said something angry, she jerked away from him as though he had raised his hand against her—"

"Mrs. Fox, had he anything in his hand?"

"In his hand? Oh, the poker you mean? No, nothing, no poker or anything. And anyway, he never raised his hand."

"He never raised his hand? You can swear to that?"

The Judge from the Bench said solemnly, "Mr. Tree, she *is* swearing to that. She is swearing to everything she says. She is under oath."

"Well, I could see it all quite clearly and I certainly can swear—well, I mean I am absolutely sure he never raised his hand at all. He said something. She stepped back and then she seemed to trip and topple over backwards. I thought to myself. 'Oh, she's skidded on that rug of theirs!' I know that rug—very treacherous it is on the parquet floor. I nearly slipped on it once myself. Well, and then I went back into my room and thought no more about it."

"It didn't occur to you that she might have injured herself?"

"I thought she might have banged her head or something but of course no more than that. As I say, I'd slipped there myself and been none the worse for it." And she made a little face and admitted that if the lady had collected a couple of bruises it would have been no more than she deserved. "I think she nagged him. But of course I didn't know them well."

Headlines, yes. But not much really and often not even on the center pages, let alone the front page. But there was a big picture of him planned for Sunday, with an interview—celebrating, a glass of champagne raised to the neighbor whose testimony had confirmed his innocence. Not perhaps in the best of taste, the picture taken right there in front of the fireplace where his wife had died. But it wasn't a best-of-taste newspaper and one settled for what one could get.

And the reporters withdrew; and at last they were alone in his apartment.

She held out her hands to him. "Well, Raymond?"

She looked about a hundred years old standing there before him, the sagging face devoid of its makeup, the ugly dull dress, the droopy hairdo, the mottled hands without their customary diamond flash. She revolted him.

"Well, Rosa, you did a beautiful job."

She did not hear the chill in his voice, or did not believe it. She said softly, "And one day soon—shall I collect my reward?"

"Reward?" he said.

"After all, my darling, I have perjured myself for you."

"Yes, so you have, haven't you?" he said.

Now the unpowdered skin took on a strange ashen color, and her eyes grew frightened and sick. "Raymond, what do you mean?"

"I mean that you perjured yourself, as you say; and you know, perhaps, what happens to perjurers?"

A clever woman, quick and clever. But still she insisted, "I don't understand."

"I need money, Rosa," he said.

"Money? But if we were married—"

He moved aside so that she looked over his shoulder and into the mirror above the fireplace.

He said, "You? And I? *Married?*"

She looked long, long at her pitiful reflection. She said at last, "Is this blackmail?"

"Wasn't it blackmail when you thought that by saving me from prison you could force me to marry you?"

"Yes," she said. "I think perhaps it was." And she thought to herself that now she was beaten at her own game. "If you give me away," she said, "you'll have to admit you murdered her."

"In fact I didn't murder her. I can say it happened almost exactly as you said in court."

"Very well then," she said swiftly, "I can change my story. Who can prove that I didn't see you murder her?"

"*I* can prove that you didn't see it. You couldn't have been out on your balcony. The plane trees were pollinating and anyone will confirm to the police what happens if you so much as open a window when the pollen's flying about. But when they first saw you, you showed no traces of any allergic reaction. I know, because I'd just seen you myself.

"Besides, they couldn't touch me. I've been 'put in peril,' as they say—*autre fois acquit* is the legal name for it. Once acquitted I can't be tried again for the same crime. I could shout from the housetops that I'd killed her and still be safe."

"And live with that reputation?"

"Well, of course I *wouldn't* say I'd been guilty—which anyway, as I keep telling you, I wasn't. I'd still claim it had been an accident. But *you* would be in the soup."

"I see." She pondered it long and carefully, still staring, but unseeingly now, at her sad reflection in the glass. "You thought all this out from the very first, didn't you? In detail, from the very first?"

"Quite a nice little bit of opportunism," he suggested, proud of it.

"All that about the publicity? The blood deliberately smeared on the poker? Yes, I see. You had to give them something, you had to get yourself accused and charged, you had to be tried and acquitted before it was safe to accuse me. Two purposes to my perjury: first to supply the evidence that would set you free and second to make me vulnerable to blackmail." She said almost curiously, almost as though she were humbled for him rather than for herself, "Did you never even like me?"

"I didn't mind you," he said indifferently. "But as for marrying you—I think I'm a trifle more particular than that." And he picked up her handbag, helped himself to the thick wad of banknotes there, stuffed them loosely into his wallet, tucked the wallet away. "Just a very, very small beginning, my dear," he said.

"I won't even ask how much you're demanding. You'll be back again and again and again of course, won't you? But by way of a start—?"

"Make it ten thousand," he said. "You can get that much quickly."

He smiled at her with cruel and ugly triumph. "And I need it quickly—for my honeymoon," he said.

Clever and quick. Clever not even to have to ask the name, to have summed it all up in one bright intuitive flash. And quick. The poker with its round brass knob lay there on the fender. She snatched it up—and struck.

Trudi burst open the door, darted forward from her listening post, slowed, then came smoothly the rest of the way and knelt beside him. For what seemed a long, long time they both stared down as only a few short months ago Raymond Gray himself had looked down at the dead body of his wife. It was his turn now.

Rosa's fat white arms retained something, it seemed, of their once splendid muscle; long-ago anatomical training had suggested the most susceptible spot. The heavy ball of the poker had smashed to a cobweb of fractures Raymond's delicate temple bone.

Trudi moved. With a small sick grimace she shifted Raymond's head a little way, so that the wound lay crushed against the round brass knob of the fender. "That rrug!" she said, getting up to her feet again. "Always so dangerous! Fancy, a second time, just the same like the poor wife!" She grinned with brutal complacence into the heavy white face with its look of dead despair. "So lucky that this time *I* was present, to see that it all was again just a terrible accident."

Raymond's jacket had fallen open. She stooped and with fastidious fingers picked out the wad of notes and stuffed them into her apron pocket.

"Just a verry, verrry small beginning," she quoted and took the poker out of Rosa's inert hand. "Go back to your flat, Madame. Collapse upon your bed. I see to everything, then I make telephone to the doctor." The Trudi shrug. "This time I know the number of him."

Rosa went back to her own apartment. She did not, however, collapse upon her bed.

"Police?" she said, holding the telephone receiver in a steady hand. She gave Raymond Gray's address. "You'd better get over there quick. I've just seen from my balcony the *au pair* girl going for him with a poker. And this time—no question of an accident."

She listened with a satisfied smile to a sharp voice cracking out orders. The voice returned to her. "Well, I wouldn't know about that—I can't see to the floor of the room. The girl disappeared from sight for a bit and when she got up she was stuffing money into her apron pocket. You'll find it, I daresay, hidden somewhere in her room. An affair going on, you know, even before the poor wife died; and now I suppose he was refusing to marry her."

FLORENCE V. MAYBERRY

A Goodbye Sound

Shut up, Joe," I said. "You bore me."

Joe looked as if he would cry. I can't stand a man who goes around all the time looking as if he could cry. Joe's that kind.

"Well—" He cleared his throat, a nasty, fluttering sound. It was too bad, I knew it was wrong, but Joe couldn't take a deep breath without irritating me. "Why can't you look at me like you do at everybody else? Like just smile nice at me sometimes. Like for instance you don't even know those guys standing over there, they're just waiting for a table and you never saw them before, just happened to look their way. And you give 'em a big smile like you were the hostess out here." A hesitation. "Or maybe you do know them."

"Whether I do or not is not your affair. Now listen, Joe, you've been after me to go out with you for months. So I'm out. With you. So why not cool it, lay off the witness-box stuff."

"Sure, okay, Lolly."

"Laura!"

"Okay, Laura."

What's a woman to do with a man like that? *Roll over and play dead, Joe, sit up and beg, Joe, fetch me my slippers, Joe.*

"Order anything you like, hon, the world's yours tonight."

"The prime ribs, please."

"Yeah, that's good, that's the ticket, best thing on the menu. Hon, you can have prime ribs every day, every night, if you'd only want it that way. I just finished a quarter-million-dollar contract, Lol—Laura. Your old man—" He choked it off, trying to laugh. "I mean your old ex-husband is in the bigtime contracting now. Kept slogging along until I made it."

"Maybe I ought to go back in court and try for alimony this time. First time it would have been like suing a four-year old kid for his nickels." *That's right, ruin his fun, be mean, you shrew.*

"I told you, if you'd only hang on a little while, maybe make me feel like I was something, I'd make it." He tried to laugh again, but it was like the laugh was hiding behind a door, afraid to come out. "I'm slow, hon. But right along with that, I'm too dumb to know how to give up."

That was for sure. He's telling me? Divorced two years and every week, regular as clockwork Joe telephoned. *Hon, let's try it again, will ya, Lolly, will ya just go out to dinner with me and talk a while? I get terrible lonesome, you gotta eat anyway. Hon, do you need any money, I gotta few bucks ahead, construction's picking up. Hon, hon,* over and over. So once in a while I gave in, like throwing a dog a bone. Damn a man like that. Who needs his money? I make plenty doing beauty work.

"Prime ribs for the lady. Medium-rare, same as usual, hon? Baked potatoes, all the fixings. Same for me. Don't give the lady no coffee till later, she drinks it with dessert. That still right, hon?"

A crawly feeling shivered my back, crept into my jaw. My teeth started to chatter. Nerves, I mean, like before a fit.

The food came, beautiful stuff because we were at Eugene's where it's maybe the best in Reno, but I looked at it like it was poison. Joe did that to me, always. He didn't mean to, but he did. Slender I always was, but by the time Joe and I broke up I was nothing but skinny. Chemical reaction, maybe. Or maybe I'm just mean. But I think it's more than that. I'm a one-man woman.

I never should have married Joe. My fault, of course, because I knew I shouldn't and he didn't. That's why I stuck it out with him for three years and then let him hang around these past two years. No woman ought to marry a man when she loves someone else she can't have.

"Joe, are you still smacking your mouth after every swallow? You come to a swell place like this and still eat like you're in a truck-stop diner."

"Sorry, Lol—Laura. Hon, I keep telling you, I need a nice woman to shape me up, make something out of me. All I do any more is hang around with guys. Honest, Laura, you're the only one. I tried going out with other women but it's no use. Not after you."

See what I mean? What he should have done was reach that big paw of his across the table, smack me hard, and walk out. Never phone again. And I tell you, that would have been a big relief, no more anticipating that call every week, trying to think up new ways to say no.

"Eat up, hon, come on, tear into that meat. Or you'll get skinny again, like you were after—"

"I don't want to talk about it, Joe."

"You should of kept the baby, Laura, maybe that's what turned you bitter. I wouldn't of cared it wasn't mine, anything yours is mine far as I'm concerned. You should never have—"

"Damn you to hell!" Whispered, so the tables around couldn't hear. "You dumb stubborn ox, you still believe I'm a murderer! That I deliberately killed my darling baby, my poor lost baby! How many times do I need to tell you I *wanted* that baby?"

"Well, hon, I wouldn't of cared it wasn't mine. I told you that when you told me about it, right from the start. You were honest with me, and I said if it's yours, why, I'd love it no matter who it looked like."

Maybe now you won't keep thinking I'm the witch you started out thinking I was. Who wouldn't act like a witch, getting reminded every day that I loved someone I couldn't have? Besides hanging onto the conviction I had murdered my unborn baby. It was a miscarriage, not an abortion. Joe was determined not to believe that, perhaps in the hope that I had deliberately rid myself of my last attachment to Chris. Well, he was wrong. It was a miscarriage. My baby's silly mother cried too much.

"I like Chris myself, Laura, I wouldn't of cared. Because I understood why you went for the guy, you just a green kid and him knowing how to handle women. Only when you found out he was married you should of broke it off. But that's the trouble, women get took in by a good line, him throwing money around, regular guys don't have a chance."

"Joe, I have to go. I don't feel well."

"Aw, hon, we barely started eating—"

"You stay, Joe. Eat yours and mine, too. And don't call me again. Ever. Just leave me alone." I got up, skimmed past the tables and waiters, fast.

It felt good in the open air, a nice warm night, the moon big and bright. The white clean moonshine seemed to shower me off, wipe away what Joe stirred up, and I stopped wanting to cry. Nevada's moon, I think, must be the most beautiful on earth, so brilliant, so white. I felt like diving into its glow, swimming in it.

"You're moon mad," Chris used to tell me. Then he would say in his soft, gentle voice, slurred by a Danish accent, "So am I, little Laura, when I see you in the moonlight and hold you in my arms." How many millions of men have said those same dumb words to how many millions of dumb girls? So it wasn't the words, it was the way Chris said it.

A taxi moved up to me, ready for a passenger. I opened the door and got in. But I couldn't close the door because Joe was holding it, all 200 pounds of him. "Hon, why take a cab when I gotta car? I'll pay the guy his fare, he won't lose nothing. Listen, hon, you gotta eat something—Listen, fella, I'm not taking your fare, here's a couple bucks, come on, Lol—Laura."

Two couples going inside the restaurant stared at us. One of the women looked like a customer of the beauty salon where I worked. And it was so dumb, squabbling in front of Eugene's. So I got out and let Joe lead me to his big car. A good one but all dusty, with rope and a can of oil in the back, and papers, chewing-gum wrappers, and gravel on the floor in front.

"I know what you're thinking, Laura, didn't wash his car before he picked me up. Well, hon, I been out on the job, way off the paved roads, in soft dirt. So I got to carry extra oil and a rope in case. And I barely got back tonight, tore back like crazy, didn't want to disappoint you, hahaha!"

The poor guy. Oh, God, the poor guy.

"How about a little run up to Virginia City, hon? It's warm down here tonight, be cooler up there. Those old ghosts chill the place off, huh, hahaha!"

"Okay."

Might as well. I wasn't going to get rid of Joe any more than you can break a bulldog's hold on something he's locked his jaws on by smacking his rump. I switched on the car radio, the knobs gritty under my fingers, put it on loud so Joe would need to shout to be heard; a man can't shout forever.

Lovely music, a great "mood" program, bittersweet, haunting. It drowned out Joe and I spun out with it, far out. It was easy to forget it was Joe beside me, he was merely a broad-shouldered male figure. But pretty soon, dreaming with the music, he was more than that. He was Chris.

Chris beside me while we zoomed along, not toward Virginia City but toward Carson City and Lake Tahoe. Five years ago. A time when I barely knew Joe— he was only one of the men who worked for Chris. Once in a while we would bump into him and other employees of Chris in some night spot. And they would all cluster around Chris as if he were a magnet and they were iron filings. The same way I did.

I try and try to figure out why Chris was so attractive to everyone. But I never can put it in words. He simply was. Sitting beside him could put me on a cloud, soft and gentle, yet somehow firm and secure at the same time. His voice was so tender. Once I heard him speak when he was angry, not to me but to a stranger who tried to dance with me. Even then his voice was tender, a velvet-covered steel trap closing gently, but unstoppably, around the man.

In size he wasn't as big as Joe. But he exuded a mountain feeling, a mountain covered with grass and the sun streaming over it. A dopey woman in love? True. Absolutely true.

Joe shouted over the music and drove away Chris and my dream. "How about you and me trying it again, Laura, whaddaya say? You're acting like you're a million miles away. Put your mind on me a little bit, hon."

"Joe, turn around. I don't want to go up to Virginia City. Tomorrow's a big day at the beauty shop and we're shorthanded. Turn back to Reno at Steamboat Springs."

"Aw-w-w-w, hon! Just when I'm feeling good, you back beside me. Listen, take tomorrow off. I'll give you whatever it takes to make up your lost pay."

"I don't need your money, Joe."

"Please." His voice was uneven, shaky. "I need to be a little happy once in a while."

So I said, okay, okay, and we went up the steep climb from the valley, around the last bend, into Virginia City. Tourists ambled up and down the long main street, gawking at the store windows, going in and out of the fake oldtime saloons, laughing as if it was a ball, you know, gay like fun. And all the time it was nothing but an old dead town, faked up for dollars. It gave me the creeps. Like watching people laugh in a funeral parlor while they ogled a fancy old-fashioned coffin.

We got out of the car and drifted with the crowd, Joe hanging onto my arm. But even with the crowd, with the tinpanny piano music coming out of a bar and Joe trying to make talk, I couldn't stop being back with Chris. The thought of him simply wouldn't go away. It wiped out Virginia City, Joe, everything.

Chris, darling, are we going to be married? Someday, I mean.

Little girl, don't worry, let me take care of that. Don't you worry your pretty head about that. I have problems. I need to handle those problems first.

I'm sorry to bother you, Chris, it's just I love you so. I suppose a girl shouldn't keep telling a man how much she loves him but it's the way I feel. I'm no good at pretending.

He had patted my hand then, tenderly, almost as a father would pat his daughter, and said that was why he loved me, my eyes so deep and true, they couldn't lie, nor those sweet lips—

"Wanta go inside one of the joints, Lol—hon? Have us a little fun?"

"Damn!" I said. "I'd as soon dance on somebody's grave."

Joe's jaw dropped and his eyes turned moist. Poor guy, poor guy. Why couldn't he just fade away, leave me alone?

"It's Chris," he finally said. "I can tell. You're thinking about Chris again. When you gonna get him out of your system? After the way he done you dirt."

"He didn't! I was twenty-one. I can take my own blame."

"Hon, you were nothing but a dumb little kid, barely twenty-one. What's twenty-one mean, it ain't magic. And Chris close to forty, smart, wheeling and dealing with Nevada's big shots, knowing all the angles."

"Take me home!"

"Okay, hon, have it your way. But I still think it was a damn shame, leaving you so mixed up you can't love nobody but him."

"Shut up, Joe!" *Shut up, shut up, shut up, why tell me what I know too well?* I'm like my great-grandmother and she was Indian, full-blooded. Outside I'm blonde as a Scandinavian, but inside of me I'm Indian. And Indians don't change loyalties easily; when they get set on an idea, that's it. Forever. At least that's what I've heard. Anyway, that's how I am. For me, Chris is it, and always will be.

Joe did what I said, shut up, led me back to the car, and we headed for Reno. The moonlight turned the night into a twilight, only more shimmering, just as it was the night Chris and I drove to Tahoe. Our last night together. I remembered I had leaned close to the windshield, let the moonlight bathe my face, smiled at Chris. So he drove off on a side road and took my face in his hands. "My beautiful little girl," he said.

"Yes, Chris."

He kissed me, then drew my face back to the windshield, into the moonlight. "No wonder you love moonlight, little Laura, you're moonbeams made flesh. This is how I want to remember you. Always."

Something was wrong about the way Chris said that. A strange inflection, a goodbye sound. As though he had dropped a pebble into a well that I had expected to be full, but there was no splash. Lost. Gone. A goodbye sound.

I swallowed hard to keep back a question about that, because something told me I didn't want the answer. I've heard, too, that Indians are psychic. Anyway, I didn't ask. I smiled instead. If some crazy thing was going to happen, if I was going to lose Chris, I didn't want him to remember ugliness.

Chris drove back to the highway, and that night I think we dropped into every nightspot around the Lake. Joe showed up in one of the clubs and then kept following us from place to place, hanging onto us like a burr. Truth is, Chris seemed to encourage him. He would have had to, otherwise Joe wouldn't have stayed. Chris knew how to get rid of people he didn't want around.

Once I whispered, "Tell Joe to get lost." But Chris only patted my hand and said, "Who can blame the man? He's in love with you. Who wouldn't be in love with you?"

Without any thought it popped out. "Maybe you wouldn't, Chris." Was that my Indian great-grandmother coming out in me, knowing the way all primitive people know?

We kept dancing, Chris silent. Finally he said, "Little girl, you've picked up the feeling of what I have to tell you tonight. Not all, but part. I do love you. But tonight is goodbye for us. Our last time together. That's why I want to remember your face, everything about you. Darling, it has to be. The end, I mean."

"Why?" It was a weak, strangled sound.

"I've learned in business, no use explaining. When the end comes, face it, quick, sharp, no turning back. It's simply I have too many involvements, business, everything. It won't work out." He bent and kissed my forehead.

My head floated up among the colored, spangly lights, my body a numbed automaton on the dance floor below. Then my head fell back on my body, and all of me was numb, too numb to be surprised that a smile had frozen on my face. Who wants to remember a tear-streaked face?

"Dance with Joe, little sweetheart, he's been waiting for that all evening," Chris said, when we went back to our table.

Joe stood up and looked at Chris as if he was going to lick his hand. My smile was still frozen as Joe led me back to the dance floor. Over his shoulder I watched Chris call the waiter, speak to him. Then he looked toward me, smiled, nodded his head approvingly, turned and left. Just left. That's all.

The numbness suddenly went away and I started falling into a black pit. I clung hard to Joe while I was doing it, and he squeezed back. "Aw, honey, what's this? Huh? You go for me a little bit?"

I shook my head.

"I sure wish you would, baby. Just a little, you know, like at least be friendly."

"Chris has left me," I said. "So I'm dead. Mind playing hearse and taking me home?" My voice sounded flat and far off, like someone else talking.

Joe's head swung toward our table. "You mean he's gone?" I nodded. A wide happy grin spread over his face. "Gone," he said with satisfaction. "Well, now let's you and me have some fun for ourselves. We don't care if—"

"I care," I said. "Please take me home."

Joe led me back to the table. The waiter came over and said, "The gentleman with you said to bring you anything you want, it's his party, all paid for."

"Laura, honey, the night's young. And for the first time, me with you, Chris doing this for us. It's like a dream, lemme dream a while."

"Take me home, Joe. Otherwise I'll call a cab."

Now, all these years later, I was telling him again, *Take me home, Joe.* Time hadn't changed anything.

We curved down the mountain from Virginia City, saw the valley spangled with lights, and Reno a shimmer of neon toward the north.

"Hon, didja hear what happened today? You musta, the way you're all sunk into yourself tonight."

"Hear what?"

"Chris got divorced today."

It couldn't be true. It was a crazy made-up daydream, an idiot fantasy that fairy tales come true.

"His wife finally got onto him. Took him for a bundle."

Good. Take every dime. That way I can prove it's Chris I want, not money.

"I'm really sorry, Lol—Laura. Honest. You may of always thought I only cared about what I wanted. Like, only wanting to hang onto you. But honest, all along I felt bad for you, the way you were hook, line, and sinker for Chris. He wasn't worth all that, not that he ain't a great guy. That is, with guys. But not worth all that grief. From you."

"Well, you don't have to be sorry for me any longer, Joe." All the sad five years of waiting for something I never expected to get wiped out! Because here it was, the pot of gold at the end of the rainbow. Laughter bubbled out of me—the first time I had laughed like that since Chris went away. "Not any more, Joe!"

"Gee, hon, that's great. Really great." I looked at Joe affectionately. He was kind, actually sweet, to be glad just because I was glad.

"You see, I was afraid you'd be all broke up. I mean, I figured you'd been holding onto the hope that someday you and Chris would finally make it. Then when he got his divorce today and right off married that kooky kid from New York. I mean, right today. I figured you'd take it hard."

The valley's lights went out. Blown out the way one blows out an oil lamp. When they came back on, they were blurred and my head was dizzy.

"But since you're taking it good like this, maybe I got a chance with you after all."

Keep talking, Joe, so I don't have to.

"Hon, I'll never stop loving you. You're so beautiful. I mean, looking at you sideways like now, you're like a beautiful statue or something. Honest, when I first saw you with Chris, it kinda made me sick, you so young and little and pretty."

To disinfect a wound, split it wide and rub salt in it. I may die from it, but the wound will be clean.

"Joe, is this true? Or are you making it up to try to make me forget Chris?"

He looked stunned. "Why would I make up a thing like that? Anyways, you could check, couldn't you? Oh, Lord, you're not taking it cool after all. But you'd have to find out sometime. Honest, I thought maybe you'd already heard."

"How did you find out?"

"Hell, I do business with Chris. See him all the time. So today late, when I first got in from the job, I went to his office about something. And Chris invited me to the party he's throwing tonight, even introduced me to the kid he just married, she was there, that's how I know she's kooky, giggling and crawling all over Chris."

"Where's the party?"

"I'm not going. Gee, hon, think I'd take you home and run off to that party?"

"I'm going to the party. Take me, Joe."

"Now, listen, that's no good, you got a bad sound in your voice, you don't want—"

"Take me to the party, Joe."

"Hell!" Joe said.

The party was at the Mapes Hotel in a private suite, the door wide open, come-one-come-all, so we walked right in. Flowers were everywhere, in baskets, in vases, gift cards thrusting from them. The room smelled like a funeral. When my father died, the funeral parlor smelled exactly like this wedding party.

The guests, laughing, milling around, were only a moving color-dotted blur. And in the center of the blur was Chris, sharp and clear, with a small blur beside him that bounced and jiggled and swung on his arm. Chris looked just the same. Smiling, eyes blue as the sky after a good clean rain. Stocky, strong. And he saw me. As Joe and I came in, he was looking toward the door.

Chirs dropped the bouncing blur off his arm and walked to us. He kept smiling. Smiles, I knew from five years before, don't really mean anything. "Hello, little girl," he said. "It's been a long time." Tender, loving voice. I had to bite my lips to keep them from trembling. "I hoped you would come to wish me happiness."

The small blur skipped over to us and caught hold of Chris. It shook its shaggy curls from its little heart-shaped face, came out of the blur, pursed its mouth into a pout, and asked, "Aren't you going to introduce wifey, hubby-doll-boy?"

Hubby-doll-boy introduced us. "Valerie, these are special friends, Laura and Joe Walker. You've already met Joe, remember? At the office. Joe used to work for me but now he's my competitor, a real great guy."

Joe stepped forward, grinning, pleased. "Congratulations, you two. Yeah. May you look as good on your fiftieth anniversary."

"Oooo, super, isn't that darling, Chrissy, just super darling!" Valerie cooed.

Chris took my hand. It shouldn't have sent an electric shock through me. But it did. "And little Laura is a very special lady I've known a long time. A lovely *lady*." Emphasis on *lady*.

Valerie's big brown eyes narrowed as she looked me over. "Oooo, lovely, just simply lovely-lovely. Chrissy angel, kiss me, I've not been kissed for five whole minutes, m-m-m!" She stood on tiptoe, holding up her face, nuzzling the air. Chris bent and kissed her, red creeping over his face. "Mm-mm-mm, not that way, Daddy, big-big kiss!"

He kissed her again and she snuggled against him. Then he did it another time, on his own, a long hard kiss. He didn't have to do that. He could have waited until I couldn't see him.

I began to hear the voice. Not a real voice. Not mine or anybody's. Just a voice in my mind. It said, *I'm going to kill Chris, then I'll kill myself.* Flat, no anger, simply a fact.

I didn't argue with the voice. Why argue with what had to be? But I began to think, how? Should I use fingernails? The heel of my shoe? Hit him with a compact, stab him with a lipstick, choke him with a five-dollar bill? Those were my weapons.

Joe grabbed my arm and led me to the buffet spread. "Eat something, hon, you're kinda sick looking, you oughta eat something."

"Maybe some water."

"It ain't healthy not to eat."

No knives on the buffet table. Forks, but can a fork stab deep enough to kill? The cake cutter? Nothing but dull prongs.

My knees started to tremble and I went to a chair and sat down. A standup ashtray was beside the chair. Light metal, hollow inside. Put a bump on the head, nothing more. I tried to think what my Indian great-grandmother would have done. Latched onto some brave's bow and arrow, or a tomahawk. A shotgun, if one was around. But her great-granddaughter wouldn't know how to pull the trigger on a gun if one was in her lap.

Chris was watching me over the top of Valerie's shaggy little head. Still smiling, but not comfortable. Uneasy. I never saw Chris uneasy before. He turned his eyes away, too quickly. Guilty.

Joe touched my shoulder, leaned down and whispered, "Hon, don't keep staring at Chris that way, you're giving the guy the creeps. After all, it's his wedding night, he ought to be let to be happy."

Why, I wanted to ask, just why? But that would have taken strength. I wanted to save all my strength to do what I had to do, before Chris left. Already he and Valerie were going around to their guests, bidding good night, Valerie giggling, snuggling. Chirs moving quickly, in a hurry, people making cracks about that. Finally they headed in my direction.

"Go away, Joe," I said. "This is between Chris and me."

"Now, Lol—Laura—"

"Go away!"

He shuffled off miserably. Then the bridal couple came to me, the last one in the room. I stood up, my weapon ready. Say it loud, scream it. *Chris, you never saw our son. I grieved about losing him as well as his father. He never drew breath, but do you suppose in some other world he wonders what happened to his father and what made his mother cry so much?*

"Good night, Laura. Please wish us well."

I opened my mouth. "How—" *How does our son feel about us?* I swallowed. "How—how nice to see you again, Chris."

It wasn't easy, but I smiled. Smiles don't mean anything but they're not ugly. It's better not to remember ugliness. "I wish you well."

They turned, walked away, out of the room, out of my life. Gone. Would that be the same as dead?

Joe shuffled back. "Come on, hon, let's go, you look all in. Hey, maybe you could eat a hamburger or something now. You know I worry about you, Lol—Laura."

"Joe, don't waste your time and feelings on me."

His face screwed up like an ugly baby's who isn't sure whether to cry or not. "I wish I could stop. But some things you can't help."

I knew about that. That I understood.

"Okay, Joe. Buy me a hamburger."

So Joe and I went downstairs to the coffee shop and had hamburgers. Like maybe a funeral feast?

"Q"

PATRICIA McGERR

A Choice of Murders

My brother Joe never was any good. When we were boys—though I was two years older—he was the ringleader in all our scrapes. We started by stealing candy and cigarettes from the corner store and progressed to socks, ties, and cuff links. When I was 18 we were caught joyriding in a stranger's car and drew a six-month suspended sentence. That scared me out of any criminal leanings, but not Joe.

His next arrest was for carting a typewriter and adding machine from the school office. That put him in the reformatory for a year. When he came out he was ready for the big time. I tried to steer clear of him, but every couple of weeks he'd drop by the restaurant where I was night manager to flash a roll of bills.

"You want to be poor all your life?" he taunted. "You like ringing up nickels and dimes for somebody else?"

"I want to stay out of jail," I answered. "You like being locked up?"

"I was a green kid," he came back. "But I learned a lot on the inside. They won't catch up with me again. And I could put you onto some good things."

"I don't want any part of it. Whatever you're doing, I don't even want to know about it."

"You always were chicken, Paul," he said. "But okay, it's your loss. When I'm king of the rackets you can pretend not to know me."

The flaw in that was our strong family resemblance. We both had corn-yellow hair, long thin faces, and what our mother always referred to as the "Garrison nose." The boss came in one night just as Joe was leaving and did a double take. The $200 suit and $40 shoes must have made him suspect for a minute that I'd been dipping into the till. Then he saw it wasn't me and breathed easier.

"The fellow who just went out," he said, "he must be your brother."

"That's right."

"So you got a rich relation. That's nice."

For a while he treated me with more respect. Which was fine until Joe was trapped with a closet full of heroin and his picture hit all the front pages. That's when I lost my job.

"Not that I hold a man's family against him," the boss apologized. "It's just that the picture looks so much like you. So the customers think I got a pusher in charge here. Well, Garrison, you see my problem."

I saw his problem and my own as well. The trial drew a lot of publicity and when I got on a bus the people would look at me and nudge each other. I was going with Lucille then and it was her idea that we should get married right away and leave town. I hadn't planned on an early marriage, but I liked the idea of a fresh start.

So we bought a license, took our tests, said the right words in front of a judge, and drove 800 miles to settle in a bigger city in another state where the Garrison name and Garrison nose were unknown. Two weeks after we left, Joe was found guilty and sentenced to ten years in a Federal prison. It was seven years before I saw him again.

I was sitting in the dining room of the Juniper Street house on Saturday evening about ten o'clock. Lucille had gone to bed early, sneezing and sniffling and complaining of a sore throat. The dinner dishes were stacked in the sink and the table was covered with papers—bills, tax forms, dunning letters. It was a bleak picture that had begun to take shape two years earlier when we bought this house.

Lucille had social aspirations she thought would be helped by moving to a more fashionable address. And that meant better furniture and more expensive clothes. But she didn't make any friends in the new neighborhood and all I got out of it was a mountain of debt. Now the mortgage payment was overdue and two stores had turned our accounts over to a collection agency. I was about to be sued, garnished, and foreclosed.

But that wasn't the worst of it. In my job I collected rents for an apartment management firm. Some of the tenants paid in cash and when I was hard pressed I used that money, then made it up from the following week's collections. Until now, by careful juggling, I'd managed to stay ahead of the game. But the auditor was about to check the books and I was nearly $1000 short. I could lose my job, maybe face criminal charges.

I'd get no sympathy from Lucille, that was certain. In her view it wasn't her extravagance that had caused our trouble but my inability to earn a decent living. So I was jotting down fresh columns of figures, adding and subtracting, and finding no hope anywhere. I was staring dismally at the numbers when the doorbell rang. Newsboy, I thought, after my last bit of change. I opened the door to find Joe on the porch.

"What—how—" Shock made me stammer.

"Call me a bad penny." He was as jaunty as ever. "I always keep turning up. Aren't you going to ask me in?"

"Yes, of course." I stepped back to let him come in, then closed the door. "What's happened? You didn't break out?"

"No way. I got my time off for being a good boy."

"Why didn't you let me know?" We'd exchanged infrequent letters. His last had been several months earlier.

"I love a surprise." He followed me back into the dining room and surveyed the clutter of papers. "Looks like you're still making it the hard way."

"If you need money," I began defensively, "I'd like to help you, but you've come at a bad time.'"

"Don't worry about little Joe." He reached inside his coat and pulled out a stack of bills. The one on the outside was a fifty. It was like old times. "To tell the truth, I had a touch in mind when I decided to look you up, but I ran into some luck on the way here. Now I'm in good shape."

"Maybe I should ask you for a loan." I tried to make it sound like a joke.

"Sorry, I need it all where I'm going." He returned the bills to his inside pocket.

"Where's that?"

"New York. I've friends there who'll put me back in business. But I can't make contact till Monday night, so I figured there was time for a family reunion."

"How did you find the house?"

"Easy. I studied the map in the railroad station and got a bus that dropped me two blocks away. Looks like a nice part of town. You're living high."

"Too high," I admitted. "I'm in way over my head. But you didn't come to hear my troubles. Are you hungry?"

"I ate on the train. But a Scotch would taste good right now. With just a little water."

"I'm sorry, but there's nothing in the house. Lucille doesn't—"

As if summoned by her name, Lucille appeared in the doorway. She was in her nightgown and held a pink cotton wrapper clutched tight around her middle.

"The bell woke me," she complained. "What's going on?" Her eyes rested on Joe's face, then narrowed in recognition. "You must be Paul's brother. When did you get out of jail?"

"Pleased to meet you, sister," he mocked. "You really know how to make a guy feel welcome."

"Don't think you can lay about here," she said. "You ruined the last town for us. You're not doing it again."

"Cool off, sister. I'm just passing through."

"He wants money, I suppose." She turned her anger on me. "Well, he's not going to get it. If you give him one single cent—"

"Damn it, I don't have one single cent." I waved at the table. "All I've got is bills and nothing to pay them with."

"Don't yell at me, Paul Garrison. I'm a sick woman. It's bad enough you're related to a convict without bringing him into my house. You send him on his way, you understand. At once!"

She spun round and headed back upstairs. Joe watched her go and the curl of his lips made me conscious of how quickly her girlish plumpness had turned to fat. Without makeup, her hair unkempt, she was an especially unlovely sight.

"You got yourself a charmer," he said. "If I had your problems I'd buy a nice big insurance policy. On the lady's life."

"I already have a policy. We're both insured."

"Then I'd take steps to collect it."

"That's not funny, Joe."

"Who's joking? Okay, big brother, I'll save my advice for somebody smart enough to listen. Now how about it? You going to throw me out?"

"You can spend the night, of course. But there's no need for Lucille to know."

We sat on talking for an hour or so. Then I made up the cot in the television room for Joe to sleep on and went upstairs. Lucille heard me coming and switched on the bedside lamp, ready to pounce, as I entered the room. "Is he gone?"

"He's my brother, Lu. I can't send him away in the middle of the night."

"I'm your wife, but that doesn't stop you from piling on aggravations. You know what my temperature is? A hundred and two! I've got fever and chills and my head is splitting. I won't be able to go to the concert tomorrow."

"That's too bad."

"Don't sound so happy. It won't get you out of going. At least you can bring home a program and tell me about the music."

"All right," I agreed, "if that's what you want. Maybe I can get a refund on your ticket."

Five bucks, I thought, to put in a pot that was $1000 short. The concert was the fourth in a series that Lucille had insisted on buying. I don't think she liked the longhair stuff any better than I did, but Culture was one of the rungs on her social ladder. So far all it had gotten her was a listing on the back of the program as a "friend" of the local symphony.

I got into bed but was a long time falling asleep. Joe's remark had put Lucille's insurance in my mind and I couldn't get it out. $10,000. More than enough to sweep away all my debts. Maybe what she had was more than a cold, worse than the flu. Maybe her temperature would keep rising, turn into pneumonia. I thought of raising the windows high to let in the March wind and help it along. But that was fantasy. Lucille was strong as a horse. She'd live to collect on my policy, not vice versa.

But the idea, having formed, kept nagging at me. By the time I dropped off, near dawn, I had worked out a plan to the smallest detail. Having a look-alike brother had caused me nothing but trouble in the past. At last I could make it work to my advantage.

By morning Lucille had added a hacking cough to her other symptoms. I carried her breakfast up on a tray and then told Joe my plan. He was all for it.

"You'll have to stay out of sight till evening," I explained, "and then sit through the first half of the concert in my place. After that the sooner you get out of town the better."

"That suits me fine," he said. "I've got my own reasons for not wanting to go out while it's light."

I divided the day between fetching and carrying for Lucille and probing my plan for possible pitfalls.

"I can pass for you among strangers," Joe pointed out. "But what if one of your seatmates tries to start a conversation?"

"They won't. There are a couple of old biddies on the aisle who don't even talk to each other. And the couple on the other side hasn't given us so much as a kind look since the series began. All you have to do is sit still and listen to the orchestra."

"That's another thing. What if the cops ask you about what they played. You can't expect music criticism from me."

"Of course not. My friends all know I can't tell Bach from Bacharach, that I just go to these things to humor Lucille. If the conductor has a fit or the cello catches fire, I'll need to know about it. Otherwise I can say I dozed through it all."

Joe spent an hour or so rubbing out his fingerprints and making sure the house showed no trace of his presence. Lucille, when she wasn't eating or sleeping or harassing me, passed her time on the phone talking to friends on the other side of town, where we used to live. When I was dressing for the concert, a dangerous thought occurred to me.

"Uh—Lu—" I approached the subject cautiously. "The people you talked to today—did you say anything about Joe's being here?"

"You think a jailbird brother-in-law is something to boast about?" She laughed hoarsely. "I've never even told anybody you have a brother."

Reassured, I shrugged into my purple and green checked sports jacket.

"You think you're going to the ballpark?" she shrilled. "That's no kind of coat for the symphony. You'll stand out like a sore thumb."

Which was exactly why I chose it. I adjusted the coat, straightened my tie, and said nothing.

Joe and I left the house at 7:30. It was a 20-minute drive to the Civic Auditorium and I had worked out a very exact timetable. At 7:50 I slid out of the car to let Joe take the wheel and circle the block. I went directly to the box office and told the man behind the wicket the sad story of my wife's illness. He had me write my name on a piece of paper, clipped it to Lucille's ticket, and said if anybody bought it I could get my money back. Then I went outside and waited for Joe to pick me up.

I traded my brightly colored jacket for his tan topcoat on a side street. Then Joe walked back to the auditorium and I drove home. I parked half a block away and walked the rest of the distance. Except for our bedroom the house was dark, just as I'd left it. I went in through the garage, which wasn't locked. It was exactly 8:22.

Like clockwork, I thought, and moved to the kitchen phone. Focusing my pocket flash on the dial, I called one of our old neighbors.

"Janet, this is Paul Garrison," I explained. "I'm at the auditorium and the concert is about to start. But Lucille's home with a bad cold and feeling pretty depressed. It might cheer her up to have a call from you."

"A fine time to be thinking about her," she responded tartly, "when you've left her all alone." Her opinion of me, based on Lucille's complaints, wasn't high. "If you're so worried, why didn't you stay with her?"

"I wanted to, but she insisted on my attending this concert. But I didn't call to argue. I just thought it would do her good to hear from an old friend. If you'd rather not be bothered—"

"Of course I'll call her," she bristled. "You just go ahead and enjoy yourself."

I put down the phone and, at the bottom of the stairs, stepped out of my shoes. As I did so, the phone rang. Good old Janet, fitting right into the plan. Up till then I'd been so absorbed in working out the minute-by-minute plan that I hadn't really thought about the end toward which it was all heading. Now suddenly it struck me. I was about to walk up these stairs and murder my wife.

It was a crazy idea, I told myself, a nightmare. I couldn't go through with it. Upstairs Lucille answered the phone. I moved higher till her voice, the whine louder than ever, was clear.

"That's right, Janet, he's gone off and left me alone. A lot he cares that I'm so sick I can hardly lift my head . . . His own pleasure, that's all that matters . . . Ho, that's not the half of it. If you knew what I put up with, day after day . . ."

The words and tone stiffened my resolve. I moved faster, crushing down thought till I was outside the bedroom door. Then I leaned against the wall, slid my gloved hand around the edge till it touched the switch, and turned off the light.

"Something's happened." Lucille's first reaction was unalarmed. "The light just went out, must be a fuse. Janet, I hear something—somebody—a burglar— oh, my God, he'd coming for me—Janet, get help—hurry!"

I was on her then, my fingers around her throat. From the receiver she dropped came squawking sounds as Janet kept asking what was wrong, what was going on. I held tight, pressed hard with both thumbs till she went limp and there was no life left in her. Then I let her fall back on the bed and stood for a minute, disoriented.

My teeth began to chatter. Got to get out, I told myself. Get away before Janet sends the police. But I couldn't move, couldn't make my body respond. I gulped air, finally got myself under control and ran from the room.

I was all the way to the garage when I remembered I was still in my stockinged feet and went back for my shoes. Then I was off again, out the door, running for my car. But when I got behind the wheel, my hand was shaking so I could hardly get the key in the ignition.

Take it easy, I told myself. Janet's got to make the call, get her message across. The nearest precinct is a mile away. All I have to do is drive two blocks and lose myself in the boulevard traffic.

But what had seemed so safe before the murder was now full of perils. There might be a squad car cruising nearby. They could get word by radio and catch me before I left the neighborhood. Even when I was on the boulevard, one car among hundreds, my imagination continued to create hazards. What if I had engine trouble, an accident, a flat tire. The way my heart was pounding, I could have an attack. The smallest mishap could prevent my getting back to the auditorium, destroy my alibi.

I drove with extraordinary care, below the posted limit, and stopped at lights that were barely yellow. Although I longed to push the accelerator to the floor, I couldn't risk a ticket. It seemed that hours must have elapsed since I parted from Joe, but when I finally turned into the auditorium's parking area my watch said 9:10.

The lot was unlighted and unattended. I stopped in the corner farthest from the building's side exit and waited. Faint sounds of music came from inside. What if I'd misjudged the time? The first half of the program might have been unusually short. Maybe the intermission was already over. Janet knew where I was. If she sent the police to the concert hall, they'd find Joe in my seat and me outside. In that interminable time of waiting, every mistake I might have made, everything that could possibly go wrong, passed through my mind.

Then there was a crescendo of sound as the music rose to a peak, faded out, and was followed by applause. Light flashed as the side door opened to let out the people in urgent need of a cigarette. Some formed in groups, others smoked alone. It was simple for Joe to ease off into the shadows and reach the far side of the car where I was waiting to give him his coat and reclaim my jacket.

"All okay at your end?" he asked.

I nodded. I didn't want to talk about it.

"Nothing to report about the music. Except it was noisy. I stepped hard on an old dame's foot getting to my seat. The one in the flowered hat. She knows you were there all right. And while I was waiting for the show to start I got a Scotch and water from the bar near the front door. Paid for it with a fifty and nearly cleaned out the girl's drawer."

"You did what?" I stared at him, aghast.

"It was a way to make an impression," he said, "and get you one more good witness. Besides, I needed change."

"Why the devil couldn't you stick to your instructions and not go off half—" I cut myself short. What was done was done and I was wasting time. "Did you add any other embellishments, talk to anybody, do anything else to attract attention?"

"Nope. All else was according to plan."

The light over the exit went off and on twice, signaling the end of the intermission. Joe stayed near the edge of the lot, moving swiftly through the dark of the street. He had plenty of time to walk to the terminal and catch an eastbound bus. I strolled casually back to mingle with the smokers and enter the building.

The woman in the seat second from the aisle pulled her feet back and glared at me as I slid past her. Her hat was heavy with cabbage roses. Unquestionably the one stepped on by Joe. I gave her an apologetic smile which she didn't return, then picked up the program Joe had left on the seat and sat down. The man on the other side ignored me as usual. I opened the program and stared at the dates of Mozart's birth and death while the musicians reassembled on stage.

I heard hardly more of the second half of the concert than I had of the first. The only thing in the hall of which I was fully aware was Lucille's empty seat. Most of my thoughts were on Juniper Street, trying to visualize what was happening there. Had the police come yet? What were they doing?

As soon as the last chord died away and the applause began, I forced my way past the rose-hatted lady and her companion. No need to stay for encores. A professed non-music lover with an ailing wife would logically be among the first to leave.

Driving home I braced myself for what lay ahead, the role I had to play. The house was a blaze of lights. Two cars were parked in front, a third was in the driveway. Blocked from the garage, I stopped behind one of the cars and walked toward the front porch with what I hoped was a suitable expression of puzzled concern. A man in uniform met me at the door.

"What's happened?" I asked him. "Where's my wife?"

"You Mr. Garrison?"

I nodded.

"Lieutenant!" He moved to the foot of the stairs and called up. "The husband's here. You want him?"

"Keep him there. I'll be right down."

The interview with Lieutenant Thurmond was easier than I feared. He broke the news gently and I reacted with shock, grief, and strong desire for vengeance. He asked for an account of my evening and I told him about the concert. His major interest, I was relieved to find, lay in the fact that, because of my job, I often kept large amounts of cash in the house over weekends.

"I do a lot of collecting on Saturdays," I explained, "when the tenants are at home. And I can't turn the money in until Monday."

"How many people know that?"

"Everyone I work with, of course. And the families I collect from. Plus anybody they tell about it." Purposely I offered him a wide field of suspects.

"And you go to these concerts on Sunday nights. Do people know that, too?"

"It's no secret."

"So somebody could have counted on coming into an empty house with a clear couple of hours to hunt for the dough. When he found your wife in the bedroom, he must have panicked."

"I suppose that's how it was," I agreed. "I should have stayed home with Lucille. I shouldn't have let her push me into going to that concert."

"You two get along okay?" The question was overly casual. "No problems?"

"We had our ups and downs." It was better for him to hear it first from me. "The usual arguments."

"I see. Well, I'll be frank with you, Mr. Garrison. We'll have to check out your story. But we know your wife was on the phone a little before half-past eight and that's when the attack came. So if we can confirm that you were in the hall when the concert started, you'll be in the clear."

"You've got to find him," I said vehemently. "Whoever did this to Lucille, he's got to be caught and punished."

For a long time people continued to come and go—police, technical men, some reporters. But at last the body was taken to the morgue, the questions were all asked, and I was alone. I went to bed thinking I was over the highest hurdle. Burglary was firmly established as a motive and the investigation would stay on that track until they finally wrote it off as one more unsolved crime.

The next afternoon, however, Thurmond returned with a changed attitude. Sympathy for a bereaved husband was displaced by harshness toward a prime suspect. The reason quickly became obvious. They'd been probing my financial affairs.

"You've held out on your firm, Garrison," he accused. "The books show you've collected $960 more than you've turned in."

"I'm a little behind," I admitted.

"You're also behind on your mortgage, your taxes, and a few other things."

"The last few months have been tough."

"But the future looks brighter, doesn't it? That ten grand insurance will solve all your problems."

"What are you insinuating?"

"Not a thing. I'm stating a fact. Your wife's death can pull you out of a deep hole. And another fact—her best friends say you had a very bad relationship."

"Even if that's true," I challenged, "what of it? You know when the murder happened and I was miles from here. Or have you been too busy listening to gossip to check on my story?"

"No, we've done that, too. The symphony subscription list gave us the names of those who hold the adjoining seats and we've seen them all. The people behind you don't recall whether your seat was occupied. The man on the right says the seat beside him was empty."

"That's Lucille's seat," I said. "I was in the next one."

"Well, neither Mr. nor Mrs. Carlson noticed you. They said they go to hear music, not to socialize."

"What about the women on my left? Haven't you been able to locate them?"

"The Misses Grant. Yes, we talked to them."

"They must remember me. Especially the one with the fancy hat. I accidentally stepped on her foot on the way in."

"She remembers that all right. But she says it happened after they came back from the intermission."

"She's crazy. It was at the beginning, before the concert started. I sat through the whole damn thing. And what about the man in the box office? He has to know I was there early. He still has the ticket I turned in."

"That's right, he does. Also a paper with your name in your own handwriting and a notation of the time you turned it in. That places you in the auditorium at 7:55. And the intermission ended at 9:35. That leaves about an hour and a half unaccounted for, Garrison. And we clocked the round trip from the auditorium at no more than forty-five minutes. So your alibi isn't worth much."

"It is if the Grant woman can get her facts straight. Look, she's old and easily confused. She's mixed up the times. Let me talk to her. I'll make her remember it the way it was."

"How do you figure to do that, Garrison? With a threat or a bribe?"

"All I want her to do is tell the truth."

"The truth is what we're after, too," he said. "But what we've got is a set of witnesses who say maybe you were there, maybe you weren't. They won't swear to it either way."

It can't be happening, I told myself. All my careful plans falling apart because of a bunch of highbrow snobs and an addlepated old woman. I wished Joe had broken her instep. As things stood, he might as well have been invisible. Unless—suddenly I remembered one other thing.

"Wait a minute," I said. "There's somebody else who saw me. The girl who sells drinks. I bought a Scotch and water to kill time before the concert."

"Yeah?" He was skeptical. "You think she remembers all her customers?"

"She should me. I gave her a big bill—a fifty. She had a hard time making change."

Thurmond made some notes and went away. I didn't hear from him again till the next morning. On the phone he was noncommittal, simply asked me to come to his office as soon as possible.

I drove downtown in a fever of emotion. Maybe the bargirl had amnesia. Maybe Joe bought the drink too soon, while there was still time for me to reach home before 8:30. Or maybe, by a return of luck, she had told her story and gotten me off the hook.

At headquarters I was taken directly to the lieutenant's office. He motioned me to a chair and looked me up and down with a hard stare I couldn't interpret.

"You got a good break, Garrison," he told me. "We've a statement from the bargirl. She said she usually opens her stand a half hour before the concert. But Sunday she was late, didn't get set up till ten past. So there was a rush of business all at once."

"And she—does she remember me?"

"She remembers having to make change for a fifty. We showed her your picture and she couldn't swear to the face. But she said the guy had on a coat with loud checks. Green and purple."

"That's me." I was nearly babbling with relief. "That's the coat I wore Sunday night. You saw it, too."

"Yes, I saw it."

"Then you know I'm innocent. If I bought a drink from her after 8:10, I couldn't have killed my wife at 8:30."

"That's right, you couldn't." He took something from a drawer and laid it on the desk in front of me. It was a fifty-dollar bill. "That was the only fifty in the girl's box. In fact, she said it's the first time she'd taken in anything bigger than a twenty. You recognize it?"

"How can I? All bills look alike."

"This one's a little different. See that corner. It got torn and somebody taped it back together."

I looked closer, saw the jagged place under transparent tape. "It must have been that way when I got it."

"Where did you get it, Garrison?"

"I was out collecting on Saturday. I told you, I take in a lot of cash."

"And appropriate it to your own use?"

"Is that what you're trying to pin on me now? Embezzling funds?"

"This is homicide, Garrison, not a case of petty graft. All I want is to make sure that fifty came from you."

"If it's the only one the girl had, it must be mine." I hesitated, stared at the bill. I was too close to safety to let myself be snagged on some technicality. And as I looked at it, the picture of the stack of bills Joe had waved came back to me. There had been, I was sure of it, a taped corner on the outside bill.

"Yes," I said, "come to think of it, there was a patch like that on my fifty."

"Then that ties the last knot." He seemed as pleased as I was by the outcome. "Your alibi is airtight. You can give us a signed statement and we'll get back on the trail of your wife's killer."

He called in a stenographer to take down my account of the events of Sunday evening.

"That's the crucial point," Thurmond prompted me when I told about buying a drink. "Better describe the bill."

So I mentioned the taped corner, sure now that I had seen it in Joe's hand, and finished the story with a sense of being home free. After that there was a short wait for the statement to be typed. I read it through, added my signature, and was ready to leave. The lieutenant came with me.

"Not that elevator," he said as I turned toward the one that had brought me up. "They're working on it. Better use the one on the south side."

We walked together down the long corridor and rounded a corner to face a bench with two people on it. One was a plump woman with straggly gray hair.

"That's him," she yelled, and was on me in a flash, pounding my chest with her fists. "You devil, you! You killed my Carl."

"All right, Mrs. Harley." The man left the bench and came up behind to pull her off me. "Take it easy, ma'am. You sure this is the man?"

"What's the matter with her?" I backed off, baffled.

Thurmond's attention was on the woman. "Take a good look, Mrs. Harley," he told her. "Can you make positive identification?"

"You think I ever forget that big nose, that dirty blond hair. I saw him hit Carl, smash him with the end of his gun." She fixed her eyes on my face and said quietly, "You didn't have to do that. He'd have let you take the money. You didn't have to kill him."

"Okay, Bruckner." Thurmond said. "You can take Mrs. Harley home. We have all we need."

"What's going on?" I demanded. "What's she got to do with me?"

"Her husband owned the liquor store by the railroad station—the one you took nine hundred bucks out of on Saturday night. You didn't know she was in the back room, but she got a clear view of you."

"You trying to frame me? I've never been near her liquor store!"

"No? You got an alibi for Saturday, too?"

"I was at home all evening with my wife."

"Unfortunately, she's not here to testify. Look, Garrison, we've got you cold. We know you were in desperate need of money. We have Mrs. Harley's identification and the fifty-dollar bill."

"The fifty—"

"You didn't collect that from a tenant. You took it out of the store's cash register. Mrs. Harley patched it up herself and put it back in the drawer a few minutes before you came in. She even showed us her roll of tape. It matches, Garrison. And that's the bill you used to pay for your drink."

"I didn't. It's all a horrible mistake."

"Maybe you've got a double?" His voice dripped sarcasm.

That's right, I wanted to shout. I've got a double. My brother Joe's the man you're looking for. He has a record, you can look it up. The liquor store robbery was the "luck" he said he'd run into on the way to my place. That's where he got the money he showed off.

Joe killed the old man, not me. How long, I wondered, would it take the police to put it all together, figure out that it was Joe, not me, who bought the drink and sat in my seat at the Sunday concert.

I had, it appeared, a choice of murders. To keep still and let them nail me with Joe's. Or speak up and be convicted of my own.

"Well, Garrison," Thurmond urged, "Why not make it easy for yourself and confess?"

I opened my mouth, closed it again. There was nothing I could say.

The Long Corridor of Time

On the evening of their first day, when they had hung their pictures and unpacked their wedding presents—tasks they hadn't cared to entrust to her mother or to the moving men—they went for a walk in the square. They walked along the pavement in the September twilight, admiring the pale gleaming facades of the terraces which, now divided into flats, had once been the London residences of the very rich. Then, when they had completed their little tour and had examined all four sides of the square, Marion took his hand and led him toward the wilderness of trees and shrubs which formed its center.

It was a gloomy place where only the tall trees—a plane, a walnut, and a catalpa—seemed to flourish. A few attenuated rosebushes struggled for life in the shadowy corners, their wan flowers blighted with mildew. Marion put her hand on the gate in the iron railings.

"It's locked," she said.

"Of course it is, darling. It's a private garden for the tenants only. The head porter gave me our key just now."

"Do let's go in and explore it."

"If you like, but there doesn't seem much to explore."

She hesitated, holding the key he had handed her, looking through the railings at the small patchy lawn, the stone table, and the wooden seat. "No," she said. "Tomorrow will do. I *am* rather tired."

He was touched, knowing how anxious she always was to please him. "It's hardly the sort of garden you've been used to, is it?"

She smiled but said nothing.

"Do you know, darling, I feel very guilty. I've taken you away from the country, from all your country things—your horses, the dogs—everything. And all I've given you is this."

"You didn't *take* me, Geoffrey. I came of my own free will."

"Hmm. I wonder how much free will we really have. If you hadn't met me, you'd be at the university now—you'd have your own friends, young people. I'm twice your age."

"Oh, no," she said seriously as they walked back to the terrace where their flat was. "I'll be eighteen next week. You were twice my age when we got engaged and I was seventeen and five months. Exactly twice. I worked it out to the day."

He smiled. The head porter came out, holding the door open for them. "Good night, madam. Good night, sir."

"Good night," said Geoffrey. So she had worked it out to the day. The earnest accuracy of this, a sort of futile playfulness, seemed to him entirely characteristic of the childhood she hadn't quite left behind. Only five or six years ago perhaps she had been writing, with comparable precision, inside exercise books: *Marion Craig, The Mill House, Sapley, Sussex, England, Europe, The World, The Universe*. And now she was his wife.

"He called me madam," she said as they went up in the elevator. "No one ever did that before." With his arm around her and her head on his shoulder she said, "You'll never be twice my age again, darling. That isn't mathematically possible."

"I know that, my love. You've no idea," he said, laughing, "what a tremendous comfort that is."

It wasn't true, of course, that he had given her nothing but a dusty scrap of London shrubbery to compensate for the loss of The Mill House. He asked himself which of her friends, those schoolgirls who had been her bridesmaids, could expect even in five years' time a husband who was a partner in a firm of stockbrokers, a five-room flat in nearly the smartest part of London, a car of her own parked in the square next to her husband's Jaguar, and a painting for her drawing-room wall that was almost certainly a Sisley.

And he wouldn't stand in her way, he thought as he looked in his bedroom glass before leaving for work, scrutinizing his dark head for those first silver hairs. She could still ride, still have parties for people her own age. And he would give her everything she wanted.

He glanced down at the fair head on the pillow. She was still asleep and on her skin lay the delicate bloom of childhood, a patina that is lighter and more evanescent than dew and is gone by twenty. He kissed her tenderly on the side of her folded lips.

"It bothers me a bit," he said to Philip Sarson who came out as he was unlocking his car. "What is Marion going to do with herself all day? We don't know anyone here but you."

"Oh, go shopping, go to the cinema," said Philip airily. "When I suggested you take the flat I thought how handy the West End would be. Besides, married women soon find their hands full."

"If you mean kids, we don't mean to have any for years yet. She's so *young*. God, you do talk like a Victorian sometimes."

"Well, it's my period. I'm steeped in it."

Geoffrey got into his car. "How's the new book coming?"

"Gone off to my publisher. Come round tonight and I'll read you some bits?"

"No, you come to see us," said Geoffrey, trying to sound enthusiastic. A jolly evening for Marion, he thought, a merry end to the day for an eighteen-year-old—coffee and brandy with a tired stockbroker of 35 and an historian of 45. He would ask her first thing he got back what she thought about it and if there were the least hesitancy in her manner, he would phone Philip and put him off.

"But I'd like to see him," she said. "I love hearing about Victorian London. Stop worrying about me."

"I expect I shall when we've settled in. What did you do today?"

"I went to Harrods and matched the stuff for the dining-room curtains and I arranged for my driving lessons. Oh, and I explored the garden."

"The garden? Oh, that bit of jungle in the middle of the square."

"Don't be so disparaging. It's a dear little garden. There are some lovely old trees and one of the porters told me they actually get squirrels in there. It's been such a hot day and it was so quiet and peaceful sitting on the seat in the shade."

"Quiet and peaceful!" he said.

She linked her arm through his and touched his cheek with one gentle finger. "I don't want to be a gadabout all the time, Geoffrey, and I've never been very wild. Don't you like me the way I am?"

He put his arms round her, emotion almost choking him. "I love everything about you. I must be the luckiest man in London."

"I know exactly what you mean," said Philip when, two hours later, Marion resumed her praises of the garden. "It *is* peaceful. I used to sit out there a lot last summer, working on my book, *Great-Grandfather's London*. I've passed many a happy hour in that garden."

"Yes, but you're practically a great-grandfather yourself," Geoffrey retorted. "I want Marion to go out with her contemporaries."

"Very few of her contemporaries can afford to live in Palomede Square, Geoff. But I'm glad you like it, Marion. I'm thinking of writing a book about the square itself. I've unearthed some fascinating stories and a lot of famous people have lived here." Philip named a poet, an explorer, and a statesman. "These houses were built in 1840 and I think that a hundred and thirty years of comings and goings ought to make a good read."

"I'd like to hear some of those stories one day," said Marion. In her long black skirt she looked like a schoolgirl dressed up for charades. She must get out and buy clothes, Geoffrey thought, spend a lot of money. He could afford it.

Philip had begun to read from his manuscript and during the pauses, while Marion asked questions, Geoffrey thought—perhaps because they had all been mentally transported back more than 100 years—of those Victorian dresses which were once more so fashionable for the very young. He imagined Marion in one of them, a ruched and flounced gown with a high, boned collar and long puff sleeves. In his mind's eye he saw her as a reincarnation of a Nineteenth Century ingenue crossing the square, her blonde hair combed high, walking with delicate tread toward the garden.

Smiling at Philip, nodding to show he was still listening, he got up to draw the curtains. But before he pulled the cords, he looked out beyond the balcony to the empty square below with its lemony spots of lamplight and its neglected, leafy, umbrageous center. Between the canopy of the ilex and the dusty yellow-spotted laurel he made out the shape of the stone table and, beside it, the seat that looked as if it had never been occupied.

The corners of the garden were now deep caverns of shadow and nothing moved but a single leaf which, blown prematurely from the plane tree, scuttered across the sour green turf like some distracted insect. He pulled the curtain cords sharply, wondering why he suddenly felt, in the company of his loved wife and his old friend, so ill at ease.

"How was your driving lesson, darling?"

"It was nice," she said, smiling up at him with a kind of gleeful pride. "He said I was very good. When I came back I sat in the garden learning the Highway Code."

"Why not sit on the balcony? If I'd been at home today I'd have sunbathed all afternoon on that balcony."

She said naively, "I do wish you could be home all day," and then, as if feeling her way with caution, "I like the garden best."

"But you don't get any light there at all. It must be the gloomiest hole in London. As far as I can see, so one else uses it."

"I'll sit on the balcony if you want me to, Geoffrey. I won't go in the garden if it upsets you."

"*Upsets* me? What an extraordinary word to use! Of course it doesn't *upset* me. But the summer's nearly over and you might as well make the best of what's left."

While they had been speaking, standing by the windows which were open onto the balcony, she had been holding his arm. But he felt its warm pressure relax and when he looked down at her he saw that her face now had a vague and distant look, a look that was both remote and secretive, and her gaze had traveled beyond the balcony rail to the motionless treetops below.

For the first time since their wedding he felt rejected, left out of her thoughts. He took her face in his hand and kissed her lips.

"You look so beautiful in that dress—sprigged muslin, isn't it?—like a Jane Austen girl going to her first ball. You didn't wear that for your driving lesson?"

"No, I changed when I came in. I wanted to put it on before I went into the garden. Wasn't that funny? I just had this feeling I ought to wear it for the garden."

"I hoped," he said, "you were wearing it for me."

"Oh, darling," she said, and now he felt that she was with him once more, "I can understand it upsets you when I go into the garden. I *quite* understand. I know it could affect some people like that. Isn't it strange that I know? But I won't go there again."

He didn't know what she meant or why his simple distaste for the place—a reasonable dislike that was apparently shared by the other tenants—should call for understanding. But he loved her too much to bother with it, and the vague unease he felt passed when she told him she had telephoned one of her brides-maid friends and been invited to a gathering of young people. It gratified him that she was beginning to make a life of her own, planning to attend with this friend a course of classes. He took her out to dinner, proud of her flounced lilac muslin, exultant at the admiring glances she drew.

But he awoke in the night to strange terrors which he couldn't at first define.

She lay with one arm about his shoulders but he shook it off almost roughly and went quickly to get a glass of water as if, distressingly, mystifyingly, he must get away from her for a moment at all costs.

Sitting in the half-dark drawing room, he tried to analyze this night fear and came up with one short sentence: I am jealous. Never in his life had he been jealous before and the notion of jealousy had never touched their marriage. But now in the night, without cause, as the result of some forgotten dream perhaps, he was jealous. She was going to a party of young people, to classes with young people. Why had he never before considered that some of those contemporaries whom he encouraged her to associate with would necessarily be young men? And how could he, though rich, successful, though still young in a way, compete with a youth of twenty?

A sudden impulse came to him to draw back the curtains and look down into the garden, but he checked it and went back to bed. As he felt her, warm and loving beside him, his fears went and he slept.

"That's a very young chap teaching Marion to drive," said Philip, who worked at home all day, gossiped with the porters, and knew everything that went on. "He doesn't look any older than she."

"Really? She didn't say."

"Why should she? He won't seem young to her."

Geoffrey went up the steps. He had forgotten his key.

"Is my wife in, Jim?" he said to the head porter. "If not, you'll have to open up for me."

"Mrs. Gilmour is in the garden, sir."

"In the *garden*?"

"Yes sir. Madam's spent every day this week in the garden. The gardener's no end pleased about it, I can tell you. He said to me only this morning, 'The young lady'—no disrespect, sir, but he called her the young lady—'really appreciates my garden, more than some others I could name.'"

"I don't get it," said Geoffrey as he and Philip went down into the square. "I really don't. She promised me she wouldn't go there again. I honestly do think she might keep the first promise she's made to me. It's a bit bloody much."

Philip looked curiously at him. "Promised you she wouldn't go into the garden? Why shouldn't she?"

"Because I told her not to, that's why."

"My dear old Geoff, don't get so angry. What's come over you? I've never known you to get into such a state over a trifle."

Through clenched teeth Geoffrey said, "I am not accustomed to being disobeyed," but even as he spoke, as the alien words were ground out and Philip stood still, thunderstruck, he felt the anger that had overcome him without any apparent will of his own seep away, and he laughed rather awkwardly. "God, what a stupid thing to say! Marion!" he called. "I'm home."

She had been sitting on the seat, a book on the table in front of her. But she hadn't been reading it, for although it was open, the pages were fast becoming covered with fallen leaves. She turned a bemused face toward him, blank, almost hypnotized; but suddenly she seemed to regain consciousness. She picked up her book, scattered the leaves, and ran toward the gate.

"I shouldn't have gone into the garden," she said. "I didn't mean to but it looked so lovely and I couldn't resist. Wasn't it funny that I couldn't resist?"

He had meant to be gentle and loving, to tell her she was always free to do as she pleased. The idea that he might ever become paternalistic, let alone auto-cratic, horrified him. But how could she talk of being unable to resist as if there were something tempting about that drab autumnal place?

"I really don't follow you," he said. "It's a mystery to me." If tempered with a laugh, if accompanied by a squeeze of her hand, his words would have been harmless. But he heard them ring coldly and—worse—he felt glad his reproof had gone home, satisfied that she looked hurt and a little cowed.

She sighed, giving the garden a backward glance in which there was some-thing of yearning, something—was he imagining it?—of deceit. He took her arm firmly, trying to think of something that would clear the cloud from her face, but all that came out was a rather sharp, "Don't let's hang about here. We're due at my cousin's in an hour."

She nodded compliantly. Instead of feeling remorse, he was irritated by the very quality that had captivated him, her childlike naïveté. A deep and sullen depression enclosed him, and while they were at his cousin's party he spoke roughly to her once or twice, annoyed because she sat silent and then, illogically, even more out of temper when she was stirred into a faint animation by the attentions of a boy her own age.

From that evening onward he found himself beginning to look for faults in her. Had she always been so vague, so dreamy? Had that idleness, that forgetful-ness, always been there? She had ceased to speak of the garden. All those jaded leaves had fallen. The thready plane twigs hung bare, the evergreens had dulled to blackness, and often in the mornings the stone table, the seat, and the circle of grass were rimed with frost. The nights drew in at four o'clock and it was far too cold to sit in the open air.

Yet when he phoned his home from his office, as he had increasingly begun to do in the afternoons, he seldom received a reply. Nothing had come of that plan to go to classes and she said she never saw her friend. Where, then, was she when he phoned?

She couldn't be having daily driving lessons, each one lasting for hours. He might have asked her but he didn't. He brooded instead on her absences and his suppressed resentment burst into flames when there was no dinner prepared for their guests.

"They'll be here in three-quarters of an hour!" He had never shouted at her before and she put up her hand to her lips, shrinking away from him.

"Geoffrey, I don't know what happened to me but I forgot. Please forgive me. Can't we take them out?"

"People will begin to think I've married some sort of crazy child. What about last week when you 'forgot' that reception, when you 'forgot' to write and thank my cousin after we'd dined there?"

She had begun to cry. "All right," he said harshly, "we'll take them to a restaurant. Haven't much choice, have we? For God's sake, get out of that bloody dress!"

She was again wearing the lilac muslin. Evening after evening when he got home he found her in it—the dress he had adored but which was now worn and crumpled, with a food spot at the waist.

He poured himself a stiff drink. He was shaking with anger. The arguments in her favor he had put forward when she forgot the reception—that there had been a dozen gatherings which she hadn't forgotten but had graced—now seemed invalid in the face of this neglect.

But when she came back into the room his rage went. She wore a dress he hadn't seen before, of scarlet silk, stiff and formal yet suited to her youth, with huge sleeves, a tight black and gold embroidered bodice, and long skirt. Her hair was piled high and she walked with an unfamiliar aloofness that was almost hauteur.

His rage went, to be replaced oddly and rather horribly by an emotion he hadn't supposed he would ever feel toward her—a kind of greedy lust. He started forward, slopping his drink.

"Damme, Isabella, but you're a fine woman!"

Incredulously, she stopped and stood still. "*What* did you say?"

He passed his hand across his brow. "I said, 'God, Marion, you're a lovely girl.'"

"I must have misheard you. I really thought . . . I feel so strange, Geoffrey, not myself at all sometimes. You do still love me?"

"Of course I love you. Kiss? That's better. My darling little Marion, don't look so sad. We'll have a nice evening and forget all about this. Right?"

She nodded but her smile was watery, and the next day when he phoned her at three there was no reply although she had told him her driving lesson was in the morning.

Philip looked very comfortable and at home in the armchair by the window, as if he had been there for hours. Perhaps he had. Was it possible that she was out with him, Geoffrey wondered, on all those occasions when he phoned and got no answer?

The dress he had come to hate was stained with mud at the hem as if she had been walking. Her shoes were damp and her hair untidy. Maybe she devoted her mornings to the "very young chap" and her afternoons to this much older one. The husband, he had always heard, was the last to know.

She sat down beside him on the sofa, very close, almost huddled with him. Geoffrey moved slightly aside. What had happened to her gracious ways, that virginal aloofness, which had so taken him when he first saw her in her father's house? And he recalled, while Philip began on some tedious story of Palomede before the square was built, how he had ridden over to Cranstock to call on her father and she had been there with her mother in the drawing room, the gray-brown head and the smooth fair one bent over their work. At a word from her father she had risen, laying aside the embroidery frame, and played to them— oh, so sweetly!—on the harpsichord . . .

He shook himself, sat upright. God, he must have been more tired than he had thought and had actually dozed off. When had she ever done embroidery or played to him anything but records? And where had he got the name Cranstock from? The Craigs lived in Sapley and her father was dead.

The brief dream had been rather unpleasant. He said sharply, "Anyone want a drink?"

"Nothing for me," said Philip.

"Sherry, darling," said Marion. "Did you say a *manor* house, Philip?"

"Remember all these inner suburbs were villages in the early part of the Nineteenth Century, my dear. The Hewsons were lords of the manor of Palomede until the last one sold the estate in 1838."

His ill temper welling, Geoffrey brought their drinks. What right had that fellow to call *his* wife "my dear," and who cared, he thought returning to catch Philip's words, if some Hewson had been a minor poet or another had held office in Lord Liverpool's government?

"The last one murdered his wife."

"In that garden," said Geoffrey rather nastily, "and they took him up the road to Tyburn and hanged him."

"No, he was never brought to trial, but there was a good deal of talk and he was never again received in society. He married a wife half his age and suspected her of infidelity. She wasn't quite sane—what we'd now call mentally disturbed—and she used to spend hours wandering in the manor gardens. They extended over the whole of this square, of course, and beyond. He accused her of having trysts there with her lovers. All imagination, of course—there was no foundation for it."

Geoffrey said violently, "How can you possibly know that? How can *you* know there was no foundation?"

"My dear Geoff! Because the young lady's diary happens to have come into my hands from a great-niece of hers."

"I wouldn't believe a word of it!"

"Possibly not, but you haven't read it. There's no need to get so cross."

"No, please don't, darling."

He shook off the small hand which touched his sleeve. "Be silent, Marion! You know nothing about such matters and shouldn't talk of them."

Philip half rose. He said slowly, "And you accuse *me* of being Victorian! What the hell's got into you, Geoffrey? I was simply telling Marion a tale of old Palomede and you fly into a furious temper. I think I'd better go."

"Don't go, Philip. Geoffrey's tired, that's all." Her lips trembled but she said in a steady voice, "Tell us what became of Mr. Hewson and his wife."

The historian said stiffly, "In the end he took her away to Italy where she was drowned."

"You mean *he* drowned her?"

"That's what they said. He took her out in a boat in the Bay of Naples and he came back but she didn't. After that he was blackballed in his clubs and even his own sister wouldn't speak to him."

"What God-awful romantic tripe," said Geoffrey. He was watching his wife, taking in every slatternly detail of her appearance and thinking now of the City banquet he and she were to attend in the week before Christmas. All summer during their engagement he had looked forward to this banquet, perhaps the most significant public occasion of his year, and thought how this time he would have a beautiful young wife to accompany him. But was she beautiful still? Could she, changed and waiflike and vague as she had become, hold her own in the company of those mannered and sophisticated women?

He phoned her on the afternoon of that dim December day, for she had had a slight cold in the morning, had awakened coughing, and he wanted to be sure, firstly that she was well enough to go, and secondly that she would be dressed and ready on time. But the phone rang into emptiness.

Alarmed and apprehensive, he called Philip, who was out, and then the driving school to be told that Mrs. Gilmour's instructor was out too. She couldn't be out with both of them and yet—

He got home by six. It was raining. A trail of wet footmarks led from the elevator to the door of their flat like the prints left by someone who has been called unexpectedly from a bath. And then, even before he saw the damp and draggled figure, still and silent in front of the balcony windows, he knew where she had been, where she had been every day.

But instead of calming his jealousy, this revelation somehow increased it and he began shouting at her, calling her a slut, a failure as a wife, and telling her he regretted their marriage.

The insults seemed to pass over her. She coughed a little. She said dully, remotely, "You must go alone. I'm not well."

"Of course you're not well, mooning your life away in that foul garden. All right, I'll go alone, but don't be surprised if I don't come back!"

Geoffrey drank more than he would have if she had been with him. A taxi brought him home to Palomede Square just after midnight and he went up in the elevator, not drunk but not quite sober either. He opened their bedroom door and saw that the bed was empty.

There were no lights on in the flat except the hall light which he had just put on himself. She had left him. He picked up the phone to dial her mother's number and then he thought, no, she would go to that driver chap or to Philip.

Philip lived in a flat in the next house. Geoffrey came down the steps into the square and was on the pavement, striding to the next doorway, when he stopped and stared into the garden. At first he thought it was only a pale tree trunk that he could see or a bundle of something dropped behind the stone table. He approached the railings slowly and clasped his hands round the cold wet iron. It was a bundle of clothes, but the clothes enwrapped the seated and utterly still figure of his wife. He began to tremble.

She wore the lilac dress, its skirt sodden with water and clinging to the shape of her legs, and over it her mink coat, soaked and spiky like a rat's pelt. She sat with her hands spread on the table, one gloved, the other bare, her face blank, wax-white, lifted to the rain which fell steadily upon her and dropped sluggishly from the naked branches.

He opened the gate and went up to her without speaking. She recoiled from him but she didn't speak either. He dragged her from the seat and brought her out of the garden and into the house, half carrying her. In the elevator she began to cough, sagging against the wall, water dripping from her hair which hung in draggles under the slackened scarf that wrapped it, water streaming down her face.

Heat met them as he unlocked the door of the flat. Transiently, he thought as he pushed her inside, what have we come to, we who were so happy? A drunken autocrat and a half-crazed slattern. What has come over us?

The warmth of the radiator against which she leaned made steam rise from her hair and coat. What have we come to, he thought, and then all tender wistfulness vanished, spiraling away down some long corridor of time, taking with it everything that remained of himself and leaving another in possession.

The lamp in the square lit the flat faintly with a sickly yellow radiance. He put on no lights. "I demand an explanation," he said.

"I cannot explain. I have tried to explain it to myself but I cannot." Beneath the coat which she had stripped off, over the soaked and filthy dress, she wore and ancient purple and black wool shawl, moth-eaten into holes.

"What is that repellent garment?"

She fingered it, plucking at the fringes. "It is a shawl. A shawl is a perfectly proper article of dress for a lady to wear."

Her words, her antiquated usage, brought him no astonishment. They sounded natural to his ears.

"Where did you obtain such a thing? Answer me!"

"In the market. It was pretty and I needed a shawl."

He felt his face swell with an onrush of blood. "To be more fitting for your low lover, I daresay? You need not explain why you absent yourself from my household, for I know why. You have assignations in that garden, do you not, with your paramours? With my young coachman and that scribbler fellow Sarson?"

"It is not true," she whispered.

"Do you give me the lie, Isabella? Do you know that I could have a Bill of Divorcement passed in Parliament and rid myself of you? I could keep all your fortunes and send you back to your papa at Cranstock."

She came to him and fell on her knees. "Before God, Mr. Hewson, I am your honest wife! I have never betrayed you. Don't send me away, oh don't!"

"Get up." She was clinging to him and he pushed her away. "You have disgraced yourself and me. You have committed the worst sin a woman can commit, you have neglected your duties and brought me into disrepute before my friends." She crept from him, leaving a trail of water drops on the carpet. "I shall think now what I must do," he said. "I want no scandal, mind. Perhaps it will be best if I remove you from this."

"Do not take me from my garden!"

"You are a married woman, Isabella, and have no rights. Pray remember it. What you wish does not signify. I am thinking of my reputation in society. Yes, to take you away may be best. Go now and get some rest. I will sleep in my dressing-room and we will tell the servants you are ill so that there may be no gossip. Come, do as I bid you."

She gathered up her wet coat and left the room, crying quietly. The lamp in the square had gone out. He searched for a candle to light him to bed but he could not find one.

Philip Sarson came into the porters' office to collect his morning paper. "A bit brighter today," he said.

"We can do with it, sir, after that rain."

"Mrs. Gilmour not out in the garden this morning?"

"They've gone away, sir. Didn't you know?"

"I haven't seen so much of them lately," said Philip. "Gone away for Christmas, d'you mean?"

"I couldn't say. Seven A.M. they went. I'd only just come on duty." The head porter looked disapproving. "Mr. Gilmour said she was ill but she could walk all right. Tried to get into the garden, she did, only he'd taken the key away from her. She got hold of the gate and he pulled her off very roughlike, I thought. It's not the sort of thing you expect in this class of property."

"Where have they gone? Do you know?"

"They took his car. Italy, I think he said. Yes, it was. I saw Naples on their luggage labels. Are you all right, sir? All of a sudden you look quite ill."

Philip made no reply. He walked down the steps, across the square, and looked through the railings into the garden. A small white glove, sodden and flat as a wet leaf, lay on the seat. He shivered, cursing the writer's imagination that led him into such strange and improbable fancies.

HUGH PENTECOST

They'll Kill the Lady

Many people in the New England town of Lakeview thought of George Crowder as a "character." As a young man George Crowder must have been Adonis-handsome. Now in his late fifties Uncle George, as he was affectionately known in the community, was iron-gray, with deep lines at the corners of his firm mouth and crow's-feet at the eyes, etched there by good humor and compassion.

Long ago George Crowder had been a brilliant lawyer, the county prosecutor, with a political future that seemed to have no limits. But there had come a day when George Crowder had convicted a man on a murder charge, seen him executed by the state, then discovered that the man had been innocent.

George Crowder took full blame for this miscarriage of justice even though no one else believed he'd been at fault. He had prosecuted on the basis of evidence provided by the police—wrong evidence. He resigned his post as prosecutor, dropped the practice of law entirely, and disappeared from Lakeview. No one knew what had happened to him, not even his sister, Esther Trimble, married to the town druggist. Rumor had it that he was drinking himself to death somewhere.

After several years George Crowder reappeared in town, built himself a shack up in the woods, and lived there with only a setter dog for company. He seemed unwilling to renew old friendships. There was only one person who came and went freely—Joey Trimble, Crowder's twelve-year-old nephew.

To Joey Uncle George was a hero, the wisest man on earth, a man who knew the woods like no one else, who could read a whole story in a broken twig, a scuffled pile of leaves, a muddied stretch of stream, and who was certainly the best man in the world with a gun. And there was Uncle George's setter, Timmy, the best bird dog in the county, maybe in the state, maybe in all fifty states. Uncle George talked to Joey as though the boy was an equal, a grown man. Joey would have walked through hellfire for Uncle George.

In the fall and early winter Joey's visits to the shack in the woods were curtailed. There was school and homework. But on Fridays, after school, Joey did his homework as soon as he got home and then, sometimes after early dark, he took off for Uncle George's and was allowed to stay late. Eventually, when Joey's eyelids grew heavy in spite of himself, Uncle George drove him home in the jeep.

On this Friday evening Uncle George had two large venison steaks ready to broil over the hearth coals. It was a little after seven, already dark, when Timmy, the setter, raised his head and his tail thumped on the hearth rug. Uncle George knew that Joey was coming up the old logging road from the main highway. He and Timmy went out onto the shack's porch and the man lit the approach with his powerful flashlight.

Joey was running, stumbling, up the logging road as if the devil was after him. Uncle George realized that something must be wrong. He and Timmy went to greet the boy.

Joey literally fell, fighting for breath, into Uncle George's arms.

"There's a man lying 'longside the highway, Uncle George—bad hurt," the boy gasped. "Blood all over. It might be a hit-and-run."

"Anyone you know, lad?"

Joey shook his head. "No, sir."

"So, let's move," Uncle George said.

The man went inside the cabin for his corduroy car coat and corduroy hat, then he, Joey, and the dog climbed into the jeep and went hurtling down the logging road. They said in town that Uncle George could handle that jeep like a race driver covering the dangerous Baja. How the boy and the dog stayed in it was a small miracle.

The man lying beside the highway was a ghastly sight. Uncle George had stopped the jeep so that its headlights were focused on him. Joey hung back, his face white, as Uncle George knelt beside the blood-stained body.

"Looks like a pig-sticking," Uncle George said.

The injured man lay on his back, his open eyes staring up at the starlit sky. With each anguished beat of his heart, blood pumped out of his mouth. His body looked crushed, almost flattened from back to front.

"Get over to the Andersons', Joey, and call the State Police," Uncle George said. "Tell 'em we need an ambulance in a hell of a hurry." The boy started off. "Take Timmy with you!"

The injured man struggled to say something and more blood came out of his mouth.

"Easy," Uncle George said gently. "We're getting help."

"Got to find George Crowder," the injured man said. It was a bubbling sound.

Uncle George's pale blues eyes were bright and hard. "I'm George Crowder," he said.

The man seemed not to have heard him. "Got to find George Crowder," he said, strangling on his own blood. "They—they'll kill the lady—"

"What lady?" Uncle George asked. If the man was ever going to talk it would have to be now. It seemed cruel to press him, but he was almost certainly not going to make it to the hospital.

"They'll kill the lady," the man said. A great sob shook his mangled body. "Got—to—find—George—Crowder . . ."

They were the last words the man ever spoke. The head turned to one side and the ditch was bloodied.

Tiremarks on the highway told a grim story. Uncle George, Sergeant Stanyer of the State Police, and Red Egan, Lakeview's Sheriff and an old friend of Uncle George's, studied them in the headlights from several cars and the searchlight on the State Trooper's car.

"Crazy man," Red Egan said. "Looks like he was hit—a skidding stop—backup at full power—then ran over him again. Three times in all." The tiremarks showed clear on the black licorice surface of the road.

"It's unbelievable he lived long enough to speak," Sergeant Stanyer said. "He was looking for you, George?"

"So he said," Uncle George said. "That—and 'they'll kill the lady.' "

"What lady?"

"Didn't say." Uncle George's face was like a marble mask. "I don't think he heard me. He didn't know he'd found me."

"You know any lady around here who's likely to be killed?"

"Know one or two who may rate it," Uncle George said. "But not the way this man meant it, I think."

"Not a shred of identification," Stanyer said. "No wallet. Cheap suit could have been bought at a thousand places—and long ago. Can't get any conclusive tiremarks off this blacktop. Doctor may be able to add something."

Uncle George drove a reluctant Joey home, then joined Stanyer and Red Egan at the police barracks. Under bright fluorescent lights Uncle George looked down at the body of the man who'd been trying to find him. Blood had been washed away from the unshaved face. Uncle George stared at it for a long time.

"You ever seen him before, Red?" he asked the Sheriff.

"No." Quite positive.

"Something itches me," Uncle George said. "I'd say 'no' like you, Red, but something bothers me. I'd swear I'd never seen this man—and yet—"

"You're not sure?" Sergeant Stanyer asked.

"Maybe—a long time ago," Uncle George said. "Twenty or thirty years ago—a young man who might have turned out to look like this. But I can't place him."

"I go back as far as you do, George," Red Egan said. "He's not from around here, young or old."

"I could be wrong," Uncle George said.

"Not your habit," Red Egan said. "Maybe it'll come back to you."

"Maybe."

"On the table is everything he was carrying," Stanyer said. "Two one-dollar bills and sixty-four cents in change. Cigarettes and a packet of matches."

Uncle George picked up the matchbook. Matchbooks are used for advertising, sometimes by local bars, restaurants, and shops. This one carried a national ad for an underarm deodorant. No indication of where it came from.

"The driver could have been some drunk—or some guy on drugs," Stanyer said. "He hit the guy by accident, saw he wasn't dead, was afraid he might be identified, so he backed up and run over him a couple more times to make sure."

Uncle George was fiddling with the matchbook. "He was looking for me to tell me 'they'll kill the lady'," he said. "I'd say it looks more as if they were trying to stop him from doing just that—telling me." He opened the matchbook and his eyes narrowed. "You miss this?" he asked Stanyer, and handed him the matches. "Telephone number written inside it."

"Local," Stanyer said.

A few minutes later Stanyer had the information. The number belonged to a Mr. and Mrs. Joshua Clement of Lakeview.

"Big place over on South Mountain. You know it, George. The Clements are in Europe and their phone is temporarily disconnected."

"So our dead friend couldn't reach them if he tried," Uncle George said. "Who, I wonder, put him on to me?" He glanced at Stanyer. "I don't think I can buy your drunken hit-and-run driver who panicked, Sergeant. This man was on his way to find me. Someone must have given him directions, because he was only a few yards from the logging road that would have taken him straight to my place. That means he talked to somebody local. Could be a start."

"You were supposed to help him stop a killing," Red Egan said. " 'They'll kill the lady.' Why, since you don't know him, George, would he be looking to you for help and not me or the State Troopers?"

"You got a reputation, Mr. Crowder," Stanyer said.

"I had a reputation a long time ago," Uncle George said. His mouth tightened. "I wish I knew what bugs me about that face."

"Maybe this guy knew you knew this 'lady'," Stanyer said. "Looking for you because he knew you were her friend."

Uncle George shook his head.

"More likely he'd heard you'd help anybody in trouble," Red Egan said.

"Some stronger tie-in than that in his mind, I think," Uncle George said. "Some connection I can't make—not yet."

"Meanwhile there can be a lady in big trouble," Red Egan said.

One of the worst things about growing older, Uncle George thought, was that your memory begins to play tricks on you. In particular you begin to forget names. He had comforted himself by the thought that his memory bank got so full that it discarded the unimportant. The dead man's face had been ejected from his memory because it no longer mattered. Now it mattered, but he couldn't bring the face into focus.

He was up at daylight and back at the scene of the accident—rather, the murder, because that was what it must have been. What a brutal business! The man had been walking hurriedly along the road, having got directions from someone. Just a few yards from the logging road a car had come up behind him. He must not have expected danger from it. The car ran him down, stopped, backed up, ran forward in another crushing assault, backed again, then ran over him a final time and took off into the night. Deliberate, cold-blooded murder.

All this to stop the man from finding George Crowder and telling him about a lady who was going to be killed. The lady couldn't be far away. She had to be in Lakeview or nearby. George Crowder couldn't have been expected to give emergency help to someone far away. If the lady was here in Lakeview, and still unharmed, then the man or men who had driven the murder car must also still be near.

Uncle George raised his head as if he could sense them or smell them on the morning air. In the woods you listened and listened and finally you heard something. Out here on the highway the sounds were mechanical, the air polluted by carbon monoxide.

The Andersons lived about a hundred yards from the murder scene. It was to their house Joey had run to get help the night before. Uncle George stopped there and got his first bit of concrete information. Yes, a stranger had knocked on their back door a little after dark, asking for the way to George Crowder's shack. They'd told him the logging road was "just a piece further," Nothing odd about the stranger, except that he was walking. In the country everybody rides in some kind of vehicle.

Uncle George told them what had happened to the man. They were shocked.

"We did hear some tires squealin' right after he left," Fred Anderson said. "But there's a corner just beyond here, George, and tires squealin' ain't unusual. Kids all drive like hell these days."

"Someone from hell was driving that car," Uncle George said.

Joey, Uncle George knew, would be bursting with curiosity about the night before. Also, there would be a pot of fresh coffee on his sister Esther's stove. He drove the jeep to the Trimble house with Timmy, the setter, sitting upright like a human passenger on the seat beside him. The boy came running across the lawn before he and Timmy could climb out of the jeep.

"Not one word until your mom has poured me a cup of coffee," Uncle George said.

When Esther had provided him with coffee and a piece of homemade cake Uncle George gave a detailed account of everything that had happened to date.

"It's not a nice thing to ask," he said to his sister, "but I wonder if you'd mind coming down to the undertaker's and taking a look at the dead man?"

"George!"

"Might be someone we grew up with, Esther. So help me, I can't place him, but I've got the nagging feeling that—"

"Uncle George!" Joey had something to say he couldn't hold in any more. "About the Clements' place. They may be in Europe, but there's someone staying in the house. A lady."

Uncle George turned his head. "Say that again, lad."

"There's a lady staying in the Clements' house. Eddie Hanson's trying to sell magazine subscriptions. He gets some kind of special school prize if he sells the most. I biked around with him for a while day before yesterday. We were riding by the Clements' place, not planning to stop because Eddie knew they were in Europe. But we saw smoke coming out of the fireplace chimney, so we thought maybe they were back. We rode up to the front door and rang the bell and this lady answered and—"

"What lady, Joey?"

"Search me. I never saw her before, Uncle George. She was real nice, but she didn't want any magazines."

"Did she explain what she was doing there?"

"Just said she was staying in the house while the owners were abroad."

"The Clements probably wanted someone in the house," Esther said.

"They've got a caretaker," Joey said. "Old Mr. Bohrer."

"He doesn't live in," Esther said. She looked at Uncle George. "You think she might be the 'lady they'll kill'?"

"No reason to think so," Uncle George said. "But tell me what she looked like, Joey."

"Well, she's older than Mom. Maybe as old as you, Uncle George."

Esther laughed. "An old lady of fifty-two or -three."

"Did she tell you her name, Joey?"

"No, sir. And we had no reason to ask."

"Well, there's no use stewing over it, George," Esther said "Mike Bohrer can tell you who she is and what she's doing there."

"I think I'll find out," Uncle George said.

Joey was added to the jeep's passenger list. They found old Mike Bohrer sitting on the post-office steps waiting for the mail to be sorted. In his salad days old Mike had been one of the best logging men in the state. He'd worked for the Lakeview Lumber Company most of his life, but arthritis and the years had slowed him down. He now mowed lawns, worked in gardens, and did odd jobs.

Mike was glad to see Uncle George. They called each other a few affectionate names and chatted a little about this and that, mostly about how much Mike envied Uncle George that setter dog, "settin' up in the jeep seat like a human bein'."

"I hear you got someone staying at the Clements' house," Uncle George said.

"Yep," Mike said, not very interested. "Friend of the folks, I guess."

"You guess?"

"Well, would she be stayin' there if she wasn't a friend? A Mrs. Chandler. Nice enough woman."

"The Clements invited her to stay in the house while they were gone?"

"Well, I suppose they did. Anyway, I had my instructions from Steve Randall. He's Josh Clement's lawyer, you know."

"Steve told you this Mrs. Chandler was going to stay in the house?"

"What's eatin' you?" Mike asked. "Never knowed you to be so nosey. You want all the i's dotted and the t's crossed? Steve didn't tell me anything. He wrote me a letter from Washington where he was—told me the Clements wanted me to open up the house for this Mrs. Chandler." He winked at Uncle George. "You got an eye out for her? She's kinda cute."

Joey snorted. Mrs. Chandler was an old lady of 52 or 53.

"It looks like a dead end, Joey," Uncle George said, as they took off for the Randall place at the far end of town.

You couldn't equate violence with Steven Randall. He was one of Uncle George's oldest friends. They'd graduated from law school together. Everyone thought George Crowder was the one who was going to make it big, but things had happened to him. Now Steve Randall was the town's celebrity. If you could believe the Gallup poll he was going to be the next Senator from the state and people said that in another six years he could well be living in the White House.

Uncle George hadn't seen much of his old friend in the last few years. Randall was a national figure, traveling around the country, preparing for the big pitch that lay ahead. Uncle George had become, at least, a part-time recluse. He couldn't recall how long ago it was he'd gone up to the big house on the hill where Steve Randall lived when he was home.

One reason for the fading of the friendship was Amy Randall, Steve's wife. Steve had married money and social position, some thought for what it would do for his political ambitions. Amy was what Uncle George called "image conscious." When Uncle George got into his trouble, way back, Amy had made it quite clear she considered his friendship with Steve Randall could only be harmful. Steve tried to explain, tried to see his friend on the side, but it was too difficult, too complicated. So they had drifted apart. And people said the Randalls' marriage had done some drifting, too. As he drove up the hill to the big house, Uncle George wondered what kind of reception he would get.

He left Joey and the setter in the jeep and approached the front door of the old Colonial house. He was reaching for the wrought-iron knocker when the door opened and he found himself faced by a young man in a natty sports jacket. He had dark hair and rather hostile dark eyes.

"Can I help you?" the man asked.

"I'd like to see Mr. Randall," Uncle George said.

"I'm afraid it isn't possible," the man said. "I'm Avery Tyler, Mr. Randall's executive secretary. If you'll tell me your business?"

"I'm an old friend, George Crowder. Just wanted a word or two with Mr. Randall."

There was flat refusal in Tyler's eyes, but a strong voice called out from behind him. "Who is it, Avery?"

"Steve!" Uncle George shouted. "It's George Crowder."

"George!"

Avery Tyler was swept away and a big handsome man with blond hair and a happy, smiling face took Uncle George in a bearhug of greeting. His eyes were a candid blue and bright with pleasure.

"You old sonofagun!" Steve Randall said. "Where the hell have you been keeping yourself?" He turned to his secretary. "Best damned lawyer you'll ever encounter, Avery. Best damned friend, too." He looked out at the jeep. "That Esther's boy?"

"Growing like a weed," Uncle George said. "Look, friend, I gather you're busy. I've got what may not be a problem at all and you might help me forget it."

"Well, come in, man!"

"I'm a little pressured for time, Steve." In a few terse sentences he told Randall about the murder victim of the night before and the victim's disjointed words before he died. "We found a matchbook on him and written inside the cover was Josh Clement's phone number. That phone's disconnected, but Joey happened to know that your Mrs. Chandler is staying at the house."

Randall's face clouded. "*My* Mrs. Chandler? Who the hell is Mrs. Chandler?"

"Mrs. Chandler is the woman you wrote Mike Bohrer about, telling him she was to be allowed to use the house."

"You've got something by the wrong end, George. I never wrote to Mike Bohrer about a Mrs. Chandler or anything else. Somebody's putting something over on somebody. We better see what's going on up there."

"I could do that for you, Mr. Randall," Tyler said. "You've got that speech to finish writing."

"To hell with the speech," Randall said. "I'll do better talking off the top of my head anyway. You've seen this woman, George?"

"No, but Joey did, trying to sell her magazines." Uncle George's mouth twitched. "She's an old lady of fifty-two or -three."

"If she says I wrote a letter for her to Mike Bohrer she's an old liar of fifty-two or -three. Let's go find out what she's up to. Get my car, will you, Avery?"

The lines in Uncle George's face seemed to be more deeply etched than normal. "If you have time we might stop at the mortuary on the way, Steve. I'd like you to look at the dead man. I have the feeling I've seen him before but I can't pinpoint him."

"Sure. It's on the way."

Tyler drove a fire-engine-red Mercedes up to the front door.

"We'll tag along behind you, Steve," Uncle George said.

Tyler still sat behind the wheel of the car.

"I won't need you, Avery," Randall said. "We've got that phone call coming from Washington. Tell 'em I'll be back in an hour or so."

They drove into town and stopped at the undertaker's. Inside they were shown the body of the murdered man. Randall, scowling, stared down at it for a long time.

"This man's name is Fred Wicks, George. You've seen him before—three or four times, I'd guess. It was a long time ago. He used to run a little lunch counter in New Haven when we were in law school. I remember a few times when we'd been studying late we went around the corner to his place for a sandwich and a glass of milk. He was just a kid then."

Thirty-odd years ago! The face of a scrawny kid swam into Uncle George's memory, a kid with a fresh mouth presiding over greasy hamburgers.

"I have reason to remember him better than you, George," Randall said. "We both enlisted in the navy the day after Pearl Harbor, took our training together, served on the same destroyer for a while. We got separated halfway through the war and I don't think I ever saw him again."

"Why would he be looking for me to help him instead of you?" Uncle George asked.

"If he knew you lived in this town he'd remember you were a lawyer."

"Maybe we can figure it out later," Uncle George said. "Right now I find myself concerned about your Mrs. Chandler."

"Not my Mrs. Chandler!" Randall said.

It was about a ten-minute drive to the Clement's place. Randall drove the red Mercedes right up to the front door. Uncle George parked the jeep a little distance away and told Joey and the setter to stay put. He felt a curious tension. He stopped and turned back to the boy.

"You see or hear anyone coming, Joey, blow the horn."

"Yes, sir."

"Especially anyone coming out of the woods."

"Yes, sir."

"And after you blow the horn you and Timmy duck out of sight. Understand?"

"Yes, sir."

Uncle George turned and headed for the house. He was about 15 yards from where Randall was waiting when the front door opened and a woman appeared. Some old woman of fifty-two or -three! She had the lush figure of a thirty-year-old woman in her prime. Her hair was red, probably not natural, but beautifully groomed. She had wide brown eyes and a generous mouth, and when she saw Randall her whole face seemed to light up like a kid's at Christmas.

"Steve!" she said. "I was beginning to think you were never coming."

Randall looked stunned. Then, in a broken voice, he said, "Maggie! Dear Maggie! What in God's name are you doing here?" She might not be his Mrs. Chandler, but he took her in his arms and held her very close.

Uncle George turned to go away. Whatever the problem was, Steve Randall could handle it now. Uncle George felt he was intruding on some kind of special privacy, yet instinct told him that there was danger somewhere around him, somewhere nearby. He was reluctant to stay, even more reluctant to go.

"George!" Randall's voice was sharp. "Please, George, don't leave."

Uncle George turned back. Steve Randall, his arm still around the smiling woman, offered an explanation. "I wasn't lying to you, George. I don't know why Maggie is calling herself Mrs. Chandler."

"Because I am Mrs. Chandler," the woman said, in a pleasant, husky voice.

"You're married, Maggie?"

"You didn't keep track of me, Steve," the woman said. "I was married. To a nice guy, a commercial airline pilot who made the mistake of piloting his ship into the side of a mountain. But what is the problem, Steve? I was about to call you in spite of the instructions in your letter. I thought something must have gone wrong, so I—"

"What do you mean, my letter, Maggie? I never wrote you any letter."

Randall and the woman stared at each other.

"I think it might be advisable to go inside," Uncle George said. He felt the small hairs prickling on the back of his neck.

They went into the house, into the pine-paneled living room.

"Do you still have the letter you say I wrote you, Maggie?" Randall asked. He was all business now.

"Of course I have it," Maggie Chandler said. She went over to a leather shoulder bag that was resting on the desk. She took a letter out of the bag and handed it to Randall.

Randall frowned at it. "My stationery," he said. "Postmarked Washington, D.C.—one week ago." He opened the envelope. "My letterhead." He read quickly, his frown deepening. Finally he looked up at the woman. "I never wrote this, Maggie." He held the letter out to Uncle George.

"You sure you want me to read it, Steve?" Uncle George asked.

"Of course I want you to read it—the damned thing is a fake."

Uncle George read the typed letter. "My very dear Maggie:—I am in deep trouble and you may be the only person who can help me out of it. I know when I ask for help that I can count on you. I enclose five one-hundred-dollar bills to cover your traveling expenses. You will please come to Lakeview and take a taxi to the home of Joshua Clement. The Clements are away, but I've arranged for the caretaker to open the house for you.

"I may not get to you right away, Maggie. Don't call me. Just wait for me to show up. I wouldn't ask this if my whole future wasn't at stake. Please don't let me down. My very best love to you, Maggie. Steve."

Uncle George glanced at the envelope. It was addressed to Mrs. Joseph Chandler, Miami Beach, Florida.

"I didn't know Maggie had married," Randall said. "How could I know her married name or where she was living?"

"If this is a phony," Uncle George said, "then you can count on it that the letter to Mike Bohrer was sent by the same person—on your stationery, Steve."

"I've always followed your career, Steve," Maggie said. "I supposed the trouble you mentioned had to do with—well, with long ago."

"I did not write the letter!" Randall said. "I am not in any trouble!"

"I have the feeling you're in very big trouble, Steve," Uncle George said. "What did happen long ago? What did Fred Wicks have to do with it?"

"Freddie Wicks?" Maggie said. "What about him?"

"He was murdered here in Lakeview last night," Uncle George said. "You people want to talk to me? If not, you'd better handle it yourselves."

They wanted to talk, and it was a strange story. Maggie Chandler told her part of it, looking steadily at Uncle George. Thirty years ago she had been working in a bordello in Panama City. The customers had been almost entirely navy personnel—young men far away from home, lonely, often a little frightened. Taking care of their loneliness had seemed almost a patriotic duty.

"I was one of those boys," Steve said in a hard, flat voice. "Could you believe I fell in love with Maggie?"

"Easily," Uncle George said.

Randall's ship was stationed at Panama City for several months. Fred Wicks was in that crew and he also patronized the bordello. One night there was a riot. A drunken sailor started to take the place apart. In the melee that followed, the sailor was knifed, killed. Military police came charging in.

"Maggie got us out of there, Fred Wicks and me," Randall said. "Down a back alley to another part of town—to her own apartment. It saved us from a court-martial, possibly a murder charge."

Maggie had never gone back to the bordello. She was in love, too. She and Randall lived together until his ship moved on. They had written to each other for a while, but the war had gone on for another four years and their love affair had died. They had seen each other once more, about a year after peace, and had mutually agreed there was no way to put it together again.

"I was still in love," Maggie said quietly. "But I knew I could never fit into Steve's lifestyle."

That was it. That was all of it, they told Uncle George.

"How much could this story hurt your political career, Steve?" Uncle George asked.

"Not much—not at all, I think. There was no crime that really involved me. I was a kid of twenty-one serving my country. My affair with Maggie?" Randall shrugged. "Thousands of boys had less than permanent relationships in those days."

"But if it was made to look as though there was something more? If now there was a crime?"

"I don't follow you, George."

"If you brought the lady here, hid her away from your wife Amy, and then—"

"Then what?"

"'They'll kill the lady,' Wicks said. Having got what she believed was a genuine letter from you, Steve, Mrs. Chandler comes here. She follows instructions and just waits. But sooner or later, when you didn't get in touch, she'd have called you. You'd have come running and killed the lady to protect yourself from scandal."

"You're crazy!" Randall said.

"You misunderstand. It would *look* as though you'd killed the lady. She would be dead, shot with your gun. There'd be the letter."

"*My* gun?"

"The person who could steal your stationery could easily steal a gun from you. You used to collect guns when I first knew you, Steve. So they'd have you cold. You could deny till you were blue in the face that you didn't write to Maggie or to Mike Bohrer. When the Panama City story came out no one in the world would believe you. You'd lured Mrs. Chandler here to kill her, to keep her quiet."

"But who knew the Panama story?" Randall asked.

"Fred Wicks, of course. Knew it all from top to bottom. Found someone who would pay him handsomely for it. We have a new look at political methods these days. Your enemies were willing to buy what Wicks had to sell, but they must have agreed with you, Steve, that the story itself wouldn't do you much harm. But if they could build on it—?"

"But why kill Fred Wicks?"

"It's a guess," Uncle George said. "He was willing enough to sell you out, Steve, but when he discovered the plan involved murder—killing Maggie—he couldn't go along with it. He was afraid to see you, Steve, but he remembered me, your friend, a lawyer. He was on his way to tell me about it when they caught up with him and ran him down."

"And who are 'they,' George?"

Uncle George shrugged. "You know who your enemies are better than I do, Steve. They have to be here in the Lakeview area, of course. Country people don't lock their houses. It would be simple enough to steal some of your stationery and one of your guns."

"But can we prove anything against anyone?" Randall asked.

"If you've got the guts," Uncle George said. "They must still think they can pull it off."

"We've got the guts," Maggie said.

She was quite a woman, Uncle George thought. "They can't stall any longer if they're going to make their plan work," he said. "They know you've headed here with me. There's just a chance we won't have figured it out. So when I leave they close in on you two. I actually become a witness for them. You were here, you probably told me the Panama City story. I'd have to testify to both those facts. Then after I've left, you kill Maggie. There'll be somebody nearby who hears the shots and before you can do anything they've got you. Cold."

"What do you want us to do, Mr. Crowder?" Maggie asked quietly.

"I leave," Uncle George said. "I set it up for them just the way they want it. You risk being alone for a little bit. Then I come back."

"You can't be sure you'll be back in time," Randall said.

"I can make an awfully good try," Uncle George said. "But as I said, it will take guts to risk it. There's nobody nearby right now. The boy's watching. He'd have signaled me if he'd even caught a glimpse of anyone."

Randall put his arm around Maggie. "We'll risk it," he said.

Uncle George went out to the jeep and joined Joey and the dog. "I'm going to drive down to the first turn in the road, Joey, and then I'm heading off into the brush. You and Timmy will lie low there till I come back."

"What's up, Uncle George?"

"I hope I run into a killer."

They started down the driveway to the front gates. Just as they were about to head out onto the highway an old station wagon confronted them. It was Mike Bohrer. Uncle George flagged him down.

"You headed for the Clements?" he asked.

"I check the place every day," old Mike said.

"Well, everything's all right up there," Uncle George said. "Steve Randall's visiting with Mrs. Chandler. I don't think you need to check today." The old man's presence might hold up the killer or head him off.

"If you say so, George," old Mike said. "Give me time to pour a couple of beers at the Falcon."

The Falcon was a roadside café about a mile away. Old Mike was a customer at most of the drinking spots around Lakeview. He turned the station wagon north on the highway. Uncle George headed south toward town.

"He was probably just as glad not to go up there," Joey said.

"Not too fond of work, I imagine." Uncle George said.

"It's not that, Uncle George. He and Mr. Randall don't get on at all. It was Mr. Randall got him fired from the lumber company before he had a pension coming. Some of the kids say Mr. Randall caught him stealing, let him off, but got him fired."

The jeep was suddenly in the ditch and Uncle George was climbing out. He reached in the back for the shotgun he always carried there.

"You just may have saved a life, Joey. Now, you're not to move unless you hear shooting. If you hear a gun you're to run like hell for help."

"But, Uncle George—"

"No time to explain, lad. Just do as you're told."

Uncle George could move through the woods with almost animal quiet. He came to the edge of the growth of trees bordering on the lawn that fronted the house. He saw what he expected to see. Old Mike Bohrer was approaching the house from the north boundary and he was carrying a rifle. He seemed to be heading toward the back door of the house.

Uncle George circled the other way, running low and fast. As he turned the corner of the house he saw old Mike with his hand on the back door. Uncle George raised the shotgun to his shoulder.

"You'd better hold it right where you are, Mike, and drop that rifle unless you want me to blow your head off where you stand," Uncle George called out.

Old Mike turned, his face working. He dropped the rifle on the grass.

"God almighty, George, you scared the hell out of me. I just came back to—"

"I know what you came back for, Mike. Now shut up, or at least keep your voice down." Uncle George moved forward and picked up the rifle. "Mighty expensive gun for you to own, Mike. Belongs to Mr. Randall, doesn't it?"

Old Mike looked as though his legs were going to give way under him.

"Let's see how she sounds," Uncle George said. He pointed the rifle skyward and fired it three times. The shots echoed and re-echoed down the valley. "Now, quick into the house, old man, quick!"

Uncle George went into the kitchen, hanging on to old Mike. He pushed open the swing door that led into the main part of the house.

He saw Steve Randall and Maggie clinging to each other.

"Everything's okay," he said. "Quick, Maggie. I want you out here. And you, Steve, play it like a guilty man. Hurry, please, Maggie."

She came without question and the door closed.

"That miserable old hulk over there was meant to be the triggerman. But I think our Number One boy is running across the front lawn right now," Uncle George said. He opened the swing door just a crack.

At that moment Avery Tyler, in his smart sports jacket, came running in from the front door.

"Oh, my God, Mr. Randall, I heard shots!" he said.

Randall just stared at him.

"I was afraid you'd do something desperate. That's why I tried to keep it from you that she was here. I tried to buy her off but she wouldn't listen to me. Is she dead?"

"You miserable worm," Randall said, in a toneless voice.

"A very good scene, but it might become a bit too corny if it's continued," Uncle George said, coming into the room and pushing old Mike ahead of him. "You've been waiting outside there quite a while—with your friend—for those shots to be fired, haven't you, Tyler? Unfortunately for you I fired those shots— into the air. If you were any kind of countryman you'd have known those shots were fired outdoors and not in the house. Okay, Maggie, you can join the party."

She came in from the kitchen, cool, unruffled. Tyler looked about to collapse.

"I'm going to take these two in," Uncle George said. "Citizen's arrest. I hope, Steve, that Maggie can help you prepare yourself for the next shock."

"Shock?"

"Take a look out those French windows, Steve."

Randall went to the windows. A woman stood at the end of the garden, gripping the top of a white picket fence.

"My wife!" Randall said.

"Waiting out there for Tyler to tell her it's all worked out just the way the two of them planned it."

"Amy and Tyler?"

"When I saw her waiting out there, Steve, I had to conclude there was nothing political about this at all. Woman in her forties, eager for the attentions of a young stud like Tyler. When Fred Wicks came to Tyler with his story, thinking he could blackmail you, Steve, he showed them the way. Your wife had the money to pay Wicks handsomely. But there were too many people involved— Wicks, who got squeamish, and old Mike who held a grudge and wanted his pension money. Your wife could take care of him, too. Now, with the ship sinking, they'll talk their heads off and probably make Tyler the villain."

"So help me God, Mr. Crowder—" Tyler began.

"You're going to need His help, friend," Uncle George said grimly.

LAEL J. LITTKE

The Bantam Phantom

Georgie's size probably had something to do with his getting fired from his job. As a matter of fact, it had everything to do with it. In the Official Rules and Regulations for Ghosting, Chapter 3, Section 17A(1), it states that an aspiring haunter must be a size befitting the area he expects to haunt, which is only logical. After all, how could a ghost the size of a napkin expect to haunt the Metropolitan Opera House or Yankee Stadium?

Georgie was very small. He was so small that instead of wearing a sheet the size of a double bed—the way Oscar, the head ghost at Mrs. Pomeroy's did—or even the size of a twin bed like the one Gwendolyn, Oscar's wife, wore, Georgie had to wear a tablecloth. And only the size of a bridge table, at that. And even then a good deal of it floated behind him.

Now, as you know, not all ghosts haunt houses. Most of the smaller ones are content with jobs like pushing out the peanuts in a vending machine or popping up the tissues in a Kleenex box. Georgie had several friends who were also too small to haunt houses—they worked in Grand Central Station lockers. They liked their jobs because it gave them a chance to meet all kinds of people.

Georgie, however, had higher ambitions. He didn't know exactly what it was he wanted to do, but he knew it had to be something impressive. Like being a house haunter. In a big house, and the larger the better. A mansion would be fine.

He never would have got the job at Mrs. Pomeroy's Fifth Avenue mansion if John and Marsha, two of the Pomeroy ghosts, hadn't eloped and left Oscar short of help. Georgie showed up the night of Mrs. Pomeroy's annual dinner party and in the confusion was hired without being measured to see if he met the specified minimum requirements.

But because of his hard work and willingness he was allowed to stay on for a whole year. His main assignment was to haunt the small bedroom in the east wing, usually given to children of visiting guests. The truth was, Oscar wasn't entirely satisfied with Georgie's work there since Georgie could not seem to carry on in the true haunting tradition. Instead of putting a good scare into the children by trailing spider webs across their faces or filling the room with hollow laughter in the dismal hours after midnight, Georgie spent his time whispering fanciful tales into their small ears after they had gone to bed. The little back bedroom became a favorite spot with the children and they cherished forever the memory of the delightful hours they spent there, although they were never quite sure what it was that had made the time so pleasant.

It was at Mrs. Pomeroy's that Georgie met Geraldine, a petite little ghost the size of a dish towel who worked in Mrs. Pomeroy's bedroom haunting one of her shoeboxes. She and Georgie fell in love and were married at a gala party in the furnace room one romantically dark and stormy night.

Georgie probably would have stayed on at Mrs. Pomeroy's forever if he hadn't tried to carry the heavy chain down the front stairs on the night of Mrs. Pomeroy's next annual dinner party, a tremendous affair which always took the entire ghosting staff. Everyone else was so busy that Oscar asked Georgie to carry the chain and follow him down to the dining room. They were planning to drag it across the waxed floors and see what that would do to the guests.

Everything went smoothly enough—even though Georgie was turning a little pink from his exertions—until he tripped. One of the stair-haunting ghosts swept past, causing a breeze that swirled Georgie's tablecloth around his feet, and down he went. He tried to scream a warning to Oscar, but it was too late. The heavy chain flattened Oscar, knocking him cold. Before he regained consciousness three days later, he had been laundered and used as a bedsheet for two nights. He fired Georgie.

Georgie broke the news to Geraldine gently, since she was expecting a handkerchief in a few months. She assured Georgie that she had great faith in him and that it wouldn't be long before he found another job, considering his abilities and brains. They bade a tearful farewell to all their friends at Mrs. Pomeroy's, pulled out the nails in the attic where they hung themselves to sleep in the daytime, and set out to look for a new position.

They could always go home to Dullsville, Pennsylvania, Georgie told Geraldine, and help haunt the coal mine in which his father worked. But they both agreed that to return to a poverty zone like Dullsville would be a step backward. Since both of them had become used to the nicer things in life they would try to find a position in another mansion.

Each day Georgie scanned the want ads in the New York edition of the *Ghost Gazette* and wrote stacks of letters of application. Geraldine found an easy job accumulating lint under the beds in a small hotel and they were allowed to live there until Georgie could find a job.

For a few weeks Georgie rented himself out as a tablecloth in a restaurant, a position he rather enjoyed although he regarded it as beneath his dignity. He whispered stories to the restaurant clientele while they ate. The place became a favorite eatery, especially with the arty set. However, when Georgie noticed that he was becoming somewhat threadbare from the constant bleachings, he left that job and worked for a while haunting a TV set in a wonderful dark gloomy little place in Greenwich Village. He wisely quit when he heard the lady of the house phoning a TV repairman to come and get rid of the ghost in her set.

Georgie drifted about for several weeks doing nothing much except call at the ghost employment office each day to see if anyone had offered him a job.

Dispiritedly he tried applying at some of the swanky apartments in Sutton Place, but was usually greeted with hoots of laughter and remarks such as, "Who needs a bantam phantom?"

Then one day there was a letter asking him to call at the home of Don Surly, the famous writer of children's stories. Georgie was elated until he found that the job was merely haunting a broom closet. But he hid his disappointment and took it. Geraldine was expecting her handkerchief just about any day and he couldn't afford to be choosy.

It can't be said that Georgie liked his new job, but he did it to the best of his ability. He was told to rattle the mop bucket and moan whenever the maid opened the closet door. Georgie discovered, however, that the maid, an elderly Finn, was practically deaf and noticed neither the rattling nor his moans. To add to his chagrin at being ignored, the maid snatched him one day, tore him in two, and used both halves of him to sop up the scrub water when she washed the floor.

Georgie was so depressed that while Geraldine patched him up in the cozy cubbyhole they had been assigned to under the stairs he told her that he was ready to go back to Dullsville and haunt the coal mine. It was either that or be a rag mop the rest of his life. In true wifely fashion Geraldine said that wherever he went she would go, since she was willing to put up with anything herself, even a coal mine; but, she added sweetly, she wanted something better for their coming little one and and certainly wanted it to have all the comforts to be found in a big city. Georgie sighed and decided to stick it out.

It was while he was on his way back to the broom closet that he heard a human voice. A loud male human voice.

"I can't go on," it was saying. "Nothing comes. I sit and stare at this dratted typewriter but my head is empty. I can't write any more."

Georgie heard gentler tones, soothing female tones. He followed the direction of the voices and slipped behind a door. Mr. Surly was striding furiously up and down his den, a booklined room dominated by a large desk on which sat an electric typewriter. Strewn about the desk were piles of crumpled paper.

"I'm drained dry," wailed Mr. Surly. "Empty. I can't conjure up a single fresh idea. I can't write any more. I think I'll kill myself."

"You don't mean that," said Mrs. Surly. "Give yourself a chance to rest and to fill up again with ideas."

"That isn't the way it works," shouted Mr. Surly. "It's been three months since I wrote a saleable story. I'm a failure, I tell you. We'll have to move out of here."

Oh, oh, thought Georgie, here's where I lose another job. He wondered if Geraldine could stand another move at this delicate time.

Mr. Surly stopped pacing and stared glumly out of the window. "I'll sell shoes," he said. "Or pump gas."

"If that was what you really wanted to do, dear," said Mrs. Surly, "I'd say all right, sell shoes or pump gas—if it were only the two of us to consider. But there are Billy and Walter and Peter and Polly and Edgar and Alice and Randy and Elizabeth and Peggy and Arthur and Jane."

Mr. Surly paled. "That many?"

Mrs. Surly nodded. She held up a little bootee she was in the process of knitting.

"Good lord," whispered Mr. Surly. He sat down at the typewriter. "I'm going to write a story today or I shall blow my brains out. At least you and the kids would have the insurance."

"Don't talk like that, dear," said Mrs. Surly.

"Go away. I've got to work." Mr. Surly sat down at the typewriter and scowled ferociously at it as Mrs. Surly tiptoed out.

Georgie crept over and hung around Mr. Surly's shoulder to see what he had been writing. It was a children's story about a garbage truck that murdered a mini-car because the dragon that lived inside the truck told him to do it.

"That's not much of a children's story," whispered Georgie.

"Actually it's not much of a children's story," said Mr. Surly to himself.

Georgie leaned closer. "The garbage truck could be an unfortunate ugly old man who is suspected of violence only because he looks like a criminal."

"And the mini-car could be a rich playboy. By George," chortled Mr. Surly, "that's the first good idea I've had for months. I knew *something* would come if I kept at it long enough."

Georgie pondered for a moment and then leaned even closer to Mr. Surly's ear. "Actually, it was the butler who committed the murder because he was jealous. The ugly old man looks mean but he is really a kind and generous man who is good to his wife. Dogs and children love him."

"Originality, that's what they want," said Mr. Surly. Gaily he began to type.

Georgie stayed right there with him for several hours until the manuscript was finished. He didn't mind when Mr. Surly reached around and grabbed one of Georgie's corners, thinking it was his handkerchief, and mopped his perspiring face. Georgie regarded it as an honor.

Finally, Mr. Surly pulled the last sheet from his typewriter. "Selma," he bellowed, "I'm a writer again! Come and read this story."

Georgie slipped out while Mrs. Surly was telling Mr. Surly how wonderful he was and that she had known all along he could do it.

"Geraldine," Georgie yelled as he floated home, "I've found out what I'm meant to be!"

Geraldine met him at the door of their cubbyhole. "What's the matter?" she said anxiously. "Did your stitches come loose?"

"I've found my niche," sang Georgie. "Geraldine, I'm going to be a ghost writer!"

"Darling, that's wonderful," Geraldine said. "I'm sure you'll be a great success."

And he is, even though only he and Geraldine know that Mr. Surly gets the ideas for all his fine stories—the mysteries, the romances, the adventure and science-fiction stories—from Georgie.

Georgie especially likes doing stories about people who persevere.

NEDRA TYRE

A Nice Place To Stay

All my life I've wanted a nice place to stay. I don't mean anything grand, just a small room with the walls freshly painted and a few neat pieces of furniture and a window to catch the sun so that two or three pot plants could grow. That's what I've always dreamed of. I didn't yearn for love or money or nice clothes, though I was a pretty enough girl and pretty clothes would have made me prettier—not that I mean to brag.

Things fell on my shoulders when I was fifteen. That was when Mama took sick, and keeping house and looking after Papa and my two older brothers—and of course nursing Mama—became my responsibility. Not long after that Papa lost the farm and we moved to town. I don't like to think of the house we lived in near the C & R railroad tracks, though I guess we were lucky to have a roof over our heads—it was the worst days of the Depression and a lot of people didn't even have a roof, even one that leaked, plink, plonk; in a heavy rain there weren't enough pots and pans and vegetable bowls to set around to catch all the water.

Mama was the sick one but it was Papa who died first—living in town didn't suit him. By then my brothers had married and Mama and I moved into two back rooms that looked onto an alley and everybody's garbage cans and dump heaps. My brothers pitched in and gave me enough every month for Mama's and my barest expenses even though their wives complained.

I tried to make Mama comfortable. I catered to her every whim and fancy. I loved her. All the same I had another reason to keep her alive as long as possible. While she breathed I knew I had a place to stay. I was terrified of what would happen to me when Mama died. I had no high school diploma and no experience at outside work and I knew my sisters-in-law wouldn't take me in or let my brothers support me once Mama was gone.

Then Mama drew her last breath with a smile of thanks on her face for what I had done.

Sure enough, Norine and Thelma, my brothers' wives, put their feet down. I was on my own from then on. So that scared feeling of wondering where I could lay my head took over in my mind and never left me.

I had some respite when Mr. Williams, a widower twenty-four years older than me, asked me to marry him. I took my vows seriously. I meant to cherish him and I did. But that house we lived in! Those walls couldn't have been dirtier if they'd been smeared with soot and the plumbing was stubborn as a mule. My left foot stayed sore from having to kick the pipe underneath the kitchen sink to get the water to run through.

Then Mr. Williams got sick and had to give up his shoe repair shop that he ran all by himself. He had a small savings account and a few of those twenty-five-dollar government bonds and drew some disability insurance until the policy ran out in something like six months.

I did everything I could to make him comfortable and keep him cheerful. Though I did all the laundry I gave him clean sheets and clean pajamas every third day and I think it was by my will power alone that I made a begonia bloom in that dark back room Mr. Williams stayed in. I even pestered his two daughters and told them they ought to send their father some get-well cards and they did once or twice. Every now and then when there were a few pennies extra I'd buy cards and scrawl signatures nobody could have read and mailed them to Mr. Williams to make him think some of his former customers were remembering him and wishing him well.

Of course when Mr. Williams died his daughters were johnny-on-the-spot to see that they got their share of the little bit that tumbledown house brought. I didn't begrudge them—I'm not one to argue with human nature.

I hate to think about all those hardships I had after Mr. Williams died. The worst of it was finding somewhere to sleep; it all boiled down to having a place to stay. Because somehow you can manage not to starve. There are garbage cans to dip into—you'd be surprised how wasteful some people are and how much good food they throw away. Or if it was right after the garbage trucks had made their collections and the cans were empty I'd go into a supermarket and pick, say, at the cherries pretending I was selecting some to buy. I didn't slip their best ones into my mouth. I'd take either those so ripe that they should have been thrown away or those that weren't ripe enough and shouldn't have been put out for people to buy. I might snitch a withered cabbage leaf or a few pieces of watercress or a few of those small round tomatoes about the size of hickory nuts—I never can remember their right name. I wouldn't make a pig of myself, just eat enough to ease my hunger. So I managed. As I say, you don't have to starve.

The only work I could get hardly ever paid me anything beyond room and board. I wasn't a practical nurse, though I knew how to take care of sick folks, and the people hiring me would say that since I didn't have the training and qualifications I couldn't expect much. All they really wanted was for someone to spend the night with Aunt Myrtle or Cousin Kate or Mama or Daddy; no actual duties were demanded of me, they said, and they really didn't think my help was worth anything except meals and a place to sleep. The arrangements were pretty makeshift. Half the time I wouldn't have a place to keep my things, not that I had any clothes to speak of, and sometimes I'd sleep on a cot in the hall outside the patient's room or on some sort of contrived bed in the patient's room.

I cherished every one of those sick people, just as I had cherished Mama and

Mr. Williams. I didn't want them to die. I did everything I knew to let them know I was interested in their welfare—first for their sakes, and then for mine, so I wouldn't have to go out and find another place to stay.

Well, now, I've made out my case for the defense, a term I never thought I'd have to use personally, so now I'll make out the case for the prosecution.

I stole.

I don't like to say it, but I was a thief.

I'm not light-fingered. I didn't want a thing that belonged to anybody else. But there came a time when I felt forced to steal. I had to have some things. My shoes fell apart. I needed some stockings and underclothes. And when I'd ask a son or a daughter or a cousin or a niece for a little money for those necessities they acted as if I was trying to blackmail them. They reminded me that I wasn't qualified as a practical nurse, that I might even get into trouble with the authorities if they found I was palming myself off as a practical nurse—which I wasn't and they knew it. Anyway, they said that their terms were only bed and board.

So I began to take things—small things that had been pushed into the backs of drawers or stored high on shelves in boxes—things that hadn't been used or worn for years and probably would never be used again. I made my biggest haul at Mrs. Bick's where there was an attic full of trunks stuffed with clothes and doodads from the twenties all the way back to the nineties—uniforms, ostrich fans, Spanish shawls, beaded bags. I sneaked out a few of these at a time and every so often sold them to a place called Way Out, Hippie Clothiers.

I tried to work out the exact amount I got for selling something. Not, I know, that you can make up for theft. But, say, I got a dollar for a feather boa belonging to Mrs. Bick: well, then I'd come back and work at a job that the cleaning woman kept putting off, like waxing the hall upstairs or polishing the andirons or getting the linen closet in order.

All the same I *was* stealing—not everywhere I stayed, not even in most places, but when I had to I stole. I admit it.

But I didn't steal that silver box.

I was as innocent as a baby where that box was concerned. So when that policeman came toward me grabbing at the box I stepped aside, and maybe I even gave him the push that sent him to his death. He had no business acting like that when that box was mine, whatever Mrs. Crowe's niece argued.

Fifty thousand nieces couldn't have made it not mine.

Anyway, the policeman was dead and though I hadn't wanted him dead I certainly hadn't wished him well. And then I got to thinking: well, I didn't steal Mrs. Crowe's box but I had stolen other things and it was the mills of God grinding exceeding fine, as I once heard a preacher say, and I was being made to pay for the transgressions that had caught up with me.

Surely I can make a little more sense out of what happened than that, though I never was exactly clear in my own mind about everything that happened.

Mrs. Crowe was the most appreciative person I ever worked for. She was bedridden and could barely move. I don't think the registered nurse on daytime duty considered it part of her job to massage Mrs. Crowe. So at night I would massage her, and that pleased and soothed her. She thanked me for every small thing I did—when I fluffed her pillow, when I'd put a few drops of perfume on her earlobes, when I'd straighten the wrinkled bedcovers.

I had a little joke. I'd pretend I could tell fortunes and I'd take Mrs. Crowe's hand and tell her she was going to have a wonderful day but she must beware of a handsome blond stranger—or some such foolishness that would make her laugh. She didn't sleep well and it seemed to give her pleasure to talk to me most of the night about her childhood or her dead husband.

She kept getting weaker and weaker and two nights before she died she said she wished she could do something for me but that when she became an invalid she had signed over everything to her niece. Anyway, Mrs. Crowe hoped I'd take her silver box. I thanked her. It pleased me that she liked me well enough to give me the box. I didn't have any real use for it. It would have made a nice trinket box, but I didn't have any trinkets. The box seemed to be Mrs. Crowe's fondest possession. She kept it on the table beside her and her eyes lighted up every time she looked at it. She might have been a little girl first seeing a brand-new baby doll early on a Christmas morning.

So when Mrs. Crowe died and the niece on whom I set eyes for the first time dismissed me, I gathered up what little I had and took the box and left. I didn't go to Mrs. Crowe's funeral. The paper said it was private and I wasn't invited. Anyway, I wouldn't have had anything suitable to wear.

I still had a few dollars left over from those things I'd sold to the hippie place called Way Out, so I paid a week's rent for a room that was the worst I'd ever stayed in.

It was freezing cold and no heat came up to the third floor where I was. In that room with falling plaster and buckling floorboards and darting roaches, I sat wearing every stitch I owned, with a sleazy blanket and a faded quilt draped around me waiting for the heat to rise, when in swept Mrs. Crowe's niece in a fur coat and a fur hat and shiny leather boots up to her knees. Her face was beet-red from anger when she started telling me that she had traced me through a private detective and I was to give her back the heirloom I had stolen.

Her statement made me forget the precious little bit I knew of the English language. I couldn't say a word, and she kept on screaming that if I returned the box immediately no criminal charge would be made against me. Then I got back my voice and I said that box was mine and that Mrs. Crowe had wanted me to have it, and she asked if I had any proof or if there were any witnesses to the gift, and I told her that when I was given a present I said thank you, that I didn't ask for proof and witnesses, and that nothing could make me part with Mrs. Crowe's box.

The niece stood there breathing hard, in and out, almost counting her breaths like somebody doing an exercise.

"You'll see," she yelled, and then she left.

The room was colder than ever and my teeth chattered.

Not long afterward I heard heavy steps clumping up the stairway. I realized that the niece had carried out her threat and that the police were after me.

I was panic-stricken. I chased around the room like a rat with a cat after it. Then I thought that if the police searched my room and couldn't find the box it might give me time to decide what to do. I grabbed the box out of the top dresser drawer and scurried down the back hall. I snatched the back door open. I think what I intended to do was run down the back steps and hide the box somewhere, underneath a bush or maybe in a garbage can.

Those back steps were steep and rose almost straight up for three stories and they were flimsy and covered with ice.

I started down. My right foot slipped. The handrail saved me. I clung to it with one hand and to the silver box with the other hand and picked and chose my way across the patches of ice.

When I was midway I heard my name shrieked. I looked around to see a big man leaping down the steps after me. I never saw such anger on a person's face. Then he was directly behind me and reached out to snatch the box.

I swerved to escape his grasp and he cursed me. Maybe I pushed him. I'm not sure—not really.

Anyway, he slipped and fell down and down and down, and then after all that falling he was absolutely still. The bottom step was beneath his head like a pillow and the rest of his body was spreadeagled on the brick wall.

Then almost like a pet that wants to follow its master, the silver box jumped from my hand and bounced down the steps to land beside the man's left ear.

My brain was numb. I felt paralyzed. Then I screamed.

Tenants from that house and the houses next door and across the alley pushed windows open and flung doors open to see what the commotion was about, and then some of them began to run toward the back yard. The policeman who was the dead man's partner—I guess you'd call him that—ordered them to keep away.

After a while more police came and they took the dead man's body and drove me to the station where I was locked up.

From the very beginning I didn't take to that young lawyer they assigned to me. There wasn't anything exactly that I could put my finger on. I just felt uneasy with him. His last name was Stanton. He had a first name of course, but he didn't tell me what it was; he said he wanted me to call him Bat like all his friends did.

He was always smiling and reassuring me when there wasn't anything to smile or be reassured about, and he ought to have known it all along instead of filling me with false hope.

All I could think was that I was thankful Mama and Papa and Mr. Williams were dead and that my shame wouldn't bring shame on them.

"It's going to be all right," the lawyer kept saying right up to the end, and then he claimed to be indignant when I was found guilty of resisting arrest and of manslaughter and theft or robbery—there was the biggest hullabaloo as to whether I was guilty of theft or robbery. Not that I was guilty of either, at least in this particular instance, but no one would believe me.

You would have thought it was the lawyer being sentenced instead of me, the way he carried on. He called it a terrible miscarriage of justice and said we might as well be back in the eighteenth century when they hanged children.

Well, that was an exaggeration, if ever there was one; nobody was being hung and nobody was a child. That policeman had died and I had had a part in it. Maybe I had pushed him. I couldn't be sure. In my heart I really hadn't meant him any harm. I was just scared. But he was dead all the same. And as far as stealing went, I hadn't stolen the box but I had stolen other things.

And then it happened. It was a miracle. All my life I'd dreamed of a nice room of my own, a comfortable place to stay. And that's exactly what I got.

The room was on the small side but it had everything I needed in it, even a wash basin with hot and cold running water, and the walls were freshly painted, and they let me choose whether I wanted a wing chair with a chintz slipcover or a modern Danish armchair. I even got to decide what color bedspread I preferred. The window looked out on a beautiful lawn edged with shrubbery, and the matron said I'd be allowed to go to the greenhouse and select some pot plants to keep in my room. The next day I picked out a white gloxinia and some russet chrysanthemums.

I didn't mind the bars at the windows at all. Why, this day and age some of the finest mansions have barred windows to keep burglars out.

The meals—I simply couldn't believe there was such delicious food in the world. The woman who supervised their preparation had embezzled the funds of one of the largest catering companies in the state after working herself up from cook to treasurer.

The other inmates were very friendly and most of them had led the most interesting lives. Some of the ladies occasionally used words that you usually see written only on fences or printed on sidewalks before the cement dries, but when they were scolded they apologized. Every now and then somebody would get angry with someone and there would be a little scratching or hair pulling, but it never got too bad. There was a choir—I can't sing but I love music—and they gave a concert every Tuesday morning at chapel, and Thursday night was movie night. There wasn't any admission charge. All you did was go in and sit down anywhere you pleased.

We all had a special job and I was assigned to the infirmary. The doctor and nurse both complimented me. The doctor said that I should have gone into professional nursing, that I gave confidence to the patients and helped them get well. I don't know about that but I've had years of practice with sick people and I like to help anybody who feels bad.

I was so happy that sometimes I couldn't sleep at night. I'd get up and click on the light and look at the furniture and the walls. It was hard to believe I had such a pleasant place to stay. I'd remember supper that night, how I'd gone back to the steam table for a second helping of asparagus with lemon and herb sauce, and I compared my plenty with those terrible times when I had slunk into supermarkets and nibbled overripe fruit and raw vegetables to ease my hunger.

Then one day here came that lawyer, not even at regular visiting hours, bouncing around congratulating me that my appeal had been upheld, or whatever the term was, and that I was as free as a bird to leave right that minute.

He told the matron she could send my belongings later and he dragged me out where TV cameras and reporters were waiting.

As soon as the cameras began whirring and the photographers began to aim, the lawyer kissed me on the cheek and pinned a flower on me. He made a speech saying that a terrible miscarriage of justice had been rectified. He had located people who testified that Mrs. Crowe had given me the box—she had told the gardener and the cleaning woman. They hadn't wanted to testify because they didn't want to get mixed up with the police, but the lawyer had persuaded them in the cause of justice and humanity to come forward and make statements.

The lawyer had also looked into the personnel record of the dead policeman and had learned that he had been judged emotionally unfit for his job, and the psychiatrist had warned the Chief of Police that something awful might happen either to the man himself or to a suspect unless he was relieved of his duties.

All the time the lawyer was talking into the microphones he had latched onto me like I was a three-year-old that might run away, and I just stood and stared. Then when he had finished his speech about me the reporters told him that like his grandfather and his uncle he was sure to end up as governor of the state.

At that the lawyer gave a big grin in front of the camera and waved goodbye and pushed me into his car.

I was terrified. The nice place I'd found to stay in wasn't mine any longer. My old nightmare was back—wondering how I could manage to eat and how much stealing I'd have to do to live from one day to the next.

The cameras and reporters had followed us.

A photographer asked me to turn down the car window beside me, and I overheard two men way in the back of the crowd talking. My ears were sharp. Papa always said I could hear thunder three states away. Above the congratulations and bubbly talk around me I heard one of those men in back say, "This is a bit too much, don't you think? Our Bat is showing himself the champion of the Senior Citizen now. He's already copped the teeny-boppers and the under-thirties, using methods that ought to have disbarred him. He should have made the gardener and cleaning woman testify at the beginning, and from the first he should have checked into the policeman's history. There ought never to have been a case at all, much less a conviction. But Bat wouldn't have got any publicity that way. He had to do it in his own devious, spectacular fashion." The other man just kept nodding and saying after every sentence, "You're damned right."

Then we drove off and I didn't dare look behind me because I was so heartbroken over what I was leaving.

The lawyer took me to his office. He said he hoped I wouldn't mind a little excitement for the next few days. He had mapped out some public appearances for me. The next morning I was to be on an early television show. There was nothing to be worried about. He would be right beside me to help me just as he had helped me throughout my trouble. All that I had to say on the TV program was that I owed my freedom to him.

I guess I looked startled or bewildered because he hurried on to say that I hadn't been able to pay him a fee but that now I was able to pay him back—not in money but in letting the public know about how he was the champion of the underdog.

I said I had been told that the court furnished lawyers free of charge to people who couldn't pay, and he said that was right, but his point was that I could repay him now by telling people all that he had done for me. Then he said the main thing was to talk over our next appearance on TV. He wanted to coach me in what I was going to say, but first he would go into his partner's office and tell him to take all the incoming calls and handle the rest of his appointments.

When the door closed after him I thought that he was right. I did owe my freedom to him. He was to blame for it. The smart aleck. The upstart. Who asked him to butt in and snatch me out of my pretty room and the work I loved and all that delicious food?

It was the first time in my life I knew what it meant to despise someone. I hated him.

Before, when I was convicted of manslaughter, there was a lot of talk about malice aforethought and premeditated crime.

There wouldn't be any argument this time.

I hadn't wanted any harm to come to that policeman. But I did mean harm to come to this lawyer.

I grabbed up a letter opener from his desk and ran my finger along the blade and felt how sharp it was. I waited behind the door and when he walked through I gathered all my strength and stabbed him. Again and again and again.

Now I'm back where I want to be—in a nice place to stay.

PHYLLIS BENTLEY

Miss Phipps Exercises Her Metier

All of a sudden Miss Marian Phipps felt lonely.

This was rather strange, for up to that moment she had been enjoying the peace of this remote Shetland isle. After the repeated discussions, the divergent human wishes, and the frequent telephonings of the morning, the present silence—the sheer absence of human voices—was restful in the extreme. The island was small, but large enough to offer considerable grassy slopes, and over the steepest of these her four companions on the excursion were now climbing rapidly.

The dark cliffs rose to fine and jagged heights; the northern sea was a rich dark blue with white surf fringes; the sun shone; the sea birds—gulls, gannets, oyster-catchers, shags, terns, puffins, what-have-you (Miss Phipps was not too well up in birds)—clamored a good deal, to be sure, as they swooped about the sky; but their various modes of flight were beautiful to watch, and their resonant tones were a pleasant change from the motor horns and airplane engines which formed her usual sound track.

The rest of the party had wanted to see the remains of the old Viking settlement for which they had indeed come to the island, but these lay on the far side of the steep hill. Miss Phipps, surveying its gradient, and perhaps, in spite of her real affection for them, a little tired of Inspector Tarrant and his wife after a fortnight's holiday together—and certainly tired of Professor Morison and *his* wife after a mere few hours—decided to remain idly in the vicinity of the tiny harbor and landing stage. A neighboring bay, gained by climbing a much slighter slope, was as far as Miss Phipps was prepared to walk.

If she felt a little less than her usual warmth toward the Tarrants this afternoon it was not, she admitted at once, their fault but just part of the usual exasperation of things in general, which so often refused to fit, to go right. Today was the last one of their stay in Shetland, and though they had seen several fine Viking remains, everyone at their hotel in the main port had assured them that those on Fersa were the finest, grimmest, most complete in existence. But to reach Fersa one had to proceed to a village on the mainland coast and there rent a boat. "Just telephone the village post office," urged their hotel acquaintances. "They keep a motor vessel for hire."

They telephoned. In fact, they seemed to spend the whole morning at the telephone. Sometimes Inspector Tarrant telephoned, sometimes his wife Mary did, sometimes Miss Phipps. All without result. At first a young man's voice had replied, saying crossly that the sea was too high, and besides, he hadn't the time. Then the wind calmed a little, so they telephoned again. This time a young woman's voice replied. Her voice had sobs in it, and cried out that she couldn't "fash" with them now.

After an hour's wait they telephoned again—and then again. The receiver was lifted and replaced, only a kind of moan being heard in the brief interim. Miss Phipps urged the Tarrants to give up Fersa and decide on some other excursion. Although disappointed as to Vikings, the Tarrants would probably have accepted her advice if it had not been for the Morisons, who now appeared to be seized by Fersa and telephone.

Professor Morison was one of those long, concave, balding academics devoted to abstruse subjects; he had a sallow complexion and sad brown eyes—the type whom Miss Phipps respected but regarded as supremely dreary. His wife, short, plump, fairhaired, bossy, appeared soft-hearted, but in defense of her husband she took on the consistency of marble. When the Tarrant party left the hotel to accompany some fellow guests to the ship about to leave the port harbor for Scotland, Mrs. Morison was again at the telephone in the hall.

"Her husband's away—her husband's out with the boat," she reported over her shoulder to the Professor. When the Tarrant party returned for lunch she was still telephoning.

Meanwhile, Miss Phipps had had a poignant experience. Indeed it was to the poignancy of this experience that she attributed her present sudden attack of loneliness; the usual well-adjusted balance of her feelings had been upset, leaving her open to alarms. (For was she, in fact, feeling "lonely" now, or was she, in reality, for some inexplicable cause merely feeling nervous? She was uncertain.)

The poignant experience was simply the sight of a face peering out from the lower deck of the ship bound for Scotland. A young man's face, dark and handsome, but fixed with such a look of agony that Miss Phipps hoped never to see the like again. As Miss Phipps was a novelist, suitable explanations of other people's feelings were naturally apt to rush into her mind.

Poor lad! she thought with genuine pity. Going away from home for the first time, I expect. The heart beholds the islands. A difficult place to leave. Mountains and sea. Poor boy.

On entering the lobby of the hotel she found Mrs. Morison again at the end of the telephone cord, and addressing her husband.

"She says her father-in-law will take us," she cried in triumph. With a sudden change of tone she added, "It'll cost enough."

"Er-hrrumph," said Professor Morison, concaving (Miss Phipps thought) almost more than before.

"Shall we go, James?" pressed Mrs. Morison.

"Er-hrrumph."

"Would you allow our party of three to join you?" said Miss Phipps, springing cheerfully into the breach. "That would lessen the—"

"Er-hrrumph!" said Professor Morison, straightening a little, hopefully.

Mrs. Morison looked eager but still doubtful.

"We have a hired car at our disposal," Miss Phipps added as bait.

Mrs. Morison beamed.

"A happy suggestion," she said. "I'm *sure* my husband will approve."

While she clinched the arrangement on the telephone, Miss Phipps flew off to tell the Tarrants of her achievement. It was not well received.

"Fancy spending an afternoon with that old stick!" growled the Inspector.

"Er-hrrumph!" said Mary peevishly.

"Very well, tell them you've changed your mind and don't want to go," said Miss Phipps, vexed.

"Of course we'll go," said Inspector Tarrant with decision.

"Er-hrrumph," said Mary in a kinder tone.

After lunch they drove down to the village, which was almost too tiny to be called a village, consisting chiefly of a post office, above which a home-painted board announced MACKAY. Near a tiny stone landing stage, just across the road from this building, tossed a small boat with an outboard motor, the boat attached to a red buoy. It tossed a good deal; looking out to sea Miss Phipps observed with interest that the waves were also tossing a good deal and were topped by quite a few whitecaps.

Professor Morison, carrying a pair of binoculars, a camera, and a notebook, with two textbooks protruding from his pockets, walked to the end of the little jetty and began to examine such birds as flew into view. Bill Tarrant, looking a little more cheerful, followed him, and Mrs. Morison trotted after them on her fat little ankles. Mary and Miss Phipps entered the post office and began to choose picture postcards. Mary, hearing the approach of a distant car, tapped sharply with a coin on the counter.

A most beautiful creature entered. A young woman, not yet 20, Miss Phipps thought; of dazzlingly smooth and unblemished complexion, with pale golden hair twined and piled about her head in thick lustrous swaths. She wore a thin white dress, so short that if another inch were subtracted it would almost be a belt, and so tightly modeled as to show every line of her lovely body except an inch or two hinted at by a few tiny scraps of lace.

She turned her head and Miss Phipps started; her beauty was marred by a heavy bruise on one temple, imperfectly concealed by a good deal of crude makeup, and her large pale blue eyes were red from crying. A wedding ring, and an engagement ring with a single no doubt much-prized pearl, decked the hand with which she pointed out, competently enough, the various categories of postcards and their prices. Her accent had none of the island lilt that Miss Phipps liked so much, and it seemed tinged with Cockney.

"What's come into ye, Zelda?" boomed an angry voice.

The post office door was thrust open vehemently, sounding its little bell, and in strode a solid grizzled figure wearing one of the patterned knit garments native to the island.

"Hae ye no sense, woman? Why can't Eric take the boat across? Dragging me all this way from ma sheep."

"Eric isn't here, Mr. Mackay," said Zelda timidly.

"Whaur's Magnus then?"

"He left."

"Did they go off together then? Whaur did they go?"

"I don't know," moaned Zelda, almost weeping.

"Women!" exclaimed Mackay. "Sons!"

"I thought you wouldn't want to miss the chance of a boatload of passengers."

"How many are ye, then?" barked Mackay, fixing Miss Phipps with an angry glare.

"Five."

"It'll cost ye two pun ten."

"Very well," said Miss Phipps shortly. "You'll give us enough time on the island to visit the broch?"

Mackay gave a prolonged growl in which might be distinguished the vowels composing an assenting "aye" or "yaas."

"Ye may nae like the sea," he said with what struck Miss Phipps as rather sinister enjoyment. "It's a wee high. Come awa' wi' ye, then."

As they followed Mackay Senior out of the post office and down the little stone pier, Mary and Miss Phipps exchanged glances indicating their unfavorable impressions of the dour boatman. Mary's raised eyebrows brought also a familiar accusation against Miss Phipps.

"I'm irritated by the way you find *a story* in everything," Mary had said not once but several times to Miss Phipps. "It seems an insult to reality."

But Miss Phipps could not help it—it was by now an inveterate habit, and usually she replied cheerfully to these accusations; and this time, as Mary suspected, Miss Phipps had been swept irresistibly into her dearly loved profession. She had begun her imaginings the moment she set eyes on Zelda and the bruise on the girl's temple. The lad with the agonized face was Zelda's husband; they had quarreled; he had struck her, then in shame and fury had left the island. And now this fierce old Mackay had come to confirm her imaginings.

Oh, yes, reflected Miss Phipps, surveying the strong aquiline features, the solid body and crisp graying hair, his older face is strongly akin to the face of the anguished lad on the ship; Zelda had said on the telephone that her father-in-law would ferry the party across to Fersa; the anguished lad is therefore this man's son and this girl's husband.

"Why will people make each other so unhappy?" murmured Miss Phipps. Eric, a good Norse name. As for Magnus, she could not fit him in; perhaps only a minor character in her burgeoning plot.

The Tarrants and Mrs. Morison stood the rough sea well; Miss Phipps enjoyed it, tossing her white curls to the breeze; the Professor turned a curious pea-green and was watched anxiously by his wife, but he yielded no further to queasiness. They landed on the island in a tiny bay, arranged a time for re-embarkation, and then the two married couples strode vigorously up the long green slope. Mr. Mackay vanished round a cliff in his chugging boat, and Miss Phipps wandered about.

It was then that Miss Phipps began to feel lonely. After all, she was apparently left by herself on a small island in the far North Sea, surrounded by a far from calm ocean. Nothing human was visible. The remains of an old cottage—empty windows, broken chimney, vacant doorway—served only to make the absence of life more obvious. The birds soared by uncaring—almost, one might think, contemptuous. Even a sheep's company would have been acceptable. But there was no sheep.

She could no longer hear the chugging of Mr. Mackay's engine. Suppose they had all gone off and left her! It was an uneasy thought. Yes, she did feel uneasy. I'll go back to the landing stage, thought Miss Phipps. She turned; and bobbing in the waters of the bay beneath her feet she saw a gray head.

"It's a seal!" exclaimed Miss Phipps, delighted. For though on Shetland they had seen the towering brochs (like huge buckets turned upside down), eider ducks, underground funeral chambers, Vikings' descendants (at a gala) agreeably rigged out as Vikings, Shetland ponies with correct shortage of height and length of mane and tail, sheep with half their fleece hanging off their backs, jumpers of many patterns knitted from this silky wool, lochs, mountains, peat hags, seas in every mood, fishing fleets—indeed, almost everything they had expected and hoped to see in Shetland—their view of seals had been singularly scanty. To return to England without having seen some of these massive northern sea mammals would, Miss Phipps believed, diminish their prestige and credibility as Shetland tourists.

"A seal!" she repeated with delight. "I wonder if it lives in the rocks of this bay? Where do seals have their lairs, if any?"

Scanning the rocks which edged the little bay, all thought was suddenly struck from her mind. For beside a low seaweed-covered ledge of rock lay Mr. Mackay's boat, its painter wound round a protruding buttress, and on the ledge knelt Mr. Mackay himself, and he was actually—yes, actually—wringing his hands and bowing back and forth as if in uncontrollable sorrow.

Miss Phipps stared—at first, amazed, then in horror. For what was it, lying amid the seaweed, urgently lapped by long waves, over which Mr. Mackay showed so much grief? He raised his face to the sky; tears coursed down his leathery cheeks. Wasn't the object over which he grieved the outstretched corpse of a young man in fisherman's jersey, a young man with dark curly hair, the image of the young man with the anguished face on the boat, and sufficiently like Mackay Senior to confirm the relationship?

"Brothers!" she exclaimed. "It must be Magnus!"

Yes, now the story was complete—in Miss Phipps's bubbling mind. The dead boy was the younger brother; he had been paying attention to the older son's beautiful wife; the older son had caught him at it, taken him off in the boat to Fersa, tipped his body over a cliff, expecting the tides to carry off the corpse; but a hand or foot had caught in a niche of the rock and the body still lay there awaiting discovery.

But heavens, what was old Mackay doing now? He pulled at a foot, released it, then heaving the body on its side, pushed it into the waters of the bay. It rolled, paused, drifted, was sucked below a nose of rock, was freed by a stronger wave, then edged its way slowly toward the open sea.

Mackay looked up; Miss Phipps quickly hid behind a rock. A pebble shot from beneath her foot. She hoped he had not heard it or seen her; but she could not feel comfortably sure, for he stood still and gazed round the bay, even shading his eyes with his hand to give himself clearer vision.

There were only two possible courses of action, thought Miss Phipps: go down and confront him, or slip away unseen. With immense relief she perceived that the cliffs were too precipitous here for an elderly lady to descend with reasonable safety, not to mention ease. For a moment which seemed an hour, Mackay gazed and Miss Phipps crouched, peering sideways round her concealing rock. Then at last the old man gave up his search, stepped down into his boat, released the painter and chugged away.

The moment he was out of sight beyond the cliff Miss Phipps flew. She climbed up the rocks behind her with no care for knees or hands, rushed up the green slope, ran down the rough path, and was sitting on a grassy knoll with her hands clasped round her knees, breathing hard but gazing serenely out to sea when Mackay in his boat came round the nose of the cliff and approached the rocks. Miss Phipps gave him a friendly wave.

"Have ye seen all the isle ye fancy?"

Miss Phipps found this inquiry a trifle sinister. Was he trying to discover if she had visited the bay which held the body?

"Enough," she replied in an off-hand but, she hoped, reassuring tone.

Mackay gave one of those northern snorts whose meaning can only be discovered by its context. He climbed out of his boat, tied it up to the iron ring provided for the purpose, and approached her.

He suspects me; I must admit, reflected Miss Phipps, that I'm afraid.

She looked with longing at the massive hillside beyond which her companions were presumably still engrossed in Viking remains.

"Wad it please ye to come round in the boat wi' me to fetch the others awa'?" suggested Mackay, obviously noting the direction of her glance.

Not on your life, thought Miss Phipps. There was a gleam in his eye which she found most disturbing. If she went out alone in the boat with him, she was sure there would be another body lost off this island. But how to put him off?

"Is there a landing stage there?" she said aloud, with an obvious note of doubt.

"There's a slab of concrete amid the rocks."

"We should probably miss them, wouldn't we?"

"We could always turn back."

"We could," began Miss Phipps, "but is it wise to take the risk of missing them?"

Mackay gave another island snort and extended his hand. Miss Phipps—

unhappily, but not able to think of further delaying tactics—took it and rose. She gave a last despairing glance toward the hillside, and there, oh, joy, came her rescuers. Just over the brow appeared Professor Morison and Inspector Tarrant.

"There they are!" she exclaimed gratefully. "Bill! Professor Morison! Cooee!"

Deep in conversation they took not the slightest notice of her appeals. She waved, she cried out, she almost screamed, but Inspector Tarrant remained bent toward the Professor, who continually talked and pointed. Obviously he was deep in his favorite subject of ornithology.

"These birdwatchers," said Miss Phipps with irritation.

"Aweel, you can get in the boat and sit," urged Mackay.

"I'll wait for them here," said Miss Phipps, reminding herself how many a slip there could be between boat and rock. That iron ring too—a nasty thing to strike one's head against. She withdrew her hand. "I'll wait for them here," she repeated.

"As ye please," said Mackay.

He withdrew to his boat, but with true Norse economy did not start the engine.

At long, long last the Viking-fans reached Miss Phipps. Professor Morison, his sad eyes beaming, was now talking about the varying coloration of puffins.

"You might have acknowledged my greetings," snapped Miss Phipps, peevish.

"I'm sorry, but we didn't hear you," said Bill Tarrant mildly.

After a further long wait Mary and Mrs. Morison arrived talking about fashions. They all got into the boat without incident, Miss Phipps taking care to descend with, and sit between, her two female companions.

The sea was rougher than before. Professor Morison's shade of green was now a darkling olive. Waves slapped overboard, and Miss Phipps, normally a lover of stormy seas, began to wish that they were safely ashore—really this tossing gave too many opportunities for an "accident." Mackay was capable of drowning the whole lot of them to save his son, she reflected.

"Hae ye bairns?" inquired Mackay suddenly.

It seemed the Morisons had none; the Tarrants admitted their two.

"And you?" said Bill politely.

"I have two sons, Eric and Magnus," said Mackay, glancing at Miss Phipps. "But they're footloose. Shetland's too small for them. They're both intending to be awa' to London."

"What will they do there?" asked Professor Morison. "No mountains, no sea, no birds."

"Zelda will like it. Eric's wife. Her at the post office. She's London-born," said Mackay, with a certain bitterness. "She came to the island on a holiday cruise."

"Oh, look, there's a seal!" cried Mary Tarrant enthusiastically.

Glancing up, Miss Phipps found Mackay's eyes fixed fiercely on her. Of course—there was a seal at the entrance of the murder bay, she thought; if he learns I saw it he'll think I saw other things in that bay too. All this passed through her mind in a flash. As if she had never seen a seal in her life and would not recognize a seal if she saw one, she cried out cheerfully, "Where?"—and conscientiously scanned the horizon.

It was a good lie—accepted, Miss Phipps noted with great relief, where acceptance was most needed.

Two mornings later, with Scottish soil safely beneath their feet and Shetland lying far behind them in the northern waves, Miss Phipps began to argue with her conscience as to whether she should tell Inspector Tarrant of her Fersa adventure. It seemed, on the one hand, her duty as a citizen to do so. But on the other hand, she thought of old broken-hearted Mackay, of that silly lovely Zelda, of the anguished Eric . . .

"They will have enough misery as it is," she murmured, "and it won't do Magnus any good."

After a few moments she smiled. "Besides, I don't *know* anything—I don't *really* know. After all, it was only an exercise of my métier!"

It was one of the rare occasions on which Miss Phipps the professional novelist triumphed over Miss Phipps the amateur criminologist.

JOE GORES

File Number 6:
Beyond the Shadow

Christmas Eve in San Francisco: bright decorations under alternating rain and mist. Despite the weather, the fancy shops ringing Union Square had been jammed with last-minute buyers, and the Santa Claus at Geary and Stockton had long since found a sheltered doorway from which to contemplate his imminent unemployment. Out on Golden Gate Avenue the high-shouldered charcoal Victorian which housed Daniel Kearny Associates was unusually dark and silent. Kearny had sent the office staff home at 2:30; soon after, Kathy Onoda, the Japanese office manager, had departed.

Sometime after 9:00, Giselle Marc stuck her shining blonde head through the open sliding door of Kearny's cubbyhole in the DKA basement.

"You need me for anything more, Dan?"

Kearny looked up in surprise. "I thought I sent you girls home."

"Year-end stuff I wanted a head start on," she said lightly. Giselle was 26, tall and lithe, with a Master's degree in history and all the brains that aren't supposed to go with her sort of looks. That year she had no one special to go home to. "What about you?"

"I've been looking for a handle in that Bannock file for Golden Gate Trust. There's a police A.P.B. out on Myra, the older girl, and since she's probably driving the Lincoln that we're supposed to repossess—"

"An A.P.B.! Why?"

"The younger sister, Ruth, was found today over in Contra Costa County. Shot. Dead. She'd been there for several days."

"And the police think Myra did it?" asked Giselle.

Kearny shrugged. Just then he looked his 44 hard driving years. Too many all-night searches for deadbeats, embezzlers, or missing relatives; too many repossessions after non-stop investigations; too many bourbons straight from too many hotel-room bottles with other men as hard as himself.

"The police want to talk to her, anyway. Some of the places we've had to look for those girls, I wouldn't be surprised at *anything* that either one of them did. The Haight, upper Grant, the commune out on Sutter Street—how can people live like that, Giselle?"

"Different strokes for different folks, Dan'l." She added thoughtfully, "That's the second death in this case in a week."

"I don't follow."

"Irma Carroll. The client's wife."

"She was a suicide," objected Kearny. "Of course, for all we know, so was Ruth Bannock. Anyway, we've got to get that car before the police impound it. That would mean the ninety-day dealer recourse would expire, and the bank would have to eat the car."

He flipped the Bannock file a foot in the air so that it fell on the desk and slewed out papers like a fanned deck of cards. "The bank's deadline is Monday. That gives us only three days to come up with the car."

He shook a cigarette from his pack as he listened to Giselle's retreating heels, lit up, and then waved a hand to dispel the smoke from his tired eyes. A rough week. Rough year, actually, with the state snuffling around on license renewal because of this and that, and the constant unsuccessful search for a bigger office. There was that old brick laundry down on 11th Street for sale, but their asking price . . .

Ought to get home to Mama and the kids. Instead he leaned back in the swivel chair with his hands locked behind his head to stare at the ceiling in silence. The smoke of his cigarette drifted almost hypnotically upward.

Silence. Unusual at DKA. Usually field men were coming in and going out. Phones were ringing, intercom was buzzing. Giselle or Kathy or Jane Goldson, the Limey wench whose accent lent a bit of class to the switchboard, calling down from upstairs with a hot one. O'Bannon in to bang the desk about the latest cuts in his expense account . . .

The Bannock Lincoln. Damned odd case. Stewart Carroll, the auto zone man at Golden Gate Trust, had waited three months before even assigning the car to DKA. That had been last Monday, the 21st. The same night Carroll's wife committed suicide. And now one of the free-wheeling Bannock girls was dead, murdered maybe, in a state park on a mountain in the East Bay. One in the temple, the latest news broadcast had said.

Doubtful that the sister, Myra, had pulled the trigger; if he was looking for a head-roller in the case he'd pick that slick friend of theirs, that real-estate man down on Montgomery Street. Raymond Edwards. Now there was a guy capable of doing anything to . . .

The sound of the front door closing jerked Kearny's eyes from the sound-proofed ceiling. He could see a man's shadow cast thick and heavy down the garage. It might have belonged to Trinidad Morales, but he'd fired Morales last summer.

The man who appeared in the office doorway *was* built like Morales, short and broad and overweight, with a sleepy, pleasantly tough face. Maybe a couple of years younger than Kearny. Durable-looking. Giselle must have forgotten to set the outside lock.

"You're looking hard for that Bannock Lincoln."

"Any of your business?" asked Kearny almost pleasantly. Not a process server: he would have been advancing with a toothy grin as he reached for the papers to slap on the desk.

"Could be." He sat down unbidden on the other side of the desk. "I'm a cop. Private tin, like you. We were hired by old man Bannock to find the daughters, same day you were hired by Golden Gate Trust to find the car."

Kearny lit another cigarette. Neither Heslip nor Ballard had cut this one's sign, which meant he had to be damned smooth.

"The police found one of the girls," Kearny said.

"Yeah. Ruth. I was over in Contra Costa County when she turned up. Just got back. Clearing in the woods up on Mount Diablo, beside the ashes of a little fire." He paused. "Pretty odd, Stewart Carroll letting that car get right up to the deadline before assigning it out."

"He probably figured old man Bannock would make the payments even though he wasn't on the contract." Then Kearny added, his square hard face watchful, "You have anything that says who you are?"

The stocky man grunted and dug out a business card. Kearny had never heard of the agency. There were a lot of them he'd never heard of, mostly one-man shops with impressive-sounding names like this one.

"Well, that's interesting, Mr. Wright," he said. He stood up. "But it *is* Christmas Eve and—"

"Or maybe Carroll had other things on his mind," Wright cut in almost dreamily. "His wife, Irma, for instance. Big fancy house out in Presidio Terrace—even had a fireplace in the bedroom where she killed herself. Ashes in the grate, maybe like she'd burned some papers, pictures, something like that."

Kearny sat down. "A fire like the one where Ruth died?"

The stocky detective gave a short appreciative laugh. "The girls got a pretty hefty allowance—so why were they three months' delinquent on their car payment? And why, the day before they disappeared—last Thursday, a week ago today—did they try to hit the old man up for some very substantial extra loot? Since they didn't get it—"

"You checked the pawnshops." It was the obvious move.

"Yeah. Little joint down on Third and Mission, the guy says that Myra, the older sister, came in and hocked a bunch of jewelry on Friday morning. Same day she and her sister disappeared. She had a cute little blonde with her at the pawnshop."

Kearny stubbed out his cigarette and lit another. The smoke filled the cramped office. Cute little blonde didn't fit the dead Ruth at all.

"Irma Carroll," he said. "You think her husband delayed assigning the Lincoln for repossession because she asked him to. Why?"

"So old man Bannock wouldn't know his daughters had financial woes," beamed the other detective. "We got a positive ident on Irma Carroll from the pawnbroker. Plus she was away from home Friday—the day the sisters disappeared."

"And on Monday she killed herself. When did Ruth die?"

"Friday night, Saturday morning, close as the coroner can tell."

"Mmmm." Kearny smoked silently for a moment. James (Jimmy) Wright—according to the name on his card—had a good breadth of shoulder, good thickness of chest and arm. Physically competent, despite his owl-like appearance. With a damned subtle mind besides. "I wonder how many *other* local women in the past year—"

Wright held up three fingers. "I started out with a list like a small-town phone book—every female suicide and disappearance in San Francisco since January first. Three of them knew the Bannock girls *and* the Carroll woman, and all three needed money *and* burned something before they killed themselves. No telling how many more just burned whatever it was they were buying and then sat tight."

Kearny squinted through his cigarette smoke. He had long since forgotten about spending Christmas Eve with Jeanie and the kids.

"I figure you've got more than just that. Another connection maybe between your three suicides and the Bannock girls and Irma Carroll—" He paused to taste his idea, and liked it. "Raymond Edwards?"

The stock man beamed again.

"Edwards. Yeah. I'd like to get a look at that bird's tax returns. Real-estate office on Montgomery Street—but no clients. Fancy apartment out in the Sunset and spends plenty of money—but doesn't seem to make any. What put you on to him?"

"Two of the hippies at that Sutter Street commune gave us a make on a cat in a Ferrari who was a steady customer for psilocybin—the 'sacred mushrooms' of the Mex Indians. On their description I ran Edwards through DMV in Sacramento and found he holds the pink on a Ferrari. A lot of car for a man with no visible income not to owe any money on. And—no other car."

"I don't see any significance in that," objected Wright.

"You don't sell real estate out of a Ferrari."

The other detective nodded. "Got you. And Edwards made it down to his office exactly twice this week—to pick up his mail. But every night he made it to a house up on Telegraph Hill—each time with a different well-to-do dame."

"But none of them the Bannock girls," said Kearny.

The phone interrupted. That would be Jeanie, he thought as he picked up. But after a moment he extended the receiver to Wright.

"Yeah . . . I see." He nodded and his eyes glistened. "Are you sure it was Myra? In this fog . . . that close, huh?" He listened some more. "Through the cellar window? Good. Yes. No. Kearny and I'll go in—what?" Another pause. "I don't give a damn about that, we need someone outside to tail her if she comes out before we do."

He hung up, turned to Kearny.

"Myra just went into the Telegraph Hill place through a cellar window. She's still in there. You heavy?"

"Not for years." You wore a gun, you sometimes used it. "And what makes you so sure I'll go along with you?"

The stocky detective grinned. "Find Myra, we find the Lincoln, right? *Before* the cops. You get your car, I get somebody who ain't shy to back my play. I'd have a hell of a time scraping up another of my own men on Christmas Eve."

Kearny unlocked the filing cabinet and from its middle drawer took out a Luger and a full clip. A German officer had fired it at him outside Aumetz in 1944, when the 106th Panzer SS had broken through to 90th Division HQ.

He dropped it into his right-hand topcoat pocket, stuck Wright's card in his left. He had another question but it could wait.

The fog was thick and wet outside, glistening on the streets and haloing the lights. They walked past Kearny's Ford station wagon, their shoes rapping hollow against the concrete. He felt twenty years old again. From a Van Ness bus they transferred to the California cable, transferred again on Nob Hill where the thick fog made pale blobs of the bright Christmas decorations on the Mark and the Fairmont. A band of caroling youngsters drifted past them, voices fog-muted. Alcatraz bellowed desolately from the black bay like an injured sea beast.

They were the only ones left on the car at the turn-around in the 500 block of Greenwich. Fog shrouded the crowded houses slanting steeply down the hill. Christmas trees brightened many windows, their candles flickering warmly through the steamy glass. The detectives paused in the light from the tavern on Grant and Greenwich.

"Which way?" asked Kearny.

"Up the hill. Then we work around to the Filbert Street steps. My man'll meet us somewhere below Montgomery."

They toiled up the steep brushy side of Telegraph beyond the Greenwich dead end, their shoes slipping in the heavy yellowish loam. Kearny went to one knee and cursed. When they paused at the head of the wooden Filbert Street steps, both men were panting and sweat sheened their faces. The sea-wet wind off the bay swirled fog around them, danced the widely-scattered street lights below.

Just as they started down, the fog eddied to reveal, beyond the shadow of clearly etched foliage, the misty panorama of the bay. Off to the left was grimly lit Alcatraz, and ahead, to the right of dark Yerba Buena Island, the 11:00 o'clock ferry to Oakland, yellow pinpoints moving against the darkness. Then foliage closed in wetly on either side. The Luger was a heavy comfortable weight in Kearny's pocket. He could see only about two yards ahead in the bone-chilling fog. When they crossed Montgomery the air carried the musty tang of fermenting grapes. The old Italians must make plenty of wine up here. There was another, more acrid scent; somewhere an animal bleated.

"They ought to pen up their goats once in a while," chuckled Kearny's companion. "They stink."

More wooden steps in the fog. They paused where a narrow path led off into the grayness.

"Catfish Row," muttered the stocky detective in Kearny's ear. "My man ought to be around some—" He broke off as a short dark shape materialized at their elbow. "Dick?"

"Right."

"She's still inside?"

"Right."

The newcomer pulled out a handkerchief to wipe the fog from his sharp-featured irritable face. Kearny got a vagrant whiff of scent.

"We're going in," breathed the stocky detective. "If the Bannock girl comes out, stick with her."

"Right," said Dick.

They started along an uneven brick path slippery with moss, then began climbing another set of narrow wooden steps which paralleled those on Filbert.

"Your man is talkative," said Kearny drily.

"Canadian," said the other. "A good detective."

"But you don't trust him on this." Kearny then asked the question he hadn't asked back in the office. "Why?"

Wright shrugged irritably. "I've got enough to do without having to watch him." He didn't elaborate.

They stopped and peered through the gloom at a three-storied narrow wooden house that looked egg-yolk yellow in the fog. Dripping bushes flanked it both uphill and down. There was a half basement; the uphill side had not been excavated from the rock. Myra Bannock must have entered by one of the blacked-out windows which flanked the gray basement door.

The two detectives climbed past it to the first-floor level. Here a small porch cantilevered out over the recessed basement. The front door and windows were decorated to echo the high-peaked roof of the house itself.

A big black man answered the bell. The hallway behind him was so dark that his face showed only highlights: brows, cheekbones, nose, lips, a gleam of eyeballs. He was wearing red. Red fez, red silk Nehru jacket over red striped shirt, red harem pants with baggy legs, red shoes with upturned toes.

"*As-salaam aleikum,*" he said.

"Mr. Maxwell, please," said Wright briskly.

The door began to close. The dumpy detective stuck his foot in it and immediately a gong boomed in the back of the house. Kearny's companion sank a fist into the middle of the red shirt as Kearny's shoulder slammed into the door.

The guard was on his hands and knees in the dim hallway, gasping. His eyes rolled up at Kearny's as the detectives stormed by him.

A door slammed up above. They climbed broad circular stairs in the gloom, guns out. Their shoulders in unison splintered a locked door at the head of the stairs. The room was blue-lit, seemingly empty except for incense, thick carpets, and strewn clothing of both sexes. Then they saw three women and a man crowded into a corner, a grotesque frightened jumble, all of them nude.

"Topless *and* bottomless," grunted Kearny.

"But no Myra," said Wright in a disgust that was practical, not moral. "Let's dust."

As they came out of the room, feet pounded down the stairs. They'd been faked out—drawn into the room by the slamming door so that someone who was trapped upstairs by their entrance could get by them. Peering down, Kearny saw Raymond Edwards' head just sliding from view around the stairs' old-fashioned newel post. Edwards. The real-estate promoter who didn't promote real estate.

Kearny went over the banister, landed with a jar that clipped his jaw against his knee, stumbled to his feet, and charged down the hall. He went through an open doorway to meet a black fist traveling very rapidly in the other direction. The doorkeeper.

"Ungh!" Kearny went down, gagging, but managed to wave Wright through the door where Edwards and the black man had just disappeared.

There was a crash within, and furious curses. A gun went off. Once more. Kearny tottered through the doorway, an old man again, to see another door across the room just closing and the stocky detective and the guard locked in a curious dance. The black man had the detective's arms pinned at his side, and the detective was trying to shoot his captor in the foot.

Kearny's Luger, swung in a wide backhand arc, made a thwucking sound against the black's skull. The black shook his head, turned, grabbed Kearny, who dropped the Luger as he was bounced off the far wall. A hand came up under his jaw and shoved. He started to yell at the ceiling. His neck was going to break.

The black shuddered like a ship hitting a reef. Again. Again. Yet again. His hands went away. Wright was standing over the downed man, looking at his gun in a puzzled way.

"I hit him with it four times before he went down. Four times."

"Edwards?" Kearny managed to gasp.

"That way." He shook his head. "Four times."

The door was locked. They broke through after several tries and went downstairs to the empty cellar. But there was another door; the durable detective kicked off the lock. A red glow and a chemical smell emerged.

"Darkroom," said Kearny.

A girl came out stiffly, her eyes wide with shock. It was Myra Bannock. A solid meaty girl in a fawn pants suit with a white ruffled Restoration blouse. Square-toed high heels made her two inches taller than either of them.

"Did you kill him, sister?"

"Y—yes."

Over her shoulder Kearny could see Edwards on the floor with one hand still stretched up into an open squat iron safe. He was dressed in 19th Century splendor: black velvet even to his shirt and shoes. Once in the temple, a contact wound with powder burns. Kearny looked at his watch automatically. They'd been in the house exactly six minutes. *Six minutes?* It seemed like a weekend.

"Why'd you come here tonight?" demanded the other detective.

"Pic-pictures. I wanted—" Her jaw started to tremble.

"What kind of scam was Edwards running?" Kearny wondered.

"Cult stuff, I'm sure," said Wright. "Turning on wealthy young matrons to the Age of Aquarius or something. Getting them up here, doping them up, taking pictures of them doing things they'd pay to keep their parents or husbands from seeing." He turned sharply to the girl. "What kind of pictures?"

"Ter-terrible. Nasty things. We—he would give us 'sacred' wine to drink. It—distorted—able to see beyond . . . beyond the shadow. At the time everything seemed *right*." A long shudder ran through her flesh like the slow roll of an ocean wave.

"You and Ruth both?"

"Yes. Both. Together, even. With my own sister, with Irma—" She drew a ragged breath. "I sneaked in to get the negatives. I found the safe—but it was locked. Then Raymond ran in. I was behind the door." She suddenly giggled, a little girl sound. "He opened the safe and I saw the pictures inside, so I walked up and—and I shot him. Just shot him."

Without warning she started to cry, great racking sobs that twisted her face and aged her. The stocky detective was on his knees at the safe, dragging out a thick sheaf of Kodacolor negatives and a heavy stack of prints.

"Where'd you get the gun?" he asked over his shoulder.

"On Third Street," she got out through her sobs. "We pawned our jewelry to pay for the pictures."

"Same gun your sister was killed with?" asked Kearny.

"Does this have to go on and on?" she demanded suddenly, with an abrupt synthetic calmness. "I killed him. Just take me in—"

"We're private," snapped Wright. "Hired by your father to find you girls. Tell us what happened up on Mount Diablo."

His tone got through and started words again.

"I—we opened the pictures we bought—Friday morning after we pawned the jewelry to pay for them. Just prints. No negatives. We knew then that he planned to ask for more money. Irma was trying to raise it, but Ruth and I decided to just—well, kill ourselves. So we drove up to the mountains to—" Her face was starting to crumple, but the detective held her with his eyes. "To do it. But then I said I wouldn't give him the satisfaction. I would burn the pictures and then come back with the gun. But when I started burning them—when I—"

"Keep going," said Kearny.

"Ruth just grabbed the gun from the glove compartment and ran across the little clearing. I ran after her but she stopped and—and—" She started to cry.

"There's no time for that now!" snarled the stocky detective to her tears. "Let's have it."

"She put the gun against her head and it made such a little noise." Her eyes were puzzled now. "Like a twig breaking. Then she fell down."

"Where have you been since then?" asked Kearny.

"I paid for a Lombard Street motel with a credit card and just stayed there. I wanted to shoot myself but I couldn't. Tonight the radio said they had found Ruth. I knew then that I had to come here and get the negatives, so she wouldn't have died for nothing."

"Just dumb luck she made it here without being spotted by the cops," said Kearny. He swung back to her. "Where did you leave the Lincoln?"

"On Montgomery. In front of Julius's Castle."

"Give me the keys." She did. He said to Wright, "The pawnbroker isn't about to identify the gun, since he sold it to her illegally in the first place. So if the cops find it here beside the body with only Edwards' fingerprints on it—"

The squat detective's eyes narrowed. He paused in his picture shuffling. "Yeah. It'll work. And they'll think Edwards burned whatever was in the safe before he did himself in. Yeah. Hand her over to Dick, tell him to take her back to her old man so his doctor can knock her out before they call in the police. I'll—"

"You'll burn the pictures," said Kearny. "While I watch."

Wright laughed, then handed a slim sheaf of them to Kearny. As Myra had said, they were indescribably nasty—acts performed by people strung out on the mind-altering psilocybin. The things people got themselves into while looking for kicks. It was lucky Edwards was dead or Kearny might have been tempted to do the job himself. He handed the pictures back.

"Burn them," he said harshly. "All of them."

The squat durable detective did. A good man, good when the trouble started. Myra drifted away into the fog with Dick's hand on her arm. The Lincoln was parked by the closed restaurant, as she had said, and the key started it. No cops spotted Kearny getting it back to the DKA garage . . .

Kearny came to with a start, found himself slumped in his chair, his head hanging over the back at an odd angle, the edge of the typing stand digging into him. He groaned. His stomach hurt, his neck was stiff. Must have fallen asleep after getting the Lincoln—

Mists of sleep and dream cleared. He dug strong fingers into the back of his neck. Midnight and after, and he and Jeanie still faced a night of trimming the tree. The kids were at an age when Santa arrived while they slept, so Christmas morning dawned to awe and delight.

He stood up. Damned neck. Sleep and dream. Dream.

Dream.

Dammit! He'd fallen asleep over the Bannock file, with Stewart Carroll's wife's suicide on his mind, and Ruth Bannock's death, and had dreamed the whole crazy thing! Fog. Cable cars. The house on Telegraph Hill.

He rubbed his neck again. So damned vivid; but there was no Greenwich Street cable car. Had there ever been? Catfish Row was now Napier Lane. And the Christmas trees now had, not candles, but strings of electric lights. Goats and the smell of wine were both long gone, fifty years or more, from Telegraph Hill.

He flipped through the big maroon *Polk Cross-Street Directory* to 491 Greenwich. *Mike's Grocery.* In the dream, a tavern. And in the dream, an Oakland ferry: they had stopped running a dozen years before. No Bay Bridge either—it had been built in the 'thirties. As had Treasure Island, also missing from the dream, man-made in 1938, '39, as a home for the San Francisco World's Fair.

All so damned vivid. Usually a dream faded in a few minutes, but this one had remained, sharp and clear.

Kearny started to sit down, frowning, then stood up abruptly and felt his topcoat hanging on the rack. Damp. It should have dried off from the rain he'd ducked through this afternoon. Well, it hadn't, that's all. A better way to check: merely pull open the middle drawer of the filing cabinet to look at the Luger—

The Luger was gone.

Kearny stood quite still with the hairs tingling on the back of his sore neck. Then he slammed the drawer impatiently shut. Hell, it could have been missing for weeks.

But what if the Luger was found in a yellow house on Telegraph Hill, a house with a dead body in the basement and a safe full of ashes? So? The gun had never been registered, and it was tougher to get fingerprints off them than people realized.

Dammit, he thought, stop it. It had been a dream, just a dream. And despite the dream he still had to find the Bannock Lincoln before the deadline. He strode around the desk, slid back the glass door, stuck his head out to look down the garage.

Kearny's face felt suddenly stiff. Bright gleam of chrome and black enamel. Correct license plate. He went out, stiff-legged like a dog getting ready to fight, rapped his knuckles on the sleek streamlined hood. Real. The Bannock Lincoln. How in hell—

Larry Ballard, of course. Larry had been working the case, had spotted the car, repo'd it, dropped it off in the garage without even knowing that Kearny was asleep in his sound-proofed cubbyhole.

But what if Ballard *hadn't* repo'd the car?

Well, then, dammit, Kearny would dummy up some sort of report for the client. They had the car, that was the important thing. And—well, there would be some rational explanation if Larry *hadn't* been the one who'd brought it in.

Kearny left the office, setting the alarms and double-locking the basement door to activate them. He walked slowly down to the Ford station wagon. What did it all add up to? A crazy dream that *couldn't* be true, because it was mixed up with San Francisco of fifty years ago. Certain things seemed to have slopped over from the dream into subsequent reality, but there was a rational explanation for all of them—there must be. He would take that rational explanation, every time. Dan Kearny was not a fanciful man.

He reached for his keys in the topcoat pocket and touched a small oblong of thin cardboard. He looked at it for a long moment, then with an almost compulsive gesture he flipped it into the gutter between his car and the curb. It had probably been in his pocket for a week—people were always handing him business cards. Especially guys in his own racket, guys with little one-man outfits sporting those impressive-sounding names.

Kearny snorted as he got into the station wagon. What was the name on his business card? Oh, yeah.

Continental Detective Agency.

AUTHOR'S NOTE

I think I have invented a new kind of procedural detective story—what might be termed a "procedural fantasy." While it uses the dream "story-within-a-story" which antedates even William Langland's *The Vision of Piers Plowman* (1550), it is also a Files Series procedural.

There are numerous clues in the story that suggest it is a dream, beginning with Kearny and Jimmy Wright walking past Kearny's car as if it doesn't exist in the time continuum the two men now inhabit. Some clues—for example, candles on Christmas trees—should be apparent to all readers; others—such as the nonexistent Bay Bridge—would obviously have more significance to those who are familiar with San Francisco.

Because the story grew out of my personal conviction that San-Francisco-in-the-fog still belongs to Dashiell Hammett, I have inserted quite a few clues pointing to the identity of Jimmy Wright.

First, the plot was frankly adapted from Hammett's masterly Continental Op story, *The Scorched Face*; even DKA's client (Golden Gate Trust) was borrowed from it, as were the first names of other characters.

Next, the detective on stakeout was obviously that old Continental hand, Dick Foley. Besides retaining his first name, I described him essentially as Hammett did in *Red Harvest*. (It was in *Red Harvest*, you'll remember, that Foley suspected the Continental Op of murder and was sent away with the remark, "I've got enough to do without having to watch you.")

As for Jimmy Wright himself, his physical description, reiterated throughout *Beyond the Shadow*, is that of the Continental Op. His slang is the Op's slang, not that of Kearny's age: "private tin" for private investigator; "bird" for a man (instead of a girl); and "let's dust" instead of today's hipper "let's split."

To those who may claim I have cheated in giving him any name at all (we know the Continental Op was nameless in Hammett's tales), I would like to point out that the name itself is the clinching proof of his identity. As evidence I submit the editorial remarks of Ellery Queen which preceded *Who Killed Bob Teal?* in the July 1947 issue of *Ellery Queen's Mystery Magazine* (also included in the Dashiell Hammett original paperback titled *Dead Yellow Women*, 1947):

"One night Dashiell Hammett and your Editor were sitting in Lüchow's Restaurant on 14th Street. We had sampled various liquids . . . Ah, those amber fluids—they set the tongue to padding. Anyway, about this character known as the Continental Op: who was he, really? And Dash gave us the low-down. The Continental Op is based on a real-life person—James (Jimmy) Wright, Assistant Superintendent, in the good old days, of Pinkerton's Baltimore Agency, under whom Dashiell Hammett actually worked . . ."

Q.E.D.

JOE GORES

JAMES HOLDING

Library Fuzz

It was on the north side in a shabby neighborhood six blocks off the interstate highway—one of those yellow-brick apartment houses that 60 years of grime and weather had turned to a dirty taupe.

The rank of mailboxes inside told me that Hatfield's apartment was Number 35, on the third floor. I walked up. The stairway was littered with candy wrappers, empty beer cans, and a lot of caked-on dirt. It smelled pretty ripe, too.

On the third landing I went over to the door of Apartment 35 and put a finger on the buzzer. I could hear it ring inside the apartment, too loud. I looked down and saw that the door was open half an inch, unlatched, the lock twisted out of shape.

I waited for somebody to answer my ring, but nobody did. So I put an eye to the door crack and looked inside. All I got was a narrow view of a tiny foyer with two doors leading off it, both doors closed. I rang the bell again in case Hatfield hadn't heard it the first time. Still nothing happened.

The uneasiness that had driven me all the way out here from the public library was more than uneasiness now. My stomach was churning gently, the way it does when I'm hung over—or scared.

I pushed the door wide open and said in a tentative voice, "Hello! Anybody home? Mr. Hatfield?"

No answer. I looked at my watch and noted that the time was 9:32. Then I did what I shouldn't have done. I opened the righthand door that led off Hatfield's foyer into a small poorly furnished living room, and there was Hatfield in front of me.

At least, I assumed it was Hatfield. I'd never met him, so I couldn't be sure. This was a slight balding man with a fringe of gray hair. He was dressed in a neat but shiny blue suit with narrow lapels. I knew the suit's lapels were narrow because one of them was visible to me from where I stood in the doorway. The other was crushed under Hatfield's body which lay sprawled on its side on the threadbare carpet just inside the living-room door.

I sucked in my breath and held it until my stomach settled down a little. Then I stepped around Hatfield's outflung arms to get a better look at him.

There wasn't any blood that I could see. Looked as though he'd fallen while coming into the living room from the foyer. Maybe a heart attack had hit him at just that instant, I thought. It was a possibility. But not a very good one. For when I knelt beside Hatfield and felt for a pulse in his neck, I saw that the left side of his head, the side pressed against the carpet, had been caved in by a massive blow. There was blood, after all, but not much.

I stood up, feeling sick, and looked around the living room. I noticed that the toe of one of Hatfield's black loafers was snagged in a hole in the worn carpet and that a heavy fumed-oak table was perfectly positioned along the left wall of the room to have caught Hatfield's head squarely on its corner as he tripped and fell forward into the room. A quick queasy look at the corner of the table showed me more blood.

Under the edge of the table on the floor, where they must have fallen when Hatfield threw out his arms to catch himself, was a copy of yesterday's evening newspaper and a book from the public library. I could read the title of the book. *The Sound of Singing*.

I thought about that for a moment or two and decided I was pretty much out of my depth here. So I called the police. Which, even to me, seemed a rather odd thing to do—because I'm a cop myself.

A "sissy kind" of a cop, it's true, but definitely a cop. And it isn't a bad job. For one thing, I don't have to carry a gun. My arrests are usually made without much fuss and never with any violence. I get a fair salary if you consider ten thousand a year a fair salary. And nobody calls me a pig, even though I am fuzz.

Library fuzz. What I do is chase down stolen and overdue books for the public library. Most of my work is routine and unexciting—but every once in a while I run into something that adds pepper to an otherwise bland diet.

Like this Hatfield thing. The day before I found Hatfield's body had started off for me like any other Monday. I had a list of names and addresses to call on. Understand, the library sends out notices to book borrowers when their books are overdue; but some people are deadbeats, some are book lovers, and some are so absent-minded that they ignore the notices and hang onto the books. It's these hard-core overdues that I call on—to get the books back for the library and collect the fines owing on them.

Yesterday the first name on my list was Mrs. William Conway at an address on Sanford Street. I parked my car in the driveway of the small Cape Cod house that had the name "Conway" on its mailbox and went up to the front door and rang the bell.

The woman who answered the door wasn't the maid, because she was dressed in a sexy nightie with a lacy robe of some sort thrown over it, and she gave me a warm, spontaneous, friendly smile before she even knew who I was. She was medium-tall in her pink bedroom slippers and had very dark hair, caught back in a ponytail by a blue ribbon, and china-blue eyes that looked almost startling under her dark eyebrows. I also noticed that she was exceptionally well put together.

What a nice way to start the day, I thought to myself. I said "Are you Mrs. Conway?"

"Yes," she said, giving me a straight untroubled look with those blue eyes.

"I'm from the public library. I've come about those overdue books you have." I showed her my identification card.

"Oh, my goodness!" she said, and her look of inquiry turned to one of stricken guilt. "Oh, yes. Come in, won't you, Mr. Johnson? I'm really embarrassed about those books. I know I should have returned them a long time ago—I got the notices, of course. But honestly, I've been so busy!" She stepped back in mild confusion and I went into her house.

It turned out to be as unpretentious as it had looked from outside. In fact, the furnishings displayed an almost spectacular lack of taste. Well, nobody is perfect, I reminded myself. I could easily forgive Mrs. Conway's manifest ignorance of decorating principles, since she was so very decorative herself.

She switched off a color TV set that was muttering in one corner of the living room and motioned me to a chair. "Won't you sit down?" she said tentatively. She wasn't sure just how she ought to treat a library cop.

I said politely "No, thanks. If you'll just give me your overdue books and the fines you owe, I'll be on my way."

She made a little rush for a coffee table across the room, the hem of her robe swishing after her. "I have the books right here." She scooped up a pile of books from the table. "I have them all ready to bring back to the library, you see?"

While I checked the book titles against my list I asked, "Why didn't you bring them back, Mrs. Conway?"

"My sister's been in the hospital," she explained, "and I've been spending every free minute with her. I just sort of forgot about my library books. I'm sorry."

"No harm done." I told her how much the fines amounted to and she made another little rush, this time for her purse which hung by its strap from the back of a Windsor chair. "The books seem to be all here," I went on, "except one."

"Oh, is one missing? Which one?"

"*The Sound of Singing.*"

"That was a wonderful story!" Mrs. Conway said enthusiastically. "Did you read it?" She sent her blue eyes around the room, searching for the missing book.

"No. But everybody seems to like it. Maybe your husband or one of the kids took it to read," I suggested.

She gave a trill of laughter. "I haven't any children, and my husband"—she gestured toward a photograph of him on her desk, a dapper, youngish-looking man with a mustache and not much chin—"is far too busy practicing law to find time to read light novels." She paused then, plainly puzzled.

I said gently, "How about having a look in the other rooms, Mrs. Conway?"

"Of course." She counted out the money for her fines and then went rushing away up the carpeted stairs to the second floor. I watched her all the way up. It was a pleasure to look at her.

In a minute she reappeared with the missing book clutched against her chest. "William *did* take it!" she said breathlessly. "Imagine! He must have started to read it last night while I was out. It was on his bedside table under the telephone."

"Good," I said. I took the book by its covers, pages down, and shook it— standard procedure to see if anything had been left between the pages by the borrower. You'd be surprised at what some people use to mark their places.

"I'm terribly sorry to have caused so much trouble," Mrs. Conway said. And I knew she meant it.

I had no excuse to linger, so I took the books under my arm, said goodbye, and left, fixing Mrs. Conway's lovely face in my memory alongside certain other pretty pictures I keep there to cheer me up on my low days.

I ticked off the last name on my list about one o'clock. By that time the back seat of my car was full of overdue books and my back pocket full of money for the library. Those few-cents-a-day book fines add up to a tidy sum when you put them all together, you know that? Would you believe that last year, all by myself, I collected $40,000 in fines and in the value of recovered books?

I went back to the library to turn in my day's pickings and to grab a quick lunch at the library cafeteria. About two o'clock the telephone in my closet-sized office rang and when I answered, the switchboard girl told me there was a lady in the lobby who was asking to see me.

That surprised me. I don't get many lady visitors at the office. And the lady herself surprised me, too. She turned out to be my blue-eyed brunette of the morning. Mrs. William Conway—but a Mrs. Conway who looked as though she'd been hit in the face by a truck since I'd seen her last.

There was a bruise as big as a half dollar on one cheek, a deep scratch on her forehead; an ugly knotted lump interrupted the smooth line of her jaw on the left side; and the flesh around one of her startling blue eyes was puffed and faintly discolored. Although she had evidently been at pains to disguise these marks with heavy make-up, they still showed. Plainly.

I suppose she saw from my expression that I'd noticed her bruises because as she sat down in my only office chair, she dropped her eyes and flushed and said with a crooked smile, "Do I look *that* bad, Mr. Johnson?" It was a singularly beguiling gambit. Actually, battered face and all, I thought she looked just as attractive now in a lemon-colored pants suit as she had in her nightie and robe that morning.

I said, "You look fine, Mrs. Conway."

She tried to sound indignant. "I fell down our stupid stairs! Can you imagine that? Just after you left. I finished making the beds and was coming down for coffee when—zap!—head over heels clear to the bottom!"

"Bad luck," I said sympathetically, reflecting that a fall down her thickly carpeted stairs would be most unlikely to result in injuries like hers. But it was none of my business.

She said, "What I came about, Mr. Johnson, was to see if I could get back *The Sound of Singing* you took this morning. My husband was furious when he came home for lunch and found I'd given it back to you."

"No problem there. We must have a dozen copies of that book in—"

She interrupted me. "Oh, but I was hoping to get the same copy I had before. You see, my husband says he left a check in it—quite a big one from a client."

"Oh. Then I must have missed it when I shook out the book this morning."

She nodded. "You must have. William is sure he left it there." Mrs. Conway put a fingertip to the lump on her jaw and then hastily dropped her hand into her lap when she saw me watching her.

"Well," I said, "I've already turned the book back to the shelves, Mrs. Conway, but if we're lucky it'll still be in. Let me check." I picked up my phone and asked for the librarian on the checkout desk.

Consulting my morning list of overdue book numbers, now all safely returned to circulation, I said, "Liz, have you checked out number 15208, *The Sound of Singing*, to anybody in the last hour?"

"I've checked out that title but I don't know if it was that copy. Just a second," Liz said. After half a minute she said, "Yes, here it is, Hal. It went out half an hour ago on card number PC28382."

I made a note on my desk pad of that card number, repeating the digits out loud as I did so. Then, thanking Liz, I hung up and told Mrs. Conway, "I'm sorry, your copy's gone out again."

"Oh, dammit anyway!" said Mrs. Conway passionately. I gathered this was pretty strong talk for her because she blushed again and threw me a distressed look before continuing, "*Everything* seems to be going wrong for me today!" She paused. "What was the number you just took down, Mr. Johnson? Does that tell who's got the book now?"

"It tells *me*," I answered. "But for a lot of reasons we're not allowed to tell *you*. It's the card number of the person who borrowed the book."

"Oh, dear," she said, chewing miserably on her lower lip, "then that's *more* bad luck, isn't it?"

I was tempted to break the library's rigid rule and give her the name and address she wanted. However, there were a couple of things besides the rule that made me restrain my chivalrous impulse. Such as no check dropping out of *The Sound of Singing* this morning when I shook the book. And such as Mrs. Conway's bruises, which looked to me more like the work of fists than of carpeted stairs.

So I said, "I'll be glad to telephone whoever has the book now and ask him about your husband's check. Or her. If the check *is* in the book, they'll probably be glad to mail it to you."

"Oh, would you, Mr. Johnson? That would be wonderful!" Her eyes lit up at once.

I called the library's main desk where they issue cards and keep the register of card holders' names and addresses. "This is Hal Johnson," I said. "Look up the holder of card number PC28382 for me, will you, Kathy?"

I waited until she gave me a name—George Hatfield—and an address on the north side, then hung up, found Hatfield's telephone number in the directory, and dialed it on an outside line, feeling a little self-conscious under the anxious scrutiny of Mrs. Conway's beautiful bruised blue eyes.

Nobody answered the Hatfield phone.

Mrs. Conway sighed when I shook my head. "I'll try again in an hour or so. Probably not home yet. And when I get him I'll ask him to mail the check to you. I have your address. Okay?"

She stood up and gave me a forlorn nod. "I guess that's the best I can do. I'll tell Ralph you're trying to get his check back, anyhow. Thanks very much." She was still chewing on her lower lip when she left.

Later in the afternoon she called me to tell me that her husband Ralph had found his missing check in a drawer at home. There was vast relief in her voice when she told me. I wasn't relieved so much as angry—because it seemed likely to me that my beautiful Mrs. Conway had been slapped around pretty savagely by that little jerk in her photograph for a mistake she hadn't made.

Anyway, I forgot about *The Sound of Singing* and spent the rest of the afternoon shopping for a new set of belted tires for my old car.

Next morning, a few minutes before 9:00, I stopped by the library to turn in my expense voucher for the new tires and pick up my list of overdues for the day's calls. As I passed the main desk, Kathy, who was just settling down for her day's work, said, "Hi, Hal. Stop a minute and let me see if it shows."

I paused by the desk. "See if what shows?"

"Senility."

"Of course it shows, child. I'm almost forty. Why this sudden interest?"

"Only the onset of senility can account for *you* forgetting something," Kathy said. "The man with the famous memory."

I was mystified. "What did I forget?"

"The name and address of card holder PC28382, that's what. You called me to look it up for you not long after lunch yesterday, remember?"

"Sure. So what makes you think I forgot it?"

"You said you had when you called me again at four-thirty for the same information."

I stared at her. "Me?"

She nodded. "You."

"I didn't call you at four-thirty."

"Somebody did. And said he was you."

"Did it sound like my voice?"

"Certainly. An ordinary, uninteresting man's voice. Just like yours." She grinned at me.

"Thanks. Somebody playing a joke, maybe. It wasn't me."

While I was turning in my voucher and picking up my list of overdues I kept thinking about Kathy's second telephone call. The more I thought about it, the more it bothered me.

So I decided to make my first call of the day on George Hatfield . . .

Well, I didn't touch anything in Hatfield's apartment until the law showed up in the persons of a uniformed patrolman and an old friend of mine, Lieutenant Randall of Homicide. I'd worked with him when I was in the dectective bureau a few years back.

Randall looked at the setup in Hatfield's living room and growled at me, "Why me, Hal? All you need is an ambulance on this one. The guy's had a fatal accident, that's all."

So I told him about Mrs. Conway and her husband and *The Sound of Singing* and the mysterious telephone call to Kathy at the library. When I finished he jerked his head toward the library book lying under Hatfield's table and said, "Is that it?"

"I haven't looked yet. I was waiting for you."

"Look now," Randall said.

It was book number 15208, all right—unmistakably the one I'd collected yesterday from Mrs. Conway. Its identification number appeared big and clear in both the usual places—on the front flyleaf and on the margin of page 101. "This is it. No mistake," I said.

"If Hatfield's killing is connected with this book, as you seem to think," Randall said reasonably enough, "there's got to be something about the book to tell us why."

I said, "Maybe there was. Before the back flyleaf was torn out."

"Be damned!" said Randall, squinting where I was pointing. "Torn out is right. Something written on the flyleaf that this Conway wanted kept private maybe?"

"Could be."

"Thought you said you looked through this book yesterday. You'd have seen any writing."

"I didn't look through it. I shook it out, that's all."

"Why would a guy write anything private or incriminating on the blank back page of a library book, for God's sake?"

"His wife found the book under the telephone in their bedroom. He could have been taking down notes during a telephone conversation."

"In a library book?"

"Why not? If it was the only blank paper he had handy when he got the telephone call?"

"So his wife gave the book back to you before he'd had a chance to erase his notes. Is that what you're suggesting?"

"Or transcribe them, yes. Or memorize them."

Lieutenant Randall looked out Hatfield's grimy window for a moment. Then he said abruptly, "I'm impounding this library book for a few days, Hal, so our lab boys can take a look at it. Okay?"

"Okay."

Randall glanced pointedly toward the door. "Thanks for calling us," he said. "Be seeing you."

I stepped carefully around Hatfield's sprawled body. "Right."

"I'll be in touch if we find anything," Randall said.

Much to my surprise he phoned me at the library just about quitting time the next day. "Did you ever see this Mr. Conway?" he asked. "Could you identify him?"

"I never saw him in the flesh. I saw a photo of him on his wife's desk."

"That's good enough. Meet me at the Encore Bar at Stanhope and Cotton in twenty minutes, can you?"

"Sure," I said. "Why?"

"Tell you when I see you."

He was waiting for me in a rear booth. There were only half a dozen customers in the place. I sat down facing him and he said, without preamble, "Conway *did* write something on the back flyleaf of your library book. Or somebody did, anyhow. Because we found traces of crushed paper fibers on the page *under* the back flyleaf. Not good enough traces to be read except for one notation at the top, which was probably written first on the back flyleaf when the pencil point was sharper and thus made a deeper groove on the page underneath. Are you with me?"

"Yes. What did it say?"

Randall got a slip of paper from his pocket and showed it to me. It contained one line, scribbled by Randall:

Transo 3212/5/13 Mi
Encore Harper 6/12

I studied it silently for a minute. Randall said, faintly smug, "Does that mean anything to you?"

"'Sure," I said, deadpan. "Somebody named Harper off Transoceanic Airlines flight 3212 out of Miami on May 13th—that's today—is supposed to meet somebody in this bar at twelve minutes after six."

"A lucky guess," Randall said, crestfallen. "The *Encore* and *Transo* gave it to you, of course. But it took us half an hour to figure the meaning and check it out."

"Check it out?"

"There really *is* a Transoceanic flight 3212 out of Miami today—and there really is somebody aboard named Harper, too. A Miss Genevieve Harper, stewardess."

"Oh," I said, "and of course there *is* an Encore Bar—could even be a couple of them in town."

"Only one that Harper can get to through rush-hour traffic within twenty minutes after she hits the airport," the lieutenant said triumphantly. "She's scheduled in at 5:52."

I glanced at my watch. It was 5:30. "You have time to check whether Conway had any phone calls Sunday night?"

"Not yet. Didn't even have time to find out what Conway looks like. That's why you're here." He grinned. "What's your guess about why they're meeting here?"

I gave it some thought. "Drugs," I said at last, "since the flight seems to be out of Miami. Most of the heroin processed in France comes to the United States via South America and Miami, right?"

Randall nodded. "We figure Conway for a distributor at this end. Sunday night he got a phone call from somebody in South America or Miami, telling him when and where to take delivery of a shipment. That's what he wrote on the flyleaf of your library book. So no wonder he was frantic when his wife gave his list of dates and places to a library cop."

I suddenly felt tired. I called over to the bartender and ordered a dry martini. I said to Randall, "So Hatfield's accident could have been murder?"

"Sure. We think it went like this: Mrs. Conway gave you the book, got knocked around by her husband when she told him what she'd done, then on hubby's orders came to you to recover the book for him. When she couldn't do that, or even get the name of the subsequent borrower, her husband did the best he could with the information she *did* get—the borrower's library card number and how you matched it up with his name and address. Conway got the name the same way you did—by phoning what's-her-name at your main desk."

"Kathy," I said.

"Yeah. Conway must have gone right out to Hatfield's when he learned his identity, prepared to do anything necessary to get that book back—or his list on the flyleaf, anyway. Conway broke the lock on Hatfield's apartment and was inside looking for the book when Hatfield must have walked in on him."

"And Conway hid behind the door and clobbered Hatfield when he walked in?"

"Yeah. Probably with a blackjack. And probably, in his panic, hit him too hard. So he faked it to look like an accident. Then he tore the back flyleaf out of your book thinking nobody would ever notice it was missing."

"You forgot something," I said.

"What?"

"He made his wife call me off by telling me he'd found his lost check."

"I didn't forget it," Randall grinned.

I said, "Of course you can't prove any of this."

"Not yet. But give us time. We get him on a narcotics charge and hold him tighter than hell while we work up the murder case."

"*If* it's Conway," I said, looking at my watch, "who shows up here in twenty-two minutes."

"He'll show." Randall was confident. "Likely get here a little early, even."

And he did, At 5:56 the original of Mrs. Conway's photograph walked in the door of the Encore Bar. Dapper, young-looking, not much chin under a mustache that drooped around the corners of his mouth.

He sat down in the booth nearest the door and ordered a Scotch-and-soda.

Randall threw me a questioning look and I nodded vigorously. Then we talked about baseball until, at 6:14, a bouncy little blonde dish came tripping into the Encore and went straight to Conway's booth, saying loud enough for everybody in the joint to hear, "Well, hello, darling! I'm so thirsty I could drink *water*!" She looked very pert in her uniform and had a flight bag over her shoulder. She sat down beside Conway with her back to us.

Randall got up, went to the bar entrance, and opened the door. He stepped out into the vestibule and casually waved one arm over his head, as though he were tossing a cigarette butt away. Then he came back in and leaned against the bar until three young huskies appeared in the doorway. Randall pointed one finger at Conway's booth and the three newcomers stepped over there, boxing in Conway and Miss Harper.

It was all done very quietly and smoothly. No voices raised, no violence. One of the narcotics men took charge of Harper's shoulder bag. The other two took charge of Conway and Harper.

When they'd gone, Randall ordered himself a bourbon and carried it back to our booth and sat down. "That's it, Hal," he said with satisfaction. "Harper had two one-pound boxes of bath powder in her flight bag. Pure heroin. This is going to look very good—*very* good—on my record."

I took a sip of my martini and said nothing.

Randall went on, "You're sure Conway's wife has nothing to do with the smuggling? That she doesn't suspect what her hubby is up to?"

I thought about Mrs. Conway's friendliness, so charming and unstudied. I remembered how the animation and pride I'd seen in her eyes yesterday morning had been replaced by distress and bewilderment in the afternoon. And I said to Lieutenant Randall, "I'd stake my job on it."

He nodded. "We'll have to dig into it, of course. But I'm inclined to think you're right. So somebody ought to tell her why her husband won't be home for dinner tonight, Hal." He paused for a long moment. "Any volunteers?"

I looked up from my martini into Randall's unblinking stare. "Thanks, Lieutenant," I said. "I'm on my way."

PATRICIA HIGHSMITH

The Nature of the Thing

Eleanor had been sewing nearly all day—sewing after dinner, too—and it was now almost midnight. She looked away from her machine, sideways toward the hall door, and saw something about two feet high, something grayish black, which after a second or two moved and was lost from view in the hall. Eleanor rubbed her eyes. Her eyes smarted, and it was delicious to rub them. But since she was sure she had not really seen something, she did not get up from her chair to go and investigate. She forgot about it.

She stood up about five minutes later, after tidying her sewing table, putting away her scissors, and folding the yellow dress whose side seams she had just let out. The dress was ready for Mrs. Burns tomorrow. Always letting out, Eleanor thought, never taking in. People seemed to grow sideways, not upward any more, and she smiled at this fuzzy little thought. She was tired, but she had had a good day. She gave her cat Bessie a saucer of milk—rather creamy milk, because Bessie liked the best of everything—then heated some milk for herself and took it in a mug up to bed.

The second time she saw it, however, she was not tired, and the sun was shining brightly. This time she was sitting in the armchair, putting a zipper in a skirt, and as she knotted her thread, she happened to glance at the door that went into what she called the side room, a room off the living room at the front of the house. She saw a squarish figure about two feet high, an ugly little thing that at first suggested an upended sandbag. It took a moment before she perceived a large square head, thick feet in heavy shoes, and incredibly short arms with big hands that dangled.

Eleanor was half out of her chair, her slender body rigid.

The thing didn't move. But it was looking at her.

Get it out of the house, she thought at once. Shoo it out the door. What *was* it? The face was vaguely human. Eyes looked at her from under hair that was combed forward over the forehead. Had the children put some horrid toy in the house to frighten her? The Rolands next door had four children, the oldest eight. Children's toys these days—you never knew what to expect!

Then the thing moved, advanced slowly into the living room, and Eleanor stepped quickly behind the armchair.

"Get out! Get away!" she said in a voice shrill with panic.

"Um-m," came the reply, soft and deep.

Had she really heard anything? Now it looked up from the floor—where it had stared while entering the room—to her face. The look at her seemed direct, yet was somehow vague and unfocused. The creature went on, toward the electric heater, where it stopped and held out its hands casually to the warmth. It was masculine, Eleanor thought; its legs—if those stumpy things could be called legs—were in trousers. Again the creature took a sidelong look at her, a little shyly, yet as if defying her to get it out of the room.

The cat, curled on a pillow in a chair, lifted her head and yawned, and the movement caught Eleanor's eye. She waited for Bessie to see the thing, straight ahead of her and only four feet away; but Bessie put her head down again in a position for sleeping. Now that was curious!

Eleanor retreated quickly to the kitchen, opened the back door and went out, leaving the door wide open. She went around to the front door and opened that wide, too. Give the thing a chance to get out! Eleanor stayed on her front walk, ready to run to the road if the creature emerged.

The thing came to the front door and said in a deep voice, the words more a rumble than articulated, "I'm not going to harm you, so why don't you come back in? It's your house." And there was the hint of a shrug in the chunky shoulders.

"I'd like you to get out please!" Eleanor said.

"Um-m." He turned away, back into the living room.

Eleanor thought of going for Mr. Roland next door; he was a practical man who probably had a gun in the house, since he was a captain in the Air Force. Then she remembered that the Rolands had gone off before lunch and that their house was empty. Eleanor gathered her courage and advanced toward the front door.

She didn't see him in the living room. She even looked behind the armchair. She went cautiously toward the side room. He was not in there, either. She looked quite thoroughly.

She stood in the hall and called up the stairs, really called to all the house, "If you're still in this house I wish you would leave!"

Behind her a voice said, "I'm still here."

Eleanor turned and saw him standing in the living room.

"I won't do you any harm. But I can disappear if you prefer. Like this."

She thought she saw a set of bared teeth, as if he were making an effort. As she stared, the creature became a paler gray, and more fuzzy at the edges. And after ten seconds there was nothing. *Nothing*! Was she losing her mind? She must tell Dr. Campbell, she thought. First thing tomorrow morning, she would go to his office and tell him honestly what had happened—what she thought had happened.

The rest of the day, and the evening, passed without incident. Mrs. Burns came for her dress and brought a coat to be shortened. Eleanor watched a television program, then went to bed at half-past ten. She had thought she would be frightened—going to bed and turning all the lights out; but she wasn't.

And before she had time to worry about whether she could get to sleep or not, she had fallen asleep.

But when she woke up he was the second thing she saw, the first thing being her cat, who had slept at the foot of the bed for warmth.

Bessie stretched, yawned, and miaouwed simultaneously, demanding breakfast. And hardly two yards away, there he stood, staring at her. Eleanor's promise of immediate breakfast to Bessie was cut short by her seeing him.

"I could use some breakfast myself," he said. Was there a faint smile on that square face? "Nothing much. A piece of bread will do."

Now Eleanor found her teeth tight together, found herself wordless. She got out of bed on the other side from him, quickly pulled on her old flannel robe, and went down the stairs. In the kitchen she comforted herself with the usual routine—she put the kettle on, fed Bessie while the kettle was heating, cut some bread. But she was waiting for the thing to appear in the kitchen doorway, and as she was slicing the bread he did appear. Trembling, Eleanor held a piece of bread toward him.

"If I give you this, would you go away?" she asked.

The monstrous hand reached out and up and took the bread. "Not necessarily," rumbled the bass voice. "I don't need to eat, you know. I thought I'd keep you company, that's all."

Eleanor was not sure, really not sure she had heard it. She was imagining telling Dr. Campbell all this, imagining the point at which Dr. Campbell would cut her short—politely, of course, because he was a nice man—and prescribe some kind of sedative.

Bessie finished her breakfast and walked so close by the creature that her fur must have brushed his leg; but the cat showed no sign of feeling or seeing anything. That was proof enough that he didn't exist, Eleanor thought.

A strange rumbling "Um-m-m" came from him. He was laughing! "Not everyone—or everything—can see me," he said to Eleanor. "In fact, very few people can see me." He had eaten the bread, apparently.

Eleanor steeled herself to carry on with her breakfast. She cut another piece of bread, got out the butter and jam, scalded the teapot. It was ten to 8:00. By 9:00 she'd be in Dr. Campbell's office.

"Maybe there's something I can do for you today," he said. He had not moved from where he stood. "Odd jobs. I'm strong." The last word was like a nasal burr, like the horn of a large and distant ship.

At first Eleanor thought of the rusty old lawn roller in her barn. She'd rung up Field's, the secondhand dealer, to come and take it away, but they were late as usual, two weeks late. "I have a roller out in the barn. After breakfast you can take it to the edge of the road and leave it there, if you will." That would be further proof, Eleanor thought, proof that he wasn't real. The roller must weigh two or three hundred pounds.

He walked, in a slow, rolling gait, out of the kitchen and into the sitting room. He made no sound.

Eleanor ate her breakfast at the scrubbed wooden table in the kitchen, where she often preferred to eat instead of in the dining room. She propped a booklet on sewing tips in front of her, and after a few moments she was able to concentrate on it.

At 8:30, dressed now, Eleanor went out to the barn behind her house. She had not looked for him in the house—didn't know where he was, in fact; but somehow it did not surprise her to find him beside her when she reached the barn door.

"It's in the back corner. I'll show you." She removed the padlock which had not been entirely closed.

He understood at once, rubbed his big yellowish hands together, and took a grip on the wooden handle of the roller. He pulled it toward him with apparently the greatest ease, then began to push it from behind, rolling it. But using the handle was easier, so he took the handle again, and in a few minutes the roller was at the edge of the road.

Billy, the boy who delivered the morning papers, was cycling along the road just then.

Eleanor tensed, thinking Billy would cry out at the sight of him; but the boy only said shyly, "Morning, Mrs. Heathcote," and pedaled on.

"Good morning, Billy," Eleanor called after the boy.

"Anything else?" he asked.

"I can't think of anything, thank you," Eleanor replied rather breathlessly.

"It won't do you any good to speak to your doctor about me," he said.

They were both walking back toward the house, up the carelessly flagstoned path that divided Eleanor's front garden.

"He won't be able to see me, and he'll just give you useless pills," he continued.

What made you think I was going to a doctor? Eleanor wanted to ask. But she knew. He could read her mind. Is he some part of myself? she asked herself, with a flash of intuition which went no further than the question. If no one *else* can see him—

"I am myself," he said, smiling at her over one shoulder. He was leading the way into the house. "Just me." And he laughed.

Eleanor did not go to see Dr. Campbell. She decided to try to ignore him, to go about her usual affairs. Her affairs that morning consisted in walking a quarter of a mile to the butcher's for some liver for Bessie and half a chicken for herself, and of buying several articles at Mr. White's, the grocer. But Eleanor was thinking of telling all this to Vance—Mrs. Florence Vansittart—who was her best friend in town. Vance and she had tea together, at one or the other's house, at least once a week—usually once every five days, in fact; so Eleanor phoned Vance as soon as she got home.

The creature was not in sight at that time.

Vance agreed to come over at 4:00. "How *are* you, dear?" Vance asked as she always did.

"All right, thanks," Eleanor replied, more heartily than usual. "And you? . . . I'll make some blueberry muffins if I get my work done in time."

That afternoon, though he had kept out of sight since the morning, he lumbered silently into the room just as Eleanor and Vance were starting on their second cup of tea, and just as Eleanor was drawing breath for the first statement, the introductory statement, of her strange story. She had been thinking that the roller at the edge of the road—she must ring Field's again first thing in the morning—would be proof that what she said was not an hallucination.

"What's the matter, Eleanor?" asked Vance, sitting up a little. She was a woman of Eleanor's age, about 55, one of the many widows in town; but unlike Eleanor, Vance had never worked at anything—she had been left enough money. And Vance looked to her right, at the side-room door, where Eleanor had been looking. Eleanor took her eyes away from the creature who was now standing inside the door.

"Nothing," Eleanor said. Vance didn't see him, she thought. Vance *can't* see him.

"She can't see me," the creature rumbled to Eleanor.

"Swallow something the wrong way?" Vance asked, chuckling, helping herself to another blueberry muffin.

The creature was staring at the muffins, but came no closer.

"You know, Eleanor—" Vance chewed "—if you're still charging only two dollars for putting a hem up, I think you need your head examined. People around here, all of them could afford to give you twice as much. It's criminal the way you cheat yourself."

Vance meant, Eleanor thought, that it was high time she had her house painted, or recovered the armchair, which she could do herself if she had the time. "It's not easy to mention raising prices, and the people who come to me are used to mine by now."

"Other people manage to mention price-raising pretty easily," Vance said as Eleanor had known she would. "I hear of a new higher price every day!"

The creature took a muffin. For a few seconds the muffin must have been visible in mid-air to Vance, even if she didn't see him. But suddenly the muffin was gone, chewed by the massive jaw.

"You look a bit absent today, my dear," Vance said. "Something worrying you?" Vance looked at her attentively, waiting for a confidence—such as another tooth extraction that Eleanor felt doomed to, or news that her brother George in Canada, who had never made a go of anything, was once more failing in business.

Eleanor braced herself and said, "I've had a visitor for the last two days. He's standing right here by the table." She nodded her head in his direction.

The creature was looking at Eleanor.

Vance looked where Eleanor had nodded. "What do you mean?"

"You can't see him? . . . He's quite friendly," Eleanor added. "It's a creature two feet high. He's right there. He just took a muffin! I know you don't believe me," she rushed on, "but he moved the roller this morning from the barn to the edge of the road. You saw it at the edge of the road, didn't you? You *said* something about it."

Vance tipped her head to one side, looking in a puzzled way at Eleanor. "You mean the handyman. Old Gufford?"

"No, he's—" But at this moment the creature was walking out of the room, so Vance couldn't possibly see him, and before he disappeared into the side room he gave Eleanor a look and pushed his great hands flat downward in the air, as if to say, "Give it up," or "Don't talk."

"I mean what I said," Eleanor pursued, determined to share her experience, determined also to get some sympathy, even some protection. "I'm not joking, Vance. It's a little—creature—two feet high, and he talks to me." Her voice had sunk to a whisper. She glanced at the side-room doorway, which was empty. "You think I'm seeing things, but I'm not, I swear it!"

Vance still looked puzzled, but quite in control of herself, and she even assumed a superior attitude. "How long have you—been seeing him, my dear?" she asked.

"I saw him first two nights ago," Eleanor said, still in a whisper. "Then yesterday quite plainly, in broad daylight. He has a deep voice."

"If he just took a muffin, where is he now?" Vance asked, getting up. "Why can't I see him?"

"He went into the side room. All right, come along."

Eleanor was suddenly aware that she didn't know his name, didn't know how to address him. She and Vance looked into an apparently empty room, empty of anything alive except some plants on the window sill. Eleanor looked behind the sofa. "Well—he has the faculty of disappearing."

Vance smiled, again in a superior way. "Eleanor, your eyes are getting worse. Are you using your glasses? That constant sewing—"

"I don't need them for sewing. Only for distance. Matter of fact, I did put them on when I looked at him yesterday across the room." She was wearing her eyeglasses now.

Vance frowned slightly. "My dear, are you afraid of him? . . . It looks like it. Stay with me tonight. Come home with me now, if you like. I can come back with Hester and look the house over thoroughly." Hester was her cleaning woman.

"Oh, I'm sure you wouldn't see him. And I'm not afraid. He's rather friendly. But I *did* want you to believe me."

"How can I believe you if I don't see him?"

"I don't know." Eleanor thought of describing him more accurately. But would that convince Vance, or anybody? "I think I could take a photograph of him. I don't think he'd mind," Eleanor said.

"A good idea! You've got a camera?"

"No. Well, I have, an old one of John's, but—"

"I'll bring mine. This afternoon. Now I'm going to finish my tea."

Vance brought the camera just before 6:00. "Good luck, Eleanor. This should be interesting!" Vance said as she left.

Eleanor could tell that Vance had not believed a single word of what she had told her. The camera said "5" on its indicator. There were eight more pictures on the roll, Vance had said. Eleanor thought two would be enough.

"I don't photograph," his deep voice said on her left, and Eleanor saw him standing in the doorway of the side room. "But I'll pose for you. Um-m-m." It was the deep laugh.

Eleanor felt only a mild start of surprise, or of fear. The sun was still shining. "Would you sit in a chair in the front garden?"

"Certainly," the creature said, and he was clearly amused.

Eleanor picked up the straight chair which she usually sat on when she worked, but he took it from her and went out the front door with it. He set the chair in the garden, careful not to tread on flowers. Then with a little boost he got himself onto the seat and folded his short arms.

The sunlight fell full on his face. Vance had showed Eleanor how to work the camera. It was a simple one compared to John's. She took the picture at the prescribed six-foot distance. Then she saw Old Gufford, the neighborhood handyman, going by in his little truck, staring at her. They did not usually greet each other, and they did not now, but Eleanor could imagine how odd he must think she was to be taking a picture of an ordinary empty chair in the garden. But she had seen him clearly in the finder. There was no doubt at all about that.

"Could I take one more of you standing next to the chair?" she asked.

"Um-m." That was not a laugh, but a sound of assent. He slid off the chair and stood beside it, one hand resting on the chair's back.

This was splendid, Eleanor thought, because it showed his height compared with that of the chair.

Click!

"Thank you."

"They won't turn out," he remarked, and took the chair back into the house.

"If you'd like another muffin," Eleanor said, wanting to be polite and thinking also he might have resented her asking him to be photographed, "they're in the kitchen."

"I know. I don't need to eat. I just took one to see if your friend would notice. She didn't. Not many do."

Eleanor thought again of the muffin in mid-air for a few seconds—it must have been—but she said nothing. "I—I don't know what to call you. Have you got a name?"

A fuzzy, rather general expression of amusement came over his square face. "Lots of names. No particular name. No one speaks to me, so there's no need of a name."

"I speak to you," Eleanor said.

He was standing by the stove now, not as high, not nearly as high as the gas burners. His skin looked dry, yellowish, and his face somehow sad. She felt sorry for him.

"Where have you been living?"

He laughed. "Um-m-m. I live anywhere, everywhere. It doesn't matter."

She wanted to ask some questions, such as, "Do you feel the cold?" but she did not want to be personal, or seem to be prying. "It occurred to me you might like a bed," she said more brightly. "You could sleep on the couch in the side room. I mean, with a blanket."

Again a laugh. "I don't need to sleep. But it's a kind thought. You're very kind."

His eyes moved to the door as Bessie walked in, making for her tablecloth of newspaper on which stood her bowl of water and her unfinished bowl of creamy milk. His eyes followed the cat.

Eleanor felt a sudden apprehension. It was probably because Bessie had not seen him. That was certainly disturbing, when she could see him so well that even the wrinkles in his face were quite visible. He was clothed in strange material, gray-black, neither shiny nor dull.

"You must be lonely since your husband died," he said. "But I admit you do well. Considering he didn't leave you much."

Eleanor blushed. She could feel it. John hadn't been a big earner, certainly. But he was a decent man, a good husband—yes, he had been that. And their only child, a daughter, had been killed in a snow avalanche in Austria when she was twenty. Eleanor never thought of Penny. She had set herself never to think of Penny. She was disturbed, and felt awkward, because she thought of her now. And she hoped the creature would not mention Penny. Her death was one of life's tragedies. But other families had similar tragedies—only-sons killed in useless wars.

"Now you have your cat," he said, as if he read her thoughts.

"Yes," Eleanor said, glad to change the subject. "Bessie is ten. She's had fifty-seven kittens. But three—no, four years ago, I finally had her doctored. She's a dear companion."

Eleanor slipped away and got a big gray blanket, an army-surplus blanket, from a closet and folded it in half on the couch in the side room. He stood watching her. She put a pillow under the top part of the blanket. "That's a little cosier," she said.

"Thank you," came the deep voice.

In the next few days he cut the high grass around the barn with a scythe and moved a huge rock that had always annoyed Eleanor, embedded as it was in the middle of a grassy square in front of the barn. It was August, but quite cool. They cleared out the attic, and he carried the heaviest things downstairs and to the edge of the road to be picked up by Field's. Some of these things were sold a few days later at auction, and fetched nearly $30.

Eleanor still felt a slight tenseness when he was present, a fear that she might annoy him in some way; and yet in another way, she was growing used to him. He certainly liked to be helpful. At night he obligingly got onto his couch bed, and she wanted to tuck him in, to bring him some cookies and a glass of milk; but he ate and drank next to nothing, and then, as he said, only to keep her company. Eleanor could never understand where all his strength came from.

Vance rang up one day and said she had the pictures. Before Eleanor could ask about them, Vance had hung up. Vance was coming over at once.

"You took a picture of a chair, dear! Does he look like a chair?" Vance asked, laughing. She handed Eleanor the photographs.

There were twelve photographs in the batch, but Eleanor looked only at the top two, which showed him seated in the straight chair and standing next to it. "Why, there he *is*!" she said triumphantly.

Vance hastily, but with a frown, looked at the two pictures again, then smiled broadly. "Are you implying there's something wrong with *my* eyes? It's only a chair, darling—an empty chair!"

Eleanor knew that Vance, speaking for herself, was right. Vance couldn't see him. For a moment Eleanor couldn't say anything.

"I told you what would happen. Um-m-m."

Eleanor knew he was behind her, in the doorway of the side room, though she did not turn to look at him.

"All right. Perhaps it's my eyes," Eleanor said. "But I *do* see him there!" She couldn't give up. Should she tell Vance about his Herculean feats in the attic? Could she have got a big heavy chest of drawers down the stairs by herself?

Vance stayed for a cup of tea. They talked of other things—everything to Eleanor was now "other" and a bit uninteresting and unimportant compared with him. Then Vance left, saying, "Promise me you'll go to Dr. Nimms next week. I'll drive you, if you don't want to drive. Maybe you shouldn't drive if your eyes are acting funny."

Eleanor had a car, but she seldom used it. She didn't care for driving. "Thanks, Vance, I'll go on my own." She meant it at that moment, but when Vance had gone, Eleanor knew she would not go to the eye doctor.

He sat with her while she ate dinner. She now felt defensive and protective about him. She no longer wanted to share him with anyone.

"You shouldn't have bothered with those photographs," he said. "You see, what I told you is true. Whatever I say is true."

And yet he didn't look brilliant or even especially intelligent, Eleanor reflected.

He tore a piece of bread rather savagely in half and stuffed one half into his mouth. "You're one of the very few people who can see me. Maybe only a dozen people in the whole world can see me. Maybe less than that. Why should the others see me?" he continued, and shrugged his chunky shoulders. "They're just like me."

"What do you mean?" she asked.

He sighed. "Ugly." Then he laughed softly and deeply. "I am not nice. Not nice at all."

She was too confused to answer for a moment. A polite answer seemed absurd. She was trying to think what he really meant.

"You enjoyed taking care of your mother, didn't you? You didn't mind it," he said, as if he were being polite himself and filling in an awkward silence.

"No, of course not. I loved her," Eleanor said readily. How could he know? Her father had died when she was 18, and she hadn't been able to finish college because of a shortage of money. Then her mother had become bedridden, but she had lived on for ten years. Her treatment had taken all the money Eleanor had been able to earn as a secretary, and a little more besides, so that everything of value they had possessed had finally been sold. Eleanor had married at 29, and gone with John to live in Boston. Oh, the gone and lovely days! John had been so kind, so understanding of the fact that she had been exhausted, in need of human company—or rather, the company of people her own age. Penny had been born when she was thirty.

"Yes, John was a good man, but not so good as you," he said and sighed. "Um-m."

Now Eleanor laughed spontaneously. It was a relief from her thoughts. "How can one be good—or bad? Aren't we all a mixture? You're certainly not all bad."

This seemed to annoy him. "Don't tell me what I am."

Rebuffed, Eleanor said nothing more. She cleared the table.

She put him to bed, thanked him for his work in the garden that day— gouging up a thousand dandelions was no easy task. She was glad of his company in the house, even glad that no one else could see him. He was a funny doll that belonged to her. He made her feel odd, different, yet somehow special and privileged. She tried to put these thoughts from her mind, lest he disapprove of them, because he was looking, vaguely as usual, at her, with a resentment or a reproach. "Can I get you anything?" she asked.

"No," he answered shortly.

The next morning she found Bessie in the middle of the kitchen floor with her neck wrung. Her head sat in the strangest way on her neck, facing backward. Eleanor seized the corpse impulsively and pressed the cat to her breast. The head lolled. She knew he had done it. But why?

"Yes, I did it," his deep voice said.

She looked at the doorway, but did not see him. "How could you? Why did you do it?" Eleanor began to weep. The cat was not warm any longer, but she was not stiff.

"It's my nature." He did not laugh, but there was a smile in his voice. "You hate me now. You wonder if I'll be going. Yes, I'll be going." His voice was fading as he walked through the living room, but still she could not see him. "To prove it I'll slam the front door, but I don't need to use the door to get out." She heard the door slam.

She was looking at the front door. The door had not moved.

Eleanor buried Bessie in the back yard near the barn, and the pitchfork was heavy in her hands, and the earth heavier in her spade. She had waited until late afternoon, as if hoping that by some miracle Bessie might come alive again. But the cat's body had grown rigid. Eleanor wept again. . .

She declined Vance's next invitation to tea, and finally Vance came to see her, unexpectedly. Eleanor was sewing. She had quite a bit of work to do, but she was depressed and lonely, not knowing what she wanted, and there was no person she especially wanted to see. She realized that she missed him, that strange creature. And she knew he would never come back.

Vance was disappointed because Eleanor had not gone to see Dr. Nimms. She told Eleanor that she was neglecting herself. Eleanor did not enjoy seeing her old friend. Vance also remarked that Eleanor had lost weight.

"That—little monster isn't annoying you still, is he? Or is he?" Vance asked.

"He's gone," Eleanor said, and managed a smile, though what the smile meant she didn't know.

"How's Bessie?"

"Bessie—was killed by a car a couple of weeks ago."

"Oh, Eleanor! I'm sorry. Why didn't you—you should've *told* me! What bad luck! You'd better get another kitty. That's always the best thing to do. You're so fond of cats."

Eleanor shook her head a little.

"I'm going to find out where there's some nice kittens. The Carters' Siamese might've had another batch." Vance smiled. "They're always nice, half-Siamese. Really!"

That evening Eleanor ate no supper. She wandered through the empty-feeling rooms of her house, thinking not only of him, but of her lonely years here, and of the happier years here when John had been alive. He had tried to work in Millersville, ten miles away, but the job hadn't lasted. Or rather, the company hadn't lasted. That had been poor John's luck. No use thinking about it now, about what might have been if John had ever had a business of his own.

But now she thought more of when *he* had been here, the funny little fellow who had turned against her. She wished he were back. She felt he would not do such a horrid thing again, if she spoke to him the right way. He had become annoyed when she had said he was not entirely bad. But she knew he would not come back, not ever.

She worked until midnight. More letting out. More hems taken up. People were becoming square, she thought, but the thought did not make her smile any more. She looked at his photographs again, half expecting not to see him—like Vance; but he was still there, just as clear as he had been before. That was some comfort to her—but pictures were so flat and lifeless.

The house had never seemed so silent. Her plants were doing beautifully. Not long ago she had repotted most of them. Yet Eleanor sensed a negativity when she looked at them. It was very curious—a happy sight like blossoming plants causing sadness. She longed for something, and did not know what it was. That was strange also, this unidentifiable hunger, this loneliness that was worse and more profound than it was after John had died. . .

Tom Roland phoned one evening at 9:00 P.M. His wife was ill and he had to go at once to an "alert" at the Air Base. Could she come over and sit with his wife? He'd be home before midnight.

Eleanor went over at once, taking a bowl of fresh strawberries sprinkled with powdered sugar. Mary Roland was not seriously ill—it was a 24-hour virus attack of some kind; but she was grateful for the strawberries. The bowl was put on the bedtable. It was a pretty color to look at, though Mary could not eat anything.

Eleanor heard herself chatting as she always did, though in an odd way she felt she was not present with Mary, not even in the Rolands' house. It wasn't a "miles away" feeling, but a feeling it was not taking place. It was not even as real as a dream.

Eleanor went home at midnight, after Tom returned. Somehow she knew she was going to die that night. It was a calm and destined sensation. She might have died, she thought, if she had merely gone to bed and fallen asleep. But she wished to make sure of it, so she took a single-edge razor blade from her shelf of paints in the kitchen closet—the blade was rusty and dull, but no matter—and cut her two wrists at the basin in the bathroom.

The blood ran and ran, and she washed it down with running cold water, still mindful, she thought with slight amusement, of conserving the hot water in the tank. Finally, she could see that the streams were lessening. She took her bathtowel and wrapped it around both her wrists, winding her hands as if she were coiling wool. She was feeling weak, and she wanted to lie down and not soil the mattress, if possible.

The blood did not come through the towel before she lay down on her bed. Then she closed her eyes and did not know if the blood came through or not. It really did not matter, she supposed. Nor did the finished and unfinished skirts and dresses downstairs. People would come and claim them.

Eleanor thought of him, small and strong, strange and yet so plain and simple. He had never told her his name. She realized that she loved him.

EDWARD D. HOCH

The Theft of the Dinosaur's Tail

The affair of the Dinosaur's Tail really began on the day of the Rockland County horse trials, when Nick Velvet met a man named Frader Kincaid. It was a gloomy October Sunday, with a definite threat of rain, and Nick had driven up because Gloria wanted to watch the jumpers.

"Nicky," she had told him, "there's nothing more exciting than watching those horses take the jumps with hardly a break in stride."

Nick who could think of several things more exciting to watch, had felt it was one of those rare occasions when he must humor Gloria, and so they'd made the trip to Rockland County. She proved to know more about horses than he'd imagined, readily explaining to his disinterested ear the features of a double oxer or of parallel bars.

"Isn't it thrilling?" she asked at one point.

"I suppose so," Nick replied. His eyes were following a tall, trimly built man on a chestnut mare. The man seemed to be one of the jump judges.

Presently there was some commotion across the field, and they could see that one of the horses had thrown its youthful rider at a water jump. The standby ambulance started toward the scene and the other riders were held at their starting point. The man on the chestnut mare watched for a time through his binoculars, then cantered over to Nick's car.

"Looks like rain," he said, smiling. "Enjoying the show?"

"We were until now." Nick motioned across the field. "Is the rider badly hurt?"

"No, no! Just had the wind knocked out of her. It's Lynn Peters, one of our new members. I'm afraid she's not up to water jumps yet." He seemed to remember that he hadn't introduced himself. "I'm Frader Kincaid, master of the hunt here. You folks coming to the open house afterwards?"

"We're not members," Nick told him.

"Don't worry about that—it's open to all. The big house at the top of the hill. I'll be looking for you."

When Kincaid had ridden away, Gloria tugged on Nick's sleeve. "I'd love to go for a little while, Nicky."

He sighed, seeing there was no way out. "We'll stop by."

When Nick and Gloria arrived at the house on the hill two hours later, the party was already in full swing. A light rain had started to fall, but it hadn't dampened any spirits. Middle-aged men and somewhat younger women in riding togs filled two large downstairs rooms, sipping cocktails while they chattered and giggled and generally relaxed. It was not Nick's sort of gathering, but he knew Gloria would enjoy it.

"Glad you could make it," Kincaid greeted them. It was obvious now that the house was his, and the party was his also. "Martinis all right?"

"Fine."

He produced two with a smile and then hooked an arm around the waist of a passing girl. "This is Lynn Peters, who scared us all with her fall this afternoon. Feeling better, Lynn?"

She was young and sandy-haired, with cheeks flushed pink from drink or embarrassment. Her riding breeches and red corduroy vest fitted her well, and she was quick with a smile that included them all. "I'm fine now, Frader. My mount just didn't like the looks of that water hole."

Kincaid smiled benevolently. "Why don't you girls talk it over while I show Mr. Velvet my den? I have a nice collection I'd like to show him."

Nick followed the tall man through a door at the far end of the room, into a book-lined study that overlooked the valley where the horse trials had been held. "Beautiful country, even on a rainy day," Kincaid commented.

Nick sipped his drink and asked, "How did you happen to know my name?"

"Oh, you noticed that? Once down at the Yacht Club someone pointed you out to me. I recognized you watching the jumps today and thought I might interest you in a business venture."

"My business activities are strictly limited."

Frader Kincaid moved around to the side of the desk, carefully resting his cocktail glass on a used envelope. "You're a professional thief, Mr. Velvet, and that's exactly the sort of venture I have in mind."

Nick's expression didn't change. He simply said, "My fee is quite large—$20,000—and I steal only objects of little or no value."

"I understand all that."

"What is the object you had in mind?"

Kincaid motioned toward the wall between the bookcases where an elaborate oil painting hung. It was an odd subject for a rich man's wall—a prehistoric scene of two dinosaurs locked in deadly combat against a dank swampy land-scape. "How much do you know of these things, Mr. Velvet?"

"Nothing I didn't learn from the monster films when I was a kid."

"I publish several lines of paperbound books, and this was the cover painting for a science-fiction novel. I liked the painting, even if the book lost money. Only one thing sells these days." He grinned and chose a book at random from the case beside him. Nick needed only a glance at the bare-bosomed model and the sex-slang title to know the kind of book it was.

"You publish pornography?" he asked Kincaid.

"I publish what the people buy. One year it's dinosaurs, the next it's derrières. Makes not a particle of difference to me."

Nick merely grunted. He was hardly in a position to comment on other men's morals. "What is it you want stolen?"

Kincaid tapped the framed painting with his index finger. "This one is a Tyrannosaurus Rex, the largest flesh-eating creature that ever existed. Its teeth alone were eight inches long, and its total length was something like fifty feet. The Brontosaurus was larger, of course, but it ate only herbs and plants."

"You seem to know a great deal about them."

"It's a hobby of mine." Kincaid smiled with satisfaction. "But to get to the point, Mr. Velvet. You are familiar with the Museum of Ancient History in upper Manhattan?"

"Of course."

"They have a fine complete skeleton of a Tyrannosaurus Rex there. I want you to steal its tail."

Nick Velvet simply stared at him, letting the words sink in. He had received some strange assignments in his career, but never anything like stealing the tail from a museum's dinosaur skeleton. "Not the whole thing? Just the tail?"

"Just the tail. The last few bones of the tail, to be exact."

"All right. How soon do you need it?"

"Before the end of the week. I do believe it was fate that brought you here today, just when I needed you." He walked a few steps to a small wall safe and returned with a packet of money. "This much in advance. The rest when you deliver the tail."

They shook hands and Nick pocketed the money. Then he left the room in search of Gloria. When he found her she was looking unhappy. "I thought you were never coming back, Nicky!"

"Didn't you enjoy your chat with Lynn Peters?"

"Not really. She doesn't actually know too much about jumping." Gloria put down her glass. "Maybe we should go now, Nicky. They really aren't our sort of people."

"No," he agreed. "I don't think they are."

On Monday morning Nick drove down to New York. He left the Major Deegan Expressway at 155th Street and crossed the Harlem River into Manhattan's northern limits. From there it was only a five-minute drive to the Museum of Ancient History, a big rambling red-brick monstrosity that reminded him of the Smithsonian on a bad day. The parking lot was nearly deserted this early, and he pulled up near the front entrance.

Inside, the place was all that its exterior promised—high ceilings with dusty skylights, marble floors, an air of mustiness that seemed to filter right through his clothes. It was everything a museum of the 1920's should have been, and if it was still that way nearly a half century later, one could only sigh with regret and remember those earlier, grander days.

Nick made his way through the Egyptian Room and the Etruscan Wing, coming at last to the Hall of Great Reptiles. And there it was, in all its baroque splendor—Tyrannosaurus Rex, towering 25 feet into the air and stretching back nearly 50 feet from head to tail. There was something sad and oddly dated about the hundreds of polished bones wired together as a memorial to this creature of long ago. After the indignities of the zoo, would modern animals be subjected to such extravagances, too? He'd read somewhere that only 600 tigers remained in the world, and he wondered if some future generation might be forced to view the skeleton of a Bengal as he now viewed this blanched relic.

He walked the full length of the great beast and paused to examine the jointed tail section. There was certainly nothing remarkable about the dozens of small bones that made up the tail. He bent closer across the rope barrier for a better look, but there was nothing to explain his assignment. He'd hardly expected a jeweled tail, for example; yet there must be some reason for the proposed theft.

Almost at once a uniformed guard appeared and called out, "Not too close there, mister. Them things are delicate!"

"Sorry. Just wanted a good look. Know where these bones came from?"

The guard moved closer, friendly now. "Out west somewhere. It tells on the sign. In most of these skeletons we have to use some fake bones. It's impossible to find one of these things complete."

Nick nodded and turned away, not wanting to show too much interest. "It sure was big," he said by way of conclusion, and drifted back to the Etruscan Wing.

He might have passed directly through to the Egyptian Room if he hadn't recognized a familiar face bent over one of the glass display cases. It was that of Lynn Peters, the girl he'd met at Kincaid's house. Her flushed cheeks and sandy hair were unmistakable, even if she was not wearing her riding costume.

"Hello there," he said. "I believe we met yesterday after the horse trials."

She turned, the fresh young smile coming naturally to her face. "Oh, it's Mr. Velvet, isn't it? I had a nice chat with your wife last evening."

"Gloria's just a friend," he corrected her amiably. "But what brings you here? I don't see a single horse in the whole place. Not a live one, anyway."

"They're having a special exhibit of antique jewelry, including some pieces from ancient Egypt." She led him to a nearby case filled with what looked to him like beaded trinkets. "That necklace of gold and jasper and amethyst is from the twelfth dynasty—two thousand years B.C.! Can you imagine?"

She seemed genuinely excited by the necklace, and Nick had to pretend a mild interest. Almost at once he noticed another guard, watching them from a high balcony that ran around the room. "This place is alive with guards, isn't it? Don't they trust anyone?"

Lynn Peters brushed the long hair from her eyes. "They've had some trouble—a number of robberies during the past couple of years. The latest one, a few months back, was the last straw, I guess. Someone stole the famous Pliny diamond, one of several brought from India to Rome about the year 60 A.D., and described by Pliny in his writings."

Nick grunted, vaguely remembering having read something about the robbery in the papers. "I don't know much Roman history, but I always thought Pliny was a politician of some sort."

"Pliny the Younger was, but his father was a naturalist. He wrote a thirty-seven-volume *Natural History*, which still survives. The diamond that bears his name is a really fabulous stone, almost priceless. Though of course it doesn't have the brilliancy of modern gems."

"Why is that?"

"The art of lapidary wasn't fully developed until the middle years of the Eighteenth Century—around 1746, to be exact. Before that, very little was known about the faceting of diamonds to give them the sparkle and brilliance we know today."

"You speak like a true authority."

She smiled at the compliment. "I'm studying to be a lapidarist. I work at the diamond exchange on West Forty-seventh Street."

"An unusual occupation for a young lady."

The grin turned impish. "Did you think I spent my life falling off horses?"

"Hardly." He was watching the guard on the balcony. "Just what happened to this Pliny diamond?"

"It was stolen from one of these showcases, just as other jewelry had been earlier. An alarm sounded when the glass was broken, of course, but by the time the guards got here there was no sign of the thief. Each of the thefts happened during the daytime hours, which is why they now have a guard assigned to every room. At night they have an elaborate alarm system, and two guard dogs patrol the place." She chuckled at the thought. "I always imagine the dogs carrying off the dinosaur bones and burying them somewhere."

"That stolen diamond would be difficult to dispose of."

"Not if it was cut up and refaceted. Pieces of a necklace from a similar robbery turned up with a fence in Boston. Museum robberies have been quite a problem around New York ever since the Star of India was stolen from the Museum of Natural History back in 1964."

Nick nodded. The watching guard made him nervous, and he didn't know how far their voices might carry in this high-ceilinged room. "Look," he decided suddenly, "I have to be going. Can I drop you anywhere?"

She shook her head. "This is part of my homework."

"Is this Egyptian stuff valuable, too?"

Lynn shrugged. "Depends on what you mean by valuable. To a collector it would be priceless, though it's not the sort of thing a fence would care to handle."

He nodded and started for the door. "I'll see you around. Don't fall off any more horses!"

* * *

Each time Nick Velvet was handed an assignment like this he reminded himself of the Clouded Tiger affair, some years back. In that one he'd been hired to steal a tiger from a zoo and it turned out to be only a means of drawing attention from the real crime being committed at the same time. The same trick had been tried with Nick on other occasions too, but he was usually able to see through the ruse and bow out in time. He didn't like being played for a patsy, and he had a suspicion that Frader Kincaid was trying to do just that.

No man, Nick felt, not even a dinosaur enthusiast, could have any use for the bones from a Tyrannosaurus tail. It seemed much more likely that Kincaid was connected with the museum thefts, and that he was using Nick simply to get by the added security precautions so he could enter the museum behind him and pull off another jewel robbery.

It made sense, in a way, and it might even explain why Lynn Peters had been at the museum. She might be working with Kincaid, watching Nick to see when he would pull the job. She might even be the lapidarist who cut up the gems for Kincaid after the robberies.

Thinking about it, Nick turned his car north and headed toward Kincaid's big house on the hill. He wanted another chat with the man before he undertook the theft of the dinosaur's tail.

When he reached it in mid-afternoon the big house was quiet. It was possible that Kincaid was in the city, but the elaborate study had indicated he did much of his work at home.

Nick was in luck. Kincaid himself answered the door on the second ring. "Well, Mr. Velvet! Don't tell me you're bringing the tail to me already!"

"No, not quite."

"Well, come in for a drink, anyway. I was just dictating some business correspondence on my machine, but I always welcome a little break. This big place gets lonely."

"That was quite a party last evening. We enjoyed it."

"My pleasure! Who would have thought that fate would bring you to me at the very moment I needed your services?" He led Nick into the study and opened a well-stocked liquor cabinet. "Is Scotch satisfactory?"

"Fine."

"What brings you here? Are there any complications?"

"Somewhat. The number of guards at the museum has been increased considerably since a recent string of thefts."

"That should present no problem to a man of your skill, Mr. Velvet."

"It doesn't, really." He accepted the drink and took a sip. It was good Scotch. Expensive. "But as you know, I never steal things of value, like cash or jewelry. Nor do I allow myself to be used as a decoy for such thefts."

Kincaid smiled indulgently. "But, Mr. Velvet, by the very nature of your chosen calling you invite people to take advantage of you. After all, what truly valueless object would be worth your fee of $20,000, even to an eccentric like myself?"

"Then you admit you haven't told me the whole truth?"

"What other explanation could there be?"

"Some jewels have already been stolen from that museum, and more are on exhibit now. You could be using me only to provide access or diversion while your own gang carried out the real theft."

"Gang, gang! Mr. Velvet, I'm a businessman, a publisher. I don't have any gang!"

"Then why do you really want the dinosaur's tail?"

Kincaid sighed and put down his drink. "Come with me, Mr. Velvet. I'm going to show you something very few people have ever seen."

Nick followed him across the study to a small door that might have led to a closet. Surprisingly, it opened to reveal a narrow staircase to the basement. In that moment, descending toward the unknown, Nick's first thought was of a velvet-lined chamber where Kincaid might act out the orgies of his pornographic books. Then he remembered a story he'd read as a boy—about a man who bred giant ants, and he wondered if some living creature from the distant past might be awaiting him in Frader Kincaid's basement.

The first thing he saw as Kincaid snapped on the lights did nothing to relieve his mind. Nick had paused only inches from the gaping jaws of a dinosaur's skull. He jerked back quickly and looked around. The entire basement work-room was filled with bones—skulls, ribs, shinbones, jawbones. They hung from the ceiling and they littered the rows of shelves that circled the room.

"What in hell is this?" Nick asked.

Frader Kincaid smiled at his reaction. "My hobby, my avocation. I told you last evening of my great interest in prehistoric creatures. Here I find a way to enjoy that interest and even make a little money out of it." He took down one of the jawbones and handed it to Nick. "This particular one is carved from wood and, as you see, highly polished. But I have others of molded plastic and even of bone. Bones made out of bone!"

"You *make* these? But what for?"

"I sell them to museums. A complete skeleton of a prehistoric reptile or mammal is very hard to come by. Many museums, especially the smaller ones, often possess only a few bones from a Mammoth or a Brontosaurus. They want to reconstruct a complete skeleton, and the only way to do it is to use a number of artificial bones. That's where I come in."

"Amazing," was all Nick could say.

"I can furnish a single bone or a dozen. Generally I go right to the museum and work on the skeleton myself, fitting the missing bones in place. They close off the room, and I do my work."

"Are there many New York museums that do this sort of thing?"

"All of them use reproductions in one form or another. I suppose the largest must be the giant blue whale at the American Museum of Natural History. Many people viewing it believe that it's stuffed, but actually it's a complete reproduction, carefully formed in every detail. I don't work on anything that complex, though. I stick to bones."

"And you need the tail of the Tyrannosaurus to serve as a model?"

"Of course! I must have it, and soon."

Nick Velvet sighed and avoided the gaping jaws. "All right," he said at last. "I'll steal it for you."

"I'd be most grateful," Kincaid said with a smile, and led the way upstairs.

Nick spent Tuesday morning checking out one more point, just to ease his mind. The Egyptian jewelry on display at the museum had little market value. It was not to be compared with the Pliny diamond and other stolen pieces. Nick now felt certain that he'd been wrong in suspecting another jewel robbery.

When the museum closed its doors at six o'clock, Nick was still inside. He'd already decided that the theft must take place after hours, despite the alarm system and the dogs. The daytime guards in all the rooms were obstacles he could not safely overcome. A quick test had shown him that they were quite professional and not the sort to be diverted by fire-crackers or an escaped mouse. Besides, Nick estimated he would need at least two or three minutes to cut through the wires that held the tail bones in place. So it had to be at night.

When the guard in the Egyptian Room turned away for an instant at the sound of the closing buzzer, Nick had simply stepped into one of the large upright sarcophagi against one wall and pulled the lid almost shut. The guard passed once, glancing around, but apparently assumed that Nick had left by the other exit. He flicked off the light switch and Nick was alone in his own dark tomb. The sarcophagus was far from comfortable, being a bit shorter than Nick's six feet, but he knew he would have to remain inside for at least an hour.

Through the crack in the lid he watched the dusky remains of daylight filter through the overhead skylight until the Egyptian Room settled into total darkness. Then at last it was night, and he slipped from his cramped hiding place to move silently through the darkened halls. It was easy to spot the electric eye alarms in each doorway, and just as easy to avoid them by bending very low. They would have trapped only the most amateur of thieves. He entered the Etruscan Wing and crossed the marble floor toward the Hall of Great Reptiles. So far, all was well.

Then he froze, hearing a guard's voice far off, echoing through the lonely building. It was answered by the barking of a dog. Nick listened and moved a bit faster.

Avoiding the electric eye at the entrance to the Hall of Great Reptiles, he made his way toward the enormous white skeleton in the center of the room. He took a moment to shine his narrow-beam flashlight at the walls, but there was nothing except the tall dusty display cases filled with fossils and petrified footprints from ages ago. He wondered why he'd done that and then realized there was something wrong. It was—what?—a feeling that he was not alone here?

He tensed his body, but no sound came. Then he allowed the flashlight to return to its target on the dinosaur's bony tail. He went under the rope and clamped the flashlight to his left wrist, leaving both hands free. As he had assumed, the individual bones were strongly wired together, but a few quick snips with his wire cutters should free them.

The ominous feeling came again, and this time he knew that someone else was in the room. He raised his left arm slightly, until the flashlight beam targeted a black-clad figure crouched like a cat some ten feet in front of him. Despite the black knit cap that covered her sandy hair, he had no trouble recognizing Lynn Peters.

"What in hell are you doing here?" he whispered harshly.

"The same thing as you," she said with a grin, sliding closer across the polished floor. "You hid somewhere after the place closed, so I did the same thing."

"But—you mean you've been following me?"

"Of course. You're the famous thief Nick Velvet, aren't you?"

"Where did you hide?" he asked, ignoring her question.

"In the Ladies' Room. The male guards never think to check it. I had this black outfit on under my raincoat, just in case. You're after the jewelry, aren't you?"

He shifted the light from her face and brought out his wire cutters. "No, I think that's your game. If you really knew anything about me, you'd know I don't steal anything valuable."

"But you're working for Kincaid," she insisted.

"I have what I want right here." He snipped away at the wires, carefully disengaging about fifteen inches of the tail section. The bones felt zero-cold in his hands.

Then suddenly they heard voices nearby, and the barking of a dog. "Come on," Nick snapped. "We've got to get out of here."

"What are you doing with those bones?"

"Stealing them." He grabbed her arm.

"But the jewelry—"

"No time for your jewels now. If those guard dogs catch our scent we're in trouble—big trouble."

He led her back through the Etruscan Wing, grasping her wrist with one hand and the dinosaur's tail with the other. The voices seemed farther off, and for a moment he relaxed, certain they were going to make it.

"Duck under here," he warned. "It's an electric eye."

She ducked, but not low enough. Instantly a clanging alarm bell shattered the silence. "Damn!"

"I'm sorry."

He tugged her and broke into a run. "A fine burglar you'd make!"

"I never pretended to be one."

"Then what in hell are you doing here?"

There were shouts and running footsteps now, and up ahead the lights were going on. "Nick, I'm scared!" she cried as the barking of the dogs sounded closer.

"You should be. Right now I'm scared myself."

They had reached the main hall of the museum, and the front exit was only a hundred feet away. But already they could see the guards converging. Someone spotted them, shouted to the others.

"Run!" Nick told her.

Their running footsteps echoed on the polished marble as they retreated toward the Egyptian Room. He remembered the mummy cases, but knew the dogs would sniff them out in a minute.

"There's no way out, Nick."

Ahead, appearing suddenly like some hound of hell, a large German shepherd blocked their path. Nick reversed direction, dragging Lynn with him.

"I—I can't—"

The dog started after them, so close they could hear its panting as it ran. "I know just how Sir Henry Baskerville must have felt," Nick gasped.

"We can't make it," Lynn moaned.

Nick slid to a sudden stop and pulled a handful of capsules from his pocket. The dog was only twenty feet away, coming fast, as Nick hurled the capsules to the floor, breaking them.

"What's that?" Lynn asked.

The dog slowed its charge, turning its nose to the floor. "Come on! That'll only divert him for a minute or two."

"But what—?"

"It's a chemical that looks like blood and has a strong meat scent. Fishermen use it to attract good catches. I thought it might distract the dogs for a minute if I got into a jam."

The German shepherd had paused, sniffing, but already it was losing interest in this new odor. It turned again toward them. "Now what, Nick? I can't run any more."

"There they are!" a guard shouted from the corridor ahead of them.

Nick sighed and braced himself. "Through the window. It's our only chance."

"The window!"

"We're on the first floor. It's no worse than falling off a horse."

Ten minutes later, bruised, cut, and out of breath, they sat in the front seat of Nick's car as he pursued a winding route through upper Manhattan.

"Do you always cut things that close?" she asked him.

He tried a relaxed smile, and it didn't feel bad at all. There was a glass cut along one cheek, but it wasn't deep. "Not usually. I hadn't counted on your being there. What about your car?"

"I parked it a few blocks away, just in case. But they'll find my raincoat in the Ladies' Room."

"Any identification in it?"

"No." She grinned at a sudden thought. "My, won't they be surprised when they discover the only thing missing is the dinosaur's tail!"

"Sorry you didn't have time for the jewels."

"Look, Nick—Mr. Velvet—I was only there because you were. I thought Kincaid hired you to steal that jewelry."

He took one hand from the steering wheel to rub a bruise on his arm. "But why would you care anyway, unless you were after the jewelry yourself?"

"Those things aren't worth much in the open market, but the diamonds that were already stolen are worth a fortune. There's a $5,000 reward for the Pliny diamond alone, and I mean to collect it."

"You mean you're—?"

She nodded. "Not a lapidarist at all, but an insurance investigator. Sorry to disappoint you."

"But what about the horses and the jumping?"

"I joined the group recently, to get close to Kincaid. I'm not much of a horsewoman—that's why I fell on Sunday. You see, Kincaid was doing some work at the museum the same day the Pliny diamond was stolen. The insurance companies are suspicious of him."

"He makes bones," Nick explained. "For dinosaurs. That's what he was doing at the museum."

"Maybe that's just a cover."

Nick ran his fingers over the length of tail bone at his side. "We'll find out soon enough. We're going to Kincaid's place."

The lights were still burning when they reached the house on the hill, and Kincaid greeted them at the door. He couldn't quite mask his surprise, though, at seeing Lynn. "Well, hello. I thought you two barely knew each other."

"We've gotten friendly," Lynn explained. "We've been through a lot together."

But Kincaid's eyes were on the length of wired bone that Nick carried in his left hand. "You did it! You stole the Tyrannosaurus tail!"

"I did it," Nick agreed.

"Splendid, splendid! This calls for a drink while I get you the rest of your money."

Nick accepted the bundle of bills and stuffed it into his pocket without counting. By now he was used to payments in cash, and it felt like the right amount. "I should tell you that Miss Peters here is an insurance investigator. If you're wise, you won't carry out your scheme to recover the Pliny diamond."

Kincaid's face went white. "What are you talking about?"

Nick saw that Lynn was listening intently, so he hurried on. "You do work for the museum. Surely they would have allowed you to take a plaster cast of the tail bones for your models. No, Mr. Kincaid, you didn't pay me $20,000 because you wanted to have the tail, but rather because you wanted the museum *not* to have it. I asked myself what they'd do without this tail segment, and the answer was obvious. They'd hire you to replace it with a reproduction."

Kincaid lowered his eyes. "You're right. I needed the work."

"Enough to pay me $20,000 so you could get a job worth maybe a few hundred? I think not. But you were working in the museum on the day the Pliny diamond was stolen. And that started me thinking. You said yourself that when you fitted an artificial bone they usually closed off that room of the museum while you did your work. That means, at least for a brief period, the guard would probably be removed—or he wouldn't be watching you too closely. The jewelry at the museum now isn't worth your trouble, but suppose the Pliny never left the building. Suppose you simply broke the display case, removed the Pliny and hid it somewhere. Somewhere, say, in the Hall of Great Reptiles."

"That's crazy!"

"Is it? You couldn't risk carrying it out of the building on your person with alarm bells ringing all around, but you could hide and return for it later—a week or a month later, if necessary. But what happened after the Pliny diamond was stolen? The museum tightened its security by placing a guard in every room. The Pliny was still there, safer now than ever, except that the museum didn't know it."

"Of course!" Lynn Peters breathed at his side. "That would explain everything."

Nick nodded. "It would certainly explain why you were so pleased to see me on Sunday, Kincaid. You knew I couldn't be hired to steal the diamond for you, but if I could steal part of the dinosaur, the museum would ask you to come down and fix it. Alone in that room you could retrieve the Pliny from its hiding place."

"You'll never convince anyone of that story, Velvet."

"I've convinced Miss Peters already, and I'm sure she'll be able to convince the museum officials. You were growing nervous and wanted me to steal the tail soon, which means the hiding place isn't too safe. I think a search of the room will turn it up quickly."

Kincaid bit his lip and looked from one to the other. "I have money. I'll pay you both well."

"I already have my pay from you," Nick said.

"A deal?"

"That's up to Miss Peters now. But if you tell us exactly where the Pliny is, I think she'd allow you enough time to catch a morning flight to South America."

"South—"

"They must read dirty books down there, too. You could start a whole new life."

Kincaid made a sudden motion toward the desk, but Nick stopped him. "No guns, please. Nothing like that."

"Where's the Pliny?" Lynn demanded.

He stared at the carpeted floor for a long moment before he answered. Then he said, so softly that they could hardly hear, "On top of one of those tall display cases along the wall. I just threw it up there. The cases are so dusty I knew they were rarely cleaned or even examined."

They left him in his house on the hill, and as they drove away Lynn asked, "Is your work always this much fun?"

"Sometimes. When there's somebody like you along."

"What are you thinking about right now?"

He turned to her and grinned. "You know, in a sense that damned dinosaur had a jeweled tail after all."

LAWRENCE TREAT

R As in Rookie

A
ll they had, there on the Homicide Squad, was what some kid said he'd heard from over on the other side of a fence. And the kid, he was just a scrawny, scared little thirteen-year-old with a runny nose and a rip in his shirt, and he was standing all alone in the squad room and just about managing to keep the tears back. And blurting out the same thing over and over again.

"What he said was, 'See that cat? I'm gonna kill him dead.' Then somebody else said what for, and the first guy, he said, 'Because I don't like his puss.' Then I heard a shot, so I beat it."

"What about the guy that got shot? Didn't he say anything? Didn't he even yell?"

"I didn't hear nothing," the kid said. Which figured, on account the victim was a mute. They called him Dummy, down in the dock section. Still, can you believe what a thirteen-year-old kid says?

Lieutenant Decker did, and that was good enough for Mitch Taylor and the rest of the Homicide Squad.

Still, with no other evidence, no other witnesses, no other anything, where were you? Everybody on the block had cotton in their ears or closed their windows and went to the backs of their apartments or else flew off into space somewhere so they wouldn't be home and hear anything that could help the cops. Which was the way things were there.

In the old days when there was river traffic, that part of town had been in the warehouse section where the carts and the trucks used to load up. They said it was prosperous then, but Mitch Taylor wouldn't know about that. What he saw was a bunch of run-down firetraps which for the past ten years they said they were going to tear down for urban renewal, except the money got lost somewhere in the city administration. So the dope pushers and the rats took over, and if there was a couple of homicides every couple of months, who cared?

There was no pressure on the Homicide Squad for this one. Lieutenant Bill Decker could forget about it if he wanted to, and leave it out of his reports; the

458

Commissioner would thank him in private for maybe helping keep down the statistics.

Only the boss wasn't that kind. To him a homicide was a homicide no matter where or who, and this one, that nobody else gave a damn about, was the same as all the others. And maybe a lot worse. Just killing a guy for no reason at all, for Pete's sake!

Still, two weeks went by and nothing happened, except Mitch got saddled with this blue-eyed, curly-haired, pink-eared rookie with a college diploma. You see, Decker had a new theory buzzing around in his head that police work ought to be a regular profession and you ought to study it in college, with special courses and even a special degree. Once you had all that under your hat, Decker claimed, you could learn the rest of it in a few months, and this kid was the experiment, and Mitch was supposed to make a real cop out of him.

The boss told Mitch to take him in tow and show him which way the wheels turned round. The kid—his name was Richard Sutton, only Mitch and everybody else called him Dicky-Boy. It seemed he was up on police administration and traffic control and lab stuff, but he'd skipped all the other police courses on account he hadn't made up his mind to be a cop until his last year in college. Decker hadn't picked him—he'd left that up to the college. So they'd come up with Dicky-Boy, and here he was.

Mitch knew pretty much what the boss was after, and Mitch felt like a father and Dicky-Boy could have been his son. Like Mitch said to Amy, maybe some day he'd be doing the same thing for Joey. Which made Amy smile, because she had other ideas for Joey. In her mind Joey was a born lawyer, and once he got to law school he'd knuckle down and those low marks of his would be gone like an ice cube in hot tea. And that's a mother for you.

Anyhow, Mitch and Dicky-Boy hit it off pretty good, except maybe at the start when Dicky-Boy called him "sir." And that kind of riled Mitch.

"Can it," he said. "The only time a cop says 'sir' is to the big brass, like the Commissioner. And while you say it out loud, what you call him to yourself is something else again. Got it?"

The kid nodded. "I guess so, except the way I was brought up—"

"That," Mitch said, "is what you're here to forget."

"I'll try," Dicky-Boy said. "I guess I have a lot to learn."

Mitch agreed.

They were tooling along real slow, with Mitch at the wheel of the patrol car and going nowheres in particular. He was kind of pointing out stuff that could be useful to the rookie, like the joint where they fenced jewelry or where some of the gangs hung out and where the boundaries were between the different political territories, so you knew whom to arrest and whom to lay off. Things like that, they ought to give the kid the feel of the place.

"What I'm going to tell you now," Mitch said, and he meant every word, "is the most important lesson you're ever going to learn, and it's this: the first thing you got to do is stay alive. Don't stick your neck out, don't take chances, don't try and be a hero. Just get along with the squad and make friends with the guys in the Records Bureau and Motor Vehicles and all the rest of them. Because you can't do nothing alone."

The kid barely missed out saying "sir," but he stopped in time. "And stoolies," he said. "I guess you need them."

"You build up a few contacts after a while," Mitch said offhand. "Now you see that guy over there? The guy with the green hat?"

"What about him?" Dicky-Boy asked.

"Name of Gosse," Mitch said. "Ernie Gosse. He's a pusher, and he'll give me a tip once in a while for letting him alone."

"You *let* him sell dope?"

"Nothing I can do about it," Mitch said. "That's up to the Narcotics Squad, and you don't want to step on *their* toes. I know he's selling the stuff, but that don't mean I got any evidence. But he thinks I could turn him in, so he calls me any time he hears something he thinks I'm interested in."

"Don't you ever see him?"

"See him?" Mitch said. "Look—if I stopped now and said hello to him, he'd be dead tomorrow."

"Shot?"

"Hell no! They don't shoot people in the narcotics racket. They all use the stuff, which is cut down with sugar and milk, so when you want to get rid of one you go and give them a hot shot. Pure H, that is. They don't know the difference when they take it, and next day they're found dead from an overdose, and what can we prove? Nothing. All this talk you hear about 'the perfect crime'—they pull one off practically every day, and there's not a thing we can do about it."

Dicky-Boy swallowed hard and concentrated, like he'd got it straight out of the barrel bung and wanted to memorize what he'd just learned. No addict ever gets shot, he just gets an overdose.

So that night Gosse went and got killed. By a bullet. Making a liar out of Mitch.

The Lieutenant had been out to the scene of the crime, along with a couple of the boys. Jub Freeman, up in the lab, had been working on ballistics and the rest of the physical evidence, with an assist from Dicky-Boy. So in the morning, when the guys sat down in the squad room, the Lieutenant briefed them.

He didn't have much to tell. Gosse had been in the dock area on his way home; he was a couple of blocks from where he lived when a black car, going kind of slow, came down the street. When it got alongside Gosse, somebody stuck a gun out of the window and let fly. Four shots, with the first three of them missing, and that was about it, except they found Gosse with a gun in his hand that he'd never had the chance to fire.

Mitch kept looking at Dicky-Boy. The rookie read a lot of books, but this was his first swing around the carousel and he just sat there without trying to grab any brass rings. But Mitch could tell the kid had lost faith in him and probably wouldn't believe another thing Mitch ever said, unless Mitch somehow picked up the ball and started pitching strikes. Which Mitch did.

"This Ernie Gosse," he said, "He was in my cheering section and I know this much about him—he was a pusher and nothing else. A strict organization man, but in none of the rackets. If they wanted to get rid of him they'd give him a hot shot, like I explained to you; so when he's gunned down it's on account of a private war, like maybe if he's been playing around with somebody else's wife.

The squad pretty much went along with that, which saved Mitch as far as Dicky-Boy went. Then Balenkey, balancing on a chair near the wall, came up with a new idea.

"What kind of a guy misses three times at short range, and then drills his man on the fourth shot? If you ask me, those first three shots were meant to scare Gosse, that's all. But when Dummy pulled a gun, then they pinked him for real. Without he pulled a gun, that car would have gone on and Gosse would still be around. So the thing is, what did they want to scare him out of telling?"

Nobody knew, so that about wrapped it up and the boss started handing out assignments. On account Mitch had known Gosse, Mitch was elected Number One in the pecking order, which meant he was the one to go see the widow and find out what he could. For the rest, Mitch would check with Decker on anything that came up.

Mitch took Dicky-Boy along. Out in the courtyard Mitch got his regular car, Number Four, and he drove, and on the way to the dock area he explained things to the kid.

"They don't like cops where we're going," Mitch warned. "We ought to be okay, but you never know. Some hophead can always go haywire, so stay a couple steps behind me and keep your eyes open. Don't take your gun out, but make sure you can get hold of it fast, just in case."

"You can count on me," Dicky-Boy said, like the fate of the world was in his hands and he wanted to measure up.

"Yeah," Mitch said. "Now get this, and a lot of rookies been killed because they wanted to be brave or something. So don't take any chances. If you think a guy's armed, take your gun out first, but if he has the draw on you, take a dive. And whenever you do have to shoot, shoot to kill. There's more cops been cut down by wounded men than any other way."

"I'm a pretty good shot," Dicky-Boy said.

"Yeah," Mitch said. "Well, I guess we're about there."

He parked in front of Gosse's building, which Mitch didn't particularly like doing. But he reported where he was and where he was going, and then he locked the car. Like he explained to Dicky-Boy, they'd obeyed regulations and so they had no further responsibility for the car.

"You want to know the rule book," Mitch said, "because if you use it right, you can make it work your side of the street. You just got to know where they put the heavy print."

"I'll remember that," Dicky-Boy said.

Then they went into the downstairs hall and Mitch found the Gosse bell and pushed it. The buzzer answered right off and Mitch and Dicky-Boy went on up. Dicky-Boy was a couple of steps behind and he held one hand inside his jacket, and anybody around who happened to look could tell right off he was hanging onto his gun and was nervous and probably hadn't been a cop for more than a couple of weeks.

None of which bothered Mitch, particularly. What got him, though, was all the smells, which started off with garlic and tomato paste, and then a little stale coffee with some dead mice thrown in. So Mitch was plenty glad he didn't have to go up more than those two flights.

The female who opened the door, she was Mrs. Gosse and she had a complexion like wrapping paper and she'd been crying. Even if she hadn't been, she looked like she'd been sat on a long time ago and never got up, so Mitch figured he was right about Gosse maybe running around with somebody else.

She took one look at Mitch and tried to slam the door in his face.

"No want you here," she said. "No want police."

"Ernie was a friend of mine," Mitch said, lowering his voice like he was telling her a secret. "He told you about me, didn't he?"

"Police!" she said, almost spitting.

"Ernie and me, we got along," Mitch said quietly. "So I want to help out."

"How you help?"

"I'll find out who did this, then tip you off. Like Ernie would want me to."

"You stand there," the Gosse female said, "and everybody hear what you say."

Which was maybe an invitation, or maybe she was scared that somebody would hear what Mitch was saying and figure out Ernie had been a stoolie. Anyhow, Mitch stepped inside, with Dicky-Boy and his gun right behind him.

The room had some fancy chairs and some photographs of guys dressed up in store clothes and looking unhappy, and some carved wooden figures of saints. The Gosse female didn't sit down.

"You know," Mitch said, friendly-like, "the last time I saw Ernie he said you were a good wife and if anything ever happened to him, would I take care of you. So here I am."

"He hate police," she said coldly.

"He hated the Narcotics Squad," Mitch said, "but me, I'm Homicide. Big difference. So, like I started to say, I want to find out things. To help you. And Ernie."

"I no know why he was killed," she said. "He was good man, he give people what they want. Not his fault they want—you know what."

"Yeah," Mitch said, still real friendly. "Ernie was all right."

"His customers, they all his friends. They like him, they depend on him. All he want was money for his family, and so he can sit home and carve. Look." She pointed to the wooden saints. "He make those. He make them fine."

"He was a real artist," Mitch said respectfully. "Now about this little fight you and him had—"

"What fight?" she asked, interrupting.

"That dame. He told me she was trouble and—"

"Liar!" Marie Gosse said sharply. "Liar-cop."

Mitch stared her down. "He wouldn't want you to call me that. Not me. Not to a friend of his."

"He no have other girl," she said angrily and proudly. "My husband a good man, we love plenty."

"Sure," Mitch said. "Now you want to get hold of the guy who did this to him, don't you? So I need your help."

She moved back like she didn't know how to handle him. Then, kind of shooing him out like a kid she couldn't get rid of without she gave him a piece of candy, she grabbed one of the wooden statues and stuck it in his hand.

"You want?" she said. "You take and you go."

Mitch nodded, accepted the statue, and holding it in front of him he went out and down the stairs.

The car was still where he'd left it. There were no new dents on it and nobody'd even spat on it; so Mitch unlocked it, picked up the two-way radio, buzzed the dispatcher, and reported back. Then Mitch put the phone down, stuck the key in the ignition, and leaned back.

"What do you think of this thing?" he said, indicating the carved saint.

"Pretty bad," Dicky-Boy said. "Did you really like the guy?"

"Him?" Mitch said, kind of shocked. "He hung around the high school and tried to drum up trade. He hooked more kids than anybody else around. That was his specialty."

"But you told his widow he was all right."

"When you want information," Mitch said, "you have to kind of butter people up, and sometimes you learn things and sometimes you don't."

"But she didn't tell us anything."

"Think so?" Mitch said. "She told us a lot. The way she said they'd loved plenty and then she gave me this piece of junk—that means there was no other dame. If there had been she'd of got sore and stayed sore." Mitch turned on the ignition and started the car. "Well, I guess there's not much we can do for a day or two, except wait for the funeral. We might find out something there."

For the next couple of days the investigation kept going. The Narcotics Squad tried to find out who had a reason for rubbing out Ernie Gosse. The local precinct cops went around trying to locate somebody who'd witnessed the shooting. The Homicide Squad questioned Gosse's friends; Jub Freeman up in the lab analyzed bullets; and the Medical Examiner did an autopsy and came up with a long technical report that nobody understood except himself.

Meanwhile Mitch kept riding around town and instructing Dicky-Boy on how to be patient and expect nothing to happen until the funeral. At which time you couldn't expect much, either.

"We gotta be there," Mitch said, "that's all. There's a chance the killer will show, and there's a chance somebody's going to try and pick a fight with us. If they do, cool it. It might be the killer, and it might be just somebody that doesn't like cops. But the thing is, stay out of trouble."

"But it's our case!" Dicky-Boy said. "We have to solve it."

"Nuts," Mitch said. "We just hang around. That's what you got to learn—how to hang around without really doing anything."

Dicky-Boy looked puzzled.

Still, he couldn't have done better at the funeral. He stood there looking like a cop and proud of it, looking like he was after somebody and nothing could stop him. And that stance of his, it made everybody so uncomfortable that Mitch wandered around and nobody noticed him. Which was how he happened to pick up a couple of scraps of conversation.

There was, for instance, the old uncle who wanted to know where Ramon was, and then a little later on Mitch heard somebody else say pretty much the same thing. So Mitch went up to some dame—he didn't know who she was, but she looked like she'd been left out of the party. She was maybe a relative who lived at the other end of town and wasn't wised up to what had really happened. So Mitch asked her where Ramon was.

She kind of stared like she didn't know Mitch was a cop and she was trying to place him. "You mean Ramon Gebba?" she said. Mitch nodded, and then she had sense enough to shut up. But he had what he wanted. Ramon Gebba had either shot Gosse, or knew something about who had.

You get a name like that and then you and the rest of the Homicide Squad pour it on. You go around asking where Ramon Gebba went, and either you're going to find him or you're going to scare him so that things begin to happen. Which maybe had something to do with the shooting the next day.

It was around three in the afternoon, and Mitch and Dicky-Boy were cruising out in the West Hills section. Mitch wanted to show the kid that junk yard where you might pick up stuff that would help out on a hit-and-run accident, like one that happened last night.

"Whoever it was," Mitch said, "He busted a headlight and he's gotta buy a new one. But he don't want to go anywheres that would report the sale, so what's left? Junk yards. And this place is the biggest. We ask the guy there if anybody bought a headlight, and if so, what he looked like, and so on. If nobody did, then we kind of look around anyhow and see what we can see."

That was when the radio phone buzzed. Dicky-Boy picked it up and it was the dispatcher calling Car Four and telling him to proceed to an address in the dock area where there's been a shooting. So Mitch backed around, and it was one of the few times he used his siren. And when he turned it on he could see Dicky-Boy's eyes light up. This was what he'd dreamed about all his life, going hell-bent with the siren blaring and on his way to the scene of a crime.

A couple of precinct cops and the precinct lieutenant were waiting there, and so was Bankhart who'd been sort of in the neighborhood, but Mitch and Dicky-Boy were the next arrivals. They found out that a car had come down the street, slowed up in front of Number 476, fired about five shots, and then beat it. The shots had busted a couple of windows and made a broken line in the plaster wall of a room that had nothing in it except a mattress propped up on an old bedstead and covered with a torn Turkish rug.

The people in the building, naturally they'd seen nothing. They didn't know who'd occupied the room—they'd never seen anybody go into it or come out of it, they said. They'd been deaf and blind, which was pretty much what you expected around here. And while Mitch didn't have any real ideas, he figured it didn't hurt to pretend he knew that Ramon Gebba was behind this or connected with it.

The main trouble was, Mitch didn't know whether to guess that this Ramon had fired the shots or been fired at, so he had to ask his questions real cagey. He asked stuff like which way had Ramon gone, or else he said Ramon wasn't going to get away with it, and where was he? You ask enough questions like that, and pretty soon somebody tells you something. But not this time.

Mitch was kind of up in the air, not getting anywheres, but neither was anybody else. They couldn't even find the janitor, name of Ned Byrne, and that gave Mitch an idea.

"Let's go down to the boiler room," Mitch said to Dicky-Boy, "and look around."

There Mitch took a gander and pointed out a few violations—like the trash piled up over in one corner, and the way the furnace was gummed up with soot and then a stuck valve on one of the steampipes, and finally you added in a few leaks—you could always find one or two. All of which he noted on his pad.

"A case like this," he said, "sometimes you got to play the angles. You take a couple of violations, you build them up, and you maybe got something on this Byrne guy. The next thing we got to do is find him."

"Where?"

"Around here," Mitch said, "every janitor's got himself a racket. It's maybe policy or maybe horses, something like that. You just got to look around a little, so let's you and me try a couple of neighborhood bars. We'll track him down easy."

In the second bar they tackled, Mitch spotted this flat-haired guy sitting on a stool at one end of the bar. He had a beer mug in front of him and two or three guys were listening to what he was saying, which was probably all about the shooting. Only when Mitch and Dicky-Boy came in, the guy clammed up, along with everybody else in the joint.

Mitch just said, "Byrne. Ned Byrne." Flat-Hair looked up, started to answer and didn't, which made him Ned Byrne, and so Mitch walked up to him.

"You and me," Mitch said, "we're going to have a little private talk. How about in back, huh?"

Mitch and Dicky-Boy followed Byrne to a table in the rear room, where Mitch sat down. But on the way he could tell from the low whispering that the guys here in the bar were expecting something. Which meant Mitch was hot, and he'd better watch out. But the thing was, how do you tip off Dicky-Boy without giving away that you heard the warning bell in your head?

It looked like there was nothing much Mitch could do right off, so he started by taking out his identification. "I got a couple of questions about that shooting," Mitch said.

Byrne said what Mitch expected him to. "What shooting?"

"Better not horse around," Mitch said. "I got a bunch of violations at your place a yard long. They're your personal responsibility and I'm going to push them if I have to." He took out his pad. "Trash in the southwest corner, violation of Fire Department Regulation 187. Too much soot in the furnace, violation of pollution code of the Sanitation Department. Leaky steampipe, violation of Building Code. You know what the penalties are?"

"What do you want from me?"

"Who rented Apartment 1-C, into which the shots were fired?"

"Party by the name of Fesco. Rick Fesco."

"How long ago did he rent it?"

"About two weeks ago."

"Who lived with him?"

"Nobody. He was kind of holed up there."

"You mean he stayed there without going out?"

"Pretty much. I brought him his food, mostly."

"Okay," Mitch said. "Now where'll I find him?"

Byrne blinked, and Mitch could tell it was one of those times when somebody wants to tell you something, only they're scared. With the guys back there in the bar, if Byrne talked to a cop and gave out with anything, he'd be through and they wouldn't even let him in here for a drink. So Mitch was racking his brains how he could save face for Byrne and at the same time get him to talk.

Then Byrne said, "Don't one of you guys have to go to the Men's Room?" Which, as far as Mitch was concerned, was telling him where this Fesco was.

Mitch took out his pad and wrote down, "Watch yourself." Then he handed the note to Dicky-Boy and said, "Maybe you better go in there, huh?"

For the first time it looked like Dicky-Boy was learning, on account there was hope for him in the way he stood up like he was bored with the conversation and the hell with it. Then he crossed over and went into the Men's Room, and the guy he came out with was Gosse. Or at least that's what Mitch thought, first off. Then he realized it was somebody else. Still, the easiest thing in the world was to mistake one of them for the other.

He said to Byrne, "Beat it." Then to the guy that looked like Gosse he said, "Sit down. Who are you?"

"Fesco."

"Sit down," Mitch said again, and Fesco did. "What's your real name?" Mitch said. "You Ernie's brother?"

"Me?" Fesco said. "Naah, he was my half brother."

"He got shot by mistake," Mitch said, guessing but pretty sure it was a good guess. "Ramon wanted to scare you and he shot at Gosse thinking it was you. When Gosse reached for a gun, Ramon killed him, but Ramon still had to throw a scare into you, which is what he did this afternoon. Okay, but what for?"

"You got it all wrong," Fesco said.

Mitch shook his head. "Why did he do it?" he said. "What have you got on Ramon?"

"Nothing. Not a thing."

It was the same business as with Byrne, and it was up to Mitch to find a way of getting Fesco's information without the guys in the bar catching on that Fesco was giving anything away. So Mitch leaned forward and spoke in a low voice.

"Look," he said. "If I let you go, you're a dead duck, because Ramon will figure either you squealed or you'll squeal next time we talk to you. He won't take a chance on you, and you know it, so why don't I put the bracelets on you and take you to a nice safe place? Then it will look like you didn't talk, so I had to bring you in. And we'll keep you under wraps until we get hold of Ramon. How about it?"

Fesco didn't say anything. He just held out his wrists and waited for the handcuffs to get snapped on. And Mitch, wanting to tell Dicky-Boy what a dope Fesco was, said, "Dummy, huh?"

Fesco, with his arms still out, kind of jerked in surprise. "Dummy," he said. "That's right. I was with Ramon when he shot Dummy, only how'd you know?"

"Easy," Mitch said, without even blinking. Then he saw the guy in the doorway and he yelled, "Duck!"

It had to be Ramon standing there. He fired, and Fesco's head got almost slapped off his neck and he went spinning around and dropped off the chair. Mitch moved with the shot and made a dive for the corner of the room and the protection of a table, where he went rolling over. And kept rolling until he was behind a screen. While it wouldn't stop any bullets, Ramon couldn't see him to take dead aim.

What Dicky-Boy did was what only a rookie cop would do. He yelled at Ramon, "Drop that gun!" Then Dicky-Boy pulled his own gun, and he stood up and waited to be obeyed, brave as hell and a perfect target. Which Mitch didn't know about until a few seconds later, after three shots that practically split his eardrums and after he poked his head out from behind the screen. He had his gun out by then and was ready to shoot, only there was nobody to shoot at any more. Because Dicky-Boy was lying there on the floor and Ramon had run out to the street, where half the Homicide Squad saw him and mowed him down in nothing flat. All of which was no help to Dicky-Boy.

Mitch put his arm around him. "You hurt?" Mitch said.

"I'm hurt bad," Dicky-Boy muttered. "I shot, but I shot too late and I aimed at his arm. Should have done what you told me to."

"Yeah," Mitch said. "You'll be okay. Next time—" Only Mitch knew there wasn't going to be any next time.

Amy heard about it over the radio, and she was quiet when Mitch came home. He didn't talk about it, either. He didn't feel much like talking about anything, and the kids, Mamie and Joey, they kind of sensed something and kept themselves out of his way. But Mitch kept looking at Joey. Eight years old and a good kid; sweet like kids are at that age, only he got bad marks at school. So what was he going to be when he grew up?

Not a cop. In a way it was like Mitch was being told that if Joey ever became a cop he'd be just like Dicky-Boy, he'd want to be brave. But as for being a lawyer, the way Amy wanted, Joey just didn't have the brains. So what was there?

Later on, just before Joey went to bed, Mitch sat the kid on his lap and started telling him a story. It was all about a parole officer; he was a nice kind of guy and he played on the parole-board baseball team, and he was a humdinger of a parole officer.

Joey's eyes sort of caught fire at that, and Mitch smiled and went on with the story. Being a parole officer wasn't bad; not as good maybe as being a detective, but not bad—not bad at all.

R. R. IRVINE

Lobster Shift

There are simple rules for survival. Keep your mouth shut, do what you're told, pay your union dues on time, and keep your canary-eating grins down to a minimum. That's what it takes to be a successful television newsman, because it's just like any other business: politics and bootlicking get you ahead. And that's why my big mouth landed me on the lobster shift Monday, May 25th.

The date is stamped on my mind. It was the first day of my exile from the living, and the beginning of my nightmare.

I had trudged into the newsroom thirty minutes early, right into the middle of a screaming match between our anchorman, Al Aarons—we called him AA because of his drinking—and the Eleven O'Clock News producer, Jerry Green.

"You idiot!" Aarons yelled, his anchorman's voice booming in the nearly deserted newsroom.

"You're drunk. You're drunk now and you were drunk on the air." Green turned to me as if I were a referee.

AA licked his lips and fired a slur of obscenity. His eyes glittered. On camera his glassy peepers gave him a kind of charisma.

"Go home and sleep it off," Green advised.

AA answered with more elaborate obscenities. Then, as if victorious, he lurched out of the newsroom. We could hear him stumbling down the hall, careening from wall to wall.

"I'm through," Green said. "I can't take any more of this, Jeff."

"You say that every time he gets drunk."

"I know." A twitch pulled at Green's pinched lips. "But one of these days he's going to pass out in front of the camera, and that will be the end of me."

"Of him, you mean," I consoled.

"You've been in this business long enough to know better than that."

Yeah, I said to myself, you've got ten years in the business, Jeff Simmons, and only the lobster shift to show for it.

"If he ever blows it on camera," Green continued, "I'll get blamed for letting him drink. I'll be the one to get canned. Aarons will end up with a raise."

I nodded. Like I said, it's politics and pretty faces in the television news business.

"Why don't you go out and get yourself a drink," I suggested. In a way that suggestion was responsible for everything that happened later.

Green tossed his stopwatch into the nearest drawer, slammed the drawer shut with a tinkle of crystal, then swore at the top of his voice, pitiful by comparison to AA's parting blast, but still formidable in the narrow confines of the newsroom. He sucked in a deep breath. "Jeff, you're right. I'm going to get out of here early. Do you mind if I leave without clearing the wires?"

"No. I'll take care of it. You get going."

"Thanks, Jeff." He forced a smile, then practically ran from the newsroom.

I sighed after him. Eight hours to go on the lobster shift, and about half a mile of teletype copy to pull for Jerry Green.

Of course, if he'd stayed I'd never have seen that first message. It had run at 11:23 P.M. Even at that I almost missed it. By the time I'd read through both United Press wires and the output from three Associated Press machines, the clatter of the wireroom had jangled my nerves and started a stabbing headache which turned me copy-blind.

I had just about decided to dump the National News Service copy and go down the hall for coffee and a couple of aspirins when my conscience caught up with me. I shrugged, clipped all twenty yards of the canary-yellow NNS paper, spun it into a tight roll, and carried it back to my already cluttered desk.

Since I had about a half hour of NNS ahead of me, I stocked up with two soggy cardboard cups of black coffee after swallowing the grimy aspirins I found loose in my pencil drawer.

Halfway through the second cup, with three feet of primary election analysis behind me, I ran across the first message.

HC
L548SR
IS FIRST STORY ACCEPTABLE? IF NOT, CONTACT SOONEST. URGENT
       M363FF

Not much at first glance, but the HC caught my attention. HC is National News Service code for our area, Los Angeles.

Ever since my big scoop last year ("What have you done lately?" Bud Murch, the news director, had asked when he sentenced me to the lobster shift) I always check the HCs closely. An innocent-looking HC had got me an exclusive interview, thirty seconds of 16-millimeter color film, with the Vice President between planes at International Airport.

So, with a deep sigh for past glories, I reread the HC URGENT, filed it in my head for future reference, and plowed on through the rest of the wire copy, soon rubbing my eyes with the full conviction that the coming California primary election was an obsession with NNS. They told me more, much more than I wanted to know about it. Besides, everyone knew the big race, the one for senator, was no contest. Bobby Lundon was a cinch for the nomination and better than even money to knock off the incumbent, Wild Bill Bronson, in the November runoff.

Even old AA, who doubled as our political editor, had sadly predicted an end to the Bronson machine and to the free booze that Bronson sent him every month. Bronson's administration had been hit hard by one scandal after another in the past year. Even so, Wild Bill was still popular, and nobody but Bobby Lundon could beat him.

The next day, Tuesday, the answer came in on my shift, at 12:20 A.M.

JN
M363FF
MONEY UNACCEPTABLE. STORY OFF IF NOT FORTHCOMING.
     L548SR

That snapped me to attention. JN was code for Las Vegas, and I always think of Vegas in terms of money.

In the news business it's rare to pay for a story. You only put out for the big ones—I mean the really big ones—and then only as a last resort.

So with a smile, figuring we were about to get a free ride on an NNS scoop, I left a note asking Jerry Green to save the early NNS copy for me. I sure as hell didn't want to miss the next message if it happened not to come through on my shift.

I spent the rest of the early hours Tuesday drinking coffee and trying to work on my novel—yes, The Great American Novel. But I kept wondering what kind of story NNS—known for its low pay and cheap attitude—would pay big money for. By the time my shift ended at eight o'clock, I had accomplished little if anything, but then the lobster man wasn't expected to do very much. Actually, he's only there in case of a big news story, like a plane crash. Then he calls a film crew and gets a pat on the back from the boss, the guy who assigned him to the lobster shift in the first place.

Some people never can adjust to lobster-shift hours. That's why they figure you'll end up quitting and save them the trouble of trying to fire you and maybe touch off a union grievance.

I'm too damned obstinate to quit, and smart enough to know all the lobster man really has to do is stay awake, weed through the wires for bulletins, and talk to every crank who calls in. It's a newsroom rule: always talk to the cranks— maybe you'll get a big story one day. But I've never known anyone to get anything that way.

Once, maybe twice a year, the lobster man earns his salary by getting film of a plane crash or some other equally visual disaster.

Friday morning at 4:22 I thought I had earned my keep for the year.

HC
L548SR
WE UP THE ANTE 10-THOUSAND
        M363FF

Now, that's big money. Too big to be anything short of exclusive rights to World War Three.

I wrote the transmission numbers down in my notebook, then decided I couldn't just sit there waiting for it to break. Without thinking it through I grabbed the phone and called the downtown office of NNS.

Their lobster man came on with a tired drinker's voice. "Williams, National News Service."

"This is Jeff Simmons at Channel Three."

"Good for you," he croaked. He rattled when he spoke, as though from a hundred cigarettes a day.

I plunged in. "I've been watching those messages between LA and Vegas and I'd like to know what's up?" As soon as the question came out I knew it was a mistake. Play it cool, I told myself.

"What messages?" He sounded annoyed.

"Hell, you're talking to a pro, you know." I lost my cool. "I'm talking about the messages offering ten thousand dollars for a story."

"You must be crazy. National wouldn't pay that kind of money for the Armageddon."

My cool boiled. "Look, I can read. What are you trying to pull?"

"Hey, you're serious, aren't you? Well, I still don't know what you're talking about."

"Look at your wire for 4:22. What do you see?" I asked.

"Just a minute." A chair scraped, accompanied by a tired grunt. A couple of minutes later he said, "It's probably about something else altogether. It doesn't say anything about money. Hell, for that matter it could even be a bet—though that's strictly against the rules—sent by one of our operators to someone in Vegas."

"Unh-unh. That message is from Vegas to LA."

"Yeah, you're right," he said. "Still, I'm just the night man. You'd better call the boss later this morning."

I agreed. It would just stir up the man's imagination to question him further. I hung up and thought about $10,000.

Since the weekend started for me at eight A.M., I typed a long note to Jerry Green outlining what I knew so far and suggesting that he contact the head of NNS. Maybe, as long as Channel Three was a paying subscriber to their news service, they would let us in on their scoop.

Jerry Green was waiting for me when I ambled into the newsroom at 12:05 Monday morning. He was perched on my desk like a quarrelsome towhee, his dangling feet thumping nervously against my typewriter stand.

"You're late," he announced.

"Either you're waiting for me," I quipped, "or you're twelve hours early for work."

"You and your big nose," he said.

"It's a nice nose," I said, fingering my snout lovingly.

"You should never stick it in where it belongs."

I grinned. "There's something wrong with the way you said that."

"I'm just quoting the law of survival in the news business."

"You're not that cynical," I said. "Not yet anyway."

"It's that story of yours. It's been bothering me all weekend. I kept dreaming about it."

"The messages, you mean?"

"Yes. National News Service claims there's nothing to them."

"What about the money?" I asked.

"They say it wasn't ten thousand dollars, but an order for a ten-thousand-word feature story on gambling in Las Vegas."

"Since when has a wire service run ten-thousand-word feature stories?"

Green waved his hands helplessly.

"Did you talk to the guy who sent the messages?" I said.

"No. I never got past the editor. Besides, how would I know who sent them?"

"Each teletype operator has a code number he signs his transmissions with."

"That's right. I'd forgotten about that," Green said. He shook his head in self-disgust.

I still couldn't figure why he'd come in to see me in the middle of the night. "Is that all you got, Jerry?"

He nodded. "That's it, Jeff."

"Why this special visit then? You could have left me a note."

Green's loud sigh ended in a shrug. "I don't know. I just don't trust NNS. I never have."

I studied Green's pinched face. The hair on the back of my neck prickled to attention; instinct means survival in the news business. With a palms-up gesture I urged him to continue.

"I don't like the way they're handling the election for one thing," Green said.

"What do you mean, Jerry?"

"Hell, you know as well as I do that they're slanting everything against Bobby Lundon. They're backing Bronson."

"I hadn't noticed they were slanting it."

"Bronson's chief aide is a major stockholder in NNS, has been for the past year or so. I thought you knew that."

"No." I shook my head. "Still—"

"Don't take my word for it," Green snapped. "Read the wires for yourself tonight and see what I mean."

It was my turn to sigh. "Okay."

He hopped down from his perch. "I'm going home and try to get some sleep. I hope I don't dream about you and your story again." He started down the hall, then came back. "Hey, Jeff, leave me a note if you get anything more on this, will you?" He waved goodbye a second time.

I hung up my coat, stalled over a cup of tepid coffee, groaning out loud when I thought of what was ahead of me that morning. I wasn't disappointed either. The wire services had produced a good hundred yards of copy in honor of election eve—everything from personal portraits, including the inevitable family dog, to complete election schedules for the candidates. Bronson was headquartered at the Hilton; Lundon had chosen the less pretentious Sheraton.

When I finally reached the NNS copy I saw what Jerry Green had been talking about. The stories about Bronson used phrases like, "Bronson declared," "Bronson stated firmly," or "Bronson affirmed," while the Lundon copy read, "Lundon alleged" or "Lundon claimed." It was too subtle to influence an election, but it galled me just the same.

As I was about to dump NNS in the circular file, I spotted a byline by an old friend, Irv Scott, who had worked with me on my first newspaper. I called him at home at 4:30 in the morning.

"Who," I asked him when he had calmed down, "is M363FF in Las Vegas and who is L548SR in Los Angeles?"

"You mean you want to know tonight?" he asked.

"Sure. It's morning already and I'm at work."

A stream of obscenities cleared the wax out of my ear. "I'll call you back," he grumbled finally.

At 4:55 I found another message.

HC
L548SR
HALF PAYMENT IN ADVANCE NOW AT PRE-ARRANGED LOCA-
TION. REMAINDER UPON COMPLETION. SUGGEST SHERATON LO-
CATION.
            M363FF

Five minutes later Irv Scott called back.

"What's all this about?" he asked, now fully awake.

I leveled with him.

"That's strange," he said. "We don't have any operators with those code numbers."

"Are you sure, Irv?"

"Well, I talked to our night man and he checked the transmission list. Half the stuff is run through a computer these days. Maybe it was just a mispunched number."

"Probably," I said. It had to be a very big story, I thought, if they weren't even letting their own people in on it. "Hell, maybe I got the numbers wrong," I lied. There didn't seem to be any reason to drag Scott in any further.

"Are you telling me everything?" Scott's voice sounded guarded.

"Yeah. You know as much as I do."

"Well, keep in touch," he said.

Forty minutes later the final message came through.

JN
M363FF
SHERATON IDEAL. THIS WILL BE LAST TRANSMISSION. SEND
FINAL PAYMENT UPON COMPLETION.
      L548SR

I stapled the last two messages together and left them in Jerry Green's mailbox.

When I walked into the newsroom shortly before midnight the next day, people were crammed everywhere. Channel Three's live election coverage was in full swing and would continue right up until the results were official.

I poked in my cluttered mailbox and found a message from Irv Scott. He'd got the break of a lifetime and had been transferred to the NNS bureau in Washington, D.C. But I didn't have time to think about what I was reading then. The newsroom's organized insanity blotted out everything else.

Jerry Green, surrounded by writers and copy boys who shuffled nervously waiting to run bulletins from the newsroom to the broadcast studio, waved me over. Every telephone was in use; everyone seemed to be yelling at once. Jerry and I conversed at a shout.

"You get anything else?" he asked.

"I think more than I bargained for," I murmured.

"What?" he yelled.

"No, nothing," I said. "But I plan to do some more checking when things quiet down around here." My eyes swept around the frenzied newsroom.

"We'll be out of your way pretty soon. Lundon's got it locked up. His victory speech is due in about ten minutes."

I nodded and then strolled over to an empty desk in the corner. The lobster man never has much to do election night, just clean up the mess after everyone else has gone home.

Feet up, coffee at my elbow, I settled back to watch the bank of big color-TV sets, each monitoring one of our competitors. The volume on Channel Three had been cranked wide open. You couldn't actually hear the words, but you could get the drift of things.

Lundon was on his way to the podium to accept the nomination.

I didn't really hear the shot, but I could tell something was wrong immediately. On the screen people moved wildly and screamed. In the newsroom there was stunned silence as veterans and copy boys alike gaped at the row of flickering screens; each showed Lundon close-up, slumped over the podium, blood spilling from his ear.

Over the picture Al Aarons' voice wavered: "The scene at the Sheraton is total chaos—"

The word screamed in my brain, echoing: "SHERATON . . . SHERATON."

The messages on NNS had been arrangements for an assassination. But I had been too stupid to see it. You're nuts, I told myself. Still, phones can be tapped, letters opened, conversations overheard. The safest way just might be right out in the open where no one would pay any attention to them—no one, that is, but a disgruntled lobster man looking for a way to get back on the day shift.

I squinted across the newsroom, now just beginning to come back to life, and caught Green's eye. His lips were pressed into a grim white line, his head canted to one side. He, too, had guessed the meaning of the messages.

I didn't have time to talk with him until eight o'clock that morning. By then Lundon was dead and a single suspect was in custody. The press knew nothing about the suspect yet, not even his name.

Jerry Green and I knew he was part of a conspiracy.

"Jerry," I said, "I think we'd better save those messages."

He nodded. "They're in your mailbox. I put them there after I read them."

"That's funny. I didn't notice them when I came in."

They weren't in my mailbox.

"Maybe they fell out and were swept up," he suggested.

"Maybe." I shook my head. Neither of us believed it; we looked around the newsroom suspiciously.

I cornered the office secretary. "Has anyone been here from NNS in the last few hours?"

"Not this morning," she said. "But there was somebody last night. A man came to fix the machine. It went on the blink about eleven o'clock."

Green stared at me helplessly.

At the arraignment and subsequent press conference District Attorney John Rasdale said, "Our investigation indicates that this was the act of a single individual, a man named Edgar Young."

I saw his statement after the fact when Green ran the 16-millimeter film of the press conference for me.

"We just can't sit on our hands and forget about it," I said. "We've got to do something."

"What? This is too big for us."

"Jerry, we're going to the D.A."

"Not me," said Green. "Bronson is a cinch for senator now. I don't want to get involved in politics."

"Politics! This is murder."

"Look, Jeff, you're already on the lobster shift. You don't have anything to lose. But it's taken me a long time to make producer."

"You should never have left the union."

"Leave me out of it," he said.

"Okay, Jerry. Okay." I waved my hands in disgust. "I'll go it alone."

The D.A. tried to intimidate me. He greeted me in a trout-gray suit and rainbow tie and shook hands like a politician, with a steady pressure to one side as if I were taking up too much of his time.

I told him about the messages.

Over the top of steel-rimmed glasses he gave me the fish-eye, shook his head doubtfully, then picked up the phone and called Wild Bill Bronson's special aide, the one who owned most of National News Service. The D.A. repeated my accusation, nodded to something I couldn't hear, and hung up quickly.

"Well," Rasdale said, swinging his big leather desk chair back in my direction, "I hope you're not trying to say Bill Bronson is somehow mixed up in this?"

"You're damn right I am," I snapped. Me and my big mouth. I'd forgotten Rasdale wanted to run for governor in two years and would need Bronson's help for that.

When he clicked his tongue derisively I got mad. "Look, I'm telling you there was a conspiracy to kill Lundon. Edgar Young may have been one of them, I don't know, but he's a small fish."

"We have witnesses who saw him shoot Lundon. It was even on television."

"I know."

"Anyone else believe your story?" the D.A. asked.

"You're damn right. Jerry Green, who produces the Eleven O'Clock News for Channel Three."

"Why isn't he here?" asked Rasdale.

"He doesn't want to get involved."

The next day they fired Jerry Green—two weeks' pay in lieu of notice and out the door. They couldn't touch me because of the union. Green left town the same day.

It was a bigger conspiracy than I thought.

The prosecution didn't want me for a witness, so I told my story to Young's attorney, a high-powered lawyer from Northern California who had been attracted by the publicity.

I don't think he believed me—at least, he never said so—but he put me on the stand just the same.

Channel Three didn't like the whole thing either; but Murch talked with me the day before I was scheduled to testify. "Simmons," he warned, "politics and news don't mix."

But what could he do? He didn't have anything worse than the lobster shift to threaten me with. (The newswriters' union is a force to be reckoned with in Los Angeles.)

I told Murch just that. Me, the big mouth again.

My testimony shook the jury momentarily. Everyone in court could see that, including the prosecution. All the newsmen covering the trial began to fidget, waiting to see what the Deputy D.A., a man in line for promotion to the top spot if and when Rasdale made governor, would try against me.

He countered with Murch. He was Channel Three's news director, the Deputy D.A. pointed out, a veteran journalist, highly respected in his profession.

"Mr. Murch," he began, "did you know about these so-called messages on National News Service?"

"No, I did not." Murch pronounced each word carefully, emphatically.

"As news director would you normally be informed about such things?"

"I certainly would. That is, if my people were doing their job."

"I take it that you mean it is policy at Channel Three to keep the news director informed about all major stories?"

"Yes, I do," Murch answered.

"Did Mr. Simmons so inform you?" The Deputy D.A. was laying it on pretty thick.

"No, he did not," Murch said.

"What kind of newsman," the Deputy D.A. asked, "do you consider Mr. Simmons to be?"

"He's on the lobster shift," Murch said. "That's where we put people who aren't good enough for the daytime operation."

Or who don't kiss your feet, I thought.

But that did it—it sunk my testimony.

However, the Deputy D.A. didn't take any chances. He called the editor of National News Service to the stand. Without a qualm the man said, "There were a couple of messages on the wire about a feature story on gambling." He produced twenty feet of yellow paper. "Here's a copy of it." He shrugged elaborately.

There was no way I could prove him a liar.

The trial dragged on through the first week of September. Even without my credibility, Edgar Young got off with diminished capacity and was sent to a state mental hospital.

I, of course, had been given a stiffer sentence—the lobster shift without a hope of parole.

With the November election only three weeks away Wild Bill Bronson is already talking victory. His press aides have leaked stories that he is in line for the Vice Presidency, or even the *big job* in two more years.

The lobster shift seems more lonely than ever. By the time I get in, the new Eleven O'Clock producer is always gone, so I never see anyone except an occasional janitor.

I feel vulnerable, alone there in the newsroom from midnight to eight, knowing they are out to get me.

So every morning I tell myself, fingers crossed, that I'm not really worth the trouble. Why kill me? I'm too small potatoes to be a threat. But with a conspiracy that may even involve the *big job* itself, the stakes are fantastic, so no threat is too small. And I have a reputation for a big mouth.

A heart attack in the newsroom wouldn't be hard to fake. They'd find me in the morning at the end of the lobster shift. NNS would report it that way, and even follow it up with a brief obit; they do that for every dead newsman.

MICHAEL GILBERT

The Curious Conspiracy

When I qualified as a solicitor, one of the first clients I took on was Grandmother Clatterwick. I did so with some trepidation. I was a young lawyer and she was a formidable old lady, as tough and straight as one of the whalebone inserts in her own corsets. Surprisingly we got on well together. My mother, who died in the same year as my father, had been her youngest and favorite daughter, and I think some of the affection washed off on me.

As the years went by, it became a source of sadness to me to see Grandmother's estate diminish. Not that there was any question of her sinking into poverty. Her husband, Herbert Clatterwick, had been a strange silent man who had known nothing about anything except South American mining shares; but he had understood them well enough to make a comfortable fortune on the Stock Exchange, all of which was left to his widow, along with Hambone Manor and its park. Unfortunately the money was all unearned income and as taxation bit into it more and more deeply, pieces of the park had to be sold, wings of the Manor shut off, and servants dismissed or not replaced.

In the end Grandmother Clatterwick lived in the south wing, attended only by the faithful McGuffog and assisted by a couple of villagers who came up by day.

McGuffog had started life at the Manor as gardener's boy, had graduated through the pantry to assistant butler, and was now butler, gardener, and handyman combined. When I went down, as I did from time to time, to talk business and stayed overnight, McGuffog would wait on the two of us, through an elaborate meal. After dinner he would bring the coffee into the drawing room, place a log on the fire, inquire whether anything else was wanted, and retire to the rooms which had been fitted out for him over the stable. There were, in fact, a dozen bedrooms he could have used in the house itself, but when the last of the resident servants left, my grandmother's sense of propriety would not allow her to sleep alone in the house with a man. She was 75 at the time.

All these thoughts and memories of my grandmother were in my mind as we sat round the desk in my office that spring morning a week after her funeral.

The aunts were all there. Aunt Gertrude, a dry and intellectual spinster; Aunt Valerie, who had married Dr. Moffat and produced two ghastly children called George and Mary; and Aunt Alexandra, who had married a Major Lumsden and bought him out of the cavalry to listen to her talk.

"*Why* did she leave no will?" said Aunt Alexandra. "You were her solicitor. It was surely your duty to see that she made one. Isn't that what lawyers are for?"

"Don't be absurd," said Aunt Gertrude. "As if anyone, let alone her own grandson, could have persuaded mother to do anything she didn't wish to do."

"Does it make any difference?" said Aunt Valerie. "As I understand the law— you must correct me if I'm wrong, dear—her money is divided into four equal shares. Not that I mind for myself. I was thinking only of George and Mary."

Aunt Gertrude cackled sardonically. It was well known in the family that Valerie excused any personal selfishness by passing it on, second-hand, to her revolting children.

I took over to prevent a fight.

"That's quite correct. The property passes to the children equally, per stirpes. That—"

"No need to explain," said Aunt Gertrude. "I haven't forgotten the Latin I learned at school"—and she shot a glance at her sisters which implied quite clearly that she suspected they had.

"How much will the estate amount to?" inquired Dr. Moffat.

"It's difficult to say. Estate duty will account for a slice of it. And the Manor will have to be sold."

"No one will give a penny for it," said Aunt Gertrude. "A rambling old place in a shocking state of repair."

"What about stocks and shares and things like that?" asked Aunt Valerie.

I said, "Granny had been using up capital quite a bit during recent years. Not so much since we bought her that annuity—that cost capital too, of course. But there must be quite a lot left. And although we may not get much for the Manor there were one or two nice things in it. It's a couple of years since I've been down there, but I remember an attributed Morland in the drawing room. That was insured for £5000. And I think there was an Etty in the dining room."

"*I* was somewhat more regular in my visits," said Dr. Moffat reprovingly.

"For George and Mary's sake," said Aunt Gertrude under her breath.

"—and I was actually there a fortnight before her decease. It struck me that she had become rather eccentric. We had a good dinner, as usual, but what do you suppose we were offered to drink with it?"

None of us could guess.

"A very large bottle of raspberry wine."

I could hardly conceal my delight. My uncle is the complete wine snob. By this I mean that he reads books about wine, belongs to all the wine societies, has a cupboard full of wine lists and the catalogues of wine auctions, talks endlessly about vintages and *crus*—and has less taste and discernment than a camel. On one occasion when we had him to dinner I emptied a bottle of red wine, which I had bought for two francs fifty at a grocer's shop in France, into an old Château Margaux bottle which I happened to have, and received the warmest commendation of my choice. "Superb bouquet, my boy. One can almost taste the violets in it." I could visualize exactly his expression when he was offered a bottle of raspberry wine.

"Apparently," said Aunt Valerie, "she had been making quite a thing of it.

McGuffog, who had been helping her to brew it, told us that she had more than two thousand bottles of it in the cellar."

"Of raspberry wine?"

"Not all raspberry. There was raspberry, plum, and turnip wine, black currant and red currant cordial, and elderflower champagne. And half a dozen other nauseating brews too, I don't doubt."

Major Lumsden was a silent man, as anyone would be who was married to my Aunt Alexandra, but he had a kind heart. He said, "Talking about that fellow McGuffog, are we going to do anything for him?"

"I was thinking about that," I said. "He looked after granny for more than forty years. If I could have persuaded her to make a will I'm sure she'd have left him something."

"But she didn't make a will," said Aunt Valerie sharply.

"All the same—" said the Major.

"As a matter of fact," I said, "I had a letter from McGuffog only this morning. I won't bother to read it all to you, although it's surprisingly well composed—"

"He must be reasonably competent," said Aunt Valerie. "After all, he used to manage a very large household. Larger than any of *us* have had to deal with."

"Quite so," I said. "Well, this is the passage I wanted to read you: 'I realize that Mrs. Clatterwick didn't approve of will making. She often told me so. There couldn't therefore be any question of a legacy. However—'"

As I turned the page I was aware of five pairs of eyes on me. One pair sardonic, one kindly, the other three pairs frankly greedy.

"'—it did occur to me to wonder whether the family would agree to me taking over the unused stock of homemade wine. I cooperated with Mrs. Clatterwick in getting together what must, I venture to think, be a unique collection of vintages—'"

"If *that's* all he wants," said Aunt Valerie, striving to keep the relief out of her voice, "I should be the first to agree."

The others nodded. Major Lumsden said, "Don't you think that some sort of pension—" But he was quickly and decisively overruled.

"All right," I said, "I'll tell him. He can store it in the old stable. And I assume you'll let him stay on in his flat until the house is sold?"

"If the people who buy the house have got an atom of sense," said Aunt Gertrude, "they'll take McGuffog with the house. Servants like that don't grow on trees."

The winding up of an intestate estate, particularly the estate of an old and secretive lady, is not a quick matter. But as the months slipped by and the answers came in from banks and stockbrokers and insurance companies, I began to feel the first stirrings of unease. There was so much less in the estate than I had expected.

It was true, as I had told her daughters, that Grandmother Clatterwick had been nibbling into capital for years. But when I finally persuaded her to put £40,000 into a life annuity, this had insured her an almost tax-free income in the high thousands—enough, one would have thought, even for a Victorian old lady who liked to double the parson's stipend and to support charities with objects as diverse as the clothing of Eskimo babies and the moral rearmament of Hottentot girls.

Moreover, when I had bought the annuity I had made a very careful check of what money and securities were left, and the total was not far short of £20,000. Now, I could locate barely half of it.

The final blow fell in the early autumn when I got the schedule of the contents of Hambone Manor. I rang up the appraiser.

I said, "Why have you left out the Morland and the Etty?"

"I left them out," said the appraiser, "because they weren't there. The old man who looks after the place—McGuffog, that's the name—told me they were put up at auction about eighteen months ago. The Morland wasn't signed, so it only fetched two thousand. The Etty went for one and a half."

It was then I decided I would have to look into the matter personally.

Hambone Street lies in the miraculously still unravaged piece of Kent to the south of the A20. It has villages which still *are* villages, which possess things like village greens on which the local cricket team plays, village halls for the Women's Institute, and not less than three public houses for a population of four hundred and fifty. Lack of a rail service has helped to keep it the way it is, and I drove down by car on a lovely autumn morning when the leaves were just beginning to turn.

I found the Manor in sad decline. The grass was uncut, the hedges were straggling, and there were unfilled potholes in the driveway. This was disappointing. The estate had continued to pay McGuffog's salary on the understanding that he did some work on the grounds. It looked as though he had fallen down on the job.

However, there was someone in the house. Smoke was coming from one of the chimneys and the front door was open. I found Annie, one of the two village women, in possession. She had been told to keep the house as clean and dry as possible, and I could see she, at least, was doing a good job of it. When I asked her about McGuffog she looked startled.

"Didn't they tell you?" she said. "He passed away. They should have let you know, sir."

"I'm terribly sorry," I said. "When did it happen?"

"Two weeks ago it was. They laid him to rest on Sunday. A nice service. Vicar's been very helpful too. He left no family, you see. Only a cousin, or some such, who lives over in Essex. If you'd like a word with Mr. Stacey I saw his car in the yard. Likely he'll be over there now."

I walked across to the stable and introduced myself to the Reverend Stacey, who was coming down the stairs which led to McGuffog's flat. He was a cheerful young man with the well-scrubbed face and no-nonsense look that Theological Colleges turn out nowadays. He said, "I'm glad you're here. I thought of getting in touch with you. Not that there's much for a lawyer to do. All the stuff in the flat was borrowed from the house, you know. With Mrs. Clatterwick's agreement, of course. But it belonged to her, not to McGuffog. Almost the only things he left were the clothes he stood up in. Oh, and the remains of the wine."

"The remains?"

"He seems to have got rather fond of it. Rather too fond, perhaps." The vicar gave an unclerical chuckle. "'People in the village used to hear him singing. Fortunately they couldn't make out the words, so they assumed it was Gaelic."

"*Can* you get drunk on raspberry wine?"

"I expect you can get drunk on anything, if you try hard enough. McGuffog certainly put his back into it. He took over nearly two thousand bottles of it—"

"Nineteen hundred and eighty-four," said Annie who had joined us. "I helped him store them in the hayracks in the stable."

"When he died there were just about fifteen hundred left."

I did some mental arithmetic. The period between my grandmother's death and McGuffog's was not much more than twenty weeks. Call it a hundred and fifty days. At three bottles a day he could just have done it.

Annie said unexpectedly, "I reckon he looked on it as a duty."

We both stared at her. She blushed and then said, rather defiantly, "Well, there's no harm in me telling you. They've both gone now. But they sometimes used to share a bottle in the evenings. I know, because I came back once and saw them. There was a bottle of raspberry wine on the table and they were taking a glass each. I reckon they used to do it most evenings, when they were alone. Being homemade wine seemed to make it all right. It wasn't really *drinking*, you see."

I saw exactly what she meant. If it had been real drink it would have been an orgy. As it was elderflower champagne or plum cordial it was simply a charming, old-fashioned ritual. I said, "I think it was a beautiful idea. You mean that McGuffog had such pleasant memories of those evenings with my grandmother that he thought it his duty to finish off the whole stock rather than let it fall into the hands of uncaring outsiders."

"Death cut him down before he could accomplish it," said the vicar. "Sad."

"Talking of outsiders, what have you done with the balance of the stuff?"

The vicar said, "The cousin from Essex suggested that we give it to the Women's Institute. They'll be selling it off at their jumble sale this afternoon. I was on my way there. Perhaps you'd like to come along."

While we were talking we had drifted into the stable—a fine old-fashioned accommodation for eight horses, with deep hayracks. Annie spotted something in the corner. She said, "There now. They've forgotten that one. It must have got hidden in the straw."

It was a claret bottle of the green-glass type used by some Bordeaux shippers for a few years after the War when supplies were scarce, but now uncommon. A label in Grandmother Clatterwick's spidery writing identified the contents as damson wine.

"Don't you think," I said, "that it would be a fitting gesture if we drank a last toast, a farewell salute to a gallant old lady?"

"An excellent idea," said the vicar, adding, "the later I arrive at that jumble sale the less I shall have to spend."

Annie fetched glasses and a corkscrew. It was while I was in the act of drawing the cork that a great many questions were posed—and a few answered.

The first thing that struck me was that the cork was remarkably firm.

Amateur bottlers do not usually manage to sink the whole of the cork into the neck of the bottle. The next was that it was an old cork, stiff with age and impregnated with the lees of the wine. Now this was really curious. Not only was the cork clearly twenty or thirty years old, but it was equally clear that it had spent those twenty or thirty years *in that bottle*.

I carried the bottle to the door to examine it more closely. Imprinted into its side was the name of one of the four finest Châteaux in the Haut-Médoc.

I went back, picked up the tumbler which Annie had filled for me, and held it up to the light.

The vicar had already tasted his. "Remarkable damsons," he said.

I gave the tumbler a twist and watched the thick dark red liquid cling to the sides of the glass and slide away. Then I tasted it—and all my suspicions became facts.

The vicar, who had put his glass down, said, "Hold on a moment. I wonder if this will help us."

He went across to his car and came back with an exercise book. "I found it in McGuffog's flat. I was going to send it on to his cousin."

I opened the book. The writing I recognized as McGuffog's. I only needed a single glance at it. "When did you say that jumble sale was due to start?"

"It's started—half an hour ago."

"Where is it being held?"

"Take you in my car. It'll be quicker than explaining."

"Thank you," I said, "and if you'll excuse the expression, padre, drive like hell."

There were half a dozen cars parked outside the Village Hall, a crowd of women, most of them with perambulators and pushcarts, and a lot of children skirmishing round the flanks. We pushed in and the vicar introduced me to a tweedy lady whose name I never got. He said, "This is Mrs. Clatterwick's grandson." I admired his tact. It was a better introduction than "her solicitor." "He's interested in his grandmother's homemade wines."

The tweedy lady beamed at me. She said, "I'd have recognized you anywhere. You've got the family nose. Yes. It was kind of McGuffog's cousin to think of us. We've been doing quite a brisk trade."

My feelings must have been apparent. The tweedy lady said, "There's a good deal left, though. I had them all put together over here."

On and under the long trestle tables normally devoted to village teas stood the bottles, rank upon rank. "I had intended," I said, "to make you an offer for the lot. As a collection, you know."

"That's a nice idea," said the tweedy lady. "This gentleman is old Mrs. Clatterwick's grandson, Cynthia. He wanted to buy all the homemade wine. In memory of his grandmother. Has much of it gone already?"

Cynthia consulted a list. "Mrs. Parkin had a bottle. And Mrs. Batchelor had two. But the only other lot was Colonel Nicholson. *He* took six dozen."

I was making a rapid count of the bottles assisted by the fact that they were arranged in orderly groups of twenty-five. I said, "That's right. Fourteen hundred and twenty-five bottles—"

"They took *hours* to arrange," said Cynthia.

"What were you selling them at?"

"We had them down at sixpence a bottle," said the tweedy lady. "But we could give you a discount if you really are taking the lot."

"Far from it," I said. "A complete collection is always worth more than its individual parts." I wrote out a check for £100. "Who shall I make it out to?"

"A *hundred* pounds," said Cynthia, who had also been doing some arithmetic. "But that's nearly three times—"

"I'm sure my grandmother—and Mr. McGuffog—would have wanted it that way," I said. "I'll make all the arrangements for transporting the bottles. Please don't think of disturbing them. Leave it just as it is. If you'll excuse me a moment—"

Outside the hall I collared two intelligent-looking small boys. I said, "Would you like to earn half a crown?" The less intelligent boy nodded at once. The brighter one said, "What for?"

"One of you find Mrs. Parkin and one of you find Mrs. Batchelor—do you know them?"

The boys nodded.

"I want to buy back the bottles of homemade wine they bought here this afternoon. Here's five shillings each. See how cheaply you can buy them back—you can keep the change."

The two boys scudded off. I went to look for the vicar.

"Last lap," I said. "Can you take me to Colonel Nicholson's house?"

"Almost as quick to walk," said the vicar. "That path through the spinney there will bring you to his back lawn. Watch out for his dog, though. He's quite all right if you don't make any sudden movements."

I arrived at the colonel's front door followed by a Doberman pinscher. I refrained from making any sudden movements and rang the bell. It was the colonel himself who opened the door. No doubt about that. A tall man with guileless light-blue eyes and a silky white mustache. When I had introduced myself he said, "Ah, yes. Come along in. I was half expecting a visit."

He led me through into the dining room. An agreeable apartment, full of polished mahogany and sparkling glass and shining silver. One of the bottles I had come for was standing on the sideboard. The cork had been drawn and there was a glass beside it.

"I don't normally drink wine at four in the afternoon," said the colonel. "But this was by way of being an experiment."

He brought out a second glass from the cupboard and proceeded to fill them both. I was glad to see that he did this properly, tilting the bottle slowly but firmly, with no sudden movements. The Doberman pinscher would have approved.

He said, "About nine months ago—it would have been around the turn of the year—I had the pleasure of having dinner with your grandmother. It must, I suppose, have been one of the very last dinner parties she gave. We drank a *remarkable* red currant cordial. I made up my mind that I must at all costs obtain the recipe from her or from her man, McGuffog, who had, I was told, assisted her in brewing it."

His eyes twinkling frostily, the colonel picked up his glass, sniffed at it, tilted it delicately, and took a sip. I followed suit.

"Unfortunately she died before I could do so. And I did not like to intrude on McGuffog who seems to have led a somewhat hermitlike if happy existence for the last six months of his life."

"Musical, too," I said.

We drank again, and the colonel continued. "When, however, I learned that the wines were for sale I hurried down and purchased some. I fully intended, if they came up to my expectations—as, indeed this one does, let me refill your glass—to go back and make an offer for the lot."

"Too late," I said. "I've bought them for the estate."

"I feared as much."

"And I'd like to buy back the six dozen you have."

The colonel considered the matter, stroking his mustache delicately with the tip of his little finger. Then he said, "I'll make a deal with you. You can buy back four dozen at the price I gave for them. I'll keep two dozen as a memento—that is, if you'll tell me the whole story."

"I'm not sure I know the whole story," I said. "A lot of it will be guessing. What I *think* happened is that my grandmother and McGuffog, both rather lonely people by that time, got into the way of splitting a bottle in the evening. But in order to avoid offending my grandmother's rather strict sense of propriety, it had to be something which sounded harmless and old-fashioned."

"Like raspberry wine?"

"Exactly. Unfortunately, the only thing they both liked and appreciated were good French and German wines."

"I wouldn't call it unfortunate," said the colonel, refilling our glasses. "Was it all as good as this?"

I took the exercise book from my brief case and showed it to the colonel, who riffled through the pages.

"Glory be," he said ecstatically, "it must have cost her a fortune."

"Not a whole fortune—nine or ten thousand pounds."

"There's a page full of Private-Estate-bottled Trockenbeeren Auslese Hock. That must have set them back fifteen pounds a bottle. What did they call that?"

"I think that was called elderflower champagne."

"They seem to have chosen their stuff very well. I see they avoided the '47 clarets and stuck to the '45's and '49's. Sound judgment that."

"It would be McGuffog who did the buying. He'd had a good deal of experience."

"Ah," said the colonel. "*That's* what I was looking for. Domaine de la Romanée Conti. They've got some of the Richebourg '29. Do you think that could possibly be what we're drinking now?"

"'29 or '34," I said. "This is certainly one of the finest Burgundies I've ever tasted."

The third glass of a triumphant Burgundy induces contemplation and dispenses with the necessity for small talk. As we drank in silence I reflected on the real motives behind that curious conspiracy between Grandmother Clatterwick and Mr. McGuffog. Undoubtedly they both liked good wine. And undoubtedly the relabeling of a princely claret as raspberry wine and watching my Uncle Moffat turn his nose up at it must have appealed sharply to their sense of humor.

But I felt there was more to it than that. Like most very old and fairly rich people my grandmother must have been conscious of her next of kin like jackals sitting around a dying lion, licking their chops and waiting to get their teeth in. As each night the log fire flickered in the grate and another great wine sank in its bottle, must there not have been a feeling akin to triumph? Another ten pounds salvaged from Gertrude, Valerie, and Alexandra. Another crust out of the mouths of little George and Mary.

A further thought occurred to me. Might this not account for the heroic efforts of McGuffog after her death? His sensibility would not, of course, have allowed him to destroy such wine, but if it could all be consumed—?

The colonel seemed to have read my thoughts.

"I'm told," he said, "that McGuffog was averaging three to four bottles a day. I suppose that's really what finished him off."

"I fear it must have been."

"What a *wonderful* way to go!"

PATRICIA HIGHSMITH

Sauce for the Goose

The incident in the garage was the third near-catastrophe in the Amory household, and it put a horrible thought into Loren Amory's head: his darling wife Olivia was trying to kill herself.

Loren had pulled at a plastic clothesline dangling from a high shelf in the garage—his idea had been to tidy up, to coil the clothesline properly—and at that first tug an avalanche of suitcases, an old lawnmower, and a sewing machine weighing God-knows-how-much crashed down on the spot that he barely had time to leap from.

Loren walked slowly back to the house, his heart pounding at his awful discovery. He entered the kitchen and made his way to the stairs. Olivia was in bed, propped against pillows, a magazine in her lap. "What was that terrible noise, dear?"

Loren cleared his throat and settled his black-rimmed glasses more firmly on his nose. "A lot of stuff in the garage. I pulled just a little bit on a clothesline—" He explained what had happened.

She blinked calmly as if to say, "Well, so what? Things like that do happen."

"Have you been up to that shelf for anything lately?"

"Why, no. Why?"

"Because—well, everything was just poised to fall, darling."

"Are you blaming me?" she asked in a small voice.

"Blaming your carelessness, yes. I arranged those suitcases up there and I'd never have put them so they'd fall at a mere touch. And I didn't put the sewing machine on top of the heap. Now, I'm not saying—"

"Blaming my carelessness," she repeated, affronted.

He knelt quickly beside the bed. "Darling, let's not hide things any more. Last week there was the carpet sweeper on the cellar stairs. And that ladder! You were going to climb it to knock down that wasps' nest!—What I'm getting at, darling, is that you *want* something to happen to you, whether you realize it or not. You've got to be more careful, Olivia.—Oh, darling, please don't cry. I'm trying to help you. I'm not criticizing."

"I know, Loren. You're good. But my life—it doesn't seem worth living any more, I suppose. I don't mean I'm *trying* to end my life, but—"

"You're still thinking—of Stephen?" Loren hated the name and hated saying it.

She took her hands down from her pinkened eyes. "You made me promise you not to think of him, so I haven't. I swear it, Loren."

"Good, darling. That's my little girl." He took her hands in his. "What do you say to a cruise soon? Maybe in February? Myers is coming back from the coast and he can take over for me for a couple of weeks. What about Haiti or Bermuda?"

She seemed to think about it for a moment, but at last shook her head and said she knew he was only doing it for her, not because he really wanted to go. Loren remonstrated briefly, then gave it up. If Olivia didn't take to an idea at once, she never took to it. There had been one triumph—his convincing her that it made sense not to see Stephen Castle for a period of three months.

Olivia had met Stephen Castle at a party given by one of Loren's colleagues on the Stock Exchange. Stephen was 35, which was ten years younger than Loren and one year older than Olivia, and Stephen was an actor. Loren had no idea how Toohey, their host that evening, had met him, or why he had invited him to a party at which every other man was either in banking or on the Exchange; but there he'd been, like an evil alien spirit, and he'd concentrated on Olivia the entire evening, and she'd responded with her charming smiles that had captured Loren in a single evening eight years ago.

Afterward, when they were driving back to Old Greenwich, Olivia had said, "It's such fun to talk to somebody who's not in the stock market for a change! He told me he's rehearsing in a play now, 'The Frequent Guest.' We've got to see it, Loren."

They saw it. Stephen Castle was on for perhaps five minutes in Act One. They visited Stephen backstage, and Olivia invited him to a cocktail party they were giving the following weekend. He came, and spent that night in their guest room. In the next weeks Olivia drove her car into New York at least twice a week on shopping expeditions, but she made no secret of the fact she saw Stephen for lunch on those days and sometimes for cocktails too. At last she told Loren she was in love with Stephen and wanted a divorce.

Loren was speechless at first, even inclined to grant her a divorce by way of being sportsmanlike; but 48 hours after her announcement he came to what he considered his senses. By that time he had measured himself against his rival—not merely physically (Loren did not come off so well there, being no taller than Olivia, with a receding hairline and a small paunch) but morally and financially as well. In the last two categories he had it all over Stephen Castle, and modestly he pointed this out to Olivia.

"I'd never marry a man for his money," she retorted.

"I didn't mean you married me for my money, dear. I just happened to have it. But what's Stephen Castle ever going to have? Nothing much, from what I can see of his acting. You're used to more than he can give you. And you've known him only six weeks. How can you be sure his love for you is going to last?"

That last thought made Olivia pause. She said she would see Stephen just once more—"to talk it over." She drove to New York one morning and did not return until midnight. It was a Sunday, when Stephen had no performance. Loren sat up waiting for her. In tears Olivia told him that she and Stephen had come to an understanding. They would not see each other for a month, and if at the end of that time they did not feel the same way about each other, they would agree to forget the whole thing.

"But of course you'll feel the same," Loren said. "What's a month in the life of an adult? If you'd try it for three months—"

She looked at him through tears. "Three months?"

"Against the eight years we've been married? Is that unfair? Our marriage deserves at least a three-month chance, too, doesn't it?"

"All right, it's a bargain. Three months. I'll call Stephen tomorrow and tell him. We won't see each other or telephone for three months."

From that day Olivia had gone into a decline. She lost interest in gardening, in her bridge club, even in clothes. Her appetite fell off, though she did not lose much weight, perhaps because she was proportionately inactive. They had never had a servant. Olivia took pride in the fact that she had been a working girl, a saleswoman in the gift department of a large store in Manhattan, when Loren met her. She liked to say that she knew how to do things for herself. The big house in Old Greenwich was enough to keep any woman busy, though Loren had bought every conceivable labor-saving device. They also had a walk-in deep freeze, the size of a large closet, in the basement, so that their marketing was done less often than usual, and all food was delivered, anyway. Now that Olivia seemed low in energy, Loren suggested getting a maid, but Olivia refused.

Seven weeks went by, and Olivia kept her word about not seeing Stephen. But she was obviously so depressed, so ready to burst into tears, that Loren lived constantly on the brink of weakening and telling her that if she loved Stephen that much, she had a right to see him. Perhaps, Loren thought, Stephen Castle was feeling the same way, also counting off the weeks until he could see Olivia again. If so, Loren had already lost.

But it was hard for Loren to give Stephen credit for feeling anything. He was a lanky, rather stupid chap with oat-colored hair, and Loren had never seen him without a sickly smile on his mouth—as if he were a human billboard of himself, perpetually displaying what he must have thought was his most flattering expression.

Loren, a bachelor until at 37 he married Olivia, often sighed in dismay at the ways of women. For instance, Olivia: if he had felt so strongly about another woman, he would have set about promptly to extricate himself from his marriage. But here was Olivia hanging on, in a way. What did she expect to gain from it, he wondered. Did she think, or hope, that her infatuation for Stephen might disappear? Or did she want to spite Loren and prove that it wouldn't? Or did she know unconsciously that her love for Stephen Castle was all fantasy, and that her present depression represented to her and to Loren a fitting period of mourning for a love she didn't have the courage to go out and take?

But the Saturday of the garage incident made Loren doubt that Olivia was indulging in fantasy. He did not want to admit that Olivia was attempting to take her own life, but logic compelled him to. He had read about such people. They were different from the accident-prone, who might live to die a natural death, whatever that was. The others were the suicide-prone, and into this category he was sure Olivia fell.

A perfect example was the ladder episode. Olivia had been on the fourth or fifth rung when Loren noticed the crack in the left side of the ladder, and she had been quite unconcerned, even when he pointed it out to her. If it hadn't been for her saying she suddenly felt a little dizzy looking up at the wasps' nest, he never would have started to do the chore himself, and therefore wouldn't have seen the crack.

Loren noticed in the newspaper that Stephen's play was closing, and it seemed to him that Olivia's gloom deepened. Now there were dark circles under her eyes. She claimed she could not fall asleep before dawn.

"Call him if you want to, darling," Loren finally said. "See him once again and find out if you both—"

"No, I made a promise to you. Three months, Loren. I'll keep my promise," she said with a trembling lip.

Loren turned away from her, wretched and hating himself.

Olivia grew physically weaker. Once she stumbled coming down the stairs and barely caught herself on the banister. Loren suggested, not for the first time, that she see a doctor, but she refused to.

"The three months are nearly up, dear. I'll survive them," she said, smiling sadly.

It was true. Only two more weeks remained until March 15th, the three months' deadline. The Ides of March, Loren realized for the first time. A most ominous coincidence.

On Sunday afternoon Loren was looking over some office reports in his study when he heard a long scream, followed by a clattering crash. In an instant he was on his feet and running. It had come from the cellar, he thought, and if so, he knew what had happened. That damned carpet sweeper again!

"Olivia?"

From the dark cellar he heard a groan. Loren plunged down the steps. There was a little whirr of wheels, his feet flew up in front of him, and in the few seconds before his head smashed against the cement floor he understood every-thing: Olivia had not fallen down the cellar steps, she had only lured him here; all this time she had been trying to kill *him*, Loren Amory—and all for Stephen Castle.

"I was upstairs in bed reading," Olivia told the police, her hands shaking as she clutched her dressing gown around her. "I heard a terrible crash and then—I came down—" She gestured helplessly toward Loren's dead body.

The police took down what she told them and commiserated with her. People ought to be more careful, they said, about things like carpet sweepers on dark stairways. There were fatalities like this every day in the United States. Then the body was taken away, and on Tuesday Loren Amory was buried.

Olivia rang Stephen on Wednesday. She had been telephoning him every day except Saturdays and Sundays, but she had not rung him since the previous Friday. They had agreed that any weekday she did not call him at his apartment at 11:00 A.M. would be a signal that their mission had been accomplished. Also, Loren Amory had got quite a lot of space on the obituary page Monday. He had left nearly a million dollars to his widow, and houses in Florida, Connecticut, and Maine.

"Dearest! You look so tired!" were Stephen's first words to her when they met in an out-of-the-way bar in New York on Wednesday.

"Nonsense! It's all makeup," Olivia said gaily. "And you an actor!" She laughed. "I have to look properly gloomy for my neighbors, you know. And I'm never sure when I'll run into someone I know in New York."

Stephen looked around him nervously, then said with his habitual smile, "Darling Olivia, how soon can we be together?"

"Very soon," she said promptly. "Not up at the house, of course, but remember we talked about a cruise? Maybe Trinidad? I've got the money with me. I want you to buy the tickets."

They took separate staterooms, and the local Connecticut paper, without a hint of suspicion, reported that Mrs. Amory's voyage was for reasons of health.

Back in the United States in April, suntanned and looking much improved, Olivia confessed to her friends that she had met someone she was "interested in." Her friends assured her that was normal, and that she shouldn't be alone for the rest of her life. The curious thing was that when Olivia invited Stephen to a dinner party at her house, none of her friends remembered him, though several had met him at that cocktail party a few months before. Stephen was much more sure of himself now, and he behaved like an angel, Olivia thought.

In August they were married. Stephen had been getting nibbles in the way of work, but nothing materialized. Olivia told him not to worry, that things would surely pick up after the summer. Stephen did not seem to worry very much, though he protested he ought to work, and said if necessary he would try for some television parts. He developed an interest in gardening, planted some young blue spruces, and generally made the place look alive again.

Olivia was delighted that Stephen liked the house, because she did. Neither of them ever referred to the cellar stairs, but they had a light switch put at the top landing, so that a similar thing could not occur again. Also, the carpet sweeper was kept in its proper place, in the broom closet in the kitchen.

They entertained more often than Olivia and Loren had done. Stephen had many friends in New York, and Olivia found them amusing. But Stephen, Olivia thought, was drinking just a little too much. At one party, when they were all out on the terrace, Stephen nearly fell over the parapet. Two of the guests had to grab him.

"Better watch out for yourself in this house, Steve," said Parker Barnes, an actor friend of Stephen's. "It just might be jinxed."

"What d'ya mean?" Stephen asked. "I don't believe that for a minute. I may be an actor, but I haven't got a single superstition."

"Oh, so you're an actor, Mr. Castle!" a woman's voice said out of the darkness.

After the guests had gone, Stephen asked Olivia to come out again on the terrace.

"Maybe the air'll clear my head," Stephen said, smiling. "Sorry I was tipsy tonight. —There's old Orion. See him?" He put his arm around Olivia and drew her close. "Brightest constellation in the heavens."

"You're hurting me, Stephen! Not so—" Then she screamed and squirmed, fighting for her life.

"Damn you!" Stephen gasped, astounded at her strength.

She had twisted away from him and was standing near the bedroom door, facing him now. "You were going to push me over."

"No! Good God, Olivia!—I lost my balance, that's all. I thought I was going over myself!"

"That's a fine thing to do, then, hold onto a woman and pull her over too."

"I didn't realize. I'm drunk, darling. And I'm sorry."

They lay as usual in the same bed that night, but both of them were only pretending sleep. Until, for Olivia at least, just as she had used to tell Loren, sleep came around dawn.

The next day, casually and surreptitiously, each of them looked over the house from attic to cellar—Olivia with a view to protecting herself from possible death traps, Stephen with a view to setting them. He had already decided that the cellar steps offered the best possibility, in spite of the duplication, because he thought no one would believe anyone would dare to use the same means—if the intention was murder.

Olivia happened to be thinking the same thing.

The cellar steps had never before been so free of impediments or so well lighted. Neither of them took the initiative to turn the light out at night. Outwardly each professed love and faith in the other.

"I'm sorry I ever said such a thing to you, Stephen," she whispered in his ear as she embraced him. "I was afraid on the terrace that night, that's all. When you said, 'Damn you'—"

"I know, angel. You *couldn't* have thought I meant to hurt you. I said 'Damn you' just because you were there, and I thought I might be pulling you over."

They talked about another cruise. They wanted to go to Europe next spring. But at meals they cautiously tasted every item of food before beginning to eat.

How could *I* have done anything to the food, Stephen thought to himself, since you never leave the kitchen while you're cooking it.

And Olivia: I don't put anything past you. There's only one direction you seem to be bright in, Stephen.

Her humiliation in having lost a lover was hidden by a dark resentment. She realized she had been victimized. The last bit of Stephen's charm had vanished. Yet now, Olivia thought, he was doing the best job of acting in his life—and a twenty-four-hour-a-day acting job at that. She congratulated herself that it did not fool her, and she weighed one plan against another, knowing that this "accident" had to be even more convincing than the one that had freed her from Loren.

Stephen realized he was not in quite so awkward a position. Everyone who knew him and Olivia, even slightly, thought he adored her. An accident would be assumed to be just that, an accident, if he said so. He was now toying with the idea of the closet-sized deep freeze in the cellar. There was no inside handle on the door, and once in a while Olivia went into the farthest corner of the deep freeze to get steaks or frozen asparagus. But would she dare to go into it, now that her suspicions were aroused, if he happened to be in the cellar at the same time? He doubted it.

While Olivia was breakfasting in bed one morning—she had taken to her own bedroom again, and Stephen brought her breakfast as Loren had always done—Stephen experimented with the door of the deep freeze. If it so much as touched a solid object in swinging open, he discovered, it would slowly but surely swing shut on its rebound. There was no solid object near the door now, and on the contrary the door was intended to be swung fully open, so that a catch on the outside of the door would lock in a grip set in the wall for just that purpose, and thus keep the door open. Olivia, he had noticed, always swung the door wide when she went in, and it latched onto the wall automatically. But if he put something in its way, even the corner of the box of kindling wood, the door would strike it and swing shut again, before Olivia had time to realize what had happened.

However, that particular moment did not seem the right one to put the kindling box in position, so Stephen did not set his trap. Olivia had said something about their going out to a restaurant tonight. She would not be taking anything out to thaw today.

They took a little walk at three in the afternoon—through the woods behind the house, then back home again—and they almost started holding hands, in a mutually distasteful and insulting pretense of affection; but their fingers only brushed and separated.

"A cup of tea would taste good, wouldn't it, darling?" said Olivia.

"Um-m." He smiled. Poison in the tea? Poison in the cookies? She'd made them herself that morning.

He remembered how they had plotted Loren's sad demise—her tender whispers of murder over their luncheons, her infinite patience as the weeks went by and plan after plan failed. It was he who had suggested the carpet sweeper on the cellar steps and the lure of a scream from her. What could *her* bird-brain ever plan?

Shortly after their tea—everything had tasted fine—Stephen strolled out of the living room as if with no special purpose. He felt compelled to try out the kindling box again to see if it could really be depended on. He felt inspired, too, to set the trap now and leave it. The light at the head of the cellar stairs was on. He went carefully down the steps.

He listened for a moment to see if Olivia was possibly following him. Then he pulled the kindling box into position, not parallel to the front of the deep freeze, of course, but a little to one side, as if someone had dragged it out of the shadow to see into it better and left it there. He opened the deep-freeze door with exactly the speed and force Olivia might use, flinging the door from him as he stepped in with one foot, his right hand outstretched to catch the door on the rebound. But the foot that bore his weight slid several inches forward just as the door bumped against the kindling box.

Stephen was down on his right knee, his left leg straight out in front of him, and behind him the door shut. He got to his feet instantly and faced the closed door wide-eyed. It was dark, and he groped for the auxiliary switch to the left of the door, which put a light on at the back of the deep freeze.

How had it happened? The damned glaze of frost on the floor! But it wasn't only the frost, he saw. What he had slipped on was a little piece of suet that he now saw in the middle of the floor, at the end of the greasy steak his slide had made.

Stephen stared at the suet neutrally, blankly, for an instant, then faced the door again, pushed it, felt along its firm rubber-sealed crack. He could call Olivia, of course. Eventually she'd hear him, or at least *miss* him, before he had time to freeze. She'd come down to the cellar, and she'd be able to hear him there even if she couldn't hear him in the living room. Then she'd open the door, of course.

He smiled weakly, and tried to convince himself she *would* open the door. "Olivia?—*Olivia!* I'm down in the *cellar!*"

It was nearly a half hour later when Olivia called to Stephen to ask him which restaurant he preferred, a matter that would influence what she wore. She looked for him in his bedroom, in the library, on the terrace, and finally called out the front door, thinking he might be somewhere on the lawn.

At last she tried the cellar.

By this time, hunched in his tweed jacket, his arms crossed, Stephen was walking up and down in the deep freeze, giving out distress signals at intervals of thirty seconds and using the rest of his breath to blow into his shirt in an effort to warm himself. Olivia was just about to leave the cellar when she heard her name called faintly.

"Stephen?—Stephen, where are you?"

"In the deep freeze!" he called as loudly as he could.

Olivia looked at the deep freeze with an incredulous smile.

"Open it, can't you? I'm in the *deep freeze!*" came his muffled voice.

Olivia threw her head back and laughed, not even caring if Stephen heard her. Then still laughing so hard that she had to bend over, she climbed the cellar stairs.

What amused her was that she had thought of the deep freeze as a fine place to dispose of Stephen, but she hadn't worked out how to get him into it. His being there now, she realized, was owing to some funny accident—maybe he'd been trying to set a trap for her. It was all too comical. And lucky!

Or, maybe, she thought cagily, his intention even now was to trick her into opening the deep-freeze door, then to yank her inside and close the door on her. She was certainly not going to let *that* happen.

Olivia took her car and drove nearly twenty miles northward, had a sandwich at a roadside café, then went to a movie. When she got home at midnight she found she had not the courage to call "Stephen" to the deep freeze, or even to go down to the cellar. She wasn't sure he'd be dead by now, and even if he were silent it might mean he was only pretending to be dead or unconscious.

But tomorrow, she thought, there wouldn't be any doubt he'd be dead. The very lack of air, for one thing, ought to finish him by that time.

She went to bed and assured herself a night's sleep with a light sedative. She would have a strenuous day tomorrow. Her story of the mild quarrel with Stephen—over which restaurant they'd go to, nothing more—and his storming out of the living room to take a walk, she thought, would have to be very convincing.

At ten the next morning, after orange juice and coffee, Olivia felt ready for her role of the horrified, grief-stricken widow. After all, she told herself, she had practiced the role—it would be the second time she had played the part. She decided to face the police in her dressing gown, as before.

To be quite natural about the whole thing she went down to the cellar to make the "discovery" before she called the police.

"Stephen? Stephen?" she called out with confidence.

No answer.

She opened the deep freeze with apprehension, gasped at the curled-up, frost covered figure on the floor, then walked the few feet toward him—aware that her footprints on the floor would be visible to corroborate her story that she had come in to try to revive Stephen.

Ka-*bloom* went the door—as if someone standing outside had given it a good hard push.

Now Olivia gasped in earnest, and her mouth stayed open. She'd flung the door wide. It should have latched onto the outside wall. "Hello! Is anybody out there? Open this door, please! At once!"

But she knew there was no one out there. It was just some damnable accident. Maybe an accident that Stephen had arranged.

She looked at his face. His eyes were open, and on his white lips was his familiar little smile, triumphant now, and utterly nasty. Olivia did not look at him again. She drew her flimsy dressing gown as closely about her as she could and began to yell.

"Help! Someone!—*police!*"

She kept it up for what seemed like hours, until she grew hoarse and until she did not really feel very cold any more, only a little sleepy.

LAWRENCE G. BLOCHMAN

Dr. Coffee and the Whiz Kid

Dr. Daniel Webster Coffee sat before his microscope diagnosing tissue from Thursday's surgery when Detective Lieutenant Max Ritter stalked into the pathology laboratory at Pasteur Hospital with another man in tow.

"Hi, Doc," said the Northbank Police Department's tallest and skinniest homicide specialist. "Meet Detective Sergeant Kendall."

Dr. Coffee looked up to behold a husky prognathous redhead twice as broad but only two-thirds as tall as Ritter. The sergeant extended a bear's paw of a hand.

"Meetcha," said the sergeant.

"Greetings." The pathologist reflected that any number of forward-passing quarterbacks would envy that hand. "What's up, Max?"

"My sister's young kid Jake," Ritter said. "He ain't here?"

"He was, but he's long gone." Dr. Coffee frowned. "He should have reached home hours ago."

"He never got there," said Ritter.

"Disappeared," said Sergeant Kendall.

Dr. Coffee arose suddenly. A feeling of vague foreboding passed over him like a breath of cold wind. He had experienced the same uneasiness the day before when he had first heard about Max's young nephew Jake. Good lord, was it really only yesterday, less than twenty-four hours ago, that Ritter had come to get him in a police car?

There had been no reason for the uneasiness, unless it was his feeling that he was not really doing Ritter a favor. When the pathologist got into the car parked in front of the hospital, Ritter had said to him, "I sure appreciate this, Doc. And my mother will kiss you. Or anyhow bake you some of that strudel you like."

"It's absolutely crazy, Max." Dr. Coffee had shaken his head. "I won't be able to do anything for the boy. He should see a good psychiatrist, or at least a clinical child psychologist. I'm a lab man, Max, and what can—?"

"Don't argue!" The detective put the car in gear. "For mama you're a wizard. Ever since you cured her black Chow-dog tongue by telling her to stop taking bismuth tablets, she thinks you can do anything. And when she heard your wife was out of town visiting relatives this week, she insisted you come to dinner, and she'll invite my sister and her husband to come and bring the kid so you can see him. You know you can't cross mama."

The car stopped for a red light.

"I don't recall your ever talking about your sister before," Dr. Coffee said.

"We've never been what you might call palsy-walsy," Ritter had said. "She's ten years older and she was always papa's pet when the old man was alive. She went east to college. She got a Pee Aitch Dee come louder, a Phi Bait key, and a husband. I'm just a high-school dropout. Besides, Esther says I'm practically a goy."

The light turned green.

Dr. Coffee had known little about the bachelor detective's family life except that he was devoted to his widowed mother. He had only then learned that Max's older sister Esther was married to a professor of comparative religion at Northbank State College—a Dr. Irving Liebman with degrees from Vienna, the Sorbonne, and Oxford; the professor had been teaching at Columbia when Esther Ritter was getting her doctorate. The couple had adopted a Vietnamese orphan named Nguyen Quong-trang who for obvious reasons became Irving Liebman, Junior on his adoption papers, but whom everyone but his parents called "Jake."

"Tell me more about Jake," said Dr. Coffee, as Ritter swung north toward the once-stylish Heights neighborhood, now rapidly becoming a Northbank backwater. The detective had obliged.

It seemed that the Liebmans had adopted Jake through the intercession of a U.S. Army chaplain, Captain Amos Misch, who had once been rabbi of Northbank's Temple Beth Israel, and who had insisted that Jake was half Jewish. His reputed and unmarried father, the chaplain had said, was a Northbank man named Joe Straus, one of the first American advisers in Vietnam. Although a noncombatant, Straus had nevertheless been blown up by a land mine.

"Myself, I got doubts about Joe Straus being Jake's father," Ritter said, "because Jake is very bright—a whiz kid, you might say—and Joe Straus wasn't. I went to school with Joe and any brains he could pass on to a kid you could put in a thimble and have room left over for a dime's worth of bubble gum. Joe was what my mother would call a first-class schlemiel, and I ain't surprised he got blown up."

"But little Jake is a genius?"

"You'll see. If only he didn't have this—this thing I'm telling you about."

"He steals?"

"He steals. He says he can't help it. He admits he knows better but he says the urge is too strong for him."

"I could recommend a behavior therapist who deals with compulsions like that," the pathologist said. "It may be a conditioned reflex he picked up in Vietnam."

Ritter shook his head as he turned into a tree-lined street. "Jake ain't one of them wild street kids. His ma died shortly after Joe was killed, but she first left the kid with a Catholic orphanage. But you'll see for yourself. Here we are, Doc."

The police car stopped in the driveway of a two-story frame house. The white paint was peeling from the clapboards and the Victorian gingerbread that garlanded the eaves, but the red geraniums in the window boxes bloomed brightly and the curtains at the windows were stiffly immaculate.

"Come in, come in, Doctor. You are an angel to come. How is your good wife?"

"She's fine, Mrs. Ritter."

Mrs. Ritter was difficult to pigeonhole. Dr. Coffee would never have taken her for the mother of a high-ranking police detective. She certainly was not the caricature of the stereotyped Jewish mother, and he could not picture her as the mother of a scholarly female doctor of philosophy whose dissertation was entitled "The Interrelation of Climate and the Russian Novel as a Major Influence on the October Revolution."

Ma Ritter was plump and rather short. Her pink scalp glowed through the bluish tinge of thinning white hair. Her old-fashioned-length dark dress was probably homemade, but it was not dowdy. She moved with a certain grace.

"Please sit down, Doctor. My daughter and her family will be a little late. She just phoned. You'll take a glass of wine in the meantime?"

"No, mama, no!" Ritter made a panic gesture. "Doc can't drink that sweet Concord grape stuff. He breaks out in hives."

"Don't talk foolishness, Max." Mrs. Ritter smiled apologetically to the pathologist. "Max is such a joker."

"No joke, mama. Kosher wine gives him boils. I got a bottle of honest poison in my room. I'll fix him up."

When the detective had disappeared, his mother said, "I hope you can help little Jake, Doctor. Did Max tell you how worried I am?"

"I'm sure he'll be all right, Mrs. Ritter."

"Unless that judge decides to send him away. Didn't Max tell you? If it wasn't for Max they would send him to some farm for juvenile delinquents."

Max Ritter returned juggling two drinks and his mother's glass of wine.

"To your good health, Mrs. Ritter." Ice tinkled as Dr. Coffee raised his glass. He scowled at Ritter reproachfully. "Max, you didn't tell me the boy had been arrested."

The detective's Adam's apple bobbed twice in his long neck, and a slow flush mounted to the tips of his outsize ears. "It's just a formality," he said. "The kid was released in my custody. Kendall couldn't help himself, so he went through the motions—"

"Who's Kendall?" Dr. Coffee interrupted.

"A detective sergeant. You don't know him. He was with the pickpocket squad in Chicago before he did a trick in Asia with the Marines. Then he came here. He catches odd jobs when he ain't karate instructor to the force."

"Karate?"

"All Northbank cops got to learn the fundamentals now," Ritter said. "And Kendall is a Black Belt. He can break two one-inch planks with a barehanded chop or an elbow smash. Anyhow, Kendall got a call from Jimmy Jamaica—"

"Hold on, Max, you've lost me again. Who's Jimmy Jamaica?"

"He's the blind man who owns this candy and stationery store across from Jake's school, the place Jake's been stealing chocolate bars from."

"You mean Jamaica called in the police just because a boy took some candy?"

"Not the first time, Doc. This is going on quite a while. At first Jimmy Jamaica boxed his ears when he caught him. Then he took him to the principal of the school and said next he'd call the cops. The principal called Jake's father and the kid promised he wouldn't do it again, but he broke his promise."

"Max, he's only a child," Mrs. Ritter interrupted. "So he forgot his promise."

"Mama, he didn't forget. He's got a brain like Einstein. Something's wrong with the kid. You know it yourself since you asked me to bring Doc to look him over. Wait till you see him, Doc."

As if on cue, the front doorbell played a lively tune and the door opened. While Irving Liebman, Junior's finger was still on the bell button, his family entered. Esther Ritter Liebman appeared first, apologizing for being late—the boy was taking a nap and they didn't want to wake him. She and her brother had obviously not inherited their dominant genes from the same parent. While Ritter was lean and angular, his sister was short and plump. She wore a blonde wig, a superior smile, and a Phi Beta Kappa key suspended on a gold chain above her ample bosom.

Professor Liebman was not much taller but he was better proportioned. His silky black beard curled slightly above his blue polka-dot bow tie and his stern eyes peered through thick spectacles with octagonal gold rims. He bowed slightly from the waist in pre-Anschluss-Vienna fashion.

The youngster was still playing a tune on the doorbell while the preliminary introductions were made. A sharp "Irving" from his foster father reminded him that he was expected inside.

"Hello," the boy said, pressing the palms of his hands together with the fingertips pointing to his chin. Then he solemnly shook hands all around. He was an appealing lad. Although his Eurasian origin was evident in some of his features, his black eyes were distinctly non-Asiatic. They were big and wondering, and the lids lacked the Mongolian fold.

"Irving, Dr. Coffee is a pathologist," said Professor Liebman. "Do you know what a pathologist is?"

"Sure," said the boy. "He tries to find out what makes people sick, and if they die anyhow, he takes them apart to find out why."

"His English has a fine American accent," said Dr. Coffee.

"He speaks French and Vietnamese, and he's learning German," said his foster mother proudly.

"He's going to study Russian next year," the professor added. "He wants to enter the foreign service."

"Last month he wanted to be a big-league ball player," said Ritter. "Did the Mets win today, Jake?"

"Not yet," the boy said. "They play the Giants on the coast tonight, but they should win. Seaver's pitching."

"Who's leading the National League in batting, Jake?" Ritter continued. "Willie Mays?"

The boy stuck his tongue out at the detective. "You're kidding me. You know Mays hasn't led the league since 1954. It's Pete Rose right now. He's hitting .348."

"In March he wanted to be an astronaut," said Professor Liebman. "How far away is the moon, Irving?"

"At its apogee, 252,710 miles."

"Don't ask him if he knows Einstein's equation," said Ritter, "because he'll tell you, and I bet even Esther don't understand it."

"As long as he doesn't grow up to be a cop like his Uncle Max," Esther Liebman said.

"Please everybody come in the dining room," said Mrs. Ritter. "Max, you'll carve the chicken. The matzo balls I made especially for you, Doctor Coffee, even if it isn't Passover. Max said you raved about them when you were here last time."

Dr. Coffee did indeed appreciate the culinary skills of Mama Ritter. Although a zealous votary of the more sophisticated aromatic spectrum of classical *haute cuisine*, he had a great liking for the subtle variations of good uncomplicated fare. After all, what could an Escoffier or a Prosper Montagné do to a roasting chicken to improve the succulence of Mama Ritter's bird?

Dr. Coffee did not let his gastronomic enjoyment distract him from the primary purpose of his visit. He watched intently every mouthful consumed by the young Eurasian kleptomaniac, if such he was. He was particularly interested by the gusto with which the boy attacked Mama Ritter's apple strudel.

"You like dessert, don't you, Jake?" he asked. "Cookies and ice cream?"

"You bet."

"And candy?"

A peculiar look came over the boy's face. He was suddenly on his guard. He nodded, but said nothing.

"Your Uncle Max tells me you've been taking candy from a store near your school," Dr. Coffee pursued, "without paying for it." Again the boy nodded. His lower lip advanced slightly. "Why is that?"

"I didn't have any money. And anyhow, other kids do the same thing and they don't get in trouble."

"Don't you get any sweets at home?"

"He gets plenty of sweets," Esther Liebman broke in. "We eat desserts regularly."

"Do you give him candy?" Dr. Coffee redirected his question.

"Certainly, once in a while," replied Professor Liebman. "Too much candy is not good for a boy whose teeth are still forming. Isn't that so, Doctor?"

Dr. Coffee made a noncommittal gesture. He seemed preoccupied with Mama Ritter's strudel.

"He certainly knows right from wrong," said Esther Liebman defensively, as if someone had accused her of faulty upbringing. "We certainly haven't neglected the moral or spiritual side of his education, have we, Irving?"

"The boy has been subjected to ethical bombardment from all sides." Professor Liebman pointed the tip of his beard in Dr. Coffee's direction as he made the announcement. "He was first brought up as a Buddhist, then as a Catholic. We want him to know something of our own faith, naturally, but he sometimes attends a Protestant Sunday school with a classmate. We want to expose him to all religions, and when he gets old enough to understand them, to choose the one he finds most compatible."

"More strudel, Doctor?"

"No, thank you, Mrs. Ritter. It's delicious, but—"

"Just a little piece. No? Then Esther, will you please serve the coffee."

Dr. Coffee watched the boy's eyes follow the strudel as it disappeared into the kitchen. He leaned across the table and said, "Jake, tomorrow's Saturday, so you don't go to school—right?"

"This Saturday we were planning to go to a Quaker meeting," Professor Liebman volunteered.

"Then perhaps, Professor, you could bring the boy to Pasteur Hospital instead?"

"Hospital?" Mama Ritter was alarmed. "Why do you have to put him in the hospital?"

"Only for an hour, Mrs. Ritter, in my laboratory. With his parents' permission I'd like to make a few tests."

"I'd be glad to bring him, Doctor."

"He doesn't have to take me," said Jake. "Like I'll come by myself. I've never seen a laboratory. What are you going to do to me?"

"Nothing that will hurt," Dr. Coffee tried his best to remember the bedside manner from his intern days—how long ago was it? Good lord, twenty, thirty years! "Maybe I'll take a sample of your blood."

"Blood?" echoed Mama Ritter. "What for?"

"Just a few drops."

"Wow!" said Jake. "Will you teach me how to do it?"

"Certainly," Dr. Coffee smiled. "Come before lunch. Say about noon, pathology lab, fifth floor, Pasteur Hospital."

"He'll be there, I promise," said Professor Liebman.

In the police car Dr. Coffee said, "Max, do you suppose that candy store is still open?"

"Could be," said Ritter. "Jimmy Jamaica lives upstairs. We can try."

"I'd like to stop off there, if you don't mind. Is the man really blind?"

"He sees a little out of one eye—enough to catch kids that swipe his Creamy Crunch and Chunky Chucknuts. And what he don't see, Maggie Dorwin sees for him. She's his housekeeper and sorta takes care of him."

"Do you think Jake is telling the truth—that Jamaica lets some kids steal candy but cracks down on Jake exclusively?"

"If you mean is Jimmy Jamaica a racist who don't like Jake because he's half Jewish and half Vietnamese, the answer is no. Jake's special playmates, the ones he says get away with swiping stuff, are mostly blacks and Latins. What are you going to test the kid for tomorrow, Doc?"

"I'd rather not speculate, Max."

"But you think he's got something wrong?"

"Let's say I suspect something's wrong physically."

"Hope it's not serious," Ritter said. "I like that kid. He's going to grow up to be really somebody if that sister of mine and her trained poodle don't ruin him."

The police car turned a corner at the Calvin Coolidge Grammar School and drew up in front of the two-story frame building that was Jimmy Jamaica's Scholastic Candy and Stationery Store. There was a light burning inside when Ritter braked to a stop, but the store went dark as he switched off the ignition. He and Dr. Coffee got out of opposite sides of the car.

The front door of the shop was locked. Ritter rattled the knob, played a toccata and fugue on the doorbell, then banged gently on the glass panel with the flashlight he was carrying. When there was no response, he sent the flashlight beam through the glass to explore the darkness inside. In about a minute an apparition loomed in the circle of light—a blue-eyed Medusa head with a frightening halo of bright red curlers.

"We're closed," shouted the Medusa through the glass. "What do you want?"

"Tell Jimmy Jamaica that Lieutenant Ritter wants to see him."

"Jimmy's gone to bed." The Medusa made no move to open the door.

"Get him down. Tell him I want to speak to him."

The apparition vanished from the circle of brightness.

"Who's the gorgon?" Dr. Coffee asked.

"Gorgon? I guess you mean Maggie Dorwin. She's Jimmy Jamaica's seeing-eye dog and whatnot. Ain't she a dish?"

The pathologist chuckled.

It was several minutes before an emaciated elderly man with an incongruously developed potbelly shuffled up to the glass door and into the field of Ritter's flashlight. He wore dark glasses. He was in his undershirt and his suspenders hung down outside his trousers.

"What do you want?" he shouted through the door.

"Open up, Jimmy. Dr. Coffee here wants to talk to you about my sister's kid."

"I got nothing more to say about that thieving little brat. He ain't my worry no more. Tell your friend to talk to Sergeant Kendall. It's his baby now."

"Quit stalling, Jimmy. Let us in."

"You got a warrant?" Maggie Dorwin's Medusa head reappeared over Jamaica's shoulder.

"Come on, Jimmy. You know we don't need a warrant to talk to you. Open up."

"You got to have a warrant this time of night. I know my constitutional rights. I got the right—"

"I know, I know. The Fourth Amendment. You got a right to be secure in your house and person against unreasonable search and seizure. Well, we ain't gonna search or seize—"

Ritter stopped when he realized he was talking to the dark. Jimmy Jamaica and Maggie Dorwin had withdrawn from the searching beam of his light.

"Shall I bust in?" Ritter asked.

"Don't bother. We can talk to him after I've run my tests. Drive me home now, Max, and I'll give you a brandy."

Jake Liebman, né Nguyen Quong-trang, arrived at Dr. Coffee's laboratory next day promptly, out of breath, and wide-eyed with excited curiosity.

"Hey, this is groovy!" he exclaimed as he looked around at the mysterious chromium apparatus and glistening glassware. "Ive never been in a lab before."

The boy leaned against a wall.

"You're all in, Jake," Dr. Coffee said. "Did you walk over here?"

"No. My father drove me to the hospital. But I missed the elevator and I was afraid I'd be late, so I ran up the stairs."

"Do you get tired like this often?"

"No. Well, sometimes before dinner I lie down and read. What's that round thing there?"

"That's a centrifuge."

"What's it for?"

"It spins test tubes around several thousand times a minute. It separates things—like a cream separator. It separates bacteria from spinal fluid, blood cells from the serum—"

"Are you going to spin some of my blood in there?"

"Not today, Jake. I'm going to put a little of your blood in that machine over there. It's a photoelectric colorimeter."

"What does it do?"

"It has an electronic eye that looks at your blood and tells us how much of everything is in it."

"Like what? Don't you already know what's in everybody's blood?"

"Not the precise amounts, Jake. For instance, I don't know exactly how much sugar you've got in your blood."

"So that's it again." The boy's face darkened. He looked at the floor. "You don't need the machine for that. I already told about stealing the candy. I think I'll go home."

"Now wait a minute, Jake—"

"You're trying to get me to, you know, squeal on somebody else, but I won't. I don't tell on other people. Not ever."

"I think we understand each other." The pathologist held out his hand. "Shake. I'm just trying to help you and I think this whole business will be cleared up this afternoon."

The boy silently took his hand.

"Jake, I want you to meet Dr. Mookerji." Dr. Coffee presented his pear-shaped resident pathologist. "He's from India."

The boy stared at Dr. Mookerji's pink turban as he shook the plump brown hand of the man from Calcutta.

"Am delighted to meet fellow Asian," said Dr. Mookerji.

"I knew a man from India," said Jake. "He was the watchman at the orphanage in Saigon. But he had, you know, a red turban and whiskers. Why don't you have whiskers?"

"Watchman was no doubt Sikh," said Dr. Mookerji. "Personally am Bengali."

"If you'll go with Dr. Mookerji, Jake," said Dr. Coffee, "he'll introduce you to that pretty girl over there in a white smock—her name is Doris Hudson. They'll take a sample of your blood and then you can go home. Should I call your Uncle Max to come by for you?"

"I'll take the bus. I've got my school tickets."

Dr. Coffee considered giving the boy an injection of glucose before he left, but instead handed him a chocolate bar to eat on the way home.

When he dialed the number of Professor Irving Liebman, Ph.D., Dr. Coffee had the colorimeter readings in front of him.

"Professor, you won't have to worry any more about your boy stealing candy. That was a purely physiological response."

"Don't you mean *psycho*logical, Doctor?"

"*Phy*siological. His body has an overwhelming hunger for sugar. He has a mild case of hypoglycemia—or hyperinsulinism."

"That sounds terrible. What is it?"

"He has an overactive pancreas—diabetes in reverse, you might call it. His blood sugar is below normal. His pancreas secretes more insulin than he can use, and it burns up too much of the blood sugar he needs for energy. And since you people probably ration his sweets at home, he instinctively replaces the missing energy by stealing and eating candy."

"Curious. But is this hypoglycemia serious?"

"Probably not, if it's treated. If you'll give me the name of your family physician I'll tell him about my preliminary findings, which are only indicative. He'll probably want to run a glucose tolerance test for a more extensive diagnosis, and of course he'll want to rule out certain other possibilities. Meanwhile let the boy eat sweets, particularly when he's tired."

"Thank you, Doctor Coffee. Is Irving still with you?"

"He should be home at any minute now. He took the bus."

But the boy did not get home "at any minute now." In fact, he had not reached home by 4:30 when Max Ritter barged into the pathology lab with Sergeant Kendall in tow.

"How long since the kid left here?" Ritter asked.

Dr. Coffee turned to Doris Hudson who sat beside him at the microscope, a notebook in her lap. "Two hours, Doris?"

"More than three, Doctor."

"Sergeant Kendall and I stopped by the place fifteen minutes ago and he wasn't home yet. My sister and that egghead she lives with are ready to climb walls."

"The juvenile probation people want to talk to him," said Sergeant Kendall. "We think we can fix things up."

"You'd better let me go along. I can explain the whole matter." The pathologist told the detectives about the boy's "diabetes in reverse," and added, "You might say his petty larceny was dictated by nature's need to correct his blood-sugar deficiency."

"Sure, come along if you want," Ritter said. "But we better find the kid first. My sister is going nuts."

"Where would you look first?" Dr. Coffee asked. "He told me he was going right home on the bus."

Sergeant Kendall made a funny face. "I know where I'd look," he said. "Jimmy Jamaica's joint."

"Why Jamaica's?"

"To get even with the old buzzard for blowing the whistle on him."

"You think a kid his age would nurse that kind of grudge?"

Sergeant Kendall's red eyebrows expressed surprise that his thesis should even be questioned. "Sure. He's half gook."

"Let's start there anyhow," Ritter said.

Jimmy Jamaica's front door was still locked. A sign inside the glass that read "Closed" offered no further explanation. "Maybe he's closed Saturdays because there's no school," Dr. Coffee suggested.

Ritter banged on the door and rattled the knob. "He must be here. He phoned me about an hour ago, a little before Kendall came by to pick me up."

"Why did he phone you?"

"I dunno. He says drop in this afternoon, I got something to talk to you about. Shall we call the Safe and Loft Squad or have you got your Open-sesame with you?"

Sergeant Kendall produced a bunch of keys and in two minutes the door was open.

In four minutes Lieutenant Ritter was telephoning to the technicians of the Homicide Squad.

Jimmy Jamaica lay on his back behind his candy counter, one hand above his head, the other hand resting in a scatter of cigarettes and Bonbon Bars. Even before Dr. Coffee had confirmed the absence of vital signs, it was obvious he was dead.

Dr. Coffee made a quick, if illegal, examination of the body before the photographers and fingerprint men arrived. He found no apparent bullet wound, no blood, no visible signs of brute force. He tried lifting the outstretched arm. It resisted him.

"Funny," Ritter commented. "He's already in rigor mortis, but he was alive only an hour ago."

"Then one of two things must have happened," said the pathologist. "Either it was someone else who phoned you, pretending to be Jamaica, or he died in a convulsion or while struggling. In the latter case rigor mortis sets in very quickly, sometimes in less than a hour."

"If you want to do an autopsy," Ritter said, "I'll fix it with the coroner. Anyhow, we still gotta find Jake."

"What about the woman who was here last night?" the pathologist asked.

"Maggie Dorwin," Ritter said. "She's got a room upstairs."

"She not there." Sergeant Kendall snapped his fingers. "I know several places she might be at. Here comes your crew, Max, so I'll go pick her up. I'll bring her to headquarters."

When the experts got into high gear with their paraphernalia, Ritter and Dr. Coffee climbed the stairs to the second-floor apartment. They did not find Maggie Dorwin there. Neither did they find Irving Liebman, Jr., né Nguyen Quong-trang. What they did find surprised and puzzled them.

In the room that was obviously Jimmy Jamaica's there was a disarray of empty bottles under an unmade bed, dirty clothes piled in corners, three white canes stuck in a wastebasket, a dozen wrist watches carelessly strewn on a dresser top. The dresser drawers revealed, in addition to socks and underwear, more wrist watches of all sorts.

On the floor of a kitchenette a bag of groceries had been dropped. The bag had burst, spilling out a carton of milk, a loaf of bread, a package of bacon, a tin of coffee, a cellophane sheath of sliced cheese.

There was a definitely feminine accent in the second bedroom—jars and bottles of cosmetic preparations on the dressing table—but both men were goggle-eyed over what they saw in the open suitcases on the bed. One of them was cluttered with nylon stockings, panty hose, women's gloves, and dozens of transistor radios. In the other was a jumble of petit-point handbags, bottles of perfume, and embroidered lingerie. On a shelf in the closet was a cardboard box full of rings, brooches, and earrings.

Dr. Coffee, bending over the suitcases on the bed, suddenly straightened and ran his long fingers through his tousled mop of sandy hair. There was a shadow of apprehension in his gray eyes as he became aware of the possible significance of what they had just discovered. He could not pinpoint all the ramifications, but the same feeling of cold foreboding he had first experienced twenty-four hours before again touched his spine.

"Max!" Dr. Coffee was giving orders now. The pathologist was directing the surgeon to proceed according to his microscopic diagnosis. "Max! Get a description of your sister's kid to the whole Northbank police force, the sheriff's office, and the State Police. The boy's in danger."

"Kidnaping, Doc?"

"An understatement, Max. Whoever killed Jimmy Jamaica—"

"You don't think Jimmy just dropped dead?"

"It's safer to assume he was murdered. Max, get moving!"

Esther Ritter Liebman was having her hysterics as quietly as she believed compatible with her status as a Doctor of Philosophy and the wife of a Professor of Comparative Religion. She lay on her chaise longue crying silently and taking an occasional sniff of smelling salts in the best turn-of-the-century manner.

The professor was taking the disappearance of his adopted son calmly— almost to the point of apathy, Dr. Coffee thought as he listened to Max Ritter question his brother-in-law. There was no use losing one's head over this contretemps, said the professor, because that's what it was—a contretemps. Why foresee a possible tragic outcome when things would probably turn out all right?

"We have always encouraged young Irving to be self-reliant," he said, "and I have every confidence he is well able to take care of himself."

No, the boy had not telephoned. No, there had been no phone call demanding ransom or making threats.

"The phone has rung only once this afternoon since you called from the hospital," the professor said. "A Mrs. Gonzalez called. She's apparently the mother of one of Irving's classmates. She complained that Irving had been at her house talking to her son—I believe his name is Paco—and that Paco was very much upset. Paco wouldn't tell her what Irving and he had been talking about and when Irving left, Paco locked himself in his room. She wanted to know if we could tell her what had disturbed her son. Of course we could not. But the call indicated that Irving made one or more stops on his way home. So, you see, there is nothing to worry about."

"I hope you're not overoptimistic, Professor," said Dr. Coffee. "Could you tell us the names of some of your son's other school friends?"

"I'm afraid not," said the professor's wife, suddenly alert to the situation. "Irving never brought them home."

"I can name four," Max Ritter volunteered. "Besides Paco Gonzalez, there's Bill Cox, Hank Werner, and Wally Block. A couple of Saturdays ago I had a day off and I took Jake and his pals to the ball game."

"That's a side of you I never knew." Dr. Coffee smiled briefly. "Do you know where Jake's pals live?"

"Sure. I picked 'em up and took 'em home."

"Could you place their homes in serial order, say between Pasteur Hospital and here?"

"I guess so. The Cox place is closest to the hospital. Then comes Gonzalez, then Werner, and Block is nearest here."

"Get on the phone, Max, and find out if the boy called on any of his other buddies besides Gonzalez. I got the impression while he was in my lab that he thought I was trying to make him betray his friends—how I don't know."

Ritter disappeared into the next room.

He was back in a few minutes with some notes scribbled on an envelope.

"I talked to Mrs. Cox," he reported. "She says Jake—par'me, Esther, Irving—came to see Bill about half-past one and the two of them went out to the backyard for a while. She don't know what they talked about but when Bill came in he made a phone call. She thinks it was to some girl because he's not talking about it, like he don't want to be considered a sissy. The Werners and the Blocks, both negative. Neither of them seen him today."

"So it looks as though the boy disappeared somewhere between the Gonzalez place and here, assuming he was coming home. Max, if you put enough men on that stretch right away you might find someone who saw what happened—if anything."

"Will do, Doc."

"Did you call the coroner?"

"I did. He says it's okay for you to do the P.M. If you want him to sign anything he'll come over."

"Then I'll get a bite to eat and run over to the hospital. If Jamaica's body is there, I'll do the autopsy tonight."

When Dr. Coffee walked into his laboratory, Dr. Mookerji and Doris Hudson were sharing sandwiches and a container of milk. A transistor radio was perched on the workbench between them.

"What are you two doing here so late?" Dr. Coffee asked. "Don't you know Pasteur doesn't pay overtime?"

"Salaam, Doctor Sahib," said the Hindu resident. "Have been hearing wireless reports of mysterious fatality in sweet shop. Believing same is perhaps client of Leftenant Ritter, staff is offering services."

"Besides, we were wondering if there was any news of that cute little boy who was here this afternoon," said Doris Hudson.

"The boy hasn't turned up yet." Dr. Coffee shook his head as he took off his jacket and slipped into a white smock. "Has that package from the coroner arrived yet?"

"Ten minutes ago, Doctor. They phoned from the basement."

"Then I'll accept your offer, Dr. Mookerji. Get our usual impedimenta together—we'll go right down and get to work. You'd better go home, Doris."

"If there's any news about the boy—"

"I'll phone you. Max has his troops mobilized. We're all worried. With reason, I'm afraid. Good night, Doris."

Max Ritter's phone call was transferred to the white-tiled room in the basement of Pasteur Hospital where the mortal remains of Jimmy Jamaica lay on a stainless-steel dissection table. Dr. Coffee had finished his external examination of the naked body and Dr. Mookerji was making notes. There were no wounds apparent.

He was about to make the first incision from the sternum through the navel when the clangor of the telephone bell shattered the solemn silence. Dr. Coffee put down his knife and picked up the instrument.

The boy was still missing, Ritter reported, but there were developments.

Among the fingerprints collected by the police experts from Jimmy Jamaica's place was a set apparently belonging to Maggie Dorwin. The Henry classification was telephoned to the F.B.I. in Washington. Within the hour the identification was made and her record telephoned to Northbank.

"Maggie got busted twice in Chicago," Ritter said. "Shoplifting. She did time and when she got out she came to Northbank. Her sister lives here."

"I suppose that's where Sergeant Kendall was going to look for her," Dr. Coffee suggested.

"She ain't there. I talked to Kendall after I got word from Washington."

"Look, Max. That shoplifting record ties in with all those watches and junk we found this afternoon. Why don't you check with Jake's pals and—"

"Already done, Doc. I talked to the Coxes, and they got Billy out of bed. He admitted Maggie was teaching the kids how to pick pockets, snatch handbags, and steal from stores. They got paid off in candy and gum and once in a while in nickels and dimes. So this afternoon Jake made the rounds of his friends to warn them he's going to blow the whistle on Jimmy and Maggie. When Jake left, Billy Cox phoned Jamaica to put him wise."

"You think Jamaica sent somebody to intercept Jake while he was making the rounds of his friends?"

"Natch. I think Maggie grabbed him after he left the Cox place. He never got any farther. But we'll find him."

"I hope," said Dr. Coffee, "before—" He did not finish the sentence. That vague feeling of uneasiness came over him again. He looked at the waxen body on the gleaming table. "Max, I'm just starting on Jamaica. It shouldn't take more than two hours. Call me then. Or before, if you have any news of Jake."

When Doctors Coffee and Mookerji returned from the basement with their Mason jars and white enamel containers, Max Ritter was already waiting in the laboratory.

"Doc, what killed Jamaica?"

"Massive hemorrhage," said the pathologist, "and shock."

"Hemorrhage? Why didn't I see any blood?" The detective pushed his hat to the back of his head.

"We found over a quart of blood in the abdominal cavity."

"Hey. How come?"

"He had a ruptured liver—technically a sagittal rupture between the two lobes. The hepatic artery was severed."

"Ain't that a funny way to die?"

"We see a ruptured liver occasionally—in an auto accident, a big fall, or anything that will smash the liver back against the spine. Have you heard from Sergeant Kendall since I spoke to you last?"

A blank expression crossed Ritter's face. He picked up the phone and dialed the police number. He asked to speak to Sergeant Kendall.

When he replaced the receiver his Adam's apple jounced twice.

"Kendall was unexpectedly called outa town," he said, almost without moving his lips. "Seems his father is dying in Chicago."

"Use your own judgment about getting out a warrant for Kendall," said Dr. Coffee, "but a man who can break two one-inch planks with a barehanded karate chop can certainly rupture a man's liver. Jamaica was apparently a heavy drinker. His liver extended several inches below his rib cage. So if our Black Belt karate expert backed him against the wall behind his candy counter—Max, do you want me to give you a hypothetical picture of what must have happened?"

"I'm all ears."

"Okay. Kendall was on the Pickpocket Squad in Chicago. Maggie Dorwin is a convicted Chicago shoplifter. When they came to Northbank they were not strangers. Here they teamed up with Jamaica and started a sort of Fagin operation."

"What's a Fagin operation?"

"Don't you remember your Charles Dickens, Max? Fagin was the villain in *Oliver Twist* who trained children to be pickpockets. Let's say Maggie was the instructor and Jamaica recruited kids who already showed larcenous tendencies by stealing candy. Only Jake refused to be blackmailed into a life of crime, but he continued to steal candy because of this pathological craving for sweets. Our three-headed Fagin thereupon put pressure on Jake to join the team—first the school principal, then the fond parent, and finally the police in the person of cop-accomplice Sergeant Kendall. Do you follow me?"

"I'm way ahead of you," said Ritter. "Jake decided he had enough, but before he sprung the trap he warned his pals to stand clear if they could. But Billy Cox panicked and spilled to Jamaica—"

"Whereupon Jamaica panicked and called you, expecting to make some sort of deal," Dr. Coffee resumed. "But Sergeant Kendall came in, overheard part of the conversation, and started a fight with Jamaica. Maybe he didn't mean to kill him—you'll probably have a hard time making anything more than manslaughter stick after you catch up with him—but he did give him the karate chop.

"Maggie had been out shopping during this time. She came in during the argument and dropped her groceries when she heard the ruckus reaching a climax. We can assume that Jamaica was putting up some kind of fight by the rapidity with which rigor mortis developed. Maggie rushed downstairs to find Jamaica dead or dying. Kendall sent her out to intercept Jake.

"Then Kendall started to set up an alibi. He locked up the candy store and got you to join him in finding your wayward nephew."

"I bet the juvenile probation people never asked to see the kid at all," said Ritter. "I'll check in the morning."

The phone rang.

"Pathology. Doctor Coffee speaking . . . Yes, he's here. Do you—is that so? . . . Well, that's good news—superlative, in fact . . . You don't say! Certainly, we'll be over."

Dr. Coffee was grinning as he hung up.

"That was your sister Esther," he said. "The prodigy has returned."

"Jake's back?"

Dr. Coffee nodded. "He just got home—in a taxi."

Irving Liebman, Junior obviously enjoyed being the center of attention. He displayed less emotion (his Oriental blood, no doubt) than his foster parents as he described the afternoon and evening he had spent with Maggie Dorwin at the Riverside Motel.

No, he said, he hadn't been afraid when she asked him to get into her car near the Gonzalez home. He was curious about where she was going to take him and what she might try to do to him. It turned out she wasn't quite sure about these points herself, because she drove around aimlessly for an hour or so, as if she couldn't make up her mind. Suddenly she said aloud, "The hell with Kendall! I'm just a minor league crook. I'm not a killer or a kidnapper. Why can't I keep on being just a dip and a shoplifter?"

The boy remembered her exact words with the total recall with which he remembered batting averages.

Maggie drove into the parking lot behind a shopping center and locked the boy in the car while she bought some chocolate bars and a bottle of whiskey. She then proceeded to the motel, where she registered, paid in advance, locked them both in the cabin, and hid the key in the bosom of her dress. She then addressed herself to the bottle seeking an answer to her dilemma.

She debated with herself in ringing tones. Should she take the kid to the rendezvous Kendall had designated? Or should she just sit here and hope Kendall wouldn't find her, because he would beat the hell out of her if he did? Or should she call the cops, turn over the kid, and tell them what Kendall did to Jimmy Jamaica, even though that would mean she'd go right back into the pokey?

As the evening wore on and the level in the bottle went steadily down, she reached no decision. Meanwhile she was dozing off for a few seconds at a time, but not enough for Jake to get at her key.

The boy had finally managed to escape by locking himself in the bathroom, standing on the toilet seat, and squeezing through the tiny window.

"How did you pay the taxi?" Dr. Coffee asked. "Would a Northbank cabbie extend credit to a small boy who hailed him in the middle of the night?"

"Oh, I had money," the boy said. "I showed the driver the ten-dollar bill I borrowed from Maggie."

"You borrowed—?"

"Well, I took it out of her handbag. I watched her one day when Maggie was, you know, teaching the kids how to open a woman's bag without the woman noticing. It looked easy, and it is. I tried it, and Maggie didn't notice." He turned to Professor Liebman. "If you want to pay it back, sir, you could take it out of my allowance—a quarter a week. I think Maggie is still at the motel. She's in Cabin Six."

She was indeed in Cabin Six when the police arrived—out cold.

In response to a broadcast by Detective Lieutenant Max Ritter of the Northbank Homicide Squad, the New York Police picked up Sergeant Kendall at Kennedy Airport as he boarded a plane for Mexico.

"What I can't understand, Irving," Professor Liebman said to Jake before sending him to bed on the night of the prodigy's return, "is the reason you got into this woman's car so readily, knowing she had been engaging in criminal activities. Why didn't you cry out or run for help? Why?"

"Well," the boy replied, "I thought this was a good chance for me to learn more about crooks, in case like I should decide I wanted to be a detective like Uncle Max."

The Crimson Coach Murders

Iit's rather step, this path," said Miss Penny. "And a little bit slippery."

"You'll be all right," said her companion reassuringly. "Just hold on to the rail."

"Oh, don't worry about me. I haven't enjoyed myself so much for years. It was such a wonderful idea, the coach tour. Everybody seems so nice. And the weather."

Miss Penny looked up, a little old birdlike woman wearing a mauve silk frock, a hat with a great deal of fruit on it, and dazzling ornamental dark glasses.

The cliff rose up, as it seemed, a long way above her, overhanging so that the top was invisible. She saw sky and sea that, through her glasses, was not dazzling but muted blue. She saw the face of her companion, smiling. And below, quite near now, was a rocky cove hollowed out of the cliff, with little pools between the rocks.

"Rather a sharp turn," said her companion. A hand was laid on her arm, on the arm that held the handrail.

"This is really a great adventure," Miss Penny said gaily.

Quite gently the hand lifted her arm from the rail, and a knee pushed her less gently in the back. Miss Penny fell helter-skelter down the last few steps, squawking like a duck. She caught her head nastily on a rock, and before she could get up, before she really knew what was happening at all, hard hands gripped her shoulders and forced her resistlessly down so that her face touched the salt and slimy water in one of the pools.

Miss Penny struggled then, and tried to speak, but when she opened her mouth, water filled it. She did not struggle for long. It was the end of her great adventure.

Her hat floated on the pool, like a toy boat laden with cherries and strawberries. Her body lay face down in the water.

There was one more thing to do, and her companion did it. The time was just after six o'clock in the evening . . .

The Crimson Coach Luxury Tour party sat in the lounge of the Barbeck Hotel and waited for dinner. The Barbeck was not the best hotel in Eastbourne, but it justified well enough, Gilbert Langham thought, the brochure's claim: 'The *hotels specially selected by our experts offer THE BEST OF EVERYTHING— food prepared by Continental chefs, smiling service, and rooms with a view of the sea.'* The room was comfortable, the service was quick, and there were pleasant smells coming from the dining room.

But back to duty. This was really a piece of field research for Gil Langham, whose fifth detective novel was to be about a murder committed on a coach tour in Southern England. With part of a plot sketched out he found himself at a loss to imagine what sort of people actually went on such a tour. What could be simpler than to go on one himself, and find out?

He took a small black notebook from his pocket and studied what he had already written, after the trip down from London with its break for a "surprise" lunch (which proved to be a picnic), and a visit to Arundel Castle.

William and Mary Blake. Married couple. Husband much older than wife. Wandered off on their own this afternoon.

Gil Langham looked at them now, sitting on a window seat with hands touching, and wondered if they were honeymooners.

At a table nearby sat the handsome gray-haired old man named Antrobus, and on a sofa Mrs. Elaine Williams lay back studying her blood-red nails and looking bored. He read what he had written.

Mr. Antrobus. Retired businessman? Made a fuss when we stopped for drinks, said he'd been charged twopence too much for tomato juice. But looks prosperous. Doesn't seem really to be enjoying himself.

Elaine Williams. Merry Widow spider? Looking for husband-fly to walk into her parlor?

A hand was placed on his shoulder, and a voice boomed in his ear. "Hello, hello! This won't do. Settling down to work while you're on holiday isn't allowed. Have a drink, old man."

Tompkins was fortyish, almost bald, and obviously destined for the part of bore of the tour. But very likely his book would have a bore in it, Gilbert Langham thought with a mental sigh as he said that he would like a drink. As they passed the Merry Widow she looked up. Her eyes telegraphed an invitation which Langham ignored.

"Not a bad looker, that," Tompkins said when they had their whiskies at the bar. "Did you notice her giving me the eye? But I always say, take it easy. You don't want to start anything you can't finish on a holiday like this."

"You've been on tours like this before?"

"I get around," Tompkins said. "Now, don't think I'm nosey, old man, but I always flatter myself I can spot a man's occupation. You're a schoolmaster, right?"

Gilbert had been prepared for this. "No. I'm a journalist, a free lance."

"Looking for copy, eh? Writing us up?"

"Of course not!" But he felt uncomfortable. The look in Tompkins' eye had been remarkably shrewd. He might be a bore, but he was far from a fool.

A young man came into the lounge, a young man with a tanned face, dark hair carefully parted, and teeth that showed dazzlingly white when he smiled.

This was Jerry Benton, the tour guide, who seemed to Gilbert Langham rather too much of a good thing. One couldn't make him a murderer in a story because it would be too obvious, but all the same—

"Don't like that chap," Tompkins said, cutting into and confirming his thoughts. "Don't trust him. 'Call me Jerry,' he says. I'll call him—" And he made a coarse joke.

Benton was going round from table to table, talking to all the members of the party, many of whom Gilbert Langham did not know. He chatted for a minute with Mr. Antrobus and then stopped beside the Merry Widow. They came over to the bar together. Benton performed introductions in a low, pleasant voice.

"There is a dance this evening at the Winter Garden. For those on the tour there is no charge."

"Don't dance," Tompkins snapped.

"And a concert at the Pavilion. Again no charge. Tomorrow morning at ten thirty there is a mystery tour that will last the morning."

"Same old South Downs mystery, I suppose," Tompkins said.

Benton was imperturbable. "Those who wish to stay here may, of course, do so. We leave the hotel after lunch."

The Merry Widow smiled at him. "Are you going to the dance?"

Benton smiled back. "Of course!"

The dinner gong sounded, and at the same moment the manager came into the lounge with a tall, hard-faced man wearing a blue serge suit. They came up to Benton together.

"Mr. Benton?" the man in the blue suit said. "My name is Lake. Detective-Superintendent Lake."

For a moment there seemed to be a break in Benton's perfect composure, then his smile was in place again. "Yes, Superintendent. What can I do for you?"

"You have a Miss Penny in your coach party?"

"That's right. But she's not here at the moment. She is a little late for dinner."

"Miss Penny won't want dinner. She's dead."

Mrs. Williams gave a little scream.

Tompkins said, "An accident?"

"It seems that she fell down by some rocks, caught her head, and drowned in a pool." The Superintendent spoke with deliberate slowness. "But there's one odd thing. A book, with all the pages torn out, was by her side. The pages were scattered around."

"What was the book?" Gil Langham asked.

Superintendent Lake stared at him. "*The Adventures of Sherlock Holmes.*"

Langham stared, and said with a gulp when asked his occupation, "I write detective stories."

A sergeant in the corner of the manager's office, where this interrogation was taking place, snorted slightly. Gilbert Langham gulped again, and decided that he might as well go on. "I'm here to get background material for a new book."

"You've been very successful." With the same grim sarcasm Lake said, "Using your no doubt exceptional faculties of observation, have you noticed anything odd on this coach tour so far?"

"I can't think of anything."

"Or about Miss Penny?"

Miss Penny, Miss Penny? They had hardly spoken. She was a face to him, no more than that—an old face inquisitive and perhaps vain, topped by a ridiculous hat. "I remember the fruit on her hat more than the face under it. Wasn't it an accident, then, Superintendent?"

"This is a queer business." Lake stared hard at him. "A crime writer might have thought it up." Langham flinched. "This little old woman goes off for a walk, climbs down some steps, slips—we can see the mark—falls, hits her head, and drowns in a pool of water. That's the way it looks. I think we might accept it as an accident.

"But then someone—someone, Mr. Langham—tears the pages out of a famous detective book, throws them all over the place, and leaves the gutted book by her body. If she was murdered, why should the murderer do that, after arranging things to look like a neat little accident? Or why should anybody else do it? This is the kind of thing that should appeal to a writer of crime stories."

The way in which these last words were spoken made Gilbert Langham gulp again. "Have you found out anything about Miss Penny? I mean, why should anybody want to kill her?"

The sergeant in the corner said, "Evelyn Penny. Spinster. Lived at 18 Cotes Avenue, Turnham Green, London. Told other members of party that she had retired from work in drapery store, had small private income, went away somewhere every year. Did not appear to know anyone else in coach party."

"And her movements, Sergeant?"

"Coach arrived Barbeck Hotel, Eastbourne, about three-thirty. Miss Penny had tea in lounge, then said she was going for a stroll. Was seen by Mr. Tompkins on front, later by Mr. and Mrs. Blake having photograph taken at the Nu-Stile-Picksher stall also on the front. This was about four forty-five. Not seen afterwards until discovery of body just before seven o'clock. Purse appeared not to have been touched and no sign of bodily violence."

"There's nothing to connect this with the coach," the Superintendent said. "But still, I'd like to keep what you might call an unofficial sort of an eye on your party. With your powers of observation, Mr. Langham, you could be a help to us in that way if you cared to."

The Superintendent smiled now. It made the request sound like an order.

"All right. But I don't really see what you want me to do."

"Just keep your eyes and ears open. We'll get in touch with you again in a day or two."

Dinner was late, but it could not be said that Miss Penny's death cast a shadow over the coach party. Rather it provided a ready-made subject of conversation which could be added to the weather and the food. Gilbert

Langham sat afterward at a table with the Blakes and listened to them talking about it.

"Honestly, you know, Mr. Langham, I don't think the poor thing was quite all there," Mary Blake said. "I mean, we saw her having her photograph taken on the parade by those people who give away prizes every day—"

"Nu-Stile-Pickshers," her husband said. He was a hearty, tweed-jacketed, pipe-smoking man in his early thirties, perhaps ten years older than his birdlike wife. "Advertising stunt, you know. As a matter of fact, we had our own pictures taken."

"But no luck with a prize," Mary Blake said. "Anyway, when the young man asked if she wanted her picture taken, she was primping and blushing like a girl of fifteen."

Mr. Blake puffed at his pipe, rustled the evening paper. "I reckon some man got hold of her—sex maniac, probably."

"But Bill," his wife said with ghoulish eagerness, "there wasn't—I mean, she wasn't *interfered with*, was she?"

Bill Blake was having trouble with his pipe. He tapped out the dottle in an ashtray. "The Superintendent didn't say so. If we're going to this dance, my girl, you ought to get ready."

Mary Blake excused herself. Her husband began to read the paper.

Gilbert Langham also went to the dance at the Winter Garden. The unattached women in the party, he saw, were beginning to pair up with men. He found himself asking the Merry Widow to dance. They talked, as seemed inevitable, about Miss Penny.

"I'm so glad it hasn't been allowed to spoil the tour," she said. "Jerry has been simply marvelous about it. You know how silly people are—they get worried; but Jerry's told them all it was just an accident."

"That was good of him."

"Yes, wasn't it? But he must have had a lot of experience in handling awkward situations. He was some sort of courier in the Middle East at one time. And then he was a smuggler."

"Really? What did he smuggle, Mrs. Williams?"

"My name's Elaine." She came close to him. The bloom of youth, he saw, had been replaced by the enamel of middle age, but she was still an attractive woman. She whispered in his ear, "Diamonds."

He wanted to ask why, if Jerry Benton was a diamond smuggler, he had this humble job of guide to a coach party, but after all it was none of his business if the guide liked to tell fairy stories to impressionable women. Instead he said, "Who was particularly worried about Miss Penny?"

"That's a funny thing. It was the man who keeps himself so much to himself. Mr. Antrobus."

Mr. Antrobus, gray-haired and really remarkably handsome, sat in the lounge drinking coffee when the party from the Winter Garden returned, gay and chattering. Tompkins also was in the lounge. He made a beeline for Gilbert Langham.

"I've had a word with the Super and told him my theory about the Penny murder—"

Jerry Benton interrupted him. "It was an accident. And anyway it's rather a gloomy subject, old man. I think it should be declared closed."

Tompkins glared at him. "It's a free country. This is my theory. That old girl, Miss Penny, had somehow got the wrong side of a chap who's a maniac about books, see. And this chap did for her, and then left the book by her side. What you might call symbolism."

There was a clatter from the other side of the lounge. Mr. Antrobus had knocked his coffee cup to the floor. He did not pick it up, but slowly rose and walked over to the lift.

"Good night," Tompkins said cheerfully.

Mr. Antrobus did not reply.

A man who is tired of Brighton is tired of life, Gilbert Langham said to himself, bringing Dr. Johnson up to date. He walked from the lawns of Hove to the Palace Pier in a trance of pleasure, leaving the promenade as he passed the Metropole to walk down beside the beach.

Here children shrieked happily; their parents bought tea trays and sticky cakes; young men in vivid shirts left the sunlight to play earnestly at pinball machines in the amusement arcades.

Behind the popular, vulgar Brighton lay the solid hotels full of money, and behind them the appropriately artificial glamor of the Prince Regent's onion domes. He stopped before a little hut that said *Nu-Stile-Pickshers*. Underneath was a sign in dashing scarlet calligraphy: *'Hav Yore Foto Takn and Win Wun of Our Munny Prizes.'* A curly-haired young man with an engaging smile was in charge.

"Step right up now, and take advantage of this stupendous offer. Three postcard size pictures for a bob, and a money prize if you get one of today's lucky numbers."

A chord was struck in Gilbert Langham's mind. "Haven't you got a place in Eastbourne?"

"Eastbourne, Littlehampton, Brighton, Worthing, Folkestone—a dozen places along the coast," the young man said. "But only one set of prizes each day, and each day at a different town. Today it's Brighton. Come along, you lucky people, we're offering you twenty-five quid to nothing."

"You were offering prizes in Eastbourne yesterday," Langham said. "Did you happen to see an old lady named Miss Penny?"

The young man looked at him sharply, then shouted inside the hut, "Just going out for a cuppa," and led the way to a self-service café twenty yards away from the hut. He put three spoonfuls of sugar in his tea, stirred, and said, "The name's Wilson, Charlie Wilson. What's yours?"

"Gilbert Langham."

"So now we know each other's monicker. I like to know who I'm talking to. Now, what's your interest?"

There was something a shade odd about the young man, Langham thought, as though he knew that working for Nu-Stile-Pickshers demanded a front of brass that was not natural to him. A university graduate seeing the other side of life?

"I'm one of the coach party she was with. I write crime stories and her death roused—well, you might call it my professional curiosity."

"Fair enough. She came along yesterday, had her picture taken. Funny old girl! I remember the way she mucked around with her hat, trying it this way and that for effect. Then she went off. I told the police." He hesitated.

"You've remembered something else." Gilbert Langham was careful not to sound too eager.

"Not exactly. It's just that they were only trying to fix a time, and I told them she came along at a quarter to five. They didn't want anything else, so I didn't tell them."

"Tell them what?"

"She seemed a bit excited, as if she was going to meet someone. And after she left the hut she did meet someone. I saw her."

"What did he look like?"

"I only caught a glimpse, mind. And side face. I'm not sure I could identify him. But he was a good-looking sort of chap, about her own age I should say. And he had a fine crop of iron-gray hair."

Mr. Antrobus.

"Superintendent Lake, please," he said into the receiver. "Tell him it's Gilbert Langham. About Miss Penny."

There was a click and he heard Lake's voice, with its faint undertone of sarcasm. "Yes, Mr. Langham?"

With attempted casualness he said, "I've been talking to a man named Wilson, who works for those Nu-Stile-Pickshers people. He saw Miss Penny walking with somebody after she had her photograph taken yesterday."

"Why didn't he tell us?"

"You were concentrating on the time," he said with a touch of complacency. "Wilson's not sure that he could identify the man, but says he had a fine crop of gray hair. From the description it might be a man on the tour named Antrobus."

There was silence. Then Lake said, "Miss Penny died between six and six thirty. Antrobus was in the hotel lounge a minute or two after six o'clock. Three or four people saw him."

"Alibis have been broken before now," Gilbert Langham said. He put down the receiver.

The telephone booth was opposite the Palace Pier. When he came out of it he hesitated. The coach party had split up, some of them going on a tour of the Royal Pavilion, and others preferring what was rather oddly called "Free Time."

They were all to meet back at the Packham Hotel at half-past six. With an hour to fill, Gilbert Langham went on to the Palace Pier.

He strolled idly, sniffing the salt air, until he saw ahead of him the gray hair and slightly shuffling walk of Mr. Antrobus. It was with a feeling that he was about to make a discovery of vital importance that he cautiously followed the gray head up the pier, and with some disappointment that he saw Mr. Antrobus turn into the Palace of Pleasure and settle down to play a game called Cup and Ball, at which he proved to be rather skillful.

He went up behind Antrobus and said, "Hello!"

The gray-haired man turned round with what might have been a look of alarm, but when he recognized Langham, it was only one of annoyance. "Good afternoon."

"You didn't go to the Pavilion?"

"Evidently not."

"You're not forced to do anything on this sort of tour—that's what I like about it."

Mr. Antrobus did not reply. He shot up a small silver ball and dexterously caught it in the cup.

"Where did you go with Miss Penny after you met her yesterday afternoon?"

Mr. Antrobus was about to catch another ball. His hand jerked, and he dropped it. He turned round and said very decidedly, "I did not meet Miss Penny. I did not even know her. You are being a nuisance. Will you please go away?"

Gilbert Langham went away.

When the tour of the Pavilion was over, the Blakes and the tour guide, Jerry Benton, went down to the beach.

"Have you made up your minds?" Jerry Benton asked.

"Let me see it again." There was something greedy in Bill Blake's voice.

They sat down. Jerry drew from an inside pocket something wrapped in tissue. As he unwrapped it, the white stone sparkled in the sunlight.

"Oh, Bill," Mary Blake breathed, "it's lovely, lovely!"

"You're asking a hundred," her husband said. "That's a lot of money."

"A quarter of what it's worth." Jerry Benton began to wrap the stone.

"Don't put it away. I told you, I don't know anything about diamonds. I'd need to have it examined by a jeweler."

"And have him asking where it came from? Not likely! I risked a five-year sentence to bring this in. I'm not having any jeweler poking his nose in."

"Bill," said Mary Blake in a small voice, "Mr. Tompkins said last night that he knew a lot about jewelry. Supposing he looked at it for us, would that—?" She left the sentence unfinished.

"That would suit me." Blake looked at Benton.

Benton hesitated, then shrugged. "Tompkins doesn't love me much. But all right. You can show it to him tonight."

He let the stone rest in his palm. Blake could not take his eyes off it.

* * *

"Another whiskey?" Bill Blake said.

"I don't mind if I do." Tompkins was wearing a brightly checked shirt, open to reveal his boiled red neck, and purplish linen trousers. He downed half the whiskey at a gulp and sighed with pleasure. "This is the life."

"Mr. Tompkins." Mary Blake put her pretty arms on the bar counter and looked at him with her birdlike head on one side. "You said you used to be an agent for a firm of jewelers."

"Correct, my dear lady. Brant and Boulding, Hatton Garden, dealers in precious stones."

"Would you look at a stone for us?"

Tompkins frowned. "Mixing business and pleasure—don't like that. Why d'you want me to look at it?"

"We'd pay you—" Bill Blake began, but his wife interrupted.

"We're thinking of buying it and wondered how much we should pay. And we're awfully stupid about these things. We thought we'd come to an expert."

The frown changed to a leer. "Anything to oblige a charming lady," Tompkins said.

Upstairs in Tompkins' room, Bill Blake took out of his pocket the stone wrapped in tissue which Jerry Benton had given him, with the remark that nobody could say he didn't trust his fellow men. Tompkins glanced at it, raised his thick eyebrows, and then took from his suitcase a jeweler's glass which he put into his eye.

He examined the stone carefully, turning it this way and that for perhaps half a minute. When he spoke his tone was professional.

"It's a diamond, and quite a fine one. Not cut as well as it might be, but still a very nice stone."

"How much is it worth?"

Tompkins took the glass out of his eye, and grinned at them conspiratorially. "You notice I haven't asked where it came from, and I don't want to know. But if you were asking me to buy it, that's the first question I'd ask."

"I'm not asking you to buy it. What's it worth?"

"I'm telling you the difficulty about selling it is that any honest jeweler will ask the same question. He'll want to be sure it came into this country legally." Now Tompkins winked.

"We shouldn't want to sell it," Mary Blake said excitedly. "It's to make into a ring for me."

Tompkins rubbed his chin. "Hard to put a value on it. Wouldn't be dear at two hundred quid."

"Oh, you darling man," Mary Blake said. She kissed Tompkins on the cheek.

The Merry Widow was telling Gilbert Langham the story of her life, as they sat in deck chairs on the front. Her husband, a colonel in the Engineers, had gone through the war unscratched, and had then died in a yachting accident shortly after his retirement, three years ago.

"No children," she said, turning on him the full force of still-lustrous eyes.

"And this rambling old house in Shropshire to look after. I'm a lonely woman, Gil."

Gilbert Langham was not much interested in her past. "You remember that yesterday evening we were sitting in the lounge of that hotel at Eastbourne. Did you happen to notice what time that man Antrobus came into the lounge?"

"I already told the police that as far as I could remember it was about six o'clock," Elaine Williams said coldly.

"You couldn't be more exact?"

"No. I must be going back to the hotel." As she got up she said, "I detest snoopers."

Gilbert Langham sighed. The way of an amateur detective is hard.

That night there was a fireworks display at the end of the Palace Pier, and tickets were free for those who wanted them.

"I must say," said Mr. Portingale, a self-important, pigeon-chested man who went about with a limp, long-nosed wife apparently permanently attached to his arm, "That young chap Benton knows how to manage things. As a businessman myself, I respect efficiency."

"He's very good," Gilbert Langham agreed. He was watching Mr. Antrobus to see if he took one of the tickets. He did, after asking whether they were free.

"My husband had thirty men under him at his retirement," Mrs. Portingale said in a melancholy voice.

"A versatile young fellow, too," Portingale resumed. "Used to be in the diamond trade, I understand. Adventurous."

"It takes all sorts to make a world," Mrs. Portingale said sadly.

"Yes, indeed." Langham took one of the tickets. The Portingales took them, too.

The night was hot, the sea still. Rockets swished up skyward, burst into patterns of stars. A set piece slowly made the pattern WELCOME TO BRIGHTON. There was a burst of clapping.

"It's simply gorgeous," Mary Blake said. "Perfect. I want it to last forever. Have you told Jerry about the ring, darling?"

"A hundred pounds is okay," her husband said. "I'll give you a check tomorrow." He produced the stone in its tissue and Benton took it.

"No checks, old man. Strictly cash. If you can let me have the money at the end of the tour I'll hand over the stone then." His teeth gleamed in a smile. "You can ask Tompkins to vet it for you again then, if you like. See you later." He waved a graceful hand.

"I wonder why he insists on cash." Blake took out his pipe and tapped it thoughtfully on the rail.

"He's just being careful, silly. Ooh!" A cascade of colored lights exploded just above their heads. The hand that she had placed over her husband's clutched at him, the nails digging gently into his palm.

"I want some cigarettes," Elaine Williams said, and opened her bag. "Oh, damn! I've forgotten my purse."

Portingale, who was sitting just behind her, took out his case. She murmured her thanks, lighted the cigarette, took a few puffs, then murmured something about going back to the hotel, and got up.

It was a few minutes afterward that Langham, who had been temporarily enthralled by a set piece depicting the battle of Trafalgar, with the *Victory*'s guns magnificently firing, noticed that Antrobus was not in his place. He got up and walked down the pier to look for him. But the man with gray hair had vanished.

Elaine Williams did not go back to the hotel. An hour later she was walking by the cliffs near Rottingdean, talking about her husband's death and the big house in Shropshire.

'Yes," her companion said. "Yes. Yes."

"The truth is that I am a very lonely woman."

"We are all lonely." Her companion took her hand and led her nearer to the cliff top.

"Sometimes—you'll think it foolish—my heart really aches." She guided his hand to her aching heart.

"You're not foolish at all." Another hand encircled her shoulder. She held up her face to be kissed.

Then she felt herself being forced backward, and opened her lips to scream, but the hand that had been on her heart quickly covered them. Her high heels scrabbled at the cliff edge before she went over . . .

It was no more than eleven o'clock in the morning, but already a fierce sun shone into the little room. The sandy sergeant he had seen before waved Gilbert Langham into a seat directly facing the window and the glare. Superintendent Lake sat in the shade.

"Now, Mr. Langham, I shall value the results of your skilled observation. What have you got to tell me?"

"I still don't know exactly what's happened," Gilbert Langham said. "There are all sorts of rumors. Nobody knew that Mrs. Williams hadn't come back to the hotel until this morning. Your people haven't really told us much."

"She's dead," Lake said. "She fell, or was pushed, off the cliffs near Rottingdean some time yesterday evening. There's a drop of about eighty feet and she was probably killed at once. She'd been dead several hours when she was found, early this morning."

Lake paused, then said, "There was a book found near the body, looked as if it had been thrown from the cliff top."

He held up a book on the desk before him, its cover spotted with damp. Gilbert Langham read the title on the back. It was *The Suicide's Grave* by James Hogg.

"That's not been gutted."

"Not this time. But the queer thing is that it should have been there at all. What sort of woman was Mrs. Williams?"

"I thought of her as the Merry Widow. She was flirtatious, particularly with young men."

"With you, for instance?"

"Yes. Though I lost favor because I didn't react properly when she said she was lonely. She seemed to like Jerry Benton, the guide. But it didn't mean anything. She'd have behaved the same way with any other young man."

"Mr. Langham." Lake leaned forward. The outlines of his face were harsh. "It seems likely that Mrs. Williams died through what you call flirtatiousness with a young man—or an old one. And since whoever killed her left a mystery book, as he did with Miss Penny, it's a fair assumption that the murderer is linked with your coach party. I want you to tell me exactly what you saw and heard after going out to watch the fireworks."

"At about nine o'clock or a little after, Mrs. Williams left us, saying she was going to the hotel. She'd left her purse there, had no money to buy cigarettes—"

Lake interrupted. "She said she had no money—you're sure of that?"

"Yes. A man named Portingale was sitting just behind her. He offered her a cigarette."

"Her handbag went over the cliff with her. There was a five-pound note in it."

"No purse?"

"Her purse was in the hotel. But a five-pound note is money. Why didn't she use it?"

A bluebottle buzzed on the windowpane. The glare of sunlight was hot on Gilbert Langham's body. He felt slightly damp.

Lake went on, "She didn't go back to the hotel—she went to meet somebody. It must all have been arranged in advance." He said sharply to Langham, "What happened after she left?"

Langham told him of Antrobus's disappearance and of his own movements.

"You say you got back to the hotel just after eleven. Nobody saw you?"

"No."

"You didn't go out again?"

"Of course not."

"I'm keeping the coach party here for the moment. Let me know if you have any intention of leaving Brighton, won't you?"

Gilbert Langham got up and said incredulously, "You mean you suspect *me*?"

"I suspect everybody." Lake smiled. "I'm still in need of suggestions, even from amateur criminologists."

"There ought to be some sort of clue in that book."

"There are no prints on it, if that's what you mean."

"No." Langham picked it up. "You see, this book is usually called *The Memoirs of a Justified Sinner*. This is a special edition, published in 1895, and it just might be possible to trace it."

"Nothing on the flyleaf, sir," said the sergeant.

"No, but—" Langham, leafing through the pages, gave an exclamation.

"What is it?" Lake came round the table, and Langham pointed out what he had found.

At the bottom of a page in the middle of the book, very small and faint, was a circular die-stamped mark. It said: *Charles Antrobus. Dealer in Rare Books. Specialist in Crime and the Occult.*

Lake said to the sergeant, "Duff, I think we'll have a word with Mr. Antrobus. No, hang on a minute. Ask Benton to come in first. I'd like to know whether he's got any details of when and how Antrobus booked for this coach tour, whether his bookings were linked with Miss Penny's and Mrs. Williams', for instance. That might help."

"Yes, sir."

"You're thinking we were stupid to have missed that," Lake said to Langham when the sergeant had left them.

"Why, no. This is a favorite book of mine. I happened to know it was an unusual edition—"

"It was careless. Two of us have looked through the book and we ought to have seen it. We've been doing fifty different things since the body was found this morning, but that's no excuse."

The Superintendent crossed to the window and stood looking out. The street was shimmering with heat.

"I don't know why people go abroad when we have weather like this in England."

"Have you found out anything more about Miss Penny?"

"Yes. It confirms that she was just what she seemed to be—a nice old lady who hadn't much money and lived a quiet life. There's no motive. Duff's taking his time." He rattled money in his pocket.

The door opened, and the sergeant came in, breathing hard. "He's not there, sir."

"Antrobus?"

"No, Benton."

Lake's face went very red. "I thought I gave instructions that nobody in the party was to leave the hotel until I'd talked to them."

"Yes, sir," the sergeant said stolidly. "We had men at the front door. Reckon he skipped down the fire escape. There are some people called Portingale looking for him—say he was in the hotel ten minutes ago."

"Right," Lake said. "Let's get up to his room."

Mr. Portingale, wife connected to him like a broken-down car being towed, was waiting for them in the passage. "Inspector, I have something I want to report to you—"

"Superintendent," Lake snapped. "It will have to wait." He turned to the sergeant. "Duff, he'll reckon on having at least half an hour's start. Chances are he'll take a train for London. Go to the station. Take someone with you who knows him by sight."

"I'll go along," Gilbert Langham said. In the car Sergeant Duff expressed himself rather scornfully about the likelihood of Benton catching a train.

"One of the Super's not so bright ideas," he said. "There's more ways out of

Brighton than out of a rabbit's burrow. If he tries the train he wants his brains tested."

"It's the quickest way of getting up to London," Langham said absently.

He was astonished by the turn of events. If Benton was the murderer, what was the meaning of the books placed by the bodies? He was pondering this problem when the police car pulled up outside Brighton Station with a screech of brakes.

The station, clean and bright, was comparatively empty at this time of the morning and Duff, who had been so skeptical in the car, was full of energy in action. Within no time at all, it seemed, he had learned that the last train for London had gone half an hour back, and that the next one left in ten minutes' time from Platform Three.

"Wouldn't have had time for the last one," Duff said as they walked along the train corridor. "Now, you look out for him. Brown face, medium height, good-looking, bit film starrish, you said. Might apply to me, eh?" He was in his forties and looked like a sandy-haired monkey.

Benton was not on the train. "Didn't suppose he would be," Duff said as they went back along the platform. "Knew it was a wild goose chase. We'll just stay around till the train goes. You get over by the departure board there and make yourself inconspicuous. I'll stay by the entrance. Give me the office if you spot him."

Langham nodded. The train left at 12:15. At exactly thirteen minutes past twelve Jerry Benton walked briskly out of the station lavatory with an attaché case in his hand, looked once round the station, and began to walk to Platform Three. Gilbert Langham raised his hand and Duff nodded.

Perhaps it was this gesture that made Benton look toward the departure board. He saw Langham, changed direction, and began to run out of the station. Duff and Gilbert Langham ran after him. Benton had several yards' start.

He was almost out of the station when a family consisting of father, mother, babe in arms, and a screaming small boy wearing a cowboy hat and carrying a spade and bucket, entered it. The small boy stuck the spade between Benton's legs and he went down with a crash. Before he could get up Duff and Langham were on him.

The small boy had stopped screaming, and looked slightly awestruck at the effect of his work. "Now, Bertie," said his mother, "you didn't ought to have done that."

"Oh yes, he did," said Duff, holding Benton's arm in a lock. "He's helped to make an important arrest. Are you Wyatt Earp?" he asked the boy.

"Nah, I'm Matt Dillon."

"Well, buy yourself another gun, Matt, will you?" He gave the boy half a crown.

"Can't buy much of a gun for 'alf a crown," the boy said.

The last words they heard as they got into the police car were his mother's. "There you are, Bertie. I told you you should have left the gentleman alone."

"She's got the right idea," Benton said, and grinned.

He did not look like a murderer, Gilbert Langham thought. But then, had he any idea at all what this particular murderer did look like?

They went back to the hotel room where Lake had conducted his interrogations. There Mr. Portingale stood, indignation filling his pigeon chest. There also, Langham saw with surprise, were the Blakes.

"All right, Benton. What have you got to say?" Lake's tone was rough.

"I don't know what this is all about." Benton smiled. "I just got fed up with the job and decided to chuck it."

Lake sighed. "Mr. Portingale."

Mr. Portingale took from his pocket something wrapped in tissue. When he unwrapped the tissue a stone gleamed in the sunlight.

"You offered me this for a hundred pounds, said it was a diamond. Then this morning you asked me for twenty pounds cash deposit, which I gave you, and handed me the stone. Later on I happened to be speaking to Mr. Blake—"

Blake produced another stone. "We took them to a jeweler. They're not diamonds, just quartz."

"How many more have you got in that case?" Lake asked.

"Six," Benton said calmly. "I don't know what they're moaning about. I never guaranteed the stones. They were sold to me as diamonds. I suggested they should contact somebody who would check on them."

"It's no good, Benton," Lake nodded to Duff.

The sergeant went outside. When the door reopened it revealed, to Gilbert Langham's astonishment, the bald head, puce face, and checkered shirt of Tompkins. The backslapping geniality was gone, however: Tompkins had no eyes for anybody but Benton.

"You rat," he said, "skipping and leaving me to hold the bag. Did you think I'd go for that?"

"All right," Benton said. "It's a cop. But I had nothing to do with those two women getting done in. That put the wind up me, I don't mind telling you."

"If I'm not much mistaken we shall find that both these boys have got records as long as my arm," Lake said. He addressed himself to the Portingales and the Blakes. "A nice little racket they ran together. You see how it worked. Benton spread a rumor about smuggling diamonds, then showed you the stone. He couldn't let you take it away and show it to a jeweler, so Tompkins meanwhile makes it known that he's an expert, and also that he dislikes Benton. He certifies the stone as genuine. If everything had gone as planned, you'd have handed over a hundred pounds each at the end of the tour and never seen either of them again. You're lucky that Benton got the wind up and tried to skip."

"We had nothing to do with the other business," Tompkins said. "You can see it queered our pitch, the police coming in."

"I believe you," Lake said, and sighed again. "Take them away."

"That leaves Mr. Antrobus," Gilbert Langham said.

It was one o'clock, just two hours since he had made that momentous discovery about the book.

"Yes. We've delayed our talk with him long enough. What's his room number, Duff?"

"Second floor. Two fourteen. But he may have come down to the lounge."

The lounge was buzzing with excited members of the coach party who had seen Benton and Tompkins taken away by the police, but Antrobus was not among them. They took the elevator up. Duff strode ahead along the corridor.

"Here we are. Two ten, two twelve." He stopped abruptly, sniffing.

"Gas." Lake put a handkerchief round his mouth and nose, and turned the door handle of Room 214. The room was not locked, the blinds were drawn. The smell of gas rushed out at them.

Lake ran across the room, pulled aside the curtain, opened the window wide, turned off the gas tap, and came out coughing. "Doctor," he said to Duff. The sergeant ran down the corridor.

Looking over Lake's shoulder, Gilbert Langham could see the body of Mr. Antrobus lying on the floor, his head near to, but not quite resting on, a pillow. The hose connecting the gas tap to a fire set into the wall had been pulled away and lay just by the man's mouth.

Lake drummed on the wall with his fingers while they waited for the gas to clear. "This looks like the end of the road."

"I suppose so." Yet Langham left queerly disappointed.

When they were able to enter the room they found further evidence. At a little writing desk in one corner of the room was a scrap of paper penciled in a fine, thin, clerkly hand: *I feel the bitterest regret for what has happened. I cannot go on . . .*"

Langham bent down to look at the note, and Lake said quickly, "Don't touch it."

"That paper has been torn off a larger sheet. I wonder why he was so parsimonious." The Superintendent was kneeling by the body, extracting a wallet from the jacket. There was a pencil beside the note, a yellow Venus 3B. Langham opened his mouth to say something else, then closed it again. Lake was going through the wallet.

"Pound notes—a wad of them. Membership cards of various societies. Check book. Nothing personal. Ah, this is interesting. Membership for the Antiquarian Booksellers' Association in the name of Charles Antrobus. He simply told me he'd retired from business. Ah, hello, Doctor."

The doctor examined the body briefly, then shook his head. "No hope, I'm afraid. He's had the gas tube in his mouth for hours."

"How many hours?"

"I wouldn't like to say. Some time last night, certainly. He's had a knock on the head at some time. Not very long ago, either."

"Enough to stun him?" Gilbert Langham asked.

"Possibly."

"Supposing he'd turned on the gas tap and sat down to write his suicide note," Lake suggested. "He might have been overcome by the gas, fallen, and struck his head on the gas fire. Could that have happened?"

"I suppose so," the doctor said, without much conviction.

"And that would explain why his head wasn't *on* the pillow but *beside* it. Suicides generally like to make themselves comfortable. But why didn't somebody find him earlier this morning? I think we might ask the reception desk. Then I suppose I should have a word with the rest of the tour party. Duff, will you get them together for me in one of the lounges?"

When they left the bedroom, the photographers and fingerprint men were at work. Downstairs, Lake said to the young receptionist,

"Did Mr. Antrobus in two fourteen leave any sort of message last night?"

"I'll find out for you, sir. Edward, the night porter, would have taken any message at that time."

Edward was old and gnarled as a tree trunk. "Mr. Antrobus? Yes, sir. He rang about eleven o'clock last night, said he had a migraine headache, and didn't want to be disturbed until after lunchtime today."

"Do you know Mr. Antrobus?" Langham asked. "Would you recognize his voice?"

The porter shook his head. "Why, no, sir. He was one of those on the coach tour, that's all I know. Wouldn't know him to speak to at all."

"You're hard to satisfy, Langham," Lake said. "You put us on to Antrobus in the first place. Now when you're proved right you're still unhappy."

"Somebody else could have been in that room, hit Antrobus on the head, put the gas tube in his mouth, and rung down to the porter."

"In theory, yes. In practice the obvious explanation is right ninety-nine times in every hundred. Just wait till we dig into Antrobus' background. You'll find he's a psycho, and that he killed those two women for some reason that doesn't make sense to you or me, and then committed suicide. Now I'm going to break the news to the rest of them. If I'm not much mistaken, with three casualties and two arrests in the party, they'll want to go home. Are you coming?"

Langham shook his head. He walked moodily toward the potted palms at the hotel entrance. The name "Antrobus," spoken behind him, made him turn. A blonde girl wearing a dark blue frock stood by the reception desk.

"Were you asking for Mr. Antrobus?" Langham said.

"Why, yes. I'm Sheila Antrobus. He's my uncle."

"I'll handle this," he said to the receptionist. And then to the girl: "You must be prepared for a shock."

She was shocked, certainly, but she did not seem deeply surprised. "Uncle Charles had been getting odder and odder ever since his wife died two years ago. It made things a bit difficult for me, because he was my guardian."

"Odd in what way?"

"He was a dealer in rare books—crime books especially. Soon after Aunt Rose died he gave all that up, and in the last few months it's sometimes seemed to me that he really hated books."

"There's something else. You'll have to know about it soon. I may as well tell you." He told her about Miss Penny and Elaine Williams. "Do you think he might have done that?"

She said in a subdued voice, "I don't know. I'd like to see him, please."

They went up to the room. She looked at the figure on the floor, shivered and turned away.

"There's something I want you to see." He led her over to the desk and showed her the note. "Is it your uncle's writing?"

"His prints are on it," one of the fingerprint men said. "And on the pencil."

"Poor uncle," the girl said. Her face was very pale.

They walked out of the hotel, along the Marine Parade and into the Old Steine. "There's something I want to ask you," Gilbert Langham said. "Did your uncle draw?"

"Sometimes. He wasn't very good, but he liked to sketch." She looked surprised. "Why?"

"I know something about pencils. That note on the desk—the one that's supposed to be a suicide note—was written with a thin fine pencil, probably a 2H. The pencil on the desk is a 3B, a drawing pencil."

She said nothing. They walked around into Church Street. The North Gate to the Royal Pavilion was in front of them. "Shall we go in?"

"All right." She stopped and faced him. "What does it mean, about the pencils?"

"I believe your uncle was murdered. And if he was, then everything that has happened has been planned, with him as the final victim. You said he made things difficult for you. How?"

"I want to get married. I'm only twenty. Uncle Charles didn't approve of Chris. In fact, he very much disapproved. So we agreed to wait."

"Chris?"

"Chris Watling. The man I'm going to marry."

They stood in the Pavilion gardens, with the statue of George IV on one side and the cupola of the dome on the other, together with those other fragments of the eccentric architectural past now transformed to respectable library and art gallery. She opened her bag and took out a photograph. He looked at it, and felt as though he had been struck between the eyes.

The photograph told him almost the whole story.

"Tell me about Chris."

There was some unfathomable expression in her blue eyes. "You wanted to go into the Pavilion. Let's go, then."

He waved a hand at the onion domes. "Do you know Sydney Smith's joke about the Pavilion architecture? That the dome of St. Paul's must have come down to Brighton and pupped? But I like it."

She made no reply. They walked in silence through the Octagon Hall and the entrance hall. In the Chinese Corridor she said, staring intently at one of the bamboo plants on the wall. "What do you want to know?"

"About Chris."

"You've seen his photograph. He doesn't find it easy to settle in a job. That's what Uncle didn't like."

"He's been in trouble?"

"His father lost all his money when Chris was about thirteen. There was trouble a couple of years ago over some bad checks."

She turned to face him, her face desperate. "But he's awfully nice—Chris—he's such fun to be with. He's always wanting to do something dashing, something that will get his photograph in the papers. He makes a joke of it—he's full of jokes. There's nothing bad about him really. You've got to believe that."

"It might be easier for you if I guessed some of the story and you filled in the details. Your uncle was quite rich, and most of the money comes to you."

"All of it. He's got no other close relations and he is—was—very fond of me."

"He disapproved of Chris, more strongly than you said. He blamed himself for letting you go about with Chris, told you to stop seeing him, threatened in the good old Victorian way to cut you out of his will. Right?"

"I told you. I'm not twenty-one yet and I didn't want to upset uncle. Do you think I cared about the money?"

"Chris cared about it, though. Didn't he?"

She turned and ran from him, ran back through the halls, while shocked respectable holiday-goers, wearing sleeveless shirts and with shorts above sun-reddened knees, looked after her. He found her in the garden.

"If your uncle died the money would come to you, and there would be no obstacle to your marriage. Uncle Charles was eccentric—he did odd things like coming on this coach tour. Why did he do that, by the way?"

"He always went on tours. He was awfully mean in little ways—said they were wonderful value for money. And this one attracted him because of going to a different place each day. All the places had piers. He loved playing the slot machines." She smiled faintly.

"Yes. Uncle Charles was eccentric, but he wasn't crazy. If Chris murdered him and tried to make it look like suicide, questions would be asked.

"But supposing it could be shown that Uncle Charles had really gone round the bend—supposing he'd killed two people and left the books he now hated beside his victims—then his suicide wouldn't be questioned. Superintendent Lake is prepared to accept it now."

"You mean that those two people, Miss Penny and Mrs. Williams, were murdered just to—"

"To convince people that your Uncle Charles was a psychopathic killer? I'm afraid so." He paused, said abruptly, "You recognized that so-called suicide note, didn't you? It was part of a letter from your Uncle to Chris."

"I don't know. There *was* a letter in which Uncle said something like that, about blaming himself for letting me go around with Chris. But I still can't believe it was the same note. What makes you so sure?"

"Why, you see," Gilbert Langham said, "I know who Chris is."

When they got back to the hotel, Mr. Portingale stood in the doorway beside the potted palms. "Have you heard the news?" he asked eagerly. "Do you know that we have been nursing a pair of scoundrelly tricksters in our midst?"

Langham had almost forgotten about Benton and Tompkins. "The Superintendent has got them under lock and key, though, hasn't he?"

"Would you believe it, my dear sir, they tried to practice their arts on me. I'm afraid they picked the wrong person there, eh, Mrs. P.?" Mrs. Portingale, firmly attached to one arm, smiled and nodded. "But as a result our happy little party is broken up. The coach company is making a very handsome refund, and Mrs. P. and I are departing for fresh fields and pastures new."

To call the party a happy one seemed to Langham an overstatement. "Where are you going?"

Mrs. Portingale beamed. "We are lucky enough to have been able to book with another coach tour. We are off to the New Forest. I believe that there are still one or two vacancies if you would care to—"

"No, thank you," Langham said hurriedly.

Sergeant Duff said cheerfully, "Where have you been? The Super's been looking for you—wants to pin a medal on your chest, I shouldn't wonder."

Langham said a little pompously. "This is Mr. Antrobus' niece, Sheila. We've got to see the Superintendent urgently. Some fresh information about the case."

Duff scratched his sandy head. "The trouble with you amateurs is you never can let well alone. The Super's round at the station."

They went to the station and found Lake. He listened impatiently, until Sheila Antrobus produced the photograph.

"That's Chris Watling," Gilbert Langham said.

Lake gasped. Then he said. "This seems to be an occasion for a little telephoning." When he put down the receiver after a telephone call to London he said, "He's in Folkestone."

"What are we waiting for?" Langham asked.

From the promenade at Folkestone you can reach the beach either by way of the two lifts that go up and down together, working in series, or, more circuitously, by the famous zigzag with its right-angled paths separated by banks of shrubs. Or you can get to the beach by going through the Old Town, emerging near the harbor. The police car came round there and stopped.

They began to walk across the shingle, past the children's playground.

"You understand what to do, Miss Antrobus?" Lake said. "If you don't feel up to it, say so now."

"I'm up to it."

"Good." Lake was brisk. "We'll follow you slowly as you walk along the lower promenade. We won't be more than a few yards away."

The lower promenade was full of people buying candy, ice cream, and cups of tea. Children were crowded round a Punch and Judy show.

Langham jumped down to the pebbled beach and watched. Sheila Antrobus threaded her way along through the people, putting one foot precisely before another, unhurried and cool-looking in her dark blue dress.

She stopped in front of a hut that stood beside an ice-cream stall, and said, "Hullo, Chris."

The young man who had called himself Charlie Wilson was talking earnestly to a prospective customer for Nu-Stile-Pickshers. He stopped speaking, and the look on his face was, for a moment, that of one who wakes to find that some private nightmare—the death of a loved child or an ordeal by fire—has come true. Then his engagingly boyish smile was in place again, and he said, "Why, Sheila ducks, whatever are you doing in Folkestone?"

"You didn't tell me you were doing this sort of thing."

"I said I was doing a job for a few weeks that was great fun. Don't you call this fun?" He said to the customer, "Do go in, madam, you'll find the photographer inside. And don't forget, if you get a lucky number you win one of today's cash prizes."

"Chris, I want to talk to you."

"Of course, ducks." He shouted—and how well Gilbert Langham, who heard it before, remembered his shouting the same words—"Just going for a cuppa." He fell into step with her and said, "There's a little place along here with an old lady running it who just loves me."

"They all love you, don't they?" Sheila Antrobus said. "I mean, the ladies."

He stared at her with what seemed unaffected surprise. "I don't know what you mean. If you don't like my doing this job, all right. You're always saying I ought to work, and there aren't so many jobs that fit my peculiar talents."

Sheila Antrobus went on talking, slowly and without expression, as though some sort of machine had been wound up inside her. "Especially the ladies who got the prizes. That was the way it happened, wasn't it? You found out the people who were on the coach tour, got into conversation as they passed you, had their photographs taken or took them yourself, and then told the ones you picked, the unattached women, that their number had come up and they'd won a prize. After that, naturally they were delighted to meet such a charming young man a little later on to receive the prize. That was where the five-pound note came from that was in Mrs. Williams' handbag, wasn't it? You left that note in her bag by mistake, didn't you? Careless, Chris."

"Sheila." He jumped back as though she had jabbed him with a needle.

"And it wasn't really a clever idea to leave that note, from the letter he wrote you. If I came down, there was a good chance I'd recognize it. But I suppose you thought I'd marry you anyway."

Very slowly now, the record dying down, she said, "After we'd married, Chris, what would have happened to me?"

He made an ineffectual gesture with his hand, still backing away. Langham began to move up the shingle and at the same time Lake and Duff, behind Sheila, quickened their steps.

Chris Watling turned, bolted for the nearest entrance to the zigzag and began to run up it.

Lake and Duff went after him. Langham paused beside the girl who stood, looking upward, with no expression at all on her face.

"That must have been terrible for you."

Her voice was harsh. "I've done what you asked, haven't I? You said I could break him down, while the police might not be able to do. Now he's running. That's what you all wanted."

"You talk as though you didn't want him to be caught. He's killed three people."

"I love him." She said it flatly. They watched the figures running up the paths between the shrubs. "He's gaining on them."

"Lake's got a man waiting at the top."

For a few moments Watling was out of sight, hidden by a turn in the path. Then he emerged, and they could see the man who stood solidly blocking the exit. Watling took something from his pocket and ran toward the man at the top.

"He's got a gun," Langham said.

They heard two small sharp cracks, and the man went down. They could see Watling now, far above, running along the front, firing backward at Lake and Duff. He reached the entrance to the lift leading down the beach, and paused.

"He's coming down." Langham began to run toward the red-brick Victorian lift house. The girl followed him.

When they reached it, Langham said to the attendant, "There's a man coming down in that lift who's wanted for murder. Can't you stop him?"

"No, sir. He can't get out, though. Door's bolted outside."

They stared up and saw the great wooden cage on wheels descending. Above it was a sign: *The Lift. Fare 3d. One Minute to Center of Town.* The two lifts moving up and down worked together, and as the wooden cage from the top descended they could see some sort of confused activity inside it. There was a crash of glass, and they saw Watling climbing out of the window, still holding the revolver. He swung out and up onto the curved lift roof.

"He's going to jump over to the other one," Langham said.

No doubt Lake and Duff were now running down the slope, and Watling thought he might get away at the top. It was almost certainly hopeless—the crowd would never let him off the lift, revolver or no revolver—but he was going to try it.

They watched him poised on the top of the sloping cage as it slowly descended and the other lift rose to meet it. When the two cages were almost level, he jumped easily from one to the other.

"He's done it," the attendant cried out.

But Watling had failed to get a proper purchase on the lift's curved top. They could see him desperately trying to get a grip with hands and feet. Like a figure in a slow motion film his body slipped away from the lift roof. Then suddenly he dropped, limp as a puppet.

Sheila Antrobus turned away her head and screamed.

The broken thing that had caught in the cable at the bottom was not quite dead when Gilbert Langham reached it. The lips moved, whispered, "Sheila."

"Yes?"

The smile was as engaging as ever. "Tell her I shall have my picture in the papers."

LAWRENCE G. BLOCHMAN

Missing:
One Stage-Struck Hippie

Detective: DR. COFFEE

Northbank lay gasping under the prickly, suffocating blanket of August. As the Northbank police station was not air-conditioned, the doors to the squad room and the office of Detective Lieutenant Max Ritter beyond were wide open, courting any vagrant breeze.

Ritter did not hear the stranger come in. When he looked up, the apparition already loomed in the doorway. The Lieutenant blinked and looked again. The apparition was still there. Implausible though it certainly seemed, it must be real.

Although the man was as tall as a basketball center and as broad as an All-American lineman, his dimensions did not strike the detective until second glance. Ritter's first impression focused on one fanatical eye gleaming above a fierce tangle of red beard. The other eye was smothered by long carroty hair combed on the bias across a bulging forehead.

Lucite buttons as big as silver dollars glittered on his emerald-green shirt. His denim trousers might have been sprayed on, and his Javanese sandals were bright with gilt. He carried a corduroy jacket over one arm.

Ritter swallowed. His Adam's apple bobbed in his long throat. When the bobbing had stopped he asked, "Can we help you, buster?"

"I sincerely hope so," said the apparition. The resonant, cultured voice emerged from his garish jester's rig like a bass organ note from a tinny harmonica. "I'm desperately in need of assistance in tracing my fiancée."

Lieutenant Ritter smiled sadly but tolerantly as though to say: errant fiancées are two for a quarter around here, but we'll do our best. "Missing Persons," he said, "is just down the hall."

"Yes, I know. I've just come from there. They've been very helpful. Checked the hospitals and that sort of thing. But they don't share my conviction that Phyllis has met with foul play. This is the Homicide Bureau, isn't it?"

Ritter nodded. When he saw that the apparition was on the point of sitting down, he stood up, but he was too late to move the extra chair out of the line of airflow from the buzzing fan. He was pleasantly surprised when the expected New Left effluvia did not materialize.

"What makes you think baby doll has been given the works?" asked the detective. "Did she, to coin a phrase, frequent unsavory characters? Did she smoke pot or sniff glue or roll drunks?"

"Please." The red beard advanced halfway across Ritter's desk. "Can I hope to convince you that I'm deadly serious? My name is Brown—Tiberius Brown. My home is in San Francisco. My fiancée's name is Phyllis Emerson."

He fumbled in the pocket of his jacket and produced a Kodacolor snapshot which dropped in front of Ritter. "She came to Northbank about six weeks ago. She wrote me every other day until suddenly, about ten days ago, her letters stopped coming. I wired her. No answer. I tried to reach her by telephone— unsuccessfully."

Ritter studied the photo. It was a full-face shot of a girl with straight blonde hair that dangled to extreme length on both sides of her head. She wore a baby-blue turtleneck sweater and earrings like something by Calder out of Brancusi. The detective was puzzled by what seemed to be conflicting traits in the girl's face: sensual lips and a stern, determined chin; wistful blue eyes and an imperious tilt of the nose; the dreamer and the activist; the romantic and the aggressive realist.

"Why would anyone want her dead?" Ritter asked bluntly.

"I can't imagine." Tiberius Brown spread his hands. "But why shoud she stop writing? Where is she?"

"Maybe she left for Hanoi or Havana or some place like that," said Ritter. He didn't smile. Neither did Tiberius Brown, who shook his head vigorously.

"She would have written me," he said.

"Did she have any connection with Northbank's boy militant who got himself arrested in San Francisco a few months ago for raising hell and inciting to riot on the campus of Farwestern University? Simon Gallick. When he got out of the clink he came back here and married a screwball heiress."

"Everybody at Farwestern knew Gallick, of course. But Phyllis was not the political type."

"Look," Ritter said. "Begin at the beginning. What was Phyllis doing in Northbank? Why did she leave the Coast without you? And who the hell are you anyhow?"

Tiberius Brown seemed to swell with dignity. His red beard rose to point directly at Ritter as he leaned farther across the desk.

"I have told you that my name is Tiberius Brown. I am an instructor in Elizabethan and Restoration drama at Farwestern University in California. I am also director of the Dionysian Little Theatre in San Francisco. I've—"

"And Phyllis Emerson was a student of yours?" Ritter interrupted.

"She was registered in my course on Wycherley and the Restoration dramatists, yes. She was also one of the Dionysian Players."

"Was she living with you?" Ritter was again blunt.

"We've been very much in love for more than a year."

"Why don't you get married then?"

"We agreed to wait until I had my Ph.D. There's no future in an academic career without a doctorate, and I'm still working on my thesis."

"But she loved you—was nuts about you?"

"Definitely."

"Then why did she hightail it to Northbank without you? Why didn't you come with her?"

"I was giving a summer course at Farwestern while writing my thesis."

"You still haven't told me what she was doing in Northbank."

"Haven't I? Well, she was offered bit parts in the summer stock company here. She's crazy about the theater, so she came."

"Who made the offer?" Ritter asked.

"Don Sutherland. He's director of the summer playhouse here."

"Doesn't Sutherland know where she is?"

"No. He says she was ailing and dropped out of the cast last week."

"Like how? Was she on acid or something? Maybe she was having withdrawal symptoms."

"Nothing like that. Sutherland said she was having nauseous spells during rehearsals. He thought it was just nerves or the hot weather. Then she stopped coming around."

"And he didn't check when she didn't show?"

"He called the hotel where she was supposed to be staying and was told she was not registered. The Northbank Hilltop. I got the same answer. Apparently she just went there to write me on the hotel's stationery. You can understand now why I'm not only apprehensive but desperate."

Ritter nodded. He picked up the photo of Phyllis Emerson and studied it again. "You still don't give me a reason why anybody should want her dead," he remarked, "but maybe I can dig up one on my own. Where can I reach you, Professor?"

"I'm at the Hilltop—just in case she should turn up there. I would appreciate any help, Lieutenant."

"Keep in touch," said Ritter. "I'll keep this snapshot."

He got up as the bearded giant strode through the squad room and watched him start down the stairs.

"Brody," he called to a detective who had looked up from his two-finger typing of a report (in triplicate) to stare at Brown, "stay on his tail." Ritter pointed. He spoke in a stage whisper. "Hilltop Hotel."

Although Ritter told himself that Tiberius Brown's fears for the life of a kook like Phyllis Emerson did not really make the girl a prime concern of the Homicide Squad, the interview had somehow left him with an uneasy feeling. Something about the person and personality of the Bearded One didn't ring true, even though it was not strange that a junior pundit of Restoration Drama (whatever that was) should take on the protective coloring of the querulous generation. He was not completely surprised, therefore, when Brody called in forty minutes later to report.

"I lost him, Chief. He didn't go to the Hilltop Hotel like you said. He headed for Southbank first thing, and I lost him in the bridge traffic. I got his license number, though. He was driving a rented car, and the rental people say he gave his address as the YMCA, not the Hilltop. The Y people say he's not registered there either. Want me to call in the Southbank cops?"

"No. Come on in."

That settled it. Inasmuch as homicide in Northbank was in the summer doldrums for the moment, Ritter decided to invade the province of the Missing Persons Bureau. If his hunch proved wrong, nothing was lost. Slipping the Kodacolor image of Phyllis Emerson into his pocket, he drove to the Northbank Summer Playhouse which was housed in a deserted schoolhouse just outside of town.

He found Donald Sutherland waving his arms at two eager but slow-witted actresses on the schoolhouse stage. Sutherland was an exceedingly pretty young man. His carefully waved golden hair rippled back from a broad unruffled brow. His smooth pink cheeks dimpled when he smiled. The way his bell-bottomed candy-striped trousers clung to his posterior could only be described as callipygian. His gestures were extravagant and fluttery as he directed the rehearsal, yet he was not even perspiring. He interrupted the scene to answer the detective's questions.

"Yes, of course I know Phyllis Emerson. Good heavens! I hope nothing has happened to her."

"That's what I want to know. When did you see her last?"

"Let's see now . . . four mornings ago. She'd been feeling seedy for several days before that. I told her to go see my doctor. She didn't go, though. I called the doctor. I called her hotel, too. No answer. She may have gone back to the Coast."

"Think she was well enough to travel?" Ritter asked.

"Oh, I think so. Probably just nerves and the hot weather. She's pretty high-strung—like a lot of stage-struck kids who have more ego than talent."

"Why'd you hire her if she's no good?"

"Oh, she's not all that bad. She's adequate for walk-ons and bit parts, but I did *not* hire her. She offered to come with me for the summer at no salary—just for the experience."

"I hear her fiancé came to see you," said Ritter.

"Fiancé?" Sutherland frowned.

"Professor Tiberius Brown of Farwestern University."

"Oh, him!" The smile was not even lip-deep.

"Is Brown a phony?"

"I wouldn't say that exactly, but he's not really a man of the theater either. Of the library, rather. He smells of old books. He's wandered into the wrong century, I think—he belongs to the Seventeenth. He tries hard to live in the Twentieth, but he's miscast. He can't create the illusion. He's just a ham in a costume play."

"But Phyllis Emerson goes for him?"

Sutherland shrugged. "I wouldn't know. I've never inquired into her private emotions. Now if you'll excuse me—"

"Just a minute. You said you tried to telephone Phyllis. Where?"

"At the Hilltop Hotel."

"Brown says she's not registered there."

"She's registered there all right, but not under her own name. She doesn't want her family to come and drag her home. I promised I'd keep her secret, but since you're from the police . . . Just ask for Ellen Terry or Minnie Maddern Fiske or Adrienne Lecouvreur."

"I'll do that," said Ritter.

Dr. Daniel Webster Coffee, chief pathologist and director of laboratories at Pasteur Hospital, squinted into the twin lenses of his binocular microscope and made small clucking sounds as he twisted the focusing knobs.

"Dr. Mookerji," he called, "will you come here and look at this section of a bile duct? I'm sure you've seen plenty like it in India."

Dr. Motilal Mookerji, rotund resident pathologist, Calcutta's gift to North-bank, waddled across the laboratory. Flicking the tail of his pink turban over one shoulder, he sat down beside his chief. His plump brown fingers moved the tiny rectangle of glass under the nose of the microscope.

"Quite!" he said. "Clonorchiasis. Am wagering deceased was G.I. Joe. Yes?"

"Yes," said Dr. Coffee. "Home a year from Vietnam. He shouldn't have died. If whatever dumbbell treated him had sent the lab the proper specimen, we'd have seen eggs by the thousands. Then we could have told his doctor to clean out the trematodes with gentian violet instead of treating the poor guy for infectious hepatitis. True, we never used to see these liver flukes here in the Middle West, but with three-quarters of a million troops eventually coming home from Asia, doctors all over the country had better learn to be on the lookout for about fifty kinds of tropical parasites they never saw before . . . Oh, hello, Max."

Lieutenant of Detectives Max Ritter had made an unannounced entrance into the pathology lab. Ritter felt very much at home in the laboratory, for he had for years considered Dr. Coffee as his private medical examiner. Northbank was still burdened with the coroner system, in which the coroner, an elected official, was always more skilled in politics than in forensic medicine. Ritter unceremon-iously parked himself on a corner of Dr. Coffee's desk, pushed his dark felt hat to the back of his head, and saluted with a casual wave of his hand.

"Hi, Doc," he said. "Hi, Swami." He pulled a sheaf of dog-eared envelopes from his pocket. "I got problems."

"More felonious homicides, no doubt," said Dr. Mookerji.

"I ain't sure," said the detective, "but I could do with some advice. It's this way." And he started to outline the strange story of the missing stage-struck hippie, her disappearing red-bearded fiancé, and the dimpled, golden-haired director of the summer playhouse.

"I checked at the Hilltop Hotel where Phyllis Emerson is registered as Adrienne Lecouvreur who they tell me died two hundred years ago," he said. "The desk clerk is new and never saw the gal, but the manager let me in her room. Nobody seems to remember when she's in it last, but one thing is sure— when she leaves it, she doesn't expect to be gone long. Her feathered mules are still under the bed, her see-through nightgown is still hanging on the back of a chair, and her toothbrush is still in a glass in the bathroom. But no sign of Phyllis."

"What's all this got to do with pathology, Max?"

"It's like this," Ritter said. "The gal quit Sutherland's troupe because she got sick. In the mornings. When I get into her room I find a couple of doctors' names scribbled on the cover of the phone book." He consulted the back of an envelope and read off two names. "Would one of these M.D.'s just happen to be an abortionist, Doc?"

The pathologist glanced at the envelope. "They're G.U. men, so I have no doubt that both have at some time done a therapeutic abortion. But they're also reputable physicians and neither would risk his license to perform a clandestine D and C. Still, she might have tried. What does she look like, this girl?"

The detective produced the Kodacolor snapshot. Dr. Coffee studied it for a moment, then phoned each of the doctors. Neither remembered a girl answering Phyllis Emerson's description coming in for a consultation.

"My advice to you, Max, is to have this picture copied and give it to all the newspapers," Dr. Coffee said.

The picture of Phyllis Emerson was in all the morning editions, blown up to two- or three-column size. It was also on the early morning television news in living color.

The phone calls were already coming in when Max Ritter reported for the morning shift. Nearly half the calls were from cranks—the usual quota of exhibitionists who are drawn to a front-page story like maggots to cheese. The other calls were from people honestly trying to be helpful, and these required patient legwork to check out. Because a news photo has a tendency to impose its own features on a remembered face, all leads wound up in dead ends—until noon.

"Homicide. Lieutenant Ritter."

"Hi, Max. This is Jerry Fry, Southbank. Remember me?"

"Sure, Jerry. Haven't seen you since we worked together on that WAC murder. What's on your mind?"

"I think I got a make on that gal you're looking for—the one in the morning papers."

"Phyllis Emerson?"

"Yeah. I saw her three-four days ago getting out of a cab on this side of the river."

"You sure?"

"I'd bet on it. She was on her way to the Love Farm—the Gallick place. Know where that is?"

"Who doesn't? Look, Jerry, that's outside my jurisdiction, but I'm coming over anyway to smell around. If I need help I'll send up a smoke signal."

Ritter had never set foot on the Gallick "Love Farm," he reflected as he drove toward the War Memorial Bridge, but he was familiar enough with its denizens who often crossed the river to burn draft cards or join protest marches. The "farm" was the creation of Mrs. Zona Billworth Gallick, a rebel in mink. She was the daughter of Jonathan Billworth, manufacturer of plumbing fixtures, who made his first million pioneering the non-white toilet bowl. She could never forgive her father for having become filthy rich exploiting the hypocrisy of a society so ashamed of its natural functions that it surrounded them with a phony self-conscious beauty.

Zona's embittered filial protest took the form of spending as much of his ill-gotten gains as she could on relevant causes, such as buying an abandoned farmhouse across the river and converting it into a communal pad for North-bank's hippies and yippies. As a further protest against the Billworth bowls in pastel shades, she refused to install indoor plumbing in the old farmhouse. Her love children got along with the original outhouse in the backyard.

Zona's crowning act of defiance of Papa Billworth and his obscene millions was her marriage to Simon Gallick, the campus extremist. Gallick had become a fledgling revolutionary when he was thrown out of Northbank University in his sophomore year. The charges against him were threefold. He had been caught cheating in an Elementary Russian exam. He had flunked resoundingly in nine hours of credits—political science, economics, and American history. He had been apprehended by campus police while planting cannabis sativa in the Dean's flower garden.

Max Ritter had seen and heard Simon Gallick in action. While he considered the young man a physical mess, he had to admit that the punk possessed a peculiar perversive charm—perhaps pervasive and persuasive as well as perversive. His high-pitched voice rose, in his most hortatory moments, to heights of demagogic frenzy. His harangues were as rich in emotion as they were empty of substance, but he could make New Left clichés sound like pearls of wisdom. And he flitted (at Zona's expense) from campus to campus and coast to coast, like a wandering dervish strewing tacks on the seats of learning—until, after his latest incarceration in San Francisco, Zona (who was terrified of flying) bailed him out, brought him home, and married him.

There was a chain across the access road to the Love Farm. Ritter dropped it and drove up to the front door of the dilapidated farmhouse. Zona had not done much rehabilitation. Paint was peeling, shutters hung at crazy angles, cardboard and tar paper patched broken windows. The arid soil was knee-deep in weeds, but paper flowers garlanded the front door. A Vietcong flag hung limp on the hot steamy air.

In the front yard half a dozen fat girls and gangling young men were busy painting signs, obviously in preparation for picketing that week's state convention of the American Legion which was to be addressed by an Assistant Secretary of Defense. Two were modeling an Uncle Sam with bloodstained hands. The group stopped work and stared at Ritter.

Ritter strode through the hostile hippies and made straight for the barn, where a red Jaguar was parked next to a black Cadillac adorned with psychedelic symbols. He looked inside the cars, then climbed a ladder to the hayloft. Nothing. The long-haired boys and ratty-looking girls were clustered about the foot of the ladder when he came down.

"You pig!" screamed one of them.

"I'm a police officer," said Ritter. "Where's your high priest?"

Silence.

"I'm looking for the Gallicks."

"They're not here."

"A lie. That's Zona's Cad and Simon's Jag over there."

"They don't talk to pigs," said a barefoot fat girl.

"They'll talk to me."

"Better put on your helmet. Si's in bad humor today," said one.

"Where's your mace?" another demanded.

There was a chorus of rude lip noises and one-syllable words as Ritter walked toward the farmhouse. The noise brought the Gallicks to the front door.

"What do you want?" demanded Zona. She was a tall gawky girl, but her skinny thighs did not deter her from wearing jeans that were scarcely more than a faded blue-fringed G-string. Her tussah silk blouse was properly grimy, but the Ban the Bomb medallion that dangled from the end of her Sicilian amber love beads—an inverted trident of rubies in a circlet of platinum-mounted diamonds—had been made to order by Cartier's or Tiffany's. She wore huge violet sunglasses that hid half her face like a wrap-around windshield and made her buttonhole mouth seem even smaller than it was.

"I'm looking for a blue-eyed blonde named Phyllis Emerson," Ritter said. "I understand she's here. I'm a police officer."

"Wrong again, pig," said Simon Gallick, releasing Zona's hand to step forward. He was nearly a head shorter than his wife despite the extra inches supplied by his hair which rose in a sooty fright wig. His face was weasel-like and the upside-down crescent of a tired dark mustache drooled dismally around the corners of his mouth. His walk was the standard slow-motion lope of his kind, hands slanted into the front pockets of his levis as though caressing his lower abdomen. "Nobody here by that name."

"Take a look at this." Ritter unfolded the front page of a morning paper.

Gallick shook his head. Zona, looking over her shoulder, said, "We've never seen her."

"Let me refresh your memories. She came here in a taxi a few days ago. She's from California."

"She's not here."

"Mind if I go in and look around? Or shall I dig up the cabbie and get a search warrant?"

"Go ahead and look," Gallick said. "Or do you want to throw in a few tear-gas grenades first?"

The detective walked in. He gingerly traversed several rooms on which mattresses and rumpled blankets were heaped on the floor. Trailing a noisome odor to the rear of the house, he found that the kitchen had been converted into a laboratory for the manufacture of stink bombs, probably to greet the Assistant Secretary of Defense. When he opened a cupboard door, a kitten-sized rat jumped out, knocking over several cans and then scurrying silently away. He climbed rickety stairs, poked into dark corners, opened doors, and discovered nothing more than another rat.

"Satisfied, pig?" Gallick said when he came down.

"No," said Ritter. "I've seen better sties."

Zona let out a string of epithets.

"Now, now. Be nice, or we'll keep the TV cameras away from your next demonstration."

"See you from the barricades"—followed by another sequence of epithets.

"A pleasure," said Ritter, grinning.

He hurried from the house while he could still control his itch to take a poke at the Love Farm's leader. He was steaming, physically and mentally, as he strode through the tall weeds. Suddenly he stopped, bent to investigate a gleam of reflected sunlight that had caught his eye. He picked up a lucite button as big as a silver dollar. He turned it over. A few green threads clung to the under side.

He hesitated, started to turn back, changed his mind. When he reached his car he switched on his radio and ordered an all-points broadcast for the Thunderbird that Tiberius Brown had rented.

Ritter had scarcely returned to his desk when his phone rang.

"This is Dan Coffee, Max. I've been trying to reach you for more than an hour. I think I've located that blue-eyed blonde."

"You think? You're not sure, Doc?"

"Well, she's here in the hospital, but she's not blonde."

"You mean she's dyed her hair?"

"I mean she hasn't any hair. She's bald."

The startled sound that Ritter made could have been a bark. "Has she been scalped, Doc? Or was she wearing a wig?"

"She's been poisoned, Max, and I'm afraid she's in pretty bad shape. Better get right over here in case she has a lucid moment."

Ritter went through six red lights with his siren going all the way to Pasteur Hospital.

"Am I too late?" he gasped as he charged into the pathology lab.

Dr. Coffee shook his head. "She's hanging on, but she's in shock and in a coma. She can't talk."

"Think she'll make it?"

Again the pathologist shook his head. "They've given her stomach lavage and tried chelation with dimercaprol, but—"

"Hold on, Doc. Translate."

"My tentative diagnosis," said Dr. Coffee, "based on the loss of hair, is selenium or thallium poisoning. Thallium, which is the more probable, is a heavy metal. When metallic ions are inactivated by some other substance, the process is called chelation. That's what was tried. I'm afraid however, that her body had already absorbed more than a toxic dose. As little as one one-hundredth of an ounce can be fatal."

"Let's go back, Doc. How did she get here?"

"I understand that emergency got an ambulance call this morning from the Northbank Summer Playhouse—"

"From a guy named Don Sutherland?"

"I think that was the name."

"Why in hell didn't he call the police?"

"I wouldn't know, Max. I'm just a pathologist, remember. He told the ambulance intern that when he came to the theater this morning he found the girl lying on the stage near the footlights. She was comatose. She had been vomiting on the proscenium and this man—Sutherland?—thought she had been sleeping off a drunk until he noticed blood in the vomitus. Then he called for an ambulance."

"Sounds fishy to me," Ritter said. "Or don't you think so?"

"That's your job, Max. My primary interest is in identifying the poison so that I can keep her alive, if possible. Luckily the ambulance intern brought me a sample of the vomitus, and Dr. Mookerji is doing a chemical analysis now. It's a complicated affair, though, and will take several days. Meanwhile I'm getting a spectrographic analysis from the lab at Northbank University. They have the equipment, and it's much quicker."

"What am I supposed to do in the meantime?"

"You know your own routine, Max. Keep in touch with me, and—" The phone rang. "Pathology," said Dr. Coffee. "Yes, Doctor . . . I see. Just now? . . . Okay, I'll get authorization for an autopsy." He replaced the instrument with great deliberation. "Max, Phyllis Emerson is dead."

"Do I get a John Doe warrant for homicide?"

"I doubt very much that it was suicide. It's such an unpleasant, messy way to die. Does she have family?"

"On the Coast. I'll pass the word."

The Missing Persons Bureau of the San Francisco police department was very much interested in Ritter's telephone call. Phyllis Emerson had indeed been on their list for weeks. Her parents hadn't reported her when she first disappeared. They thought she had simply gone off on one of her periodic demonstrations to prove that she belonged to another generation and was beholden to no one. They weren't worried. She had left home before, but had come back after holing up for a week or so in the Haight-Fillmore district.

"When we couldn't locate her there, we sent out queries to Los Angeles, Chicago, New York—all the hippie meccas. We never thought of Northbank."

"Did her parents say anything about her possible love life?" Ritter asked. "Wasn't she supposed to be engaged? Did she have any boy friends?"

The voice at the other end of the transcontinental line gave a cultured chuckle. Its owner was probably a recent graduate of the Criminology Department at Berkeley. He chose his words carefully. "According to her father, there was no romantic attachment, but of course the parents are always the last to know. Phyllis Emerson, said her father, was heart-loose and fancy-free. Her only love affair was with her generation. She was infatuated with the disillusioned, the dispossessed, the bewildered. I'm sure her father will fly out as soon as I give him the bad news."

"Try to hold him until after the autopsy," Ritter said, "so we can get the girl a wig. She was poisoned bald-headed. Call me if you dig up anything."

He had scarcely finished his conversation when the phone rang.

"You the fella looking for that blonde cutie who had her pitcher in the papers this morning?" a man's voice asked.

"I was," said Ritter, "but we've found her."

"Oh. Then you tell her when she comes back to pick up her stuff that she owes me three bucks for cleaning up the mess in her cabin."

"Who's this speaking?"

"I'm Sam Tullinger, manager of the Riverside Motel out on River Road and Garfield."

"I'm afraid Miss Emerson won't be back, Mr. Tullinger—"

"Emerson? She registered as Minnie Fiske."

"Same gal, I'm sure. Have you cleaned up the cabin yet?"

"Not yet. I just looked inside when I seen her pitcher. She wasn't there."

"Then don't touch a thing. Don't let anybody in the cabin. I'll be right out," Ritter said.

He took off as soon as he could assemble a crew of technicians. He knew the Riverside Motel, having, with Dr. Coffee's help, once solved a particularly diabolic murder there. The motel had changed hands in the interim, the former manager having been the last man to die in the electric chair before the state abolished capital punishment.

Sam Tullinger, the present manager, was prepared to be uncooperative until Lieutenant Ritter paid the three-dollar cleaning fee out of his own pocket.

"What about the rent?" Ritter wanted to know.

"Miss Fiske paid a week in advance."

"Mrs. Fiske died thirty-odd years ago. Miss Emerson just died today. When did she rent the cabin?"

"Two-three days ago. Want the exact date?"

"Later. Who brought her here?"

"A taxi."

"Nobody with her? No man?"

"Nope. She was alone when she came in."

"No men came to see her while she was here?"

"I wouldn't know. I don't play Big Brother to my tenants."

"You never noticed a man with a big red beard?"

"I said I mind my own business. I—now wait a minute. Last night a hippie type with a red beard and a green shirt drove up in a Thunderbird while I was looking after some Legionnaires. He started to get out of the car, then changed his mind and got back in and drove off."

"Did he have a girl with him?"

"I didn't see nobody else in the car. This guy with a beard acted drunk to me, but I didn't pay too much attention. We been pretty busy these days with the state Legion convention starting tomorra."

"When did Miss Emerson—or Fiske, as you call her—leave?"

"I wouldn't know. I didn't know she was gone when I saw her pitcher in the paper. Then I went down to look in Cabin Fourteen and she wasn't there. So I called you."

Ritter accompanied Sam Tullinger to Cabin Fourteen where the photographers and fingerprint men were already busy. He noted the meager store of staples in the kitchenette and the few dirty dishes in the sink. The bed was unmade. There were no bottles or cosmetics in the bathroom, but there was evidence on the floor that the occupant had been sick on the way to the bathroom. He was only mildly interested in the cheap plastic suitcase—empty, of course—but he was fascinated by the tufts of long blonde hair strewn about the place—on the pillow, the back of a chair, on the floor.

Ritter collected the hair into a neat bundle which he gave to the chief of the technical squad to deliver to Dr. Coffee at Pasteur Hospital.

On his way back to police headquarters the detective mused that while the pieces were beginning to fall into place, there were still too many pieces missing.

The phone was ringing when he walked into his office. State Highway Patrol was on the wire. "We just found that rental Thunderbird you're looking for," said the trooper at the other end.

"Good. Where? Southbank?"

"No, just off Lilac Lane. That's a side road runs into Interstate Seventy-five north of town."

"Anywhere near the Summer Playhouse?"

"About half a mile."

"No sign of the driver?"

"Nope. Car was wrecked. Left the road on a turn and smacked into a tree. Blood on the windshield and an empty bourbon bottle on the floor. You sending your lab men out?"

"It's your backyard," Ritter said, "but I'll come over just to watch you boys work."

Half an hour later Ritter was watching but saw little he considered significant. There were, as he expected, a few coarse red hairs clinging to the bloodstains on the windshield. There were also what appeared to be dried drops of blood trailing footsteps that crossed the road and disappeared into the weeds and scrub growth. Troopers who had tried to follow the trail farther up the hillside found nothing.

Ritter watched several moulage men spraying shellac on tracks apparently made by a heavy car beyond the spot where the Thunderbird had left the road, as they prepared to make casts of the tire patterns. Then he drove back to Interstate 75 and proceeded to the Summer Playhouse.

Don Sutherland was busy tidying up last-minute details for the evening performance. He repeated for the detective the circumstances of his finding the dying Phyllis on the stage, but he could offer no explanation of her presence there. He was the last one to leave the night before, near midnight, and she was certainly not there then.

No, Sutherland said, there was no sign of a forced entrance. He was sure he had locked the front door when he went home, but someone must have left the stage door unlocked. No, he had not seen Tiberius Brown since the previous day, dead or alive. He offered to escort Ritter on a backstage tour to satisfy him that there were no corpses or near-corpses concealed in the scenery or dressing rooms. There were none.

On his way back to town Ritter realized that he hadn't eaten since breakfast. He stopped at a roadside diner and had two rare hamburgers and coffee.

Ritter was waiting in the pathology lab next morning when the Drs. Coffee and Mookerji came up from the basement carrying Mason jars and enamelware pails.

"What gives, Doc?" was the detective's greeting. "Developments?"

"Some," the pathologist replied. "At least we know that the late Miss Emerson did not patronize an abortionist, legal or otherwise, as you suspected."

"You mean I'm a bum diagnostician, Doc?"

"No, no, Max." Dr. Coffee chuckled. "You were quite right in guessing the cause of her morning sickness. But her pregnancy was not terminated. In fact, she was about two months along."

"That long?"

"Yes. Is it a clue?"

"Offhand," said Ritter, "it practically eliminates Sutherland. I'd say Phyllis wasn't his type anyway—or any other girl."

"Another thing. The spectroscopist at Northbank U. came up with the characteristic bright green line that confirms my diagnosis of thallium poisoning. Now the most probable and most easily accessible source of thallium would be rat poison containing thallium sulfate. I seem to remember there is some sort of restriction on the sale of this. Give me a few hours and I'll have some information that will narrow the field when you start looking for the man who sold it. So—"

Dr. Mookerji interrupted. "Phone for you, Leftenant." He passed the instrument to Ritter.

"Speaking. Oh, hello, Brody . . . You did? Where? . . . For the love of—he is? Still passed out? No, look. It may not be just booze. Better bring him over to Pasteur. Sure. The emergency entrance."

Ritter turned from the phone. "One of my suspects just turned up," he said. "Tiberius Brown. Missing since Wednesday. Just staggered into a barber shop, asked to have his red beard shaved off, and passed out in the barber chair."

"Drunk?" Dr. Coffee asked. "Or an injury?"

"I don't know." Ritter shrugged. "The barber told Brody he stank of whiskey, but he had a nasty gash on his forehead. He also had a pistol in his pocket, so the barber called the police. I told Brody to bring him here for diagnosis. Okay?"

"Why not? We'll intercept him in Emergency."

Tiberius Brown might have been a refugee from the Augean stables when he was carted into the Pasteur emergency ward. His magnificent beard, still unshaved, had accumulated so many leaves and other extraneous rubbish that it was as untidy as a sparrow's nest. He had not only slept in his clothes but had wallowed in them. Ritter was happy to note that one lucite button had been torn from his emerald-green shirt.

Dr. Coffee guided the admitting intern in making a differential diagnosis of Brown's coma. Was it concussion or merely alcoholic? After ten minutes of tests they concluded that the patient was suffering from complete exhaustion, lack of sleep, emotional trauma, and the remnants of a cataclysmic hangover. A nurse was summoned to give Tiberius Brown a cold bath, intravenous caffeine, and a few whiffs of oxygen.

Half an hour later the Bearded One opened his eyes, sat up, blinked, then fixed Ritter with a dismayed stare. "You!" he said. "I knew it would be you!"

"You're under arrest, Brown, for carrying a concealed and unlicensed weapon and for—"

"I know, I know." Brown closed his eyes again. "For murder. I killed her all right. Poor Phyllis! Okay, I'll go quietly." He held out his arms for handcuffs which were not there.

"Why have you been lying to me?" Ritter demanded. "Why have you been handing out phony addresses? What did you have against that girl, anyhow? Your fiancée, my eye! Missing, my foot! You knew where she was. You knew—"

"Ah-ee-ee-ee!" The red beard parted in an agonized cry that ended in a fit of sobbing. When he had pulled himself together, Brown said softly without looking at anyone, "Yes, I lied. Had I told you the truth Phyllis might still be alive. But no, I had to be the big hero, the knight in shining armor who alone would rescue the princess in distress. True, she was never my fiancée. Phyllis didn't give a damn for me, but she knew how crazy I was about her and she used me when it suited her. I lied when I let you think I'd been living with her."

"Then who was?" Ritter demanded. "She was two months' pregnant."

"I wouldn't know." The Bearded One shook his head bewilderedly.

"Guess."

"Well . . ." Brown swallowed hard. "Logically, and I am not logical at this moment, I should say it was someone she followed to Northbank."

"Like who?"

"Don Sutherland."

Ritter executed five cynical ha's in perfect rhythmic succession. "You must be kidding," he said.

"I lied when I said he offered her a job. *She* offered to join *him* without compensation."

"You really think Sutherland could make her pregnant?"

"Oscar Wilde could and did beget children, despite the Marquess of Queensbury and his son."

"Why did you go to see Gallick on Wednesday?"

Brown winced. "You're very clever at your trade, Lieutenant. Let me tell it my way. I'd been to see Sutherland to upbraid him for luring Phyllis to Northbank. He laughed at me. He suggested it was more likely that Phyllis had followed Simon Gallick. I didn't believe him."

"Why not?"

"I was sure he was diverting suspicion from himself. Furthermore, he seemed more Phyllis' type. She was a true hippie in the original sense. The flower child.

Gentleness and love. Withdrawal from society, not revolt against it. Phyllis was not at all militant."

"But she did know Gallick when he was making trouble out there?"

"Everyone did. He saw to that. But as far as getting involved with him—" Brown shook his head. "Incredible."

"So you went to see Gallick on Wednesday," said Ritter, "and he had you thrown out?"

"Forcibly. How did you know?"

"I found one of your buttons in the weeds at the Love Farm. Torn off. Did he deny knowing Phyllis?"

"He said he couldn't remember the names of every coed who fought for the privilege of sitting at his feet."

"Why did you give me the routine of being frantic about the gal's disappearance when you knew she was at the Riverside Motel?"

"I didn't know it then, I swear," said Brown, mopping his brow. "I lied when I said she wrote me twice a week. I had only one letter from her. And then this telegram. I should have showed it to you. It read, 'Ty dear I'm in trouble. Please come to Northbank. Look for letter general delivery. Philomela.' That was my pet name for her. She hated it.

"When I saw you I'd been to general delivery. There was nothing. After my encounter with Gallick I was desperate. I dropped in at a bar and had a few drinks. Then I went back to the post office. There was a letter for me, with postage due on it. Someone had apparently dropped it in a box without a stamp on it. The envelope bore the return address of the Riverside Motel. Inside there was just a scrap of paper on which were two words: 'Help. Ty.' I went out to the motel and found there was no Phyllis Emerson registered."

"Didn't Sutherland tell you that she was using names like Ellen Terry and Minnie Maddern Fiske?" Ritter asked.

"Sutherland wouldn't tell me the right time. I believe he is allergic to professors of classical drama. In a word, Sutherland does not like me."

"What did you do when you were told the girl was not registered?"

"I had a few more drinks, I'm afraid," said Brown. "I worked myself into a state of great indignation, high courage, and firm resolution. I then bought a bottle of bourbon and a hand gun, which you have confiscated. I returned to the Riverside Motel. The lobby was still crowded with Legionnaires with potbellies and ridiculous garrison caps on their bald heads. I couldn't break through the mob. I was about to drive off when, at the end of the row of cabins, I saw a man helping a woman into a car. It was dark. I couldn't swear the girl was Phyllis, but the resemblance was certainly close, even at that distance."

"So you followed them?"

"Yes. The car turned north on Interstate Seventy-five, which convinced me that the man driving was Sutherland—the road leads past the Summer Playhouse. The driver must have seen that I was following, because he speeded up and took a side road in an effort to shake me off. He knew the road better than I did. I missed a turn and crashed into a tree."

"That was Wednesday night," Ritter said. "This is Friday morning. Where were you all day yesterday?"

"I'm not sure." Brown dug his fists into his eyes. "I managed to stagger uphill into the trees before I passed out on Wednesday night. I must have slept around the clock. It was dark when I awoke. I had no idea what time it was. Somehow I made my way to Sutherland's theater. It was deserted. I thumbed a ride into town. The driver had his radio on, and I heard the news—that Phyllis was dead. I jumped out at the first stoplight and got drunk all over again.

"This morning I decided to quit playing the hippie. I would revert to being a square—get my beard shaved off, throw away my masquerade, and rejoin my generation from which I had temporarily seceded in the hope of pleasing Phyllis. In that, too, I apparently failed."

"Pretty glib," Ritter said. "Don't you wish half of it was true? Because I'm holding you on the weapons charge while I check every damned thing you've been telling me."

"Max, I've got to get back to the lab and read today's surgicals," said Dr. Coffee, breaking his long silence. "When you've finished the homework I've laid out for you, why don't you round up your cast of characters and bring them up to my lab—say, at five this afternoon? I'd like to kibitz. I might even help a little."

Lieutenant Ritter had a busy schedule after leaving the hospital. First he booked Tiberius Brown on the weapons charge. He next deployed a dozen detectives to canvass pharmacies and hardware stores for information on buyers of such thallium-sulfate-based pesticides as Dyratt and Pestkill. He had Zona Billworth Gallick's Cadillac towed to police headquarters for a thorough examination and vacuum cleaning. The Jaguar—Zona's wedding present to Simon—was no longer at the Love Farm. Neither were the two Gallicks.

When picked up, the Gallicks were casing all probable sites for television cameras at American Legion Hall so that their planned reception for the Assistant Secretary of Defense would get maximum exposure. They were, of course, indignant at being interrupted.

Don Sutherland was indignant too, but he came quietly.

When the last of Ritter's perspiring candidates for a first-degree murder indictment had found a seat in the laboratory, Dr. Coffee spoke.

"All this may seem somewhat irregular to you," he said, "but the circumstances are not exactly usual. I asked Lieutenant Ritter to bring you here because Phyllis Emerson died in this hospital, and I have certain medical findings bearing on her death. You are all in some way a part of Miss Emerson's past."

"Not I," Zona Gallick interrupted. "I never laid eyes on her, living or dead."

"Your husband has," said Ritter. "That makes you a member of the club, too."

"What the hell club are you talking about?" Gallick demanded.

"The Damn Liars Society," said Ritter. "Mrs. Gallick says she's never seen Phyllis Emerson, but a Southbank police officer sees the dead girl getting out of a taxi at Mrs. Gallick's so-called Love Farm. Professor Brown is lying his head off since Wednesday morning, but is he lying when he says Don Sutherland drove Phyllis away from the Riverside Motel on Wednesday night? We got evidence that Phyllis was at the motel, all right, and Sutherland can't explain how she gets to the stage of his theater, passed out and baldheaded, to start dying."

"You might at least tell us what she died of," said Zona Gallick.

"She was poisoned," said Dr. Coffee, "by thallium sulfate almost surely obtained from rat poison."

"I can't think of anybody stupid enough to swallow rat poison without a struggle," Sutherland broke in. "It must be pretty nasty. Even Phyllis would balk at that."

"She might not have," said Dr. Coffee, "if somebody had told her she was taking an abortifacient. She was eight weeks' pregnant, you know, and there are indications she was seeking to terminate her pregnancy. In that case she might very well have held her nose and taken anything that she was told would solve her problem."

The pathologist paused. The silence was broken only by the hum of the air conditioner and the rustle of people shifting in their seats. He continued, "It has been relatively easy to locate the source of the rat poison that killed Phyllis Emerson. In 1965 the U.S. Department of Agriculture banned the interstate shipment of thallium-based pesticides for home use because of an increasing number of cases of accidental poisoning of children. However, the Department made no effort to recall old stocks on the shelves of retail outlets until prodded by a Congressional Committee four years later—last month, in fact. So Lieutenant Ritter had relatively few stores to canvass before finding those still selling thallium sulfate pesticide. Max?"

Ritter got up and opened the door leading to Dr. Coffee's private office. A wizened little man in a seersucker suit emerged, blinking through thick spectacles as he smiled at the group.

"Mr. Stone is a pharmacist who owns a drug store on Taft Avenue," Ritter said. "Do you see any of your customers here, Mr. Stone?"

"Only one," replied the old man, squinting at each face in turn. "The lady over there." He pointed at Zona Gallick. "She bought the last six cans of DyRatt I had in stock. Just last week."

"Of course I buy rat poison." Zona was on her feet. Crimson flooded her cheeks. "And with good reason. The farm would be overrun with the filthy beasts if we didn't keep the rodent population explosion under control. I repeat, I've never seen the dead woman in my life."

"Where were you on Wednesday night, Zona?" asked Ritter.

"None of your business," snapped Zona's husband.

"Oh, stop it, Si. It's no secret. I was addressing a meeting of the American Legion Auxiliary, trying to persuade the women to join our anti-war demonstration against the Assistant Secretary tomorrow."

"Did you drive your own car, Mrs. Gallick?" Dr. Coffee asked.

"I—no." Zona turned suddenly to stare at Gallick. "Si needed the big car that night."

"I had to pick up some signs and banners and other heavy protest material that wouldn't fit in my Jag," said Gallick.

"I bring this up, Mrs. Gallick," the pathologist continued, "because Lieutenant Ritter has been exploring the upholstery of your Cadillac with a vacuum cleaner this afternoon and he has brought me a handful of long blonde hair."

"So what?" Zona's cheeks were losing color. "We have many fair-haired friends."

"I'm sure you have," said Dr. Coffee, "but this particular hair was once Phyllis Emerson's, no doubt about it. You see, thallium has the peculiar property of causing human hair to fall out. It also has the property, when ingested, of being absorbed by all tissues of the body, including the hair. The hair found in your car has been shown by photospectrographic analysis to contain thallium. Likewise, the hair lost at the Riverside Motel. Likewise, on the stage of the Northbank Summer Playhouse."

"Are you implying, Doctor, that my husband transported this woman to or from a motel while I was addressing the Legion wives?"

"The evidence indicates that one of you did."

"But why? Why?" Zona's cheeks were chalky white.

"In your own case, Mrs. Gallick, you may have wanted to remove a threat to your marriage."

"Don't make me laugh, Doctor. Do you think Si would jeopardize his marriage, his career, and his whole life for some fawning little trollop from nowhere?" She glared at her husband who seemed to shrink visibly.

"You said it, Zona baby," said Max Ritter. "Your Si knows which side his bed is buttoned on. He wouldn't stop at a little thing like murder if he thought a trusting little girl he'd made pregnant was going to come between him and your old man's millions."

"Don't listen to that dirty fink, Zona."

Zona had not stopped staring at her husband. "Si," she said, "did you? With that little tramp? Not that I really care, of course—"

"Of course not," said Gallick.

"In the interests of justice," said Dr. Coffee, "I'm going to propose a little scientific experiment. Dr. Mookerji here will take a few drops of blood from each of you gentlemen, and then—"

"What for?" Sutherland asked.

"A paternity exclusion test," said the pathologist smoothly. "I've already typed the blood of the late Miss Emerson. She is type O. Now by comparing the blood types of possible fathers with that of Miss Emerson's unborn child, we may be able to exclude all you gentlemen from the responsibility of having been the sire. For example, since Miss Emerson was an O, and if the unborn child has AB blood, any one of you three who has type A, B, or O is positively excluded. Any objection, Professor Brown?"

"None whatever."

"And you, Mr. Sutherland?"

"Will it hurt?"

"No more than a pinprick."

"Okay then."

"You can go to hell!" Simon Gallick shouted before Dr. Coffee could put the question to him. "Not one drop!"

"But, Si," said Zona, "if this test will put a stop to these silly accusations—"

"I know my rights!" Gallick's tiny eyes bulged and his lips were contorted as though he was about to foam at the mouth. "I refuse to give my blood to or for anyone in this stinking society anywhere—here, or in Vietnam or Korea or Northbank or any place. I'll go to jail first."

Dr. Coffee made a helpless gesture with both hands. "Draw your own conclusions, Max. I suggest you get a court order."

"I'm going to hold every screwball of this whole screwy lot as material witnesses," said Ritter.

"Don't start reciting that stupid rigamarole about my right to remain silent and all that jazz." Gallick stuck out his lower jaw at the detective. "I know it all by heart. Phone your lawyer, Zona. We're entitled to that."

When Ritter and his gaggle of bizarre characters had departed, Dr. Mookerji held out a chubby brown hand to Dr. Coffee. "Felicitations, Dr. Sahib," he said.

"For what, Doctor?"

"You are doubtless preparing paper for medical journals describing unique Coffee method of securing agglutination reaction from blood of unborn embryos," said the Hindu.

Dr. Coffee laughed. "Nonsense, Dr. Mookerji. You know as well as I do that a two-months' embryo has not yet developed agglutinins in its blood. A baby may not even have agglutinogens sensitive enough for testing several months after birth."

"Nevertheless—" Dr. Mookerji wagged his turbaned head twice to the left "—was able to detect overt symptoms of dismay, consternation, and second-degree panic in person of Simon Gallick when asked to volunteer blood sample."

"I hope you noted," said Dr. Coffee, grinning broadly, "that I promised no actual result from an agglutination test. I merely said 'if the unborn child had AB blood.' I was only trying to inspire the young man with the fear of God— Whom he doubtless doesn't even believe exists."

Dr. Mookerji frowned. "Am somewhat nonplused," he said, "regarding focus of suspicions upon violent young gent with sad mustache when poisonous hairs belonging to deceased were retrieved from motor car belonging to wife. Please elucidate, Dr. Sahib."

"I think it's fairly obvious," Dr. Coffee explained, "that Gallick was scattering red herrings all over the place—assuming, of course, that he's the culprit. First of all, he went to great lengths to keep the California girl away from his wife. I'm inclined to believe Mrs. Gallick when she says she never laid eyes on Miss Emerson, who stayed meekly put in her hotel until she found herself in trouble.

When she came over to the Gallick Love Farm for a confrontation with Gallick, Mrs. Gallick was probably not there, and he whisked the girl away to isolation in that motel. The motel also had the advantage over the Hilltop Hotel in that she would be unable to call a house physician when she began to suspect that she might not survive the supposed abortifacient.

"What inspired him to move the girl from the motel to the Summer Playhouse I can only imagine. When she did not die at once, I suppose he panicked and thought that somehow he could implicate Sutherland by leaving the girl to die in the Playhouse."

"Am further nonplused and perplexed." Dr. Mookerji's frown persisted. "You are therefore of opinion that fear of God will impel confession from youthful iconoclast? Or that courts will accept godly fear as legal evidence of guilt?"

"Not at all. But we have reached a point in this case where police science must now take over. Pathology has determined the cause of death, furnished a likely motive for murder, and pointed a way to unmasking the culprit. From here on it's up to Max."

The phone rang as if on cue.

"Pathology. Dr. Coffee . . . You have? Good, Max . . . You did? Fine. Yes, of course I'll testify."

"Leftenant Ritter has no doubt unmasked culprit?" said Dr. Mookerji.

"Max's technical crew has developed a fine set of fingerprints from Cabin Fourteen at the Riverside Motel. Simon Gallick, standing on his civil rights, refuses to be printed unless charges are placed against him. However, he was printed in California when jailed for inciting to riot at Farwestern. The Henry classification has just been telephoned in, and the match is perfect."

The Hindu resident beamed. "Am greatly gratified," he said, "that native land has contributed to solving criminous enigma of lady with poisoned hair."

"Really?" Dr. Coffee smiled with tolerant disbelief. "And what, may I ask, is India's contribution to this case?"

"Both essential and copious," replied Dr. Mookerji. "Fingerprints first used to trap felonious wrongdoers by Sir William Herschel while Calcutta police functionary in 1877. Furthermore, classification system just cited by San Francisco was invented by Sir Edward Henry while Inspector-General of Bengal Police at turning of century. Okey doke?"

"Okey doke," said Dr. Coffee. "I'll inform Lieutenant Ritter of his debt to Bengal."

ROBERT L. FISH

Double Entry

I don't like it," George Morton said stubbornly.

There was something almost petulant in his tone, like that of a child being driven to a task against his will. He was a middle-aged, nondescript, balding man, growing too fat. His wrinkled suit bagged at the ankles, bunched itself across his stomach, straining the buttons. He turned from his position near the windows of the swank apartment where he had been staring morosely down at the snow-covered meadows of Central Park, and walked over to the small bar that furnished one corner of the elegant room. He seated himself on one of the stools, frowned across the counter at his host, and repeated: "I don't like it."

His words made no visible impression on the other. Jerry Reed was a tall dapper man with a hairline mustache and an almost military haircut. He continued to carefully measure gin and vermouth into the ice-filled pitcher and then to stir it even more carefully. He slowly decanted the contents into a tall stemmed glass, and smiled. It was a faintly sardonic smile.

"Who said you had to like it?" Jerry Reed poured a glass of beer for his guest and pushed it across the bar together with a bottle of bourbon. A two-ounce shot glass was added to the collection. "Who ever said you had to like any of them?"

He picked up his martini and carried it to the coffee table, lowering himself into an easy chair and holding his drink protectively as he sat. His eyes came up to the face of the man at the bar and he raised his glass slightly.

"Cheers."

"Cheers." Morton poured himself a shot of bourbon, downed it, then sipped at his beer.

"Now, then," Jerry said briskly, leaning forward and setting his partially emptied glass on a coaster on the table. "Why don't you like it?"

"I never killed a woman before."

Jerry sighed. When he spoke his voice had lost its amusement, had turned flat. "When they're dead, they're not men or women any more. They're just bodies. Sexless. Clay. Mud. And you've seen enough of them. And produced enough of them."

"But I never hit a woman before."

"So this time it's a woman. She won't be any less dead for that. Or any deader,

556

either." Reed studied the other man emotionlessly. "You like the money, don't you?"

"Of course I like the money."

"And your wife doesn't think all that nice spendable money just comes from your so-called job as a bookkeeper, does she?"

"My wife doesn't know about the money," Morton said, and reached for the bottle, pouring himself another drink. "I don't even lay out all the dough I earn at the office. She thinks we're broke and I let her think so." His voice was emotionless. "If she knew how much money we really have I'd never get another minute's peace. When it's time for me to retire she'll know."

Reed smiled, pleased to allow the subject to drift from the assignment, satisfied to wait until Morton was in the proper mood. "That's smart. Keep them barefoot, ignorant, and pregnant, I always say."

"Janie never could get pregnant," Morton said absently, and shrugged. "I don't mind. I'm too old to stand the noise of kids, anyway, I guess."

"And how does she feel about your drinking?"

"She doesn't know about that, either. And she better not." The second drink had brought a touch of truculence into the heavy man's voice. Jerry watched him calmly as the glass on the counter top was replenished for the third time and then allowed to sit. Morton always followed the same pattern: the third drink, when finally taken, would eliminate the hostility, bring him back to normal. And Jerry Reed knew from long experience that the alcohol was not to build up false courage. Morton was the best there was. It was simply habit.

"I chew some gum and suck on some drops I've got before I go home," George said, and dismissed the subject, getting back to another statement of Reed's that his present mood rejected. "And don't call it any 'so-called book-keeping job.' We hire accountants, not bookkeepers. And I'm the assistant office manager down there. It's a real enough job, all right."

"You're also a professional killer," Reed reminded him gently. "Working for me." He smiled, continuing to avoid the subject of Morton's next hit, still waiting for the proper mood to be established. The third drink would do it. The dapper man's tone was idle. "How do you manage to get those afternoons off when you have a job to do?"

Morton shrugged. "The place is owned by my brother-in-law. He probably thinks I'm sneaking out for a dame." He shook his head. "He doesn't care. He only thinks I'm doing it. I know he is." He took his last drink.

"And you never do?"

"As a matter of fact, I don't." The third drink was already working; Morton smiled. "One woman gives me all the grief I need."

He finished the beer, pushed both glasses from him, and swung about on the stool, facing Reed. The last drink had acted as usual; he seemed calm, thoughtful, almost detached. Jerry stared at him curiously.

"So if your wife gives you grief, and she doesn't know about the money, why not just do a disappearing act? In a town this size you could do it right here and still keep doing jobs for me."

"Oh, Janie isn't so bad," Morton said, and then added patiently, "Besides, I told you. I like the job. Old Thomason—he's the office manager now—isn't going to last forever. Two, three years and I ought to be holding down his job."

Jerry Reed studied the fleshy face a moment. It certainly took all kinds! Yet he knew that no professional gun in New York City could hold a candle to Morton. Nor did any other command—and get—as high a fee. He shrugged.

"About the hit—"

Morton was ready. He relaxed against the bar. "Yes?"

"It's Marcia Collingswood."

"What?" Morton sat straighter, surprised. "But why—" He cut the question off as soon as he started it; only his amazement had made him begin to ask it in the first place. The whys were not his department. "The movie actress? I didn't even know she was in town."

"Well, she is. She's staying at the Hotel Belleville. Room 509."

Morton snorted. "The Belleville? You've got to be kidding! That fleatrap? Kept dames, quick rentals, and floating crap games—I know the place. That's where I hit Quinleven just last month. Remember?"

"I remember," Reed said dryly. "Anyway, that's where she's staying. Incognito."

Morton considered this. "So," he said at last, simply. "Incognito. Except everybody in the world seems to know where she is."

"Nobody knows where she is. Except you, me, and the man who's paying his good money for the job."

"The Belleville, eh?" Morton considered, then nodded slowly. "Fifth floor . . . Well, that shouldn't be any great chore. When does the curtain go up?"

"Tomorrow evening, between five and six," Reed said.

"Between five and six?" Morton shook his head decisively. "We're doing our annual audit today and tomorrow. I took this afternoon off to come up here and see you, but I told my brother-in-law I'd stay late tomorrow to make up for it. I ask him for tomorrow off, even one minute, and he's going to scream bloody murder." His tone became accusing. "I've just been telling you I've got a job I like and I'd rather not get canned, if you don't mind."

"Tomorrow evening," Reed said with no change in his voice. "Between five and six. She's meeting somebody for cocktails and dinner at seven—or at least she thinks she is—and she's scheduled to fly back to the coast on a midnight flight. But she'll be in her room between five and six, and expecting a caller." He studied Morton calmly. "There'll be a bonus for this one."

The heavy man sighed unhappily. "I'll have to say I'm sick, which means I can't even go back to the office afterwards. Which means I'll not only miss the time at the office, but I'll have to catch the seven o'clock train to Jersey. Which also means I miss the bus, and either wait half an hour, or walk. In all this snow—"

"Tough," Reed said evenly, and came to his feet, indicating the conference was over. He stood while Morton climbed down from the stool, walked Morton to the door, waited while the heavy-set man struggled into his overcoat.

"Marcia Collingswood," Reed said. "Hotel Belleville, Room 509. Between five and six." He didn't give the name under which she was registered; Morton would know her by sight. Actually, the repetition was merely force of habit; George Morton, he knew, had the information stored unforgettably in his mind. He smiled at the heavy man in friendly fashion. "If you make it close enough to five you might still catch your regular train."

"Not a chance," Morton said mournfully, and opened the apartment door. "You ever try to get a cab up near the Belleville at that hour? Even in good weather? Not a hope." He shook his head dispiritedly, and closed the door behind him.

George Morton glanced at his watch and nodded. The smoke-filled bar a block down from the Belleville was infinitely more comfortable than the freezing weather outside—the bar was too warm, in fact, since he was standing, one foot on the rail, still wearing his overcoat. But then, he wasn't being paid to be comfortable. He picked up the small change before him, finished his beer, and moved toward the door.

It had begun to sleet heavily when he emerged. Morton smiled faintly. Good! True, he would have greater trouble getting to the station afterward, but at least in this kind of weather heads were bent against the driving wind, eyes buried in coat collars, minds preoccupied with their owners' discomfort rather than the faces of strangers. And, too, the Belleville suited his purpose better than any other hotel he knew. Privacy being the sole reason for the hotel's continued existence, and hence propriety, the lobby and desk were around a corner from the entranceway, and both the staircase and self-service elevator could be reached without a person necessarily being seen.

Morton paused before the entrance, under the canopy flapping in the icy wind, and glanced through the heavy glass of the swinging doors. The immediate vicinity of the elevator was deserted; the door of the small cab was open, electrically awaiting custom; the light streaming obliquely from it added to the weaker illumination of the corridor.

Morton nodded in satisfaction, pushed through into the area, and stepped quite routinely into the empty elevator, pushing the button for the sixth floor. If one considered walking a flight a necessary precaution, George preferred it to be down rather than up.

The door slid shut; the cab slowly began its whining climb. Morton removed his gloves, opened his overcoat, and brought out a revolver from one jacket pocket and a silencer from another. He carefully screwed the silencer into place, stuffed the lethal assembly into his overcoat pocket, then pulled one glove on. His bare hand was placed into the pocket over the gun, hiding its projection. It made one side of his coat bulge suspiciously, but he knew that the only person who might possibly notice would be in no condition to report it.

At the sixth floor the elevator paused, considered, and then allowed its doors to slide jerkily open. Morton stepped out quite naturally, moving down the hallway with assurance. There was nobody to be seen. From behind most of the doors there was an almost watchful silence, but he did not allow this to disturb him in the least. The other rooms projected muffled music from cheap radios.

Morton pushed beneath the red light illuminating the entrance to the stair- way, trotted down the uncarpeted stairs, his face calm and assured. He paused at the fifth-floor landing, glancing through the small glass window set in the upper part of the door. Like the sixth floor, the fifth was also deserted; he was not particularly surprised, nor did he allow it to detain him. With a nod he thrust the door aside and walked with confidence to the door marked 509, rapping on it evenly, loud enough but not too loud, with aplomb. Confidence was everything. It removed suspicion from his victims until it was too late; it added to his anonymity in case he was ever noticed. Confidence, but not overconfidence . . .

The door opened. Instantly he recognized the woman facing him, although in person, without makeup, she appeared much older than her publicity photo- graphs. He spoke quickly, before she could recover from her evident surprise at the strange face.

"Miss Collingswood? I'm from the *Daily News*. Chamberly is my name. We heard that you—"

The surprise and disappointment had disappeared; her face had turned hard. "You heard what? What are you doing here? If I wanted to see reporters I wouldn't be staying at this—this—"

She clamped her jaws shut, starting to close the door. It caught on his heavy shoe, wedged in the opening.

George Morton was extremely apologetic. The important thing was that nobody appear from another room, or from the elevator, before he gained entrance.

"Look, Miss Collingswood, we're a newspaper. I've got an editor who eats reporters alive. When a good story breaks—"

"Take your foot out of the door. Do you hear?" Her white face studied his for a moment and seemed to see something in it. She came to a decision. "If you don't I'm going to call the desk and have them send a policeman up here. And if you print one word about my being here, I'll deny it and sue your newspaper for more money than it's got. Do you hear? Is that clear?"

The foot remained. "Look, Miss Collingswood—"

But the girl had had enough. She marched to the small table beside the bed, swinging about to hide the sight of him, reaching for the telephone. Morton stepped inside, closing the door quickly behind him. Her hand didn't have time to raise the receiver; he shot her through the nape of the neck, and then once more slightly higher, even as the body was crumpling helplessly to the bed. The only sounds were the coughs of the silencer.

Morton unscrewed the silencer, put the gun in one jacket pocket and the silencer in the other, and walked to the door, pressing his ear against the thin panel. He didn't even look back. He could hear no voices; he straightened up, buttoning his overcoat, slipping on the other glove. He opened the door slowly, calmly, walking out and carelessly closing it behind him. The elevator was in use, the pointer moving. He walked to the stairway, backing into the door to open it, and then trotted down the steps.

The entranceway was empty when he made the last turn at the final landing and descended to the street level. He stared through the glass with a frown. The sleet had stopped beating down, but the hazards of walking were evident in the figures lurching past. The seven o'clock train? He'd probably be lucky to make even the eight o'clock!

He pulled his coat collar up over his ears and pushed his way to the street. A thin figure, face hooded in a fur collar, hunched in the protection of the doorway, partially blocked his passage. He pushed past and then heard the familiar voice.

"Hello, George."

He swung about, staring, and then smiled in unbelieving amazement. Whatever had brought Janie to the city that day, she couldn't have picked a better time, because no matter where she went, Janie always drove. So she'd have the car, and, slippery or not, a car was always better than walking. His smile suddenly faded. Janie? Here?

"Janie! What are you doing here?" A further question came to him, disturbing, inexplicable. "And how did you know where I was?"

"Because I followed you here about a month ago when I called you at the office and my brother said you were going to be away for the afternoon." Her voice was spiteful, scathing. "I followed you from the office when you left. And when I called to talk to you today and my brother told me he was fed up with your taking time off, I knew where you were. Do you understand? *I knew!*"

She stared up at him, her thin face almost wolfish. "I know what kind of hotel this is. You think I'm a fool, but I know what goes on here—"

"But you don't understand, Janie—"

She fumbled in her purse as for a handkerchief; her hand emerged with a small gun. Morton stared at her incredulously. She raised the weapon evenly.

"I said—I know—what kind—of hotel—this is."

Her words were soft although half strangled, punctuated by the sharp splat of the gun. Morton's eyes had widened in amazement at the sight of the weapon; now they suddenly squeezed closed.

Two bullets drove him back inexorably, relentlessly; he struck the glass doors leading into the hotel as if in relief for their support, collapsing, sliding slowly down to the small step before the entrance, then leaning sideways as if resting against the doorjamb, lifeless.

She moved to him, bending over the rigid figure with its grotesquely open mouth, oblivious of the tableau of startled spectators frozen in their tracks by the sight, oblivious of the shrill whistle from the corner of the street and the figure of the policeman running toward her, sliding, slipping; oblivious of everything but her all-consuming bitterness and her recognition of her failure as a woman. The revolver dangled from her hand, unnoticed, like an admonishing finger, scolding.

"And you've been drinking, too," she said, and suddenly began to cry.

The Adventure of the Honest Swindler

W ho leads off this evening?" asked Ellery. It was his turn to crack the mystery.

"My gambit." Syres was the Founder of The Puzzle Club. The regular meetings took place in his Park Avenue penthouse, and his chef's *cordon bleu* dinners were never served until the challenged member had either triumphed or failed. So a hungry Ellery took the inquisitional armchair facing four of his five comembers—the fifth, Arkavy the Nobel biochemist, was in Glasgow attending one of his interfering symposiums—and was fortifying himself from the steam tray of Charlot's canapé works of art.

"The villain of tonight's Puzzle," began the multimillionaire who had made his oily pile in the Southwest, "is an old scamp, one of those legendary prospectors the West used to brag could live for months on beans and jerky in temperatures that would frazzle an ordinary man's gizzard or turn his blood to mush-ice."

"Old Pete's life," Darnell, the criminal lawyer, took up the tale, "has been one uninterrupted washout. Although he's tracked a hundred El Dorado-type rumors thousands of miles in his time, he's never once made the big strike. Only an occasional miserable stake scratched out of hardpan has kept Pete alive. Doctor?"

The psychiatrist, Vreeland, tapped the ash surgically off his two-dollar cigar. "Finally the mangy old fox becomes desperate. Frustration, loneliness, advancing years have whittled his wits to a fine edge; he plots a cunning—no, why plagiarize the shrinking violet? a brilliant!—scheme. To carry it off he sells just about everything in the world he owns. It brings him enough to pay for a display ad in *The Wall Street Journal*."

"*The Wall Street Journal*?" Ellery helped himself to the Scotch, looking delighted. "What imagination, what panache! Exactly how does your villain word his ad, by the way?"

Little Emmy Wandermere, who had just won the Pulitzer Prize for poetry, offered him a sheet of paper. On it she had penciled in her swashy hand:

Finance My Uranium Hunt!
Impossible to Lose!!

5-Year Money-Back Guarantee!
Complete Refund
Even If Uranium
Is Never Found!
Old Prospector, Box 1313

"Hardly a *Wall Street Journal*-type ad," Ellery said. "I'll put it down to poet's license, Miss Wandermere. And the response to Pete's pitch?"

"Heavy," the oil tycoon said. "You know what I always say—a sure thing gathers no moss. The dough comes rolling in."

"Can you give me a figure, Mr. Syres?"

"Well, let's say five hundred suckers invest $100 each to stake the old skunk for five years. That's $50,000. Agreeable, Miss Wandermere, gentlemen?"

The poet, the lawyer, and the psychiatrist nodded solemnly.

"In short, Mr. Queen," Dr. Vreeland said, "if Pete should strike uranium, the investors can realize many times their investments—"

"Would you believe like five thousand percent on their money?" winked the oil man.

"But even if he should fail," Lawyer Darnell chipped in, "every last investor at least gets back his original investment. That was Pete's offer."

"Do you mean that if I'd staked Pete to $100 of my money and he didn't find uranium, he'd give me my hundred back?"

"Your money, and that of every other investor."

Ellery meditated. The company waited. Finally Ellery said, "Did the old fellow find uranium, or didn't he?"

"If I may embroider the obvious, gentlemen?" The lady-poet's wicked blue eyes took on a faraway look. "Prospector Pete, better provisioned and outfitted than he's ever been outside his most beautiful dreams, sets out on his uranium quest. With the euphoria of his breed he spends years—in the deserts, the plains, the mountains, the glaciers, from Baja, California, to the Rockies to Alaska and all stops between—patient years of foot-slogging, climbing, chipping, digging, panning, or whatever it is you do when you're looking for uranium. The sun fries him, the rain waterlogs him, snow and ice make a Father Frost out of him. Many times he nearly dies of thirst. He runs the risks of bear and cougar and, worst of all, of loneliness. It does seem as if he deserves a happy ending, Mr. Queen, but he doesn't get it. He finds absolutely nothing. Not a squawk or a wiggle in his Geiger counter. Until finally the time limit in his guarantee is up and he hasn't a cent left."

"Whereupon," Syres said, "old Pete makes good the promise in his ad."

To which Darnell added, with magnificent simplicity, "End of story."

There was a tranquil hush.

"Well," Ellery muttered. "I see. His money's gone, he's failed to find uranium, and still he manages to pay back every one of his backers. In full?"

"In full."

"Then and there? Not ten years later?"

"Within twenty-four hours," Dr. Vreeland said. "Question: How does Pete do it?"

"I suppose I had better rule out the obvious. He hadn't found something else of value? Gold, say? Diamonds? Platinum?"

Emmy Wandermere looked sad. "Alas, as they used to say, Mr. Queen. He found nothing."

"Or just before the five years were up, his long-lost uncle—on his mother's side, of course—died in Poona, Illinois, and left him ten billion lakhs?"

"Please," Lawyer Darnell said, pained. "Our man Pete is penniless when he runs the ad, his prospecting efforts produce an unrelieved zero, he doesn't have an uncle, and at the expiration of the five years he can't claim a single negotiable asset. His equipment is worn out and not worth the match to set it on fire, and even his burro has died of exhaustion."

"Yet every investor gets his money back *in toto*."

"Every investor, every dollar."

"Hm," Ellery said, reaching for the Scotch again.

"You have the usual one hour, Queen," Syres said briskly. "After that, as you know, Charlot's dinner—"

"Yes, won't be edible, and I'm declared Nitwit of the Month." Ellery took an elegant swallow. "To avert both disasters I'd better solve your puzzle right now."

"How did old Pete manage to repay the entire $50,000 after five years in spite of his failure to find anything of value and winding up dead broke?

"The answer has to be," Ellery said gently, "that *he never touched the $50,000 in the first place*. Didn't spend a dime of it. So when the time limit expired he was naturally able to give the whole sum back.

"But if he never touched the principal, how did he manage to finance five years of prospecting?

"Simplest way in the world," Ellery went on. "When he first collected the $50,000 from his backers, he deposited the entire amount in a savings bank. At, say, five percent interest the $50,000 would bring him an income of $2500 a year. $2500 a year was a sumptuous grubstake to a desert rat with one ancient burro to his name and a lifetime's practise in living on next to nothing.

"Old Pete was no swindler, and he certainly wasn't the scoundrel you deliberately painted him to set me off the track. He was simply a businessman following time-honored business practice. And now, fellow-puzzlers, shall we partake of Charlot's goodies?" Ellery flourished his empty glass. "I'm ready to eat Pete's burro."